Praise for the long-awaited return of *New York Times*
bestselling author Robert McCammon and . . .

SPEAKS THE NIGHTBIRD

"Thoughtful as well as entertaining—think *Burn, Witch, Burn*
crossed with Arthur Miller's *The Crucible*. . . . The week I spent
listening to the nightbird every evening between eight and
eleven was a very fine one."

—Stephen King

"[This] story is as timely as today. It's about superstition, preju-
dice, good and evil, hatred and love. Told with matchless insight
into the human soul, this novel makes for a deeply satisfying
read."

—*New York Times* bestselling author Sandra Brown

"A decade's hiatus has done nothing to dull McCammon's abilities as a storyteller or a literary craftsman. . . . Will keep readers
glued to the pages."

—*Denver Rocky Mountain News*

"A trial for witchcraft proves the tip of an iceberg of intrigues in
this absorbing historical mystery. . . . A compulsively readable
yarn. McCammon's loyal fans will find his resurfacing reason to
rejoice."

—*Publishers Weekly*

"*SPEAKS THE NIGHTBIRD* is a welcome return of a master
who keeps his audience spellbound with every sentence. . . .
Powerful and tense, thrilling and atmospheric . . . reads like a
rocket on a witch hunt. Once you hear the Nightbird sing,
you'll never be the same."

—*Clarion-Ledger* (Jackson, MS)

"For sheer screwball storytelling exuberance, McCammon's book is hard to top. There will be times when most adults will find themselves faintly embarrassed to be gobbling the thing like hot buttered popcorn, but gobble they will all the same."

—Entertainment Weekly

"McCammon captures the joys and fears of late childhood with sure strokes, ably conveying his love for the time, the place and all the attendant forms of pop culture. . . . As an affecting paean to the magical possibilities of boyhood . . . the novel works exceedingly well."

—San Francisco Chronicle

"A tour de force of storytelling, it is a powerful story about the magic inherent in everyday life, about the many wonders and pains of growing up, about the strange beauty around us that we so often miss. . . . One of the most entertaining books in a long time."

—BookPage

And Robert McCammon's classic work

SWAN SONG

"A broad, compelling story. . . . A long, satisfying look at hell and salvation."

—Publishers Weekly

"A wild ride into terror. . . . A grand and disturbing adventure."

—Dean R. Koontz

"A chilling vision that keeps you turning pages to the shocking end."

—John Saul

Speaks the Nightbird

ROBERT McCAMMON

POCKET BOOKS

New York London Toronto Sydney

POCKET BOOKS
A Division of Simon & Schuster, Inc.
1230 Avenue of the Americas
New York, NY 10020

First Pocket Books trade paperback edition July 2007

POCKET and colophon are registered trademarks
of Simon & Schuster, Inc.

For information about special discounts for bulk
purchases, please contact Simon & Schuster Special Sales
at 1-800-456-6798 or business@simonandschuster.com

Designed by Suet Chong

Manufactured in the United States of America

10 9 8 7 6 5 4 3 2 1

ISBN-13: 978-1-4165-5250-5
ISBN-10:   1-4165-5250-2

To Hunter Goatley

Think where man's glory most begins and ends
And say that my glory was I had such friends.

—*William Butler Yeats*

one

CAME THE TIME when the two travellers knew night would catch them, and shelter must be found.

It had been a joyful day for frogs and mudhens. For the human breed, however, the low gray clouds and chill rain coiled chains around the soul. By the calendar the month of May should by all rights and predictions be charitable if not merry, but this May had entered like a grim-lipped miser pinching out candles in church.

Waterfalls streamed through the thick branches that interlocked forty feet above the road. The leaves of ancient oaks and elms, and the needles of the lofty pines, were more ebon than green, the huge trunks bearded with moss and blotched by brown lumps of fungus the size of a blacksmith's fist. To say that there was a road beneath those branches would be taking liberties with language: it was a canchre-colored mudhole emerging from the mist and disappearing into the mist.

"Steady, steady," said the wagon's driver to the pair of laboring nags as they pulled southward, breath steaming and skinny flanks trembling against the weight of wooden wheels through slop. He had a small stinger of a whip close at hand, but he declined to use it. The horses, which along with the wagon had been afforded him from the municipal stable of Charles Town, were doing all they could. Beneath the wagon's soaked brown burlap canopy, and behind the raw pinewood plank that occasionally fired splinters into the travellers' rear ends, were two unmatched trunks, a valise, and a wig box, all four pieces of luggage bearing scars and gouges that betrayed lives of undignified shipment.

Thunder rumbled overhead. The horses struggled to lift their hooves in the muck. "Get up, there," the driver said, with not a smudge of enthusiasm. He gave the reins a half-hearted flick, his hands protected by a pair of gray cloth gloves, then he sat without further comment as raindrops fell from the furled edges of his black, mud-spattered tricorn hat and added more soggy bulk to his raven's-hue fearnaught coat.

"Shall I take them, sir?"

The driver glanced at his fellow sufferer, who was offering to hold the reins. By no idylls of the imagination could the two be called bookends; the driver was fifty-five years of age, the passenger fresh of twenty. The older man was big-boned and had a heavy-jowled and ruddy face, with thick and bristling gray eyebrows set like ramparts over deeply cast ice-blue eyes that were as congenial as newly primed cannon barrels. His nose—as a polite Englishman might say—was well-dimensioned. A forthright Dutchman might say its owner had bloodhound in his lineage. The driver's chin was also a sturdy piece of sculpture, a square bulwark scored with a cleft that could have sheltered a small musket ball. Usually his face was scraped clean by scrupulous passes of the razor, but today the salt-and-pepper beard was making an appearance.

"Yes," he said. "Thank you." He passed the reins over, one of the many times they'd exchanged this duty in the past hours, and worked some feeling back into his fingers.

The younger man's lean, long-jawed face had courted more candle glow than sunlight. He was thin but not frail, rather sinewy like a tough garden vine. He wore square-toed shoes, white stockings, olive-green breeches, and a short, tight-fitting brown jacket made of cheap kerseymere over a plain white linen shirt. The knees of his breeches and the elbows of his jacket had been patched at least as often as the older man's clothing. On his head was a dun-colored woolen cap, pulled down over finely textured black hair that had recently been cropped close to the scalp to combat an infestation of lice in Charles Town. Everything about the younger man—nose, chin, cheekbones, elbows, knees—conveyed the impression of sharp angles. His eyes were gray, flecked with dark blue, the colors of smoke at twilight. He did not urge on the horses nor spank them with the reins; he only intended to guide. He was if anything a stoic. He understood the value of stoicism, for already in his life he'd endured such trials as might break someone who did not.

As he worked his hands, the older man mused that if he saw fifty-six after this ordeal then he should put aside his vocation and become a samaritan in thanks to God. He was not cut from the crude frontier cloth. He considered himself a man of taste and refinement, an urban denizen ill-suited to pierce this wilderness. He appreciated clean brickwork and painted fences, the pleasing symmetry of manicured hedges, and the solid regularity of the lamplighter's rounds. He was a civilized man. Rain was down his neck and in his boots, the light was fading, and he had but a single rusty saber in the wagon with which to protect their belongings and their scalps. The village of Fount Royal lay at the end of this mudtrack, but that was cold comfort. His task at that place would not be a gentle one.

But now a touch of mercy! The rain was tapering off, the sound of thunder more distant than before. The older man thought that the worst of the storm must be moving over the ocean, which they'd glimpsed as a frothy gray plain through brief breaks in the forest. Still, a nasty drizzle continued to sting their faces. The hanging folds of mist had curtained the treelimbs, giving the forest a phantasmagoric pall. The wind had stilled, the air thick with a swampy green smell.

"Carolina spring," the older man muttered, his husky voice carrying the melodic accent of well-bred English generations. "There'll be many new flowers in the graveyard come summer."

The younger man didn't answer, but inwardly he was thinking that they might perish on this road, that a stroke of evil could befall them and they'd vanish from the face of the earth just as Magistrate Kingsbury had vanished on this same journey not two weeks ago. The fact that wild Indians haunted these woods, along with all manner of savage animals, was not lost on his imagination. Even with its lice and plague deaths, Charles Town looked like paradise compared to this dripping green hell. The settlers of Fount Royal must be insane to stake their lives and fortunes on such a territory, he'd decided.

But what now was Charles Town had itself been wilderness twenty years ago. Now it was a city and a thriving port, so who could say what Fount Royal might become? Still, he knew that for every Charles Town there were dozens of other settlements that had been devoured by misfortunes. Such too might be the eventual fate of Fount Royal, but at present it was the physical reality of someone's hard-worked dream, and the problem there must be tended to like any problem of a civilized society. But the question remained: why had Magistrate Kingsbury, en route from Charles Town to Fount Royal on this same—and only—road, never reached his destination? The older man had supplied a number of answers to the younger's inquiry—that Kingsbury had run afoul of Indians or highwaymen, that his wagon had broken down and he'd been set upon by beasts. But though the older man had the nose resembling a bloodhound's, it was the younger man who had the bloodhound's instinct. Any lingering scent of a question was strong enough to keep him pondering in pale candle glow long after the older man had retired and was snoring in his bedchamber.

"What's that?"

A gray-gloved finger pointed toward the mist ahead. In a moment the younger man saw what his companion had spied: the pitch of a roof off to the right side of the road. It was the same dark green and wet black as the woods, and might be as ruined a place as the trading post at which they'd expected to rest the horses and break bread in early afternoon, but instead had found only charred timbers and collapse. But there on the roof before them was a pretty sight: a stone chimney flying a flag of white smoke. The mist moved, and the rough-hewn lines of a log cabin took shape.

"Shelter!" said the older man, with exultant relief. "God's grace on us, Matthew!"

It was a fairly new structure, which explained why it hadn't been marked on the map. The nearer they got, the stronger was the smell of freshly axed pinelogs. Matthew noted, perhaps ungraciously, that the cabin's builder had not been the most skilled nor neatest of craftsmen. Copious amounts of red mud had been used to seal the cracks and chinks in crooked walls. The chimney was more mud than stones, spitting smoke through its fissures. The roof sat at a precarious angle, like a tilted cap on the head of a blowzy drunk. The cabin was unadorned by any paint or decoration, and the small narrow windows were all sealed by plain plankboard shutters. Behind the cabin was an even more slovenly looking structure that must be a barn, beside which stood three swaybacked horses in a fenced enclosure. A half-dozen pigs snorted and grumbled in the nasty mire of a second pen nearby. A red rooster strutted about, followed by a number of wet hens and their muddy chicks.

A stake had been driven into the ground beside a hitching rail. Nailed to the stake was a green pinewood placard with the words *Tavern Ye Trade* scrawled on it in thick eggwhite paint.

"A tavern too!" the older man said, taking the reins from Matthew as if his hands could speed them to that hitching rail any faster. "We'll get a hot meal tonight after all!"

One of the horses back by the barn began nickering, and suddenly a shutter opened and an indistinct face peered out. "Hello!" the older man called. "We're in need of shel—"

The shutter slammed closed.

"—ter," he finished. Then, as the horses made their last slog to the rail, "Whoa! Hold up!" He watched the shutter. "Inhospitable for a tavern-keeper. Well, here we are and here we'll stay. Right, Matthew?"

"Yes, sir." It was said with less than firm conviction.

The older man climbed down from his seat. His boots sank into the mud up to his ankles. He tied the reins to the hitching post as Matthew eased himself down. Even losing two inches to the mud, Matthew was taller than his companion; he stood ten inches over five feet, an exceptionally tall young man, whereas his companion was a more normal height at five feet seven inches.

A bolt was thrown. The cabin's door opened with dramatic flourish. "Good day, good day!" said the man who stood on the threshold. He wore a stained buckskin jacket over a brown shirt, gray-striped breeches and gaudy yellow stockings that showed above calf-high boots. He was smiling broadly, displaying peg-like teeth in a face as round as a chestnut. "Come in and warm y'selves!"

"I'm not certain about it being a good day, but we will surely enjoy a fire."

Matthew and the older man scaled two steps to the porch. The tavern-keeper stepped back and held open the door for their entry. Before they reached him, both wished the pungence of the pinewood was stronger, so as to mask the appalling smell of their host's unwashed body and dirty clothes. "Girl!" he hollered to someone inside the tavern, just as Matthew's left ear got in the path of his pewter-melting voice. "Put another log on that fire and move y'self quick!"

The door closed at their backs and gone was the light. It was so gloomy in the place that neither of the two travellers could see anything but the red glimmer of fitful flames. Not all the smoke was leaving through the chimney; a duke's portion of it had made its home in the room, and hung in greasy gray layers. Matthew had the sensation of other shapes moving around them, but his eyes were blurred by smoke. He felt a knotty hand press against his back. "Go on, go on!" the tavern-keeper urged. "Get the chill out!"

They shuffled closer to the hearth. Matthew banged into a table's edge. Someone—a muffled voice—spoke, someone else laughed and the laugh became a hacking cough. "Damn ye, mind your manners!" the tavern-keeper snapped. "We got gentlemen among us!"

The older man had to cough several times too, to relieve his lungs of the tart smoke. He stood at the flickering edge of the firelight and peeled off his wet gloves, his eyes stinging. "We've been travelling all day," he said. "From Charles Town. We thought we'd see red faces ere we saw white."

"Yessir, the red demons are thick 'round here. But you never see 'em 'less they wants to be saw. I'm Will Shawcombe. This is my tavern and tradin' post."

The older man was aware that a hand had been offered to him through the haze. He took it, and felt a palm as hard as a Quaker's saddle. "My name is Isaac Woodward," he replied. "This is Matthew Corbett." He nodded toward his companion, who was busy rubbing warmth into his fingers.

"From Charles Town, do y'say?" Shawcombe's grip was still clamped to the other man's hand. "And how are things there?"

"Livable." Woodward pulled his hand away and couldn't help but wonder how many times he would have to scrub it before all the reek was gone. "But the air's been troublesome there these past few weeks. We've had hot and cold humours that test the spirit."

"Rain won't quit 'round these parts," Shawcombe said. "Steam one mornin', shiver the next."

"End a' the world, most like," someone else—that muffled voice—spoke up. "Ain't right to wear blankets this time a' year. Devil's beatin' his wife, what he is."

"Hush up!" Shawcombe's small dark eyes cut toward the speaker. "You don't know nothin'!"

"I read the Bible, I know the Lord's word! End a' time and all unclean things, what it is!"

"I'll strop you, you keep that up!" Shawcombe's face, by the flickering red firelight, had become a visage of barely bridled rage. Woodward had noted that the tavern-keeper was a squat, burly man maybe five-foot-six, with wide powerful shoulders and a chest like an ale keg. Shawcombe had an unruly thatch of brown hair streaked with gray and a short, grizzled gray beard, and he looked like a man not to be trifled with. His accent—a coarse lowborn English yawp—told Woodward the man was not far removed from the docks on the river Thames.

Woodward glanced in the direction of the Bible-reader, as did Matthew, and made out through the drifting smoke a gnarled and white-bearded figure sitting at one of several crudely fashioned tables set about the room. The old man's eyes caught red light, glittering like new-blown coals. "If you been at that rum again, I'll hide you!" Shawcombe promised. The old man started to open his mouth for a reply but had enough elder wisdom not to let the words escape. When Woodward looked at the tavern-keeper again, Shawcombe was smiling sheepishly and the brief display of anger had passed. "My uncle Abner," Shawcombe said, in a conspiratorial whisper. "His brain pot's sprung a leak."

A new figure emerged through the murk into the firelight, brushing between Woodward and Matthew to the edge of a large hearth rimmed with black-scorched stones. This person—slim, slight, barely over five feet tall—wore a patched moss-green woolen shift and had long dark brown hair. A chunk of pinewood and an armload of cones and needles were tossed into the flames. Matthew found himself looking at the pallid, long-chinned profile of a young girl, her unkempt hair hanging in her face. She paid him no attention, but moved quickly away again. The gloom swallowed her up.

"Maude! What're you sittin' there for? Get these gentlemen draughts of rum!" This command had been hurled at another woman in the room, sitting near the old man. A chair scraped back across the raw plank floor, a cough came up followed by another that ended in a hacking gasp, and then Maude—a skinny white-haired wraith in clothes that resembled burlap bags stitched together—dragged herself muttering and clucking out of the room and through a doorway beyond the hearth. "Christ save our arses!" Shawcombe hollered in her miserable wake. "You'd think we never seen a breathin' human before in need of food 'n drink! This here's a tavern, or ain't you heard?" His mood rapidly changed once more as he regarded Woodward with a hopeful expression. "You'll be stayin' the night with us, won't you, sirrah? There's a room right comfortable back there, won't cost you but a few pence. Got a bed with a good soft mattress, ease your back from that long trip."

"May I ask a question?" Matthew decided to say before his companion could respond. "How far is Fount Royal?"

"Fount Royal? Oh, young master, that's a two, three hour ride on a good road. The weather bein' such, I'd venture it'd take you double that. And dark's comin' on. I wouldn't care to meet Jack One Eye or a red savage without a torch and a musket." Shawcombe focused his attention once more on the older traveller. "So you'll be stayin' the night then?"

"Yes, of course," Woodward began to unbutton his heavy coat. "We'd be fools to continue on in the dark."

"I suspect you have luggage in need of cartin'?" His smile slipped off as his head turned. "*Abner*! Get your arse up and fetch their belongin's! Girl, you go too!"

The girl had been standing motionlessly with her back against a wall, her face downcast and her bare arms crossed over her chest. She made no sound, but walked at Shawcombe's drumbeat toward the door, her feet and legs clad in knee-high deerskin boots. "Ain't fit for a pig out there!" Abner complained, holding firm to his chair.

"No, but it's just right for a hog like you!" Shawcombe countered, and daggers shot from his eyes again. "Now get up and get to it!" Muttering under his beard, Abner pulled himself to his feet and limped after the girl as if his very legs were stricken by some crippling disease.

Matthew had wanted to ask Shawcombe who "Jack One Eye" was, but he hated the thought of that girl and the old man—the girl, especially—struggling with the heavy trunks. "I should help." He started toward the door, but Shawcombe gripped his arm.

"No need. Those two sops sit 'round here too long, they get lazy. Let 'em stir a bone for their supper."

Matthew paused, staring into the other man's eyes. He saw something in them—ignorance, pettiness, pure cruelty perhaps—that sickened him. He had seen this man before—with different faces, of course—and he knew him to be a bully who revelled in power over the weak of body and feeble of mind. He saw also a glint of what might have been recognition of his perceptions, which meant Shawcombe might be more intelligent than Matthew had surmised. Shawcombe was smiling slightly, a twist of the mouth. Slowly but forcefully, Matthew began to pull his arm away from Shawcombe's hand. The tavern-keeper, still smiling, would not release him. "I said," Matthew repeated, "that I should help them."

Shawcombe didn't surrender his grip. Now at last Woodward, who had been shrugging out of his coat, realized some small drama was being played out before him. "Yes," he said, "they will need help with the trunks, I think."

"Yessir, as you say." Shawcombe's hand instantly left the young man's arm. "I'd go m'self, but my back ain't no good. Used to lift them heavy bales, port a' Thames, but I can't do it no—"

Matthew gave a grunt and turned away, walking out the door into the last blue light and what was now blessedly fresh air. The old man had hold of Woodward's wig box, while the girl was around behind the wagon trying to hoist one of the trunks up on her back. "Here," Matthew said, slogging through the mud to her. "Let me help you." He took hold of one of the leather handles, and when he did the girl skittered away from him as if he were a leper. Her end of the trunk smacked down into the muck. She stood there in the rain, her shoulders hunched over and the lank hair covering her face.

"Ha!" Abner chortled. In this clearer light, his skin was as dull gray as wet parchment. "Ain't no use you talkin' to her, she don't say nothin' to nobody. She's one step out of Bedlam, what she is."

"What's her name?"

Abner was silent, his scabby brow furrowing. "Girl," he answered. He laughed again as if this were the most foolish thing any man had ever been asked, and then he carried the wig box inside.

Matthew watched the girl for a moment. She was beginning to shiver from the chill, but yet she made no sound nor lifted her gaze from the mud that lay between them. He was going to have to heft the trunk—and the second one as well, most likely—in by himself, unless he could get Abner to help. He looked up through the treetops. The rain, strengthening now, pelted his face. There was no use in standing here, shoes buried in the mire, and bewailing his position in this world; it had been worse, and could yet be. As for the girl, who knew her story? Who even gave a spit? No one; why then should he? He started dragging the trunk through the mud, but he stopped before he reached the porch.

"Go inside," he told the girl. "I'll bring the other things."

She didn't move. He suspected she'd remain exactly where she was, until Shawcombe's voice whipped her.

It was not his concern. Matthew pulled the trunk up to the porch, but before he hauled it across the threshold he looked again at the girl and saw she had tilted her head back, her arms outflung, her eyes closed and her mouth open to catch the rain. He thought that perhaps—even in her madness—it was her way of cleansing Shawcombe's smell off her skin.

two

"MOST INCONVENIENT," Isaac Woodward said, just after Matthew had looked under the straw-mattressed pallet of a bed and found there to be no chamberpot. "An oversight, I'm sure."

Matthew shook his head with dismay. "I thought we were getting a decent room. We'd have been better served in the barn."

"We won't perish from one night here." Woodward motioned with a lift of his chin toward the single shuttered window, which was being pelted by another heavy downpour. "I dare say we would perish, if we had to continue out in that weather. So just be thankful, Matthew." He turned his attention back to what he was doing: getting dressed for dinner. He'd opened his trunk and taken from it a clean white linen shirt, fresh stockings, and a pair of pale gray breeches, which he'd laid carefully across the bed so as not to snag the material. Matthew's trunk was open as well, a clean outfit at the ready. It was one of Woodward's requirements that, wherever they were and whatever the circumstances, they dress like civilized men for the dinner hour. Matthew often saw no point in this—dressing like cardinals, sometimes for a pauper's meal—but he understood that Woodward found it vitally important for his sense of well-being.

Woodward had removed a wigstand from his trunk, and had placed it upon a small table which, along with the bed and a pinewood chair, comprised the room's furnishings. On the wigstand Woodward had set one of his three hairpieces, this one dyed a passable shade of brown with curling ringlets that fell about the shoulders. By the smoky candlelight from the hammered-metal lantern that hung on a wallhook above the table, Woodward examined his bald pate in a silver-edged handmirror that had made the journey with him from England. His white scalp was blotched by a dozen or more ruddy agespots, which to his taste was a thoroughly disagreeable sight. Around his ears was a fragile fringe of gray hair. He studied the agespots as he stood in his white undergarments, his fleshy belly overhanging the cinched waistband, his legs pale and thin as an egret's. He gave a quiet sigh. "The years," he said, "are unkind. Every time I look in this mirror, I see something new to lament. Guard your youth, Matthew. It's a precious commodity."

"Yes, sir." It had been said without much expression. This topic of conversation was not unfamiliar to Matthew, as Woodward often waxed poetic on the tribulations of aging. Matthew busied himself by shrugging into a fresh white shirt.

"I was handsome," Woodward wandered on. "Really I was." He angled the mirror, looking at the agespots. "Handsome and vain. Now just vain, I suppose." His eyes narrowed slightly. There were more blotches this time than the last time he'd counted them. Yes, he was sure of it. More reminders of his mortality, of his time leaking away as water through a punctured bucket. He abruptly turned the mirror aside.

"I do go on, don't I?" he asked, and he gave Matthew a hint of a smile. "No need to answer. There'll be no self-incrimination here tonight. Ah! My pride!" He reached into his trunk and brought out—very carefully and with great admiration—a waistcoat. But by no means an ordinary one. This waistcoat was the dark brown color of rich French chocolate, with the finest of black silk linings. Decorating the waistcoat, and glinting now in the candlelight as Woodward held it between his hands, were thin stripes woven with golden threads. Two small and discreet pockets were likewise outlined with woven gold, and the waistcoat's five buttons were formed of pure ivory—a rather dirty yellow now, after all the years of use, but ivory just the same. It was a magnificent garment, a relic from Woodward's past. He had come to breadcrumbs and briars on several occasions, facing a bare larder and an even barer pocketbook, but though this garment would procure a pretty sum in the Charles Town marketplace he had never entertained a notion of selling it. It was, after all, a link to his life as a gentleman of means, and many times he'd fallen asleep with it draped over his chest, as if it might impart dreams of happier years in London.

Thunder boomed overhead. Matthew saw that a leak had begun, over in the corner; water was trickling down the raw logs into a puddle on the floor. He had noted as well the number of rat droppings around the room and surmised that the rodents here might be even larger than their urban cousins. He decided he would ask Shawcombe for an extra candle, and if he slept at all it would be sitting up with the lantern close at hand.

As Matthew dressed in a pair of dark blue trousers and a black coat over his shirt, Woodward pulled on his stockings, the gray breeches—a tight squeeze around the midsection—and then his white blouse. He thrust his legs into his boots, which had been scraped of mud as much as possible, and then put on and buttoned up his prized waistcoat. The wig went on, was straightened and steadied with the aid of the handmirror. Woodward checked his face for stubble, as he had shaved with the benefit of a bowl of rainwater Shawcombe had brought in for their washing. The last piece of apparel to go on was a beige jacket—much wrinkled but a sturdy traveller. Matthew ran a brush through the cropped and unruly spikes of his black hair, and then they were ready to be received by their host.

"Come in and set y'selves!" Shawcombe brayed as Woodward and Matthew came into the main room. If anything, the smoke from the hearth seemed thicker and more sourly pungent. A few candles were set about, and Maude and the girl were at work over a pot that bubbled and steamed on a hook above the red coals. Shawcombe was on his feet with a wooden tankard of rum in one hand, motioning them to a table; his balance, or lack of same, indicated the liquor was finding its target. He blinked and let out a low whistle that rose in volume. "Lord fuck the King, is that gold you're wearin'?" Before Woodward could draw back, Shawcombe's dirty hand had snaked out and fondled the glittering waistcoat. "Ah, that's a fine piece of cloth there! Maude, look at this! He's wearin' gold, have you ever seen the like?"

The old woman, revealed by the firelight to have a face like a mask of cracked clay under her long white hair, peered back over her shoulder and made a noise that could have been either mangled English or a wheeze. Then she focused again on her cooking, stirring the pot and snapping what sounded like orders or criticism at the girl.

"You two look the birds!" Shawcombe said, grinning widely. His mouth appeared to Matthew like a wet-edged cutlass wound. "The gold bird and the black bird! Ain't you the sights!" He scraped back a chair from the nearest table. "Come on, sit down and rest your feathers some!"

Woodward, whose dignity had been affronted by this performance, pulled out his own chair and lowered himself into it with as much grace as he could muster. Matthew remained standing and, looking Shawcombe directly in the face, said, "A chamberpot."

"Huh?" The grin stayed, crooked, on Shawcombe's mouth.

"A chamberpot," the younger man repeated firmly. "Our room lacks one."

"Chamberpot." Shawcombe took a swig from the tankard, a rivulet of rum dribbling down his chin. His grin had vanished. The pupils of his eyes had become dark pinpoints. "Chamber fuckin' pot, huh? Well, what do you think the woods are for? You want to shit and piss, you go out there. Wipe your arse with some leaves. Now sit down, your supper's 'bout ready."

Matthew remained standing. His heart had begun beating harder. He could feel the raw tension in the air between them, as nasty as the pinewood smoke. The veins in Shawcombe's thick neck were bulging, gorged with blood. There was a defiant, churlish expression on his face that invited Matthew to strike him, and once that strike was delivered the response would be triplefold in its violence. The moment stretched, Shawcombe waiting to see what Matthew's next move would be.

"Come, come," Woodward said quietly. He grasped Matthew's sleeve. "Sit down."

"I think we deserve a chamberpot," Matthew insisted, still locking his gaze with the tavern-keeper's. "At the very least a bucket."

"Young master"—and now Shawcombe's voice drooled false sentiment—"you should understand where you are. This ain't no royal palace, and you ain't in no civilized country out here. Maybe you squat over a fancy chamberpot in Charles Town, but here we squat out behind the barn and that's how things is. Anyway, you wouldn't want the girl to have to clean up behind you, would you?" His eyebrows lifted. "Wouldn't be the gentlemanly thing."

Matthew didn't answer. Woodward tugged at his sleeve, knowing this particular skirmish wasn't worth fighting. "We'll make do, Mr. Shawcombe," Woodward said, as Matthew reluctantly surrendered and sat down. "What may we look forward to supping on this evening?"

Bang! went a noise as loud as a pistol shot, and both men jumped in their chairs. They looked toward the hearth, at the source of the sound, and saw the old woman holding a hefty mallet in one hand. "Eyegots at 'am bigun!" she rasped, and proudly raised her other hand, two fingers of which pinched the long tail of a large, crushed black rat that twitched in its death throes.

"Well, toss the bastard!" Shawcombe told her. Both Woodward and Matthew expected her to throw the rat into the cookpot, but she shambled over to a window, unlatched the shutter, and out went the dying rodent into the stormy dark.

The door opened. A wet rat of another breed came in trailing a blue flag of curses. Uncle Abner was soaked, his clothes and white beard dripping, his boots clotted with mud. "End 'a the damn world, what it is!" he pronounced, as he slammed the door and bolted it. "Gonna wash us away, d'rectly!"

"You feed and water them horses?" Shawcombe had previously commanded Abner to take the travellers' horses and wagon to shelter in the barn, as well as tend to the three other swaybacked steeds.

"I reckon I did."

"You bed 'em down all right? If you left them nags standin' in the rain again, I'll whip your arse!"

"They're in the damn barn, and you can kiss my pickle if you're doubtin' me!"

"Watch that smart mouth, 'fore I sew it up! Go on and get these gents some rum!"

"I ain't doin' nothin'!" the old man squalled. "I'm so wet I'm near swimmin' in my skin!"

"I believe I'd prefer ale," Woodward said, remembering how his earlier taste of Shawcombe's rum had almost burned his tongue to a cinder. "Or tea, if you have it."

"Myself the same," Matthew spoke up.

"You heard the gentlemen!" Shawcombe hollered at his hapless uncle. "Go on and fetch 'em some ale! Best in the house! *Move,* I said!" He took a threatening two steps toward the old man, lifting his tankard as if he were about to crown Abner's skull with it, in the process sloshing the foul-smelling liquor onto his guests. Matthew shot a dark glance at Woodward, but the older man just shook his head at the base comedy of the situation. Abner's soaked spirit collapsed before his nephew's ire and he scurried off to the storage pantry, but not without leaving a vile, half-sobbed oath lingering in his wake.

"Some people don't know who's the master of this house!" Shawcombe pulled a chair over and sat without invitation at their table. "You should pity me, gents! Everywhere I look, I have to rest my eyes on a halfwit!"

And a halfwit behind his eyes too, Matthew thought.

Woodward shifted in his chair. "I'm sure running a tavern is a troublesome business."

"That's God's own truth! Get a few travellers through here, but not many. Do some tradin' with the trappers and the red-skins. 'Course, I only been here three, four months."

"You built this place yourself?" Matthew asked. He had noted a half-dozen sparkles of water dripping from the shoddy roof.

"Yep. Every log and board, done it all."

"Your bad back allowed you to cut and haul the logs?"

"My bad back?" Shawcombe frowned. "What're you goin' on about?"

"Your bad back that you injured lifting the heavy bales. Didn't you say you worked on the river Thames? I thought your injury prevented you from carrying anything like . . . oh . . . a trunk or two."

Shawcombe's face had become a chunk of stone. A few seconds passed and then his tongue flicked out and licked his lower lip. He smiled, but there was a hardness in it. "Oh," he said slowly, "my back. Well . . . I *did* have a partner. He was the one did the cuttin' and haulin'. We hired a few redskins too, paid 'em in glass beads. What I meant to say is . . . my back's in pain more when it's wet out. Some days I'm fit as a fiddle."

"What happened to your partner?" Woodward inquired.

"Took sick," came the quick response. His stare was still fixed on Matthew. "Fever. Poor soul had to give it up, go back to Charles Town."

"He didn't go to Fount Royal?" Matthew plowed on. His bloodhound's instinct had been alerted, and in the air hung the definite smell of deceit. "There's a doctor in Fount Royal, isn't there?"

"I wouldn't know. You asked, I'm answerin'. He went back to Charles Town."

"Here! Drink 'til your guts bust!" Two wooden tankards brimming with liquid were slammed down in the center of the table, and then Abner withdrew—still muttering and cursing—to dry himself before the hearth.

"It's a hard country," Woodward said, to break the tension between the other two men. He lifted his tankard and saw, distressingly, that an oily film had risen to the liquid's surface.

"It's a hard *world*," Shawcombe corrected, and only then did he pull his stare away from Matthew. "Drink up, gents," he said, uptilting the rum to his mouth.

Both Woodward and Matthew were prudent enough to try sipping the stuff first, and they were glad at their failure of courage. The ale, brewed of what tasted like fermented sour apples, was strong enough to make the mouth pucker and the throat clench. Matthew's eyes watered and Woodward was sure he felt prickles of sweat under his wig. Even so, they both got a swallow down.

"I get that ale from the Indians." Shawcombe wiped his lips with the back of his hand. "They call it a word means 'snakebite.'"

"I feel soundly bitten," Woodward said.

"Second swaller's not so bad. Once you get halfway done, you'll be a lion or a lamb." Shawcombe took another drink and sloshed the liquor around in his mouth. He propped his feet up on the table beside them and leaned back in his chair. "You don't mind me askin', what business do you have in Fount Royal?"

"It's a legal matter," Woodward answered. "I'm a magistrate."

"Ahhhhhh." Shawcombe nodded as if he understood perfectly. "Both of you wear the robes?"

"No, Matthew is my clerk."

"It's to do with the trouble there, am I right?"

"It *is* a matter of some concern, yes," Woodward said, not knowing how much this man knew about the events in Fount Royal, and unwilling to give him any more rope with which to bundle a tale for other travellers.

"Oh, I know the *particalars*," Shawcombe said. "Ain't no secret. Message riders been back and forth through here for the last couple a' months, they gimme the story. Tell me this, then: you gonna hang her, burn her, or cut her head off?"

"Firstly, the accusations against her must be proven. Secondly, execution is not one of my duties."

"But you'll be passin' the sentence, won't you? C'mon! What'll it be?"

Woodward decided the only way to get him off this route was to run the distance. "If she's found guilty, the penalty is hanging."

"Pah!" Shawcombe waved a disapproving hand. "If it was up to my quirt, I'd cut her head off and burn her to boot! Then I'd take them ashes and throw 'em in the ocean! They can't stand salt water, y'know." He tilted his head toward the hearth and hollered, "Hey, there! We're waitin' for our suppers!"

Maude snapped something at him that sprayed an arc of spittle from her mouth, and he yelled, "Get on with it, then!" Another swig of rum went down his hatch. "Well," he said to his guests' silence, "this here's how I see it: they ought to shut Fount Royal down, set fire to everything there, and call it quits. Once the Devil gets in a place, ain't no remedy but the flames. You can hang her or whatever you please, but the Devil's took root in Fount Royal now, and there ain't no savin' it."

"I think that's an extreme position," Woodward said. "Other towns have had similar problems, and they survived—and have flourished—once the situation was corrected."

"Well, *I* wouldn't want to live in Fount Royal, or any other place where the Devil's been walkin' 'round town like he's made hisself at home! Life's damn hard enough as it is. I don't want conjures bein' put on me while I'm sleepin'!" He grunted to emphasize his point. "Yessir, you talk pretty, but I'll wager you wouldn't care to turn down an alley and see ol' Scratch waitin' in the dark! So my advice to you, sir—lowly tavern-keeper that I am—is to cut the head off that Devil's whore and order the whole town burnt to the ground."

"I will not pretend that I know any answers to mysteries—holy or unholy," the magistrate said evenly, "but I do know the situation in Fount Royal is precarious."

"And damn dangerous too." Shawcombe started to say something else, but his open mouth expelled no words; it was obvious to Woodward and Matthew that his attention, made imprecise by strong drink, had been diverted from the matter of Fount Royal. He was admiring the gold-threaded waistcoat once more. "I swear, that's a fine piece a' work," he said, and dared to run his grimy fingers over the material again. "Where'd you get that? New York?"

"It . . . was a present from my wife. In London."

"I was married once'st. And once'st was enough." He gave a gruff, humorless laugh. His fingers continued to caress the fabric, much to Woodward's discomfort. "Your wife is in Charles Town?"

"No." Woodward's voice had thickened. "My wife . . . remains in London."

"Mine's at the bottom of the bloody Atlantic. She died on the passage, shit herself to death. They rolled her up and rolled her over. Y'know, a waistc't like this . . . how much is somethin' like this worth?"

"More than any man should have to pay," Woodward said, and then he pointedly moved his chair a few inches away from Shawcombe and left the tavern-keeper's fingers groping the air.

"C'lear room! Watchyer elbows, there!" Maude slapped two wooden bowls, both filled with a murky brown stew, onto the table in front of Shawcombe and the magistrate. Matthew's bowl was brought by the girl, who set it down and quickly turned away to retreat to the hearth again. As she did, her clothes brushed his arm and the wind of her passage brought a strong scent to Matthew's nostrils: the scent of an unwashed body, yes, but another odor that overpowered the first. It was musky and sweetly sour, a compelling pungency, and it hit him like a fist to the chest that it was the aroma of her private region.

Shawcombe inhaled deeply, with a raucous noise. He looked at Matthew, whose eyes had widened slightly and were still tracking the girl. "Hey, there!" Shawcombe barked. "What're you gawkin' at?"

"Nothing." Matthew averted his gaze to the stew bowl.

"Uh huh."

The girl returned, bringing with her their wooden spoons. Once more her skirt brushed his arm, and he moved it with a twitch as if his elbow had been hornet-stung. That smell wafted to his nostrils. His heart was beating very hard. He picked up his spoon and realized his palm was damp. Then he realized Shawcombe was staring intensely at him, reading him like a broadsheet.

Shawcombe's eyes glittered in the candlelight. He wet his lips before he spoke. "She's a fair piece, do y'think?"

"Sir?"

Shawcombe smiled slightly, a mean and mocking smile. "A fair piece," he repeated. "You fancy a look at her oyster basket?"

"Mr. Shawcombe!" Woodward grasped the situation, and it was not acceptable to him. "If you don't mind—"

"Oh, you both can have a go at her, if you please. Won't cost you but a guinea for the two of you."

"Certainly not!" Woodward's cheeks had flamed. "I told you, I'm a married man!"

"Yeah, but she's in London, ain't she? Don't mean to tell me you got her name tattooed on your cock now, do you?"

If the storm had not been raging outside, if the horses had not been in the barn, if there were anywhere else in the world to spend this night, Woodward might've gotten to his feet with all the dignity he could summon and bade farewell to this coarse-minded lout. What he really wanted to do, deep in his soul, was to strike an openhanded blow across Shawcombe's leering face. But he was a gentleman, and gentlemen did no such things. Instead, he forced down his anger and disgust like a bucketful of bile and said tersely, "Sir, I am faithful to my wife. I would appreciate your understanding of that fact."

Shawcombe replied by spitting on the floor. He riveted his attention on the younger man again. "Well, how 'bout you then? You care for a toss? Say ten shillin's?"

"I . . . I mean to say—" Matthew looked to Woodward for help, because in truth he didn't know what he meant to say.

"Sir," Woodward said, "you force us into a difficult position. The young man . . . has lived in an almshouse for much of his life. That is . . ." He frowned, deciding how to phrase the next thing. "What you must realize is . . . his experience is very limited. He hasn't yet partaken of—"

"Great sufferin' mother!" Shawcombe broke in. "You mean he ain't never been fucked?"

"Well . . . as I say, his experience hasn't yet led him to—"

"Oh, quit that foamin' at the mouth! He's a fuckin' *virgin,* is that what you're tellin' me?"

"I believe your way of expressing that is a contradiction of terms, sir, but . . . yes, that's what I'm telling you."

Shawcombe whistled with amazement, and the way he regarded Matthew made the younger man blush blood-red. "I ain't never met one of your breed before, sonny! Damn my ears if I ever heard such a thing! How old are you?"

"I'm . . . twenty years old," Matthew was able to answer. His face was absolutely on fire.

"*Twenty* years and no pussy? How're you able to draw a breath without bustin' your bag?"

"I might ask how old that girl is," Woodward said. "She's not seen fifteen yet, has she?"

"What year is this?" Shawcombe asked.

"Sixteen ninety-nine."

Shawcombe began counting on his fingers. Maude brought to their table a wooden platter laden with chunks of brown cornbread, then scurried away once more. The tavern-keeper was having obvious difficulty with his digital mathematics, and finally he dropped his hand and grinned at Woodward. "Never you mind, she's ripe as a fig puddin'."

Matthew reached for the snakebite and near guzzled it.

"Be that as it may," Woodward countered, "we shall both pass on your invitation." He picked up his spoon and plunged it into the watery stew.

"Wasn't no invite. Was a business offer." Shawcombe drank some more rum and then started in on his stew as well.

"Damnedest thing I ever heard!" he said, his mouth full and leaking at the corners. "I was rogerin' the girls when I was twelve years old, m'self!"

"Jack One Eye," Matthew said. It had been something he'd wanted to ask about, and now seemed as good a time as any to get Shawcombe's mind off the current subject.

"What?"

"Earlier you mentioned Jack One Eye." Matthew dipped a chunk of cornbread into his stew and ate it. The bread tasted more of scorched stones than corn, but the stew wasn't at all objectionable. "What were you talking about?"

"The beast of beasts." Shawcombe picked up his bowl with both hands and slurped from it. "Stands seven, eight feet tall. Black as the hair on the Devil's ass. Had his eye shot out by a redskin's arrow, but just one arrow didn't stop him. No sir! Just made him meaner, is what they say. Hungrier, too. Swipe your face off with a claw and eat your brains for breakfast, he would."

"Jack One Eye's a fuckin' *bear!*" spoke up Abner, from where he stood steaming by the hearth. "Big one, too! Bigger'n a horse! Bigger'n God's fist, what he is!"

"Hain't no *burr.*"

Shawcombe looked toward the speaker of this last declaration, stew glistening on his grizzled chin. "Huh? What're you sayin'?"

"Sayin' he hain't no burr." Maude came forward, silhouetted by the firelight. Her voice was still a mangled wheeze, but she was speaking as slowly and clearly as she could. This subject, both Woodward and Matthew surmised, must be of importance to her.

"'Course he's a bear!" Shawcombe said. "What is he, if he ain't no bear?"

"Hain't *jus'* a burr," she corrected. "I seen 'im. You hain't. I know 'hut he is."

"She's as addle-brained as the rest of 'em," Shawcombe told Woodward with a shrug.

"I *seen* 'im," the old woman repeated, a measure of force in her voice. She had reached their table and stood next to Matthew. Candlelight touched upon her wizened face, but her deep sunken eyes held the shadows. "I 'as at the door. Right *they,* at the door. Me Joseph was comin' home. Our boy too. I watch 'em, comin' out of the woods, over the field. Had a deer hangin' 'tween 'em. I lift up me *laneturn,* and I start ta holler 'em in . . . and all suddens that thang behind 'em! Jus' rose up, out of nowhar'." Her right hand had raised, her skinny fingers curled around the handle of a spectral lantern. "I try ta scream me husband's name . . . but hain't get nothin' out," she said. Her mouth tightened. "I try," she croaked. "I try . . . but God done stole me voice."

"Most like it was rotgut liquor stole it!" Shawcombe said, with a rough laugh.

The old woman didn't respond. She was silent, as rain battered the roof and a pineknot popped in the hearth. Finally she drew a long ragged breath that held terrible sadness and resignation. "Kilt our boy 'fore Joseph could tarn 'round," she said, to no one in particular. Matthew thought she might be looking at him, but he wasn't certain of it. "Like take his head off, one swang o' them claws. Then it fell on me husband . . . and weren't nothin' to be dun. I took a'running, threw me laneturn at 'im, but he 'as *big.* So awful big. He jus' shake them big black shoulders, and then he drag that deer off and leave me with what 'as left. Joseph 'as a-split open from 'is windpipe to 'is gullet, his innards a-hangin' out. Took 'im three days ta die." She shook her head and Matthew could see a wet glint in her eye sockets.

"My Lord!" Woodward said. "Wasn't there a neighbor to come to your aid?"

"*Naybarr?*" she said, incredulously. "Hain't no naybarrs out 'chere. Me Joseph 'as a trapper, dun some Injun tradin'. Tha's how we live. What I'm tellin' you is, Jack One Eye hain't jus' a burr. Ever'thin' dark 'bout this land . . . ever'thin' cruel and wicked. When you think your husband 'n son are comin' home and you liftin' a light and 'bout to holler 'em in. Then that thang rises up, and all sudden you hain't got *nothin'* no more. Tha's what Jack One Eye is."

26 • Robert McCammon

Neither Woodward nor Matthew knew how to respond to this wretched tale, but Shawcombe, who had continued slurping stew and pushing cornbread into his mouth, had his own response. "Aw, *shit!*" he cried out and grasped his jaw. His face was pinched with pain. "What's in this bloody bread, woman?" He reached into his mouth, probed around, and his fingers came out gripping a small dark brown object. "'Bout broke my tooth on this damn thing! Hell's bells!" Realization had struck him. "It *is* a fuckin' tooth!"

"I 'spect it's mine," Maude said. "Had some loose 'uns this mornin'." She grabbed it from his hand, and before he could say anything more she turned her back on them and went to her duties at the hearth.

"Damn ol' bitch is fallin' to pieces!" Shawcombe scowled. He swigged some rum, swished it around his mouth, and started in on his supper once more.

Woodward looked down at a chunk of cornbread that he'd placed in his stewbowl. He very politely cleared his throat. "I believe my appetite has been curtailed."

"What? You ain't hungry no more? Here, pass it over then!" Shawcombe grabbed the magistrate's bowl and dumped it all into his own. He had decided to disdain the use of his eating utensils in favor of his hands, stew dripping from his mouth and spattering his shirt. "Hey, clerk!" he grunted, as Matthew sat there deciding whether to risk chewing on a rotten tooth or not. "You want a go with the girl, I'll pay you ten pence to watch. Ain't like I'll see a virgin ridin' the wool every day."

"Sir?" Woodward's voice had sharpened. "I've already told you, the answer is no."

"You presumin' to speak for him, then? What are you, his damn father?"

"Not his father. But I am his guardian."

"What the hell does a twenty-year-old man need with a fuckin' guardian?"

"There are wolves everywhere in this world, Mr. Shawcombe," Woodward said, with a lift of his eyebrows. "A young man must be very careful not to fall into their company."

"Better the company of wolves than the cryin' of saints," Shawcombe said. "You might get *et* up, but you won't die of boredom."

The image of wolves feasting on human flesh brought another question to Matthew's mind. He pushed his stewbowl toward the tavern-keeper. "There was a magistrate travelling to Fount Royal from Charles Town two weeks ago. His name was Thymon Kingsbury. Did he happen to stop here?"

"No, ain't seen him," Shawcombe answered without pause in his gluttony.

"He never arrived at Fount Royal," Matthew went on. "It seems he might have stopped here, if he—"

"Prob'ly didn't get this far," Shawcombe interrupted. "Got hisself crowned in the head by a highwayman a league out of Charles Town, most like. Or maybe Jack One Eye got him. Man travellin' alone out here's a handshake away from Hell."

Matthew pondered this statement as he sat listening to the downpour on the roof. Water was streaming in, forming puddles on the boards. "I didn't say he *was* alone," Matthew said at last.

Shawcombe's chewing might have faltered a fraction. "You just spoke the one name, didn't you?"

"Yes. But I might not have mentioned his clerk."

"Well, shit!" Shawcombe slammed the bowl down. The fury had sparked in his eyes again. "Was he alone or *not?* And what does it matter?"

"He was alone," Matthew said evenly. "His clerk had taken ill the night before." He watched the candle's flame, a black thread of smoke rising from its orange blade. "But then, I don't suppose it really matters."

"No, it don't." Shawcombe darted a dark glance at Woodward. "He's got an itch to ask them questions, don't he?"

"He's an inquisitive young man," Woodward said. "And very bright, as well."

"Uh huh." Shawcombe's gaze turned on Matthew again, and

Matthew had the distinct and highly unsettling sensation of facing the ugly barrel of a primed and cocked blunderbuss. "Best take care somebody don't put out your lamp." Shawcombe held the penetrating stare for a few seconds, and then he started in on the food Matthew had pushed aside.

The two travellers excused themselves from the table when Shawcombe announced that Abner was going to play the fiddle for their "entertainment." Woodward had tried mightily to restrain his bodily functions, but now nature was shouting at him and he was obliged to put on his coat, take a lantern, and venture out into the weather.

Alone in the room, rain pattering from the roof and a single candle guttering, Matthew heard Abner's fiddle begin to *skreech*. It appeared they would be serenaded whether they liked it or not. To make matters worse, Shawcombe began to clap and holler in dubious counterpoint. A rat scuttled in a corner of the room, obviously as disturbed as was Matthew.

He sat down on the straw mattress and wondered how he would ever find sleep tonight, though he was exhausted from the trip. With rats in the room and two more caterwauling out by the hearth, it was likely to be a hard go. He decided he would create and solve some mathematics problems, in Latin of course. That usually helped him relax in difficult situations.

I don't suppose it really matters, he'd told Shawcombe in regard to Magistrate Kingsbury's travelling alone. But it seemed to Matthew that it did matter. To travel alone was exceptional and—as Shawcombe had correctly stated—foolhardy. Magistrate Kingsbury had been drunk every time Matthew had seen the man, and perhaps the liquor had enfeebled his brain. But Shawcombe had assumed that Kingsbury was alone. He had not asked *Was he alone* or *Who was travelling with him.* No, he'd made the statement: *Man travellin' alone . . .*

The fiddling's volume was reaching dreadful heights. Matthew sighed and shook his head at the indignity of the situation. At least, however, they had a roof over them for the night. Whether the roof held up all night was another question.

He could still smell the girl's scent.

It came upon him like an ambush. The scent of her was still there, whether in his nostrils or in his mind he wasn't sure.

Care for a toss?

Yes, Matthew thought. Math problems.

She's ripe as a fig puddin'.

And definitely in Latin.

The fiddle moaned and shrieked and Shawcombe began to stomp the floor. Matthew stared at the door, the girl's scent summoning him.

His mouth was dry. His stomach seemed to be tied up in an impossible knot. Yes, he thought, sleep tonight was going to be a hard go.

A very, very hard go.

three

MATTHEW'S EYES OPENED with a start. The light had dwindled to murky yellow, the candle having burned itself to a shrunken stub. Beside him on the harsh straw, Woodward was snoring noisily, mouth half ajar and chinflesh quivering. It took Matthew a few seconds to realize that there was a wetness on his left cheek. Then another drop of rainwater fell from the sodden ceiling onto his face and he abruptly sat up with a curse clenched behind his teeth.

The sudden movement made a rodent—a very large one, from the sound—squeal in alarm and scurry with a scrabbling of claws back into its nest in the wall. The noise of rain falling from the ceiling onto the floor was a veritable tenpence symphony. Matthew thought the time for building an ark was close at hand. Perhaps Abner was right about it being the end of the world; the year 1700 might never be marked on a calendar.

Be that as it may, he had to add his own water to the deluge. And a bit more as well, from the weight of his bowels. Damned if he wouldn't have to go out in that weather and squat down like a beast. Might try to hold it, but some things could not be constrained. He would relieve himself in the woods behind the barn like a civilized man while the rats did their business on the floor beside the bed. Next trip—God forbid—he would remember to pack a chamberpot.

He got out of the torture apparatus that passed as a bed. The tavern was quiet; it was a slim hour, to be sure. Distant thunder rumbled, the storm still lingering over the Carolina colony like a black-winged vulture. Matthew worked his feet into his shoes. He didn't have a heavy coat of his own, so over his flannel nightshirt he donned the magistrate's fearnaught, which was still damp from Woodward's recent trek behind the barn. The magistrate's boots, standing beside the bed, were clotted with mud and would bear the administrations of a coarse hog's bristle brush to clean. Matthew didn't want to take the single candle, as the weather would quickly extinguish it and the wall-dwellers might become emboldened by the dark. He would carry a covered lantern from the other room, he decided, and hope it threw enough illumination to avoid what Woodward had told him was "an unholy mess" out there. He might check on the horses, too, while he was so near the barn.

He placed his hand on the door latch and started to lift it when he heard the magistrate cease snoring and quietly moan. Glancing at the man, he saw Woodward's face wince and contort under the freckled dome of his bald head. Matthew paused, watching in the dim and flickering light. Woodward's mouth opened, his eyelids fluttering. *"Oh,"* the magistrate whispered, very clearly. His voice, though a whisper, was wracked with what Matthew could only describe as a pure and terrible agony. *"Ohhhhh,"* Woodward spoke, in his cage of nightmares. *"He's hurting Ann."* He drew a pained breath. *"Hurting he's hurting oh God Ann . . . hurting . . ."* He said something more, a jumble of a few words mingled with another low awful moan. His hands were gripping at the front of his nightshirt, his head pressed back into the straw. His mouth released a faint sound that might have been the memory of a cry, and then slowly his body relaxed and the snoring swelled up once again.

This was not something new to Matthew. Many nights the

magistrate walked in a dark field of pain, but what its source was he refused to talk about. Matthew had asked him once, five years ago, what the trouble had been, and Woodward's response had been a rebuke that Matthew's task was learning the trade of judicial clerking, and if he did not care to learn that trade, he could always find a home again at the orphans' refuge. The message—delivered with uncharacteristic vinegar—had been clear: whatever haunted the magistrate by night was not to be touched upon.

It had something to do with his wife in London, Matthew believed. Ann must be her name, though Woodward never mentioned that name in his waking hours and never volunteered any information about the woman. In fact, though Matthew had been in the company of Isaac Woodward since turning fifteen years old, he knew very little about the man's past life in England. This much he did know: Woodward had been a lawyer of some fame and had found success in the financial field as well, but what had caused his reversal of fortune and why he had left London for the roughhewn colonies remained mysteries. At least Matthew understood from his readings and from what Woodward said about London that it was a great city; he'd never set foot there, or in England either, for he'd been born aboard a ship on the Atlantic nineteen days out of Portsmouth.

Matthew quietly lifted the latch and left the room. In the darkened chamber beyond, small flames still gnawed at black bits of wood in the hearth, though the largest of the coals had been banked for the night. Bitter smoke lingered in the air. Hanging from hooks next to the fireplace were two lanterns, both made of hammered tin with small nail-holes punched in the metal for the light to pass through. One of the lanterns had a burnt candle stuck on its inner spike, so that was the illuminator Matthew chose. He found a pine twig on the floor, touched it alight in the remains of the fire, and transferred the flame to the candle's wick.

"What are *you* about? Eh?"

The voice, cutting the silence as it did, almost lifted Matthew out of his shoes. He twisted around and the lantern's meager but spreading light fell upon Will Shawcombe, who was sitting at one of the tables with a tankard before him and a black-scorched clay pipe clenched in his teeth.

"You up prowlin', boy?" Shawcombe's eyes were deepsunken and the skin of his face was daubed dirty yellow in the candle-light. A curl of smoke oozed from his mouth.

"I . . . have to go out," Matthew replied, still unnerved.

Shawcombe drew slowly on his pipe. "Well," he said, "mind your legs, then. Awful sloppy out there."

Matthew nodded. He started to turn toward the door, but Shawcombe spoke up again: "Your master wouldn't want to part with that fine waistc't, would he?"

"No, he wouldn't." Though he knew Shawcombe was baiting him, he couldn't let it go past. "Mr. Woodward is not my master."

"He ain't, huh? Well then, how come he tells you what you can do and what you cain't? Seems to me he's the master and you're the slave."

"Mr. Woodward looks out for my interest."

"Uh huh." Shawcombe tilted his head back and fired a dart of smoke at the ceiling. "Makes you cart the baggage, then he won't even let you dip your wick? All that shit about wolves and how you ought to be guarded. And you a twenty-year-old man! I'll bet he makes you scrape the mud off his boots, don't he?"

"I'm his clerk," Matthew said pointedly. "Not his valet."

"Does he clean his own boots, or do you?"

Matthew paused. The truth was that he did clean the magis-trate's boots, but it was a task he did without complaint. Some things over the years—such as organizing the judicial paperwork, keeping their living quarters in order, darning the clothes, pack-ing the trunks, and arranging sundry other small affairs—had fallen to Matthew simply because he was much more efficient at taking care of details.

"I knew you did it," Shawcombe went on. "Man like that's got blue blood in his veins. He don't want to get them hands too dirty, does he? Yeah, like I said, he's the master and you're the slave."

"You can believe what you like."

"I believe what I *see*," Shawcombe said. "Come over here, lemme show you somethin'. You bein' a slave and all, you might well want to have a look." Before Matthew could decline and go on his way, Shawcombe lifted his right fist and opened it. "Here's somethin' you ain't never seen before and ain't like to see again."

The lantern's light sparked off the surface of a gold coin. "Here!" Shawcombe offered it to Matthew. "I'll even let you hold it."

Against his better judgment—and the urge to pee pressing on his bladder—Matthew approached the man and took the coin from him. He held it close to the lantern and inspected the engraving. It was a well-worn piece, much of the lettering rubbed off, but at its center was a cross that separated the figures of two lions and two castles. Matthew could make out the faint letters *Charles II* and *Dei Grat* around the coin's rim.

"Know what that is?" Shawcombe prodded.

"Charles the Second is the King of Spain," Matthew said. "So this must be Spanish."

"That's right. Spanish. You know what that means, don't you?"

"It means a Spaniard was recently here?"

"Close. I got this from a dead redskin's pouch. Now what's a redskin doin' with a Spanish gold piece?" He didn't wait for Matthew to venture a guess. "Means there's a damn Spanish spy 'round here somewhere. Stirrin' up some trouble with the Indians, most like. You know them Spaniards are sittin' down there in the Florida country, not seventy leagues from here. They got spies all in the colonies, spreadin' the word that any black crow who flies from his master and gets to the Florida country can be a free man. You ever heard such a thing? Them Spaniards are promisin' the same thing to criminals, murderers, every like of John Badseed."

He swiped the coin from Matthew's hand. "If you was to run to Florida and your master was to want you back, them Spaniards would jus' laugh at him. Same's true of somebody done a stealin' or a murder: get to Florida, them Spaniards would protect him. I tell you, once them blackamoors start runnin' to Florida by the scores and gettin' turned into free men, this world's gonna roast in Hell's fires." Shawcombe dropped the coin into the tankard, which still had liquid in it, judging from the sound of the wet *plop,* then sat smoking his pipe with his arms crossed over his chest. "Yeah," he said with a knowing nod, "a Spanish spy's out there, payin' the redskins to get up to some mischief. Hell, he might even be livin' in Fount Royal, an Englishman turned black-coat!"

"Possibly." Matthew's need for relief was now undeniable. "Excuse me, I have to go."

"Go on, then. Like I say, watch where you step." Shawcombe let Matthew get to the door and then said, "Hey, clerk! You sure he wouldn't part with that waistc't?"

"Absolutely sure."

Shawcombe grunted, his head wreathed with blue pipesmoke. "I didn't think so," he said in a quiet voice.

Matthew unlatched the door and went out. The storm had quietened somewhat, the rain falling now as misty drizzle. In the sky, though, distant lightning flashed through the clouds. The mud clasped hold of Matthew's shoes. A half-dozen steps through the mire, Matthew had to lift up his nightshirt and urinate where he stood. Decorum, however, dictated that he relieve his bowels in the woods behind the barn, for there were no leaves or pine needles nearby with which to clean himself. When he finished, he followed the lantern's glow past the barn, his shoes sinking up to the ankles in a veritable swamp. Once beyond the forest's edge, he gathered a handful of wet leaves and then crouched down to attend to his business. The lightning danced overhead, he was soaked, muddy, and miserable, and all in all it was a nasty moment. Such things, however, could not be rushed no matter how fervently one tried.

After what seemed an eternity, during which Matthew cursed Shawcombe and swore again to pack a chamberpot on their next journey, the deed was completed and the wet leaves put to use.

He straightened up and held the lantern out to find his path back to the so-called tavern. Once more the waterlogged ground opened and closed around his shoes, his kneejoints fairly popping as he worked his legs loose from the quagmire. He intended to check on the horses before he returned to the so-called bed, where he could look forward to the magistrate's snoring, the rustling of rats, and rainwater dripping on his—

He fell.

It was so fast he hardly knew what was happening. His initial thought was that the earth had sucked his legs out from under him. His second thought, which he barely had an eyeblink of time to act upon, was to keep the lantern from being extinguished. So even as he fell on his belly and the mud and water splashed around him and over the magistrate's fearnaught coat, he was able to lift his arm up and protect the light. He spat mud out of his mouth, his face aflame with anger, and said, "Damn it to Hell!" Then he tried to sit up, mud all over his face, his sight most blinded. He found this task harder than it should have been. His legs, he realized, had been seized by the earth. The very ground had collapsed under his shoes, and now his feet were entangled in something that felt like a bramble bush down in the swampy muck. Careful of the lantern, he wrenched his right foot loose but whatever held his left foot would not yield. Lightning flared again and the rain started falling harder. He was able to get his right leg under him, and then he braced himself as best he could and jerked his left leg up and out of the morass.

There was a brittle cracking sound. His leg was free.

But as he shone the lantern down upon his leg, Matthew realized he'd stepped into something that had come out of the earth still embracing his ankle.

At first he didn't know what it was. His foot had gone right through what looked like a mud-dripping cage of some kind. He could see the splintered edges, one of which had scraped a bleeding gouge in his leg.

The rain was slowly washing mud off the object. As he stared at it, another flash of lightning helped aid his recognition of what held him, and his heart felt gripped by a freezing hand.

Matthew's anatomy studies did not have to be recollected to tell him that he'd stepped into and through a human-sized rib cage. A section of spinal cord was still attached, and on it clung bits of grayish-brown material that could only be decayed flesh.

He let out a mangled cry and began frantically kicking at the thing with his other shoe. The bones cracked, broke, and fell away, and when the last of the rib cage and vertebrae had been kicked loose Matthew crawled away from it as fast as the mud would allow. Then he sat up amid leaves and pine needles and pressed his back against a treetrunk, the breath rasping in his lungs and his eyes wide and shocked.

He thought, numbly, how distraught the magistrate was going to be over the fearnaught coat. Such coats were not easy to come by. It was ruined, no doubt. *A rib cage. Human-sized.* Ruined beyond all hope of cleaning. Damn this rain and mud, damn this wild land, and damn Shawcombe and the chamberpot he should have had.

A rib cage, Matthew thought. Rain was running down his face now. It was cold, and the chill helped him organize his mind. Of course, the rib cage might've belonged to an animal. Mightn't it?

The lantern was muddy but—thank providence!—the candle was still burning. He stood up and made his way over to the broken bones. There he knelt down and shone the light upon them, trying to determine what animal they might've come from. While he was so occupied, he heard a soft slithering sound somewhere to his right. He angled the lantern toward it and in a few seconds saw that a gaping hole some four feet across had opened in the boggy ground; the slithering sound was mud sliding down its sides.

Matthew thought it might have been what had collapsed under his feet and caused him to fall, for the earth itself was rebelling against this incessant downpour. He stood up, eased to the edge of the hole, and directed the lantern's light down into it.

At first he saw what looked like a pile of sticks lying in the hole. Everything was muddy and tangled together into an indistinct mess. The longer he stared, however, the more clear came the picture.

Yes. Horribly clear.

He could make out the bones of an arm, thrown across what might've been a half-decayed, naked torso. A gray kneejoint jutted up from the muck. There was a hand, the fingers shriveled to the bones, grasping upward as if in a begging gesture for help. And there was a head, too; mostly a mud-covered skull, but some of the flesh remained. Matthew, his mouth dry of saliva and his heart pounding, could see how the top of the skull had been crushed inward by a savage blow.

A hammer could've delivered such a death, he realized. A hammer or a rat-killing mallet.

Perhaps there were more corpses than one in that burial pit. Perhaps there were four or five, thrown in and entangled together. It was hard to tell how many, but there were a great number of bones. None of the bodies seemed to have been buried with their clothing.

Hey, clerk! You sure he wouldn't part with that waistc't?

Matthew felt the earth shift and slide around his feet. There was a noise like a dozen serpents hissing and, as the ground began to collapse around him, Matthew saw more human bones being pushed up to the surface like the muddy spars of ships wrecked on vicious shoals. Dazed as if locked in a nightmare, Matthew stood at the center of the sinking earth as evidence of murders revealed themselves under his shoes. Only when he was about to be sucked under into an embrace with the dead did he turn away, pulling his feet up and struggling toward the barn.

He fought his way through the rain in the direction of the tavern. The immediacy of his mission gave flight to his heels. He slipped and fell once again before he reached the door, and this time the lantern splashed into a puddle and the candle went out. Red mud covered him from head to toe. When he burst through the door, he saw that Shawcombe was no longer sitting at the table, though the tankard was still in its same position and the bitter-smelling pipesmoke yet wafted in the air. Matthew restrained the urge to shout a warning to the magistrate, and he got into the room and latched the door behind him. Woodward was still stretched out and soundly asleep.

Matthew shook the man's shoulders. "Wake up! Do you hear me?" His voice, though pinched with fright, was strong enough to pierce the veil of the magistrate's sleep. Woodward began to rouse himself, his eyelids opening and the bleary eyes struggling to focus. "We have to get out!" Matthew urged. "Right now! We've got to—"

"Good God in Heaven!" Woodward croaked. He sat upright. "What happened to you?"

"Just listen!" Matthew said. "I found bodies out there! Skeletons, buried behind the barn! I think Shawcombe's a murderer!"

"*What?* Have you lost your senses?" Woodward sniffed the younger man's breath. "It's that damn Indian ale, isn't it?"

"No, I found the bodies down in a hole! Shawcombe may have even killed Kingsbury and thrown him in there!" He saw the magistrate's expression of bewilderment. "Listen to me! We have to leave as fast as we—"

"Gentlemen?"

It was Shawcombe. His voice beyond the door made Matthew's blood go cold. There came the rap of knuckles on the wood. "Gentlemen, is all well?"

"I think he means to kill us tonight!" Matthew whispered to the magistrate. "He wants your waistcoat!"

"My waistcoat," Woodward repeated. His mouth was dry. He looked at the door and then back to Matthew's mud-splattered face. If anything was true in this insane world, it was that Matthew did not lie, nor was he servant to flights of fantasy. The shiny fear in the younger man's eyes was all too real, and Woodward's own heart began beating rapidly.

"Gents?" Now Shawcombe's mouth was close to the door. "I heard you talkin'. Any trouble in there?"

"No trouble!" Woodward replied. He put a finger to his

lips, directing Matthew to be silent. "We're very well, thank you!"

There was a few seconds' pause. Then: "Clerk, you left the front door open," Shawcombe said. "How come you to do that?"

Now came one of the most terrible decisions of Isaac Woodward's life. His saber, as rusted and blunt as it was, remained in the wagon. He had neither a dirk nor a prayer to protect them. If Shawcombe was indeed a killer, the time had arrived for him to deliver death. Woodward looked at the room's single shuttered window and made the decision: they would have to leave everything behind—trunks, wigs, clothing, all of it—to save their skins. He motioned Matthew toward the window and then he eased up out of the damp straw.

"What's got your tongue, boy?" Shawcombe demanded. His voice was turning ugly. "I asked you a question!"

"Just a moment!" Woodward opened one of the trunks, lifted a pair of shirts, and put his hands on the golden-threaded waistcoat. He could not leave this, even with a murderer breathing down his neck. There was no time to work his feet into his boots nor grab his tricorn hat. Grasping the waistcoat, he straightened up and motioned for Matthew to unlatch the window's shutter.

Matthew did. The latch *thunked* out of its groove and he pushed the shutter open into the falling rain.

"They're comin' out the winda!" Uncle Abner yelled, standing just beneath it. Matthew saw he was holding a lantern in one hand and a pitchfork in the other.

Behind Woodward, there was a tremendous crash as the door burst inward. He twisted around, his face bleached of blood, as Shawcombe came across the threshold with a grin that showed his peglike teeth. Behind him, Maude carried a double candlestick that held two burning tapers, her white hair wild and her wrinkled face demonic.

"Oh, oh!" Shawcombe said mockingly. "Looky here, Maude! They're tryin' to get gone without payin' their bill!"

"What's the meaning of this outrage?" Woodward snapped,

putting on a mask of anger to hide his true emotion, which was raw and naked terror.

Shawcombe laughed and shook his head. "Well," he said, lifting up his right hand and inspecting the mallet with which Maude had earlier crushed the black rat, "the meanin' of it, you bloody ass, is that you and the clerk ain't goin' nowhere tonight. 'Cept Hell, I reckon." His eyes found the prize. "Ahhhhh, there 'tis. Give it here." He thrust out his grimy left hand.

Woodward looked at the dirty fingers and then at the waistcoat he held so dearly. His gaze returned to Shawcombe's greedy hand; then Woodward lifted his chin and took a long breath. "Sir," he said, "you'll have to kill me to take it."

Shawcombe laughed again, more of a piggish grunt this time. "Oh, indeed I'll kill you! " His eyes narrowed slightly. "I 'spected you'd go out like a mouse 'stead of a man, though. 'Spected you might give a squeal like that other little drunk titmouse did when I whacked him." He abruptly swung the mallet through the air past Woodward's face, and the magistrate flinched but did not retreat. "Gonna make me take it, huh? Allrighty then, ain't no skin off my bum."

"They'll send someone else," Matthew spoke up. "From Charles Town. They'll send—"

"Another fuckin' magistrate? Let 'em, then! They keep sendin' 'em, I'll keep killin' 'em!"

"They'll send the militia," he said, which was not nearly as fearsome as it sounded and was probably untrue anyway.

"The *militia!*" Shawcombe's teeth gleamed in the murky light. "They're gonna send the militia all the way from Charles Town? But they didn't come lookin' for Kingsbury or none of them others I laid to rest, did they?" His grin began to twist into a snarl. He lifted the mallet up to a striking position. "I think I'm gonna kill you first, you skinny son of a bi—"

Woodward made his move.

He whipped the waistcoat sharply across Shawcombe's eyes and rushed the man, grabbing his wrist before the mallet could begin its descent. Shawcombe hollered a curse and Maude started shrieking, a sound that surely scared the wall-dwelling rats into flight. Shawcombe's left hand came up—a fist now instead of a palm—and smacked into the magistrate's chin. Woodward's head rocked back, his eyes clouding, but he kept his grip on Shawcombe's right wrist. *"Abner! Abner!"* the old woman was yelling. Woodward fired his own blow at Shawcombe's face, a fist that grazed the man's cheekbone when Shawcombe saw it coming and twisted to avoid it. Then Shawcombe clamped his free hand around the magistrate's throat and squeezed as they fought in the little room, one trying to get the mallet into action and the other intent on restraining it.

They staggered back against the bed. Shawcombe's eye caught a movement to his side and he looked in that direction a second before Matthew slammed him in the head with one of the magistrate's boots he'd picked up from the floor. Another swing of the boot struck Shawcombe on the shoulder, and now Matthew could see a glint of desperation in the man's eyes. Shawcombe, who had realized that the magistrate was more formidable than he appeared, gave a roar like an enraged beast and drove his knee upward into Woodward's genitals. Woodward cried out and doubled over, clutching himself. Suddenly the mallet was free. Shawcombe lifted it high, a two-handed grip, in preparation to bash in the back of the other man's skull.

"No!" said Matthew. The boot was already swinging forward, and with every ounce of strength he could muster, Matthew hit Shawcombe across the bridge of the nose with its wooden heel.

The noise of the blow was like an axeblade striking oak; somewhere in it was the *crunch* of Shawcombe's nose breaking. Shawcombe gave a strangled cry and stumbled backward, intent on grabbing at his wounded face instead of seeing the color of the magistrate's brain. Matthew stepped forward to wrest the mallet away, but suddenly he was attacked by the shrieking old hag, who grabbed at his coat collar with one hand and with the other shoved the candleflames toward his eyes.

Matthew reflexively struck at her, hitting her in the face, but he had to retreat to get away from her, and now Abner was coming into the room with his lantern and his pitchfork.

"Kill 'em!" Shawcombe whined, a nasal sound; he'd met the wall and slid down to the floor, his hands clamped across his face and the mallet lying beside him. Blood, black in the ochre light, was leaking between his fingers. "Abner! Kill 'em both!"

The old man, rain dripping from his beard, lifted the pitchfork and stepped toward Woodward, who was still groaning and trying to straighten himself up.

Matthew was aware of the open window behind him. His mind worked, faster than his body could react. He said, "Thou shalt not kill."

Abner stopped in his tracks. He blinked as if stunned. "What?"

"Thou shalt not kill," Matthew repeated. "It's in the Bible. You do know the Lord's word, don't you?"

"I . . . the Lord's word? Yeah, I reckon I—"

"Abner! Goddamn it, kill 'em!" Shawcombe bawled.

"It's in the Bible, is it not? Mr. Woodward, would you go out the window, please?" The magistrate had tears of pain streaming down his face. He'd regained enough sense, however, to realize he should move quickly.

"Shit! Lemme up!" Shawcombe tried getting to his feet, but both eyes were already turning purplish and starting to swell. He had a harder time than he'd expected finding his balance, and it yet eluded him. He sank back down to the floor. "Maude! Don't let 'em get out!"

"Gimme 'at damn pigsticka!" Maude grabbed the pitchfork and tugged at it, but Abner resisted her.

"The boy's right," Abner said; his voice was calm, as if a great truth had been revealed to him. "It's in the Bible. Thou shalt not kill. That's the Lord's word."

"Ya damn fool! Give it 'ere!" Maude tried, unsuccessfully, to wrench the pitchfork out of his hands.

"Hurry," Matthew said, as he helped the magistrate over the

windowsill and out. Woodward fell into the mud like a flour sack. Then Matthew started climbing out.

"You ain't gettin' far!" Shawcombe promised, his voice tight with pain. "We'll hunt ya down!"

Matthew glanced back into the room to make sure Maude didn't have the pitchfork. Abner was still holding on to it, his face furrowed with thought. Matthew figured the old man wouldn't remain in that state of religious piety much longer, though; he was as much of a murderer as the other two, and Matthew had only rolled a stone in his path. Before Matthew let go of the sill, he saw another figure standing in the doorway. It was the girl, her face pale, the dark and dirty hair hanging in her eyes. Her arms were clasped around herself, a protective gesture. He had no idea if she was as mad as the rest of them, or what would become of her; he knew for certain, though, that she was beyond his help.

"Go on and run like a dog!" Shawcombe taunted. The blood was dripping between his fingers to the floor, his eyes becoming narrow, puffed slits. "If you're thinkin' to get that sword was in your wagon, it's done been got! Damn blade ain't sharp enough to cut a fart! So go on and see how far ya get!"

Matthew released the sill and jumped down into the mud beside Woodward, who was struggling to his feet. Maude began flailing Abner with curses, and Matthew knew they'd better put as much distance between them and the tavern as they could before the pursuit started. "Can you run?" he asked the magistrate.

"Run?" Woodward looked at him incredulously. "You might ask if I could *crawl!*"

"Whatever you can do, you'd best do it," Matthew said. "I think we should get into the woods, first thing."

"What about the horses and the wagon? We're not just going to leave them here!"

"There's no time. I expect they'll be after us in a few minutes. If they come at us with an axe or a musket—"

"Say no more." With an effort, Woodward began slogging toward the woods across the road from the tavern. Matthew followed close at his side, watchful in case he staggered.

The lightning flashed, thunder clapped, and rain fell upon their heads. Before they reached the forest, Matthew looked back at the tavern but saw no one yet following. He hoped Shawcombe had lost—at least for the moment—the desire to rouse himself and come out in this storm; he doubted if the old man and woman were very self-motivated without him. Probably Shawcombe was too busy dealing with his own pain to inflict it on anyone else. Matthew thought about going back for the horses, but he'd never saddled and bridled a mount in his life and the situation was volatile. No, he decided, it was best to head into the forest and follow the road in the direction they'd been going.

"We left everything," Woodward said disconsolately as their feet sank into the quagmire of mud and pine needles at the forest's edge. "Everything! My clothes, my wigs, my judicial robes! Dear Christ, my *waistcoat!* That animal has my waistcoat!"

"Yes, sir," Matthew answered. "But he doesn't have your life."

"And a sorry thing that will be, from this day forward! Ahhhhh, that man almost made me a soprano!" He peered into the utter darkness that lay ahead. "Where are we going?"

"Fount Royal."

"What?" The magistrate faltered. "Has that man's madness impressed you?"

"Fount Royal is at the end of the road," Matthew said. "If we keep walking, we might be there in a few hours." An optimistic appraisal, he thought. This swampy earth and the pelting rain would slow them considerably, but it would also hinder their pursuers. "We can return here with their militia and retrieve our belongings. I think it's our only choice."

Woodward was silent. It was indeed their only choice. And if he could get his waistcoat back—and see Shawcombe kicking at the end of a noose—it would be worth a few hours of this vile indignity. He could not help thinking that once a man fell into the pit of disfavor with God, the hole was bottomless. He had no shoes, his balls were bruised and aching, his head was naked to the world, and his nightshirt was sopping and covered with mud. But at least they did both have their lives, which was more than he could say of Thymon Kingsbury. *Execution is not one of my duties,* he'd told Shawcombe. Well, that just might have to be amended.

He would come back here and get that waistcoat if it was the last thing he did on this earth.

Matthew was moving a little faster than the magistrate, and he paused to wait for Woodward. In time, the night and the storm swallowed them up.

four

A T LAST THE AFTERNOON SUN had cleaved a path through the clouds and shone now on the drenched earth. The weather had warmed considerably, compared to the chill of the night before. This was more like the usual May, though the clouds—dark gray and swollen with more ghastly rain—were still looming, slowly converging together from all points of the compass to overtake the sun again.

"Go on," said the heavyset, lavishly bewigged man who stood at a second-floor window of his house, overlooking the vista. "I am listening."

The second man in the room—which was a study lined with shelves and leather-bound books, a gold-and-red Persian rug on the pinewood floor—sat on a bench before a desk of African mahogany, a ledger book open in his lap. He was the visitor here, however, as the bewigged man had recently lifted his 220-pound bulk from his own chair, which stood on the other side of the desk facing the bench. The visitor cleared his throat and placed a finger upon a line written in the ledger. "The cotton plants have again failed to take root," he said. "Likewise the tobacco seedlings." He hesitated before he delivered the next blow. "I regret to say that two-thirds of the apple trees have been blighted."

"Two-*thirds?*" said the man at the window, without turning away from the view. His wig, a majesty of white curls, flowed down around the shoulders of his dark blue, brass-buttoned suit. He wore white ruffles at his sleeves, white stockings on his thick calves, and polished black shoes with silver buckles.

"Yes, sir. The same is true of the plum trees, and about half of the pears. At present the blackcherries have been spared, but it is Goode's opinion that a parasite of some kind may have laid eggs in all the fruit trees. The pecans and the chestnuts are so far unblemished, but the fields have been washed to the extent that many of their roots are now aboveground and vulnerable to harm." The speaker halted in his recitation of agricultural maladies and pushed his spectacles up a little further on his nose. He was a man of medium height and stature, also of medium age and appearance. He had light brown hair, a lofty forehead, and pale blue eyes, and he bore the air of a wearied accountant. His clothes, in contrast to the other man's finery, consisted of a plain white shirt, brown cloth waistcoat, and tan trousers.

"Continue, Edward," the man at the window urged quietly. "I am up to the hearing."

"Yes, sir." The speaker, Edward Winston, returned his attention to the items quilled in the ledgerbook. "Goode has made a suggestion regarding the fruit trees that he felt important for me to pass to you." Again, he paused.

"And that suggestion is?"

Winston lifted his hand and slowly ran two fingers across his mouth before he went on. The man at the window waited, his broad back held straight and rigid. Winston said, "Goode suggests they be burned."

"How many trees? Only those afflicted, yes?"

"No, sir. All."

There was a long silence. The man at the window pulled in his breath and let it slowly out, and when he did so his shoulders lost their square set and began to sag. "*All,*" he repeated.

"Goode believes that burning is the only way to kill the parasite. He says it will do no good in the long run to destroy only the trees presently showing ill. Furthermore, he believes that the site of the fruit orchards should be moved and the earth itself cleansed with seawater and ashes."

The man at the window made a soft noise that had some pain in it. When he spoke, his voice was weak. "How many trees are to be burned, then?"

Winston consulted his ledger. "Eighty-four apple, fifty-two plum, seventy-eight blackcherry, forty-four pear."

"And so we start over yet again, is that it?"

"I fear it is, sir. As I always say, it's better to be safe than sorry."

"*Damn,*" the man at the window whispered. He placed his hands on the sill and stared down through red-rimmed hazel eyes at his endangered dream and creation. "Is *she* cursing us, Edward?"

"I don't know, sir," answered Winston, in all candor.

Robert Bidwell, the man at the window, was forty-seven years old and scarred with the marks of suffering. His deeply lined face was strained, his forehead furrowed, more lines bracketing his thin-lipped mouth and cutting across his chin. Many of those markings had afflicted him in the past five years, since the day he had been presented with official papers deeding him 990 acres on the coast of the Carolina colony. But this was his dream, and there before him, under the ochre sunlight that slanted through the ominously building clouds, lay his creation.

He'd christened it Fount Royal. The reason for the name was twofold: one, to thank King William and Queen Mary for their fount of faith in his abilities as a leader and manager; and two, as a geographic waypoint for future commerce. Some sixty yards from the front gate of Bidwell's house—which was the sole two-story structure in the community—was the fount itself: an oblong-shaped spring of fresh, cold aquamarine-colored water that covered an expanse of nearly three acres. Bidwell had learned from a surveyor who'd been mapping the area several years ago and who'd also plumbed the spring that it was more than forty feet deep. The fount was of vital importance to the settlement; in this country of salt marshes and stagnant black ponds, the spring meant that fresh water would always be in abundance.

Bulrushes grew in the spring's shallows, and hardy wildflowers that had endured the intemperate chill grew in clumps on the grassy banks. As the spring was the center of Fount Royal, all streets—their muddy surfaces made firmer by sand and crushed oyster shells—radiated from it. The streets were four in number, and had been named by Bidwell: Truth ran to the east, Industry to the west, Harmony to the north, and Peace to the south. Along those streets were the whitewashed clapboard houses, red barns, fenced pastures, lean-to sheds, and workshops that made up the settlement.

The blacksmith toiled at his furnace on Industry Street; on Truth Street stood the schoolhouse, across from the general store; Harmony Street was host to three churchhouses: Anglican, Lutheran, and Presbyterian; the cemetery on Harmony Street was not large, but was unfortunately well-planted; Peace Street led past the slave quarters and Bidwell's own stable to the forest that stood just short of the tidewater swamp and beyond that the sea; Industry Street continued to the orchards and farmland where Bidwell hoped someday to see bounties of apples, pears, cotton, corn, beans, and tobacco; on Truth Street also stood the gaol, where *she* was kept, and near it the building that served as a meeting-house; the surgeon-barber was located on Harmony Street, next to Van Gundy's Publick Tavern; and a number of other small enterprises, scattered about the fledgling town in hopes that Bidwell's dream of a southernmost city might come to fruition.

Of the 990 acres Bidwell had purchased, little more than two hundred were actually built upon, tilled, or used as pasture. A wall made of logs, their uptilted ends shaved and honed by axes into sharpened points, had been constructed around the entire settlement, orchards and all, as protection against Indians. The only way in or out—notwithstanding the seacoast, though a watchtower built in the forest there was occupied day and night by a musket-armed militiaman—was through the main gate that opened onto

Harmony Street. A watchtower also stood beside the gate, allowing its militiaman a view of anyone approaching on the road.

So far in the existence of Fount Royal, the Indian element had offered no trouble; in fact, they'd been invisible, and Bidwell might have questioned whether there were indeed redskins within a hundred miles, if Solomon Stiles hadn't discovered strange symbols painted on the trunk of a pinetree during a hunting expedition. Stiles, a trapper and hunter of some regard, had explained to Bidwell that the Indians were marking the wilderness beyond the tree as territory not to be trespassed upon. Bidwell had decided not to press the issue, though by the royal deed all that land belonged to him. No, best to let the redskins alone until it was time to smoke them out.

Looking down upon the current decrepit condition of his dream hurt Bidwell's eyes. There were too many empty houses, too many gardens gone to weed, too many broken fences. Untended pigs lay about in the muck and dogs wandered, snapping and surly. In the past month five hard-built structures—all deserted at the time—had been reduced to piles of ash by midnight fires, and a burnt smell still tainted the air. Bidwell was aware of whom the residents blamed for these fires. If not her hand directly, then the hands—or claws, as the case might be—of the infernal beasts and imps she invoked. Fire was their language, and they were making their statements very clear.

His dream was dying. *She* was killing it. Though the bars of her cell and the thick walls of the gaol confined her body, her spirit—her phantasm—escaped to dance and cavort with her unholy lover, to plot more wreckage and woe to Bidwell's dream. To banish such a hydra into the judgment of the wilderness was not enough; she had plainly said she would not go, that no power on earth could make her leave her home. If Bidwell hadn't been a lawful man, he might have had her hanged at the beginning and been done with it. Now it was a matter for the court, and God help the judge who must sit in attendance.

No, he thought grimly. God help Fount Royal.

"Edward," Bidwell said, "what is our present population?"

"The exact figure? Or an estimate?"

"An estimate will do."

"One hundred or thereabouts," Winston offered. "But that will change before the week is done. Dorcas Chester is ill onto death."

"Yes, I know. This damp will fill up our cemetery ere long."

"Speaking of the cemetery . . . Alice Barrow has taken to bed as well."

"Alice Barrow?" Bidwell turned from the window to face the other man. "Is she ailing?"

"I had cause to visit John Swaine this morning," Winston said. "According to Cass Swaine, Alice Barrow has told several persons that she's been suffering dreams of the Dark Man. The dreams have so terrified her that she will not leave her bed."

Bidwell gave an exasperated snort. "And so she's spreading them about like rancid butter on scones, is that it?"

"It seems to be. Madam Swaine tells me the dreams have to do with the cemetery. More than that, she was too fearful herself to say."

"Good Christ!" Bidwell said, the color rising in his jowls. "Mason Barrow is a sensible man! Can't he control his wife's tongue?" He took two strides to the desk and slapped a hand down upon its surface. "This is the kind of stupidity that's destroying my town, Edward! *Our* town, I mean! But by God, it'll be ruins in six months if these tongues don't cease wagging!"

"I didn't mean to upset you, sir," Winston said. "I'm only recounting what I thought you should know."

"*Look* out there!" Bidwell waved toward the window, where the rain-swollen clouds were beginning to seal off the sunlight once again. "Empty houses and empty fields! Last May we had more than three hundred people! Three *hundred!* And now you say we're down to *one* hundred?"

"Or thereabouts," Winston corrected.

"Yes, and how many will Alice Barrow's tongue send running? Damn it, I cannot stand by waiting for a judge to arrive from Charles Town! What can I do about this, Edward?"

Winston's face was damp with perspiration, due to the room's humid nature. He pushed his spectacles up on his nose. "You have no choice but to wait, sir. The legal system must be obeyed."

"And what legal system does the Dark Man obey?" Bidwell planted both hands on the desk and leaned toward Winston, his own face sweating and florid. "What rules and regulations constrain his mistress? Damn my eyes, I can't watch my investment in this land be destroyed by some spectral bastard who shits doom in people's dreams! I did not build a shipping business by sitting on my bum quaking like a milksop maid." This last had been said through gritted teeth. "Come along or not as you please, Edward! I'm off to silence Alice Barrow's prattling!" He stalked toward the door without waiting for his town manager, who hurriedly closed his ledger and stood up to follow, like a pug after a barrel-chested bulldog.

They descended what to the ordinary citizens of Fount Royal was a wonder to behold: a staircase. It was without a railing, however, as the master carpenter who had overseen the construction of the stairs had died of the bloody flux before its completion. The walls of Bidwell's mansion were decorated with English pastoral paintings and tapestries, which upon close inspection would reveal the treacheries of mildew. Water stains marred many of the whitewashed ceilings, and rat droppings lay in darkened niches. As Bidwell and Winston came down the stairs, their boots loudly clomping, they became the focus of Bidwell's housekeeper, who was always alert to her master's movements. Emma Nettles was a broad-shouldered, heavyset woman in her mid-thirties whose hatchet-nosed and square-chinned face might've scared a redskin warrior into the arms of Jesus. She stood at the foot of the stairs, her ample body clad in her customary black cassock, a stiff white cap enforcing the regimented lie of her oiled and severely combed brown hair.

"May I he'p you, sir?" she asked, her voice carrying a distinct Scottish burr. In her formidable shadow stood one of the servant girls.

"I'm away to business," Bidwell replied curtly, plucking from a rack on the wall a navy blue tricorn hat, one of several in a variety of colors to match his costumes. He pushed the hat down on his head, which was no simplicity due to the height of his wig. "I shall have toss 'em boys and jonakin for my supper," he told her. "Mind the house." He strode past her and the servant girl toward the front door, with Winston in pursuit.

"As I always do, sir," the madam Nettles said quietly an instant after the door had closed behind the two men, her flesh-hooded eyes as dark as her demeanor.

Bidwell paused only long enough to unlatch the ornate white-painted iron gate—six feet tall and shipped at great expense from Boston—that separated his mansion from the rest of Fount Royal, then continued along Peace Street at a pace that tested Winston's younger and slimmer legs. The two men passed the spring, where Cecilia Semmes was filling a bucket full of water; she started to offer a greeting to Bidwell, but she saw his expression of angry resolve and thought it best to keep her tongue sheltered.

The last of the miserly sunlight was obscured by clouds even as Bidwell and Winston strode past the community's brass sundial, set atop a wooden pedestal at the conjunction of Peace, Harmony, Industry, and Truth streets. Tom Bridges, guiding his oxcart to his farmhouse and pasture on Industry, called a good afternoon to Bidwell, but the creator of Fount Royal did not break stride nor acknowledge the courtesy. "Afternoon to you, Tom!" Winston replied, after which he had to conserve his wind for keeping up with his employer as Bidwell took a turn onto the easterly path of Truth.

Two pigs occupied a large mud puddle in the midst of the street, one of them snorting with glee as he rooted deeper into the mire while a mongrel dog blotched with mange stood nearby barking his indignation. David Cutter, Hiram Abercrombie, and Arthur Dawson stood not far from the pigs and puddle, smoking their clay pipes and engrossed in what appeared to be stern conversation. "Good day, gentlemen!" Bidwell said as he passed them, and Cutter removed his pipe from his mouth and called out, "Bidwell! When's that judge gettin' here?"

"In due time, sir, in due time!" Winston answered, still walking.

"I'm talkin' to the string puller, not the puppet!" Cutter fired back. "We're gettin' tired a' waitin' for this thing to be resolved! You ask me, they ain't gonna never send us a judge!"

"We have the assurances of their councilmen, sir!" Winston said; his cheeks were stinging from the insult.

"Damn their assurances!" Dawson spoke up. He was a spindly red-haired man who served as Fount Royal's shoemaker. "They might assure us the rain will cease, too, but what of it?"

"Keep walking, Edward," Bidwell urged sotto voce.

"We've had a gutful of this dawdlin'!" Cutter said. "She needs to be hanged and done with it!"

Abercrombie, a farmer who'd been one of the first settlers to respond to Bidwell's broadsheets advertising the creation of Fount Royal, threw in his two shillings: "The sooner she hangs, the safer we'll all sleep! God save us from bein' burnt up in our beds!"

"Yes, yes," Bidwell muttered, lifting a hand into the air as a gesture of dismissal. His stride had quickened, sweat gleaming on his face and darkening the cloth at his armpits. Behind him, Winston was breathing hard; the air's sullen dampness had misted his spectacles. With his next step, his right foot sank into a pile of moldering horse apples that Bidwell had just deftly avoided.

"If they send us anybody," Cutter shouted as a last riposte, "it'll be a lunatic they plucked from the asylum up there!"

"That man speaks knowingly of asylums," Bidwell said, to no one in particular. They passed the schoolhouse and next to it Schoolmaster Johnstone's house. A pasture where a small herd of cattle grazed stood next to Lindstrom's farmhouse and barn, and then there was the meeting-house with a flagpole before it from which drooped the British colors. Just a little further on, and Bidwell's pace hastened even faster; there loomed the rough and windowless hardwood walls of the gaol, its single entrance door secured with a chain and iron lock. In front of the gaol was a pillory where miscreants who thieved, blasphemed, or otherwise incurred the wrath of the town council found themselves bound and sometimes pelted with the same substance that currently weighted Winston's right boot.

Past the gaol, a number of houses with barns, gardens, and small fieldplots occupied the last portion of Truth Street. Some of the houses were empty, and one of them had dwindled to a charred shell. Weeds and thorns had overtaken the forlorn gardens, the fields now more frightful swamp than fruitful earth. Bidwell walked to the door of a house almost at the very end of the street and knocked solidly while Winston stood nearby, blotting the sweat from his face with a shirtsleeve.

Presently the door was opened a crack and the grizzled, sunken-eyed face of a man who needed sleep peered out. "Good afternoon to you, Mason," Bidwell said. "I've come to see your wife."

Mason Barrow knew full well why the master of Fount Royal was at his door; he drew it open and stepped back, his black-haired head slumped like that of a dog about to be whipped. Bidwell and Winston entered the house, which seemed the size of a wig box compared to the mansion they'd recently left. The two Barrow children—eight-year-old Melissa and six-year-old Preston—were also in the front room, the older watching from behind a table and the younger clinging to his father's trouser leg. Bidwell was not an ungracious man; he removed his hat, first thing. "She's to bed, I understand."

"Yes sir. Sick to the soul, she is."

"I shall have to speak to her."

"Yes sir." Barrow nodded numbly. Bidwell noted that the two children also looked in need of sleep, as well as in need of a good hot meal. "As you please." Barrow motioned toward the room at the rear of the house.

"Very well. Edward, come with me." Bidwell walked to the open door of the other room and looked in. Alice Barrow was lying in the bed there, a wrinkled sheet pulled up to her chin. Her eyes were open and staring at the ceiling, her sallow face gleaming with sweat. The room's single window was shuttered, but the light was strong because seven tallows were aflame, as well as a clay bowl full of pine knots. Bidwell knew it was a re-markable extravagance for a farmer such as Mason Barrow, whose children must be suffering due to this surplus of illumination. As Bidwell stepped across the threshold, a loose plank squeaked un-derfoot and the woman looked at him; her eyes widened, she sucked in her breath as if she'd been struck, and shrank away from him deeper into the confines of the bed.

Bidwell immediately halted where he stood. "Good after-noon, madam," he said. "May I have a word with you?"

"Where's my husband?" the woman cried out. "Mason! Where's he gone?"

"I'm here!" Barrow replied, standing behind the other two men. "All's well, there's naught to fear."

"Don't let me sleep, Mason! Promise me you won't!"

"I promise," he said, with a quick glance at Bidwell.

"What's all this nonsense?" Bidwell asked him. "The woman's feared to sleep?"

"Yes, sir. She fears fallin' asleep and seein'—"

"Don't speak it!" Alice Barrow's voice rose again, tremulous and pleading. "If you love me, don't speak it!"

The little girl began to cry, the little boy still clinging to his father's leg. Barrow looked directly into Bidwell's face. "She's in a bad way, sir. She ain't slept for the past two nights. Cain't abide the dark, not even the day shadows."

"This is how it begins," Winston said quietly.

"Rein yourself!" Bidwell snapped at him. He produced a lace-rimmed handkerchief from a pocket of his jacket and wiped beads of sweat from his cheeks and forehead. "Be that as it may, Barrow, I must speak to her. Madam? May I enter?"

"No!" she answered, the damp sheet drawn up to her terror-stricken eyes. "Go away!"

"Thank you." Bidwell walked to her bedside and stood there,

looking down at her with both hands gripping his hat. Winston followed behind him, but Mason Barrow remained in the other room to comfort the crying little girl. "Madam," Bidwell said, "you must desist in your spreading of tales about these dreams. I know you've told Cass Swaine. I would ask—"

"I told Cass 'cause she's my friend!" the woman said behind her sheet. "I told others of my friends too! And why shouldn't I? They should know what *I know,* if they value their lives!"

"And what is it that makes your knowledge so valuable, madam?"

She pushed the sheet away and stared defiantly up at him, her eyes wet and scared but her chin thrust toward him like a weapon. "That whoever lives in this town is sure to *die.*"

"That, I fear, is only worth a shilling. All who live in any town are sure to die."

"Not by *his* hand! Not by fire and the torments of Hell! Oh, he told me! He *showed* me! He walked me through the graveyard, and he showed me them names on the markers!" The veins in her neck strained, her brown hair lank and wet. She said in an agonized whisper, "He showed me Cass Swaine's marker! And John's too! And he showed me the names of my *children!*" Her voice cracked, the tears coursing down her cheeks. "My own children, laid dead in the ground! Oh, sweet Jesus!" She gave a terrible, wrenching moan and pulled the sheet up to her face again, her eyes squeezed shut.

With all the candle flames, the pine knot smoke, and the humidity seeping in, the room was a hotbox. Bidwell felt as if drawing a breath was too much effort. He heard the rumble of distant thunder, another storm approaching. A response to Alice Barrow's phantasms was in order, but for the life of him Bidwell couldn't find one. There was no doubt a great Evil had seized upon the town, and had grown in both murky day and blackest night like poisonous mushrooms. This Evil had invaded the dreams of the citizens of Fount Royal and driven them to frenzies. Bidwell knew that Winston was correct: this indeed was how it began.

"Courage," he offered, but it sounded so very weak.

She opened her eyes; they had become swollen and near-scarlet. *"Courage?"* she repeated, incredulously. "Courage again' *him?* He showed me a graveyard full of markers! You couldn't take a step without fallin' over a grave! It was a silent town. Everybody gone . . . or dead. He told me. Standin' right at my side, and I could hear him breathin' in my ear." She nodded, her eyes staring straight through Bidwell. "Those who stay here will perish and burn in Hell's fires. That's what he said, right in my ear. Burn in Hell's fires, forever and a day. It was a silent town. Silent. He said *Shhhhhhhh, Alice.* He said *Shhhhhhhh, listen to my voice. Look upon this,* he said, *and know what I am."* She blinked, some of the focus returning to her eyes, but she still appeared dazed and disjointed. "I did look," she said, "and I do know."

"I understand," Bidwell told her, trying to sound as calm and rational as a man at the bitter end of his rope possibly could, "but we must be responsible, and not so eager to spread fear among our fellows."

"I'm not wantin' to spread fear!" she answered sharply. "I'm wantin' to tell the truth of what was shown me! This place is cursed! You know it, I know it, every soul with sense knows it!" She stared directly at one of the candles. The little girl in the other room was still sobbing, and Alice Barrow said with small strength in her voice, "Hush, Melissa. Hush, now."

Bidwell, again, was lost for words. He found himself gripping his tricorn with a force that made his fingers ache. The distant thunder echoed, nearer now, and sweat was crawling down the back of his neck. This hotbox room seemed to be closing in on him, stealing his breath. He had to get out. He abruptly turned, almost bowling Winston over, and took the two strides to the door.

"I saw his face," the woman said. Bidwell stopped as if he'd run into a brick wall. "His face," she repeated. "I saw it. He *let* me see it."

Bidwell looked at her, waiting for the rest of what she had to say. She was sitting up, the sheet fallen aside, a terrible shiny anguish in her eyes. "He was wearin' *your* face," she said, with a savage and half-crazed grin. "Like a mask, it was. Wearin' your face, and showin' me my children laid dead in the ground." Her hands came up and covered her mouth, as if she feared she might let loose a cry that would shatter her soul.

"Steady, madam," Bidwell said, but his voice was shaky. "You must tend to reality, and put aside these visions of the nether-world."

"We'll all burn there, if he has his way!" she retorted. "He wants her free, is what he wants! Wants her free, and all of us gone!"

"I'll hear no more of this." Bidwell turned away from her again, and got out of the room.

"Wants her free!" the woman shouted. "He won't let us rest 'til she's with him!"

Bidwell kept going, out the front door, with Winston follow-ing. "Sir! Sir!" Barrow called, and he came out of the house after them. Bidwell paused, trying mightily to display a calm de-meanor.

"Beg pardon, sir," Barrow said. "She meant no disrespect."

"None taken. Your wife is in a precarious condition."

"Yes, sir. But . . . things bein' as they are, you'll understand when I tell you we have to leave."

A fine drizzle was starting to fall from the dark-bellied clouds. Bidwell pushed the tricorn down on his head. "Do as you please, Barrow. I'm not your master."

"Yes sir." He licked his lower lip, plucking up the courage to say what was on his mind. "This *was* a good town, sir. Used to be, before . . ." He shrugged. "It's all changed now. I'm sorry, but we cain't stay."

"Go on, then!" Bidwell's facade cracked and some of his anger and frustration spilled out like black bile. "No one's chain-ing you here! Go on, run like a scared dog with the rest of them! *I* shall not! By God, I have planted myself in this place and no phantasm shall tear me——"

A bell sounded. A deep-tolling bell. Once, then a second and third time.

It was the voice of the bell at the watchman's tower on Harmony Street. The bell continued to sound, announcing that the watchman had spied someone coming along the road.

"—shall tear me out!" Bidwell finished, with fierce resolve. He looked toward the main gate, which was kept closed and locked against Indians. New hope blossomed in his heart. "Edward, it must be the judge from Charles Town! Yes! It *has* to be! Come along!" Without another word to Mason Barrow, Bidwell started off toward the junction of the four streets. "Hurry!" he said to Winston, picking up his pace. The rain was beginning to fall now in earnest, but not even the worst deluge since Noah would've kept him from personally welcoming the judge this happy day. The bell's voice had started a chorus of dogs to barking, and as Bidwell and Winston rushed northward along Harmony Street—one grinning with excitement and the other gasping for breath—a number of mutts chased round and round them as if at the heels of carnival clowns.

By the time they reached the gate, both men were wet with rain and perspiration and were breathing like bellows. A group of a dozen or so residents had emerged from their homes to gather around, as a visitor from the outside was rare indeed. Up in the watchtower, Malcolm Jennings had ceased his pulling on the bellcord, and two men—Esai Pauling and James Reed—were readying to lift the log that served as the gate's lock from its latchpost.

"Wait, wait!" Bidwell called, pushing through the onlookers. "Give me room!" He approached the gate and realized he was trembling with anticipation. He looked up at Jennings, who was standing on the tower's platform at the end of a fifteen-foot-tall ladder. "Are they white men?"

"Yes sir," Jennings answered. He was a slim drink of water with a shockpate of unruly dark brown hair and perhaps five teeth in his head, but he had the eyes of a hawk.

"Two of 'em. I mean to say . . . I *think* they be white."

Bidwell couldn't decipher what that was supposed to mean, but neither did he want to tarry at this important moment. "Very well!" he said to Pauling and Reed. "Open it!" The log was lifted and pulled from its latch. Then Reed grasped the two wooden handgrips and drew the gate open.

Bidwell stepped forward, his arms open to embrace his savior. In another second, however, his welcoming advance abruptly stopped.

Two men stood before him: one large with a bald head, one slender with short-cropped black hair. But neither one of them was the man he'd hoped to greet.

He presumed they were white. With all the mud they wore, it was difficult to tell. The larger—and older—had on a mud-covered coat that seemed to be black under its earth daubings. He was barefoot, his skinny legs grimed with muck. The younger man wore only something that might serve as a nightshirt, and he appeared to have recently rolled on the ground in it. He did wear shoes, however filthy they might be.

The mutts were so excited by all the commotion that they began to snarl and bark their lungs out at the two arrivals, who seemed dazed at the appearance of people wearing clean clothing.

"Beggars," Bidwell said; his voice was quiet, dangerously so. He heard thunder over the wilderness, and thought it must be the sound of God laughing. His welcoming arms fell heavily to his sides. "I have been sent *beggars,*" he said, louder, and then he began to laugh along with God. Soft at first it was, and then the laughter spiraled out of him, raucous and uncontrollable; it hurt his throat and made his eyes water, and though he ardently wanted to stop—ardently *tried* to stop—he found he had as much power over this laughter as if he'd been a whirligig spun by the hand of a foolish child. *"Beggars!"* he shouted through the wheezing. "I . . . have . . . run . . . to admit beggars!"

"Sir," spoke the larger man, and he took a barefooted step forward. An expression of anger swept across his mud-splattered features. *"Sir!"*

Bidwell shook his head and kept laughing—there seemed to be some weeping in it as well—and he waved his hand to dismiss the wayfaring jaybird.

Isaac Woodward pulled in a deep breath. If the night of wet

hell had not been enough, this crackerjack dandy was here to test his mettle. Well, his mettle broke. He bellowed, *"Sir!"* in his judicial voice, which was loud and sharp enough to silence for a moment even the yapping dogs. *"I* am Magistrate Woodward, come from Charles Town!"

Bidwell heard; he gasped, choked on a last fragment of laughter, and then he stood staring with wide and shocked eyes at the half-naked mudpie who called himself a magistrate.

A single thought entered Bidwell's mind like a hornet's sting: *If they send us anybody, it'll be a lunatic they plucked from the asylum up there!*

He heard a moan, quite close. His eyelids fluttered. The world—rainstorm, voice of God, green wilderness beyond, beggars and magistrates, parasites in the apples: ruin and destruction like the shadows of vulture wings—spun around him. He took a backward step, looking for something to lean against.

There was nothing. He fell onto Harmony Street, his head full of cold gray fog, and there was cradled to sleep.

five

A KNOCK SOUNDED on the door.
"Magistrate? Master Bidwell sent me to tell you the guests are arrivin'."

"I'll be there directly," Woodward answered, recognizing the housekeeper's Scottish brogue. He recalled that the last time he'd heard a knock on a door, his life had been near snuffed. Of course the mere thought of that wretch wearing the gold-striped waistcoat was enough to make him fumble in buttoning the clean pale blue shirt he had recently put on. "Damn!" he said to his reflection in the oval wall mirror.

"Sir?" Mrs. Nettles inquired beyond the door.

"I said I'd be there directly!" he told her again.

She said, "Yes sir," and walked with a heavy gait along the corridor to the room Matthew occupied.

Woodward completed the task of buttoning his shirt, which was a bit short at the sleeves and more than a bit tight across the belly. It was among a number of clothes—shirts, trousers, waistcoats, stockings, and shoes—that had been collected for himself and Matthew by their host, once Bidwell's fainting spell had been overcome and the man made aware of what had happened to their belongings. Then Bidwell, realizing his providence was at hand, had been most gracious in arranging two rooms in his mansion for their use, as well as gathering up the approximately sized clothing for them and making sure they had such necessities as freshly stropped razors and hot water for baths. Woodward had feared he'd never be able to scrub all the mud from his skin, but the last of it had come off by the administrations of a rough sponge and plenty of elbow oil.

He had previously put on a pair of black trousers—again, a shade snug but wearable—and white stockings and a pair of square-toed black shoes. Over his shirt he donned a pearl-gray silk waistcoat, loaned to him from Bidwell's own wardrobe. He checked his face again in the mirror, lamenting that he would have to meet these new people in a bareheaded and age-spotted condition, as a wig was such a personal item that asking the loan of one was out of the question. But so be it. At least he still had a head upon his neck. If truth be told, he would rather have slept the night away than be the centerpiece at Bidwell's dinner, as he was still exhausted; but he'd slumbered for three hours after his bath, and that would have to do until he could again stretch himself out on that excellent feather-mattressed four-poster behind him.

As a last precaution he opened his mouth and checked the condition of his teeth. His throat felt somewhat parched but nothing that a draught of rum couldn't satisfy. Then, smelling of sandalwood soap and lemon-oil shaving lotion, he opened the door of his spacious room and ventured out into the candle-illumed hallway.

Downstairs, he followed the sound of voices into a large wood-panelled room that stood just off the main entrance vestibule. It was arranged for a gathering, the chairs and other furniture shunted aside to afford space for movement, a polite fire burning in a white stone hearth as the rainy night had turned cool. A chandelier made of antlers hung overhead, a dozen candles flickering amid the points. Bidwell was there, wearing another opulent wig and a velvet suit the color of dark port. He was standing with two other gentlemen, and as Woodward entered the room Bidwell interrupted his conversation to say, "Ah, there's the magistrate now! Sir, how was your rest?"

"Not long enough, I fear," Woodward admitted. "The rigors of last night haven't yet been eased."

"The magistrate tells a remarkable tale!" Bidwell said to the other gentlemen. "It seems he and his scribe were almost murdered at a tavern on their way here! The rogue was evidently well versed in murder, isn't that right sir?" He lifted his eyebrows, prompting Woodward to take over the story.

"He was. My clerk saved our skins, though that's all we came away with. By necessity, we abandoned our belongings. Oh, I look forward to the morrow, Mr. Bidwell."

"The magistrate has asked me to send a party of militia there in order to regain his worldly goods," Bidwell explained to the two others. "Also to arrest that man and bring him to justice."

"I'll be going, too," Woodward said. "I wouldn't miss seeing the expression on Shawcombe's face when the iron's slapped on him."

"Will Shawcombe?" One of the gentlemen—a younger man, perhaps in his early thirties—frowned. "I've stopped at his tavern before, on my trips back and forth to Charles Town! I had my suspicions about that man's character."

"They were well founded. Furthermore, he murdered the magistrate who was on his way here two weeks ago. Thymon Kingsbury was his name."

"Let me make introductions," Bidwell said. "Magistrate Isaac Woodward, this is Nicholas Paine"—he nodded toward the younger man, and Woodward shook Paine's outstretched hand— "and Elias Garrick." Woodward grasped Garrick's hand as well. "Mr. Paine is the captain of our militia. He'll be leading the expedition to secure Mr. Shawcombe in the morning. Won't you, Nicholas?"

"My duty," Paine said, though it was obvious from the glint in his iron-gray eyes that he might resent these plans of arrest being made without his representation. "And my pleasure to serve you, Magistrate."

"Mr. Garrick is our largest farmholder," Bidwell went on. "He was also one of the first to cast his lot with me."

"Yes sir," Garrick said. "I built my house the very first month."

"Ah!" Bidwell had glanced toward the room's entrance. "Here's your scribe!"

Matthew had just walked in, wearing shoes that pinched his feet. "Good evening, sirs," he said, and managed a wan smile though he was still dog-tired and in no mood for convivialities. "Pardon my being late."

"No pardon necessary!" Bidwell motioned him in. "We were hearing about your adventure of last night."

"I'd have to call it a *mis*adventure," Matthew said. "Surely not one I'd care to repeat."

"Gentlemen, this is the magistrate's clerk, Mr. Matthew Corbett," Bidwell announced. He introduced Matthew to Paine and Garrick, and hands were again shaken. "I was telling the magistrate that Mr. Paine is the captain of our militia and shall be leading—"

"—the expedition to secure Mr. Shawcombe in the morning," Paine broke in. "As it's a lengthy trip, we shall be leaving promptly at sunrise."

Woodward said, "It will be a pleasure to rise early for that satisfaction, sir."

"Very well. I'll find another man or two to take along. Will we need guns, or do you think Shawcombe'll give up without violence?"

"Guns," Woodward said. "Definitely guns."

The talk turned to other matters, notably what was happening in Charles Town, and therefore Matthew—who was wearing a white shirt and tan trousers with white stockings—had the opportunity to make quick studies of Paine and Garrick. The captain of militia was a sturdy-looking man who stood perhaps five-ten. Matthew judged him to be in the vicinity of thirty years; he wore his sand-colored hair long and pulled into a queue at the back of his head, secured with a black cord. His face was well balanced by a long, slender-bridged nose and thick blond brows that settled low over his gunmetal gray eyes. Matthew surmised from Paine's build and economy of motion that he was a no-nonsense type of man, someone who was no stranger to strenuous activity and probably an adept horseman. Paine was also no clotheshorse; his outfit consisted of a simple gray shirt, well-used leather waistcoat, dark brown trousers, gray leggings, and brown boots.

Garrick, who listened far more than he spoke, impressed Matthew as an earthy gentleman who was probably facing the dusk of his fifties. He was slim and rawboned, his gaunt-cheeked face burnt and weathered by the fierce sun of past summers. He had deeply set brown eyes, his left brow slashed and drawn upward by a small scar. His gray hair was slicked with pomade and combed straight back on his skull, and he wore cream-colored corduroy trousers, a blue shirt, and an age-buffed waistcoat that was the bright yellowish hue of some spoiled cheese Matthew once had the misfortune to inhale. Something about Garrick's expression and manner—slow-blinking, thick and labored language when he did deem to speak—made Matthew believe that the man might be the salt of the earth but was definitely limited in his selection of spices.

A young negress servant appeared with a pewter tray upon which were goblets—real cut glass, which impressed Woodward because such treasures of luxury were rarely seen in these rough-edged colonies—brimming with red wine. Bidwell urged them all to partake, and never did wine flow down two more appreciative throats than those of the magistrate and his clerk.

The ringing of a dulcet-toned bell at the front door announced the arrival of others. Two more gentlemen were escorted into the room by Mrs. Nettles, who then took her leave to attend to business in the kitchen. Woodward and Matthew had already made the acquaintance of Edward Winston, but the man with him—who limped in his walk and supported himself on a twisted cane with an ivory handle—was a stranger.

"Our schoolmaster, Alan Johnstone," Bidwell said, introducing them one to another. "We're fortunate to have Master Johnstone as part of our community. He brings to us the benefit of an Oxford education."

"Oxford?" Woodward shook the man's hand. "I too attended Oxford."

"Really? Which college, may I ask?" The schoolmaster's elegant voice, though pitched low and quiet, held a power that Woodward felt sure would serve him well securing the respectful attention of students in a classroom.

"Christ Church. And you?"

"All Souls'."

"Ah, that was a magnificent time," Woodward said, but he rested his eyes on Bidwell because he found the schoolmaster more than a little strange in appearance. Johnstone wore a dusting of white facial powder and had plucked his eyebrows thin. "I remember many nights spent studying the bottom of ale tankards at the Chequers Inn."

"I myself preferred the Golden Cross," Johnstone said with a slight smile. "Their ale was a student's delight: very strong and very cheap."

"I see we have a true scholar among us." Woodward returned the smile. "All Souls' College, eh? I expect Lord Mallard will be drunk again next year."

"In his cups, I'm sure."

As this exchange between fellow Oxfordians had been going on, Matthew had been making his own cursory study of Alan Johnstone. The schoolmaster, slim and tall, was dressed in a dark gray suit with black striping, a white ruffled shirt and a black tricorn. He wore a simple white wig, and from the breast pocket of his jacket protruded a white lace handkerchief. With the powder on his face—and a spot of rouge highlighting each sharp cheekbone—it was difficult to guess his age, though Matthew reasoned he was somewhere between forty and fifty. Johnstone had a long, aristocratic nose with slightly flared nostrils, narrow dark blue eyes that were not unfriendly but rather somewhat reserved in expression, and the high forehead of an intellectual. Matthew glanced quickly down and saw that Johnstone wore polished black boots and white stockings, but that a misshapen lump on his right leg served him as a knee. When he looked up again, he found the schoolmaster staring into his face and he felt a blush spreading across his cheeks.

"As you're interested, young man," Johnstone said, with an uplift of his finely plucked eyebrows, "it is a defect of birth."

"Oh . . . I'm sorry. I mean . . . I didn't—"

"Tut tut." Johnstone reached out and patted Matthew's shoulder. "Observance is the mark of a good mind. Would that you hone that quality, but be a shade less direct in its application."

"Yes, sir," Matthew said, wishing he might sink through the floor.

"My clerk's eyes are sometimes too large for his head," Woodward offered, as a poultice of apology. He, too, had noted the malformed knee.

"Better too large than too small, I think," returned the schoolmaster. "In this town at this present time, however, it would be wise to keep both eyes and head in moderation." He sipped his wine, as Woodward nodded at Johnstone's sagacity. "And as we are speaking of such things and it is the point of your visit here, might I ask if you've seen her yet?"

"No, not yet," Bidwell answered quickly. "I thought the magistrate should like to hear the particulars before he sets sight on her."

"Do you mean particulars, or *peculiars?*" Johnstone asked, which brought uneasy laughter from Winston and Paine but only a slight smile from Bidwell. "As one Oxford man to another, sir," he said to the magistrate, "I should not wish to be in your shoes."

"If you were in my shoes, sir," Woodward said, enjoying this joust with the schoolmaster's wit, "you would not be an Oxford man. You would be a candidate for the noose."

Johnstone's eyes widened a fraction. "Pardon me?"

"My shoes are in the custody of a murderer," Woodward explained, and then proceeded to paint in detail the events at Shawcombe's tavern. The judge had realized that such a tale of near-tragedy was as sure a draw to an audience as was a candle-flame to inquisitive moths, and so began to bellows the flame for all it was worth. Matthew was intrigued to find that in this go-round of the tale, the judge was certain from the beginning that Shawcombe was "a scoundrel of evil intent," and that he'd made up his mind to guard his back ere Shawcombe sank a blade into it.

As the clay of history was being reshaped, the doorbell again rang and presently Mrs. Nettles reappeared escorting another guest to the gathering. This gentleman was a slight, small-boned man who brought to Matthew's mind the image of a bantam owl perched atop a barn's beam. His face was truly owlish, with a pale pursed mouth and a hooked nose, his large pallid blue eyes swimming behind round-lensed spectacles and arched brown brows set high on his furrowed dome. He wore a plain black suit, blue shirt with ruffled cuffs, and high-topped boots. His long brown hair—streaked with gray at the temples—overhung his shoulders, his head crowned by an ebon tricorn.

"Dr. Benjamin Shields, our surgeon," Bidwell announced. "How goes it, Ben?"

"An unfortunate day, I fear," the doctor said, in a voice very much larger than himself. "Forgive my tardiness. I just came from the Chester house."

"What is Madam Chester's condition?" Winston asked.

"Lifeless." Shields removed his tricorn and handed it to Mrs. Nettles, who stood behind him like a dark wall. "Sad to say, she passed not an hour ago. It's this swamp air! It clogs the lungs and thickens the blood. If we don't have some relief soon, Robert, our shovels will see much new work. Hello!" He strode forward and offered his hand to Woodward. "You're the magistrate we've been waiting for. Thank God you've finally come!"

"As I understand it from the council in Charles Town," Woodward said after he'd shaken the doctor's hand, which he noticed was more than a little cold and clammy, "I am actually the third magistrate involved in this situation. The first perished by the plague back in March, before he could leave the city, and the second . . . well, Magistrate Kingsbury's fate was unknown until last night. This is my clerk, Matthew Corbett."

"A pleasure, young man." The doctor shook Matthew's hand. "Sir," he said, addressing Woodward again, "I care not if you are the third, thirteenth, or thirty-third magistrate involved! We just want this situation resolved, and the sooner the better." He punctuated his statement with a fiery glare over the rims of his spectacles, then he sniffed the air of the aroma that had been creeping into the room. "Ah, roasted meat! What's on the table tonight, Robert?"

"Toss 'em boys in peppercorn sauce," Bidwell said, with less vitality than a few moments previously; he was pained by the death of Dorcas Chester, a grandly aged lady whose husband Timothy was Fount Royal's tailor. Indeed, the cloth of things was unravelling. The doctor's remark about the work of shovels also made Bidwell think—uncomfortably so—of Alice Barrow's dreams.

"Dinner will be a'table presently," Mrs. Nettles told them, and then she left the room, carrying the doctor's tricorn.

Shields walked to the fireplace and warmed his hands. "A pity about Madam Chester," he said, before anyone else could venture off into new territory. "She was a fine woman. Magistrate, have you had much of a chance to inspect our town?"

"No, I haven't."

"Best hurry. At this rate of mortality, Fount Royal will have to soon be renamed Grave Common."

"Ben!" Bidwell said, rather more sharply than he'd intended. "I don't think there's any purpose in such language, do you?"

"Probably not." Shields rubbed his hands together, intent on removing from them the chill of Dorcas Chester's flesh. "Unfortunately, though, there's much truth in it. Oh, the magistrate will find out these things for himself soon enough; we may as well speed his knowledge." He looked at the schoolmaster, who stood nearby. "Alan, are you finished with that?" Without waiting for a response, he plucked the half-full wineglass from Johnstone's hand and took a hearty swallow. Then he fixed his baleful gaze full upon Isaac Woodward. "I didn't become a doctor to bury my patients, but lately I should wear an undertaker's shingle. Two last week. The little Richardson child, bless his soul, was one of them. Now Dorcas Chester. Who shall I be sending off next week?"

"This does no good," Bidwell said firmly. "I urge you to restrain yourself."

"Restrain myself." The doctor nodded and gazed into the glass's shallow pond of red wine. "Robert, I've restrained myself too long. I have grown weary of restraining myself."

"The weather is to blame," Winston spoke up. "Surely these rains will pass soon, and then we'll—"

"It's not just the weather!" Shields interrupted, with a defiant uplift of his sharp-boned chin. "It's the *spirit* of this place now. It's the darkness here." He drank again, finishing off the glass. "A darkness at noon the same as at midnight," he said, his lips wet. "These sicknesses are spreading. Sick of spirit, sick of body. They're linked, gentlemen. One regulates the other. I saw how Madam Chester's sickness of spirit robbed her body of health. I saw it, and there wasn't a damned thing I could do. Now Timothy's spirit has been blighted with the contagion. How long will it be before I'm attending *his* demise?"

"Pardon me, sir," Garrick said, before Bidwell could deliver a rebuke. "When you say the sickness is spreadin' . . . do you mean . . ." He hesitated, as he fit together exactly what he desired to say. "Do you mean we're facin' the *plague?*"

"Careful, Benjamin," the schoolmaster cautioned in a quiet voice.

"No, that's not what he means!" Bidwell said heatedly. "The doctor's distraught about Madam Chester's passing, that's all! Tell him you're not speaking of plague, Ben."

The doctor paused and Matthew thought he was about to announce that plague indeed had come to Fount Royal. But instead, Shields released his breath in a long weary sigh and said, "No, I'm not speaking of plague. At least, not plague caused by any *physical* power."

"What the good doctor means, I believe," said Johnstone to Garrick, "is that the town's current spiritual . . . um . . . vulnerability is affecting the physical health of us all."

"You mean the witch is makin' us sick," Garrick said, thick-tongued.

Bidwell decided it was time to stop these floodwaters, ere the dam break when Garrick—who was a proficient farmer but whose intellect in less earthy things was lacking—repeated these musings around the community. "Let us look to the future and not to the past, gentlemen! Elias, our deliverance is at hand in the magistrate. We should put our trust in the Lord and the law, and forbid ourselves of these destructive ramblings."

Garrick looked to Johnstone for translation. "He means not to worry," the schoolmaster said. "And I'm of the same opinion. The magistrate will resolve our difficulties."

"You put great faith in me, sirs." Woodward felt both puffed and burdened by these attentions. "I hope I meet your expectations."

"You'd better." Shields had put aside the empty glass. "The fate of this settlement is in your hands."

"Gentlemen?" Mrs. Nettles loomed in the doorway. "Dinner's a'table."

The banquet room, toward the rear of the house next to the kitchen, was a marvel of dark-timbered walls, hanging tapestries, and a fieldstone fireplace as wide as a wagon. Above the hearth was the mounted head of a magnificent stag, and displayed on both sides of it was a collection of muskets and pistols. Neither Woodward nor Matthew had expected to find a mansion out here on the coastal swampland, but a room like this—which might have served as the centerpiece in a British castle—rendered them both speechless. Above a huge rectangular table was an equally huge candlelit chandelier supported from the ceiling by thick nautical chains, and upon the floor was a carpet as red as beef-blood. The groaning board was covered with platters of food, principal among them the roasted toss 'em boys still asizzle in their juices.

"Magistrate, you sit here beside me," Bidwell directed; it was clear to Matthew that Bidwell relished his position of power, and that he was obviously a man of uncommon wealth. Bidwell had the places already chosen for his guests, and Matthew found himself seated on a pewlike bench between Garrick and Dr. Shields. Another young negress servant girl came through a doorway from the kitchen bringing wooden tankards of what proved to be—when Woodward tried a tentative sip, remembering the bite of the Indian ale—cold water recently drawn from the spring.

"Shall we have a prayer of thanks?" Bidwell asked before the first blade pierced the roasted and peppercorn-spiced chicken. "Master Johnstone, would you do the honors?"

"Surely." Johnstone and the others bowed their heads, and the schoolmaster gave a prayer that appreciated the bounties of the table, praised God for His wisdom in bringing the magistrate safely to Fount Royal, and asked for an abatement to the rains if that was indeed in God's divine plan. While Johnstone was praying, however, the muffled sound of thunder heralded the approach of another storm, and Johnstone's "Amen" sounded to Matthew as if the schoolmaster had spoken it through clenched teeth.

"Let us sup," Bidwell announced.

Knives flashed in the candlelight, spearing roasted toss 'em boys—a title rarely used in these modern days except by sportsmen who recalled the gambler's game of setting dogs upon chickens to bet upon which dog would "toss" the greatest number. A moment of spirited jabbing by Bidwell's guests was followed by tearing the meat from its bones with teeth and fingers. Hunks of the heavy, coarse-grained jonakin bread that tasted of burnt corn and could sit in a belly like a church brick found use in sopping up the greasy juices. Platters of steaming beans and boiled potatoes were there for the taking, and a servant girl brought a communal, beautifully worked silver tankard full of spiced rum with which to wash everything down the gullet.

Rain began to drum steadily on the roof. Soon it was apparent to Matthew that the banquet had drawn a number of unwelcome guests: large, buzzing horseflies and—more bothersome—mosquitoes that hummed past the ears and inflicted itching welts. In a lull of the idle conversation—which was interrupted quite frequently by the slapping at an offensive fly or mosquito—Bidwell took a drink from the rum tankard and passed it to the magistrate. Then Bidwell cleared his throat, and Woodward knew it was time to get to the heart of the matter.

"I should ask you what you know of the situation here, sir," Bidwell said, with chicken grease gleaming on his chin.

"I know only what the council told me. In essence, that you have in your gaol a woman accused of witchcraft."

Bidwell nodded; he picked up a bone from his plate and sucked on it. "Her name is Rachel Howarth. She's a mixed breed, English and Portuguese. In January, her husband Daniel was found dead in a field with his throat cut."

"His head almost severed from the neck," the doctor added.

"And there were other wounds on the body," Bidwell went on. Made by the teeth or claws of a beast. On his face, his arms, his hands." He returned the naked bone to his plate and picked up another that still held a bit of meat. "Whatever killed him . . . was ferocious, to say the least. But his was not the first death in such a fashion."

"The Anglican minister, Burlton Grove," Johnstone spoke up, reaching for the silver tankard. "He was murdered in a similar way in November. His corpse was found in the church by his wife. Widow, I should say. She very soon afterward left town."

"Understandable," Woodward said. "You have a minister at present?"

"No," Bidwell said. "I've been presenting sermons from time to time. Also Dr. Shields, Master Johnstone, and several others. We had a Lutheran here for a while, to serve the Germans, but he spoke very little English and he left last summer."

"The Germans?"

"That's right. At one point, we had a number of German and Dutch families. There are still . . . oh . . ." He looked to Winston for help. "How many, would you say?"

"Seven German families," Winston supplied. He swung a hand at a mosquito that drifted past his face. "Two Dutch."

"Edward is my town manager," Bidwell explained to the

magistrate. "He takes care of the accounting, a position in which he served for my shipping company in London."

"Would I know the name of your company?" Woodward asked.

"The Aurora. You might've come over on one of my ships."

"Possibly. You're a long way from the center of commerce here, aren't you?"

"Not so far. My two sons are now at the helm, and my wife and daughter remain in London also. But I trust the young men to do what has to be done. In the meantime, I am busy in furthering the future of my company."

"In Fount Royal? How?"

Bidwell smiled slightly, like a cat that has swallowed the canary. "It must be apparent to you, sir, that I hold the southernmost settlement in these colonies. You must be aware that the Spaniards are not too far from here, down in the Florida land." He beckoned for Dr. Shields to pass him the rum tankard. "It is my intent," he said, "to create a city out of Fount Royal that will rival . . . no, *surpass* Charles Town as a point of trade between the colonies and the Indies. In time, I shall base my company here to take advantage of such trade. I expect to have a military presence here in the future, as the King is interested that the Spanish don't pursue their territorial greed in a northerly direction." He grasped the tankard's handle and downed a swig. "Another reason to create a naval base at Fount Royal is to intercept the pirates and privateers who regularly attack ships carrying freight from the Indies. And who should build those naval vessels, do you think?" He cocked his head to one side, awaiting Woodward's reply.

"Yourself, of course."

"Of course. Which also means the construction of docks, warehouses, lumberyards, homes for the officers . . . well, you can see the profit in the picture, can't you?"

"I can," Woodward said. "I presume you would build a better road between here and Charles Town, as well?"

"In time, Magistrate," Bidwell answered, "the councilmen of Charles Town will build the road. Oh, I expect I'll meet them halfway and we'll make some kind of compromise." He shrugged. "But it will be obvious to them that Fount Royal is better situated as a port city and naval base, and they'll need the trade I send them."

Woodward grunted softly. "Lofty ambitions, sir. I suspect the councilmen must already know your plans. That may be part of why it took so long to get a magistrate here."

"Likely so. But I'm not planning on running Charles Town out of the shipping business. I simply saw an opportunity. Why the founders of Charles Town didn't elect to build as far south as possible, I don't know. I expect it had to do with the rivers there, and their need for fresh water. But the spring, you see, gives us all the fresh water we need. Plenty enough to fill barrels for thirsty sailors from the Indies, that's a certainty!"

"Uh . . . sir?" Matthew said, scratching at a mosquito bite on his right cheek. "If these plans of yours are so clear . . . then why is it you haven't yet begun building your docks and warehouses?"

Bidwell glanced quickly at Winston. Matthew thought it was a glance of nervous communication. "Because," Bidwell said, directing a hard stare at Matthew, "first things are first." He pushed his plate of bones aside and folded his hands on the table. "It is just like the building of a ship, young man. You do not mount the mast first, you lay the keel. As it will take several years to drain the swampland and prepare the necessary details *before* construction of the docks can begin, I must make sure that Fount Royal is self-supporting. Which means that the farmers"—here he gave a nod of acknowledgment to Garrick—"are able to raise sufficient crops; that the cobbler, tailor, blacksmith, and other craftsmen are able to work and thrive; that we have a sturdy schoolhouse and church and an atmosphere of purpose and security; and that we have a yearly increase in population."

He paused after this recitation, and regarded the plate of bones as darkly as if they were the ribs of the burned houses that littered Fount Royal. "I regret to speak the truth," he said after a few seconds of grim silence, "but very few of those conditions have come to pass. Oh, our farmers are doing the best they can, as the weather is doing its worst, but the fight is all uphill. We have the staples—corn, beans, and potatoes—and the game is abundant. But as far as producing a commerce crop such as cotton or tobacco . . . the attempts have not met with success. We are losing our population at a rapid rate, both to illness and . . ." Again, he hesitated. He took a pained breath. "And to fear of the witch," he went on. Then he looked into Woodward's eyes.

"It is my passionate dream," Bidwell said, "to create a town here. To build from it a port city that shall be the pride of my possessions. In truth, sir, I have strained my accounts to see that dream become a reality. I have never failed at anything. *Never.*" He lifted his chin a fraction, as if daring a blow from the fist of fate. Woodward noticed that on it was a large, reddening insect bite. "I am not going to fail here," he said, with iron in his voice, and this time he swept his gaze around the table to take in the rest of his audience. "I *refuse* to fail," he told them. "No damned witch, warlock, nor cloven-hooved ass shall destroy Fount Royal so long as I have a drop of blood in my body, and that's my vow to all of you!"

"Your vow finds a brother in mine, sir," Paine said. "I won't run from a *woman,* even if she *is* licking the devil's buttocks."

"More like sucking his cock," the doctor said. His voice was a little slurred, indicating that the wine and rum had together overrun his fortifications. "Isn't that right, Elias?"

The attention of the magistrate and his clerk turned toward Garrick, whose weathered face had blushed a shade red. "Yes sir, it is," the farmer agreed. "I seen the witch on her knees, tendin' to her master in such a way."

"One moment." Woodward had felt his heart give a kick. "You mean to say . . . you actually *witnessed* such a thing?"

"I did," came the answer without hesitation. "I seen Rachel Howarth on her knees, in the dirt. He was standin' in front of her, with his hands on his hips. She had hold of . . ." He stopped, and squirmed uneasily on the bench.

"Go on," Bidwell urged. "Tell the magistrate exactly what you saw."

"It . . . it was . . . awful *big,*" Garrick struggled onward, "and . . . it was black and shiny. Wet-lookin', like a snail. And . . . the worst thing was that . . . it . . ." He glanced for help first to Johnstone and then to Shields, but both those gentlemen had chosen to stare at their plates. Garrick forced himself to look at the magistrate and finish what he'd begun. "It was covered with *thorns,*" he said, and instantly he dropped his gaze to his own plate.

"Thorns," Woodward repeated; he felt a little lightheaded himself, whether from the rum or the impact of this testimony he didn't know.

"Mr. Garrick?" Matthew leaned forward. "What did the man's face look like?"

"His *face?*"

"Yes, sir. I presume you saw his face?"

"Well . . ." Garrick frowned, his eyes downcast. "I was might scared. I don't reckon I got a good look at that part of him."

"Hell's bells, boy!" Shields said, with a harsh laugh. "If you'd taken a gander at a woman sucking a foot-long black pecker covered with thorns, would *you* have looked at the face hanging over it?"

"I don't know," Matthew replied calmly. "I've never been in that position before."

"He was wearing a cloak and a cowl over his head. Isn't that what you told me, Elias?" Bidwell prompted.

"Yes sir, that he was. A black cloak, with gold buttons on the front. I seen 'em shine in the moonlight." Garrick paused once more; he swallowed thickly, his eyes glassy from the memory of what he'd witnessed. "Where his face was . . . was just dark, that's all. Like a hole you could look into and not see the bottom of. I was might scared, 'bout to wet my britches. I stood there, starin' at 'em. Both of 'em, right there behind the barn. Then all of a sudden he musta spied me . . . 'cause he said my name. Spoke it like he knew me. He said, 'Elias Garrick, do you like what you see?'" Garrick lifted trembling fingers and ran them across his lips. "I . . . wanted to run. I *tried,* but he had me rooted. He made me open my mouth. Made me say 'Yes.' Then he . . . laughed, and he let me go. I ran home, but I was too scared to wake up my 'Becca. I didn't tell her . . . I couldn't bear to tell her. But I did go to Mr. Paine, and then he took me to see Mr. Bidwell."

"And you're positive the woman you saw . . . uh . . . in service to this creature was Rachel Howarth?" Woodward asked.

"Yes sir, I am. My farm's right next to the Howarth land. That night I had me some stomach trouble, and I woke up and went outside to spew. Then I seen somebody walkin' 'cross the Howarth cornfield, near where Jess Maynard found Daniel's body. I thought it was might strange, somebody walkin' in the dark with no lantern, so I crossed the fence and followed. Went behind the barn, and that's where I seen what I did."

"You saw the woman's face, then?" Matthew asked.

"Back to the face he goes again!" Dr. Shields scoffed.

"I seen her hair," the farmer went on. "I seen . . . well . . . by the time I'd got there, she was out of her clothes."

"The woman was *naked?*" Woodward, on an impulse, reached for the tankard. There was a single drink left in it, which he made disappear.

"Naked, yes sir." Garrick nodded. "It was her, all right. Rachel Howarth, the witch." He looked from Woodward to his host and then back again to the magistrate. "Who *else* would it've been?"

"No one else," Bidwell said flatly. "Magistrate, you *do* know your daemoniacals, do you not?"

"I do."

"The witch has all but admitted a hand in murdering Reverend Grove and her husband. She has the marks, and she cannot recite the Lord's Prayer. She has the evil eye, and—most telling of all—a number of straw poppets that she fashioned to trance her victims were found hidden beneath a floorboard in her house. Rachel Howarth is most certainly a witch, and she along with her black-cocked master have almost succeeded in destroying my town."

"Mastuh Bidwell?" The voice had come from the kitchen doorway. A man with flesh as black as polished ebony stood there, peering into the dining room. The sight of such a crow coming on the heels of the discussion was startling enough to drive spikes of alarm through both Woodward and his clerk.

"Yes, Goode! Come in, we need your talents!"

The black man entered the room. He was a carrying a wooden box and something bound in a burlap wrapping. Matthew watched as the man—white-haired and ancient but moving with strong purpose and youthful posture—set the wooden box down in a corner. His coarse-clothed suit of thin gray stripes against darker gray was damp, indicating a walk of some distance through the rain. He unwrapped the burlap, exposing a wheaten-colored violin and its bow; then he stood upon the box and began to pluck and tune the violin's strings, his lean black face tilted to one side to cup the notes in an ear. As the instrument was being tuned, two negress servants came in to clear away the plates, while a third carried a burning candle.

Bidwell had produced a golden snuffbox from his jacket. He opened it and placed a pinch into both nostrils. "Now," he said after he'd snorted, "I think she should be hanged here, instead of transported to Charles Town. I believe it will do the citizens well to see her swing, and know she's good and gone. Magistrate, I'll give you the day tomorrow, to go about your business of reclaiming your property from that villain tavern-keeper. But might you see fit to pass sentence on the following day?"

"Well . . ." Woodward looked around the table. Dr. Shields was involved in his own ritual of snuff-pinching, both Johnstone and Garrick were lighting up pipes—the former a smooth briar and the latter a corncob—from the servant girl's candleflame, and Paine had drawn a leather holder from within his waistcoat. Only Winston watched the magistrate with full attention. "Well," Woodward repeated, "I . . . don't know if—"

"Mr. Bidwell, sir?" Garrick interrupted, as one of the girls reached for his plate. "Could I ask you to let me take this here piece a' chicken home to 'Becca? She sure would like a taste of it."

"Yes, of course. Naomi, take that chicken and have it wrapped for Mr. Garrick. Put some beans and potatoes in with it as well, also a slice of the vanilla cake. Our excellent dessert shall be out shortly, gentlemen." Bidwell's eyes, still watering from the snuff's sting, swung back toward the magistrate. "Will you pass sentence on the witch day after tomorrow, sir?"

"I . . . I'm afraid I can't." He felt the beginnings of a terrible itch at the back of his neck, and placing his fingers there he found he'd been pierced at least twice by a true leviathan.

"What, then? You need another day to compose yourself?"

"No, sir," Woodward said; he saw a quick flash of flame in the other man's stare. "I am a servant of the law," he continued. "I am compelled to speak to the witch—the woman, I mean—and also to witnesses both against her and in her favor."

"There's no one here in her favor!" Winston said, rather loudly; he too was feeling the rum sway his decks. "Excepting *one,* and I doubt you'd be pleased to be visited by such a witness!"

"Not only that," spoke Paine, who had withdrawn from his leather holder a slim brown cylinder, "but many of the people who saw her in the act of communion with her master have already fled." He put the cylinder into his mouth and leaned toward the offered candle, touching its tip to the flame. Blue smoke puffed from his lips. "Possibly there are two or three witnesses left, but that's all."

"She's a damn witch, and I seen her with my own good eyes!" Garrick said forcefully to Woodward. "Nicholas was the one found the poppets! I was right there with James Reed and Kelvin Bonnard, we seen him bring them poppets out of the floor! She can't speak the Lord's Prayer, and she's got the Devil's marks on her! What more do you need to hang her?"

"What more, indeed?" Shields's nostrils were flecked with snuff. The brown powder had dusted his lapels. "My God, man! The sooner she dances on the rope, the better we'll all—"

Scrrrowlllll, went a noise like a cat whose tail had been stomped. So loud and disagreeable was the sound that all present jumped in their seats and one of the servant girls dropped her plates. A silence remained, punctuated only by the rain on the roof.

"Beg pardon," Goode said, staring at the floor. His bow was poised over the quivering strings. "A bad note." Without waiting for a response, he lowered the bow and began to play in earnest—quietly this time, and much more tunefully as well. Tones as sweet as butterscotch wafted through the smoky room, and as Goode played he closed his eyes to commune with the music.

Johnstone cleared his throat and removed the pipe from between his teeth. "The magistrate is correct, Robert. If the woman is to be hanged, it must be done by the letter of the law. I say bring the witnesses forward and let them speak. Let the magistrate interview Madam Howarth as well, and divine for himself whether she's a witch or not."

"Foolishness!" Garrick scowled. "It's just givin' her time to do more harm!"

"Elias, we are not uncivilized men." The schoolmaster's voice had softened. "We are in the process of building a vital city here, so the more reason not to sully its future with our present actions." He inserted the pipestem into his mouth again and drew on it, as Goode continued to display a wondrous pleasing knowledge of harmony and timing. "I suggest the magistrate handle this situation as he sees fit," Johnstone said. "How long can it take? A week? Am I correct?" He looked at Woodward for a response.

"You are," Woodward said, with a brief nod of thanks for Johnstone's smoothing of these rough waters.

Bidwell started to say something, his face blighted with frustration as well as with insect bites, but then he thought twice about it and his mouth closed. He dug out his snuffbox again and once more indulged. "Damn," he said quietly. "You're right." He snapped the box shut. "We don't want to become a mob here, do we? Then that black-cocked bastard would have the last laugh on us."

The violin's melody never faltered. Goode's eyes were still closed.

"Very well, then." Bidwell smacked the table's edge with his palm as a way of enforcing his judgment, much as Woodward would've used his gavel. "I grant you one week to interview the witch and the witnesses."

"Kindly appreciated," Woodward answered, not without a hint of sarcasm at being rushed into what he considered an odious task.

While this small contest of wills had been going on, Matthew had been interested in watching Nicholas Paine. In particular, Paine's method of partaking tobacco by lighting up a tightly rolled leaf. Matthew had seen this only twice before, as it was very rare in the English kingdom of snuff-pinchers and pipesmen; it was called, as he understood it, smoking in the "Spanish style."

Paine took a puff, released the blue smoke into the thickened air, and suddenly turned his head to look directly into Matthew's face. "Your eyes have gotten large, young man. Might I ask what you're staring at?"

"Uh . . ." Matthew resisted the urge to avert his gaze. He decided in another second that he didn't care to make an issue of this, though he didn't quite understand why his mind told him to make a note of it. "Nothing, sir," he said. "My pardon."

Paine lowered the smoking stick—Matthew thought it was called a "cigar"—and directed his attention to his host. "If I'm going to lead this expedition at sunrise, I'd best find two or three other men to go along." He stood up. "Thank you for the dinner and the company. Magistrate, I'll meet you at the public stable. It's behind the blacksmith's shop on Industry Street. Good night to you all." He nodded, as the other men—excepting Bidwell and Dr. Shields—stood as a matter of courtesy, and then he left the dining room with a brisk stride, the "cigar" gripped between his teeth.

"Nicholas seemed ill at sorts," Johnstone said after Paine was gone; he grasped his deformed knee for extra support as he eased himself onto the bench again. "This situation has gotten the best of all of us."

"Yes, but the dawn of our dark night has arrived." Bidwell

looked over his shoulder. "Goode!" The black man immediately stopped playing and lowered the violin. "Are there any more turtles in the spring?" Bidwell asked.

"Yes, suh. They be some big ones." His voice was as mellow as the violin's.

"Catch us one tomorrow. Magistrate, we'll have turtle soup in our bowls for dinner. Would that suit you?"

"Very much," Woodward said, scratching another massive welt on his forehead. "I pray that all goes well with our hunting party on the morrow. If you want a hanging in your town, I'd be glad to pass sentence on Shawcombe as soon as we return."

"That might be splendid!" Bidwell's eyes lit up. "Yes! To show the citizens that the wheels of justice are indeed in motion! That would be a fine sippet before the main course! Goode, play us something merry!"

The black servant lifted his violin again and began another tune; it was faster and more lively than the one previous, but Matthew thought it was still more tinged with melancholy than merriment. Goode's eyes closed again, sealing himself off from his circumstances.

The vanilla cake arrived, along with another tankard of rum. Talk of Rachel Howarth dwindled, while Bidwell's talk of his plans for Fount Royal increased. Matthew found himself drifting, itching in a dozen places and longing for the embrace of the bed in his room. The candles burned low in the overhead chandelier. Garrick excused himself and went home, followed soon afterward by the schoolmaster. Dr. Shields, after imbibing much of the fresh tankard, laid his head upon the table and so departed the company. Bidwell dismissed Goode, who carefully wrapped the violin in the burlap before he braved the weather. Winston also began to drowse in his chair, his head thrown back and his mouth open. Woodward's eyes were heavy, his chin dropping. At last their host stood up, yawned, and stretched.

"I'll take my leave of you," Bidwell announced. "I hope you both sleep well."

"I'm sure we shall, thank you."

"If there's anything you need, Mrs. Nettles will be at your service. I trust your endeavors tomorrow will be successful." He started out of the room, then halted on the threshold. "Magistrate, don't put yourself at risk. Paine can handle a pistol. Let him and his men do the dirty work, as I require you for a higher purpose. Understand?"

"Yes."

"Good night then, gentlemen." Bidwell turned and left the dining room, and in a moment could be heard tromping up the staircase to his own quarters.

Woodward regarded the two sleepers, to make sure they were both unconscious, and then said to Matthew, "Nothing like a command performance to sharpen the wits, eh? One week to decide the fate of a woman I've never met. Even the coldhearted murderers in Newgate prison are afforded more time than that. Well . . ." He stood up, his vision bleary. "I'm to bed. Good night."

"Good night, sir," Matthew replied. After the magistrate had trudged out, Matthew got up from the bench and retrieved the empty tankard near Dr. Shields's outstretched hand. He stared into it, recalling the tankard in which Shawcombe had dropped the gold coin. A Spanish coin, taken from an Indian. What was an Indian doing with a Spanish coin? This question had needled him all day, daring him to find an answer. It was still there, something that required clearing away before he could fully concentrate on his clerking duties and the case of the witch. Possibly Shawcombe could be persuaded to shed more light on it, before he swung.

Tomorrow was sure to be an interesting day. Mathew returned the tankard to the table, then wearily climbed the stairs to his room. Within a few minutes he was asleep in his borrowed clothes.

six

Fɪʀsᴛ Pʀᴏᴠɪᴅᴇɴᴄᴇ had brought the magistrate and his clerk to Shawcombe's wretched little tavern, and now necessity had returned them.

There stood the place, festering alongside the muddy track. As he saw it come into view, Woodward felt his guts tighten. He and Matthew were sitting in a wagon whose team of horses was guided by Malcolm Jennings, he of the hawkish eye and toothless mouth. On the left, Nicholas Paine sat easily astride a burly chestnut stallion while on the right a third militiaman named Duncan Tyler—an older man, his beard gray and face seamed with wrinkles but his attitude right and eager for the job at hand—mounted a black horse. The journey from Fount Royal had taken well over three hours, and even though the rain had ceased before dawn the sky was still pale gray with clouds. The onset of an oppressive, damp heat had caused steam to rise from the muck. All the travellers were wet with sweat under their shirts, the horses ill tempered and stubborn.

Still fifty yards from the tavern, Paine lifted his hand as a signal for Jennings to halt the wagon. "Wait here," he commanded, and he and Tyler rode their horses on to the tavern's door. Paine reined his steed and dismounted. He brought his wheel-lock pistol from his saddlebag and inserted a spanner to properly wind and prepare the mechanism. Tyler got off his horse and, a readied wheel-lock pistol also in hand, followed the captain of militia up onto the tavern's porch.

Matthew and the magistrate watched as Paine balled up his fist and pounded the door. "Shawcombe!" they heard him call. "Open up!"

There was no response. Matthew expected at any second to hear the ugly *crack* of a pistol shot. The door was unlatched, and the force of Paine's fist had made it creak open a few inches. Inside was not a glimmer of light. "Shawcombe!" Paine shouted warily. "You'll be better served by showing yourself!" Still no response.

"They're like to get they heads blowed off," Jennings said, both hands gripping the reins and his knuckles white.

Paine put one boot against the door and kicked it wide open.

"Careful," Woodward breathed.

Paine and Tyler entered the tavern. The others waited, Matthew and Woodward expecting to hear shouts and shots. But no such things happened. Presently Paine reappeared. He held his pistol down at his side and motioned for Jennings to bring the wagon and the passengers the rest of the distance.

"Where are they?" Woodward asked as he climbed down from the wagon. "Didn't you find them?"

"No sir. It appears they've cleared out."

"Damn it!" Heat rose into Woodward's face. "That cunning bastard! But wait, there's the barn to be searched!"

"Duncan!" Paine called into the tavern's gloom. "I'm going back to the barn!" He started off, slogging through the mud, and Matthew followed at a distance respectful of any gunfire that might erupt from the barn or the forest. Matthew quickly noted that things had indeed changed: the horses were no longer in their corral, which was wide open, and the pigs were gone as well. The rooster, hens, and chicks were likewise vanished. The barn door was slightly ajar, its locking timber lying in the mud nearby. Paine lifted his pistol again. "Come out of there!" he called toward the entrance. "I won't hesitate to shoot!"

But again, no one replied. Paine glanced sharply back at

Matthew as a warning to remain where he was, then he walked forward and pulled the barn door open wider. He peered in, his pistol ready for any sudden movement. He drew a breath to steel himself and walked inside.

Matthew waited, his heart pounding. Presently, Paine emerged with his pistol lowered. "Not in there," he said. "I found two wagons, but no horses."

Then they *were* well and truly fled, Matthew thought. Probably when Shawcombe realized his intended victims might reach Fount Royal, he knew his reign had ended. "I'll show you where Shawcombe buried the bodies," he told Paine, and led him around behind the barn toward the woods. Back there, where the watersoaked earth had given way and revealed Shawcombe's misdeeds, a small storm cloud of flies swirled above the grisly remains. Paine put one hand over his mouth and nose to stifle the smell and approached the gravepit, but only close enough for a quick look before he retreated.

"Yes," he said, his face gone pasty-gray. "I see the picture."

Matthew and Paine returned to the tavern. Tyler had opened most of the shutters, allowing the daylight to overrun Shawcombe's sorry domain. With the onset of such illumination, the rats that had been making carnival in every room put up a fierce and indignant squealing and fled for their holes, save one large individual that bared its teeth and might've attacked had not Tyler's right boot dealt the first and bone-breaking blow. Jennings was happily busying himself by collecting such items as lanterns, wooden bowls, spoons and knives, and other small utensils that could be easily carted home. Matthew found the magistrate standing in the room from which they'd escaped; the light revealed the shattered door and on the floorboards the dark brown stains of Shawcombe's blood.

"Gone," Woodward said grimly. "Everything, gone."

And so it was. Their luggage—the two trunks and the wig box, the valise containing Matthew's writing quills, inkpot, and tablet—had disappeared.

"My waistcoat." Woodward might've sunken down onto the

straw pallet, but evidence of rodent habitation prevented him, even though he felt weak enough to faint. "That animal Shawcombe has taken my waistcoat, Matthew." He looked into the younger man's face, and Matthew saw that his eyes were damp with soul-deep anguish. "I'll never get it back now," he said. "Never."

"It was just a garment, " Matthew answered, and instantly he knew it was the wrong thing to say because the magistrate winced as if he'd been physically struck.

"No." Woodward slowly shook his head; he stood stoop-shouldered, as if crushed by a tremendous sadness. "It was my *life.*"

"Magistrate?" Paine called. He looked into the room before Woodward could rouse himself to respond. "They haven't been gone very long. The fire's still banked. Did you find your belongings?"

"No. They've been taken."

"Oh, I'm sorry. You had some items of value?"

"Very much value, yes. Shawcombe took everything."

"This is a strange state of affairs," Matthew said, after a moment of thought. He went to the open window and stared toward the barn. "There are no horses here, but Shawcombe left two wagons. I presume one of those is ours. Shawcombe took our luggage and his pigs and chickens, but he left behind the lanterns. I'd say a good lantern is as valuable as a hen, wouldn't you?"

"Hey, hey! Looky what I done found!" came a happy cry from the front room. Paine hurried to see what the discovery was, followed by the magistrate and Matthew.

Jennings, who'd uncovered a burlap sack in which to deposit his booty, was holding a wooden tankard. His lips were wet, his eyes shiny. "Rum!" he said. "This was a-settin' right on that table over there! Might be a bottle 'round somewhere. We oughta hunt it down a'fore we—"

"One moment," Matthew said, and he approached the man and took the tankard from him. Without another word, Matthew held the tankard over the nearest table and upended it.

"Great God, boy!" Jennings squalled as the drink poured out. "Are you cra—"

Plink!

A gold coin had fallen from the bottom of the murky brown liquid. Matthew picked it up and looked closely at it, but he already knew what it was. "It's a Spanish piece," he said. "Shawcombe told me he got it off a dead Indian. I saw him drop it in that tankard."

"Let me see that!" Paine reached out for it, and Matthew gave it up. Paine walked closer to a window, the better to inspect the coin's details. Tyler stood behind him, looking at the coin over Paine's shoulder. "You're right, it *is* Spanish," the militia captain said. "You say Shawcombe got it from a dead *Indian?*"

"That's what he claimed."

"Strange. Why would an Indian be in possession of Spanish gold?"

"Shawcombe believed there was—" Matthew suddenly stopped. *A Spanish spy hereabouts,* he had been meaning to say. But he had the mental image of Paine lighting his cigar at the banquet last night. Smoking in the Spanish style. Who had taught Paine to take his tobacco in that fashion?

Matthew recalled, as well, something else that Shawcombe had said about this Spanish spy: *Hell, he might even be livin' in Fount Royal, an Englishman turned blackcoat!*

"Believed what?" Paine's voice was quiet and controlled; his fist had closed around the gold piece.

"He . . . said . . ." Matthew hesitated, thinking furiously. He couldn't make out the expression on Paine's face, as the steamy light held Paine in silhouette. "He . . . believed the Indians might have found pirate's gold," Matthew finished, lamely.

"Pirate's gold?" Jennings had sniffed a new intoxication. "Where? 'Round here?"

"Steady, Malcolm," Paine warned. "One coin does not make a fortune. We've had no squall with pirates, nor do we wish to." He cocked his head to one side and Matthew could tell his brainwheels were turning. "Shawcombe was wrong," he said. "No black-flagger in his right mind would bury his loot in redskin wilderness. They hide their gold where they can easily get to it, but it would be a poor pirate whose winnings could be found and unearthed by savages."

"I imagine so," Matthew said, unwilling to dig his grave of deceit any deeper.

"Still . . . how *else* would an Indian get hold of this? Unless there was a shipwreck, and somehow this washed up. Intriguing, wouldn't you say, Magistrate?"

"Another possibility," Woodward ventured, "that a Spaniard *gave* it to the Indian, down in the Florida country."

"No, the redskins around here wouldn't travel that far. The tribes in the Florida country would make sure to part the scalps from their skulls."

"Stranger still," Matthew spoke up, wanting to divert this line of discourse, "is the fact that Shawcombe left that coin in the tankard."

"He must'a been in an almighty hurry to get out," Jennings said.

"But he took the time to gather up our luggage and his pigs and chickens? I think not." Matthew swept his gaze around the room. Nothing was disturbed; no tables overthrown, no blood nor evidence of violence. The hearth was still warm, the cooking kettles still in the ashes. There was no hint of what had happened to Shawcombe or the others. Matthew found himself thinking about the girl; what had become of her, as well? "I don't know," he said, thinking aloud. "But I *do* know Shawcombe would never have left that coin. Under ordinary circumstances, I mean."

Paine gave a soft grunt. He worked the coin with his fingers for a few seconds, and then he held it out to Matthew. "This is yours, I suppose. It's most likely all the revenge you'll have from Shawcombe."

"Revenge is not our aim, sir," Woodward said curtly. "Justice is. And I must say that justice has been cheated this day."

"Well, I don't think Shawcombe's going to return here." Paine bent down and picked up the burnt stub of a candle from the floor. "I would offer to stay the night and keep watch, but I don't care to be eaten alive." He looked uneasily around at the room's shadowy corners, from which some agitated squeaking could still be heard. "This is a place only Linch could abide."

"Who?" the magistrate asked.

"Gwinett Linch. Our ratcatcher in Fount Royal. Even *he* might wake up with his legs chewed off in this damn hovel." Paine tossed the candlestub into one of the dark corners. Something large scuttled for safety. "I saw tack and harness in the barn. Duncan, you and I can hitch our horses to the magistrate's wagon and let them take it back. Is that agreeable to you, Magistrate?"

"Absolutely."

"All right, then. I say we quit this place." Paine and Tyler went outside to discharge their pistols into the air, because the firing mechanisms, once wound, were as dangerous as coiled vipers. Tyler's pistol fired immediately, but Paine's threw sparks and went off only after a sputtering delay.

Within a half hour, the horses were harnessed to the recovered wagon and Woodward was at the reins, following the first wagon on the swampy trail back to Fount Royal. Matthew occupied the uncomfortable plank beside the magistrate, while Paine and Tyler rode with Malcolm Jennings; he looked back at Shawcombe's tavern before they left it from sight, imagining what the place would be like in a few days—or, forbid the thought, a few *weeks*—of uninterrupted rodent dominion. The image of the young girl, who had seemed to be only a bystander to her master's crimes, again came to him, and he couldn't help but wonder why God could be so cruel. But she was gone to her fate—as they all were—and there was nothing more to be done. With that thought he turned his gaze from the past and aimed it toward the future.

Matthew and Woodward were alone together for the first time since their arrival at Fount Royal, as their walk from Bidwell's mansion to the public stable this morning had been escorted by a young black servant boy on Mrs. Nettles's command. It was, therefore, the first opportunity Matthew had to make remarks about their dinner companions of the night before without the ears of strangers between them.

But it was the magistrate who first grasped the chance to speak freely. "What do you make of Paine, Matthew?"

"He seems to know his work."

"Yes, he does. He seems also to know the work of . . . That term he used: a 'black-flagger' . . . Interesting."

"How so?"

"In New York some years ago . . . I believe it was 1693 or thereabouts . . . I sat at the docket on a case involving a man who had come up on charges of piracy. I recall the case because he was a learned man, a timber merchant who'd lost his business to creditors. His wife and two children had died by the plague. He was not at all the kind of man you might expect would turn to that life. I remember . . . he referred to his compatriots as 'black-flaggers.' I'd never heard that term before." Woodward glanced up at the sky, making judgment on how long it might be before the thick gray clouds let loose another torrent. "I'd never heard the term since, until Paine spoke it." He returned his attention to the road ahead. "Evidently, it's a term used with respect and more than a little pride. As one member of a society speaking about another."

"Are you suggesting that Paine—"

"I'm suggesting nothing," Woodward interrupted. "I'm only saying that it's of interest, that's all." He paused to emphasize his position. Then he said, casually, "I should like to know more about Mr. Paine's background. Just for interest's sake, of course."

"What happened to the timber merchant?"

"Ex–timber merchant," the magistrate corrected. "He committed murder on the high seas, as well as piracy. He was guilty, no matter what the circumstances of his fall from grace. I ached for his soul, but I had no recourse other than to sentence him to hanging. And so it was done."

"I was going to ask you what you thought of the guests last night," Matthew said. "Take Schoolmaster Johnstone. What do you make of his face powder?"

"Such fashion is currently popular in Europe, but I've seen it in the colonies on occasion. Actually, though, I believe I have another explanation for his appearance."

"What might that be?"

"He attended Oxford, yes? All Souls' College. Well, that college had a reputation as being the plaything of young dandies and gamblers who were certainly not there for spiritual enlightenment. The core of the debauchers at All Souls' was an organization called the Hellfire Club. It was a very old gathering, closed to all but a select few within the college, those with wealthy families and debased sensibilities. Among Hellfire Club members the custom was to wear daubings of white ashes the morning after their bawdy banquets." He looked quickly at Matthew and then focused on the road once more. "There was some strange pseudo-religious significance to it, I think. As in washing their faces clean of sin, that sort of thing. Unfortunately, they couldn't powder their hearts. But perhaps Johnstone is simply aware of European fashion and wishes to mimic it, though why one would care to do so in this forsaken wilderness is beyond me."

Matthew said nothing, but he was thinking about the magistrate insisting they dress for dinner at that wretched tavern.

"It *is* peculiar, though," Woodward mused. "If Johnstone was a member of the Hellfire Club—and I'm not saying he *was,* though there are indications—why would he care to carry on its custom so long after he left Oxford? I mean to say, I used to wear a crimson jacket with green tassels dangling from the sleeves when I was a college student, but I wouldn't dream of putting on such an item today." He shook his head. "No, it must be that Johnstone has embraced the European trend. Of course, I doubt if he wears his powder in the daytime. Such would only be for nocturnal festivities."

"He seems an intelligent man," Matthew said. "I wonder why a schoolmaster who'd earned his education at Oxford would consent to come to a settlement like Fount Royal. One would think he might prefer more civilized surroundings."

"True. But why are *any* of them in Fount Royal? For that matter, why does anyone in his or her right mind consent to go live in a place that seems poised on the edge of the earth? But they do. Otherwise there would be no New York or Boston, Philadelphia or Charles Town. Take Dr. Shields, for instance. What prompted him to leave what was probably a well-established urban practise for a task of extreme hardship in a frontier village? Is Bidwell paying him a great deal of money? Is it a noble sense of professional duty? Or something else entirely?" Woodward tilted his gaze upward once more; his eyes had found the slow, graceful circling of a hawk against the curtain of clouds. It occurred to him that the hawk had spied a victim—a rabbit or squirrel, perhaps—on the ground.

"Dr. Shields seems to me an unhappy man," Woodward went on, and he cleared his throat; it had been moderately sore and scratchy since his awakening this morning, and he resolved to gargle some warm salt water to soothe it. "He seems also to want to drown his sorrows in strong drink. I'm sure that the high rate of deaths in Fount Royal does nothing to ease the doctor's depression. Still . . . one would hope Dr. Shields does not rely too much on the cup when he's making his professional rounds." He watched the hawk wheel around and suddenly dive for its prey, and he had the thought that death was always close at hand in this world of tumults and cataclysms.

That thought led into another, which also involved death: he saw in his mind small fingers curled around the iron frame of a bedpost. The knuckles—so perfect, so fragile—were bleached white from the pressure of a terrified grip.

Woodward squeezed his eyes shut. The sounds had almost come to him again. Almost. He could not stand hearing those sounds, even from this distance of time and place. From the deep green thicket on his left he thought he heard the shrill, triumphant cry of a hawk and the brief scream of some small animal.

"Sir?" He opened his eyes. Matthew was staring at him. "Are you all right?"

98 • Robert McCammon

"Yes," Woodward said. "A little weary, perhaps. It will pass."

"I'll take the reins, if you like."

"Not necessary." Woodward gave them a flick across the horses' haunches to show he was in full command. "I would be just as weary riding as a passenger. Besides, at least this time we know Fount Royal is not very far."

"Yes, sir," Matthew answered. After a moment, he reached into the pocket of his trousers and took out the gold coin he'd put there. He held it in his palm and studied the markings. "I told an untruth to Mr. Paine," he admitted. "About this coin. Shawcombe did take it from the body of an Indian . . . but he told me he believed there might be a Spanish spy hereabouts who was paying the Indians for their loyalty."

"What? He said nothing about pirate's gold, then?"

"No, sir. I made that up because of the fashion in which Paine took his tobacco after dinner last night. He smoked a roll called a 'cigar.' It's—"

"A Spanish custom, yes." Woodward nodded; his eyes narrowed, a sign that told Matthew he was intrigued by this new information. "Hmmm. Yes, I understand your fiction. Very few Englishmen that I know of have taken to smoking in such a manner. I wondered about it last night, but I said nothing. But there's the question of how Paine might have become introduced to it."

"Yes, sir. Shawcombe also made mention that the Spanish spy might be an Englishman. Or at least an Englishman in appearance. And that he might be living in Fount Royal."

"Curious. What would be the purpose of such a spy? Ah!" he said, answering his own question. "Of course! To report on the progress of Fount Royal. Which may yet turn out to be known as Bidwell's Folly, I might add. But what part would the Indians play in this, that they would have to be tamed by Spanish gold?"

Matthew had already formulated this question and given it some thought. He ventured his opinion, something he was never reluctant to do: "One of Bidwell's motives behind the creation of Fount Royal is as a fort to keep watch on the Spanish. It might be that they're already much nearer than the Florida country."

"You mean living with the Indians?"

Matthew nodded. "A small expeditionary force, possibly. If not living *with* the Indians, then close enough to want to seek their good graces."

Woodward almost reined the horses in, so hard did this speculation hit him. "My God!" he said. "If that's true—if there's any possibility of it being true—then Bidwell's got to be told! If the Spaniards could incite the Indians to attack Fount Royal, they wouldn't have to lift a finger to destroy the whole settlement!"

"Yes, sir, but I don't think Mr. Bidwell should be alarmed in such a way just yet."

"Why not? He'd want to know, wouldn't he?"

"I'm sure he would," Matthew agreed calmly. "But for now you and I are the only ones making these suppositions. And that's what they should remain, until some proof can be found."

"You don't think the coin is proof enough?"

"No, I don't. As Mr. Paine said, one coin does not make a fortune. Nor does it give proof that Spanish soldiers are encamped out in the wilderness. But if such an idea flew out of Mr. Bidwell's mouth and into the ears of the citizens, it would mean the certain end of Fount Royal."

"Do you propose we do nothing?" Woodward asked, rather sharply.

"I propose we watch and listen," Matthew said. "That we make some discreet inquiries and—as far as we are able—monitor Mr. Paine's activities. If indeed there *is* a spy, he might be waiting to see what develops concerning the witchcraft case. After all, with Satan walking the fields, Fount Royal may simply continue to shrivel up and soon dissolve."

"Well, it's a damnable thing!" the magistrate snorted. "You raise these speculations, but you don't wish to act on them!"

"Now is not the time. Besides, sir, I believe we both have a more pressing engagement with Rachel Howarth."

Woodward started to respond, but sealed his mouth. The wagon's wheels continued to turn through the mud, the two horses keeping a slow but steady pace. After a spell of deliberation, Woodward cleared his throat again. "Rachel Howarth," he said. "I can't say I look forward to making her acquaintance tomorrow. What did you make of Garrick's story?"

"Very strange."

"A grand understatement, I should think. I don't believe I've ever heard anything quite like it. In fact, I know I haven't. But is it *believable?*"

"Unless he's one of the best liars I've ever heard, *he* believes it."

"Then he did see someone or something behind that barn, yes? But that act he described . . . how in the name of all that's holy could a woman perform in such a way?"

"I don't think we're dealing with a holy situation," Matthew reminded him.

"No. Of course not. Two murders. It seems reasonable that the first murder should've been a minister. The diabolic would seek to destroy first and foremost a man who could wield the sword of God."

"Yes, sir, it does. But in this instance, it appears the blade of Satan was a stronger weapon."

"I'd keep such blasphemies chained, before you're summoned to a higher court by a bolt of lightning," Woodward cautioned.

Matthew's eyes regarded the green, steamy wilderness that loomed beside the road, but his mind had turned to other sights: namely, the finding of truth in this matter of witchcraft. It was a blasphemous thought—and he knew he risked eternal damnation for thinking it—but sometimes he had to wonder if there was indeed a God who reigned over this earthly arena of fury and brutality. Matthew could sing the hymns and mouth the platitudes with the best of them, in the stiffly regimented Sabbath church services that basically consisted of the minister begging for five or six hours that Jehovah show mercy on His wounded and crippled Creation. But in his life Matthew had seen very little real evidence of God at work, though it seemed he'd seen much of Satan's fingermarks. It was easy to sing praise to God when one was wearing a clean white shirt and eating from china platters, much less easy when one lay on a dirty mattress in an almshouse dormitory and heard the shrill scream of a boy who'd been summoned after midnight to the headmaster's chambers.

SOMETIMES HE DID DREAM of his mother and father. Not often, but sometimes. In those dreams he saw two figures that he knew were his parents, but he could never clearly see their faces. The shadows were always too deep. He might not have recognized them even if he had been able to see their faces, as his mother had died of poisoned blood when he was three years old and his father—a taciturn but hardworking Massachusetts colony plowman who had tried his best to raise the boy alone—succumbed to the kick of a horse to the cranium when Matthew was in his sixth year. And with the flailing of that fatal equine hoof, Matthew was thrust into a pilgrimage that would both mold and test his mettle. His first stop on the journey was the squalid little cabin of his uncle and aunt who ran a pig farm on Manhattan island. As they were both drunks and insensate much of the time, with two imbecile children aged eight and nine who thought of Matthew as an object to be tormented—which included regular flights into a huge pile of pig manure beside the house—Matthew at seven years of age leaped upon the back of a southbound haywagon, burrowed into the hay, and so departed the loving embrace of his nearest relatives.

There followed almost four months of living hand-to-mouth on the New York waterfront, falling in with a group of urchins who either begged from the merchants and traders in that locale or stole from them when the fires of hunger became too hot. Matthew knew what it was like to fight for a few crumbs of hard bread and feel like a king when he came away from the battle bloody-nosed but his fists clenching sustenance. The finale to that episode in his life came when one of the harbor merchants roused the constable to action and men of the law subsequently raided the beach-wrecked ship where Matthew and the others were sheltered. They were caught in nets and bound up like what they were—kicking, spitting, frightened, vicious little animals.

And then a black wagon carried them all—still bound and now gagged to contain the foul language they'd gleaned from the merchants—over the city's hard dirt streets, four horses pulling the load of snot-nosed criminals, a driver whipping, a bell-ringer warning citizens out of the way. The wagon pulled to a halt in front of a building whose bricks were soot-dark and glistening with rain, like the rough hide of some squatting lizard yellow-eyed and hungry. Matthew and the others were taken none too gently out of the wagon and through the iron-gated entrance; he would always remember the awful sound that gate made as it clanged shut and a latchpin fell into place. Then under an archway and through another door into a hall, and he was well and truly in the chill embrace of the Sainted John Home for Boys.

His first full day in that drear domain consisted of being scrubbed with coarse soap, immersed in a skin-stinging solution meant to kill lice and fleas, his hair shorn to the scalp, his nails trimmed, and his teeth brushed by the eldest of the boys—the "fellows," he was to learn they were called—who were overseen by an eagle-eyed "commander" by the name of Harrison, aged seventeen and afflicted with a withered left hand. Then, dressed in a stiff-collared gray gown and wearing square-toed Puritan shoes, Matthew was taken into a room where an old man with sharp blue eyes and a wreath of white hair sat behind a desk awaiting him. A quill pen, ledgerbook, and inkwell adorned the desktop.

They were left alone. Matthew looked around the room, which held shelves of books and had a window overlooking the street. He walked directly across the bare wooden floor to the window and peered out into the gray light. In the misty distance he could see the masts of ships that lay at harbor. It was a strange window, with nine squares set in some kind of metal frame. The shutters were open, and yet when Matthew reached toward the outside world his hand was stopped by a surface that was all but invisible. He placed his palm against one of the squares and pressed, but the surface would not yield. The outside world was there to be seen, the shutters were open, but some eerie force prevented him from pushing his hand through.

"It's called 'glass,'" the man behind the desk said in a quiet voice.

Matthew brought his other hand up and pressed all his fingers against this strange new magic. His heart was beating hard, as he realized this was something beyond his understanding. How could a window be open and closed at the same time?

"Do you have a name?" the man asked. Matthew didn't bother answering. He was enraptured in studying the mysterious window.

"I am Headmaster Staunton," the man said, still quietly. "Can you tell me how old you are?" Matthew pressed his face forward, his nose pushing against the surface. His breath bloomed before him. "I suspect you've had a difficult time. Would you tell me about it?"

Matthew's fingers were at work again, probing and investigating, his young brow furrowed with thought.

"Where are your parents?" Staunton asked.

"Dead," Matthew replied, before he could think not to.

"And what was your family name?"

Matthew tapped at the window with his knuckles. "Where does this come from?"

Staunton paused, his head cocked to one side as he regarded the boy. Then he reached out with a thin, age-spotted hand, picked up a pair of spectacles on the desk before him, and put them on. "The glazier makes it."

"Glazier? What's that?"

"A man whose business is making glass and setting it in lead window frames." Matthew shook his head, uncomprehending. "It's a craft not long introduced into the colonies. Does it interest you?"

"Never seen the like. It's a window open and shut at the same time."

"Yes, I suppose you might say that." The headmaster smiled slightly, which served to soften his gaunt face. "You have some curiosity, don't you?"

"I don't got nothin'," Matthew said adamantly. "Them sons-abitches come and now we ain't got nothin', none of us."

"I have seen six of your tribe so far this afternoon. You're the only one who's shown interest in that window. I think you do have some curiosity."

Matthew shrugged. He felt a pressure at his bladder, and so he lifted the front of his gown and peed against the wall.

"I see you've learned to be an animal. We must unlearn some things. Relieving yourself without benefit of a bucket—and in privacy, as a gentleman—would earn you two stings of the whip given by the punishment captain. The speaking of profanity is also worthy of two lashes." Staunton's voice had become solemn, his eyes stern behind the spectacles. "As you're new here, I will let this first display of bad habits pass, though you *shall* mop up your mess. The next time you do such a thing, I will make certain the lashes are delivered promptly and—believe me, son—the punishment captain performs his task very well. Do you understand me?"

Matthew was about to shrug again, dismissing the old man's complaint; but he was aware of the fierce gaze that was levelled at him, and he had some idea that he might be doing himself future harm not to respond. He nodded, and then he turned away from the headmaster to once more direct his full attention to the window's glass. He ran his fingers over it, feeling the undulating ripples and swells of its surface.

"How old are you?" Staunton asked. "Seven? Eight?"

"'Tween 'em," Matthew said.

"Can you read and write?"

"I know some numbers. Ten fingers, ten toes. That makes twenty. Double that's forty. Double again's . . ." He thought about it. His father had taught him some basic arithmetic, and they'd been working on the alphabet when the horse's hoof had met skullbone. "Forty and forty," he said. "I know *a-b-c-d-e-f-g-h-i-j-n-l-o-p-k* too."

"Well, it's a beginning. You were given a name by your parents, I presume?"

Matthew hesitated; it seemed to him that telling this headmaster his name would give the man some power over him, and he wasn't ready to do that. "This here window," he said. "It don't let the rain in?"

"No, it doesn't. On a windy day, it allows sunlight but turns away the wind. Therefore I have more light to read by, but no fear of my books and papers being disturbed."

"Damn!" Matthew said with true wonder. "What'll they think of next?"

"Watch your language, young man," Staunton cautioned, but not without a hint of amusement. "The next profanity will raise a blister on your hide. Now, I want you to know and remember this: I want to be your friend, but it is your choice whether we are friends or adversaries. Enemies, I mean to say. In this almshouse there are sixty-eight boys, ages seven to seventeen. I do not have the time nor resources to coddle you, nor will I overlook bad manners or a troublesome attitude. What the lash does not cure, the dunking barrel remedies." He paused to let that pronouncement sink to its proper depth. "You will be given studies to achieve, and chores to perform, as befits your age. You will be expected to learn to read and write, as well as calculate arithmetic. You will go to chapel on the Sabbath and learn the holy writ. *And* you shall comport yourself as a young gentlemen. But," Staunton added in a gentler tone, "this is not a prison, and I am not a warden. The main purpose of this place is to prepare you for leaving it."

"When?" Matthew asked.

"In due time, and not before." Staunton plucked the quill from the inkwell and poised it over the open ledgerbook. "I'd like to know your name now."

Matthew's attention had wandered back to the window's glass once more. "I sure would like to see how this is made," he said. "It's a puzzle how it's done, ain't it?"

"Not such a puzzle." Staunton stared at the boy for a moment, and then he said, "I'll strike a deal with you, son. The glazier has a workshop not far from here. You tell me your name and your circumstances, and—as you're so interested in the craft—I'll ask the glazier to come and explain it. Does that sound reasonable?"

Matthew considered it. The man, he realized, was offering him something that set a spark to his candle: knowledge. "Reason'ble," he repeated, with a nod. "My name's Matthew Corbett. Two *t*'s and two *t*'s."

Headmaster Staunton entered the name into the ledger in small but precise handwriting, and thus was Matthew's life greatly altered from its previous muddy course.

Given books and patient encouragement, Matthew proved to be a quick study. Staunton was true to his word and brought the glazier in to explain his craft to the assembly of boys; so popular was the visit that soon followed a shoemaker, a sailmaker, a blacksmith, and other honest, hardworking citizens of the city beyond the almshouse walls. Staunton—a devoutly religious man who had been a minister before becoming headmaster—was scrupulously fair but set high goals and expectations for his charges. After several encounters with the lash, Matthew's use of profanity ended and his manners improved. His reading and writing skills after a year were so proficient that Staunton decided to teach him Latin, an honor given only to two other boys in the home, and the key that opened for Matthew many more volumes from Staunton's library. Two years of intense Latin training, as well as further English and arithmetic studies, saw Matthew leave the other scholars behind, so sharp and undivided was his power of concentration.

It was not a bad life. He did such chores as were required of him and then returned to his studies with a passion that bordered on religious fervor. As some of the boys with whom he'd entered the almshouse left to become apprentices to craftsmen, and new boys were brought in, Matthew remained a fixed star—solitary, aloof—that directed his light only toward the illumination of answers to the multitude of questions that perplexed him. When Matthew turned twelve, Staunton—who was now in his sixty-fourth year and beginning to suffer from palsy—began to teach the boy French, as much to sow a language he himself found fascinating as well as to further cultivate Matthew's appreciation of mental challenges.

Discipline of thought and control of action became Matthew's purpose in life. While the other boys played such games as slide groat and wicket, Matthew was likely to be found dredging through a Latin tome on astronomy or copying French literature to improve his handwriting. His dedication to the intellectual—indeed his slavery to the appetite of his own mind—began to concern Headmaster Staunton, who had to encourage Matthew's participation in games and exercise by limiting his access to the books. Still, Matthew was apart and afar from the other boys, and had grown gangly legged and ill-suited for the rough-and-tumble festivities his compatriots enjoyed, and so even in their midst he was alone.

Matthew had just seen his fourteenth birthday when Headmaster Staunton made a startling announcement to the boys and the other almshouse workers: he had experienced a dream in which Christ appeared, wearing shining white robes, and told him his work was done at the Home. The task that remained for him was to leave and travel west into the frontier wilderness, to teach the Indian tribes the salvation of God. This dream was to Staunton so real and compelling that there was no question of disobedience; it was, to him, the call to glory that would assure his ascent into Heaven.

Before he left—at age sixty-six and severely palsied—Headmaster Staunton dedicated his library of books to the almshouse, as well as leaving to the Home's fund the majority of the money he'd banked over his service of some thirty years. To Matthew in particular he gave a small box wrapped in plain white paper, and asked the boy not to open it until he'd boarded a wagon and departed the following morning. And so, after wishing every boy in his charge good fortune and a good life, Headmaster Staunton took the reins of his future and travelled to the ferry that would deliver him across the Hudson River into his own personal promised land, a Bible his only shield and companion.

In the solitude of the Home's chapel, Matthew unwrapped

the box and opened it. Within it was a palm-sized pane of glass, especially made by the glazier. Matthew knew what Headmaster Staunton had given him: a clear view unto the world.

A short time later, however, the Home had a new headmaster by the name of Eben Ausley, who in Matthew's opinion was a rotund, fat-jowled lump of pure vileness. Ausley quickly dismissed all of Staunton's staff and brought in his own band of thugs and bullies. The lash was used as never before, and the dunking barrel became a commonplace item of dread employed for the slightest infraction. Whippings became beatings, and many was the night that Ausley took a young boy into his chambers after the dormitory's lamps were extinguished; what occurred in that chamber was unspeakable, and one boy was so shamed by the deed that he hanged himself from the chapel's belltower.

At fifteen, Matthew was too old to attract Ausley's attentions. The headmaster left him alone and Matthew burrowed ever deeper into his studies. Ausley didn't share Staunton's sense of order and cleanliness; soon the place was a pigsty, and the rats grew so bold they seized food off the platters at suppertime. Several boys ran away; some were returned, and given severe whippings and starvation diets. Some died and were buried in crude pinewood boxes in a cemetery beside the chapel. Matthew read his books, honed his Latin and French, and in a deep part of himself vowed that someday, somehow, he would bring justice to bear on Eben Ausley, as a grinding wheel on a piece of rotten timber.

There came the day, toward the midst of Matthew's fifteenth year, that a man arrived at the Home intent on finding a boy to apprentice as his clerk. A group of the five eldest and best educated were lined up in the courtyard, and the man went down the line asking them all questions about themselves. When the man came to Matthew, it was the boy who asked the first question: "Sir? May I enquire as to your profession?"

"I'm a magistrate," Isaac Woodward said, and Matthew glanced at Ausley, who stood nearby with a tight smile on his mouth but his eyes cold and impassive. "Tell me about yourself, young man," Woodward urged.

It was time to leave the Home. Matthew knew it. His view upon the world was about to widen further, but never would he lose sight of this place and what he'd learned here. He looked directly into the magistrate's rather sad-eyed face and said, "My past should be of little interest to you, sir. It is my usefulness in the present and future that I expect you wish to ascertain. As to that, I speak and write Latin. I'm also fluent in French. I don't know anything about law, but I am a quick study. My handwriting is legible, my concentration is good, I have no bad habits to speak of—"

"Other than being full of himself and a bit too big for his britches," Ausley interrupted.

"I'm sure the headmaster prefers smaller britches," Matthew said, still staring into Woodward's eyes. He felt rather than saw Ausley go rigid with barely controlled anger. One of the other boys caught back a laugh before it doomed him. "As I was saying, I have no bad habits to speak of. I can learn whatever I need to know, and I would make a very able clerk. Would you get me out of here, sir?"

"The boy's unsuitable for your needs!" Ausley spoke up again. "He's a troublemaker and a liar! Corbett, you're dismissed."

"One moment," the magistrate said. "If he's so unsuitable, why did you even bother to include him?"

Ausley's moon-shaped face bloomed red. "Well . . . because . . . that is to say, I—"

"I'd like to see an example of your handwriting," Woodward told the boy. "Write for me . . . oh . . . the Lord's Prayer. In Latin, if you're such a scholar." Then, to Ausley, "Can that be arranged?"

"Yes sir. I have a tablet and quill in my office." Ausley cast Matthew a look that, had it been a knife, would've plunged between the eyes, and then he dismissed the other boys and led the way to his chamber.

When it was done, the magistrate satisfied as to Matthew's value, and the papers of transferral drawn up, Woodward announced he had some business to attend to elsewhere but that he would return the next morning and take the boy away. "I do expect the young man will be in good condition," Woodward told the headmaster. "As he is now my charge, I shouldn't like it that he might suffer an accident in the night."

"You needn't be concerned, sir," was Ausley's rather chill reply. "But I require the sum of one guinea to house and feed him until your return. After all, he *is* your charge."

"I understand." The gold guinea coin—worth twenty-one shillings, an exorbitant price to pay—was removed from Woodward's wallet and placed into Ausley's outstretched hand. Thus was the agreement sealed and Matthew's protection bought.

At supper, however, one of Ausley's thuggish helpers entered the dining hall. A silence fell as the man walked directly to Matthew and grasped his shoulder. "You're to come with me," he said, and Matthew had no choice but to comply.

In the headmaster's chamber, Ausley sat behind the same desk that Staunton had occupied in happier times. The place was dirty, the window's glass panes filmed with soot. Ausley lit a church-warden pipe with the flame of a lamp and said, "Leave us," to his accomplice. When the other man had retreated, Ausley sat smoking his pipe and staring with his small dark eyes at Matthew.

"My supper's getting cold," Matthew said, daring the lash.

"Oh, you think you're so *smart,* don't you?" Ausley drew on the pipe and expelled smoke from his nostrils. "So damned *clever.* But you're not near as clever as you take yourself to be, boy."

"Do you require a response from me, sir, or do you wish me to be silent?"

"*Silent.* Just stand there and listen. You're thinking that because you're off to be the ward of a magistrate you can cause some trouble for me, isn't that right? Maybe you think I've done some things that ought to be called to his attention?"

"Sir?" Matthew said. "Might I suggest a book on logic for your bedtime reading?"

"*Logic?* What's that got to do with anything?"

"You've told me to be silent, but then posed questions that require an answer."

"Shut your mouth, you little bastard!" Ausley rose to his feet on a surge of anger. "Just mark well what I say! My commission gives me absolute authority to run this institution as I see fit! Which includes the administering of order and punishments, as I see fit!" Ausley, realizing he was on the edge of losing all control, settled back into his chair and glared at Matthew through a blue haze of pipesmoke. "No one can prove I have been remiss in that duty, or overzealous in my methods," he said tersely. "For a very simple reason: I have *not* been so. Any and all actions I have taken here have been to benefit my charges. Do you agree with that, or do you disagree?"

"I presume you wish me to speak now?"

"I do."

"I have small qualm with the method of your punishments, though I would consider some of them to have been delivered with a sickening sense of joy," Matthew said. "My objections concern your methods after the dormitory lamps have been put out."

"And what methods are you referring to? My private counseling of wayward, stubborn boys whose attitudes are disruptive? My willingness to take in hand these boys and guide them in the proper direction? Is that your reference?"

"I think you understand my reference very clearly, sir."

Ausley gave a short, hard laugh. "You don't know anything. Have you witnessed with your own eyes any impropriety? No. Oh, you've heard things, of course. Because all of you despise me. That's why. You despise me, because I'm your master and wild dogs cannot bear the collar. And now, because you fancy yourself so damned *clever,* you think to cause me some trouble by way of that black-robed magpie. But I shall tell you why you will *not.*"

Matthew waited while Ausley pushed more tobacco into the bowl of his pipe, tamped it down, and relit it with deliberately slow motions.

"Your objections," Ausley said acidly, "would be very difficult to prove. As I've said, my commission gives me absolute authority. I know I've delivered some harsh punishments; too harsh perhaps. That is why you might wish to slander me. And the other boys?

Well . . . I like this position, young man, and I plan on staying here for many years to come. Just because *you're* leaving does not mean the others—your friends, the ones among whom you've grown up—will be departing anytime soon. Your actions might have an effect on their comfort." He drew on the pipe, tilted his head upward, and spewed smoke toward the ceiling. "There are so many *young* ones here," he said. "Much younger than you. And do you realize how many *more* the hospitals and churches are trying to place with us? Hardly a day goes by when I don't receive an enquiry concerning our available beds. I am forced to turn so many young ones away. So, you see, there will always be a fresh supply." He offered Matthew a cold smile. "May I give you some advice?"

Matthew said nothing. "Consider yourself fortunate," Ausley continued. "Consider that your education concerning the real world has been furthered. Be of excellent service to the magistrate, be of good cheer and good will, and live a long and happy life." He held up a thick finger to warrant Matthew's full attention. "And never—*never*—plot a war you have no hope of winning. Am I understood?"

Matthew hesitated; his mind was working over the planes and angles of this problem, diagramming and dissecting it, turning it this way and that, shaking it in search of a loose nail that might be further loosened, stretching it like a chain to inspect the links, and hoping to find one rust-gnawed and able to be broken.

"Am I *understood?*" Ausley repeated, with some force.

Matthew was left with one response. At least for the moment. He said, "Yes, sir," in his calmest voice.

"Very good. You may go back to your supper."

Matthew left the headmaster's office and returned to his food; it was, indeed, cold and quite tasteless. That night he said goodbye to his friends, he climbed into his bunk in the dormitory, but he found sleep elusive. What should have been an occasion of rejoicing was instead a time for reflection and more than a little regret. At first light, he was dressed and waiting. Soon afterward, the bell at the front gate rang and a staff member came to escort him to Magistrate Woodward in the courtyard.

As the magistrate's carriage pulled away, Matthew glanced back at the Home and saw Ausley standing at the window, watching. Matthew felt the tip of a blade poised at his throat. He looked away from the window, staring instead at his hands clenched together in his lap.

"You seem downcast, young man," the magistrate said. "Are you troubled by something?"

"Yes, sir, I am," Matthew had to admit. He thought of Ausley at the window, the carriage wheels turning to take him far away from the almshouse, the boys who were left behind, the terrible punishments that Ausley could bring down upon them. For now, Ausley held the power. *I plan on staying here for many years to come,* the headmaster had said. In that case, Matthew knew where to find him.

"Is this a matter you wish to talk about?" Woodward asked.

"No sir. It's my problem, and mine alone. I will find a way to solve it. I *will.*"

"What?"

Matthew looked into the magistrate's face. Woodward no longer wore his wig and tricorn, his appearance much aged since that day he'd driven Matthew away from the almshouse. A light rain was falling through the thick-branched trees, steam hanging above the muddy track they were following. Ahead of them was the wagon Paine drove.

"Did you say something, Matthew?" the magistrate asked. *I will,* he thought it had been.

It took Matthew a few seconds to adjust to the present from his recollections of the past. "I must have been thinking aloud," he said, and then he was quiet.

In time, the fortress walls of Fount Royal emerged from the mist ahead. The watchman on his tower began to ring the bell, the gate was unlocked and opened, and they had returned to the witch's town.

seven

T HE DAY HAD COME, with the announcement of a cock's crow.

It was dark-clouded and cool, the sun a mere specter on the eastern horizon. From the window of his room, which faced away from Fount Royal, Matthew could see Bidwell's stable, the slaves' clapboard houses beside it, the guard tower, and the thick pine forest that stretched toward the swamp beyond. It was a dismal view. His bones ached from the continual damp, and because of a single mosquito that had gotten past the barrier of his bed-netting, his sleep had been less than restful. But the day had come, and his anticipation had risen to a keen edge.

He lit a candle, as the morning was so caliginous, and shaved using the straight razor, soap, and bowl of water that had been left in the hallway outside. Then he dressed in black trousers, white stockings, and a cream-colored shirt from the limited wardrobe Bidwell had provided him. He was blowing out the candle when a knock sounded at his door. "Breakfast is a'table, sir," said Mrs. Nettles.

"I'm ready." He opened the door and faced the formidable, square-chinned woman in black. She carried a lantern, the yellow light and shadows of which made her stern visage almost fearsome. "Is the magistrate up?"

"Already downstairs," she said. Her oiled brown hair was combed back from her forehead so severely that Matthew thought it looked painful. "They're waitin' for you before grace is said."

"Very well." He closed the door and followed her along the hallway. Her weight made the boards squeal. Before they reached the staircase, the woman suddenly stopped so fast Matthew almost collided into her. She turned toward him, and lifted the lantern up to view his face.

"What is it?" he asked.

"May I speak freely, sir?" Her voice was hushed. "And trust you na' to repeat what I might say?"

Matthew tried to gauge her expression, but the light was too much in his eyes. He nodded.

"This is a dangerous day," she said, all but whispering. "You and the magistrate are in grave danger."

"Of what nature?"

"Danger of bein' consumed by lies and blasphemies. You seem an able-minded young man, but you nae understand this town and what's transpirin' here. In time you might, if your mind is na' poisoned."

"Poisoned by whom? The witch, do you mean?"

"The *witch*." It was said with more than a hint of bitterness. "Nay, I'm na' speakin' of Rachel Howarth. Whatever you hear of her—however you perceive her—she is na' your enemy. She's a victim, young man. If anythin', she needs your he'p."

"How so?"

"They're ready to hang her," Mrs. Nettles whispered. "They'd hang her this morn, if they could. But she does na' deserve the rope. What she needs is a champion of truth. Somebody to prove her innocent, when ever'body else is again' her."

"Madam, I'm just a clerk. I have no power to—"

"You're the only one *with* the power," she interrupted. "The magistrate is the kind of man who plows a straight furrow, ay? Well, this field's damn crooked!"

"So you contend that Madam Howarth is *not* a witch? Even

though her husband was brutally murdered, poppets were found in her house, she can't speak the Lord's Prayer, and she bears the Devil's marks?"

"Lies upon lies. I think you're a man of some education: do you believe in witchcraft?"

"The books on demonology are well founded," Matthew said.

"Hang the books! I asked if *you* believe." Matthew hesitated; the question had never been posed to him. Of course he knew the Salem incident, which had occurred only seven years ago. He'd read Cotton Mather's *Memorable Providences* and Richard Baxter's *Certainty of the Worlds of Spirits,* both of which secured witchcraft and demon possession as fact. But he'd also read John Webster's *The Displaying of Supposed Witchcraft* and John Wagstaffe's *The Question of Witchcraft Debated,* and both of those volumes held that "witchcraft" was either deliberate fraud or that "witches" were insane and should be bound for an asylum rather than the gallows. Between those two poles, Matthew hung suspended.

"I don't know," he said.

"Mark this," Mrs. Nettles told him. "Satan does walk in Fount Royal, but Rachel Howarth's na' the one beside him. Things that nae want to be seen are plentiful here. And that's God's truth."

"If you believe so, why don't you speak to Mr. Bidwell?"

"What? And then he'll be thinkin' I'm bewitched too? Because any woman or man who speaks up for Rachel Howarth would have a noose ready for—"

"*Mrs. Nettles!*" came a shout from the bottom of the stairs. "Where's Mr. Corbett?" It was Bidwell and he sounded quite irritated. "We're awaiting our breakfast, woman!"

"I'm at your mercy!" she whispered urgently to Matthew. "Na' a word about this, please!"

"All right," he agreed.

"We're here, sir!" Mrs. Nettles called to the master of the house, as she started toward the staircase again. "Beg pardon, the young man was late a'risin'!"

Their breakfast was slices of ham and cornmeal porridge, biscuits and locally gathered honey, all washed down with mugs of strong amber tea. Matthew was still full from last night's dinner of turtle soup, turtle steaks, and cornbread, so he ate only sparingly. Woodward, who'd awakened with a raw throat and clogged nostrils after a restless night, drank as much tea as he could and then sucked on a lemon. In ravenous appetite, however, was Bidwell; the master of the house consumed slice after slice of ham and a whole serving bowl full of porridge, as well as a platter of biscuits.

At last Bidwell leaned back in his chair, expelled air, and patted his bulging stomach. "Ahhhh, what a breakfast!" His gaze fell upon an unclaimed soul amid the carnage. "Magistrate, are you going to finish that biscuit?"

"No, sir, I'm not."

"May I, then?" Bidwell reached for it and pushed it into his mouth before an assent could be made. Woodward swallowed thickly, his throat very painful, and afforded himself another drink of the tart tea.

"Magistrate, are you not feeling well?" Matthew asked; it would have been difficult not to notice the man's pallor and the dark circles beneath his eyes.

"I didn't sleep very soundly last night. The mosquitoes here seem to favor me."

"Tar soap," Bidwell said. "That's what you should bathe in this evening. Tar soap keeps them away. Well . . . most of them, that is."

"I thought the insects were particularly greedy in Charles Town." Woodward scratched at a reddened welt on the back of his right hand, one of a dozen bites he'd suffered already this morning. "But your mosquitoes, sir, have no compare."

"You have to get used to them, that's all. And the tar soap does help."

"I look forward, then, to being tarred." He knew he appeared rather peaked, as the shaving mirror had told him. He was miserable in these borrowed clothes, which might have been a plowman's pride but were ill-suited for his elegant tastes. Also, he felt near naked without his wig, and terribly conscious of his age-spots. Never in his life had he felt so old, and such a prisoner of fate. Without the wig, it seemed to him that his entire face drooped near off the skull bones, his teeth appeared chipped and crooked, and he feared he looked more of a country bumpkin than an urban sophisticate. His sore throat and swollen air passages further tortured him; on any other morning, he might have returned to bed with a cup of hot rum and a medicinal poultice but on this morning he had major work ahead. He realized Matthew was still staring at him, the young man's sense of order disturbed. "I'll be fine directly," Woodward told him.

Matthew said nothing, unwilling to embarrass the magistrate by appearing overly concerned. He poured some tea for himself, thinking that Woodward's bare-headed exposure to the raw swamp humours was certainly not beneficial to his health. Not very far from the forefront of his mind, however, was the encounter he'd had with Mrs. Nettles. Her passion on the subject had been undeniable, but was her purpose to cloud his mind instead of clear it? Indeed, if she were bewitched she would be in the employ of Rachel Howarth's master as well. Was that master trying to use him, to taint the magistrate's judgment? He couldn't help but ponder the vastly different opinions on the subject of witchcraft by the authors of the tomes he'd read. He'd spoken the truth to Mrs. Nettles; he honestly didn't know *what* he believed.

But Matthew didn't have time for much reflection, because suddenly Mrs. Nettles appeared in the dining room's doorway. "Sir?" she said, addressing Bidwell. "The carriage is ready." Her visage was stern again, and she gave not even a glance in Matthew's direction.

"Excellent!" Bidwell stood up. "Gentlemen, shall we go?"

Outside, the carriage's team was reined by the elderly black servant, Goode, who had played the violin at the first dinner and caught the turtle for the second. Bidwell, Woodward, and then Matthew climbed into the carriage and under tumultuous clouds were taken away from the mansion and past the spring along Peace Street. A few citizens were out, but not many; the quality of light—or lack of such—made for a gloomy morning, and Matthew saw clearly that life was fast ebbing from this forsaken village.

At the useless sundial, Goode turned the carriage's team eastward onto Truth Street. A fit of nerves seemed to affect Bidwell as they neared the gaol, and he eased his mounting tension with a doubleshot of snuff up the nostrils. Goode steered them around the pigs that wallowed in Truth's mud, and in a moment he reined the horses to a halt before the grim and windowless wooden walls of the gaol. Two men were awaiting their arrival; one was Nicholas Paine, the other a stocky, barrel-chested giant who must have stood six feet tall. The giant wore a tricorn, but the hair that could be seen was flaming red, as was his long and rather unkempt beard.

Upon departing from the carriage, Bidwell made introductions between the magistrate, Matthew, and the red-bearded giant. "This is Mr. Hannibal Green, our gaol-keeper," he said. When Woodward shook the man's red-furred hand, he had the feeling that his fingers might be snapped like dry sticks. Green's eyes, an indeterminate dark hue, were deeply sunken into his head and held no expression other than—in Matthew's opinion—a promise to do bodily harm to anyone who displeased him.

Bidwell drew a long breath and released it. "Shall we enter?"

Green, a man of no words, produced two keys on a leather cord from a pocket of his buckskin waistcoat and inserted a key into the padlock that secured the gaol's entry. With one sharp twist, the lock opened and Green removed a chain that the lock had held fastened across the door. He pulled the door open to reveal a dark interior. "Wait," he rumbled, and then he walked inside, his boots pounding the rough planked floor.

Staring into the gaol's darkened recesses, both the magistrate and his clerk felt the gnaw of anxiety. The bittersweet smells of damp hay, sweat, and bodily functions came drifting out into their faces, along with the sense of what it must be like to be caged in that stifling and humid environment. Green soon returned, carrying a lantern that shed only paltry light through its filmed glass. "Come in," he told them. Bidwell took another quick snort of snuff and led the way.

It was not a large place. Past the entrance room there were four iron-barred cells, two on each side of a central corridor. The floor was covered with hay. Matthew presumed it had been a small stable before its conversion. "Thank Christ you're here!" called a man's voice, off to the right. "I was startin' to believe you'd forsaken me!"

Green paid him no mind. The gaol-keeper reached up to the utter height of his outstretched hand and caught hold of a chain that dangled from the ceiling. He gave it a good firm pull and with the sound of ratchets turning a hatch opened up there, allowing in more fresh air and much-needed illumination.

The light—gray and murky yet still much better than the dirty lamp—afforded a view of the man who stood in the nearest cage on the right, his hands gripping the bars, his beard-grizzled face pressed against them as if he might somehow squeeze himself to freedom. He was young, only five or six years elder than Matthew, but already thick around the middle. He had husky forearms and a stout bull's neck, his unruly black hair falling over his forehead, and a pair of gray eyes glittering on either side of a bulbous nose that was—as were his cheeks—covered with pock-marks. "I'm ready to go home!" he announced.

"She's in the cell back here," Bidwell said to the magistrate, ignoring the young man.

"Hey! Bidwell!" the man hollered. "Damn you, I said I'm ready to go—"

Wham! went Green's fist into one of the man's hands gripping the bars. The prisoner howled with pain and staggered back holding his injured fingers against his chest.

"You speak with *respect,*" Green said, "or you don't speak at all. Hear me?"

"Ahhhh, my hand's near broke!"

"Noles, you have one more day and night on your sentence," Bidwell told the prisoner. "You'll be released tomorrow morning, and not one minute sooner."

"Listen! Please!" Noles, now apologetic, came to the bars again. "I can't bear another night in here, sir! I swear before God, I can't! The rats are terrible! They et up most all my food, and I near had to fight 'em off my throat! Ain't I paid my penance yet, sir?"

"Your sentence was three days and three nights. Therefore: no, you have not yet paid your penance."

"Wait, wait!" Noles said, before Bidwell and the others could move along. "It ain't just the rats I'm feared of! *It's her.*" He'd whispered the last sentence, and motioned with a tilt of his head toward the last cage on the left of the corridor. His eyes were wide and wild. "I'm feared she's gonna kill me, sir!"

"Has she threatened you?"

"No sir, but . . . well . . . I've *heard* things."

"Such as?" Bidwell's interest had been fully secured now, and he gave Noles a long ear.

"Last night . . . in the dark . . . she was talkin' to somethin'," Noles whispered, his face once more pressed against the bars. "I couldn't hear much of it . . . but I heard her speak the word 'master.' Yessir, I did. 'Master', she said, three or four times. Then she started a'laughin', and by Christ I hope to never hear such a laugh as that again, because it was nothin' but wickedness."

"And what happened after that?"

"Well . . . she talked some more, to whatever it was. Just jabberin', like to scare the moon." He ran his tongue across his lips; his eyes flickered across Woodward and Matthew and then returned to Bidwell. "Then . . . I saw a light back there. Like fire, but it was cold blue. Yessir. Cold blue, and it was burnin' in her cage. Well, I drew myself back and laid down, 'cause I didn't want to see what it was."

"Go on," Bidwell urged, when Noles paused again.

"Well sir . . . there came a hummin' and a buzzin'. And I seen what I took to be a fly, leavin' the witch's cage. Only it was burnin' blue, makin' the air spark. Then it flew into here and started flittin' 'round my head, and I swatted at it but to tell the truth I didn't really care to touch it. It flew 'round and 'round, and I crawled over there in that corner and threw some hay at it to keep it away from me. After a while it flew on out of here and went away."

"Went away? To where?"

"I don't know, sir. It just vanished."

Bidwell looked gravely at the magistrate. "You see what we're up against? The witch's master can transform himself—itself—into shapes that have no equal on this earth."

"Yessir, that's right!" Noles said. "I'm feared for my life, bein' in here with her! I seen what I seen, and she's like to kill me for it!"

"Might I ask a question?" Matthew proposed, and Bidwell nodded. "What offense has this man committed?"

"He whipped his wife bloody with a carpet-beater," Bidwell said. "Dr. Shields had to attend to her. As it was Noles's second offense, I ordered him here."

"And what was his first offense?"

"The same," Bidwell said.

"She's a liar and a nag!" Noles spoke up adamantly. "That woman don't know when to shut her mouth! I swear, even a saint would pick up an ax and cleave her head when she starts that damn prattlin'!" The man's attention fixed on Bidwell once more. "Will you let me out then, to save my life?"

"Well—" He looked to Woodward for aid in this question. "Richard Noles *is* a good Christian fellow. I shouldn't want to leave him to the mercy of the witch. What do you propose I do, sir?"

"Has his wife recovered?"

"She is abed at Dr. Shields's infirmary. Her arm was broken during the incident, and her back much bruised. But . . . after all, sir . . . she is his property, by the writ of marriage."

"I have a suggestion," Matthew said, which relieved Woodward of a difficult decision. "Since Mr. Noles last night defeated the Devil with a handful of hay, surely he can hold off the demons of Hell with a carpet-beater. Why not bring him one with which he might defend himself."

Bidwell slowly blinked. "Are you joking, young man?"

"No, sir. He seems to be proficient with such a weapon, doesn't he?"

"What kind of damned horseshit is this?" Noles said, almost hollering again. "I want out of here, right now!"

"I won't have this man's blood on my hands, if the witch strikes him dead tonight." Bidwell nodded at Green. "Let him loose."

"Sir?" Matthew said, as the gaol-keeper found the proper key from his ring. "If the witch strikes Mr. Noles dead tonight, I don't believe there'll be need to interview the other witnesses."

"He's right," said Paine, standing behind Matthew. "It would put the rope around the witch's neck, pure and simple!"

"Hold." Bidwell grasped Green's arm before the key could be inserted in its lock.

"Have you lost your damned *minds?*" Noles bellowed. "She'll kill me tonight if you don't let me out!"

Matthew said, "I don't think she will. It would be against her interests."

"*You!*" Noles stared at Matthew, his eyes hot. "I don't know who you are, but you'd best beware me when I get out!"

"That loose tongue might earn you a further sentence," Woodward warned. "I'm a magistrate, and the young man is my clerk."

Bidwell added, "Constrain your speech, Noles! That is, if you value your freedom come morning!"

"Damn you *all,* then!" the prisoner shouted. Turning, he picked up from the floor a bucket above which several flies of the non-demonic variety were circling. His face purple with anger, Noles braced his body to fling the bucket's contents at his tormentors.

"*Noles!*" Green's voice seemed to shake the gaol's walls. "Your teeth in trade!"

The bucket hung poised on the edge of being thrown. Even in his rage, Noles realized it was a bad bargain. He paused, shaking, his face contorted in a sneer that might have cracked a mirror. He lowered the bucket to his side and finally let it drop into the hay.

"Tomorrow morning you shall be free," Bidwell said. "If you so wish, I'll . . . have brought to you a carpet-beater, with which you might—"

Noles laughed harshly. "Give it to that skinny whelp and he can stick it up his arse! Go on, I've nothin' more to say to you!" He sat down on the bench and turned his face toward the wall.

"All right." Bidwell motioned Green on. "Let's see to Madam Howarth."

They moved along the corridor, to the final cell on the left-hand side. From the occupant of this cage there was no outburst of noise or apparent movement. A hooded figure wrapped in coarse gray clothing lay huddled in the hay.

Bidwell's voice was tight when he spoke. "Open it."

Green used the second key on the leather cord, which evidently unlocked all the cells. The key turned, the lock clinked, and the gaol-keeper pulled the barred door open.

"Madam?" Bidwell said. "Stand up." The figure did not move. "Do you hear me? I said, stand up!" Still, there was no response.

"She tests me," Bidwell muttered, grim-lipped. Then, louder, "Will you stand up, madam, or will Mr. Green pull you to your feet?"

At last there was a movement, but slow and deliberate. Woodward thought it was as dangerously graceful as the uncoiling of a serpent. The figure stood up and remained standing against the far wall, head fully cloaked and arms and legs shrouded by the gray sackcloth.

"I've brought visitors," Bidwell announced. "This is Magistrate Isaac Woodward and his clerk, Matthew Corbett. The magistrate desires to ask you some questions."

Again there was no reaction. "Go ahead, sir," Bidwell said.

Woodward stepped forward, into the cage's doorway. He took note of the cell's furnishings: a refuse bucket, the same as afforded Noles; another smaller bucket that held water; a bench, and upon it a wooden tray with some scraps of bread and what appeared to be chicken bones. "Madam Howarth?" Woodward said. "I am here to ascertain the facts concerning your situation. Do I have your compliance?"

Nothing, from the hooded woman.

Woodward glanced quickly at Bidwell, who nodded for him to continue. The magistrate was aware that Green and Paine were flanking him, presumably to catch the woman should she fling herself at him. Matthew watched with acute interest, his hands clenching the bars. Woodward said, "Madam Howarth, would you please speak the Lord's Prayer?"

Again, nothing. Not a word, not a nod, not even a curse.

"Do you *know* the Lord's Prayer?"

"Of course she does!" Paine said. "But speaking it would scorch her tongue!"

"Please." Woodward held up a hand to beg the man's silence. "Madam, on these matters I do need your response. Your unwillingness to repeat the Lord's Prayer can be taken as your *inability* to speak it. Do you not understand how important this is?"

"She'll understand the noose, all right!" Bidwell said.

Woodward paused, putting his thoughts in order. "Silence is guilt, madam," he continued. "I want you to listen well to what I say. There is much talk here of nooses and hangings. You know of what you stand accused. Many witches in these colonies have met their deaths by hanging . . . but since you stand accused of murdering your husband, to whom by law you owed obedience, this is also a case of what is called 'petty treason.' The punishment for such treason is not the rope, but death by fire at the stake. Therefore it does you no good whatsoever to remain mute to my questions."

He may as well have been speaking to a gray-gowned statue. "This is absurd!" he protested to Bidwell. "It's all useless, if she refuses to speak! "

"Then we ought to get a stake ready, yes?"

"Sir?" Matthew said. "May I pose her a question?"

"Yes, go ahead!" Woodward answered, disgusted with the whole thing.

"Madam Howarth?" Matthew kept his voice as quiet and un-threatening as possible, though his heart was beating very hard. "Are you a witch?"

Bidwell gave an abrupt, nervous laugh that sounded like an ill-tuned trumpet. "That's a damned foolish question, boy! Of *course* she's a witch! None of this would be necessary if she wasn't!"

"Mr. Bidwell?" Matthew speared the man with a cold gaze. "It was a question I posed to the *woman,* not to you. I'd appreciate if you would not presume to answer for her."

"Why, you're an impudent young cock!" The blood flushed to the surface of Bidwell's jowls. "If you were more than half a man, I'd require satisfaction for that sharp tongue of—"

"I," spoke the woman, loud enough to command attention. Bidwell was immediately silent. ". . . am . . . *judged* a witch," she said, and then nothing more.

Matthew's heart was now at full gallop. He cleared his throat. "Do you judge yourself one?"

There was a long pause. Matthew thought she wouldn't reply, but then the hooded head tilted a fraction. "My husband has been taken from me. My house and land have been taken." Her voice was wan but steady; it was the voice of a young woman, not that of a wizened crone as Matthew had expected. "My innocence has been taken from me, and my very soul has been beaten. Before I answer your question, you answer mine: what more do I possess?"

"A voice. And knowledge of the truth."

"Truth," she said acidly. "Truth in this town is a ghost, its life long departed."

"There, listen!" Bidwell said, his excitement rampant. "She speaks of ghosts!"

Hush! Matthew almost snapped, but he restrained himself. "Madam, do you commune with Satan?"

She took a long breath and let it go. "I do not."

"Did you not create poppets for use in spells of witchcraft?" Woodward asked, feeling he should endeavor to take command of this questioning.

The woman was silent. Woodward realized, uncomfortably, that she was indeed making a statement: for whatever reason, she would only speak to Matthew. He looked at his clerk, who was also discomfited by the woman's behavior, and gave a shrug of his shoulders.

"The poppets," Matthew said. "Did you make them?" Bidwell let out an exasperated snort, but Matthew paid him no heed.

"No, I did not," the woman answered.

"Then how come they to be found in the floor of her house?" Paine asked. "I myself found them!"

"Madam Howarth, do you know how the poppets came to be in your house?"

"I do not," she said.

"This is a fool's court!" Bidwell was about to burst with impatience. "Of course she's going to deny her wickedness! Do you expect her to *confess* her sins?"

Matthew turned to the captain of militia. "How did you know to investigate the floor of her house?"

"The locality of the poppets was seen in a dream by Cara Grunewald. Not the exact locality, but that the witch had something of importance hidden underneath the floor of her kitchen. I took some men there, and we found the poppets beneath a loosened board."

"Was Madam Howarth still living there when you made this discovery?"

"No, she was here in the cell by then."

"So this Cara Grunewald told you where to look?" Woodward asked. "According to the dictates of a vision?"

"That's correct."

"I should think we might want to speak to Madam Grune-wald, as well," the magistrate decided.

"Impossible!" Bidwell said. "She, her husband, and four children left Fount Royal two months ago!"

Matthew frowned, rubbing his chin. "How long was Madam Howarth' s house empty before these poppets were discovered?"

"Oh . . . two weeks, perhaps." Now it was Paine's turn to wear a furrowed brow. "What's your direction, young man?"

"No direction yet." Matthew offered a faint smile. "I'm only testing the compass."

"Magistrate, I protest this ridiculous behavior by your *clerk!*" Bidwell had nearly snarled the word. "It's not his place to be posing these questions!"

"It *is* his place to be *helping* me," Woodward said, his temper beginning to fray from the man's insinuations. "As we all desire to find the truth in this situation, anything my well-versed scrivener can add to that process is—to me, at least—entirely welcome."

"The truth is already clear as glass, sir!" Bidwell retorted. "We should put the witch to death—fire, hanging, drowning, whatever—and be done with it!"

"It seems to me there are too many questions yet to be answered," Woodward said steadfastly.

"You want proof of her witchcraft, do you? Well, here it is then, and she won't have to speak a word! Green, remove the witch's clothing!" The burly gaol-keeper started into the cage. Instantly the gray-cloaked figure backed against the wall, so tightly as if to press herself into it. Green didn't hesitate; in another two strides he was upon her, reaching out to grasp a handful of sackcloth.

Suddenly the woman's right hand came up, its palm lodging against the man's chest to restrain him. *"No,"* she said, and the force of her voice stopped Green in his tracks.

"Go on, Green!" Bidwell insisted. "Strip her!"

"I said *no!*" the woman repeated. Her other hand came up from the folds, and suddenly her fingers were working at the wooden buttons of her cloak. The gaol-keeper, realizing she had elected to disrobe herself, retreated to give her room.

Her fingers were nimble. The buttons came undone. Then she reached up, pushed the hood back from her face and head, shrugged quickly out of her clothes, and let the sorry garment slide into the hay.

Rachel Howarth stood naked before the world.

"Very well," she said, her eyes defiant. "Here is the witch."

Matthew almost fell down. Never in his life had he seen a naked woman; what's more, this woman was . . . well, there was no other description but *belle exotique.*

She was no wizened crone, being perhaps twenty-five years or thereabouts. Whether by nature or due to the gaol's diet, she was lean to the point of her rib cage being visible. Her flesh was of a swarthy mahogany hue, her Portuguese heritage. Her long, thick hair was black as midnight but in dire need of washing. Matthew couldn't help but stare at her dark-nippled breasts, his face reddening with shame but his eyes wanton as those of a drunken seaman. When he removed his gaze from that area, he instantly was attracted to the mysterious triangle of black curls between her slim thighs. His head seemed to be mounted on a treacherous swivel. He gazed into the woman's face, and there found further undoing of his senses.

She was staring at the floor, but her eyes—pale amber-brown, verging on a strange and remarkable golden hue—burned so fiercely they might have set the hay aflame. Her face was most pleasing—heartshaped, her chin marked with a small cleft—and Matthew found himself imagining how she would appear if not in such dire circumstances. If his heart had been galloping before, now it was a runaway. The sight of this lovely woman naked was almost too much to bear; something about her was frail, deeply wounded perhaps, while her expression conveyed an inner strength the likes of which he'd never witnessed. It hurt him to view such a creature in this ignoble fashion and he sought to rest his eyes somewhere else, but Rachel Howarth seemed the center of the world and there was nowhere he could look without seeing her.

"Here!" Bidwell said. "Look here!" He strode toward the woman, grasped her left breast in a rough grip, and lifted it. He pointed at a small brown blotch underneath. "This is one. Here is another!" He pressed a forefinger against a second mark on her right thigh, just above the knee. "Turn around!" he told her. She obeyed, her face blanked of emotion. "The third one, here!" He put his finger against a dark blotch—a bit larger than the others, though not by very much—on her left hip. "Devil's marks, one and all! This third one here even seems to be the impression of her master! Come, look closer!"

He was speaking to Woodward, who was having as difficult a time in the presence of this compelling nudity as was Matthew. The magistrate stepped forward to get a better view of the skin blotch that Bidwell was showing. "You see? Right here? And there too?" Bidwell asked. "Don't those appear to be horns growing from a devil's head?"

"I . . . well . . . I suppose so," Woodward answered, and then decorum dictated that he retreat a few paces.

"Her right arm," Matthew said, with an uptilt of his chin. He'd recognized two small, blood-crusted wounds near the elbow. "Rat bites, I think."

"Yes, I see. Another on the shoulder." Bidwell touched the shoulder wound, which was gray-rimmed with infection, and the woman winced but made no sound. "The rats have been after you, Madam?" She didn't reply, nor did she need to; it was obvious the rodents had been visiting. "All right, we can't have you eaten up in your sleep. I'll have Linch catch the bastards. Put your clothes back on." He walked away from her and immediately she bent down, picked up her sackcloth, and covered herself. Then, shrouded once more, she huddled in the hay as she'd been at the beginning.

"There you have it!" Bidwell announced. "She cannot speak the Lord's Prayer, she created those poppets to enchant her victims, and she has the marks. For some unholy reason known only to herself and her master, she murdered or caused the murder of Burlton Grove and Daniel Howarth. She and her hellish kin are responsible for the fires we've been lately enduring. She conjures phantasms and demons and I believe she's cursed our orchards and fields as well." He placed his hands on his hips, his chest bellowing out. "It is her plan to destroy Fount Royal, and on that account she has made great and terrible progress! What more remains to be said?"

"One question," Matthew said, and he saw Bidwell visibly flinch. "If indeed this woman commands such awesome and unholy powers—"

"She does!" Bidwell asserted, and behind him Paine nodded.

"—then why," Matthew went on, "can she not strike mere rodents dead with a touch?"

"What?"

"The rats, sir. Why is she bitten?"

"A good point," Woodward agreed. "Why would she allow herself to be bitten by common rats, if she's joined with such a demonic league?"

"Because . . . because . . ." Bidwell looked for help from Green and Paine.

The militia captain came to his rescue. *"Because,"* Paine said forcefully, "it's a trick. Would you not think it more peculiar that Noles was attacked by the rodents, but the witch was spared? Oh, she knows what she's doing, gentlemen!" He looked directly at Matthew. "She is attempting to blind you, young man. Her evil is well planned. If she has the bites of rodents on her flesh, it was done by her will and blasphemous blessing."

Woodward nodded. "Yes, that sounds reasonable."

"Then there's no disagreement of the fact that she *is* a witch?" Bidwell prompted.

Matthew said, "Sir, this is a matter for careful consideration."

"What damned consideration? Who else has poisoned my town but her? Who else murdered her husband and the reverend? Boy, the facts are there to be seen!"

"Not facts. Contentions."

"You push me, boy! Remember, I'm your host here!"

"Would you take my clothes and turn me out into the forest if I refuse to view contentions as facts?"

"Please, please!" the magistrate said. "Nothing is being accomplished by this."

"My point exactly!" Bidwell steamed. "Your clerk seems determined to blunt the weapon you were brought here to wield!"

"And what weapon might that be, sir?" Woodward's raw throat and this dank gaol had combined to inflame his nerves. He felt his self-control slipping.

Bidwell's face might have been a pickled beet. "The *law*, of course!"

"Listen well to me." The magistrate's voice was calm but strained, and the power of it seized Bidwell like a hand around the scruff of a cur. "My clerk and I have come to this place to discover the *truth*, not to use the privilege of law as a battering ram." Bidwell glowered at him but didn't speak. "You may be the master of Fount Royal, but I am the master of a larger realm. I will decide whether Madam Howarth is a witch or not, and I will determine her fate. And no man shall rush or shove me to judgment. You may take that as a fact. If you have some problem with it, Matthew and I will be glad to find other lodgings."

"Let me understand this fully, then!" Bidwell said. "Who is the magistrate and who is the clerk?"

Woodward clenched his teeth to restrain what he'd really like to say. "I need some air," he told Matthew. "Will you join me in walking back to Mr. Bidwell's house?"

"Yes, sir."

"Is that all?" Paine asked. "Aren't you going to interview the witch further?"

"Not today." Woodward motioned toward the woman's crumpled form. "I don't believe she's in a communicative mood, and I'm damned certain *I'm* not! Matthew, come along!" He turned away and started for the exit.

"She needs a hot iron to loosen her tongue, is what she

needs!" Bidwell shouted after them as they went along the corridor between the cages. Noles gave a snort and a spit as they passed. His senses still shaken by his introduction to Rachel Howarth, Matthew knew he would win no contests of popularity hereabouts, and especially that he should beware making further enemies in the uncertain days to come.

eight

OUTSIDE THE GAOL, the humid air and clouded light seemed the breath and glow of paradise. Woodward disdained the carriage, where Goode sat on the driver's seat whittling a piece of wood with a small blade, and began walking in the direction of the spring. Matthew followed close behind.

"That man galls me!" Woodward said. "I may be a servant of the law, but I'm not his slave and neither are you!"

"No, sir. I mean, yes, sir." Matthew got beside him and kept pace. "As much as his manner grates, however, I can understand his anxiety."

"Well, aren't you the generous soul!"

"I might be as eager for an execution if I'd put so much money into Fount Royal, and now saw my investment near ruin."

"To the Devil with his investment!"

"Yes, sir," Matthew said. "I think that's what he fears."

Woodward slowed his pace and then stopped. He mopped beads of sweat from his face with his shirtsleeve, looked up at the ominous sky and then at his clerk. "That's why you're so invaluable to me, you know," he said, his anger dissolving. "At a glance you see the picture, the frame, the nail, and the wall."

"I see only what's there to be seen."

"Yes, and surely we've today seen a bit too much of Madam Howarth. She was . . . younger than I suspected. Much more handsome, as well. One might say lovely, if in different circumstances. When she disrobed, I . . . well, I haven't judged very many female defendants. Never have I stood and seen a woman disrobe willingly before strangers."

"Not willingly," Matthew said. "She knew her clothes would be taken from her, so she elected to remove them herself."

"Yes. What does that say about the woman?"

"That she wishes to retain some measure of control over herself. Or, at least, deny that control from Bidwell."

"Hmm." Woodward began walking west along Truth Street again, and Matthew walked alongside. Though the village still seemed very quiet, there were residents going about their daily business. Two women were crossing the street ahead, one of them carrying a large basket. A man at the reins of an oxcart passed, hauling bales of hay and a few barrels. "I should like to know," the magistrate said, ". . . what intrigues you have with Mrs. Nettles."

"Sir?"

"You may wear that expression of innocent surprise with everyone but me. I know you too well. On this day, of all days, you would never have been late rising from bed. In fact, I suspect you were up early in anticipation. So why did Mrs. Nettles say such a thing to Bidwell?"

"I . . . promised her I wouldn't betray her confidence."

Woodward pulled up short again, and this time when he looked at Matthew his gaze was more penetrating. "If it has to do with Madam Howarth, I should like to be informed. In fact, it's your requirement as my clerk to inform me."

"Yes, sir, I know. But—"

"Promise her anything you please," Woodward said. "But tell me what I ought to be told."

"She did ask that I not speak a word to Mr. Bidwell."

"Well, neither shall I. Tell me."

"In essence, she requested that you and I both approach this case with an open mind. She believes Madam Howarth to be falsely accused."

"And she told you why she believes this?"

"No, sir. Just that she fears our minds will be poisoned."

Woodward stared off across Truth Street at a small pasture where several cows grazed. A woman wearing a straw hat was on her knees in a beanfield, pulling up weeds, while her husband was at work nailing shingles atop their farmhouse. Nearby, on the other side of a split-rail fence, stood a farmhouse that had been abandoned by its previous tenants, its field now a swampy thicket. Three crows perched on the roof of the forlorn house, looking to Woodward like a trio of black-robed magistrates. Perhaps, he mused, they were awaiting the departure of the next-door neighbors.

"You know," he said quietly, "that if Rachel Howarth is a witch, then she has powers of influence that are much beyond our perception."

"Mrs. Nettles asked me not to mention our conversation to Bidwell, for the reason that he might think her so influenced."

"Hmm," Woodward said, a sound of thought. "Poison can be served from many cups, Matthew. I'd beware the one from which I chose to drink. Come, let's walk." They started off once more. "What did you make of Noles's story?"

"Hogwash. He wants out of his cage."

"And the Devil's marks on the woman's body?"

"Inconclusive," Matthew said. "Such marks are common on most people." He didn't have to mention the blotches that marked Woodward's pate.

"Granted. What, then, of the poppets?"

"I think you should see them for yourself."

"Agreed. I'm sorry Madam Grunewald is no longer available."

"You should ask Bidwell for a list of witnesses who *are* available," Matthew suggested. "Then you should secure some place to interview them where Bidwell can't interfere."

"Yes." He nodded, then darted a sidelong glance at Matthew. "We will have to interview Madam Howarth again, of course. At length. She seems to be acceptable to your questions, but mute to anyone else. Why do you think that is?"

"I don't know."

Woodward let them stride a few more paces before he spoke again. "You don't think it's possible that she *knew* Mrs. Nettles would speak to you this morning? And that by only addressing your questions she might . . . how shall I put this? . . . Win some favor from you?"

"I'm just a clerk. I have no—"

"—powers of influence?" Woodward interrupted. "You see my point, don't you?"

"Yes, sir," Matthew had to admit. "I do."

"And her unwillingness or inability to speak the Lord's Prayer is especially damning. If she would or could speak it, then why won't she? Do you have any theories?"

"None," Matthew said.

"Except for the obvious, that—as Paine said—her tongue would be scorched by mention of the Holy Father. It's happened before in witchcraft trials that the accused made an attempt at speaking the prayer and fell convulsed with agony to the courtroom floor."

"Has it ever happened that anyone accused of witchcraft spoke the prayer and was set free?"

"Of that I can't say. I'm far from an expert in these matters. I do know that some witches are able to speak the name of God without ill effect, being somehow shielded from harm by their master. That much I've read in court dockets. But if Madam Howarth *did* speak the prayer—in its entirety, with proper holy attitude and without fainting or crying out in pain—then it would go a distance in helping her cause." The magistrate frowned, watching another crow circling above their heads. It came to him that the Devil could take many forms, and he ought to be wary of what he said and where he said it. "You do realize, don't you, that Madam Howarth today made a confession of sorts?"

"Yes, sir." Matthew knew what he meant. "When she disrobed, she said, 'Here is the witch.'"

"Correct. If that's not a confession, I never heard one. I could order the stake to be cut and the fire to be laid this afternoon, if I had a mind to." He was silent for a moment, during which they neared the conjunction of Fount Royal's streets. "Tell me why I should not," he said.

"Because the witnesses should be heard. Because Madam Howarth deserves the right to speak without pressure from Bidwell. And because . . ." Matthew hesitated, "I'd like to know why she murdered her husband."

"And I the—" *same,* Woodward was about to say, but before he could finish he was interrupted by the high-pitched voice of a woman.

"Magistrate! Magistrate Woodward!"

It was so sharp and startling that for an instant Woodward thought the crow had spoken his name, and if he were to look up he would see the evil bird about to sink its talons into his scalp. But suddenly a woman came into view, hurrying across the square where Fount Royal's streets met. She wore a simple indigo blue dress, a blue-checked apron, and a white bonnet, and she carried a basket that held such household items as candles and blocks of soap. The magistrate and Matthew halted as the woman neared.

"Yes, madam?" Woodward asked.

She gave him a sunny smile and a quick curtsey. "Forgive me, but when I saw you walking I had to come and introduce myself. I am Lucretia Vaughan. My husband is Stewart, who owns the carpentry shop." She nodded in the direction of Industry Street.

"My pleasure. This is my clerk, Matthew—"

"Corbett, yes, I know. Oh, you two gentlemen are quite the talk hereabouts. How you defied that mad innkeeper and fought off his brood of murderers with a single sword! It's made for a welcome tale of bravery among us!" Matthew had to hold ba :k a laugh; it seemed their midnight flight from Shawcombe's tavern was being transformed by the residents of Fount Royal into something akin to Ulysses's monumental battle with the Cyclops.

"Well," Woodward said, unconsciously puffing out his chest a bit, "it did take all our wits to escape that gang of killers." Matthew was forced to lower his head and study the ground.

"But how *exciting* that must have been!" the woman went on, almost breathless. It had already registered to Woodward that she was a very handsome figure, in her thirties perhaps, with clear blue eyes and a friendly, open demeanor. Curls of light brown hair escaped her bonnet, and her face—though lined by time and the rigors of the frontier life—was as pleasing as a warm lantern on a chill, dark night. "And to have found such a treasure, as well!"

Woodward's smile faltered. "A treasure?"

"Yes, the sack of gold coins you discovered! Spanish gold, wasn't it? Come, sir, please don't be coy with a simple country lady!"

Matthew's heart was beating somewhere in the vicinity of his Adam's apple. He said, "May I ask a question?" then waited for Mrs. Vaughan to nod. "Who informed you of this sack of gold coins?"

"Well, I heard it from Cecilia Semmes, who heard it from Joan Baltour. But *everyone* knows, Mr. Corbett! Oh!" Her eyes widened, and she put a finger to her lips, "Was it supposed to be a *secret?*"

"I fear you've been misinformed," Woodward said. "My clerk found a single coin of Spanish gold, not a sackful."

"But Cecilia promised me it was God's truth! And Cecilia's not one to pass on tales that aren't true!"

"In this case, your friend has erred. Grievously," Woodward added.

"But, I can't understand why—" She stopped, and a knowing smile spread over her face. Her eyes gleamed with delight. "Ohhhh, I see! The cat jumped out of the bag, didn't it?"

"I beg your pardon?"

"You can trust me, sir! Mum's the word!"

"I'm afraid mum is *not* the word. If you're thinking that we have a sack of gold coins that we wish to keep a secret, you're sadly mistaken."

The coin was in the pocket of Matthew's breeches, and he would've taken it out to show her but he doubted it would do any good but simply set more tongues in motion. "I really did only find one," he told her.

"Yes." Her smile remained constant. "Of course you did. That's what I certainly shall tell anyone who asks me . . ." She looked hopefully at the magistrate. "When will the witch swing, sir?"

"Well, I—"

"I would like to know in advance, so I might make some pies to sell. There will be a great number of people there to see it, I'm sure. The whole town, most likely. Where will the gallows be constructed?"

It took Woodward a few seconds to recover from the jarring shock of the woman's rather brusque questions. "I really don't know, Mrs. Vaughan. But at the moment there are no plans to construct a scaffold."

"Oh?" Her smile began to fade, a frown tugging at the edges of her cupid's-bow mouth. "I presumed you were here to carry out an execution."

"You and many others, evidently. I am here to satisfy justice."

"I see. So you're saying there *will* be an execution, but it may be delayed for several days?"

Now it was Woodward's turn to study the ground.

"The witch must swing," Mrs. Vaughan plowed on. Her initial sweetness had given way to something more sour. "For the sake of this town and everyone in it, she must be executed as soon as possible. I mean to say, as soon as justice is satisfied. Do you have any idea when that might be?"

"No, I do not."

"But . . . you're in charge, aren't you? Surely you're not going to suffer the witch to live and keep cursing us too much longer, are you?"

"Magistrate!" Woodward and Matthew saw that Bidwell's carriage had stopped nearby, before it made the turn onto Peace Street. Bidwell had removed his tricorn and held it between both hands, a gesture that Woodward took as contrition. "Good day there, Mrs. Vaughan! I trust you and your family are well?"

"I'm feeling quite ill after learning Rachel Howarth won't swing anytime soon!" the woman replied, her comely face now stitched tight with disgust. "What's wrong with this magistrate? Has the witch already claimed him?"

Bidwell decided, at this combustible moment, to deny the powder its flame. "Magistrate Woodward has the situation well in hand, madam. He operates in a considered and proper judicial manner. Magistrate, may I have a word with you?"

"Good day, Mrs. Vaughan," Woodward said, and she gave an indignant grunt, lifted her pinched nose in the air, and strode away in the direction she'd come. He walked to the carriage. "Yes?"

Bidwell stared at his tricorn, his fingers working the curled brim. "I . . . must make a deepfelt apology, sir. Sometimes I let my impatience guide my tongue." He glanced quickly up to gauge the magistrate's reaction, then lowered his eyes once more. "I'm very sorry to have caused you grief. I know this is a difficult situation as it is for all of us. But you do understand my responsibility here, don't you?"

"I do. I trust you understand and will respect mine."

"Absolutely."

"In that case, I accept your apology. I'd also like you to know I will do my best to resolve your predicament as soon as possible, within the bounds and necessities of the law."

"I ask nothing more," said Bidwell, and then he put his tricorn back on and gave a visible exhalation at the fact that this distasteful business of apology was concluded. "Might I offer you and your clerk a ride?"

"Yes, I'd certainly accept one. It *is* terribly humid this morning, isn't it?" Woodward was also grateful that the air had been cleared, since any difficulty with their host would be painful to endure. He stepped up on the carriage's footclimb as Bidwell opened the door for him, and then he eased himself into the seat that faced the other man. He realized that Matthew hadn't moved an inch from his previous position.

"Matthew? Aren't you coming?"

"No, sir, I am not."

"My apology," Bidwell said, and now the word tasted like spoiled cheese, "was directed to your clerk as well as to you, sir." He was staring at Woodward, not even bothering to lay eyes on the boy.

"I'd rather walk," Matthew said, before the magistrate was put in the position of having to be a diplomat passing chilly responses between warring powers. "I would like the chance to think awhile. Also to explore the town."

"If your clerk desires to walk, he shall walk." Bidwell raised his voice to deliver a command to his servant: "Goode! Drive on!"

At once Goode gave the reins a flick, the team of horses responded, and the carriage moved away from Matthew. It turned left onto Peace Street, running out of its path a couple of scruffy-looking dogs who were growling over a muddy bone. Matthew watched with amusement as a third dog—much smaller than the other two—darted in just behind the carriage's wheels, grabbed up the bone, and fled at speed while its rivals seemed to gape in an amazed stupor before they took pursuit.

Matthew was on his own. He began walking again, going no particular place and certainly in no hurry. He crossed the intersection of streets and headed westward on Industry. Strolling past more fields and farmhouses, picket fences and barns, he greeted and was greeted by several people who were either at work on their various labors of living or who were walking to other destinations. Here and there stood groups of oak trees, massive shapes that overhung their branches above the roofs and yards. The number of large treestumps told Matthew that it had been an endeavor of some sweat and toil to clear this land for any kind of use, but the fallen trees had been put to good service in the walls that protected Fount Royal. It had been no easy job to build this town to its present condition, that was a surety; the sheer willpower of the people to settle what not long ago had been thick woods at the edge of a seaboard swamp greatly impressed Matthew, and seeing the number of houses and plowed fields, greened pastures, and gardens made him fully realize the hopes that humans held to be masters of an untamed land.

"Good mornin' to you!" called a man who was mending a broken fence.

"Good morning," Matthew answered.

"Your magistrate's gonna deliver us from the witch, I hear," the man said, straightening up from his work.

"The problem is being considered," was all Matthew felt free to say.

"I hope he does more'n consider it! Sooner she hangs, sooner we can sleep well at night!"

"Yes, sir. I'll be sure to pass that along to the magistrate." He kept walking, continuing on his westward trek. He expected another response, but the man had returned to his task.

They're ready to hang her, Mrs. Nettles had said. *They'd hang her this morn, if they could.*

He thought of the shape wrapped in gray sackcloth, huddled in the hay.

What she needs is a champion of truth.

He thought of the way she'd risen to her feet, the slow and sinuous movement that had started his heart beating harder.

Somebody to prove her innocent . . . He thought of the sackcloth coming open, and what was revealed beneath. He saw her lean taut body, her raven-black hair, her heartshaped face and strange gold-hued eyes . . . *when ever'body else is again' her.*

He had to stop thinking. The thoughts were causing him distress. He heard the dark growl of distant thunder and realized, not without a sense of humor, that he'd grown his own lightning rod. That was a damnable thing, and to be ashamed of. The woman was, after all, a widow. But still she was a woman, and he a man; though he often wore a lightning rod at the sight of some female that might be passing by, he had devised methods of deflating the issue. Reciting by memory Bible verses in Latin, mentally working complex mathematics problems, or observing the patterns of nature; all those had sufficed at one time or another. In this instance, however, neither Deuteronomy nor geometry had the least effect. Therefore he steered himself by the foremast toward the nearest mighty oak and sat down beneath it to ease his passions in study of grass, clouds, and anything else that needed studying.

More rain, that gift of life the people of Fount Royal certainly could live without for a time, was coming. Matthew saw the charcoal-gray clouds against the lighter gray, and could smell the scent of water in the air. It would soon be above the town, and Matthew welcomed it because it would wash some of this nonsense out of him. And it *was* nonsense, really, to let himself be so bothered, so discomforted, by the sight of a woman's nudity. He was the clerk—the *trusted* clerk—of an important magistrate, and by that office and responsibility he should be above these transgressions of thought.

He watched the storm clouds fast approaching. In a pasture nearby, the cows began lowing. A man on horseback rode past, his steed visibly nervous and fighting the bit. The smell of rain was stronger now, and the next boom of thunder was like the sound of a kettledrum being pounded. Still Matthew stayed where he was, though he'd begun to wonder about finding better shelter. Then the wind came and made the oak's branches shiver over his head, and so he got up and started walking eastward along Industry Street.

Lightning flared across the sky. Within another moment, large drops of rain began pelting Matthew's back. He picked up his pace, realizing he was in for a thorough soaking. The severity of the rainfall rapidly increased, as did the hard-blowing wind. Matthew had not yet reached the conjunction of streets when the bottom fell out of the bucket with a boom and crash, and the rain descended in a gray torrent that all but blinded him. In a matter of seconds he was as wet as a carp. The wind was fierce, almost shoving him headlong into the mud. He looked desperately around, rain slapping his face, and saw in the aqueous gloom the square of an open doorway. There was no time to beg invitation; he ran toward the shelter, which proved to be a small barn, and once inside he stepped back from the windblown entrance and shook the rain from himself like one of Fount Royal's bone-chasing mongrels.

Matthew surmised he would be captive here for a while. On a wallpeg hung a lantern, a flame aglow within its bell; Matthew realized someone had been recently here, but where that someone now was he didn't know. There were four narrow stalls, two of them each confining a horse; both horses stared at him, and one rumbled a greeting of sorts deep in the throat. Matthew ran a hand through the stubble of his wet hair and watched the deluge at a prudent distance from the doorway.

The barn was well put together. There were a few pattering raindrops falling from the roof, but not enough to be bothersome. He looked about for a place to rest and saw a pile of hay over against the far wall; going to it, he sat down and stretched his legs out to await the storm's finale. One of the horses nickered, as if asking him what he was doing. Matthew hoped that whoever owned this barn would not be too troubled by his presence here, but he didn't care to drown on the way to Bidwell's mansion. A boom of thunder and flash of lightning made the horses jump and whinny. The rain was still pouring down—if anything, harder than before—and Matthew figured that his stay here would be, unfortunately, longer than he'd planned.

A drop of rain plunked him on the top of the head. He looked up in time to receive another raindrop between his eyes. Yes, he was sitting directly beneath a leak. He moved two feet or so to the left, nearer the wall, and stretched his legs out before him again.

But then he became aware of a new discomfort. Something was pressing into his spine. He reached back, his hand winnowing into the hay, and there his fingers came into contact with a surface of rough burlap. A sack of some kind, he realized as his fingers did their exploring. A sack, buried in the hay.

He pulled his hand away from it. Whatever the sack contained, it was not his business. After all, this was private property. He should be gracious enough not to go looking through private piles of hay, shouldn't he?

He sat there for a moment, watching the rain. Perhaps it had lessened somewhat, perhaps not. The leak that had moved him aside was still dripping. He reached back, almost unconsciously, sank his hand into the hay, and felt the sack's surface once more. Then again withdrew his fingers. Private property, he told himself. Leave it alone.

But a question had come to him. This was indeed private property, so why had its owner felt the need to hide a burlap sack at the bottom of a haypile? And the next question, of course— what did the sack contain that merited hiding?

"It's not my business," he said aloud, as if saying it could convince him.

He recalled then something else that Mrs. Nettles had said: *Satan does walk in Fount Royal, but Rachel Howarth's na' the one beside him. Things that nae want to be seen are plentiful here. And that's God's truth.*

Matthew found himself wondering if that burlap sack held one of the things that, as Mrs. Nettles had expressed it, nae wanted to be seen.

If that was so, might it have some bearing on the case of witchcraft? And if it did, was he not bound to investigate it as a representative of Magistrate Woodward?

Perhaps so. Then again, perhaps not. He was torn between his curiosity and his respect for private property. Another moment passed, during which the frown of deliberation never left Matthew's face. Then he made his decision: he would clear away enough hay to get a good look at the sack, and thereafter dictate his actions.

When the job was done, Matthew saw that it was simply a plain dark brown grainsack. Touching it, however, indicated that its content was not grain; his fingers made out a circular shape that seemed to be made of either wood or metal. More study was needed. He grasped the sack and, in attempting to dislodge it, quickly learned how heavy it was. His shoulders protested the effort. Now all reluctance to pierce this mystery had fled before the attack of Matthew's desire to know; he gave the sack a mighty heave and succeeded in pulling it free about half of its length. His hands felt another circular shape, and the folds and creases of some unknown material. He got a firm grip on the thing, in preparation of dragging it out so he might inspect its other—and presumably open—end.

One of the horses suddenly gave a snort and a whuff of air. Matthew felt the small hairs move on the back of his neck and he knew in an instant that someone else had just entered the barn.

He started to turn his head. Before he could, he heard the crunch of a boot on the earthen floor and he was grasped by two hands, one around the back of the neck and the other seizing his right arm just above the elbow. There was a garbled cry that might have been a curse with God's name in it, and an instant after that Matthew was picked up and thrown through the air with terrifying force. He had no time to prevent a bad landing; on the journey his right shoulder grazed a wooden post and then he collided with the gate that secured one of the empty stalls. The breath was knocked from his lungs and he fell to the floor, his bones having suddenly become unjointed and less solid than as objects of pliable putty.

He was struggling to get his breath when his attacker loomed over him again, and now a hand took hold of his shirt and pulled him up and another hand clamped upon his throat. The pressure was such that Matthew feared his eyeballs would explode from their sockets. "You sneakin' bastard, you!" the man was shouting. With a violent twisting motion the man threw Matthew once more, this time into the wall with such force that the entire barn trembled and old dust blew from the chinks. The stunned clerk felt his teeth bite into his tongue, and as he sank to the ground again in a haze of pain he tasted bitter blood.

The man came after him. "I'll kill you, you damn sneak!" he raged, and he swung a booted foot directly at Matthew's head. Matthew knew in a flash that if he didn't move, his skull would be bashed in, so he scrabbled forward and at the same time threw up an arm to ward off the blow. The kick got him on the right shoulderblade, bringing a cry of pain from his bloody lips, but he kept frantically crawling and pulled his legs underneath himself before the man could get balanced to kick him again. Matthew staggered up, his knees buckled, but he forced them to hold true with sheer willpower, and then he turned to face his attacker, his back pressed against the wallboards.

By the lantern's light he recognized the man. He'd seen this fellow in passing yesterday morning, when he and the magistrate had met Paine at the public stables behind the blacksmith's foundry. It was indeed the blacksmith; by name, according to the sign of his business, Seth Hazelton. The smithy was a squat, round-bellied man of middle age, with a wet gray brush of hair and a coarse and dripping gray beard. His face was as rugged as weathered rock, his nose a hooked precipice. At the moment his intense blue eyes were lit with the fire of sheer, white-hot fury, and the knotty veins stood out in relief on his bull-thick neck. He paused in his onrush, as if recognizing Matthew as the magistrate's clerk, but the respite was only for a few seconds; his face flamed anew and, bellowing a cry of mingled wrath and anguish, he hurtled forward again.

Matthew was fast when he needed to be. He gauged Hazelton's swinging blow, ducked under the fist, and ran for the way out. The smithy, however, was also quick of foot when it deemed him to be so; he bounded after Matthew like a corpulent hound and caught the boy's shoulder in a grip fashioned hard by the contest with iron. Matthew was spun around, two hands set upon his throat, he was lifted off his feet and carried backward to slam once more into the wall with a force that near shattered his spine. Then the hands began to squeeze with deadly intent.

Matthew grasped the man's wrists and tried to unhinge those killing hands, but even as he fought he knew it was in vain. Hazelton's sweating face was pressed right into his, the man's eyes glazed from the heat of this—rather onesided—combat. The fingers were digging deep into Matthew's throat. He couldn't breathe, and dark motes were beginning to dance before his eyes. He was aware, strangely, that one horse was whinnying piteously and the other was kicking in its stall.

He was going to die. He knew it. In a few seconds, the darkness was going to overcome him and he would die right here by this blacksmith's crushing hands.

This was the moment he should be rescued, he thought. This was the moment someone should come in and tear Hazelton away from him. But Matthew realized it wasn't likely to happen. No, his fate would be interrupted by no samaritan this sorry day.

The lantern. Where was the lantern?

On his right, still hanging from its peg. With an effort he angled his head and eyes and found the lamp several feet away. He reached for it; he had long arms, but the lantern was at the very limit of his grasp. Desperation gave him the strength to lurch the two or three extra inches. He plucked the hot lamp from its peg. Then he smashed it as hard as he could into the side of Hazelton's face.

An edge of unsmoothed tin did its work. A cut opened across the blacksmith's cheek from the corner of the eye to the upper lip, and crimson rivulets streamed down into his beard. Hazelton blinked as the pain hit him; there was a pause in which Matthew feared the man's fit of rage was stronger than the desire to preserve his face, but then Hazelton let out a howl and staggered back, his hands leaving Matthew's throat to press against the tide of blood.

Matthew sucked air into his lungs. His head swimming, he half-ran, half-stumbled toward the barn's open doorway. The rain was still falling, but not near with its previous velocity. Matthew didn't dare to look behind to see if the smithy was gaining on him, as that glance would surely slow him down a precious step. Then he was outside the barn. The rain hit him and the wind swirled about him, his left foot snagged a treeroot that almost sent him sprawling, but he recovered his balance and ran on into the tumult, aiming his flight in the direction of Bidwell's mansion. Only when he'd reached the conjunction of streets did he slow his pace and look over his shoulder. If the blacksmith had followed, he had been left behind.

Still, Matthew didn't care to tarry. He spat blood into a mud-puddle and then tilted his head back, opened his mouth to wash it with rain, and spat again. His back and shoulders felt deeply bruised, his throat savaged by Hazelton's fingers. He would have quite a tale to tell the magistrate, and he knew he was damned lucky he was alive to tell it. He started off again, walking as fast as he could, toward Bidwell's house.

Two questions remained in his mind: what had been in the burlap sack? And what had the blacksmith concealed that he would kill to protect?

nine

T HAT'S A DAMNABLE STORY!" Bidwell said, when Matthew had finished telling it. "You mean Hazelton tried to strangle you over a *grainsack?*"

"Not just a grainsack." Matthew was sitting in a comfortable chair in the mansion's parlor, a pillow wedged behind his bruised back and a silver cup of rum on a table next to him. "There was something in it." His throat felt swollen, and he'd already looked into a handmirror and seen the blacksmith's blue fingermarks on his neck. "Something he didn't want me to see."

"Seth Hazelton has a cracked bell in his steeple." Mrs. Nettles stood nearby, her arms crossed over her chest and her dark gaze positively frightening; it was she who had fetched the cup of rum from the kitchen. "He was odd 'fore his wife died last year. Since then, he's become much the worse."

"Well, thank God you weren't killed!" Woodward was sitting in a chair across from his clerk, and he wore an expression of both profound relief and concern. "And I thank God you didn't kill *him,* either, or there would surely be Hell to pay. You know you were trespassing on private property, don't you?"

"Yes, sir."

"I understand your desire to find shelter from that storm, but what on earth prompted you to dig into the man's hidden possessions? There was no reason for it, was there?"

"No, sir," Matthew said grimly. "I suppose there wasn't."

"I *tell* you there wasn't! And you say you struck him a blow to the face that brought the blood flowing?" Woodward winced at the gravity of the legal wheels that might have to turn because of this. "Was he on his feet the last you saw him?"

"Yes, sir."

"But he didn't come out of the barn after you?"

Matthew shook his head. "I don't think so." He reached for the rum and downed some of it, knowing where the magistrate was headed. His wounded tongue—which was so enlarged it seemed to fill up his mouth—had already been scorched by the liquor's fire and was mercifully numbed.

"Then he could have fallen after you left." Woodward lifted his gaze to Bidwell, who stood beside his chair. "The man could be lying in that barn, severely injured. I suggest we see to him immediately."

"Hazelton's as tough as a salt-dried buzzard," Mrs. Nettles said. "A wee cut on the face would nae finish 'im off."

"I'm afraid it was more than a wee . . . I mean, a small cut," Matthew admitted. "His cheek suffered a nasty slice."

"Well, what did he expect?" Mrs. Nettles thrust out her chin. "That you should let 'im choke you dead without a fight? You ask me, I say he deserved what he got!"

"Be that as it may, we must go." Woodward stood up. He was feeling poorly himself, his raw throat paining him with every swallow. He dreaded having to leave the house and travel in the drizzling rain, but this was an extremely serious matter.

Bidwell too had recognized the solemnity of the situation. His foremost thought, however, was that the loss of the town's blacksmith would be another crippling hardship. "Mrs. Nettles," he said, "have Goode bring the carriage around."

"Yes sir." She started out toward the rear of the house. Before she'd gotten more than a few steps, however, the bell that announced a visitor at the front door was rung. She hurried to it, opened it—and received a shock.

There stood the blacksmith himself, hollow-eyed and gray-faced, a bloody cloth secured to his left cheek with a leather strap that was knotted around his head. Behind him was his horse and wagon, and in his arms he held a dark brown burlap sack.

"Who is it?" Bidwell came into the foyer and instantly stopped in his tracks. "My God, man! We were just on our way to see about you!"

"Well," Hazelton said, his voice roughened by the pain of his injury, "here I be. Where's the young man?"

"In the parlor," Bidwell said.

Hazelton came across the threshold without invitation, brushing past Mrs. Nettles. She wrinkled her nose at the combined smells of body odor and blood. When the blacksmith entered the parlor, his muddy boots clomping on the floor, Matthew almost choked on his rum and Woodward felt his hackles rise like those of a cat anticipating the attack of a large and brutish dog.

"Here." Hazelton threw the sack down at Matthew's feet. "This is what you were sneakin' to see." Matthew stood up—carefully, as his back's stability was precarious.

"Go on, open it," Hazelton told him. "That's what you wanted to do, ain't it?"

Matthew got his mouth working. "I'm sorry, sir. I shouldn't have invaded your priva—"

"Swalla that shit and have a look." Hazelton bent down, lifted the stitched end of the sack, and began to dump its contents out onto the floor. Bidwell and Mrs. Nettles had come in from the foyer, and they witnessed what Hazelton had fought so viciously to protect.

Clothes spilled from the sack, along with two pairs of scuffed and much-worn shoes. A woman's wardrobe, it was: a black dress, an indigo apron, a few yellowed blouses, and a number of patched skirts that at one time had fit a pair of very broad hips. A small, unadorned wooden box also slid from the sack, and came to rest against Matthew's left shoe.

"Sophie's clothes," the blacksmith said. "Ever'thin' she owned. Pick up that box and open it." Matthew hesitated; he was feeling at the moment like a complete horse's ass.

"Go on, open it!" Hazelton commanded. Matthew picked it up and lifted the lid. Within the box were four ivory hairpins, a comb fashioned from golden-grained wood, a silver ring that held a small amber stone, and another silver ring etched with an intricate rope-like design.

"Her ornaments," the blacksmith said. "Weddin' ring, too. When she passed, I couldn't bear to throw them things away. Couldn't bear to have 'em in the house, neither." He pressed a hand against the bloody cloth. "So I put 'em in a sack and hid 'em in my barn for safekeepin'." Hazelton's dark-rimmed eyes stared furiously at Matthew. "Thought it was someplace nobody'd go pokin'. Then I come in and there you be, tryin' to drag it out." He turned his gaze upon Woodward. "You be the magistrate, huh? A man of the law, sworn to uphold it?"

"That's correct."

"If it be so, I want some satisfaction. This whelp come in my barn uninvited and go to diggin' out my dear wife's belongin's. I ain't done nothin' wrong, I ain't tryin' to hide nothin' but what's mine and nobody else's business." Hazelton looked at Bidwell for a response. "Maybe I did go some crazy, like to try to kill that boy, but damn if I didn't think he was tryin' to steal my Sophie's things. Can you blame me, sir?"

"No," Bidwell had to admit, "I cannot."

"This boy"—Hazelton lifted an accusing, bloodstained finger to point at Matthew—"cut my face wide open, like to blinded me. I'm gonna lose work over it, that's for sure. A wound like I've suffered won't bear the furnace heat 'til it's near mended. Now you tell me, Mr. Bidwell and Mr. Magistrate, what you're gonna do to give me my satisfaction."

Bidwell stared at the floor. Woodward pressed his fingers against his mouth, realizing what had to come out of it, and

Matthew closed the lid of Sophie Hazelton's ornament box. At last the magistrate had to speak. "Mr. Hazelton, what would you consider a proper satisfaction?"

"If it was up to my quirt, I'd lash 'im," the blacksmith said. "Lash 'im until his back was laid open good and proper."

"His back has already received injury," Woodward said. "And he'll have your fingermarks on his throat for some time to come, I'm sure."

"Don't make no mind! I want him whipped!"

"This is a difficult position you put me in, sir," the magistrate said, his mouth tightening. "You ask me to sentence my own clerk."

"Who else'll sentence 'im, then? And if he wasn't your clerk, what would your judgment be?"

Woodward glanced quickly at Matthew and then away again; the younger man knew what torments of conscience Woodward was fighting, but he also knew that the magistrate would be ultimately compelled to do the correct thing.

Woodward spoke. "One lash, then," he said, almost inaudibly.

"Five!" the blacksmith thundered. "And a week in a cell, to boot!"

Woodward drew a long breath and stared at the floor. "Two lashes and five days."

"No sir! Look at *this!*" Hazelton tore the bloody bandage away from his face, revealing a purple-edged wound so ugly that Bidwell flinched and even Mrs. Nettles averted her eyes. "You see what he done to me? Tell me I ain't gonna wear a pretty scar the rest of my life! Three lashes and five days!"

Matthew, dazed at all this, sank down into the chair again. He reached for the rum cup and emptied it.

"Three lashes," Woodward said wearily, a vein beating at his temple, "and three days." He forced himself to meet the power of Hazelton's stare. "That's my judgment and there will be no addition or reversal to it. He will enter the gaol at six o'clock in the morning and will receive his lashes at six o'clock on the third morning. I expect Mr. Green will administer the whip?" He looked at Bidwell, who nodded. "All right, then. As a magistrate under the King of England and the governor of this colony, I have made my decree."

The blacksmith scowled; it was an expression fierce enough to scare the shine from a mirror. But then he pushed the cloth back against his injury and said, "I reckon it'll have to do, then, you bein' such a *fair-minded* magistrate and all. To Hell with that sneakin' bastard, is what I say."

"The decree has been made." Woodward's face had begun to mottle with red. "I suggest that you go pay a visit to the physician."

"I ain't lettin' that death-doctor touch me, no sir! But I'll go, all right. It smells like a pigsty in here." He began to quickly stuff the clothes back into the burlap sack. The last item in was the ornament box, which Matthew had set down upon the table. Then Hazelton held the sack in his thickly corded arms and looked defiantly from Woodward to Bidwell and back again. "It's a damn bad world when a man has to wear a scar for defendin' his wife's memory, and the law won't lay the lash on good and proper!"

"The lash *will* be laid on good and proper," Woodward said coldly. "Three times."

"You say. Well, I'll be there to make sure, you can mark it!" He turned around and started out of the parlor.

"Mr. Hazelton?" Matthew suddenly said. The blacksmith stopped and cast a brooding gaze upon his antagonist.

Matthew stood up from the chair. "I wish to say . . . that I'm very sorry for my actions. I was grievously wrong, and I beg your pardon."

"You'll have my pardon after I see your back split open."

"I understand your emotions, sir. And I must say I am deserving of the punishment."

"That and *more*," Hazelton said.

"Yes, sir. But . . . might I ask something of you?"

"What?"

"Might you let me carry that sack for you to your wagon?"

Hazelton frowned like five miles of bad road. "Carry it? *Why?*"

"It would be a small token of my repentance." Matthew took two steps toward the man and extended his arms. "Also my wish that we might put this incident behind us, once my punishment is done." Hazelton didn't speak, but Matthew could tell that his mind was working. It was the narrowing of the smithy's eyes that told Matthew the man knew what he was up to. Hazelton, for all his brutish behavior and oxlike countenance, was a crafty fox.

"That boy's as crazy as a bug in a bottle," Hazelton said to Woodward. "I wouldn't let 'im loose at night, if I was you." And with that pronouncement the blacksmith turned his back on the company, strode out of the parlor and through the front door into the drizzling rain. Mrs. Nettles followed behind him, and closed the door rather too hard before she returned to the room.

"Well," Woodward said as he lowered himself into his chair like a suddenly aged invalid, "justice has been served."

"My regrets over this situation," Bidwell offered. "But to be truthful about it, I would have imposed the five lashes." He looked at Matthew and shook his head. "You knew better than to disturb a man's private property! Boy, you delight in causing grief wherever you wander, don't you?"

"I have said I was wrong. I'll repeat it for you, if you like. And I'll take the lashes as I deserve . . . but you must understand, Mr. Bidwell, that Hazelton believes he's made a fool out of all of us."

"*What?*" Bidwell made a face, as if he'd tasted something foul. "What're you going on about *now?*"

"Simply that what Hazelton revealed to be in that sack was not its contents when it was hidden beneath the hay."

There was a silence. Then Woodward spoke up. "What are you saying, Matthew?"

"I'm saying that the weight of the sack when I tried to dislodge it was much heavier than old clothes and some shoes. Hazelton knew I was trying to ascertain its weight, and of course he didn't want me touching it."

"I should say not!" Bidwell dug into a pocket of his waistcoat for his snuffbox. "Haven't you had enough of Hazelton for one day? I'd mind my step around him!"

"It's been . . . oh, about forty minutes since our meeting," Matthew went on. "I believe he used the time to either remove what was originally in that sack and replace it with the clothes, or he found another similar sack for the purpose."

Bidwell inhaled a pinch of snuff and then blinked his watering eyes. "You never quit, do you?"

"Believe what you like, sir, but I know there was something far more substantial than clothing in the sack I uncovered. Hazelton knew I'd tell the tale, and he knew there might be some suspicion about what he would hide and then kill to protect. So he bandaged himself, got in his wagon, and brought the counterfeit sack here before anyone could go *there* and make inquiries about it."

"Your theory." Bidwell snorted snuff up his nose again, then closed the box with a *snap*. "I'm afraid it won't do to save you from the lash and the cage. The magistrate's made his decree, and Mrs. Nettles and I have witnessed it."

"A witness I may be," Mrs. Nettles said with frost in her voice, "but I tell you, sir, that Hazelton's a strange bird. And I happ'n to know he treated Sophie like a three-legged horse 'fore she died, so why should he now treat her mem'ry the better? Most like he kept her clothes and ornaments to sell 'em after a space a' time."

"Thank you, Mrs. Nettles," said Bidwell sarcastically. "It seems the 'theory tree' is one plant that's taken firm root in Fount Royal!"

"Whatever the truth of this matter is," the magistrate observed, "what cannot be altered is the fact that Matthew will spend three nights in the gaol and take the lashes. The blacksmith's private property will not be intruded upon again. But in reference to your statement, Mr. Bidwell, that you would've insisted on five strikes of the whip, let me remind you that the proceedings against Rachel Howarth must be delayed until Matthew has paid his penance and recovered from it."

Bidwell stood like a statue for a few seconds, his mouth half-open. Woodward continued in a calm tone, anticipating another storm from the master of Fount Royal, and bracing himself for it. "You see, I require a clerk to take notation when I interview the witnesses. I must have in writing the answers to my questions, and Matthew has developed a code that I can easily read. If I have no clerk, there is no point in scheduling the interviews. Therefore, the time he spends in your gaol and the time spent in recuperation from being lashed must be taken into account."

"By God, man!" Bidwell blustered. "What're you telling me? That you won't get to questioning the witnesses tomorrow?"

"I would say five days at the least."

"Damn it all, Woodward! This town will wither up and blow away before you get to work, won't it?"

"My clerk," the magistrate said, "is indispensable to the process of justice. He cannot take notation from a cage, and I dare say he won't be up to the task of concentration with fresh whip burns on his back."

"Well, why *can't* he take notation from a cage?" Bidwell's thick brows lifted. "There are three witnesses on the list I've given you. Why can you not set up your office in the gaol and have the witnesses brought there to testify? As I understand the law, they would be required to speak in the presence of the accused anyway, am I correct?"

"Yes, you are."

"All right, then! They can speak in the gaol as well as in the meetinghouse! Your clerk can be given a table and scribing materials and he can do the work while he carries out his sentence!" Bidwell's eyes had a feverish gleam. "What say you to that?"

Woodward looked at Matthew. "It *is* a possibility. Certainly it would speed the process. Are you agreeable?"

Matthew thought about it. He could feel Mrs. Nettles watching him. "I'd need more light in there," he said.

Bidwell waved an impatient hand. "I'll get you every lantern and candle in Fount Royal, if that's what you require! Winston has quills, ink, and foolscap aplenty!"

Matthew rubbed his chin and continued to contemplate. He rather enjoyed having Bidwell lapping at his feet like a powdered spaniel.

"I might point out one thing to you," Bidwell said quietly. His voice had some grit in it again, proving he was nobody's cur. "Mr. Green owns three whips. One is a bullwhip, the second is a cat-o'-nine, and the third is a leather braid. The magistrate may have decreed the punishment, but as master—governor, if you will—of Fount Royal it is *my* right to choose the implement." He paused to let Matthew fully appreciate the situation. "Now ordinarily in a violation of this nature I would ask Mr. Green to use the bullwhip." Bidwell gave the merest hint of a cunning smile. "But if you are employed in, shall we say, a noble task to benefit the citizens of my town whilst imprisoned, I should be gratified to recommend the braid."

Matthew's contemplation came to an end. "You make a persuasive argument," he said. "I'd be happy to be of service to the citizens."

"Excellent!" Bidwell almost clapped his hands together with joy. He didn't notice that Mrs. Nettles abruptly turned and walked out of the room. "We should notify the first witness, then. Who shall it be, Magistrate?"

Woodward reached into a pocket and brought out the piece of paper upon which were quilled three names. Bidwell had given him the list on his request when they'd returned from the gaol. "I'll see the eldest first, Jeremiah Buckner. Then Elias Garrick. Lastly the little girl, Violet Adams. I regret she must be questioned in the gaol, but there is no recourse."

"I'll have a servant go inform them all directly," Bidwell offered. "I presume, since your clerk is going to the gaol at six o'clock, that we may have Mr. Buckner appear before you at seven?"

"Yes, if Matthew's table and scribing materials are present and I have a comfortable place to preside."

"You shall have it. Well, now our horses are getting some-where, are they not?" Bidwell's smile would have paled the glow from his chandelier.

"The poppets," Woodward said. He remained cool and com-posed, unwilling to share Bidwell's ebullience. "Who has them?"

"Nicholas Paine. Don't worry, they're in safekeeping."

"I should like to see those and speak to Mr. Paine concerning them after the first three witnesses."

"I'll arrange it. Anything else?"

"Yes, there *is*." Woodward glanced quickly at Matthew and then returned his gaze to Bidwell. "I would request that you not be present during the interviews."

The man's buoyant mood instantly sagged. "And why not? I have a right to be there!"

"That, sir, is debatable. I believe your presence might have some undue influence on the witnesses, and certainly on Madam Howarth when she gives her testimony. Therefore, in fairness to all, I wish no spectators in my court. I understand that Mr. Green must be present, as he has the keys to the gaol, but he may sit at the entrance until he is required to lock the gaol again at the end of the hearing."

Bidwell grunted. "You'll want Mr. Green closer at hand the first time the witch throws her slopbowl at you!"

"It will be explained to her that if she disrupts the proceed-ings in any way, she shall be bound and—as much as I detest to do so—gagged. Her opportunity to respond to the charges will come when the witnesses have been heard."

Bidwell started to protest once more, but he decided to let it go in favor of moving the witch nearer the stake. "Regardless what you think of me and my motives," he said, "I am a fair-minded man. I will go reside in Charles Town for a week, if that's what you need to hold your court!"

"That won't be necessary, but I do appreciate your coopera-tion."

"Mrs. Nettles!" Bidwell hollered. "Where did that woman get off to?"

"I think she went to the kitchen," Matthew said.

"I'll have a servant go inform the witnesses." Bidwell started out of the parlor. "It will be a happy day when this ordeal is over, I can assure you that!" He walked toward the kitchen, intent to have Mrs. Nettles choose a servant to carry out the necessary errands.

When Bidwell had gone, the magistrate ran a hand across his forehead and regarded Matthew with a stony stare. "What *ever* possessed you to invade a man's privacy in such a fashion? Didn't you stop to consider the consequences?"

"No, sir, I didn't. I know I should have, but . . . my curiosity was stronger than my good sense."

"Your *curiosity,*" Woodward said in a chill tone, "is like strong drink, Matthew. Too much of it, and you're drunk beyond all reason. Well, you'll have time to repent in the gaol. And the three lashes are mild punishment indeed for such an injury as you did Hazelton." He shook his head, his lips grim. "I cannot believe it! I had to sentence my own clerk to the cage and the whip! My God, what a weight you put on me!"

"I suppose," Matthew said, "this is not the proper time to *insist* to you that what was originally in the sack was not what Hazelton revealed it to be."

"No! Certainly not!" Woodward swallowed painfully and stood up. He was feeling weak and listless, and he thought he might have a touch of fever. It was the humidity, of course. The swamp air, contaminating his blood. "There is no way to prove your theory. And I don't think it really matters, do you?"

"Yes, sir," came the firm reply. "I do think it matters."

"It does not because I say it doesn't! That man is within his rights to have you horsewhipped until your back is split to the bone, do you understand? You'll keep your nose out of his barn, his sacks, and his business!"

Matthew didn't respond. He fixed his gaze to the floor, waiting for the magistrate's anger to ebb. "Besides," Woodward said after another moment, his voice softer, "I should need your help in this case, and having you behind bars or suffering in bed from the stripes will do nothing to advance our progress." There was sweat on his brow. He felt near faint, and had to retire. "I am going upstairs to rest."

Instantly Matthew was on his feet. "You're not well, are you?"

"A sore throat. Some weakness. I'll feel better once I'm accustomed to these swamp humours."

"Do you wish to see Dr. Shields?"

"No! Heavens, no. It's a matter of acclimation, that's all. I should want to rest my voice, too." He hesitated before he went to the stairs. "Matthew, please restrain your investigations for the remainder of the day, will you promise me that?"

"Yes, sir."

"Very good." Woodward turned away and took his leave.

The day's hours passed. Outside, the rain fell in fits and spits. Matthew discovered a small library room that held a few shelves of books on subjects such as the flora and fauna of the New World, European history, some well-known English plays, and the business of shipbuilding. Only the latter tomes showed any kind of wear whatsoever. The library also held two chairs that faced each other on opposite sides of a chessboard, its squares formed of beautiful pale and dark wood, the chesspieces of the same materials. A map of Fount Royal was fixed to a wall. Upon closer study, Matthew saw the map was a fanciful representation of what Bidwell proposed the town to be in the future, with elegant streets, orderly houses, huge quiltwork farms, spreading orchards, and of course the precise pattern of the naval yards and docks.

Matthew chose a book on the history of Spain, and when he opened it the leather binding popped like the report of a pistol. He read until a late lunch of corncakes and barley-and-rice soup was served in the dining room. Bidwell was absent from the table, and when one of the servant girls went upstairs to fetch the magistrate she reported to Matthew that he had decided to decline eating. So Matthew lunched alone—his concern for Woodward's health beginning to gnaw at him—after which he returned to reading in the library.

He noted that Mrs. Nettles didn't make another appearance, and he judged that either she was busy on some errand for her master or she was avoiding him because she regretted her confidences. That was fine with him, as her opinions surely clouded what should be based solely on fact. Several times the image of Rachel Howarth opening her cloak came to him, and the vision of her lovely though stern-eyed face. It had occurred to him that, as Noles would be released on the morrow, he would be the woman's lone gaol-mate for the next three days. And then, of course, there was the braid's kiss awaiting him. He set to translating Spanish history into the French tongue.

Darkness fell, the house's lamps were lighted, and a dinner of chicken pie was presented. Both Bidwell and Woodward did attend this meal, the former light in spirits and the latter more heavily cloaked in responsibility. Attending the dinner, as well, was another contingent of mosquitoes that hummed about the ears and did their damnedest to swell their bellies. The master of the mansion offered up a bottle of Sir Richard and made toast after toast congratulating Woodward's "sterling abilities" and "clear sight of the harbor ahead," among other pufferies. The magistrate, who was hollow-eyed, feeling quite ill, and not at all receptive to a celebration, endured this falderal with stoicism, sipped the rum sparsely and picked at his food, but truly ate only a third of his portion. Though Woodward's demeanor was noticeably poor, Bidwell never inquired as to his health—probably because, Matthew surmised, the man feared a further delay in the witch's trial.

At last, over a dessert of egg custard that Woodward deigned to touch, Matthew had to speak. "Sir, I believe you're in need of Dr. Shields."

"Nonsense!" Woodward said hoarsely. "I told you, it's the swamp air!"

"You don't look very well, if you'll pardon my saying so."

"I look like what I am!" The magistrate had neared the raw edge of his nerves, what with his painful throat, swollen nasal passages, and this plague of biting insects. "I'm a bald-headed old man who's been robbed of his wig and waistcoat! Thank you for your flattery, Matthew, but please constrain your opinions!"

"Sir, I only meant to say—"

"Oh, the magistrate seems fit enough to me," Bidwell interrupted, a false smile frozen upon his face. "The swamp air *does* take some getting used to, but it's nothing a good toss of rum can't cure. Isn't that right, sir?"

Woodward was unwilling to be gracious. "Actually, no. The rum inflames more than it cures."

"But you *are* well, are you not?" Bidwell pressed. "I mean, well enough to carry out your duties, yes?"

"Certainly I am! Perhaps I do feel a shade under the weather—"

"Who does not, with all this rain?" Bidwell said, and uttered a quick and nervous laugh.

"—but I have never in my entire career been unfit to carry out my duties, and I won't blemish that record here and now." He gave Matthew a pointed glance. "I have a sore throat and I'm a little weary, that's all."

"I would still like for you to see Dr. Shields."

"Damn it, boy!" Woodward snapped. "Who is the father here?" Instantly his face bloomed red. "I mean . . . who is the *guardian* here?" He lowered his eyes and stared at his fingers, which gripped the table's edge. Silence reigned in the room. "Forgive me," Woodward said quietly, "I misspoke. Of course I am my clerk's guardian, not his father." The blood was still scorching his cheeks. "It seems my mind is rather slipshod. I believe I should retire to my room now and try to rest." He stood up from his seat and Matthew and Bidwell also rose as a measure of respect. "I require to be awakened at five o'clock," he told his host. Then, to Matthew, "And I suggest you get to sleep early, as you will find the gaol ill-suited to comfort. Good night, gentlemen." So saying, the magistrate stiffened his spine and left the room with as much dignity as he could muster.

Silence again held sway as Matthew and Bidwell returned to their places. The older man hurriedly finished his custard, drank a last swallow of rum, and departed the table with a chill "I'll take my leave now. Good night," leaving Matthew alone with the ruins of the meal.

Matthew decided it would be wise to follow the magistrate's advice, and so he went upstairs, traded his clothes for a nightshirt, and climbed into bed under the mosquito netting. Through the closed shutters of his window he heard the distant sound of a woman singing, accompanied by the double-quick plucks of a violin. He realized the music was coming from the servants' quarters, and it had to be Goode playing his instrument in a much more relaxed manner than his recital on the first evening. It was a pleasant, lively sound, and it distracted Matthew from thoughts of the gaol, Rachel Howarth, and the braid awaiting him. Therefore he pushed aside the netting, got out of bed, and opened the shutters to allow the music in.

Lanterns were aglow down in the small village of clapboard houses where the servants resided. Now Goode's tune altered itself, and the woman—who had a truly regal voice—began to sing a different song. Matthew couldn't make out any of the words; he thought it must be in some kind of African dialect. A tambourine picked up the rhythm and another, deeper-toned drum began to beat counterpoint. The woman's voice rose and fell, wandering around the tune, jesting with it, then returning to its arms. Matthew leaned his elbows against the windowframe and looked up at the sky; the clouds were too thick to see any stars or the moon, but at least the drizzle that had aggravated the afternoon had ceased.

He listened to the music, enjoying the moment.

Who is the father here? What a strange thing for the magistrate to say. Of course he wasn't feeling well, and his mind was indeed somewhat disordered, but . . . what a strange thing to say.

Matthew had certainly never thought of the magistrate as his father. His guardian, yes; his mentor perhaps. But father? No. Not to say that Matthew didn't feel an affinity for the man. After all, they'd been working and living together for five years. If Matthew had not been performing his duties in a satisfactory manner, he felt sure he never would have lasted so long in the magistrate's employ.

And that's what the arrangement was, of course. An employment. Matthew had hopes to continue his obligation for as many years as Woodward needed him, and then perhaps to make a study of law himself. Woodward had told him he might even make a magistrate someday, if he decided to enter that field.

Father? No. There were so many things that Matthew didn't know about the magistrate, even after five years. What Woodward's past had been in London, and why he'd come to the colonies. Why he refused to talk about this mysterious "Ann" he sometimes mentioned when he was enthralled in a bad dream. And the great significance of the gold-striped waistcoat.

Those were all things a father would explain to a son, even one secured from an almshouse. They were, likewise, things of a highly personal nature that an employer would not discuss with his employee.

After a short while the music came to a melodic conclusion. Matthew stared toward the swamp and the sea, both veiled by night, then he drew the shutters closed, returned to bed, and found sleep waiting.

When he awakened—with a jarring, frightful start—he knew immediately what had roused him. He could still hear the echo of a tremendous blast of thunder. As it receded, dogs began to bay and bark all across Fount Royal. Matthew turned over, intending to return to the land of Somnus, and was no sooner drifting in that direction when a second thunder cannon went off seemingly above his head. He sat up, unnerved, and waited for the next detonation. The flash of lightning could be seen through the shutters' slats, and then the entire house quaked as Vulcan hammered on his forge.

Matthew got up, his bruised back considerably stiff, and opened the window to view the storm. It was an uncertain hour somewhere between midnight and dawn. The lanterns were all extinguished down in the servants' village. No rain had yet begun to fall, but the wind was thrashing through the forest that stood at the swamp's edge. The lightning flared again, the thunder spoke, and Matthew heard the dogs answer.

He was thinking how Fount Royal might conquer the Devil, only to be washed away by God, when something caught his attention. A furtive movement, it was, down amid the Negro shacks. He peered into the dark, watching that area. In another moment the lightning streaked overhead once more, and by its fierce illumination he saw a figure depart the corner of a house and begin to walk briskly toward Fount Royal. Then the night rolled in again, like ocean waves. Matthew was left with the impression that the figure was a man——or, at least, had a masculine stride—wearing dark clothes and a monmouth cap. Had there been something swinging from the right hand? Possibly, but it was difficult to say. Also impossible to determine was if the person had been white-skinned or black. The next bolt of lightning revealed that the figure had gone from the window's viewpoint and thus out of Matthew's sight.

He closed the shutters and latched them. How very peculiar, he thought. Someone skulking around the servants' village in this slim hour, taking care—or certainly it appeared—not to be seen. How very, very peculiar.

Now: was this his business, or not? An argument might be made for either position. It was not unlawful for a person to walk where they pleased at whatever time they pleased . . . but still, it seemed to Matthew that the blacksmith was not the only person in Fount Royal who might have something to hide.

The boom and bluster of the storm—which yet held its torrents in check—in addition to this new intrigue made Matthew anything but sleepy. He scraped a sulphur match across a flintstone and lit the lamp he'd been afforded, then he poured himself a cup of spring water from the clay pitcher atop the dresser and downed it. The water, he'd already decided, was most certainly the best thing about Fount Royal. After his drink he decided to go to the library and fetch a book with which to beckon sleep, so he took the lantern before him and ventured out into the hallway.

The house was silent. Or so Matthew thought, until he heard a faint voice speaking somewhere nearby. He stopped, listening; more thunder came and went, and the voice was quiet. Then it began again, and Matthew cocked his head to judge its origin.

He knew that voice. Even though it was muffled by the thickness of a door, it was recognizable to him. The magistrate, a heavy sleeper, was speaking to his own demons.

Matthew approached the man's room. The voice faded and became a snore that would have shamed a sawblade fighting ironwood. As the next peal of thunder rang out, the snoring seemed to increase in volume as if in competition with nature's cacophony. Matthew was truly concerned for Woodward's health; indeed, the magistrate had never allowed illness to prevent him from doing his work, but then again the magistrate was rarely under the weather. This time, however, Matthew felt sure he should seek assistance from Dr. Shields.

The snoring abruptly stopped. There was a silence, and then a groan from beyond the door. *"Ann,"* the magistrate said. *"Ann, he's hurting."*

Matthew listened. He knew he should not. But this, he thought, was somehow a key to the man's inner torment.

"In pain. Pain." The magistrate drew a quick, rattling breath. "Ann, he's hurting. Oh dear God . . . dear God . . ."

"What's going on in there?" The voice, spoken so close to his ear, almost made Matthew leap not only from his nightshirt but the very skin his bones were bound up in. He twisted around, his mouth agape—and there stood Robert Bidwell, wearing a robe of crimson silk and holding a lantern.

It took Matthew a few seconds to regain his voice, during which the thunder crashed mightily again. "The magistrate," Matthew managed to whisper. "He's having a difficult night."

"He's snoring down the house, is what he's doing! I could sleep through the storm, but *his* noise trepanned my skull!"

Even as Bidwell spoke, the magistrate's snoring began anew. It was never so loud and disagreeable as this, Matthew knew; probably it was due to his ill health.

"My bedroom's next to his," Bidwell said. "I'm damned if I can get a wink!" He reached for the doorknob.

"Sir?" Matthew grasped his wrist. "I would ask that you leave him be. He'll snore again, even if you disturb him. And I do think he needs his rest for tomorrow."

"What about *my* rest?"

"You won't be interviewing the witnesses, as the magistrate will be."

Bidwell made a sour face. Without his lavish and expensive wig, he seemed a diminished presence. His hair, the color of sand, was cropped to the scalp. He pulled his arm away from Matthew's grip. "A second-rate citizen in my own house!" he fumed.

"I thank you for your understanding."

"Understanding be damned!" He flinched as Woodward sputtered and moaned.

"Hurting," the magistrate said. "Dear God . . . hurting . . ." His voice was overcome once more by the darktime sawing.

Bidwell released the breath from between his teeth. "I suppose he ought to see Dr. Shields, then, if he's suffering so grievously."

"He's speaking to a dream," Matthew explained.

"A *dream?* Well, he's not the only one in Fount Royal with evil dreams! Satan plants them in the mind like bad seeds!"

"It isn't something new. I've heard him this way on many occasions."

"My pity on your ears, then!" Bidwell ran a hand across his coarse-cut hair, his vanity making him realize how much an opulent wig added to his stature. "What're you doing up? Did he awaken you?"

"No, it was the thunder. I looked out my window and saw—" Matthew hesitated. Saw what? he asked himself. A man or woman? Negro or white? Carrying something or not? This news might add to Bidwell's impression of him as a wolf-crier. He decided to let the matter pass. "The storm approaching," he said.

"Ha!" Bidwell grinned. "You're not as smart as you fancy yourself, clerk!"

"Pardon?"

"Your window faces the sea. The storm's approaching from the west."

"Oh," Matthew said. "My mistake, then."

"Hell's bells!" Bidwell growled as the thunder crashed again. "Who can sleep in *this?*"

"Not I. In fact, I was on my way down to your library for something to read."

"To *read?* Do you know what time it is? Near three o'clock!"

"The lateness of the hour never stopped me from reading before," Matthew said. He had a sudden thought. "Of course . . . since you're unable to sleep, you might indulge me."

"Indulge you in what?"

"A game of chess. I saw your board and the pieces there. Do you play?"

"Yes, I certainly do!" Bidwell thrust out his chin. "And very well too, I might say!"

"Really? Well enough to beat me?"

"Well enough," Bidwell said, and offered a slight smile, "to grind you into a powder and puff you to the winds!"

"I should like to see that."

"Then see it you shall! After you, my swell-headed clerk!"

In the library, as the storm continued to bellow and boom outside the shuttered windows, they set the lamps down to give light upon the board and Bidwell announced his choice of the white pieces. Once seated, Bidwell advanced a pawn with ferocious alacrity. "There!" he said. "The first soldier who seeks to have your head!"

Matthew moved a knight. "Seeking," he said, "is a long distance from having."

Another pawn entered the fray. "I was schooled in chess by an expert, so don't be alarmed at the speed with which you're conquered."

"I suppose I *am* at a disadvantage, then." Matthew studied the board. "I was self-taught."

"Many evenings I played on this same board with Reverend

Grove. In fact, this was his chess set. Now surely you're not going to tarry very long over what must be a simple move, are you?"

"No," Matthew said. "Not very long." His next move was a minute more in being placed. Within twelve moves, Bidwell saw his queen impaled between a bishop and a rook.

"Go on, then! Take her, damn it!" he said.

Matthew did. Now it was Bidwell's turn to study the board. "You say Reverend Grove taught you?" Matthew asked. "He was a chess scholar as well as a minister?"

"Are you being witty?" Bidwell's tone had turned sharp.

"No, not at all. I asked an honest question."

Bidwell was silent, his eyes searching for moves but registering the fact that his king would soon be threatened by the very same knight with which Matthew had begun his game. "Grove wasn't a chess scholar," Bidwell said, "but he did enjoy playing. He was a bright man. If he was a scholar at anything, it was Latin."

"Latin?"

"That's right. He loved the language. So much that when he played—and this never failed to infuriate me, which I suppose was partly the point—he announced his moves in Latin. Ah! There's my savior!" Bidwell started to take the offending knight with a bishop.

"Uh . . . if you move that piece," Matthew said, "your king will be in check from my queen."

Bidwell's hand stopped in midair. "I knew that!" he snapped. "Do you think I'm blind?" He quickly altered the destination of his hand to move a knight toward Matthew's king.

Which Matthew instantly killed with a pawn that had been lying in wait. "Did Reverend Grove have any enemies?" he asked.

"Yes. Satan. And the witch, of course." Bidwell frowned, rubbing his chin. "I must need spectacles, to have missed that little bastard!"

"How long had the reverend been here?"

"Since the beginning. He offered himself the very first month."

"Where did he come from?"

"Charles Town. Winston and Paine met him on a trip to buy supplies." Bidwell looked into Matthew's face. "Are you playing at chess or playing at magistrate?"

"It's your move, I believe."

"Yes, and here it is!" A rook was picked up and slammed down, taking Matthew's second knight.

The rook died by the sword of Matthew's queen. "Mr. Paine," Matthew said. "From where did he come?"

"He answered my placard for citizens, which was placed in Charles Town. Most of the first residents came from there. Why are you asking?"

"Curious," Matthew told him, staring at the board. "Was Mr. Paine ever a sailor?"

"Yes, he was. He served as the first mate on an English brigantine in his younger years. Many times we've talked of ships and the sea." He narrowed his eyes. "How come you to ask that question?"

"Mr. Paine . . . strikes me as having a seaman's knowledge. What exactly is a brigantine?"

"A ship, of course!"

"Yes, sir." Matthew gave a polite, if fleeting, smile. "But what kind of ship?"

"It's a two-masted square-rigger. Fast ships, they are. Used in coastal commerce. And brigantines, because of their speed, have unfortunately found favor with the more brutal element."

Matthew lifted his eyebrows. "Sir?"

"Pirates and privateers," Bidwell said. "Brigantines are their vessels of choice. They can get in and out of tight harbors. Well, when my naval port is complete we're going to run those dogs down and hang them from their skins." His hand flashed out and moved his remaining rook to threaten Matthew's queen between it and a bishop.

"Check," Matthew said, as he moved a lowly pawn next to Bidwell's king.

"There, then!" The king slayed the pawn.

"Check," Matthew said, as he moved his queen into a position of attack.

"Not so easily, you don't!" Bidwell placed a pawn in the queen's path.

"Mate," Matthew said, as he picked up his first knight and executed the pawn.

"Just a moment!" Bidwell near shouted, frantically studying the board.

He didn't have long to complete his fruitless study. A bell began clamoring outside. A shout came through the shutters; it was a fearsome word, and struck terror like a blade into Bidwell's heart.

"Fire! Fire!"

At once Bidwell was on his feet and had thrown the shutters open. There was the glow of flames against the night, the conflagration being whipped back and forth by the wind, orange sparks flying.

"Fire! Fire!" was the shout, and the alarm bell at the watchman's tower continued to ring.

"My God!" Bidwell cried out. "I think it's the gaol!"

ten

THERE WERE SHOUTS to hurry the buckets. Another wagon pulled up, carrying two barrels full of water, and instantly a man climbed up beside the barrels and began to fill the buckets that were offered to him. Then, moving rapidly, he returned each bucket to the line of men to be passed along until the water was thrown upon the flames. It was clear to Matthew and the other onlookers, however, that the buckets were no match against a wind-tossed fire; the structure was already almost eaten by the flames, and would soon be beyond all redemption.

Matthew thought that nearly all of Fount Royal's citizens had been roused by the watchman's cries, and had come to Truth Street to either help the line of firemen or watch the flames do their work. Most of them had come to the scene as had Matthew and Bidwell: still clad in their nightshirts, with hurriedly donned trousers and shoes, or in the case of the women, robes and cloaks over their night apparel. Matthew had run upstairs, put on his breeches, and then gone to awaken the magistrate but heard the awesome snoring before he'd reached the door. Not even the cries of the crowd nor the alarm bell had pierced Woodward's sleep, though as the shutters were surely closed in his room the sounds would not have overcome his own nasal rhapsody. Therefore Matthew had decided not to take the time to hammer at his door, but had instead run down the stairs to follow Bidwell.

The heat was ferocious, the wind whipping the fire into a frenzy. It was now the zenith of irony, Matthew realized. Though thunder still rumbled and lightning flashed over the sea, this time the clouds hadn't opened above Fount Royal. He knew that Bidwell would wish for a downpour to smother this conflagration, but it was not to be. The farmhouse—the very same deserted farmhouse upon which three crows had been sitting the previous morning as Matthew and Woodward had paused to talk—was doomed.

But there wasn't much danger of the fire spreading. Certainly the firemen knew it, which was why they had formed only a single line instead of a double or triple. Yesterday's torrential rain had soaked the occupied house that stood opposite a split-rail fence from the burning structure, and other houses—and the gaol, as well—were distant enough from the flying embers. It was a fierce fire in appearance and it was gnawing down its victim quickly, but it would not leap to any other roof.

Which had started Matthew thinking. Everything had been so thoroughly wet; how had this fire started? A lightning strike, perhaps? He wasn't sure if even lightning had the power to burn drenched wood. No, the fire had to have begun *inside* the house. Even so, *how?*

"That one's gone," a man said, standing to Matthew's right.

Matthew glanced at the speaker. He was a tall, slim man wearing a brown cloak and a woolen cap. It took Matthew a few seconds to register the man's face: a long, aristocratic nose and lofty forehead, narrowed and reserved dark blue eyes. Without his white wig, his face powder, and rouge the schoolmaster looked—at least at first glance—a different person altogether. But Johnstone leaned on his twisted cane with its ivory handle, the flames daubing his face red and orange. "It was William Bryerson's house," he said. "His two sons used to come to school."

"When did the family leave?"

"Oh, William didn't leave. He lies in the cemetery yonder.

But his widow took the boys and they left . . . I suppose it was early last year." Johnstone turned his gaze upon Matthew. "I understand your magistrate is beginning his interviews tomorrow?"

"Yes, sir."

"I heard so from Mr. Winston. I also heard that you got into some trouble with Seth Hazelton?" Matthew nodded. "Talk is a great currency in this town," Johnstone said. "Everyone knows everyone else's business. But you happened to have stumbled onto a secret, is that correct?"

"Who told you this?"

"Winston, again. Mr. Bidwell confides everything in him. He visits me of an afternoon. We play a few hands of all fours and a game or two of chess, after which I am completely educated as to current events." He stared at the burning house again. Bidwell was shouting orders, trying to get more barrels of water to the scene, but the energy of the firemen was dwindling. "You're going to spend three days in the gaol and receive three lashes, I understand."

"Correct."

"And the interviews are to be held in the gaol? That will be a novel setting."

"It was on Mr. Bidwell's request."

"Mr. Bidwell," Johnstone said, his face showing not a shade of emotion, "is a bastard hungry for coin, young man. He presents himself as an altruistic gentleman, concerned for the future of safe shipping to this colony, when indeed his one single goal is the further stuffing of his pockets. And for that purpose he will have Rachel Howarth executed."

"He believes she's a witch." Matthew paused a few seconds. "Don't you?"

Johnstone gave a faint half-smile. "Do *you?*"

"It remains to be seen."

"Ah, diplomacy in action. It's to be commended in this day and age, but I'd request a more honest answer." Matthew was silent, not knowing what more he should reveal. "The magistrate," Johnstone said, looking around. "Where is he?"

"I left him asleep at the house. He's not easily awakened."

"Evidently not. Well, since he's not within earshot, I'd like to know what you honestly think about Rachel Howarth."

"It would be betraying my office, sir."

Johnstone thought about that for a moment, and then nodded. He tilted his head to one side, intently watching the fire. "Thank you; you've told me what I needed to know. I assumed you were an educated young man, freed from the bondage of ancient thinking. You have your doubts about witchcraft, as I do. Rachel Howarth is in a cage because of several reasons, not the least of which being she is a beautiful woman and threatens the sensibilities of the more portly cows in this town. Her Portuguese blood is also a mark against her. Too close to being a Spaniard. Add to that the fact that Daniel Howarth was a man of Bidwell's stripe, without his charm. He had enemies here, without a doubt."

"What, then?" Matthew had to take a glance around to make sure no one was standing close enough to overhear. "You believe someone else murdered him?"

"Yes, I do. Not Satan. A *man.* Or a woman who has a man's strength, of which there are some hereabouts."

"But Mr. Garrick saw Madam Howarth and . . . *something* . . . behind the barn."

"Mr. Garrick," Johnstone said calmly, "has a mind like an iron sieve. I would question if not his eyesight, then his soundness of sanity."

"Why did you not speak out at our dinner, then?"

"Yes, and then I might find myself a cellmate with Rachel Howarth. That's an honor I would not wish to have."

"This is a merry damnation, isn't it?" someone else spoke up, stepping beside the schoolmaster. The small-framed Dr. Shields was in his nightshirt, his long hair wild and wind-whipped, his pale blue eyes large behind the oval spectacles. "It's no use the waste of good water!"

"Hello, Benjamin." Johnstone gave a slight nod. "I should

think you'd stay in bed, these fires being such a commonplace nowadays."

"I could say the same for you. In truth, this is much more exciting than watching crops fail to grow." He steadied his gaze at Matthew. "Hello there, young man. In some trouble yesterday, I hear."

"A little," Matthew said.

"Three days in the gaol and three lashes is a modicum, not a minimum. Favor me, as I shall be applying liniment to your stripes before long. Where's the magistrate?"

"In bed," Johnstone said before Matthew could answer. "He's a sensible sleeper, it seems, not given to excitement over the burning of abandoned houses."

"Yes, but he's a man of the city, and therefore has learned how to sleep through all manner of holocausts." Shields faced the fire, which was now totally beyond control. Bidwell was still hollering orders, trying to rouse the firemen to further action but some of the urgency had gone from his demeanor. Matthew saw Nicholas Paine conferring with Bidwell, who waved an impatient arm in the direction of his mansion. Then Paine merged into the onlookers again and was gone from sight. Matthew noted also the presence of Mrs. Nettles, who was wrapped up in a long black robe; there was the giant gaol-keeper, Mr. Green, standing off to one side smoking a corncob pipe; Garrick was there, looking mightily worried; Edward Winston, wearing a gray shirt and wrinkled brown trousers that appeared hastily climbed into, stood beside Garrick. Winston glanced back over his shoulder and his eyes locked for a second or two with Matthew's. Then he too moved off into the throng of onlookers.

"I'm going home to bed," Johnstone announced. "The dampness gives my knee the devil of an ache."

"I'll give you some more liniment, if you like," Shields offered.

"You and that liniment! Matthew, if it's the same hogsfat preparation for your stripes as it is for my knee, you have my sincerest condolences. I suggest you practise wearing a clothes pin on your nose." Johnstone started to limp away, but then paused. "You think on what I've said, young man," he entreated. "When your time is served, I should like to talk to you further on this subject."

"What, are these secrets I shouldn't be hearing?" Shields asked.

"No secrets, Benjamin. I'm just attempting to advance the young man's education. Good night." So saying, he turned and followed his cane through the crowd.

"Well," Shields said with a sigh, "I should be returning to bed myself. I have a long hard day of watching another patient die." He gave a twisted smile. "Life in the New World, indeed."

A few minutes after the doctor had gone, the house's red-glowing roof collapsed. Sparks shot to the heavens and spun 'round and 'round in the whirlwinds. Bidwell had ceased giving orders; now he just stood back, his arms hanging at his sides. One of the firemen threw a final bucket of water, but then he retreated from the conflagration and suddenly the entire front wall buckled and caved in.

"It's the Devil, speakin' to us!" a man shouted. Matthew saw Bidwell's head snap around, the dark-circled eyes hunting the shouter like a hawk after a rodent. "It's Satan hisself, tellin' us to leave this damn town 'fore we all burn up!"

Someone else—a woman with reddish hair and a gaunt, long-chinned face—took up the cry. "Neal Callaway's right!" she hollered. "Satan's warnin' us to get out!"

"Stop that!" Bidwell's voice made the thunder sound meek. "I won't hear such talk!"

"Hear it or don't, as you please!" another man yelled, standing a few feet to Matthew's left. "I've had enough! I'm takin' my wife and children out of here before we all end up in caskets!"

"No, you're not!" Bidwell fired back. He was silhouetted by the flames and looked the part of a demon himself. "Cutter, don't be a fool!"

"It's a fool who stays when the Devil wants him gone!" Cutter shouted. "First light, my Nora and me are packin' up!" He surveyed the crowd, his eyes glittering with fire. "Anybody with sense oughta do the same! This town ain't worth livin' in no more, 'cause that *bitch* and her master want it!"

That statement caused a ripple of reactions: many shouting their accord, a few—a very few—trying to holler him silent. Bidwell spread his arms, a patronly gesture. "Listen to me!" he yelled. "The magistrate's going to start the hearings this very day! I promise to you, by my very soul, that the witch shall be dealt with and out of our lives before much longer!" Matthew said nothing, but he thought that Bidwell had just placed his soul in jeopardy.

"One *day's* too long for me!" Cutter was playing the crowd now, like an actor upon a stage. "No, sir! First light, we're gettin' out 'fore our skins are burnt off or the plague gets us!"

"Hush, hush!" Bidwell shouted anew, trying to quash that evil word. "There's no plague here!"

"You dig up them bodies fresh buried in the graveyard!" a woman near shrieked.

"You ask 'em what kilt 'em, 'cause that doctor a'yours sure did 'em no good!"

WHILE THIS UGLY SCENE was unfolding and Bidwell fought for control of the crowd, Isaac Woodward had awakened in a cold sweat. His throat, however, was aflame. He lay in bed on his back, staring up through the insect net at the ceiling; the net had not prevented at least one new intruder from leaving a welt on his grizzled cheek. The particulars of his nightmare—that common, cruel visitor—remained in his mind like the details of a woodcut. He saw small fingers clenched around the bars of an iron bed, and he heard a soft and terrible gasping. *Ann,* his voice had spoken. *Dear God, he's . . .*

A light! A strange light was in the room.

Woodward was aware of it now. It was not part of the nightmare, and he thought he had passed the purple edge of sleep into full reality again. But the strange light was indeed real; it was a leaping, writhing luminescence ruddy-orange in hue. He looked at the window and realized the light was coming between the shutters. The morning sun—would that there would be a morning sun!—never appeared so drunk before. And now he could smell it, and he thought that this was what might have awakened him: the bitter scent of smoke.

Still somewhat hazed in the mind, Woodward got up out of bed and opened the shutter. And there was the view of a house afire, down along Truth Street. Dangerously close to the gaol, he thought; but it looked to be on the opposite side of the street. In the phantasmagoric light he could see a crowd of onlookers, and the swirling wind brought him the crackle of the flames and the noise of shouts that sounded raised in more anger than alarm. He didn't know how long this had been going on, but it seemed his sleeping must have been a little death. He lit his lamp with its sulphur match and left the room, going across the hall to Matthew's door.

Just as he lifted his hand to knock, he heard a soft *click* from within.

The latch, he realized. Matthew must have either locked or unlocked the door.

He knocked. "Matthew! There's a fire outside, did you know?" There was no response.

"Matthew? Open, please!" Still, nothing. "Are you feeling well?" A fine question for him to ask, he thought; his voice sounded like sawblades and bloody bones.

Matthew did not speak, nor did he open the door. Woodward placed his hand on the knob and started to turn it, but he hesitated. This was so unlike Matthew, but then again . . . the young man was going to a cage shortly, so who could predict what his emotions and actions might be? But why would he not even speak through the door?

"Matthew, I'm going downstairs. Do you know if Bidwell's up?" Woodward waited, and then said with some exasperation, "I do think you should at least answer my question, don't you?"

But no answer was forthcoming.

"As you please!" Woodward turned away and stalked along the corridor toward the staircase. That was so strange and rude for Matthew, he thought. The young man was if nothing always courteous. But he was probably brooding in there, mad at the world. Woodward stopped. Well, he decided, I shall pound on that door until he opens it! I shall pound it down, because if his frame of mind is dark he'll be no use to me when the first witness arrives! He started to turn again to retrace his steps.

A hand reached out from behind him and viciously swept the lamp from Woodward's grasp. The candle was extinguished. A shoulder hit the magistrate's body and shoved him aside, and he shouted and stumbled and went down upon the floor. Then the figure was past him, the sound of footsteps running down the stairs in the dark. Though stunned, Woodward knew what he was dealing with. "Help!" he hollered. "Thief! Thief!"

AT THE FIRE, Matthew decided it was time to return to Bidwell's mansion. The shouts and accusations were still being flung about and Bidwell had been reduced to a croaking hoarseness attempting to answer all the discord. A further incentive to vacate the scene was the fact that Matthew had spied Seth Hazelton—bandage still strapped to his face—standing in the throng watching the commotion. It flashed through Matthew's mind—his wicked, wicked mind—to run over to the blacksmith's barn and find the *other* sack that must be hidden somewhere in there. But he dashed that idea for the sake of his skin and turned to leave the area.

He collided with a man who'd been standing right behind him. "'Ere, 'ere!" the man bawled, his accent reeking of London's backstreets. "Watch yer clumsy self."

"I'm sorry." Matthew's next impression was that the accent was not the only thing that reeked. He wrinkled up his nose and drew back, getting a good look at the man.

He was a short, fatbellied toad; at least, that was Matthew's first thought. The man's skin was even a toadish shade of gray, but Matthew realized it was the color of grime. This dirty citizen was perhaps in his early forties, with tousled brown hair from which was rising a bald dome at the crown. His face was round, with a beard that had streaks of gray running through it. He wore a loose-fitting garment that looked like nothing so much as rags sewn together by a drunken seamstress. The man was repellent to Matthew's sensibilities, but one feature snared his attention: the grimy toad had eyes so clear gray as to be nearing the white shade of ice on a January morning, and yet their centers seemed to be as fiery as any smith's furnace. Those compelling eyes were lodged beneath matted tufts of brows that appeared in need of brushing. Suddenly the nostrils of the man's wide, rather coarsely shaped nose flared and he looked down at the ground.

"Don't move," he said; it carried the force of a shouted command, and yet it was not a shout. He lifted his right arm. In it was a long wooden stick. The arm plunged down, and then he grinned a mouthful of yellow teeth and raised the business end of the stick up to Matthew's face.

Impaled upon a blade was a black rat, kicking in its agony. "They like to be near people," the man said.

Matthew looked down, and now he saw dark scurrying shapes running hither and yon between the shoes and boots—and bare feet, in some cases—of the assembly.

"Think they can get 'em some crumbs, a crowd like this." The man was wearing deerskin gloves stained with the fluids of previous executions. With his free hand he adroitly unfastened the leather strap of a long brown seedbag that hung from his belt, and he pushed the stick's blade and the writhing rat into it. Then he reached down into the bag and Matthew saw his hand give a sickening twist before the blade was withdrawn minus its victim. The bag, Matthew couldn't fail to notice, bulged with a number of carcasses. At least one that had not yet given up the ghost was still twitching.

Matthew realized he'd just witnessed Gwinett Linch—the ratcatcher—at his noble profession.

"*Somebody's* got to do it," Linch said, reading Matthew's expression. "A town may live without a magistrate, but it ain't no place to live without a ratcatcher. *Sir.*" He gave an exaggerated bow and walked past Matthew, making sure his bag of booty brushed along the young man's hip.

And now it was surely time to move on. The burning house had become a pile of seething embers and fiery spits. An old woman had begun hollering about how Rachel Howarth should be hauled from the gaol and beheaded with an axeblade bathed in the blood of a lamb. Matthew saw Bidwell standing staring into the waning flames, his shoulders slumped, and truly the master of Fount Royal appeared to have lost his foundations.

Matthew watched his footing as he walked back to the mansion. He also watched his back, taking care that Seth Hazelton wasn't stalking him.

He returned to find a number of lanterns illuminating the parlor, and Mrs. Nettles in attendance to the magistrate. Woodward was in the room's most comfortable chair, his head back, eyes closed, and a compress laid against his forehead. At once Matthew deduced that something very serious had happened. "What's wrong?"

Woodward's eyes immediately opened. He sat bolt upright. "I was attacked, Matthew!" he said forcefully, though his voice was strained and weak. "By someone I took to be you!"

"Took to be *me?*"

"Someone was in your room." Mrs. Nettles took the compress from Woodward's head and wet it again in a bowl of water nearby. "The magistrate heard your door bein' latched."

"In my room?" Matthew was aware he sounded all at sea, which he was. "Who was it?"

Woodward shook his head. Mrs. Nettles replaced the wet compress. "Didn't see his face," Woodward said. "It happened so swiftly. He knocked the lantern from my hand and near broke my shoulder. I heard him run down the stairs, and then . . . gone."

"This happened only a short time ago?"

"Twenty minutes a' th' most," Mrs. Nettles said. "I'd just returned from the fire, and I heard him hollerin' *'Thief.'*"

"You mean the man stole something?"

"I don't know." Woodward lifted a hand and held it against the compress. "It was all I could think of at the moment. That he was a thief trying to ransack your room."

"Well, I'm sure he was quite disappointed. Everything I have is borrowed." And then it struck Matthew like a musketball. "Except for one thing." He picked up a lantern and hurriedly ascended the stairs. He found his room to be neat and orderly, not a trace of an intruder. Except for one thing, and this was what he'd suspected.

Before going to bed, he'd placed the gold coin upon the dresser top. The coin was now gone, and Matthew doubted that it would be found in this room.

A thief indeed, Matthew thought. He spent a moment searching the floor for a gold glint, but it was not to be. "Damn!" he swore softly.

"Anythin' missin'?" Mrs. Nettles asked when Matthew returned to the parlor.

"Yes. My gold coin."

"Oh my Lord! Mr. Bidwell keeps some coins in a box next to his bed! I'd best go up and see if they've been plucked too!" She took a lamp and went up the stairs with a speed that Matthew would never have assigned to her.

He stood next to the magistrate's chair. Woodward was a pasty color and his breathing was very harsh. "You're not well at all," Matthew said.

"Who would be, after such an encounter? Goode's gone to fetch me some rum. I'll be better presently."

"It's more than the encounter. Your health concerns me."

Woodward closed his eyes, his head tilted back. "I'm under the weather. I told you, it's this swamp ai—"

"No, sir," Matthew interrupted. "I think the swamp air is the least of it. I'm going to have one of the servants go get Dr. Shields."

"No, no, no!" Woodward swatted a hand at that idea as if it

were one of the bothersome insects. "I have a job to do, and I intend to do it!"

"You can still do your job. But Dr. Shields needs to be informed of your condition. Perhaps he can prescribe a tonic."

"Sir?" It was Goode, bringing a tray upon which sat a tankard of West Indies tonic. Woodward took it and put down two swallows that made his throat feel as if scraped with a razor.

Mrs. Nettles returned to the parlor. "Everythin's there. At least, that box a' coins hasn't been touched. Must be you scared him off 'fore he could get to Mr. Bidwell's room."

"Likely someone who thought . . . because of the attention drawn to the fire . . . he could rob at his leisure." Woodward dared to take another drink; the pain was severe, but bearable.

"There are some people jealous of what Mr. Bidwell has, for sure."

"Did this thief carry a lantern?" Matthew asked the magistrate.

"No. I told you . . . the lantern was knocked from my hand. Quite forcibly."

Goode, who was standing behind Woodward's chair, suddenly spoke, "Seems to me it had to be somebody knew this house." All eyes stared at him. "What I mean is . . . whoever it was had to know his way up and down them stairs in the dark. No rail to hold on to, you could break your neck if you misstepped."

"And you say you heard the man *run* down the stairs?" Matthew returned his attention to Woodward.

"Yes. Definitely."

"If I may ask, sir . . . was nothin' stolen, then?" Goode asked of Matthew.

"One thing only, at least from *my* room. A Spanish gold coin."

"A gold coin," Goode repeated, and he frowned. "Uh . . . if I may ask another question, sir?" He paused.

"Yes, go ahead."

"Uh . . . where might you got this coin from, sir?"

"It was in the possession of a tavern-keeper on the road from Charles Town." He saw the black servant's frown deepen, and this perplexed him. "Why?"

"No reason, sir." Instantly Goode's frown relaxed. "No reason, just curious 'bout such a thing. Forgive an old man's boldness, sir."

"I understand." What Matthew understood was that Goode might know somewhat more about this incident than he was willing to say, but now was not the time to pursue it.

"Is there anythin' else I'm required for, ma'am?" Goode asked Mrs. Nettles, and she told him he was free to go. The servant left the parlor, moving rather hurriedly for his age.

Presently Bidwell returned to the house. His face was damp with sweat and streaked dark by ashes, and his regal bearing had been reduced to a pauperly state by the grievances of the crowd. Though he was bone-tired and sick at heart, still his presence of mind was sharp enough to immediately see from the gathering of Mrs. Nettles, Woodward, and Matthew that something untoward had occurred.

"We've suffered a thief," Mrs. Nettles said, before the master of the mansion could speak. "A man was in Mr. Corbett's room. He knocked the magistrate to the floor on escapin'."

"Near broke my shoulder," Woodward added.

"A thief? Did you recognize the man? What was taken?"

"I didn't see his face," the magistrate said. "But the man evidently stole Matthew's gold coin."

"The coin you found at Shawcombe's tavern?" Bidwell had heard about it from Paine just after they'd returned from their expedition.

Matthew nodded. "Yes, sir."

"I have to say I'm not surprised!" Bidwell put a hand into the bowl of water and wiped it across his sooty face. "I understand the tales that were spreading magnified that single coin into a treasure box full! Small wonder some poor farmer didn't dare to come in here and make off with the fortune!"

"Sir?" Matthew said. "Goode has advanced the theory that

whoever did it might have been a frequent visitor to your house, in that he could negotiate the stairs without benefit of a candle. Do you have many poor farmers as your guests?"

"No. Excepting Garrick, of course. But he's only been here twice, and the second time was at our dinner." Again he wet his face with a handful of water. It dawned upon him what Matthew was getting at. "You believe the thief was a common acquaintance of mine?"

"A probability. I found no lantern in my room. The man may have entered in the dark and been familiar enough with your house not to need illumination."

"A servant, then!" Bidwell looked at Mrs. Nettles. "Have you seen to my bedchamber yet?"

"Yes sir, I have. Your coin box is undisturbed. I took the liberty also of inspectin' your study. Nothin' missin' there, as far as I could tell. And—if I ma' speak my mind, sir—the servants know where your coin box is. There're Dutch gold pieces a'plenty in it." She lifted her eyebrows. "You follow what I'm sayin', sir?"

"Mr. Bidwell?" Matthew said. He had come to a conclusion of sorts. "Whoever entered your house had been here before, probably many times. I believe he specifically wanted the coin that was in my possession. He knew I wouldn't be in the room. He knew also that the magistrate was a hard sleeper. Because *I* told him."

"*You* did?"

"Yes, sir. Except this theory is somewhat flawed. Schoolmaster Johnstone couldn't have run down the stairs."

Bidwell stared at him, mouth agape. And then from that open mouth came a laugh like donkey's bray. "Now you've shown your true intellect, boy!" he said, with more than a touch of glee. "Schoolmaster Johnstone a *thief!* Put this in your broken pipe and puff on it: the man's even unable to *climb* stairs, much less run down them! He has a deformed knee, in case it's escaped you!"

"I've seen what appears to be a deformed knee," Matthew said calmly. "I've not seen the knee itself."

"By God, you are a right brash set of bones!" Bidwell grinned savagely. "Have you lost whatever mind you brought to this town?"

"I am only telling you, sir, that I informed the schoolmaster that Magistrate Woodward was asleep in his room."

"Well, Hell's burnin' bells! *I* told the same thing to Nicholas Paine, when he asked where the magistrate was!"

"And Mr. Winston asked *me,*" Mrs. Nettles said. "I told him I thought the magistrate was still abed."

"Mrs. *Nettles* knew it!" Bidwell brayed on. "I think she could knock a man down, don't you?" His wet face flushed when he realized what he'd just said. "No offense, Mrs. Nettles."

"None taken, sir. I once threw my dear departed husband through a winda."

"There, you *see?*" Bidwell turned his glare upon Woodward. "Sir, if this was the most able clerk you could discover, I pity the judicial world!"

"He's able enough," was the magistrate's rather frosty reply. "Even if he does sometimes put his cart before his horses."

"In this case, his cart is lacking not only horses but *wheels!*" Bidwell shook his head, disgusted with the whole business. "Oh, if I live to see the new year I shall count it as a miracle! Here, what's that you're drinking?"

"Rum," Woodward answered.

"What's rum for one is rum for two, then!" Bidwell took the tankard from him and swigged the rest of it down.

"There is another thing," Matthew said; he'd remembered it, just as Bidwell had mentioned living to see the new year. "Dr. Shields."

"Yes? What about him? Was he in here with the schoolmaster, both of them thieving?"

"He also inquired as to the whereabouts of the magistrate, and Mr. Johnstone told him what I'd said. The doctor excused himself from my presence just after Mr. Johnstone left."

"Oh, so now we have a gang of thieves! The schoolmaster, Dr. Shields, Mr. Paine, Winston, and Mrs. Nettles! A fearsome five, indeed!"

"Make light as you wish," Matthew said, "but I think one of those five entered this house and took my gold coin."

"Not me!" the woman said sharply. "Surely you don't mean *me!*"

"Of course he means you!" Bidwell assured her. "If he can accuse a cripple of running down a staircase in the dark, he can accuse whomever the hell he pleases!"

"It wasn't the doctor." Woodward placed his hand against his bruised shoulder. "The man who hit me had some size to him. Six feet he was, at least. A giant, possibly. And he moved as swiftly as a snake."

"Yes, sir." Matthew gave a faint smile. "And we fought off Shawcombe with candles versus daggers, didn't we?"

Woodward understood his meaning, and tucked his head down an inch or so. Bidwell slammed the tankard down upon the nearest tabletop. "I'm going back up to bed, for whatever sleep I can find! I daresay it won't be much!" He focused his gaze directly at Matthew. "First light will be here in two hours. I'll expect you to be ready to carry out your sentence."

"I shall be."

Bidwell picked up a lantern and took three weary steps toward the staircase. Then he abruptly stopped and looked back, his face daubed yellow in the glow. "Is there something in particular about that coin I should know?"

Matthew recalled the conversation he'd had with Woodward, concerning the theory that there might be an encampment of Spanish soldiers near the Indians' village. Now, however, seemed not the moment to bring it up with Bidwell, his being in such a fractious temperament.

"What I'm asking is," Bidwell continued, "why would someone risk entering my house for one gold coin?"

Matthew said, "I don't know."

"No ideas? Have your theories failed you?"

"For the moment, yes."

"I think," Bidwell said bluntly, "that you know much more about this than you wish to say. But I'll let it go, as I'm in no

mood for a fencing match with you. Good night, gentlemen."
Bidwell ascended the stairs, and Mrs. Nettles gave the two men a
crisp good night—her face a solemn mask that told Matthew she
was quite offended at his accusation of thievery—and went about
her business.

Woodward waited until he was positive they were alone.
Then he gave a quiet laugh. "Of course you have a theory, don't
you? You have a theory for everything under the sun."

"If you mean I fervently desire to know the *why* of things,
you're correct."

"The *why* of things," Woodward repeated, and there was a
bitter edge in his voice. "Knowing the why of things can kill a
man, Matthew." He put his hand to his throat and massaged it.
"Sometimes it's best not to ask too many questions. Haven't you
learned that yet?"

"It's not my nature, sir," Matthew replied; he felt sure that
Woodward's attitude in this matter of the *why* had to do with the
man's past life in London.

"You are young. I am old. That makes all the difference." He
let go a long, pained sigh. "All right, then. Tell me what you're
thinking."

"We may have had a visit tonight," Matthew said quietly,
"from the Spanish spy." Woodward didn't respond. He scratched
the mosquito bite on his cheek. "That coin may be evidence of
the Spanish presence near the Indians' village, wherever it might
be," Matthew continued, keeping his voice hushed. "The spy may
have felt it necessary to remove it from sight."

"But the damage has been done. Bidwell already knows
about the coin. The entire population does, it seems."

"Yes, sir, but—as Bidwell might say—a hole in a ship must
be patched, regardless how much water has already flooded the
hull. The thief didn't expect to be interrupted. Perhaps he hoped
I might believe the coin to be misplaced. But removing it from
sight would also remove it as an object of Bidwell's interest."

"And of course," Woodward added, "the spy wouldn't know
your suspicions."

"Exactly."

"What action do you propose, then?"

"I propose . . . to serve my sentence and scribe the answers of the witnesses. Then I propose to endure the whip as best I can, and hope I neither weep in public nor soil my breeches. I propose for you to visit Dr. Shields and ask for a tonic."

"Matthew, I told you that I'm—"

"You're ill, sir," Matthew said firmly. "And you might worsen, without help. I shall not retreat on this subject."

Woodward made a sound of exasperation. He knew the young man could be as tenacious as a dockside dog trying to gnaw through a crab's shell. "All right," he relented. "I'll go."

"Tomorrow."

"Yes, yes. Tomorrow."

"Your visit should be twofold," Matthew said. "One, to aid your health. Two, to make some inquiries—subtle, of course—about Mr. Paine, Mr. Winston, and Schoolmaster Johnstone."

"The schoolmaster? It can't be him, Matthew! His deformed knee!"

"I should like to know if Dr. Shields has ever inspected it."

"You're accusing an Oxford brother," Woodward said, with an uptilt of his chin. "I find that objectionable."

"I'm accusing no one, sir. But I would wish to know the schoolmaster's history, just as I would wish to know the histories of Mr. Winston and Mr. Paine."

"And what of Dr. Shields's history?"

"His, too. But I think the doctor may be less than candid about his own life, therefore other sources will have to be tapped."

"All this is well and good." Woodward eased himself to his feet. "However, we can't forget our main purpose here. We're primarily concerned with a witch, not a spy."

"A woman *accused* of witchcraft," Matthew corrected. He had spoken it a little too sternly, and he had to amend his tone. "Sir," he said.

"Of course." The magistrate nodded, his eyelids drooping. "Good night."

"Good night, sir." Matthew let him start walking away before he decided, on an impulse, to say the next thing that left his lips. "Magistrate? Who is in pain when you call to Ann?"

Woodward stopped as if he had collided with a wall. He stood very still.

"I couldn't help but overhear. But it's not something I haven't heard before, sir." There was no response. "Forgive my intrusion. I had to ask."

"No." Woodward's voice was tight. "You did not have to ask." He remained standing exactly as he was, his back toward the young man. "This is one *why* you should leave be, Matthew. Heed what I say. Leave it be."

Matthew said nothing more. He watched as the magistrate walked out of the parlor, his back ramrod-straight.

And thus the night ended, with more questions and no answers.

eleven

A SMALL BUT IMPORTANT MIRACLE greeted Matthew as he awakened, responding to the insistent fist of Robert Bidwell upon his chamber door: the sun had appeared.

It was a weak sun, yes, and in imminent danger of being clouded over by the jealous sky, but there it was all the same. The early light, a misty golden sheen, had brought forth Fount Royal's roosters in fine trumpeting form. As Matthew shaved and dressed, he listened to the orchestra of cocks vying for vocal dominance. His gaze kept slipping down to where the Spanish coin had been resting atop the dresser, and he couldn't help but wonder whose boots had crossed the floor to steal it. But today another matter was supreme. He would have to forswear his mind from the subject of the coin and the spy and concentrate fully on his task—which was, after all, his raison d'être.

A breakfast of eggs, fried potatoes, and corncakes filled Matthew's belly, all washed down with a cup of sturdy dark brown tea. Woodward was late to the table, his eyes swollen and his breathing harsh; he appeared to have either slept not at all for the remainder of the night or suffered dreams that prevented rest. Before Matthew could speak, Woodward lifted a hand and said in a croaking voice, "I promised I would visit Dr. Shields today, and I shall. As soon as we have interviewed Mr. Buckner."

"Surely you're going to interview more than one witness today, aren't you? As tomorrow is the Sabbath, I mean." Bidwell was sitting at the head of the table, his breakfast platter already scraped clean. Though he'd been severely tried by the recent events, he was clean-shaven, freshly washed, and dressed in a tan-colored suit. The ringlets of his lavish wig cascaded down around his shoulders.

"I will interview Mr. Buckner this morning." Woodward seated himself on the bench across the table from Matthew. "Then I'm going to visit Dr. Shields. If I am up to the task, I will interview Mr. Garrick in the afternoon."

"All right, then. Just so there is some movement, I should be satisfied."

"I, too, should be satisfied with a movement," Woodward said. "My system has been clogged by these country meals." He pushed aside his breakfast dish, which had been loaded with food by a servant girl in preparation for his arrival. Instead he reached for the green ceramic teapot and poured a cup, which he drank down with several noisy swallows.

"You'll be feeling better before long," Bidwell assured him. "The sun cures all ills."

"Thank you, sir, but I do not desire platitudes. Will we have the proper furnishings on hand when we reach the gaol?"

"I've arranged for Mr. Winston and Mr. Green to take care of what you need. And I must say, there's no reason to be snappish. This is a great day, sir, for the history of Fount Royal."

"No day is great when murder is involved." Woodward poured a second cup of tea and that, too, went down his hatch.

It came time to leave. Bidwell announced that Goode was already waiting in front with the carriage, and he wished them both—as he put it—"good hunting." Woodward felt positively feeble as he left the house, his bones heated and flesh clammy, his throat paved by Hell's burning brimstone. It was all he could do to suck in a breath, as his nostrils were so constricted. But he would have to carry on, and hopefully Dr. Shields could relieve his discomfort later in the day.

Clouds had moved in, obscuring the blessed sun, as Goode flicked the reins and the carriage wheels began to turn. But as they passed the spring—where two women were already drawing water into buckets—the sun's rays slipped their bondage and shone down upon the surface. Matthew saw the spring suddenly glow golden with a marvelously beautiful light. Around the water, the green tops of oak trees were cast with the same gilded lumination, and for a moment Matthew realized the power that Fount Royal held over its citizens: a place carved from the wild, fenced and tamed, baptized in sweat and tears, made useful by sheer human will and muscle. It was a dream and a damnation too, this desiring to control the wilderness, to shape it with axe-blade and shovel. Many had perished in the building of this town; many more would die before it was a harbor city. But who could deny the temptation and challenge of the land?

In some old Latin tome on philosophy he'd read, Matthew recalled that the author had assigned all reflection, peace, and piety to God; to the Devil had been assigned the need of man to go forth and conquer, to break asunder and rework, to question and reach beyond all hope of grasping.

It seemed to him, then, that according to that philosophy the Devil was indeed at work in Fount Royal. And the Devil was indeed at work in him, because the question of *why* was rooted in the tree of forbidden fruit. But what would this land——this world—be without such a question? And where would it be without those instincts and needs—seeds from the Devil, some might say—that caused men to wish for more than God had given them?

The clouds shifted, and suddenly yet again the sun had vanished. Matthew looked up and saw patches of blue amid the gray, but they were becoming slimmer and smaller. In another moment, the gray clouds held dominion once more.

"So much for the healing properties of the sun," Woodward said.

Smoke was still drifting from the charred ruins of what had yesterday been a farmhouse. Along Truth Street the acrid odor of burning remained strong. Presently Goode bade the horses slow and reined them in before the gaol. The giant redhaired and redbearded Mr. Green was waiting outside for them, along with Edward Winston.

"Your wishes have been met," Winston said, eager to please. "I've even donated my own desk and Bible to the cause."

Green took them all inside. Matthew was relieved to see that Noles had been released and had fled his coop. The roof hatch was open, allowing in the hazy gray light, and Green had lit several lanterns and hung them from wallhooks. Back in the last cell, the woman was huddled in the straw, her sackcloth clothing bundled about her.

"This is where you'll be," Green rumbled, opening the door of the cage opposite the one in which Noles had been confined. Clean straw had been laid down. In a corner had been placed two buckets, one empty and the other brimmed with fresh water. At the center of the cell stood a desk and chair, a leatherbound Bible (suitable for swearing truth upon) atop the desk, and the chair holding a comfortable-looking blue cushion. Before the desk was a stool for the witness. To the right of the magistrate's position was a second, smaller combination desk and chair—removed from the schoolhouse, Matthew presumed—and atop it another blotter and a rectangular wooden box. Matthew's first act upon entering the cell was to lift the box's lid; he found within it a thick sheaf of rather yellowed paper, a well of black ink, three quills, a small brush, and a square of coarse brown cloth with which to clean clots of ink from the writing instruments.

"Is everything satisfactory?" Winston asked, waiting at the cell's threshold as Matthew inspected his tools and the magistrate tested the firmness of the cushion with the palm of his hand.

"I believe it is," Woodward decided. "One request, though: I'd like a pot of tea."

"Yes sir, I'll see to it."

"A large pot, please. With three cups."

"Certainly. Mr. Paine has gone to fetch Jeremiah Buckner, and should be returning presently."

"Very good." Woodward was loath to sit down yet, as he didn't fancy these surroundings. In his career there'd never been an equal to this set of circumstances. He heard the rustling of straw, and both he and Matthew saw Rachel Howarth rise up from her repose. She stood at the middle of her cage, her head and face hooded by her garment.

"Not to be alarmed, madam," Winston told her. "Your court is about to convene." She was silent, but Matthew sensed she was well aware of what was in preparation.

"There'll be no disruptions from you, hear?" Green warned. "Mr. Bidwell's given me the authority to bind and gag you if I must!"

She made a sound that might have been a bitter laugh. She said, "Aren't you feared to touch me? I might conjure you into a frog and stomp you flat!"

"Did you hear?" Green's eyes had widened; he looked from Woodward to Winston and back again. "She's threatenin' me!"

"Steady," Woodward said. "She's talking, nothing more." He raised his voice to address the woman. "Madam, I would suggest to you that such claims of ability are not helpful to your position."

"My *position*? What position?" Now she reached up, pulled back her hood, and her fiercely beautiful face was fully exposed, her black hair dirty and wild, her amber eyes aflame. "My position is already hopeless! What lesser depth can there be?"

"Mind that tongue!" Green shouted, but it seemed to Matthew that he was trying to make up in volume for what he might be lacking elsewhere.

"No, it's all right." The magistrate walked to the bars and peered through them into the woman's face. "You may speak your mind in my court. Within reason of course."

"There is no reason here! And this is not a court!"

"It *is* a court, because I have *decreed* it so. And as for the matter of reason, I am here to find it. I am going to be questioning witnesses who have some knowledge of your activities, and it will be for your benefit if you don't attempt to make a mockery of the proceedings."

"A *mockery*," she repeated, and she laughed again. Some of her fire, however, had been extinguished by the magistrate's calmness of tone. "Why don't you go ahead and pronounce me guilty? Put me to the rope or the stake, or whatever. I can't receive a fair trial in this town."

"On the contrary. I am sworn before the law to make certain you *do* receive a fair trial. We are holding court here because my clerk has been sentenced to three days—"

"Oh?" Her gaze fixed on Matthew. "Have they pronounced you a warlock?"

"Three days," Woodward repeated, shifting his position so that he stood between the woman and his clerk, "for a crime that does not concern you. If I were not interested in the fairness of your trial, I should have you taken to some other location and kept confined. But I wish for you to be present and hear the accusations, under the tenets of English law. That does *not* mean, however"—and here he lifted a finger for emphasis—"that you will be suffered to speak during the questioning." He had to pause for a moment, to clear his ravaged throat of what felt like a slow, thick stream of phlegm. He was going to need the acidity of the tea to get through this day. "Your time to speak will come, and you shall have all the opportunity you need to refute, explain, or otherwise defend yourself. If you choose the path of disruption, you shall be bound and gagged. If, when the opportunity of your speaking arrives, you choose silence as the cornerstone of your defense, that is your privilege. Now: do we have an understanding?"

She stared at him, saying nothing. Then, "Are you really a magistrate?"

"Yes, I really am."

"From where?" Her eyes narrowed, like those of a suspicious cat.

"Charles Town. But I originally served the bench in London for many years."

"You have experience in witch trials?"

"No, I do not. I do, however, have much experience in murder trials." He offered a faint smile. "All the jurists I know who have experience in witchcraft trials are either writing books or selling lectures."

"Is that what you hope to do?"

"Madam, I hope to find the truth," Woodward said. "That is my profit."

"And where's Bidwell, then? Isn't he attending?"

"No. I've instructed him to keep his distance." She cocked her head to one side. Her eyes were still slightly narrowed, but Woodward could tell that this last bit of information had cooled her coals.

"If you please?" Winston said, desiring the magistrate's attention. "I'll go fetch your tea now. As I said, Nicholas should be here shortly with Mr. Buckner. Three cups, did you say?"

"Three. For me, my clerk, and the witness. Wait. Make that four. A cup for Madam Howarth as well."

"This is a gaol!" Green protested. "It ain't no social club!"

"Today it's a court," Woodward said. "*My* court, and I'll preside over it as I please. At the end of the day, it will be a gaol again. Four cups, Mr. Winston."

Winston left without another word, but Green shook his red-maned head and grumbled his disapproval. The magistrate paid him no further heed, and sat down in the desk's chair. Likewise, Matthew situated himself at his clerk's station. He took a sheet of paper from the box, set it before him, and then shook the inkwell to mix the pigments and opened it. He chose a quill, dipped the nib, and made some circles so as to get the feel of the instrument; all quills might look similar, he'd learned, but some were far more suited for the task of writing than others. This one, he found directly, was a wretched tool. Its nib was much too broad, and unevenly split so that the ink came out in spots and dollops rather than a smooth flow. He snapped it in two, dropped it to the floor, and chose a second quill. This one was better; it was a neater point and the ink flowed sufficiently well, but its shape was so crooked that the hand would be paralyzed before an hour's work was finished.

"Horrible," Matthew said, but he decided not to break the second one before he tested the third. His regular quills—the ones carried in a leather holder that had been lost back at Shaw-combe's tavern—were precision instruments that, not unlike fine horses, required only the lightest of touches to perform their task. He longed for them now, as he tried the third quill and found it to be the sorriest of the batch, with a crack down its center that caused ink to bleed into the feathers. He broke it at once, and therefore was wed to the handkiller.

"Are the tools unsuitable?" Woodward asked as Matthew practised writing a few lines of Latin, French, and English on the rough-skinned paper.

"I'd best accept what I've got." He was leaving blotches of ink on the paper, and so he further lightened his pressure. "This will do, once I've tamed it."

Within a few moments Nicholas Paine entered the gaol with the first witness. Jeremiah Buckner walked slowly and unsteadily even with the use of a cane. His beard, far more white than gray, trailed down his chest, and what remained of his snowy hair hung about his frail shoulders. He wore loose-fitting brown breeches and a faded red-checked shirt. Both Woodward and Matthew stood as a show of respect for the aged as Paine helped the old man across the threshold. Buckner's watery brown eyes marked the presence of Rachel Howarth, and he seemed to draw back a bit but allowed Paine to aid him in sitting on the stool.

"I'm all right," he said; it was more of a gasp than speech.

"Yes sir," Paine said. "Magistrate Woodward will protect you from harm. I'll be waiting just outside to take you home when you are done here."

"I'm all right." The old man nodded, but his eyes kept returning to the figure in the next cage.

"Where do you want me, Magistrate?" Green inquired, with more than a little sarcasm in his voice.

"You may also wait outside. I'll ask you to return if it's necessary."

The two men left, and Buckner positioned his cane so as to

give himself balance on the stool. He swallowed nervously, his knotty fingers working together, his face gaunt and blotched with the dark spots of advanced age.

"Are we ready to begin?" Woodward asked of Matthew, and the clerk dipped his quill and nodded. The first thing was for Woodward to stand and offer the Bible to Buckner, instructing him to place his right hand upon it and swear before God that he would tell the truth. Buckner did, and Woodward put the Good Book aside and settled himself back in his chair.

"Your full name and age, please, for the record."

"Jeremiah Buckner. I shall be sixty-and-eight year come August."

"Thank you. Mr. Buckner, how long have you been a citizen of Fount Royal?"

"Ever since it begun. Five year, I reckon."

"You're a farmer, is that correct?"

"*Was*. My son brung Patience and me here to live with 'em. He did some farmin'. Wasn't no good at it, though. Two year ago, he an' Lizabeth lit out, took the boys. Gonna come back an' fetch us, once they's settled."

"Yes, sir, thank you," Woodward said. "So you and your wife occupy a farm? On which street?"

"Industry."

"And what is your source of income?"

Buckner wet his lips with his tongue. "Patience an' me get by on the lovin' kindness of our fellows, sir. Our farm ain't worth nothin'. Just got a roof o'er our heads, that's all. But when Ezra comes to get us, everythin'll be paid back. I'll swear that on the Lord's Book, too. He writ me a letter, come by the post rider from Charles Town. Said he was lookin' for some good land up Virginia way."

"I see. Now I presume you have an accusation to make concerning Madam Howarth?"

"Well . . ." Buckner glanced quickly through the bars into the next cell.

"Sir?" Woodward said sternly. "Look at me, please, not at anyone else. If you have an accusation to make, now is the proper time."

Matthew waited in the silence that fell, his quill poised. On the paper was written every utterance up to the moment, penned in the code of shortened words, abbreviations, and alphabetic memory-devices of his own creation.

Buckner stared at the floor. A blue vein at his temple throbbed. With an obvious effort he opened his mouth and spoke. "She . . . the witch . . . she come to me. In the night. She come to me . . . naked, she was. Wearin' a . . . serpent 'round her neck. A black serpent, with yella eyes. Like hers. She come to me, stood right at the foot of my bed, and Patience sleepin' a'side me."

"You're referring to Rachel Howarth?"

"She's the one."

"You have that down?" Woodward asked his clerk, but he needn't have because he knew Matthew's ability. Matthew just nodded grimly and dipped his quill once more.

"May I speak?" Rachel asked sharply.

"No, you may not!" The answer was delivered with an even-sharper point. "I told you, I'll have no disruptions in my court!"

"I would just like to say that I—"

"Madam!" Woodward shouted, and his raw throat paid the price for it. "One more word and the gag shall be delivered!"

Matthew had been scribing all this down as well. Now he stared at her, his quill's nib resting at the end of a letter, and he said quietly, "It would be wise not to speak further. Believe me."

Her mouth had already begun to open to test the magistrate's will. Now, however, she paused in her intent. Woodward waited, his fists clenched in his lap and his teeth gritted behind his lips. Slowly Rachel Howarth closed her mouth and then seated herself on the bench.

Woodward returned his full attention to Buckner. "When did this event occur? Was it before or after the murder of Daniel Howarth?"

"After. I believe Daniel had been laid down a week or two, so I reckon it was early February."

"All right. Tell me then, as clearly as you recall, exactly what happened."

"Yes sir." Buckner spent a moment putting it together in his mind, his head lowered. "Well . . . I don't recollect so good as I used to, but that kinda thing you don't forget. Me and Patience went to bed just like usual that night. She put out the lamp. Then . . . I don't know how long it was . . . I heard my name spoke. I opened my eyes. Everythin' was dark, and silent. I waited, a'listenin'. Just silent, like there was nothin' else in the whole world makin' a sound but my breathin'. Then . . . I heard my name spoke again, and I looked at the foot of the bed and seen her."

"By what light, if there was none?" Woodward asked.

"Well, I've put my mind to that but I can't answer it. The winda's were shuttered, 'cause it was might cold outside, so there wasn't no moonlight. But she was there, all right. I seen her, clear as I see you."

"You're positive it was Rachel Howarth?"

"I am."

Woodward nodded, staring at his hands spread out on the desktop before him. "And what else transpired?"

"I was scairt half out of my wits," Buckner said. "Any man would've been. I started to wake up Patience, but then that woman—the witch—said I wasn't to. She said if I woke up Patience I would be sorry for it."

"But your wife wasn't roused by Madam Howarth's voice?"

"No sir. I've puzzled on that, too, but I can't make no sense out of it. Patience slept deep as usual. Only thing I figure is that the witch put a conjure on her."

Matthew heard the woman give a muffled grunt of frustration; he was tempted to lift his head to glance at her, but the quill demanded his absolute concentration.

"All right. Then what occurred?"

"The witch . . . said I was to keep her visit a secret. Said if I spoke it to anyone, they would be killed on the spot. Said I was to meet her two nights hence, in the orchard behind my house. Just said be there betwixt midnight and two, she would find me."

"Madam Howarth was nude, you say?"

"Yes sir, she wore not a stitch."

"But she had a serpent around her neck?"

"Yes sir. Black, it was. With yella eyes."

"Had you latched your doors and windows before retiring to bed?"

Buckner nodded. "We had. Never used to, but . . . with somebody a'killin' Reverend Grove and then Daniel like that . . . Patience felt easier with the latches throwed after dark."

"Therefore in your estimation there was no possible earthly way for Rachel Howarth to have entered your house?"

"Well sir . . . after she was gone, I lit the lantern and checked them latches. They was all still throwed. Patience woke up and asked me what I was doin'. I had to tell her a lie, say a barkin' dog stirred me up. She went on back to sleep, but I couldn't near close my eyes."

"I can understand," Woodward said. "Tell me this, then: exactly how did Madam Howarth leave your house?"

"I don't know, sir."

"Oh? You didn't see her leave?"

"Soon as she told me where to meet her . . . she was just gone. Didn't fade nor nothin', like you might think a phantasm would. She was there and then not."

"And you immediately lit the lantern?"

"I think so. Maybe it was a minute or two. It was kinda hazy what I did just after she left. I believe I was still conjured, myself."

"Uh . . . Magistrate?" The voice made Matthew jump, the quill scrawling across two neat lines above it before he could rein it in.

"Yes?" Woodward snapped, looking toward the gaol's entrance. "What is it?"

"I've brought your tea, sir." Winston carried a wicker basket with a lid. He came into the cell, put the basket down upon the magistrate's desk, and opened it, revealing a white clay teapot and four cups, three of the same white clay but the fourth a dark red-dish-brown. "Compliments of Mrs. Lucretia Vaughan," Winston said. "She sells pies, cakes, and tea from her home, just up Harmony Street, but she graciously offered to brew the pot free of charge. I felt it my duty, however, to inform her that the witch would be drinking as well, therefore Mrs. Vaughan asks that Madam Howarth use the dark cup so that it may be broken into pieces."

"Yes, of course. Thank you."

"Is there anything else I might do for you? Mr. Bidwell has put me at your disposal."

"No, nothing else. You may go, and thank you for your assistance."

"Yes sir. Oh . . . one more thing: Mrs. Vaughan would like Madam Howarth herself to break the cup, and then she asks that you gather the pieces and return them to her."

Woodward frowned. "May I ask why?"

"I don't know, sir, but it was her request."

"Very well, then." Woodward waited for the other man to leave, and then he removed the teapot from the basket and poured himself a cup. He drank almost all of it immediately, to soothe his throat. "Tea?" he offered Buckner, but the farmer declined. Matthew took a cup, taking care not to spill any upon his papers. "Madam Howarth?" Woodward called. "I should be lacking in manners if I failed to offer you a cup of tea."

"Lucretia Vaughan brewed it?" she asked sullenly. "I wonder if it's not poisoned."

"I have drunk some that I would swear *was* tainted, but this is quite good. I'd daresay it's been a while since you've had a taste." He poured some into the dark cup and handed it to Matthew. "Put this through the bars, please."

Matthew stood up to do so, and the woman rose from her bench and approached. In a moment Matthew found himself face-to-face with her, the compelling amber eyes staring fixedly at him. Curls of her thick ebony hair had fallen across her forehead, and Matthew was aware of tiny beads of sweat glistening on her upper lip, due to the gaol's damp heat. He saw her pulse beating in the valley of her throat.

He pushed the cup through; it was a tight fit, but it did scrape between the bars. She reached to accept it, and her fingers pressed across his. The sensation of her body heat was like a wildfire that burned through his flesh and flamed along the nerves of his hand. He let go of the cup and jerked his arm back, and he didn't know what his expression had revealed but the woman was looking at him with curious interest. He abruptly turned his back to her and resumed his place.

"Let us continue," Woodward said, when his clerk was once more situated. "Matthew, read back to me the last question and answer, please."

"The question was: *And you immediately lit the lantern?* Mr. Buckner's reply was: *I think so. Maybe it was a minute or two. It was kind of hazy what I did just after she left. I believe I was still conjured, myself.*"

"All right. Mr. Buckner, did you later that day inform your wife of what had occurred?"

"No sir, I did not. I was a'feared that if I told her, the witch's curse might kill her on the spot. I didn't tell nobody."

"Two nights hence, did you go to the orchard at the pre-scribed time?"

"I did. Betwixt midnight and two, just as the witch com-manded. I got out of bed slow and quiet as I could. I didn't want Patience hearin' and wakin' up."

"And when you went to the orchard, what transpired?" Woodward sipped at a fresh cup of tea and waited for the man to respond.

This question obviously troubled Jeremiah Buckner, as the farmer shifted uneasily on his stool and chewed at his lower lip. "Sir?" he at last said. "I'd . . . beg not relate it."

"If it has to do with Madam Howarth, I must insist that you relate it." Again, Buckner shifted and chewed but no words were forthcoming. "I would remind you that you have taken an oath on the Bible," Woodward said. "Also, that this is a station of the law just as much as any courthouse in Charles Town. If you're fearful of your safety, let me assure you that these bars are solid and Madam Howarth cannot reach you."

"The walls of my house are solid, too," Buckner muttered. "She got through 'em, didn't she?"

"You came here to testify of your own free will, did you not?"

"Yes sir, I did."

"Then you will leave here with your testimony incomplete if you fail to respond to my questions. I need to know what occurred in the orchard."

"*Oh Lord,*" Buckner said softly; it was a supplication for strength. He bowed his head, staring at the floor, and when he lifted it again the lamplight sparkled from the sheen of sweat on his face. "I walked into the orchard," he began. "It was a cold night, and silent. I walked in, and directly I heard . . . a woman laughin', and another noise too. Somethin' that sounded . . . sounded like a beast, a'gruntin'." He was quiet, his head once again lowered.

"Go on," Woodward said.

"Well . . . I followed them sounds. Followed 'em, deeper in. I 'member I stopped to look back at my house. It seemed such an awful long way off. Then I took to walkin' again, tryin' to find the woman. Wasn't a few minutes passed 'fore I did." Buckner paused and took a deep breath, as if fortifying himself for the rest of it. "She was a'layin' on her back, under one of them apple trees. She was a'layin' with her legs spread wide, 'bout to split her down the middle. And on top a'her was . . . that *thing* I seen. It was goin' at her, like the drivin' of a spike. It was a'gruntin' ever'time it come down, and she had her eyes closed and was laughin'."

"A *thing?*" Woodward said. "What kind of *thing?*"

Buckner looked directly into the magistrate's eyes, his jaw slack and the sweat gleaming on his forehead. "It was somethin' that . . . kinda 'sembled a man, but . . . it had a black hide, and leathery. I couldn't see its face . . . I didn't *want* to. But it was big. A beast the likes I'd never set eye on before. It just kept poundin' her. That woman's legs open wide, and that beast comin' down a'top her. I saw its back movin' . . . it had some kinda spines or the like up and down its backbone. Then all a'sudden it whipped its head side to side and let out an awful moan, and the woman gave a cry too. It got up off her . . . must'a been seven, eight feet tall. I could see . . ." Buckner hesitated, his eyes glazed with the memory of it. "I could see the woman was all bloody, there in her private parts. The beast moved away, and then . . . then somethin' else come out of the orchard, and it got down on its knees a'side her."

"What was it?" Woodward had gripped his teacup in his hand, his palm damp.

"I don't know. It had white hair and a child's face. But it was a dwarf-thing, its skin all gray and shrivelled like a dead fish. It got down on its knees a'side her. It leaned its head down, and then . . . then a terrible long tongue slid out of its mouth, and . . ." He stopped, squeezed his eyes shut and shook his head. "Can't say," he gasped. "Can't say."

Woodward took a drink of tea and put the cup down. He restrained himself from casting a glance in Rachel Howarth's direction. He could feel Matthew tensed and ready to resume his scrivening. Woodward spoke quietly, "You must say."

Buckner released a noise that sounded like a sob. His chest was trembling. He said painfully, "I'll be damned to Hell for these pi'tures in my head!"

"You are acting as a proper Christian, sir. You were an observer to these sins, not a participant. I would ask you again to continue."

Buckner ran a hand across his mouth, the fingers palsied. The hue of his flesh had become pasty, and dark hollows had taken form beneath his eyes. He said, "That dwarf-thing . . . looked like a child. White hair. A falled angel, is what I thought. All shrunk up when it was cast in the Pit. I saw it . . . saw that tongue come out . . . saw it wet and shiny, like raw beef. Then . . . that tongue went up *in* the woman. In her bloody parts. She took to thrashin' and cryin' out, and the tongue was a'movin' inside her. I wanted to hide my face, but I couldn't near move my arms. I had to stand there and watch it. It was like . . . somebody was a'makin' me watch it, when I wanted to hide my face and call to God to take them sights away." His voice cracked, and for a moment Woodward feared the old man would collapse into sobbing. But then Buckner said, "When that thing . . . slid its tongue back out again . . . there was blood all over it. Drippin' blood, it was. And that woman grinned like she was a new bride."

"Matthew?" Woodward's throat felt so constricted that clear speaking had become an effort of will. "Are you getting all this?"

"If I weren't," Matthew answered tersely, "I would have to be deaf."

"Yes. Of course. This represents a new threshold in your experience of clerking, I am sure." Woodward used his sleeve to mop the moisture from his face. "It certainly opens a new door for me, one that I might wish had remained latched."

"Then there was the third one," Buckner said. "The one that was man and woman both."

Neither Woodward nor Matthew moved nor spoke. In the silence they heard Buckner's hoarse breathing. Through the open roof-hatch came the sound of a crow cawing in the far distance. Matthew dipped his quill into the inkwell and waited.

"Let us not say," spoke the magistrate, "that in our interview we failed to turn over all rocks, regardless of what might be coiled underneath them. Tell us of the third creature, Mr. Buckner."

twelve

BUCKNER'S EYES WERE SHINY now, as if these sights had burned the vision from them. "It came out of the orchard, after the dwarf-thing had gone," he related. "I took it to be a naked woman at first. Taller than most women, though, and terrible thin. She—it—had long dark hair. Brown or black, I couldn't say. The thing had tits, I seen 'em clear enough. Then I seen what else it had, and I near staggered and fell." Buckner leaned his head forward, the veins standing out in his neck. "Stones and a yard. Right there where a woman's basket oughta be. That yard was ready for work, too, and when the witch seen it she smiled so wicked it near froze my heart. The creature laid down a'side her, and then she started to . . . started to lickin' the creature's spike."

"By 'she,' you are referring to whom?" Woodward asked.

"Her. In the cage there. The witch, Rachel Howarth."

"All right." Woodward again mopped the sweat from his face. The walls of the gaol seemed to be closing in on him. The one saving grace was the open hatch, through which he could see a square of gray clouds. "Continue."

"There was just . . . more sin and vileness after that. The witch turned over, on her hands and knees, so her rear quarters was showin'. Then that half-man, half-woman took its spike in hand

and squatted down atop her. I saw . . . things no Christian should e'er have to witness, sir. I tell you, before I seen them sights I was all right in the head. Now I ain't. You ask my Patience. She'll tell you, I'm no good for nothin' no more."

"This creature—the half-man, half-woman—penetrated Madam Howarth with its penis?"

"Yes sir. The creature pushed its yard in from behind."

"Let us move past those particulars," Woodward said, his face blanched. "What was the aftermath of this incident?"

"The *what*, sir?"

"The aftermath. What happened after the creature had . . ." He paused, seeking the proper word, ". . . finished?"

"It got up off her and walked away. Then the witch stood up and took to dressin' herself. All a' sudden I heard my name spoke, right up next to my ear, and I whipped 'round to see who it be."

"And did you see?"

"Well . . . I was mighty scairt. There was a man standin' behind me . . . but I don't think he had no face. 'Cept a mouth. He did have a mouth . . . I 'member that. He said, 'Jeremiah Buckner, run home.' That's all. I must'a done what he said, 'cause next thing I knew I was a'layin' in bed, sweatin' and shakin'. Patience was hard asleep, conjured most likely. I heard a cock crow, and I knew then that the demons of the night was passin'."

"Did you in the morning, then, tell your wife what had happened?"

"No sir, I didn't. I was shamed to tell Patience such things. And I was scairt, too, that the witch might kill her for hearin'. I didn't tell nobody, not even after I heard what Elias Garrick seen. Then Lester Crane told me Stephen Dunton seen such a thing— them three creatures with the witch, 'cept they was doin' their wickedness inside the house where the Poole family used to live, right next to Dunton's farm. Still I held my tongue."

"What made you decide to tell what you'd seen?" Woodward asked. "And who did you tell?"

"I decided . . . after they found them poppets in the witch's house. I went straight to Mr. Bidwell and told him all of it."

"I should like to speak to Mr. Dunton," Woodward said to Matthew. "Make a note of that, please."

"Cain't," Buckner said. "He took his family and they left, back two month ago. Dunton's house since burnt down. Lester Crane and his brood lit out 'bout the same time."

Woodward paused for a moment, ordering his thoughts. "Did you know Daniel Howarth?"

"Yes sir."

"What kind of man was he?"

"Oh, he was but a youngster. Maybe forty, forty-five year old. Big man, he was. Took a right demon to lay him low, I'll grant you!"

"Did you have occasion to see Mr. Howarth and his wife together?"

"No, not much. Daniel kept to hisself. Wasn't a social kind of man."

"And what about his wife? Was she social?"

"Well . . . I don't know about such. Daniel and that woman been here maybe three year. He had a sizable piece a' land, bought it from a Dutchman named Niedecker. That man's wife had passed in childbirth, the child died too, so he decided to give it up. Daniel was always a quiet man. Never needed much help at anythin', seemed like." Buckner shrugged. "The woman . . . well, mayhap she did *try* to be social. But it just caused a stir."

"A stir? What kind of stir?"

"Look at her, sir. If you can bear it, after what I've told you. She's betwixt a nigger and a Spaniard. Would you care to share a pew with her?"

"The witch attended church?" Woodward raised his eyebrows.

"That was 'fore she took to witchcraft," Buckner explained. "She only come to church two or three Sabbaths. Wouldn't nobody sit near her. Them Port'a'geeze got a whiff about 'em."

"So she was not welcome in church, is that correct?"

"She could do and go as she pleased. Wasn't nobody gonna stop her from enterin' Our Lord's house. But I recall the last time she showed up, somebody—and I know who it was, but I ain't sayin'—pelted her with a rotten egg a'fore she could come in. Hit her right a'side the face. You know what she done?"

"What?"

"She sat down in a pew with that egg smellin' as it did, that mess all in her hair, and she nary made a move 'til Reverend Grove said the last Praise and Amen 'bout four hours later. 'Course, he did rush it some, that smell in the church as it was."

Matthew was aware of a movement from the corner of his eye. He looked up as he finished scribing the last line—and there was Rachel Howarth, standing next to the bars, her teeth gritted and an expression of sheer ferocity on her face. Her right arm was lifted and swinging forward, a gesture of violence that made Matthew shout, "Magistrate!"

The shout itself most possibly caused Woodward to lose the remaining few hairs on his scalp. He twisted his head around as well, and Buckner gave a garbled cry of terror and raised a hand to protect his face from what he was sure would be Satanic flame.

There was a loud *crack!* at the end of the woman's blow against the bars. Fragments of dark reddish-brown clay fell into the straw. Matthew saw that in her right hand was the cup's grip, the rest of it smashed to smithereens.

"I am done with my tea," Rachel said. She opened her hand and dropped the largest bit of the cup into their cell. "That *is* how Lucretia Vaughan wanted it returned, is it not?"

"Yes, it is. And thank you, Matthew, for your help in emptying my bladder. Will you collect those pieces for me, please?" The magistrate blotted his face with his sleeve and attempted mightily to control his galloping heart. Matthew had to bend down on his knees and reach into the woman's cell to gather up all the shards. She stood over him, an intimidating presence to begin with but now—due to farmer Buckner's tale—absolutely fearsome, even though Matthew had the benefit of clear-headed reasoning.

"Wait," she said as he started to rise. Her hand came down and plucked up a small piece he'd missed. "Take this one, too."

She placed it in his outstretched palm, which he immediately withdrew between the bars.

Woodward put the fragments into Madam Vaughan's basket. "Let us continue, please, though my mind is as shambled as that broken cup." He rubbed his temples with both hands. "Matthew, do you have any questions for the witness?"

"Yes, sir, I do," he answered readily, and then he prepared to scribe his own inquiry. "Mr. Buckner, how long have you depended on that cane?"

"My cane? Oh . . . eight, nine year. My bones are poorly."

"I understand that you were terrified that night in the orchard. Terror can strengthen a man's legs, I know. But when the person behind you said, 'Jeremiah, run home,' did you actually *run?*"

"I don't know. But I must'a, 'cause I got back to my bed."

"You don't recall running? You recall no pain to your legs?"

"No," Buckner said. "I don't recall."

"By which door did you enter your house?"

"Which door? Well . . . I reckon the back door."

"You don't *remember* which door?"

"Jus' two doors," Buckner said with a snort. "Back 'n front. I was behind the house, so I must'a gone in the back 'un."

"Was it cold that night?" Matthew asked, as he dipped the quill once more.

"It was February, like I say."

"Yes, sir. But my question to you is: was it cold that night?"

"Sure it was. Had to be cold, a February night!"

"You don't know for certain whether it was cold or not? You don't *recall* it being cold?"

"*I'm* not on trial here, am I?" Buckner looked to the magistrate for help. "What's he poundin' the nail for?"

"Is there some point to this, Matthew?"

"Yes, sir, there is. If you'll bear with me?"

"All right, then." Woodward nodded. "But please remember that Mr. Buckner is a witness, not a defendant."

"Mr. Buckner, when you rose from bed to go outside in the

cold February night, did you pause to put on any outer garments?"

"Outer garments? What're you goin' on about?"

"A coat," Matthew said. "A cloak. A hat. Gloves. Surely you
paused to at least put on *shoes.*"

Buckner scowled. "Well . . . of *course* I put on shoes!"

"And a coat?"

"Yes, I reckon I put on a coat too! Do you think me a fool?"

"No, sir, I do not. But you don't sound very certain about
those details. Tell me this, then: when you heard the cock crow,
were you lying in bed with your shoes and coat still on?"

"What?"

"You testified that you were lying in bed, sweating and shaking. Did you pause at some point to *remove* your shoes and coat
before you got into bed?"

"Yes." It was said with faint conviction. "I must'a."

"You don't recall?"

"I was scairt. Like I said, scairt half dead!"

"What about your cane?" Matthew asked. "You did take your
cane outside with you, did you not?"

"I did. I cain't hardly get 'round without it."

"Where did you put your cane when you returned from the
orchard?"

"I . . . put it . . ." He pressed his fingers against his mouth. "I
put it . . . in the corner next to the bed, I reckon. Where it always
is put."

"Then that's where it was when morning came?"

"Yes. Right there in that corner."

"Where did you put your coat and shoes?"

"I . . . took off my coat, and laid it and my shoes . . . at the
foot of the bed, I believe."

"That's where they were the next time you had need of
them?"

"Wait," Buckner said, his forehead deeply creased. "No. I
must'a hung up my coat on the hook by the front door. That's
where it was."

"By the front door? Yet you entered by the back door? Was there a lantern lit within the house, or was it dark?"

"Dark. I don't recall no light."

"You were—as you put it—scared half dead, a witness to demonic wickedness, and yet you walked from one side of the house to the other in the dark to hang your coat on its proper hook?" Matthew held up a finger before Buckner could respond. "Ah! You did so because you didn't wish your wife to know you'd been outside, could that be correct?"

"Yes, it could." He nodded vigorously. "That must be the why of it."

"Sir, if you had decided to do so, why did you believe you took it off and laid it at the foot of the bed? Is it so unclear in your mind where you left your coat?"

"I was conjured! Must'a been. Like I say, after what I seen I ain't right in the head no more."

"Mr. Buckner?" Matthew stared forcefully into the man's eyes. "You have given us a story of amazing details, seen without the benefit of illumination. Why is it, then, that your grasp of details is so hazy both before and after the incident in the orchard?"

Buckner's face tightened. "You think I'm lyin', don't you?"

"Mr. Buckner," Woodward spoke up, "no one has said that."

"Don't have to say it! I can read it in these damn questions you're askin' me! All this 'bout coats and shoes, and did I have my cane and whatnot! I'm a honest man, you can ask anybody!"

"Please, sir, there's no need for an outburst."

"I ain't no *liar!*" Buckner had fairly shouted it. He hobbled to his feet and pointed at Rachel Howarth. "*There's* the witch I seen with them three demons from Hell! I seen it was her, no mistakin' it! She's evil to her black heart, and if you think I'm lyin' she's conjured *you,* too!"

"Sir," Woodward said quietly, trying to calm the man. "Please. Won't you sit down and—"

"No, I will not! I won't be called a liar, not even by a magistrate! God knows I'm tellin' the truth, and He's the only judge matters!"

"In Heaven, yes," Woodward said, feeling a bit wounded by this last remark. "In the courts of Earth, however, justice is the responsibility of mortals."

"If justice is served, that witch'll be dead 'fore another day goes past!" Buckner had white spittle on his lips, his eyes enraged. "Or hav'ya already decided it's the town that dies and the witch that lives?"

"I still have a few questions to ask, sir." Woodward motioned toward the stool. "Won't you sit down?"

"I've had a fill of this! I ain't answerin' nothin' more!" The old man abruptly turned and walked out of the cell, leaning heavily on his cane.

Woodward also stood up. "Mr. Buckner! Please! Just a few moments longer!" His entreaties were in vain, however. Buckner stalked away and was gone from the gaol altogether.

"He can be convinced to return," Matthew said. "He'll listen to Bidwell."

"I only had two or three more questions to ask." Woodward cast a dark glare at his clerk. "What was the meaning of badgering the man like that?"

"I don't think I was badgering, sir. I was clarifying."

"You took that man to task, Matthew! You just as well said you believed him a liar!"

"No, sir," Matthew replied evenly, "I never said such a thing. I simply desired to know why he couldn't recall some specific details, when other specifics were so very clear. I should think he would remember putting on and removing his coat and shoes, no matter what kind of fright he'd experienced."

"Well, the man's not a liar!" Woodward vowed. "Confused, possibly. Frightened, certainly. But I don't believe him the stripe of man who would make up such phantasms, do you? I mean . . . dear God, if he *was* concocting such a tale, I'd fear his mind was diseased beyond all salvation!"

There came a laugh. Matthew and Woodward looked into the next cage. Rachel Howarth was sitting on her bench, her back against the rough wall and her head uptilted.

"You find this amusing, madam?" Woodward inquired.

"No," she said. "I find it sad. But as I am far past tears, I must laugh instead of weep."

"Laugh or weep as you please. This is damning evidence."

"*Evidence?*" Again, she laughed. "What evidence is there? An insane tale told by an old man? Oh, there *is* some truth in what he told you."

"Are you admitting your concordance with the Devil, then?"

"Not at all. I'm admitting that I attended church on three Sabbaths, and the third time I sat with a rotten egg in my hair. But I was *not* going to give them the pleasure of watching me run home, or seeing me sob like a wounded child. That's the only truth in Buckner's story."

"Of course you would deny the incident in the orchard. I wouldn't expect you to do otherwise."

"What was the point of it, then?" She turned her amber gaze upon him. "If I am such a witch, why did I choose to invite Buckner to watch my . . . indiscretions? Why would I not want to do such things in *private?*"

"I don't know, madam. Why did you not?"

"Evidently, according to Buckner, I can walk through latched doors. Why am I still here in this cage, then?"

"It would be an admission of witchcraft to leave this gaol."

"And allowing Buckner to witness that profanity was *not* an admission?" She shook her head. "If I really were a witch, I'd be much more clever than that."

"Oh, I think you're clever enough. Besides, madam, who is to say you do *not* leave this gaol at night, and roam where you please with your master? Possibly you inhabit some spectral world of which God-fearing citizens dare not imagine.'"

"You might ask your clerk tomorrow morning," Rachel said. "He'll find out tonight if I have the power to walk through walls."

"I doubt that you would show any such power while Matthew is present," Woodward parried. "Again, it would be an admission of guilt that would lead to your appointment at the stake."

She suddenly stood up. "You must be as insane as the rest of them! Do you honestly think, after what you heard today, that I am *not* going to burn? There are other witnesses—other liars—yet to speak against me, I know. But who will speak *for* me? No one. Oh, they hated me here before they took me to be a witch, so they made me into one, the better to hate all the stronger!"

"They *made* you into a witch? How could you be made into what you are not?"

"Hear me well, Magistrate. Someone murdered Reverend Grove and my husband, and then fashioned me into the blackest witch south of Salem. Someone made poppets and hid them in the floor of my house. Someone spread these filthy lies about me, so that now the people here don't know their own minds!"

"I believe Mr. Buckner," Woodward said. "I've seen liars before, in many courtrooms. I've seen them spin webs from which they cannot escape. Mr. Buckner may be confused about some small details, due to his advanced age and the experience of that night, but he is *not* lying."

"If he's not lying," Rachel answered, "then he's either in need of an asylum or he's been cursed by some witch *other* than the one I am painted to be. I never set foot in his house or that orchard. I swear it before God."

"Beware your mouth, madam! A bolt of holy fire might end your games."

"If it would be a quicker death than the stake, I would welcome it."

Matthew said, "There's a simple way to end all of this. Madam, if you would recite the Lord's Prayer, I think the magistrate might consider your case in a different light."

"I'll speak for myself, thank you!" Woodward said. "After what I've heard here today, I think even a recitation of the Lord's Prayer might be a trick provided by this woman's master!"

"I will save you the wondering," Rachel said, "because I refuse to speak such a thing that has no meaning in this town. Those who babble the Lord's Prayer day and night would be first to grin when I'm set afire. Like Lucretia Vaughan, for instance. Oh, there's a fine Christian example! She would've given Christ on the cross a drink of vinegar and called it honey!"

"She was kind enough to provide you a cup for tea. I didn't find it vinegared."

"You don't know her as I do. I believe I know why she wanted the cup broken and returned. Ask her yourself. You might be enlightened."

Woodward busied himself by putting the teapot and the remaining cups back into the basket. "I think that will do for today, Matthew. I'm off to visit Dr. Shields. On Monday morning we shall resume our interviews."

"I'd suggest, sir, that our next witness be Mrs. Buckner. I have some questions I'd like to pose."

"Do you, now?" Woodward paused, his cheeks showing a flame. "Who is presiding over this court, you or me?"

"You are, of course."

"Then shouldn't I be the one who determines the next witness? And since *I* do not have any questions for Mrs. Buckner, I suggest Mr. Garrick come to court on Monday morning."

"I understand that you are the authority in this court, as in any other," Matthew said, with a slight bow of his head, "but shouldn't Mrs. Buckner be asked to describe her husband's mental state during the period of time that—"

"Mrs. Buckner should be left *alone,*" the magistrate interrupted. "She was asleep during both incidents her husband related. I daresay Mr. Buckner has never told her what he saw. Would you bring a decent Christian wife into this gaol, within earshot of Madam Howarth?"

"She would be brought into any other courtroom."

"At the discretion of the judge. In my opinion, she has nothing to add, and indeed might even suffer harm by being called to appear."

"Magistrate," Matthew said quietly, "a wife knows her husband. I would like to learn whether Mr. Buckner has had . . . shall we say . . . delusions of any kind in previous years."

"If you're saying that what he witnessed was a delusion, remember that it was a delusion shared by another person. Stephen Dunton, wasn't that the man's name?"

"Yes, sir. But as Mr. Dunton is no longer present, we only have Mr. Buckner's word."

"Sworn on the Bible. Delivered in a rational manner. Told in as stomach-churning detail as I ever hope to hear. His word is good enough for me."

"But not good enough for *me*," Matthew said. The rawly honest thought had left his mouth before he could constrain it. If Woodward's teeth had been false, they might have dropped to the floor. The silence stretched, as the magistrate and his clerk stared at each other.

Woodward's throat was ravaged, his air passages swollen, and his bones aching in the damp, close heat. He had just heard a reliable witness relate a story of both fascination and horror that brought a woman—a human being, even if she was a notorious witch—nearer the stake. He felt sick to his very marrow, and now this audacity added to his freight was enough to lay him low. "You've forgotten your place," he rasped. "You are a clerk, not a magistrate. Not even—though you seem to wish it—an attorney. Your duty is as a scrivener, not a questioner. The former you do very well, the latter undoes you."

Matthew didn't respond except for the flush of shame on his face. He realized that he'd spoken completely out of turn and was better off embracing silence.

"I will ascribe this incident to our surroundings and the miserable weather," Woodward decided. "Therefore we shall put this behind us like gentlemen. Agreed?"

"Yes, sir," Matthew said, though he still thought it was appropriate—no, *vital*—to interview Buckner's wife.

"Very good, then." Woodward picked up the basket in preparation of leaving. "I'll ask Mr. Green to come in and move you to one of the cells over there." He nodded toward the opposite cages. "I would prefer that you not be in such close proximity to Madam Howarth."

"Uh . . . I'd like to stay where I am, sir," Matthew countered quickly. "I'd appreciate the benefit of the desk."

"Why? You won't be needing it."

"It . . . makes the place seem not such a cage."

"Oh. Yes, I see. Then I'll have Madam Howarth moved."

"There's no need for that, sir," Matthew said. "The distance of one or two cages hardly matters, if indeed she employs such witchcraft. And I do have *this*." He held up the leatherbound Bible. "If this isn't strong enough to protect me, nothing can."

The magistrate paused, glancing from his clerk to Rachel Howarth and back again. This whole situation—Matthew being forced to remain in this wretched place with a woman who'd known such wickedness—gnawed at his nerves. Who knew what Matthew would witness in the dead of night? He damned himself for passing sentence on the boy, but what other choice had there been? It crossed his mind to occupy one of the other cages for the night, on some pretext of keeping an eye on Madam Howarth's activities, but he knew Bidwell and everyone else would see through the flimsy gauze and realize him to be quite less the taskmaster than he appeared.

At the bottom of his pond, far down from the light of public inspection, he was afraid. Fearful of Rachel Howarth, and of what she might do to the boy. Fearful also that once he left Matthew alone with this Devil's doxy, the boy might never again be the same. The witch's pleasure would be in destroying innocence, would it not?

"I shall be all right," Matthew said, reading some of these thoughts in the magistrate's anguished expression. "Just go to Dr. Shields and ask for a tonic."

Woodward nodded, but still he couldn't bear to leave. The time, however, had come. "I'll return this afternoon and see to you," he said. "Can I bring you anything? Books from Mr. Bidwell's library?"

"Yes, that would be fine. Any books will do."

"I'm sure you will be fed before long. If you're displeased at the meal, I'll be glad to bring you—"

"Whatever the meal is, it will be good enough," Matthew told him. "Just go see Dr. Shields."

"Yes, I shall." Woodward turned his attention to the woman, who had resumed sitting on her bench. "Your actions toward my clerk will be watched and noted, madam," he said sternly. "I strongly suggest you keep your distance."

"My actions needn't cause you worry," she replied. "But the rats in here are not subject to strong suggestions."

There was nothing more that Woodward could do. Matthew would have to fend for himself, and the Lord God be with him. Woodward, basket in hand, left the gaol. In another moment Green entered, closed and locked the door of Matthew's cage, and then he too retreated.

Matthew stood at the bars, staring up toward the open hatch. His fingers were gripping the iron. The sound of the cell's door being shut had made him think of the iron gate clanging at the almshouse, and sickness roiled in his stomach.

"You've not been in here very long to feel the loss of freedom," Rachel said quietly. "What is your sentence?"

"Three days."

"An age!" She gave a harsh laugh that sounded biting.

"I've never been in a gaol before. At least, not on this side of the bars."

"Neither had I. It's not so bad here, in the daylight. But the darkness is not kind."

"Three days," Matthew repeated. "I can bear it."

"What kind of foolishness is this?" Her tone had sharpened. "Do you think I don't know you've been placed in here to spy on me?"

"You're wrong. I am here because I . . . offended the blacksmith."

"Oh, of course you did! Well, what shall I do to conjure you tonight? Shall I become a raven and flit from cage to cage? Shall I dance a jig on the air, while Satan plays the fiddle? Ah! Why don't

I turn you into a piece of cheese and let the rats tear you apart! Would that impress your magistrate?"

"I'm sure it might," Matthew said evenly. "But it would do neither of us any good, for if I were crumbs by dawn you would be ashes by noon."

"Some noon I *shall* be ashes. Why should it not be tomorrow?"

Matthew looked through the bars at Rachel Howarth, who had drawn her legs up beneath herself. "Not all in this town believe you to be a witch."

"Who does not?"

"One, at least. As for the name, I don't feel I should betray the confidence."

"*One.*" She smiled thinly. "That one is not the magistrate, is it?"

"No."

"Well then? It is *you?*"

"I have an open mind on such subjects."

"And your magistrate does not?"

"Magistrate Woodward," Matthew said, "is a man of honor and conviction. No matter his reaction today, he will act in a tempered fashion. You'll notice no flames around your feet yet, and after Mr. Buckner's tale I think the magistrate might be justified in lighting the torch."

"Buckner!" Rachel spoke it like a spit. "He's insane. I was neither in his home nor in the orchard. I hardly know the man; perhaps I've spoken a dozen words to him altogether."

Matthew walked over to his desk and began to arrange the papers into a neat stack. "He seems to know *you* well enough. After your display here yesterday, I must wonder if your natural inclination is not to shed your clothing and walk the town."

"I shed my clothing for my husband," she said. "No one else. Certainly not in public, and certainly not . . . for the vile purposes Buckner imagined."

"Was that it, then? The imaginings of an old man?"

"Yes! Of course."

Matthew located a particular sheet of paper and read from it. "Regarding the incident in the orchard, Mr. Buckner says as follows: *I didn't tell nobody, not even after I heard what Elias Garrick seen. Then Lester Crane told me Stephen Dunton seen such a thing— them three creatures with the witch, 'cept they was doin' their wickedness inside the house where the Poole family used to live, right next to Dunton's farm.*" He looked up at her. "How could it be the imaginings of two men, at two different times and two different places?"

She didn't answer; her face seemed darker and she stared straight ahead.

"The testimony of Elias Garrick on Monday morning will add more sticks to your pyre," Matthew said. "Are you aware of what he's going to say?" There was no reply. "I take it that you are. Then we shall hear from a child by the name of Violet Adams. I have no knowledge of what she will testify. Do you?" Silence met his question. "Whatever it is, it will be doubly damning coming from a child. The magistrate is very sensitive to the testimony of children, and I would advise you to hold your tongue when she is speaking."

"No matter what lies she spews?" Rachel asked, still staring blankly ahead.

"No matter if she swears she witnessed you in a privyhouse accommodating three hundred and three demons. Keep your tongue shackled."

"You might care to know," Rachel said, "that the child's mother is the person who anointed my head with such a perfumed present before the church. Constance Adams made no secret of her feelings toward me." Rachel's head turned, and her eyes found Matthew's. "You're the magistrate's clerk, sworn to abide by his law. If you're not here to spy for him, then why are you in the least interested in what I might say or not say?"

Matthew continued straightening the sheets of paper. When he was done, he returned them to the box and closed the lid. It had taken him that long to formulate an answer. "I have a curiosity for puzzles," he said, refusing to meet her gaze. "I am satisfied only when all the pieces fit to perfection. In this instance . . . I feel there are many pieces that have been forced into the wrong positions, and thus are ragged of edge. There are missing pieces that must be found. There are pieces that seem to be correct . . . but are, to me at least, of false shape. That is my interest."

A long silence followed, during which Matthew set about cleaning the quill. Then, "Do you think I am a witch?" Rachel asked pointedly.

"I think," he replied after some deliberation, "that this town is the host to a very cunning evil. Whether it is demon or man, it does seem Satanic. More than that, I can't say."

"Neither can I," she said. "But no matter who—or what—cut my husband's throat and masqueraded as me in these filthy performances, I'll be the one to burn for it." Matthew couldn't deny her statement. That conflagration now seemed very near indeed.

Lies upon lies, Mrs. Nettles had said.

What she needs is a champion of truth.

Just as truth was sparse here, Matthew thought, so were champions. He was a clerk, nothing more. Not a magistrate, not an attorney . . . certainly not a champion.

He was certain of one thing, though; it had become clear to him, after the sickening ordeal of Buckner's testimony and the magistrate's forceful reaction. At the conclusion of these interviews, Woodward would be compelled to immediately order Rachel Howarth put to death. She would burn to the bone in a matter of days after that order had been read to the prisoner. And whose hand would scribe the sentence of death?

Matthew's own, of course. He had done it several times before; it was nothing new.

Except in this instance, he would go to his own grave pondering the pieces that did not fit, and agonized over the missing *why.*

He finished cleaning the quill and put it and the inkwell into the box, and then the box went into one of the desk's drawers—which Winston had obviously cleaned out before carting to the gaol, since the desk was absolutely empty—to await further need.

Then he stretched himself out in the straw—which was fresh thanks be to Mr. Green—closed his eyes, and tried to rest. It came to him only after a moment that he had reclined as far as possible from the bars that stood between his cage and Rachel Howarth's, and that in his right hand he gripped the Bible across his chest.

thirteen

BY THE TIME THE MAGISTRATE reached Dr. Shields's infirmary, which was a chalkwhite painted house on Harmony Street, he felt as if he were walking in a fog cloud. This dazed, opaque sensation was more than his physical distress; it was his mental burden, as well.

Woodward had just left the house of Lucretia Vaughan. Mrs. Vaughan had been summoned to the door by a lovely blonde girl of sixteen or thereabouts, whom the elder lady had introduced as her daughter Cherise. Upon returning the basket containing teapot and cups, Woodward had inquired why Mrs. Vaughan had wished the reddish-brown cup to be broken to pieces by Rachel Howarth.

"Surely you understand, being a sophisticated man of the city," Mrs. Vaughan had said, "that now the cup is much more valuable than before."

"Valuable?" he'd asked. "How is it that fragments of a cup are worth more than the whole?"

"Because *she* broke it," came the reply, which only further puzzled the magistrate. It must have shown on his face, because Mrs. Vaughan explained, "After the witch is put to death and Fount Royal is steadied again, the citizens of this town might wish to possess some token of the terrible ordeal we have been strong enough to endure." She gave a smile that Woodward could only describe as chilling. "It will take time, of course, but with the proper presentation the bits of broken cup might be sold as charms of good fortune."

"Pardon me?" Woodward had then felt the fog closing in around his head.

"I chose the nearest hue to blood-red that I could find," Mrs. Vaughan said, her tone of voice that of a sharper to a dimwit. "The blood of the witch. Or the scarlet tears of the witch. I haven't yet settled on one or the other. It's a matter of imagination, do you see?"

"I . . . fear my imagination isn't as developed as yours," Woodward said, a thick knot seemingly clogged in his throat.

"Thank you for returning these so promptly. At the appropriate time I can advertise that the pieces of cup broken by the witch were given to my own hand by the magistrate who executed her." Mrs. Vaughan now exhibited a slight frown. "Tell me—what's to become of the straw poppets?"

"The straw poppets?" he'd echoed.

"Yes. Surely you'll have no need of them after the witch is dead, will you?"

"Excuse me," Woodward had said. "I really must go."

And so he found himself—fogheaded under the gray-plated sky—reaching for the bellcord at Dr. Shields's door. Above the door, a sign painted in the medical colors of red, white, and blue announced this to be the shop of *Benj. Shields, Surgeon Barber.* Woodward pulled the cord and waited, and presently the door was opened by a portly, broad-faced woman with curly dark brown hair. He introduced himself, asked to be seen by Dr. Shields, and was admitted into a sparsely appointed parlor, the most notable feature of it being a gilded birdcage that held two yellow canaries. The woman, whose ample figure was contained by a beige dress and apron that might have served as a settler's tent, went through a door at the other side of the room and Woodward was left with the birds.

But not for very long, however, as within a minute or two the door opened again and the doctor appeared, his clothing a white blouse with sleeves rolled up, a wine-colored waistcoat, and charcoal-gray breeches. He wore his round-lensed spectacles, his long hair trailing over his shoulders. "Magistrate!" he said, and offered his hand. "To what do I owe this pleasure?"

"Would that pleasure was the purpose," Woodward answered, his voice—though quite husky—now in a fragile condition. "I fear I've been visited by ill health."

"Open your mouth, please," Shields instructed. "Angle your head back a bit, if you will." He peered in. "Oh my," he said, after the briefest of inspections. "Your throat appears quite swollen and aflame. You're in some pain, I would presume."

"Yes. Very much."

"No doubt. Come with me, let's have a better look."

Woodward followed the doctor through the door and along a hallway, past one room where there stood a basin of water, a chair, and a leather strop to keen the razor for the barbering duties, and past a second room that held three narrow beds. A young female with a plaster bandage around her right arm and her torpid face discolored by bruises lay in one of the beds, being fed a bowl of soup by the woman who'd admitted Woodward. He realized it must be Noles's unfortunate wife, who'd suffered the wrath of his carpet-beater.

A door into a third room further down the hallway was opened, and Shields said, "Sit there, please," as he motioned toward a chair positioned near the single window. The magistrate seated himself. Shields opened the shutters to let in the misty gray illumination. "My soul rose at the dawn," the doctor said, as he turned away to prepare the examination. "Then it fell back to earth and resides now in a puddle of mud."

"Myself the same. Will a full day of sun never again shine on the New World?"

"A debatable question, it seems."

Woodward considered the room into which he'd been led. It appeared to be both the physician's study and his apothecary. On one side of the chamber stood a timeworn desk and chair, next to which was a bookcase of what looked to be old medical tomes, by their thickness and the dark solemnity of their bindings. Opposite those furnishings was a long workbench built to the height of Dr. Shields's waist. Atop the bench, which had perhaps a dozen small drawers with ivory pulls constructed along its length, was a glassblower's nightmare of arcane bottles, beakers, jars, and the like; along with a set of measuring scales and various other instruments. On the wall, too, were mounted shelves that held more bottles and jars, many of the vessels murky with fluids and potions.

Shields scrubbed his hands with soap in a waterbowl. "You've just recently come into this condition? Or was it bothersome before you reached Fount Royal?"

"Just recently. It began as a slight soreness, but now . . . I can hardly swallow."

"Hmmm." He dried his hands upon a cloth and then opened one of the bench's drawers. "We must go down into your throat." He turned toward the magistrate again, and Woodward saw with a start that Shields was holding a pair of clippers suitable for shearing treelimbs.

"Oh," Shields said with a slight smile at Woodward's alarm. "What I mean to say is, we must *look* down into your throat." With the clippers he snipped a candle in two, then laid the dread shears aside and fitted one of the candle stubs into a small metal holder with a mirror fixed behind the flame so as to amplify its light. He lit the candle from a match, then took another instrument out of a drawer and positioned the desk's chair in front of his patient. "Open wide, please."

Woodward did. Shields held the candle near the magistrate's mouth and studied the scene. "Quite raw, it appears. Are you having difficulty breathing as well?"

"It *is* a labor, yes."

"Lean your head back, let me inspect your nostrils." Shields gave a grunt as he peered up that formidable proboscis. "Yes, quite swollen there, too. The right much more than the left, but the passage of air is equally endangered. Your mouth open again."

This time when Woodward obeyed, the doctor inserted a long metal probe that at its end held a square of cotton secured by a clamp. "Refrain from swallowing, please." The cotton swabbed along the back of Woodward's throat, and the magistrate was compelled to squeeze his eyes shut and fight the urge to gag or cry out as the pain was so acute. At last the probe was withdrawn, and Woodward saw—through a veil of tears—that a pasty yellow fluid had soaked the cotton.

"I've seen this ailment before, in varying degrees of severity," the doctor said. "Your condition lies at about the midpoint. Such is the price one pays for habitation at the edge of a swamp, enduring fetid air and damp humours. This constriction and drainage is therefore inflicting extreme irritation to your throat." He stood up and laid the probe and yellow-soaked cotton on the benchtop. "I'll paint your throat with a tonic that should relieve much of the pain. I have also a remedy for the breathing obstruction." As he was speaking, he removed the tainted cotton and inserted a fresh square into the clamp.

"Thank God I can find some relief!" Woodward said. "It was sheer torture having to speak at the testimony today!"

"Ah, the testimony." Shields selected a bottle from the wall-shelf and removed its stopper. "Jeremiah Buckner was the first witness? Mr. Winston told me you were beginning with him."

"That's correct."

"I know his story." Shields returned to his chair, carrying bottle and probe but minus the mirrored candle this time. "It's enough to shock the hair off a wigstand, isn't it?"

"I've never heard anything more sickening."

"Open, please." Shields dipped the cotton into the bottle and brought it out wet with a dark brown liquid. "This may sting a bit, but it's the rawness being soothed." He slid the probe in and Woodward braced himself. "Steady, now." The liquid-soaked cotton made contact. Woodward almost bit down on the probe, so fierce was the pain. New tears sprang to his eyes, his hands curled into fists, and he found himself thinking that this must be akin to a burning at the stake but without the smoke. "Steady, steady," the doctor said, pausing to dip the cotton into the bottle again. The contest with agony began once more, and Woodward realized his head was starting to twist on his neck in an involuntary effort to escape; thus it was akin, he thought in a fevered sort of humor, to being hanged as well as being burnt.

In another moment, though, the awful pain did begin to subside. Shields kept redipping the cotton into the bottle and swabbing liquid liberally over the back of Woodward's throat. "You should be feeling some relief by now," Shields said. "Are you?" Woodward nodded, tears streaking his face.

"This is my own mixture: Jesuit's Bark, limonum, and opium, made more firm by a base of oxymel. It's shown very excellent results in the past. I'm even considering applying for a label." He made a few more applications of the tonic and then, satisfied that the magistrate's throat was well done, sat back with a smile. "There! I wish all my patients were as sturdy as you, sir! Ah, just a moment!" He got up, went to one of the drawers, and returned with a linen cloth. "You might wish to use this."

"Thank you," Woodward croaked. He used the cloth as it was intended, to blot his tears.

"If your condition worsens in the next few days, we shall apply the tonic again at a greater strength. But I expect you'll feel much more yourself by tomorrow evening. . . . Elias Garrick is to be your next witness?"

"Yes."

"He's already told you his story. Why do you need to see him?"

"His testimony must be spoken onto the record."

Dr. Shields peered over his spectacles, looking every bit the barn owl. "I must warn you that prolonged speaking will further harm your throat. You should rest it, by all means."

"I'm seeing Garrick on Monday. I'll have the Sabbath to rest."

"Even Monday might be too soon. I'd recommend a week of as little speech as absolutely necessary."

"Impossible!" Woodward said. "I'd be a fine magistrate who couldn't speak!"

"Be that as it may, I'm simply giving you my advice." He again went to the workbench, where he put aside the probe and opened a blue ceramic jar. "This remedy will aid your air passages," he said, returning to Woodward with the jar. "Take one."

Woodward looked into the jar and saw what appeared to be a dozen or so small brown sticks, each perhaps two inches in length. "What are they?"

"A botanical remedy, from the hemp plant. I grow and cure the weed myself, as it seems to be one of the few crops that will thrive in this atrocious climate. Go ahead; you'll find it quite a useful drug."

Woodward selected one of the sticks, which had a rather oily texture, and started to slide it into his mouth, intending to chew it. "No, no!" Shields said. "It's smoked, much as one would puff a pipe."

"Smoked?"

"Yes. Except for one difference: the smoke is pulled deeply into the lungs, let settle, and then slowly exhaled." Shields brought the candle over. "Put it between your lips and draw on it." The magistrate obeyed, and Shields touched the candle's flame to the stick's slightly twisted end. A thin plume of bluish smoke began to rise. "Draw it in," Shields instructed. "It will do you no good if you don't."

Woodward inhaled as deeply as possible. He felt the bitter-tasting smoke sear his lungs, and then the bout of coughing that burst forth from him brought fresh tears. He bent over, coughing and weeping.

"The first several inhalations *are* difficult," the doctor admitted. "Here, I'll show you how it's done." He seated himself, chose one of the hemp sticks, and lit it. Then he inhaled with a familiar ease. After a slight pause, he let the smoke exit his mouth. "You see? It does take some practise."

Even so, Woodward noted that Shields's eyes were glistening. He tried it again, and again was attacked by a coughing fit.

Shields said, "You may be taking in too much smoke. Small doses are the better."

"Do you insist I suffer this remedy?"

"I do. You'll breathe so much more freely." Shields inhaled again, uptilted his chin, and let the smoke drift toward the ceiling.

Woodward tried it a third time. The coughing was not so severe. The fourth time, he coughed only twice. By the sixth inhalation, there did seem to be some lessening of the pressure in his head.

Dr. Shields had almost smoked his down to the halfway point. He regarded the burning tip, and then he stared fixedly at Woodward. "You know, Magistrate," he said after a long silence, "you're a very fine man."

"And why is that, sir?"

"Because you take Robert Bidwell's bluff and bluster without complaint. You must be a fine man. By God, you must be verging on sanctity."

"I think not. I'm just a servant"

"Oh, more than a servant! You're master of the law, which makes you Bidwell's superior, since he so desperately needs what only *you* can supply."

"But I might say the same for you, sir," Woodward answered. He inhaled deeply, let settle, and then exhaled. The smoke, as it rose, seemed to him to break apart, merge, and break apart again like the movement of a beautiful kaleidoscope. "You are master of the healing arts."

"Would that I were!" Shields gave a hollow laugh, then leaned forward to give a conspiratorial whisper: "Most of the time, I don't know what the hell I'm doing."

"Oh, you're joking!"

"No." Shields drew again and the smoke spooled from his mouth. "It's quite pitifully true."

"I think your honesty has lost its brindle. I mean . . ." Woodward had to pause to collect the words. The lessening of the pressure in his head also seemed to have shaken the proper vocabulary from his brain. "Your *modesty* has lost its *bridle,* I think."

"Being a physician here . . . in this town, at this time . . . is a depressing occupation, sir. I have occasion to stroll past the cemetery in visiting my patients. Sometimes I feel I should set up office amid the graves, as there would not be as much travel required." He held the hemp stick between his lips and pulled rather violently on it. The amount of smoke that poured from his mouth was copious. Behind his spectacles, his eyes had become reddened and sad. "It's the swamp, of course. Human beings were not meant to live so near to such a miasma. It burdens the soul and weakens the spirit. Add upon that dismal picture the continual rain and the presence of the witch, and I cannot for the life of me see how Bidwell's town can thrive. People are leaving here every day . . . one way or the other. No." He shook his head. "Mark Fount Royal as doomed."

"If you really believe so, why don't you take your wife and leave?"

"My *wife?*"

"Yes." Woodward blinked heavily. His air passages were feeling so much clearer, but his mind seemed befogged. "The woman who admitted me. Isn't she your wife?"

"Oh, you mean Mrs. Heussen. My nurse. No, my wife and two sons—no, *one* son—live in Boston. My wife is a seamstress. I did have two sons. One of them . . ." He inhaled in a way that struck Woodward as being needful. ". . . the eldest, was murdered by a highwayman on the Philadelphia Post Road. That would be . . . oh . . . eight years ago, I suppose, but still some wounds refuse the remedy of time. To have a child—no matter what age—snatched away from you in such a fashion . . ." He trailed off, watching the blue smoke swirl in currents and eddies as it rose toward the ceiling. "Pardon me," he said presently, lifting a hand to rub his eyes. "My mind wandered."

"If I may ask," Woodward ventured, "why does your wife remain in Boston?"

"You're not suggesting that she come *here* to live, are you? Christ's Blood, I wouldn't hear of it! No, she's much better off in

Boston, where the medical facilities are modern. They've tamed their salt marshes and tidepools up there, as well, so the damp humours aren't so vengeful." He took a quick sip of the hemp and slowly spewed out the smoke. "For the same reasons, Winston left his family in England and Bidwell wouldn't dream of having his wife make the voyage—not even on one of his own ships! You know, Johnstone's wife so detested the place that she returned to England and refused to make the crossing again. Do you blame her? This isn't a woman's land, that's a surety!"

Woodward, though this fog was rapidly overcoming his mind, remembered what he had intended to ask Dr. Shields. "About Schoolmaster Johnstone," he said, his tongue thick and seemingly coated with cat fur. "I have to inquire about this, and I know it must sound very strange, but . . . have you ever seen his deformed knee?"

"His knee? No, I haven't. I'm not sure I would care to, since deformation is not my area of interest. I *have* sold him bandages and liniment for his discomfort, though." Shields frowned. "Why do you ask such a question?"

"My curiosity," he replied, though it was more Matthew's curiosity that his own. "Uh . . . would it be unlikely that Mr. Johnstone could . . . for instance . . . run or climb stairs?"

The doctor looked at Woodward as if the magistrate's senses had flown the coop.

"I take it that he could not," Woodward said.

"Most certainly not. Well, he might be able to climb stairs one at the time, but I think the effort would be considerable." He cocked his head to one side, his owlish eyes bright. "What are these questions about, Isaac? May I call you Isaac?"

"Yes, of course. And may I call you Benjamin?"

"Absolutely. So: Isaac, my friend, why these questions pertaining to Johnstone's knee?"

"A thief entered Mr. Bidwell's house early this morning," Woodward said, leaning his head forward. Smoke moved sinuously between himself and the doctor. "Whoever it was, he stole a gold coin from my clerk's room—"

"Ah, yes." Shields nodded. "The famous coin. I heard about it from Malcolm Jennings when he came to have a boil lanced."

"I encountered the thief in the hallway," Woodward continued. "He was a big man, with the strength of a bull. I fought him as best I could, but as he had caught me from behind I was at the disadvantage." It seemed more true now in his recollection that this had occurred, and who was to say it had not? "Everything happened so quickly," Woodward said. "I didn't see his face. He knocked a lamp from my hand and fled down the staircase. Of course I know Mr. Johnstone's deformity is severe, but . . . my clerk wanted to learn whether you've inspected his knee, and if he's capable of such an action."

Shields laughed. "Surely you're not serious! Alan Johnstone a *thief!* I should say that in all of Fount Royal there's no one who'd be less a thief! The man's from a wealthy family!"

"I presumed so, since he did attend All Souls' College at Oxford, but one never knows."

"I've personally seen his gold pocket watch, inscribed with his initials. He owns a gold ring with a ruby in it the size of a man's fingernail!" Shields laughed again, rather giddily. "A thief indeed! No, it wouldn't be possible for Alan to run down a staircase. You've seen how he depends on his cane."

"Yes, I have. But the theory that I believe my clerk is advancing—and understand, please, that he's young and his imagination roams unrestrained—is that Mr. Johnstone's knee *appears* to be malformed, but is in truth—*his* theory, now—as normal as yours or mine."

Shields blinked, took a sip of smoke, blinked again, and then his face broke into a merry grin. "Oh, you're wearing a jester's cap now, is that it?"

Woodward shrugged. "My clerk is quite serious. Therefore I had to make the inquiry."

The doctor's grin faltered. "This is the most . . . unbalanced thing I've ever heard! You can see the deformity of his knee through his stocking! He's been in Fount Royal for three years! Why in the world would it serve him to devise such a pretense?"

"I have no idea. Again, please understand that Matthew is a very intelligent young man, but that sometimes his mind is un-fettered by common sense."

"I should say so!" Shields smoked his remedy some more, and so did the magistrate. Woodward was feeling quite better now, most of the pain having left his throat and his breathing passages much clearer. The movement of the smoke entranced him, and the quality of the light entering the room was like gray silk. "I *will* tell you something about Alan that you might find of interest," Shields suddenly confided. "About his wife, I mean." He pitched his voice a little lower. "Her name was Margaret. She was . . . how shall I say this . . . of a peculiar character."

"In what way?"

"A lovely woman, no doubt. But . . . her bell was somewhat cracked. I never witnessed any of her outbursts, but I heard from reliable sources that she was quite the hellion, with a penchant for throwing whatever came to hand. Winston witnessed it, one night at Bidwell's house. The woman flew into a rage and smashed a platter of chicken against the wall. And there was the other thing." Shields let his sentence hang while he puffed his hemp stick, which was beginning to burn down between his fin-gers. "One moment." He got up, went to the workbench, and returned with the small stub of hemp clamped in the probe as the cotton had been. He sat down again, a mischievous shine in his eyes. "Mrs. Johnstone and the husband of that poor woman in the infirmary . . ." He motioned with an angling of his head in the direction of the other room. "They had a number of assignations."

"Noles and Johnstone's wife?"

"Correct. And quite bold about it, as I recall. Many knew what was going on—including Noles's wife. In time someone told Alan, but I think it came as no surprise to him. Well, Mar-garet despised Fount Royal anyway—she made no secret of that—and so Alan took her back to England to live with her parents. She was of wealthy stock too—her father was in the tex-tile business—but I believe she was a trifle overbred. A few months later, Alan returned here and the matter was forgotten."

"Adultery is a serious offense," Woodward said. "Did he not wish to press charges?"

"I honestly think he was relieved to be rid of the woman. She was a menace to his reputation, and certainly lacking in decorum. Alan is a quiet, thoughtful man who keeps to himself for the most part, but he does have a cutting wit."

"He must be a dedicated teacher, to have returned so soon to Fount Royal."

"That he is. He's taken it upon himself to educate not only the children here, but many of the farmers who can't read. And of course the salary Bidwell pays him is hardly enough to buy a needle and thread, but as I say the schoolmaster has money of his own."

Woodward nodded, drawing once more on his hemp stick; it had burned quite well down, and he could feel its heat between his fingers. In fact, he felt very warm all over now, and was perspiring. This was a good thing, he thought. It must mean that he was sweating out the bad humours. His eyes felt heavy-lidded, and without much prompting he could lie down and take a nap. "What about Winston?" he asked.

"What of him?"

"I mean, what do you know about him?"

Shields grinned, smoke leaking between his teeth. "Am I on the witness stand, sir?"

"No, and I don't intend to sound like a magistrate. I'd simply like to know more about the people here."

"I see," Shields said, though from his tone of voice it was clear he still believed court was in session. After a pause of deliberation, he said, "Edward Winston is a loyal mule. You know that Winston was Bidwell's office manager in London, don't you? He's an excellent administrator, organizer, and bean counter. He, too, keeps quite to himself. I think in his case he's a bit uncomfortable around people. But it *was* his idea to bring the maskers here."

"The maskers?"

"Yes. The actors, that is. Bidwell's fond of the theater. For the past three summers, a travelling company has come to enact a morality play. It does seem to bring some culture and civilization out here in the wilderness. At least, the citizens have something to look forward to every year. They come in mid-July, so it's a pity you won't be present to see them." Shields took one last puff and realized he had reached the end of his stick. "Then again," he said, "Fount Royal may not be here in mid-July, either."

"What of Nicholas Paine?" Woodward asked. "Do you know him well?"

"Nicholas Paine," the doctor repeated. He smiled slightly. "Yes, I do know him well."

"He seems an able man." Woodward was thinking of that term Paine had used: *black-flagger.* "What do you know of his history?"

"I know he has one. A history, I mean."

"I'd call that a cryptic remark," Woodward said when Shields lapsed into silence.

"Nicholas is a very private man," Shields offered. "He has been a jack-of-all-trades. Was a seaman for a number of years, I understand. But he's not open to discussing his past at much length."

"Is he married? Does he have a family?"

"He *was* married, when he was a younger man. His wife perished from an illness that caused her to suffer fits until she died."

Woodward had lifted the small stub to his mouth for a final inhalation; now, however, his hand froze. "Fits?" he said. He swallowed thickly. "What kind of fits?"

"Convulsions, I suppose." The doctor shrugged. "Some form of fever, most probably. Or the plague. But it was long ago, and I'm sure Paine wouldn't care to speak about it. In fact, I know he would not."

"The plague," Woodward repeated. His eyes had become glazed, not entirely from the bitterly compelling smoke of his remedy.

"Isaac?" Shields, noting the other man's vacant stare, touched the magistrate's sleeve. "What is it?"

"Oh, forgive me." Woodward blinked, waved some of the fumes away from his face, and brought himself back to his surroundings. "I was thinking, that's all."

Shields nodded, a sly smile twisting his mouth. "Yes. Thinking of whom you might ask questions about *me*, is that correct?"

"No. About something else entirely."

"But you *are* planning on inquiring about me, are you not? It would only be fair, since you've pumped the well concerning the schoolmaster, Mr. Winston, and Mr. Paine. Ah, I believe you're done with that! May I?" He took the burnt-down stub from Woodward's hand and placed it, along with the remnant of his own, into a small pewter jar, which he then closed with a hinged lid. "Are you feeling better now?"

"Yes. Remarkably so."

"Good. As I said, you might have to repeat the treatment according to your constitution. We shall see." Shields stood up. "Now allow me to escort you to Van Gundy's tavern for a cup of his excellent hard cider. Also he has a stock of peanuts on hand, as I'm feeling quite hungry. Will you join me?"

"I would be honored."

When the magistrate stood from his chair, his legs almost betrayed him. His head was swimming and strange lights seemed to dance behind his eyes. But the pain in his throat had all but vanished, and his breathing was miraculously cleared. The doctor's remedy, he thought, was surely a wonder drug.

"Sometimes the smoke does play tricks with the balance," Shields said. "Here, take my arm and a'tavern we shall go!"

"A tavern, a tavern!" Woodward said. "My kingdom for a tavern!" This struck him as riotously funny, and he began to laugh at his own wit. The laughter was a little too loud and a little too harsh, however, and even in his lightened state of mind he knew what he was trying to cloak.

fourteen

WITH THE FADING of the light, the rats grew bold.

Matthew had heard their squeakings and rustlings all the afternoon, but they'd not yet made an appearance. He'd been relieved to find that the rodents had not emerged to attack either his lunch or supper—meager beef broth and two slices of black bread, humble but stomach-filling—but now, ever since Green had closed the roof hatch and left only a single lantern burning on its hook, the creatures were creeping out of their nooks and crannies to claim the place.

"Watch your fingers," Rachel told him, sitting on her bench. "They'll give you a bite if you try to strike them. If one crawls on you tonight, it's best to lie perfectly still. They'll be sniffing at you, that's all."

"The one that bit your shoulder," Matthew said. He was standing up, his back against the wall. "Was it only sniffing?"

"No, I tried to get that one away from my waterbucket. I found out they can jump like cats, and I also learned they're going to have your water no matter what you do."

Matthew picked up his own bucket of water, which Green had recently filled from a larger container, and he drank copiously from it. Enough, he hoped, to quench his thirst for the night.

Then he placed the bucket on the floor in the opposite corner, as far away from his bed of straw as possible.

"Green only brings fresh water every other day," Rachel said, watching him. "You won't mind drinking after the rats when you get thirsty enough."

Another quandary had presented itself to Matthew, far worse than the problem of the rodents and the waterbucket. Green had also brought in a fresh bucket to be used for elimination. Matthew had realized he was going to have to pull down his breeches and use it—sooner or later—right in front of the woman. And, likewise, she would be using her own without benefit of a shade or screen. He thought he might endure two more lashes added to his sentence if he could have at least a modicum of privacy, but it was not to be.

Suddenly a dark shape darted from a small crevice in the wall of Matthew's cell and went straight for the bucket. As Matthew watched, the rodent—black-furred, red-eyed, and as long as his hand—climbed swiftly up the bucket's side and leaned over its rim to lap the water, its claws gripping the wood. A second one followed, and then a third. The things interrupted their drinking to chatter like washerwomen trading gossip at the common well, and then they broke ranks and squeezed their bodies again into the crevice.

It was going to be a very long night.

Matthew had several books on hand, courtesy of the magistrate, who'd brought the tomes from Bidwell's library that afternoon, but as the light was so meager there would be no reading tonight. Woodward had told him he'd had an interesting conversation with Dr. Shields, and would reveal more when Matthew was set free. Now, though, Matthew felt the walls and bars closing in upon him; without proper light by which to read or write, and with rats scratching and scurrying in the logs, he feared he might lose his grip on his decorum and shame himself before Rachel Howarth. It shouldn't matter, of course, because after all she was an accused murderess—and much worse—but still he desired to present himself as a sturdy oak, not the thin willow he felt to be.

It was warm and steamy in the gaol. Rachel cupped her hands into her waterbucket and dampened her face, washing off the salty perspiration that had collected on her cheeks and forehead. She cooled her throat with the water as well, and paid no heed when two rats squeaked and fought in the corner of her cage.

"How long is it that you've been here?" Matthew asked, sitting on his bench with his knees pulled up to his chin.

"This is the second week of May, is it not?"

"Yes."

"I was brought here on the third day of March."

Matthew flinched at the very thought of it. No matter what she might have done, she was made of sterner stuff than he. "How do you stand it, day after day?"

She finished bathing her throat before she replied. "Do I have any choice but to stand it? I suppose I could become a gibbering fool. I suppose I could break down, fall to my knees, and confess witchcraft at the boots of fine Mr. Bidwell, but should I go to my death that way?"

"You could recite the Lord's Prayer before him. That might win you some mercy."

"No," she said, and she aimed those fierce amber eyes at him, "it would not. As I told you, I refuse to recite something that has no meaning in this town. And my recitation of it would change no one's mind about my guilt." She cupped her hands again and this time let the water flow through her wild mane of ebony hair. "You heard what the magistrate said. If I spoke the Lord's Prayer, it might be a trick of the Devil to save my skin."

Matthew nodded. "I grant you, you're right. Bidwell and the others have made their opinions about you, and nothing will shake them."

"Except one thing," she said firmly. "Discovering who really murdered the reverend and my husband, and who plotted this evil against me."

"Discovery is only half the solution. The other half would be the presentation of proof, without which discovery is hollow."

When Matthew was silent again he was aware of the noises the rats were making, so he chose to speak in an effort to keep his mind busied. "Who would have cause to commit those crimes? Do you have any idea?"

"No."

"Did your husband anger someone? Did he cheat someone? Did he—"

"This is not about Daniel," she interrupted. "It is about *me*. I was chosen as the object of this farce because of the very reasons I was hounded from their church. My mother was Portuguese, my father a dark Irishman. But I have my mother's color and her eyes. They mark me as surely as a raven among doves. I alone am of this color, here in this town. Who would not look upon me as someone different . . . someone to be *feared*, because I am different?"

Matthew had thought of another reason, as well: her exotic beauty. He doubted that a woman more comely than Rachel Howarth had ever set foot in Fount Royal. Her nigrescent coloring was surely objectionable to many—if not most—in this society of pallid whitebreads, but that very same hue was as the burnished flesh of a forbidden fruit. He'd never in his life seen anyone the equal of her. She seemed more proud animal than suffering human, and he thought that this quality too could stir the fire of a man's lust. Or fan the crackling embers of another woman's jealousy.

"The evidence against you," he said, and quickly amended himself: "The *apparent* evidence against you is overwhelming. Buckner's story may be riddled with holes, but he believes what he said today to be true. The same with Elias Garrick. He firmly believes he witnessed you in . . . shall we say . . . intimate accord with Satan."

"Lies," she said.

"I have to disagree. I don't think they're lying."

"So you *do* believe me to be a witch, then?"

"I don't know what I believe," he said. "Take the poppets, for instance. They were found under a floorboard of your kitchen. A woman named Cara—"

"Grunewald," Rachel said. "She pinched her husband's ear for speaking to me, long before any of this happened."

"Madam Grunewald saw the location of the poppets in a dream," Matthew continued. "How do you account for that?"

"Simply. She made the poppets and put them there herself."

"If she hated you so deeply, then why did she leave Fount Royal? Why did she not stay to testify before the magistrate? Why did she not satisfy her hatred by remaining here to watch your execution?"

Now Rachel was staring at the floor. She shook her head.

Matthew said, "If *I* had made the poppets and hidden them beneath the floorboard, I would make certain to be in the crowd on the day of your departure from this earth. No, I don't believe Madam Grunewald had a hand in creating them."

"Nicholas Paine," Rachel said suddenly, and looked again at Matthew. "He was one of the three men who broke down my door that March morning, bound me with ropes, and threw me into the back of a wagon. He also was one of the men who found the poppets."

"Who were the other two men who took you into custody?"

"Hannibal Green and Aaron Windom. I never shall forget that dawn. They dragged me from my bed, and Green locked his arm around my throat to stop my screaming. I spat in Windom's face and got a slap for it."

"Paine, Garrick, James Reed, and Kelvin Bonnard discovered the poppets," Matthew said, recalling what Garrick had said on the night of their arrival. "Can you think of any possible reason Paine or any of those others might have fashioned them and hidden them there?"

"No."

"All right, then." Matthew saw another dark streak go across the floor. He watched the rat climb up the side of the waterbucket and drink. "Let us say that Paine, for whatever reason, did make the poppets and put them under the floorboard. Why should it be Madam Grunewald who saw their location in a dream? Why should it not be Paine himself, if he was so eager to present physical evidence against you?" He pondered the question and thought he might have an answer. "Did Paine have . . . uh . . . a relationship with Madam Grunewald?"

"I don't think so," Rachel replied. "Cara Grunewald was as fat as a pig and had half her nose eaten away by the pox."

"Oh." Matthew pondered some more. "Less reason she should leave Fount Royal, then, if she had made the poppets and knew you to be falsely accused. No, whoever fashioned them is still here. Of that I'm positive. A person who would go to the effort of such deceit would make sure he—or she—had the satisfaction of watching you die." He glanced through the bars at her. "Pardon my bluntness."

Rachel said nothing for a while, as the rats continued to squeak and scurry in the walls. Then, "You know, I'm really beginning to believe you've not been sent here to spy on me."

"You should. I'm here—unfortunately—on a criminal offense."

"Involving the blacksmith, did you say?"

"I entered his barn without permission," Matthew explained. "He attacked me, I injured his face, and he desired satisfaction. Therefore the three-day sentence and three lashes."

"Seth Hazelton is a very strange man. I wouldn't doubt that he attacked you, but what was the reason?"

"I discovered a sack hidden in the barn that he desired not to have brought to light. According to him, it was full of his wife's belongings. But I think it was something else altogether."

"What, then?"

He shook his head. "I don't know, but I do intend to find out."

"How old are you?" she asked suddenly.

"Twenty years."

"Have you always been so curious?"

"Yes," he answered. "Always."

"From what I saw today, the magistrate doesn't appreciate your curiosity."

Matthew said, "He appreciates the truth. Sometimes we arrive at it from different routes."

"If he chooses to believe what's claimed about me, he is lost in the wilderness," she said. "Tell me why it is that you—a clerk—seem to grant me more innocence than does a learned magistrate of the law."

Matthew thought about this point before he gave a reply. "Perhaps it's because I never met a witch before."

"And the magistrate has?"

"He's never tried a witch, but he does know judges who have. I think also that he was more impressed by the Salem trials than I, since I was only thirteen years at the time and still in an almshouse." Matthew rested his chin upon one of his knees. "The magistrate has in his sphere of learning all the accumulated knowledge of English law," he said. "Some of that knowledge is built on a framework of medieval belief. As I am a lowly clerk and have not yet been immersed in such knowledge, I do not hold so strongly to its conceptions. You should realize, however, that Magistrate Woodward is indeed a liberal jurist. If he were entirely of the medieval mind, you would be burnt by now."

"What's he waiting for, then? If I'm going to burn anyway, why hear these witnesses?"

"The magistrate wants to give you an opportunity to answer all the charges. It's the proper way of procedure."

"Damn the procedure!" Rachel snapped, and she stood up. "Damn the charges! They're all lies!"

"Profanity will not help your position," Matthew said calmly. "I'd suggest you refrain from it."

"What *will* help my position?" she demanded, approaching the bars. "Shall I fall on my knees and beg mercy for crimes I haven't committed? Shall I sign over my husband's land and all my possessions and swear upon the Bible that I shall never bewitch the citizens of Fount Royal again? Tell me! What can I possibly do to save my life?"

It was a good question. So good, in fact, that Matthew was unable to supply an answer. The best he could manage was: "There is some hope."

"Ah, *hope!*" Rachel said bitterly. Her hands curled around the bars. "Perhaps you're not a spy, but you're a liar and you know you are. There is no hope for me. There never was any hope, not since that morning I was dragged from my house. I am going to be executed for crimes I have not committed, and the murderer of my husband will go free. Where's the hope in *that?*"

"Hey, there! Quiet down!" It was Hannibal Green, thundering from the entrance. He came into the gaol, bearing a lantern, and behind him trudged the filthy, ragged figure Matthew had last seen by the light of a burning house. Gwinett Linch had his ratsack at his side, a cowhide bag over his shoulder, and his sticker in his hand.

"Brought you some company," Green rumbled. "Gonna clean this hole up a bit."

Rachel didn't respond. Tight-lipped, she returned to her bench and sat down, then she covered her head and face with her cowl again.

"Which one'll do ye?" Green asked of the ratcatcher, and Linch motioned toward the cage opposite Matthew's. Linch entered the cell and used his foot to brush aside the layer of dirty straw from the floor in a small circle. Then he reached into a pocket of his breeches and his hand emerged to throw a few dozen dried kernels of corn into the circle. Again his hand went into his pocket, and then a number of small pieces of potato joined the corn kernels. He produced a wooden jar from the cowhide bag, out of which he shook a brown powdery substance around the circle's perimeter. The same brown powder was shaken here and there in the straw, and applied at the base of the cell's walls.

"You gonna need me?" Green asked.

Linch shook his head. "I mi' be a while."

"Here, I'll give you the keys. You can lock up when you're done. Remember to put out the lantern."

The exchange of the keys was made, after which Green hurried out. Linch shook more of the brown powder into the straw, making trails between the corners of the walls and the circle.

"What is that?" Matthew inquired. "Some kind of poison?"

"It's most ground sugar," Linch answered. "With a teech of opium mixed to it. Got to get them rats drowsy, slow 'em down some." He returned the lid to the wooden jar and put it back in the cowhide bag. "Why? You thinkin' of robbin' my job?"

"I think *not*."

Linch grinned. He was listening to the squeakings and squealings of the rats, which had obviously caught scent of the feast that was being offered to them. Linch put on his deerskin gloves and then with smooth familiarity removed the piece of wood that secured the single blade at the end of his sticker. From his bag he brought out a fearsome appliance that had five curved blades, much like small scythes, and this he twisted into position on the sticker's tip. Two metal clips were forced into grooves to lock the ugly implement, and then Linch regarded it with obvious pride. "Ever see such a thing, boy?" he asked. "I can strike two or three at a time with this. Thought it up myself."

"An artful device, I'm sure."

"A *useful* device," Linch corrected. "Hazelton fashioned it for me. He's an inventor, once he puts his mind to a task." He cocked his head toward a rustling in the corner.

"Ah, listen to 'em! Fightin' to eat their last meal!" His grin widened. "Hey, witch!" he called to Rachel. "You gonna give me a tumble 'fore you burn?"

She didn't dignify his request with a reply or even a movement.

"You get over close to her, boy, and stick out your cock," Linch said. "She mi' suck it for you." He laughed as Matthew's face bloomed red, and then he pulled the cell's bench next to the cleared-off circle. When it was situated as he pleased, Linch left the cell to pluck the lantern from its hook and he brought it into the cage with him. He put it down on the floor a few feet away from the circle, then he sat upon the bench with his legs crossed beneath him and the five-bladed sticker held in a two-handed grip. "Won't be long now," he announced. "They're gettin' 'emselves a taste of that sweet stupidity."

Matthew saw the ratcatcher's luminous pale gray eyes glitter in the dim candlelight. They might have been the icy eyes of a specter rather than those of a human being. Linch spoke again, in a low, soft, almost singsong cadence: *"Come out, come out, my dames and dandies. Come out, come out, and taste my candies."* He repeated it twice more, each time becoming softer and more song than speech.

And then, indeed, a large black rat did enter the deadly circle. It sniffed at a piece of potato, its tail twitching; then it grabbed up a corn kernel between its teeth and fled for the darkness again.

"Come out, come out," Linch sang, all but whispering. He stared at the circle, waiting for the rodents to appear in his field of vision. "Come out, come out, and taste my candies."

Another rat appeared, grabbed up a corn kernel, and fled. But the third rat that entered the circle moved more sluggishly, and Matthew knew it must be feeling the effects of Linch's sugared opium. This benumbed rodent chewed on one of the potatoes for a moment, then stood up on its hind legs to stare at the candleflame as if it were a celestial light.

Linch was very fast. The sticker whipped down in a blur of motion and there was a high-pitched squeal as the rat was impaled. At once Linch snapped the small beast's neck, then plucked the carcass from its blade and made a deposit in his sack. All of this had taken only a very few seconds, and now Linch held the sticker ready again and he was softly singing. "Come out, come out, my dames and dandies. Come out, come out, and taste my candies . . ."

Within a minute, Matthew had witnessed two more executions and a near-miss. Linch might be disgusting, Matthew thought, but he was certainly proficient at his task.

The rats that were entering the circle now showed signs of lethargy. Feasting on the sugar and opium had clearly robbed them of much of their survival instinct. A few of them still had the speed to escape Linch's blades, but most perished before they could turn tail. Several died so bewildered they didn't even squeal as they were pierced.

After twenty or more executions there was quite a lot of rodent blood in the circle, yet the rats kept coming, too drug-fogged to be daunted from the promise of such treats. Every once in a while Linch would repeat in that soft, singsong tone his little ditty about dandies and candies, but it was such an easy massacre that it seemed a waste of breath. Down came the sticker, and rarely did Linch misjudge his aim. Soon the ratcatcher was killing them two at a time.

In forty minutes or so, the number of rodents began to subside. Matthew presumed that either Linch had killed the majority of gaolhouse rats, or that at last the odors of blood and carnage were strong enough to warn them away even through the numbing effects of the—as Linch had put it—"sweet stupidity." The ratcatcher, too, seemed thoroughly fatigued by the slaughter, which had bloodied his gloves and bulged his sack.

One small gray specimen, weaving around like a drunken lord, entered the circle. As Matthew watched, intrigued not by the grisly spectacle but by Linch's speed and surety of dispatch, the little rat nibbled at a kernel of corn and then began to chase its tail with ferocious intent. Around and around it went in a mad spin, with Linch's sticker poised above it waiting to strike. At last the rat gave up the chase and lay on its belly as if exhausted. Matthew expected the sticker to flash down and a blade to bite deep, but Linch stayed his hand.

The ratcatcher gave a long, weary sigh. "You know," he said quietly, "they ain't such terrible creatures. Got to eat, just like anybody. Got to *live*. They came over on the ships, same as the people did. They're smart beasts; they know that where the people are, that's where they'll find food. No, they ain't so terrible." He leaned over and touched a finger to some of the sugared opium he'd scattered on the floor, and then he pressed the finger to the rat's mouth. Whether it ate the offering or not,

Matthew couldn't tell, but the rodent was far too stupified to flee.

"Hey, watch this trick," Linch said. He reached over, picked up the lantern, and began to move it in a slow, sinuous circle above the gray rat. The rodent just lay there, seemingly uninterested, its body stretched out next to a gnawed lump of potato. Linch kept the movement slow and steady, and presently Matthew saw the rat's tail twitch and its head angle up toward the mysterious glow that was circling its theater of night. A minute passed. Linch kept moving the lantern around and around, with no discernible reduction or addition of speed. The candlelight glinted red in the eyes of the rat, and ice-white in the eyes of the ratcatcher.

Linch whispered, "Up, my pretty. Up, up, my pretty." The rat's tail continued to twitch, its eyes followed the light, but otherwise it remained stationary.

"Up, up," Linch whispered, again almost in a singsong cadence. *"Up, up, my pretty."* The lantern went around and around again. Linch bent his head toward the rodent, his untamed brows knitting with concentration. "Up, up," he spoke, a compelling note entering his voice. "Up, up."

Suddenly the rat gave a shiver and stood on its hind legs. Balancing on its tail, it began to circle with the progress of the lantern, like a tiny dog begging for a bone. Matthew watched with absolute fascination, realizing the rat in its bewildered state was transfixed by the candle. The rodent's eyes were directed to the flame, its stubby front legs clawing at the air as if desiring union with that which made such a strange and beautiful illumination. Who knew what the rat was seeing—by benefit of the sugared opium—there at the center of the fire?

"Dance for me," Linch whispered. "A reel, if you please." He circled the lantern a bit faster, and it seemed the rodent turned faster as well, though this might have been Matthew's imagination. Indeed, one might imagine the rat had become a dancer in accord with Linch's command. Its hind legs were shivering, about to collapse, yet still the rat sought communion with the flame.

"Pretty, pretty one," Linch said, in a voice as soft as a touch of mist on the cheek. And then he brought the sticker down, not hurriedly but rather with an air of resignation. Two of the blades pierced the rat's exposed belly and the rodent stiffened and shrieked. It bared its teeth and gnashed at the air, as most of its brothers and sisters had done in their death agonies. Linch put the lantern aside, broke the rat's neck with a quick jerk of his right hand, and the bloody carcass went into the sack with the others.

"How'd you like that?" he asked Matthew, his grin wide and expectant of praise.

"Quite impressive," Matthew said. "You might find employ in a circus, if you would spare the life of your partner."

Linch laughed. He removed a dark-stained cloth from his bag and began to clean the sticker's five blades, which meant the executions had come to an end. "I *was* in the circus," he said as he blotted away the blood. "Nine, ten years ago back in England. Used rats in my act. Dressed 'em up in little suits, made 'em dance just as you saw. They have a taste of ale or rum—or stronger—and a candle makes 'em think they're seein' God. Whatever God is to a rat, I mean."

"How come you to leave the circus?"

"Didn't get on so well with the bastard who owned it. I was makin' the lion's share of money for him, but he was payin' me lamb's wages. Anyhow, the plague's got so bad over there your audience is all ribs and teeth." He shrugged. "I found me a better way to earn my livin'."

"Ratcatching?" Matthew realized he'd spoken it a shade distastefully.

"Gainful elimination of pests," Linch answered. "Like I told you, every town's got to have a ratcatcher. If there's anythin' on earth I know about, it's *rats*. And people, too," he added. "I know enough about people to be happy I spend most of my time with rats." He shook the heavy sack full of carcasses. "Even if they *are* dead ones."

"A delightful sentiment," Matthew said.

Linch stood up, the ratsack attached to his belt. He returned the bloodied cloth to the cowhide bag and slipped its strap around his shoulder. "I been here near two years," he said. "Long enough to know this is a good town, but it ain't got a chance while that witch stays alive." He nodded toward Rachel in her cage. "Ought to take her out come Monday mornin' and finish her off. Put her out of her misery and the rest of us out of ours, too."

"Has she done anything against you?" Matthew asked.

"No. Not yet, I mean to say. But I know what she's done, and what she's like to do 'fore it's over." He held the sticker in his right hand and picked up the lantern with his left. "If I was you, boy, I'd watch my back tonight."

"Thank you for your concern, sir."

"You're so very welcome." Linch gave a mocking bow. When he had straightened up, he narrowed his eyes and looked around the cell. "Believe I've cleaned the place might fairly. Maybe a few more still hidin', but none much to worry about. I'll say good night to you and the witch, then." He left the cell and started off, still carrying the lantern.

"Wait!" Matthew said, his hands clenching the bars. "Aren't you going to leave the light?"

"What, this stub of a candle? Ain't an hour of burnin' left in it. Anyway, how am I supposed to see to lock up? No, I'm takin' it with me." Without a further word Linch walked out of the gaol and the darkness was total. There was the sound of a chain rattling as Linch secured the entrance, and then the awful silence descended.

Matthew stayed exactly where he was for a minute or more, still gripping the bars. He stared toward the gaol's doorway, hoping beyond hope that Linch, or someone, would return with a lantern, because this darkness was a brutally terrible thing. He could smell the blood of rats. He felt his nerves starting to unravel like axe-hacked ropes.

"I told you," Rachel said in a quiet but very calm voice. "The darkness is bad. They never leave a lantern in here at night. You might have known that."

"Yes." His voice sounded thick. "I might have."

He heard her stand up from her bench. He heard her foot-steps through the straw. Then there came the rustling of her sack-cloth gown and the scrape of a bucket. What followed next was the noise of a stream of water.

One problem, he realized grimly, had been solved.

He would have to bear the dark, though it was almost be-yond endurance. He would have to bear it anyway, because if he did not fight its pressure upon his mind, then he might scream or weep, and what good would come of those actions? Surely he could bear it for three nights, if Rachel Howarth had borne it for three months. Surely he could.

From the logwall behind him he heard a squeaking and scur-rying. He knew full well that now had come the night that would test his mettle, and if his mettle be found cracked he was lost.

Rachel's voice suddenly came from just beyond the bars that parted them. "Try to sleep, if you can. There's no use in standing up all night."

At last Matthew reluctantly loosened his grip on the iron and made his way past the desk to the place in the straw where he'd decided to sleep. That had been before the light had been taken, of course. He knelt down, feeling around to make sure no rats were waiting to attack him. There were none, though they sounded alarmingly near. He lay on his side and curled himself up into a tight ball, his arms around his knees. It seemed eons until the dawn.

He heard the woman lie down in the straw. Then silence reigned, except for the rodents. He clenched his teeth together and squeezed his eyes shut. Perhaps he made a noise of despair—a gasp, a moan, something—but he wasn't sure.

"May I call you Matthew?" Rachel asked.

It wasn't proper. Wasn't proper at all. He was the magis-trate's clerk, and she the accused. No, such familiarity was not proper.

"Yes," he said, his voice strained and near cracking.

"Good night, Matthew."

"Good night," he answered, and he almost said *Rachel* but he closed his mouth before the name could emerge. He did speak it, though, in his innermost voice.

He waited, listening. For what, he did not know. Perhaps the buzz of a luminous, witch-directed fly. Perhaps the cold laughter of a demon who had come to visit for obscene purposes; perhaps the sound of raven's wings flitting in the dark. None of those sounds occurred. There were just the furtive noises of the surviving rodents and then, a while later, the soft breathing of Rachel Howarth in sleep.

What she needs is a champion of truth, he thought.

And who in this town could be that champion but himself? But the evidence . . . the apparent evidence . . . was so damning.

Damning or not, there were so many questions. So many *whys,* he could scarce list them all in his mind.

One thing was certain: if the woman was not a witch, someone in Fount Royal—perhaps more than a single person—had gone to great and evil effort to paint her as one. Again the question: *why?*

In spite of his trepidations, his body was relaxing. He felt sleep coming nearer. He fought it by going over in his head the testimony of Jeremiah Buckner. At last, though, sleep was the victor, and he joined Rachel in the land of forgetting.

fifteen

THE POWER OF GOD was the subject of Robert Bidwell's lecture at the Anglican church on Sabbath morn, and during its second hour—as Bidwell paused to drink a cup of water and renew his vigor—the magistrate felt his eyes drooping as if drawn down by leaden weights. It was a sensitive situation, as he was seated in the front pew of the church, and thus being in the seat of honor Woodward was subject to the stares and whispers of the congregation. Such would not be worrisome to him if he were in firmer health, but as he'd slept very poorly and his throat was once more ravaged and swollen, he might have chosen a rack-and-wheel over the torture of this predicament.

Bidwell, to be so eloquent and forceful face-to-face, was a wandering wastrel at the pulpit. Between half-cooked pronouncements simmered long pauses, while the congregation steamed in the close, hot room. To add even more injury, Bidwell didn't know his Good Book very well and continually misquoted what to Woodward were passages every child had memorized by the age of baptism. Bidwell asked the congregation to join him in prayer after prayer concerning the well-being and future of Fount Royal, a task which became truly laborious by the fifth or sixth amen. Heads nodded and snores grumbled, but those who dared to sleep were slapped awake by the glove that Mr. Green—who was acting just as much gaol-keeper here as at the gaol—had fixed to a long wooden pole capable of reaching the cheek of any sinner.

At last Bidwell came to his dutiful conclusion and went to his seat. Next arose the schoolmaster, who limped up to the pulpit with his Bible beneath his arm, and asked that there be another prayer to secure the presence of God among them. It went on for perhaps ten minutes, but at least Johnstone's voice had inflection and character and so Woodward was able—with an effort of will—to avoid the glove.

Woodward had risen from his bed at first light. From his shaving mirror stared the face of a sick man, hollow-eyed and gray-fleshed. He opened his mouth wide and caught sight in the glass of the volcanic wasteland his throat had become. Again his air passages were thickened and blocked, which proved that Dr. Shields's remedy was less a cure than a curio. Woodward had asked Bidwell if he might see to Matthew before the beginning of Sabbath service, and a trip to Mr. Green's house had secured the key, which had been returned to him after its use by the rat-catcher.

Fearing the worst, Woodward discovered that his clerk had actually enjoyed a better rest in the harsh straw than he himself had endured at the mansion house. Matthew had had his tribulations, to be sure, but except for finding a drowned rodent in his waterbucket this morning he'd suffered no lasting harms. In the next cage, Rachel Howarth remained cloaked and impassive, perhaps a pointed response to Bidwell's presence. But Matthew had come through the first night without being transformed into a black cat or a basilisk, and seemed to have undergone no other entrancements, as Woodward had feared might happen. Woodward had vowed he would return again in the afternoon, and so had reluctantly left his clerk in the company of the cloaked harridan.

The magistrate had expected to smell the dust of a hundred dry sermons when the schoolmaster took the pulpit to speak, but Johnstone was at ease before the congregation and therefore earned more ears than had Bidwell before him. In fact, Johnstone was quite a good speaker. His message was faith in the mysterious ways of God, and over the course of an hour he skillfully wove that topic into a parallel with the situation faced by the citizens of Fount Royal. It was clear to Woodward that Johnstone relished public speaking, and used his hands in grand gestures to illustrate the verses of scripture that were his emphasis. Nary a head nodded nor a snore sounded while the schoolmaster held forth, and at the end of Johnstone's lesson the prayer that followed was short, concise, and the final "Amen" delivered like an exclamation point. Bidwell rose to say a few more words—perhaps feeling a bit upstaged by the schoolmaster. Then Bidwell called upon Peter Van Gundy, proprietor of the tavern, to dismiss the service, and at long last Mr. Green rested his glove-on-a-pole in a corner as the congregation took their leave of the sweatbox.

Outside, beneath the milky sky, the air was still and damp. Beyond Fount Royal's walls mist hung low over the forest and draped the taller treetops with white shrouds. No birds sang. As Woodward followed Bidwell to the carriage where Goode waited to drive them home, the magistrate's progress was interrupted by a tug on his sleeve. He turned to find Lucretia Vaughan standing there, wearing her somber black Sabbath gown as did the other women, yet hers had a touch of lace decorating the high bodice that seemed to Woodward a bit ostentatious. Behind her stood her blonde daughter Cherise, also in black, and a slim man of short stature who wore a vacant smile and had equally vacant eyes.

"Magistrate?" the woman said. "How goes the case?"

"It goes," he answered, his voice little more than a raspy croak.

"Dear me! You sound in need of a salt gargle."

"The weather," he said. "It disagrees with me."

"I'm very sorry to hear that. Now: I would like—that is, my husband and I would like—to offer an invitation to our table on Thursday night."

"Thursday? I'll have to wait and see how I'm feeling by then."

"Oh, you misunderstand!" She flashed him a bright smile. "I mean an invitation to your *clerk*. His sentence will be done by Tuesday morning, as I hear. He'll receive his lashes at that time, am I correct?"

"Yes, madam, you are."

"Then he should be up to joining us on Thursday evening. Say at six o'clock?"

"I can't speak for Matthew, but I will pass your invitation along."

"I would be oh so grateful," she said, with a semblance of a curtsey. "Good day, then."

"Good day."

The woman took her husband's arm and guided him along— a shocking sight, especially on the Sabbath—and the daughter followed a few paces behind. Woodward pulled himself up into the waiting carriage, lay back against the cushioned seat across from Bidwell, and Goode flicked the reins.

"You found the service of interest, Magistrate?" Bidwell asked.

"Yes, very much."

"I'm pleased to hear it. I feared my sermon was rather on the intellectual side, and most of the citizens here are—as you know by now—charmingly rustic. It wasn't too deep for them, was it?"

"No, I think not."

"Ah." Bidwell nodded. His hands folded in his lap. "The schoolmaster has an agile mind, but he does tend to speak in circles rather than to a point. Wouldn't you agree?"

"Yes," Woodward said, realizing what Bidwell desired to hear. "He does have an agile mind."

"I've told him—*suggested* to him—that he keep his message more grounded in reality than abstract concepts, but he has his own way of presentation. I myself find him somewhat tiresome, though I do try to follow his threads."

"Um," Woodward said.

"You would think that, being a teacher, he might be also a

better communicator. But I suspect his talents lie in other areas. *Not* thievery, however." He gave a brief laugh and then attended to the straightening of his ruffled cuffs.

Woodward was listening to the creak of the wheels when another sound intruded. The signal bell at the front gate's watchtower began to ring. "Hold, Goode!" Bidwell commanded, and he looked toward the tower as Goode reined in the horses. "Someone's approaching, it seems." He frowned. "I can't think of anyone we're expecting, though. Goode, take us to the gate!"

"Yes sir," the servant answered, and he maneuvered the team around to change direction.

On this afternoon, Malcolm Jennings was again atop the watchtower. A group of citizens had already assembled to see who the visitor might be. As Jennings saw Bidwell's carriage stop on the street below, he leaned over the railing and shouted, "A covered wagon, Mr. Bidwell! Young man at the reins!"

Bidwell scratched his chin. "Well, who could it be? Not the maskers; it's way too early yet for them." He motioned toward a rawboned pipesmoker who wore a straw hat. "Swaine, open the gate! You there, Hollis: help him with the timber!"

The two men Bidwell had spoken to drew the latching log from its position of security and pulled the gate open. When the gate was drawn wide, the covered wagon Jennings had announced rumbled across the threshold, hauled by two horses—a piebald and a roan—that appeared but several ragged breaths away from the pastepot. The wagon's driver reined in the team as soon as the vehicle had cleared the entrance, and he surveyed the onlookers from beneath a battered brown monmouth cap. His gaze settled on the nearest citizen, which was John Swaine. "Fount Royal?" he inquired.

"That it is," Swaine answered. Bidwell was about to direct a question of his own about who the young man might be, when suddenly the wagon's canvas was whipped open with the speed of revelation and another man emerged from the interior. This man, who wore a black suit and a black tricorn hat, stood on the seat-plank next to the driver, his hands on his hips, and scanned the vista from left to right with the narrowed eyes of an arrogant emperor.

"At last!" The thunder of his voice made the horses jump. "The Devil's own town!"

This statement, delivered so loudly and imperially, sent a terror through Bidwell. Instantly he stood up in the carriage, his face flushed. "Sir! Who might you be?"

The dark eyes of this new arrival, which were hooded with flesh in a long-jawed, gaunt face that seemed a virtual patchwork quilt of deep lines and wrinkles, fixed upon Bidwell. "Who might *thee* be?"

"My name is Robert Bidwell. I am the founder of Fount Royal, as well as its mayor."

"Mine condolences, then, in thy time of tribulation." He removed his hat, displaying a shockpate of white hair that was much too unruly to be a wig. "I am known by the name God hast given me: Exodus Jerusalem. I have come many a league to this place, sir."

"For what reason?"

"Need thou ask? I am brought here by the might of God, to do God's bidding." He returned the tricorn to his head, his show of manners finished. "God hast compelled me to this town, to smite thy witch dead and do battle with demons infernal!" Bidwell felt weak in the knees. He had realized, as had Woodward, that the gates had been opened to allow the entrance of a travelling preacher, and this one sounded steeped in the blood of vengeance.

"We have the situation in hand, Mr. . . . uh . . . Jerusalem. Well in hand," Bidwell said. "This is Magistrate Woodward, from Charles Town." He pointed a finger at his companion. "The witch's trial is already under way."

"*Trial?*" Jerusalem had snarled it. He looked across the faces of the assembled citizens. "Dost thou not know the woman is a witch?"

"We know it!" shouted Arthur Dawson. "We know she's

cursed our town, too!" This brought up a chorus of angry and frustrated voices, which Woodward noted made the preacher smile as if he were hearing the sweet refrains of chamber music.

"Then of what need is a *trial?*" Jerusalem asked, his voice becoming something akin to a bludgeoning instrument. "She is in thy gaol, is she not? But whilst she lives, who may say what evil she performs?"

"One moment!" Bidwell hollered, motioning with both arms for the onlookers to settle themselves. "The witch *will* be dealt with, by the power of the law!"

"*Foolish man!*" Jerusalem, a human cannon, blasted at the top of his leathered lungs. "There is no power greater than the law of God! Dost thou deny that God's law is greater than the law of fallen Adam?"

"No, I do not deny it! But—"

"Then shall thou depend upon the law of fallen Adam, knowing it to be tainted by the Devil himself?"

"No! I mean . . . we have to do this thing the correct way!"

"And allowing evil to live in thy town for one more *minute* is, in thy opinion, the correct way?" Jerusalem grinned tightly and shook his head. "Thyself hath been blighted, sir, along with thy town!" Again his attention went to the assembly, which was growing larger and more restless. "I say God is the truest and purest of lawgivers, and what doth God say in regards to witchcraft? Thou shalt not suffer a witch to live!"

"That's right!" George Bartow shouted. "God says to kill a witch!"

"God doth not say tarry, nor wait upon the tainted law of humankind!" Jerusalem plowed on. "And any man who serveth such folly is doomed himself to the brimstone pit!"

"He's rousting them!" Bidwell said to the magistrate, and then he called out, "Wait, citizens! Listen to—" but he was hollered silent.

"The time of God's judgment," Jerusalem announced, "is not tomorrow, nor is it the day after! The time is *now!*" He reached back into the wagon, and his hand emerged clamped to the grip of an axe. "I shall rid thee of thy witch, and afterward we shall pray for God's blessing upon thy homes and families! Who amongst thee will lead me to mine enemy?"

At the sight of the axe, Woodward's heart had started pounding and he was now on his feet. He gave a shout of "No! I won't have such a—" *blasphemy against the court,* he was going to say, but his tormented voice collapsed and he was left speechless. A half dozen men yelled that they would lead the preacher to the gaolhouse, and suddenly the crowd—which had grown to twenty-five or more—seemed to Woodward to have been seized by a raging fit of bloodlust. Jerusalem climbed down from the wagon, axe in hand, and surrounded by a veritable phalanx of human hounds he stalked down Harmony Street in the direction of the gaol, his long thin legs carrying him with the speed of a predatory spider.

"They won't get in, the fools!" Bidwell snorted. "I have the keys!"

Woodward managed to croak, "An axe may serve as a key!" He saw it, then, in Bidwell's face: a smug complacency, perhaps, or the realization that Jerusalem's blade might end the witch's life much quicker than the flames of the law. Whatever it was, Bidwell had made his decision on the side of the mob. "Stop them!" Woodward demanded, sweat glistening on his cheeks.

"I tried, sir," came the reply. "You witnessed that I tried."

Woodward thrust his face toward Bidwell's. "If the woman's killed I'll charge every man in that crowd with murder!"

"A difficult charge to prosecute, I would think." Bidwell sat down. He glanced toward the preacher's wagon, where a dark-haired woman of slim build and middle years had emerged from the interior to speak with the young driver. "I fear it's out of my hands now."

"But not out of *mine!*" Woodward climbed down from the carriage, his blood aboil. Before he could take out after the preacher and the pack, he was stopped by a voice that said, "Magistrate, suh?" He looked up at Goode.

The Negro was offering a thin lash that usually sat in a

leather pouch next to the driver's seat. "Protection 'gain the wild beasts, suh," he said.

Woodward accepted the lash, fired a glance of disgust at Bidwell, and then—aware that time was of the essence—turned and ran after Preacher Jerusalem and the mob as fast as his suffering bones would allow.

The voracious stride of Jerusalem's legs had already taken him halfway down Harmony Street. Along the way he had attracted more moths to his bonfire. By the time he made the turn onto Truth Street, the crowd trailing him had swelled to forty-six men, women, and children, four dogs, and a small pig that was scurrying about to avoid being trampled. Chickens fluttered and squawked, feathers flying, as the mass of shouting humanity and barking mongrels passed in their vengeful parade, and at the forefront Exodus Jerusalem—his sharp-boned chin thrust forward like the prow of a warship—brandished his axe as if it were a glorious torch.

Within the gaol, Matthew and Rachel heard the oncoming mob. He stood up from his bench and rushed to the bars, but Rachel remained seated. She closed her eyes, her head tilted slightly back and her face damp with perspiration.

"It's some kind of uproar!" Matthew said; his voice cracked, for he knew full well what it must mean: the citizens of Fount Royal were about to attack the gaol.

"I might have known"—Rachel's voice was calm, but it did tremble—"they would kill me on a Sabbath."

Outside, Exodus Jerusalem spied the chain that secured the entry, and lifted his axe high. When it came down upon the chain, the iron links held but sparks flew like hornets. Again he lifted the axe, and again it fell with tremendous strength. Still the chain held, however, though two of the links had received severe damage. Jerusalem braced himself, gave a mighty swing, and once more sparks flew. He was lifting the axe for a fourth and what might be a final blow, as one link was near parting from its brothers, when suddenly a figure came out of the mob and raised a walking-stick up across Jerusalem's arms.

"What is this?" Schoolmaster Johnstone demanded. He wore the wine-colored suit and black tricorn that had served him at church. "I don't know who you are, sir, but I ask you to put aside that axe!"

"And I do not know who *thee* may be, sir," Jerusalem said, "but if thou stand between me and yonder witch, thee must answer for it to God Almighty!"

"Stop him, Johnstone!" Woodward pushed through the crowd, his breathing ragged. "He intends to kill her! "

"That's right!" Arthur Dawson, who stood at the front of the mob, cried out. "It's time to put her to death!"

"Kill her!" shouted another man, standing beside Dawson. "We're not gonna dawdle no longer!"

The crowd responded with more shouts and cries for the witch's death. Jerusalem said loudly, "Thy people have spoken!" and he brought the axe down again, even more furiously than thrice before. This time the chain broke. Johnstone, hobbling on his bad knee, grabbed at the preacher's arm in an attempt to get the axe away from him. Woodward attacked him from the other side, also trying to gain possession of the axe. Suddenly someone caught Woodward around the throat from behind and pulled him away from the preacher, and another citizen struck at Johnstone's shoulder with a closed fist. The magistrate twisted around and flailed out with the lash, but now the mob was surging forward and several men were upon Woodward before he could use the lash again. A fist caught him in the ribs, and a hand seized the front of his shirt and near tore it from his back. A sea of bodies lifted him from his feet and then he was thrown down to the ground amid the shoals of dangerous boots. He heard thuds and grunts and knew Johnstone was striking in all directions with his cane.

"Go on! Into the gaol!" someone yelled. A boot narrowly missed stomping Woodward's wrist as he tried to gain his footing again.

"Stand back!" he heard a man shout. "Stand back, I said!" There was the sound of a horse's whinny, followed by the sudden jarring crack of a pistol shot. At that noise of authority, the crowd fell back and at last Woodward found space to pull himself up.

He saw Johnstone on the ground, the schoolmaster's body blocking Jerusalem's entrance to the gaol. Johnstone's tricorn hat lay crushed at his side and the preacher stood over him, Jerusalem's own hat also knocked awry but the axe still in his grip.

"Damn, what a sorry sight you are!" Gunsmoke swirled over the head of Nicholas Paine, who had ridden his chestnut stallion into the midst of the vengeful congress. He held aloft the pistol he'd just fired. "What is this insanity?"

"It's no insanity, Nicholas!" spoke an older man Woodward recognized as Duncan Tyler. "It's time for us to come to our senses and put the witch to death!"

"The preacher's gonna do it!" Dawson said. "One blow from that axe and we're free of her!"

"No!" Johnstone had regained his hat, and now he was trying to stand but was meeting great difficulty. Woodward reached down and helped his Oxford brother to his feet. "We agreed to honor the law, like civilized men!" Johnstone said when he was balanced on his cane.

Paine stared disdainfully at Jerusalem. "So you're a preacher?"

"Exodus Jerusalem, called by God to set thy town on the righteous path," came the reply. "Dost thou not wish it to be so?"

"I wish for you to put down that axe," Paine said, "or I'll knock your damn brains out."

"Ah, here is a bewitched soul!" Jerusalem yelled, his gaze sweeping the crowd. "He threatens a man of God and protects the whore of Satan!"

"I look at you, sir, and see only a common fool attempting to enter Fount Royal's gaol without the proper authority, a situation to which I am held accountable," Paine replied, with what seemed to Woodward marvelous restraint and dignity. "I'll ask you once more to put down the axe."

"Nicholas!" Tyler said, and he grabbed hold of Paine's breeches leg. "Let the man do what has to be done!"

"I have the power of God in me!" bellowed the preacher. "No evil shall stand against its justice!"

"Don't let him do it, Nicholas!" Johnstone implored. "It wouldn't be justice, it would be murder!"

Paine moved his horse, breaking Tyler's grip. He guided his mount through the crowd that stood between him and Jerusalem and pulled up barely three feet from the man's daggerblade of a nose. Paine leaned toward him, the saddle's leather creaking. "Preacher," he said quietly, "my next word to you will be presented at your graveside." He let the solemn promise hang for a few seconds as he and Jerusalem engaged in a staring duel. "Magistrate, will you please accept the gift of the preacher's axe?"

"I will," Woodward rasped, and carefully held out his hand. He was prepared to jump aside if Jerusalem took a swing at him.

Jerusalem didn't move. Woodward saw a muscle twitch in the preacher's gray-grizzled jaw. Then a smile that was part sneer and most mockery stole across his face, and in truth that smile was more fearful to look upon than the preacher's expression of righteous anger. "Mine compliments to thee," Jerusalem said, as he turned the axe around and placed its wooden handle into the magistrate's palm as gently as mist might settle to the earth.

"Go home, all of you!" Paine commanded the assembly. "There's nothing more to be seen here!"

"One question for you, Nicholas Paine!" shouted James Reed, who stood next to Tyler. "You and I both saw them poppets in the floor of her house! You know what she's been doin' to this town! Are you bewitched, like the preacher says? You must be, to turn aside an axe from killin' her!"

"James, if you were not my friend I'd have to strike you down!" Paine shouted back at him. "Now listen to me, every one of you!" He wheeled his horse around so he was facing the crowd, which by now numbered near sixty. "Yes, I know what the witch has done to us! But this I know, as well, and mark it: when Rachel Howarth dies—and she *will*—her wicked life shall be ended by the torch of legal decree, not by a preacher's axe!" He paused, almost daring any man to speak out against him. There were a few halfhearted shouts from the crowd, but they dwindled and perished like little fires. "I too believe she should die for the good of Fount Royal!" he continued. "As long as she lives, there is great danger of further corruption. Some of you may wish to leave before she burns, and that is your right and privilege to do so, but . . . listen, listen!" he commanded another heckler, who fell silent.

"We're building more than a town here, don't you understand that?" Paine asked. "We're building new lives for ourselves, in what will someday be a *city!* A city, with a courthouse of its own and a permanent magistrate to occupy it!" He scanned the crowd from one side to the other. "Do we wish to say in the future that the very first trial held in Fount Royal was interrupted by a preacher's axe? Let me tell you, I have seen mob justice before, and it is a sight to sicken a dog! Is that the first timber we wish to lay for our courthouse?"

"There'll be no courthouse!" Reed hollered. "There'll be no town, no city, nothin' here but ruins unless she's put to death!"

"There'll be ruins aplenty if she's hauled out and murdered!" Paine answered, just as vehemently. "The first thing to fall to ruin will be our honor! That I've seen men lose as well, and once lost they are as weak as scarecrows against the wind! We have agreed to allow Magistrate Woodward to carry out the trial and sentencing, and we cannot now give over that task to Artemis Jerusalem!"

"*Exodus* Jerusalem, if thy please!" The preacher had an astounding gift, Woodward thought; he could mimic thunder with hardly an effort. "I would remind thee, citizens," Jerusalem stormed on, "that the Devil's tongue is formed of silver!"

"You!" Paine snapped at him. "Shut . . . your . . . hole."

"Best heed my hole, or thou shalt perish in one that has no bottom!"

"I think yours has no bottom!" the schoolmaster said. "Or perhaps it's your bottom that's become confused with your top!"

Woodward knew this statement could not have been delivered with better timing or in better elocution on the Shakespearian stage. Its effect was to visibly cause the preacher to stumble in his search for a suitable riposte, his jaw working but no words yet formed; and at the same time, it urged laughter from several persons who had a moment earlier been scowling. The laughter rippled out across the crowd, breaking the aura of solemnity, and though most did *not* crack a smile, the mood of all had definitely been changed.

To his credit, Exodus Jerusalem recognized the value of a dignified retreat. He made no further entreaties to the assembly, but rather crossed his slim arms over his chest and glowered at the ground.

"Go home!" Paine presently repeated to the citizens. "The afternoon's entertainment has ended!"

Glances were exchanged, words were spoken, and the mob found its passions diminished. At least for today, Woodward thought. The crowd began to drift apart. The magistrate saw that Bidwell sat in his carriage just up the way, his legs crossed at the ankles and one arm resting across the seatback. Now, as it was apparent Rachel Howarth would not die this afternoon, Bidwell got down from the carriage and began to approach the gaol.

"Thank you, Nicholas," Johnstone told him. "I dread to think what might have happened."

"You." Paine was speaking to the preacher, and Jerusalem looked up at him. "Did you really intend to go in there and kill her?"

"I intended to do just what was done," he answered, his normal voice much more restrained.

"What? Cause a commotion?"

"Thy citizens know Exodus Jerusalem has arrived. That is well enough for now."

"I think we've been honored by the performance of a thespian," Johnstone said.

He saw Bidwell approaching. "Robert, here stands someone you should meet."

"We *have* met." Bidwell frowned as he regarded the broken chain. "There's work for Hazelton, I see. *If* his injury permits it." His eyes speared the preacher. "Damage to the property of Fount

Royal is a serious offense, sir. I would say the payment of a guinea should be in order."

"Alas, I am simply a poor travelling man of God," Jerusalem replied, with a shrug. "The Lord provideth food, clothing, and shelter, but English gold not a pence."

"You're a beggar, you mean!"

"Oh, not a beggar. A diviner, if thy will. I divine that my stay here shall be of great importance."

"Your *stay* here? I think not!" Bidwell said. "Nicholas, will you escort this man to the gate, make sure he boards his wagon and—"

"One moment." Jerusalem lifted a long, thin finger. "I have journeyed here from Charles Town, whence I learned of thy plight. The witch is being discussed there on the streets. A visit to the council office also told me thy have need of a preacher."

"The council office? In Charles Town?" Bidwell's brow wrinkled. "How did they know we don't have a minister?"

"They know of Grove's murder," Johnstone supplied. "It was all written out in the request for a magistrate that Nicholas and Edward carried to them."

"That may be so, but they received that letter in March. The council presumes we haven't found a minister to replace a man who was murdered last November?" His frown deepened. "It seems to me someone has loose lips concerning our business."

"Dost thou have a preacher or *not?*" Jerusalem asked.

"We do not. But we don't need one at the present time, thank you."

"Oh, it is quite apparent thou dost not need a preacher." Jerusalem gave a slim smile. "A witch in the gaol and Satan in the town. God only knows what other wickedness thrives. No, thou dost not need a *preacher*. Thou art in need of a second coming." His dark, flesh-hooded eyes in that grotesquely wrinkled face pierced Bidwell. "Thy fellow on horseback dost make a pretty point concerning laws, houses of court, and cities. But let me ask this: who speaketh here over the dead and the newborn?"

"Whomever wishes to!" Paine answered.

"Yet whomever wishes cannot walk into thy gaol and deliver the stroke of an axe? Is the life of a witch to be valued more than the burial services of thy Christian citizens and the redemption of thy little infants? Thou sendeth the dead and the newborn alike off on journeys of dark despair without proper blessings? The shame of it!"

"We'll find a minister after the witch is dead!" Bidwell said. "But I won't have anyone in my town who within five minutes of their arrival causes a near-riot! Nicholas, would you please show this man to the—"

"Thou shalt weep bitter tears," Jerusalem said, so quietly that it caught Bidwell by surprise. "Dost thou not know the power of a witch to rise from the grave?"

"From the *grave?* What are you jabbering about?"

"When thou dost kill the witch and bury her without the proper rite of sanctimony, thou shalt be jabbering aplenty thyself. In mortal terror, I might add."

"Sanctimony?" Johnstone said. "I've never heard of such a thing!"

"Are thee a preacher, sir? Dost thou have experience with witches, the Devil, and the demons of night? I have administered the rite over the graves of the notorious witches Elizabeth Stockham, Marjorie Ballard, and Sarah Jones, as well as the infamous warlocks Andrew Spaulding and John Kent. In so doing, I sealed them into the depths of Hell where they might enjoy the ticklings of the eternal fires. But without such a rite, sirs, thy witch will flee the grave and continue her wickedness as a phantasm, hellhound, or . . ." He shrugged again. "Who can say? Satan has a creative mind."

"I think it's not only Satan whose mind is creative," Johnstone said.

"Wait!" A sheen of sweat had begun to glisten on Bidwell's face. "You mean to say the witch could be put to death and we'd still not be rid of her?"

"Not," Jerusalem said grimly, "without the rite of sanctimony."

"That's pure nonsense!" the schoolmaster scoffed, and then he said to Bidwell, "I suggest you run this man out of town at once!"

From his pained expression, Bidwell was obviously caught on the horns of a dilemma. "I've never heard of such a rite," he said, "but that's not to say it doesn't exist. What's your opinion, Magistrate?"

"The man has come here to cause difficulty," Woodward croaked. "He's a flame in a powderhouse."

"I agree!" Paine spoke up.

"Yes, yes, I also agree." Bidwell nodded. "But what if such a rite *is* needed to secure the witch's phantasm in her grave?"

"It most surely is, sir," Jerusalem said. "If I were thee, I should wish all possible precautions to be taken."

Bidwell reached for a handkerchief from his pocket and blotted the moisture from his face. "I'll be damned!" he finally said. "I'm feared to let him stay and feared to make him leave!"

"If I am made to leave, it is not only thee who should be damned but thy entire enterprise." Jerusalem, with theatrical drama, motioned with a sweeping gesture across the vista of Fount Royal. "Thou hast created a most pleasing town here, sir. The work that hast gone into its creation is most evident. Why, building that fortress wall must have consumed untold energies, and these streets are far better laid than those in Charles Town. I did note, in passing, that thy cemetery is also well laid. It would give a sadness to God for all that work to have been done, and all those souls to have perished, for naught."

"You can dismount the podium now, preacher," Johnstone told him. "Robert, I still say he should go."

"I must think on it. Better to err on the side of God than against Him."

"Whilst thee is thinking," Jerusalem said, "might I view mine enemy?"

"No!" Woodward said. "Certainly not!"

"Magistrate," he answered in a silken voice, "from the sound of thee, I should say the witch hath already struck thee ill. Might she also hath struck ill your judgment?" He turned his attention again to Bidwell. "I request to view her, please. So that I may know the depth of Satan's infestation in her soul."

Woodward thought that Bidwell looked near fainting. The master of Fount Royal had come to his weakest moment. He said, "All right. I cannot see the harm in it."

"*I* can!" Woodward protested, but Bidwell moved past him and pulled open the gaol's door. Jerusalem bowed his head slightly to acknowledge Bidwell's gesture and then walked inside, his boots clumping on the boards.

At once Woodward followed him, desirous to contain whatever damage the preacher might do. Bidwell entered too, as well as Johnstone, while Paine seemed to have come to the end of his interest in the matter and remained on horseback. The gaol's dim interior was illuminated only by the milky light that came through the roof's hatch, which Woodward himself had opened that morning.

Matthew and Rachel had heard the commotion, Paine's speech, and the voices of the men outside the door, so they knew what to expect. Exodus Jerusalem first paused before Matthew's cage and peered through the bars. "Who art thee?"

"My clerk," Woodward said, his voice all but vanished.

"He is present to keep watch o'er the witch?"

"I'm present," Matthew said, "because I have been sentenced for three days due to an incident I regret."

"What?" Jerusalem pursed his lips. "A magistrate's clerk hast become a criminal? This too must be the witch's doing, to undermine the trial." Before Matthew could reply, Jerusalem's head swivelled toward the other cell and his gaze fell upon Rachel, who sat on her bench with her sackcloth cloak pulled around her but her face exposed.

There was a long silence.

"Ah, yes," Jerusalem said at last. "I see a deep pool of sin in that one." Rachel gave no reply, but she did return his stare.

"Look how she glowers," Jerusalem said. "Like a hot flame, eager to burn mine heart to a cinder. Wouldst thou delight in flying me to Hell on the wings of a crow, woman? Or wouldst thou be content to drive nails through mine eyes and split mine tongue in two?" She didn't answer, choosing to shift her gaze to the straw. "There! Dost thou see? The evil in her quakes before me, and she cannot bear to look longer upon mine face."

"You are half right, " Rachel said.

"A taunt, it seems! She's a witty bitch." Jerusalem walked past Matthew's cell and stood next to the bars of the other cage. "What is thy name?"

"A witty bitch," she answered. "You have already named me."

"Her name is Rachel Howarth," Bidwell said, standing behind the preacher. "Needless to say, she is very uncooperative."

"They always are." Jerusalem curled his long, slender fingers around the bars. "As I say, I have had much experience with witches. I know the evil that hath eaten their hearts and blackened their souls. Oh yes, I know." He nodded, his eyes fixed on Rachel. "This one hath committed two murders, is that correct?"

"Yes. She first murdered our Anglican reverend and then her own husband," Bidwell answered.

"No, thou art wrong. This witch became the bride of Satan when she spilled the blood of a reverend. She hath also bewitched thy crops and the minds of thy citizens?"

"Yes."

"Conjecture," Matthew had to say. "So far unproven."

Jerusalem looked sharply at him. "What sayest thou?"

"The evidence is not yet complete," Matthew said. "Therefore the charges against Madam Howarth are still unproven."

"*Madam* Howarth, didst thou say?" Jerusalem gave a slight, chilly smile. "Thou dost refer to the witch with respect?"

Woodward managed to speak: "My clerk has a liberal mind."

"Thy clerk may well have a *diseased* mind, made infirm by the power of this witch. It is quite dangerous to leave him here, in such close quarters. Wouldst there not be another place to confine him?"

"No," Bidwell said. "Nowhere else."

"Then the witch should be confined elsewhere. In strict solitude."

"I would have to protest that action," Matthew said quickly. "As the trial is taking place here, it is Madam Howarth's right to be present during the questioning of witnesses."

The preacher was silent, staring at Matthew. Then he said, "Gentlemen, I fear *we* are witnesses to the corruption of a young man's soul. No clean Christian wouldst protect the *rights* of a witch." He let that sentence linger before he went on. "It is a witch's evil desire to drag into Hell as many persons as demonically possible. In the Old World, entire towns were burned to the ground and their citizens hanged because they were corrupted by a single witch."

"That may be so," Matthew replied, "but this is the New World."

"Old World or New, the eternal battle between God and Satan remaineth the same. There is no middle ground. Either thou art a Christian soldier on one side . . . or a pawn of the Devil on the other. Where dost thou stand?"

It was a nice trap, Matthew realized. He also, for the first time, realized the convolutions of warped logic that had been brought to bear against Rachel. "If I say I stand on the side of truth," he answered, "does that make me a soldier or a pawn?"

Jerusalem gave a quiet laugh. "Now here, gentlemen, thy see the beginnings of Adam's fall: to emulate the serpent, first in thought, then in word, and finally in deed. Young man, be wary. Executions allow no such slippery maneuvers."

"If you please!" Woodward rasped. "My clerk is not on trial!"

"Thy clerk," Jerusalem said, "may no longer be truly thine." He directed his attention once more to Rachel. "Witch!" he said, with the thunder returning to his voice. "Hast thou willed a spell on this young man's tender soul?"

"I've willed no spell on any soul," she replied. "Tender or otherwise."

"Time shall tell, I think. Oh, thou art a brassy whore, full of lies and enchantments! But thou art caged now, art thy not? And every day's dusk is one less day remaining for thy sin to take root!" He looked at Bidwell. "This one shalt not go easy to the gallows, that is a surety."

"Her death will be by burning," Bidwell told him. "The magistrate's decreed it."

"Ahhhhh, *burning.*" Jerusalem spoke it with such reverence it might be the very balm of life. "Yes, that would be suitable. Still, even ashes need the rite of sanctimony." He gave Rachel another chilly smile. "Enemy mine," he said, "thy face changeth from town to town, but thou art always the same." Then, to Bidwell again, "I have seen enough now. Mine sister and nephew wait for me. Art we free to camp on some available plot of land?"

"Yes," Bidwell said, with only a minor hesitation. "I'll direct you."

"I'm against it!" Johnstone spoke up. "Is there nothing I can say to dissuade you, Robert?"

"I think we need Jerusalem as much as we need the magistrate."

"You'll think differently when he sets off another riot! Good day to you!" Johnstone, obviously angry and frustrated, limped out of the gaol with the aid of his cane.

"Alan will come 'round," Bidwell said to the preacher. "He's our schoolmaster, but he's also a sensible man."

"I trust thy schoolmaster is not being led astray in the same fashion as this clerk. Well sir, I am at thy disposal."

"All right, then. Come with me. But we'll have no further . . . uh . . . disturbances, I hope?"

"Disturbance is not mine cause, sir. I am here in the cause of deliverance."

Bidwell motioned for Jerusalem to proceed from the gaol, and then he followed. Just short of the doorway, he turned back toward Woodward. "Magistrate? I suggest you come along, if you wish to ride in my carriage."

Woodward nodded. He cast a sad-eyed look at Matthew and said weakly, "I shall have to rest, and so won't be back before the morning. Are you all right?"

"I am. You should ask Dr. Shields for another tonic, I think."

"I plan to." He stared grimly at Rachel. "Madam?" he said. "Do not believe that because my voice is weak and my body impoverished that I shall not continue this trial to the best of my ability. The next witness will be heard on schedule." He took two steps toward the door and hesitated again. "Matthew?" he said, in an agonized whisper. "Take care that your senses not become as feeble as my health." Then he turned away and followed Bidwell.

Matthew sat down on his bench. The arrival of Exodus Jerusalem added a highly combustible element to this tinderbox. But Matthew found himself most presently concerned about the magistrate's failing health. It was clear that Woodward should be abed, under the care of a physician. And certainly he shouldn't be spending any time in this rank gaol, but his pride and sense of duty dictated that he see this trial through without delay. Matthew had never known the magistrate to be so fragile of voice and spirit, and it frightened him.

"The magistrate," Rachel suddenly said, "is very sick, isn't he?"

"I fear he is."

"You've been serving him a long time?"

"Five years. I was a child when I met him. He has given me great opportunity to make something of myself."

Rachel nodded. "May I be forward?" she asked.

"As you please."

"When he looks at you," she said, "it is a father looking at a son."

"I'm his clerk, nothing more," Matthew answered curtly. He clasped his hands together, his head bent down. There was a hollow pain in the vicinity of his heart.

"Nothing more," he said again.

sixteen

NEAR FOUR-THIRTY on Monday morning, the lamps were lit in Robert Bidwell's mansion. Soon afterward a negress servant girl emerged from the house into the drizzling rain and quickly walked to the home of Dr. Shields on Harmony Street. Hers was an errand of urgency, and she wasted no time in ringing the bell at the doctor's door. Within fifteen minutes—long enough for Dr. Shields to dress himself and gather the necessary implements into his carrying case—the doctor was hurrying through the rain, his tricorn hat pulled low over his eyes and water dripping from the curled brim.

He was admitted to Bidwell's house by Mrs. Nettles. Bidwell was in the parlor, still wearing his silk nightclothes, an expression of deep concern on his face. "Thank God!" Bidwell said when Shields crossed the threshold. "Upstairs! Hurry!"

Mrs. Nettles climbed the stairs with the speed of a mountain goat, all but carrying the diminutive doctor in the wake of her black skirt. Before Shields reached the magistrate's closed door, he could hear the man gasping for air. "A pan of hot water and a cloth!" he commanded Mrs. Nettles, who relayed the order to a servant girl. Then Mrs. Nettles opened the door and Shields entered the chamber, where three lamps had been lit around the bed. Instantly Shields picked up one of them and shone the candlelight onto Woodward's face. What he saw made him flinch, if only imperceptibly.

The magistrate's face was the yellowish-gray hue of old parchment. Darker hollows had formed beneath his eyes, which were glassy and wet with the labor of breathing. But by no means was the effort going well; crusted mucus had all but sealed his nostrils, and a foam of saliva had gathered in the corners of his gaping mouth and glistened on his chin. His hands gripped the sodden sheet that lay around him, beads of sweat standing on his cheeks and forehead.

"Be calm," was the first thing that Dr. Shields could think to say. "It's going to be all right."

Woodward trembled, his eyes wild. He reached up and caught the sleeve of Shields's coat. "Can't breathe," he gasped. "Help me."

"I shall. Mrs. Nettles, will you hold this lamp?" He gave it to her and quickly shrugged out of his coat. He took his tricorn off as well, and put his leather carrying case atop a stool next to the bed.

"I heard him cry out." Bidwell had entered the room, and stood near the door. "Wasn't but a little while ago. I had the girl go fetch you as soon as I realized he was so ill."

Shields had removed a small blue bottle and a spoon from the case. He shook the bottle well and then proceeded to pour some oily dark brown liquid from it onto the spoon. "You did the proper thing. Magistrate, drink this please." He poured the liquid into Woodward's mouth, then loaded up the spoon again and repeated the dose. The magistrate, who was just on the edge of panic, could neither taste nor smell anything but he was aware of the thick fluid sliding down his tortured throat.

His chest hitched as he fought to find air, his fingers once more entwined in the sheets. "Am I . . . am I dying?"

"No! Of course not! Lie easy now. Mrs. Nettles, might I have that lamp, please?" He took it from her and held the light toward Woodward's mouth. "Open as wide as you can, magistrate."

Woodward did, the effort making a tear run from each eye.

Shields held the lamp as close as possible to the magistrate's face and peered down into the man's throat.

First of all, there was the smell. Shields knew the sickly sweet odor of pestilence, and here it was on the magistrate's breath. The candlelight showed him what he had already expected to find, yet much worse: the interior of Woodward's throat was red—blood-red, the red of seething caverns in the infernal landscape of Hell. Down in the folds of crimson flesh, which had swollen to such a degree as to almost completely close together over the esophagus, were ugly yellow blisters of pus and yellow streaks where previous blisters had burst. It was like viewing a platter of raw meat that had become infested with vermin, and Shields knew the pain of such a condition must be absolutely horrendous.

"Mrs. Nettles," he said, his voice tight, "please go and hurry the hot water. Also fetch me a drinking cup with two hands of salt in it."

"Yes sir." Mrs. Nettles left the room.

"Easy, there," Shields said, as the magistrate began to groan with the effort of breathing. "We shall have your air passages cleared directly." He clasped his free hand to Woodward's shoulder to give him some measure of comfort.

"Ben?" Bidwell came to the bedside. "He *will* live, won't he?"

"Yes, yes!" Shields had seen the magistrate's watery eyes tick toward Bidwell. "This is a serious condition, but treatable. No need to be concerned with mortality here." He looked at Bidwell over the rims of his spectacles. "The magistrate will be abed for quite some time, however."

"What do you mean, 'quite some time'? Exactly how long?"

"I can't say. A week, perhaps. Two weeks." He shrugged. "It depends on the strength of the patient."

"Two *weeks?*" Bidwell had spoken it in a tone of horrified amazement. "Are you saying he can't continue the trial for two *weeks?*"

"I am, yes. Please keep your voice down; it does no good to heighten the magistrate's discomfort."

"He *can't* stay in bed! He has to finish the trial and have Rachel Howarth burned and done with!"

"Impossible, Robert. I doubt he's able to sit upright in a chair, much less pose questions to witnesses."

Bidwell pushed his face toward the doctor's, whorls of red flaring in his cheeks. "Then *make* him able!"

Woodward—though his throat was afire, his lungs starved for air, and his very bones and tendons ached as if stretched on a medieval torture wheel—was not oblivious to the words being spoken about him, even if the pressure in his ears muffled the voices. "I can do my job!" he roused himself to whisper.

"I will suspect delirium has set in if you repeat such a declaration," Shields told him sternly. "You just lie there and quiet yourself."

Bidwell grasped the doctor's arm. "Come here a moment." He guided Shields over to a far corner of the room and stood with his back toward the magistrate. Bidwell pitched his voice low, but he might have been shouting for the force of it: "Ben, listen to me! We can't afford to let him lie in bed for two weeks! Not even *one* week! Did you know that Winston told me we lost three more families after that house burning the other night? One of them was the Reynolds clan, and you know Franklin had vowed he wouldn't let a witch run him off his farm! Well, Meredith talked him into going and now it's empty over there! He was the last tobacco planter! Do you realize what that means?"

"I do," Shields said, "but that does not alter the fact that Magistrate Woodward is gravely ill."

"We are scraping bottom, and our sails are near collapse. In two more weeks, we may have a ghost town! And who will come to live here, with those bastards in Charles Town spreading tales of the witch far and wide?"

"My sentiments are with you, Robert, but—"

"Give him something," Bidwell said.

"Pardon me?"

"Give him something to get him on his feet. Something

strong enough to allow him to finish the trial. Surely in your bag of tricks there's a potion to shock a man out of bed!"

"I'm a doctor, not a magician."

"You know what I mean. Give him drugs powerful enough to stand him up."

"I have no stimulants. I have only opium, which is a calming drug. Besides, I just gave him a dose of opium in that tonic."

"Ben, I am *begging* you. Get that man on his feet, no matter what it takes!"

"I can only do what I'm able."

"You can do much *more*," Bidwell said, his face only a few inches away from the doctor's. "How much money would you like to be sent to your wife?"

"What?"

"Your wife. A seamstress in Boston. Surely she is in need of some money? And your ledger at Van Gundy's tavern has become quite heavy, I understand. I shall be glad to erase your debt and arrange that your thirst for rum not be interrupted. Be a good friend to me, Ben, and I shall be a good friend to you."

"I . . . can't just—"

"Who is this magistrate to *us*, Ben? A tool, that's all! Only a tool. Brought here for a specific purpose, just as any shovel or axe." He heard the door opening and glanced around as Mrs. Nettles entered, bringing a drinking cup with the salt in it, followed by a servant girl carrying a pan of steaming water and a clean white cloth. "Money for your wife and all the rum you please," Bidwell whispered to the doctor, his eyes fierce. "All you need do is patch the tool well enough to work."

Shields had a reply on his lips, but he paused before he spoke it. He blinked slowly, a pulse beating at his temple, and then he said in a wan voice, "I . . . must see to my patient." Bidwell stepped out of his way.

"Hold the pan steady," Shields directed the servant girl. The water had just come off the fire, and so was near scalding. Shields took the drinking cup and dipped it in, then used the spoon to stir the salt until the mixture was well clouded. His hand hesitated near the blue bottle. His eyes narrowed, but only Bidwell saw it. Then the doctor picked up the bottle and poured most of its contents into the cup. He stirred the mixture again, after which he put the cup to Woodward's mouth.

"Drink," he said. Woodward accepted the liquid and swallowed. What ensued next, when the hot salt water came into contact with the ravaged flesh and ripe blisters, was not a pretty moment. The pain that ripped through Woodward's throat was blinding in its savagery, and caused him to convulse and cry out in a grotesquely mangled voice that Bidwell feared would wake the citizens before the first rooster's crow. The servant girl fairly jumped back from the bedside, almost spilling the pan's contents, and even stalwart Mrs. Nettles retreated a pace before she could steady her courage.

Tears streamed down the magistrate's cheeks. He shuddered and looked up through his reddened eyes at Dr. Shields.

"I'm sorry," the doctor said, "but you'll have to drink again."

"I can't," Woodward whispered.

"The salt must do its work. It will be painful, yes, but not as much so. Here, clasp my hand and hold tight. Robert, will you grip his other hand?"

"Me? Why me?"

"If you *please,*" Shields said, not without some vexation, and Bidwell with great reluctance took the magistrate's other hand. "Now," Shields said to the magistrate, "you must hold the salt water in your throat for as long as possible and allow it to burn the infection. Are you ready?"

Woodward gasped a breath. He squeezed his eyes shut and then opened them again to the blurred world. Knowing there was no other way, he nodded and stretched open his mouth.

Shields poured some more of the opium-spiked brine onto Woodward's whitened tongue. Again, when the salt touched its nemesis, Woodward groaned and convulsed but he did hold the water in his throat as long as he was humanly able, the sweat shining slickly upon his face and scalp.

"There, that's very good," Shields said when Woodward had

swallowed. He put aside the cup and soaked the cloth in the hot water, then wrang it out and immediately put it over Woodward's face. The magistrate trembled, but the sensation of the hot cloth against his flesh was of no consequence after what he'd just endured. Shields began to vigorously massage Woodward's cheeks through the cloth, to open up the sinus passages through a combination of heat and friction. He paused in the massage to attack the crusted mucus that blocked the magistrate's nostrils, his fingers still working through the cloth. The heat had softened the obstructions, and Shields was successful in breaking loose most of the clots. He returned to massaging Woodward's face again, concentrating on the areas on either side of the nose. In another moment he removed the cloth, dowsed it in the pan of hot water and then applied it once more to the magistrate's face, continuing the hard pressure of his fingers on the areas that he knew must be severely inflamed and swollen deep beneath the flesh.

Quite suddenly, his brain still reeling from the pain he'd suffered, Woodward realized he could breathe again through his nostrils. His air passages were slowly opening. His throat simply felt dead but that was a far better cry than before. He drew a breath in through his nose and mouth, inhaling steam from the cloth as well.

"An improvement!" Shields said, his fingers tirelessly working. "I think we're bringing the swelling down."

"God be praised!" Bidwell exclaimed.

"God may be praised," Shields told him, "but the magistrate's blood has been fouled by the swamp's evil humours. It's the thickening of the blood that's caused the closure of his throat and sinuses." He peeled the cloth away from Woodward's face, which now was as pink as a boiled ham, and put it into the pan. "Your breathing is easier?"

"Yes." Woodward's voice, however, had been reduced to a whisp and a rattle.

"Very good. You may lay the pan aside and step out of my way," he told the servant girl, who immediately obeyed. "Now," he said to the magistrate, "you realize this condition will most likely recur. As long as your blood is so thickened to affect the tissues, there's danger of the air passages again closing. Therefore . . ." He paused to remove from his carrying case a small pewter bowl, its interior marked by rings that indicated a measurement of ounces. Also from the case Dr. Shields brought a leather sheath, which he opened to display a number of slim rectangular instruments made from tortoiseshell. He chose one of them and unfolded from the tortoiseshell grip a thin blade two inches in length.

"I shall have to bleed you," he said. "When was the last time you were bled?"

"Many years," Woodward answered. "For a touch of fever."

"A flame, please," Shields requested. Mrs. Nettles opened a lamp and offered the burning wick. The doctor put the blade of his lancet into the fire. "I'll make the cuts behind your left ear," he told Woodward. "Therefore I shall need you to overhang your head off the bedside. Will you help him, Robert?"

Bidwell summoned the servant girl, and together they got Woodward's body turned on the bed so his head was in the proper position. Then Bidwell retreated to the door, as the sight of blood made his stomach queasy and the jellied eels and oysters he'd consumed for dinner seemed to be locked in combat down below.

"You might wish to bite on this." Shields put into Woodward's right hand a piece of sassafras root that still held the fragrant bark. Woodward couldn't help but note that it was marked by the grooves of previous teeth. Still, it was better than gnashing on his tongue. He put the sassafras into his mouth and fixed his teeth upon it.

The blade was ready. Shields stood beside the magistrate's head with the lancet poised at the point he wished to open, just at the base of Woodward's left ear, and the pewter bleeding bowl held beneath it. "Best to grasp the sheet and keep your fists closed," he suggested. Then he said quietly, "Courage, sir," and his hand designed the first cut.

Woodward stiffened and bit into the sassafras root as the hot lancet pierced his flesh. To the doctor's credit, the first cut was done quickly. As blood began to drip into the bowl, Shields made a second incision and then a third. Now the crimson drops were falling faster, and Shields refolded the lancet's blade back into its tortoiseshell grip. "There," he told the magistrate. "The worst is over." He took the root from Woodward's mouth and put it into his pocket, all the while holding the bleeding bowl directly beneath the three leaking wounds.

All that could be done now was wait. The sound of the blood dripping into the widening pool at the bowl's bottom was terribly loud to Woodward, who closed his eyes and also tried to close his mind. Bidwell, still standing at the door, had watched the procedure with a kind of sickened fascination, though the process of bleeding was certainly nothing novel and he himself had been bled several years ago when he'd been suffering stomach cramps.

Shields used the pressure of his fingers on the area behind Woodward's ear to keep the wounds open. In a few moments Shields said, "Mrs. Nettles, I shall need a pan of cool water and another cloth, please. Also a cup of rum would do the magistrate well, I think."

Mrs. Nettles directed the servant girl to get what Dr. Shields had requested. The blood kept falling, drop after drop, into the red pond.

Bidwell cleared his throat. "Magistrate? Can you hear me?"

"He hears you," Shields said, "but let him be. He needs no bothering."

"I only wish to ask him a question."

Woodward opened his eyes and stared at the ceiling. Up there he could see a brown waterstain. "Go ahead," he rasped.

"What did he say?" Bidwell asked, coming nearer to the bed.

"He said to ask your question," the doctor told him, looking down at the bowl to see that almost two ounces of life's fluid had so far been collected.

"Good. My question, sir, is this: what time will you be able to commence the trial today?"

Woodward's eyes found the face of Dr. Shields above him.

"What say you?" Bidwell stood beside the bed, keeping his gaze averted from the dripping blood. "This afternoon, perhaps?"

Woodward swallowed thickly; the raw pain in his throat was returning with a vengeance. "I . . . don't know . . . if I can—"

"Actually," Dr. Shields spoke up, "you might consider returning to your task, sir. Lying abed too long does no soul any good." He glanced toward Bidwell, and Woodward saw the other man's face doubly reflected in the doctor's spectacles. "We wish to keep your circulation from stagnating. It would also do you good, I think, to put your mind to proper use."

"Yes!" Bidwell said. "My sentiments exactly!"

"*However,*" the doctor amended, "I would not suggest you sit in that putrid gaol without some protection from the vapors. Robert, do you have a coat that might fit the magistrate?"

"If not, I can find one."

"All right. I'm going to prepare a liniment for you that should be smeared liberally upon your throat, chest, and back. It will stain your shirt and coat beyond hope, so give them up for lost. I wish you to wear a scarf around your throat after the liniment has been applied." He looked at Mrs. Nettles. "The magistrate will require a diet of soup and pap. Nothing solid until I give the word. Understood?"

"Yes sir."

"I'll send a servant to inform Elias Garrick he won't be needed at the gaol until . . . what time would you say, Ben?" Bidwell asked with all innocence. The doctor didn't answer, but instead watched the blood that continued to collect in the cup. "What say, Ben?" Bidwell lifted his eyebrows.

Woodward heard Dr. Shields give a heavy sigh. Then the doctor answered, "Two o'clock would be sufficient. Depending, of course, on the magistrate's desire to return to his task."

"Well, that's most of nine hours from now!" Great exultation was evident in Bidwell's voice. "Surely you can be rested and ready to continue the trial by then, Magistrate?"

"I'm not sure. I feel so poorly."

"Well of course you feel poorly at the moment, but a few hours of sleep will do wonders for you! Isn't that right, Ben?"

"He may feel stronger later in the day, yes," Shields said, with lackluster enthusiasm.

Bidwell grinned broadly. "There you have it! I should want to get out of this room and do something constructive, myself."

Woodward was hurting and his mind was fogged, but he knew precisely what Bidwell's prime interest in his health concerned. He was of the opinion that the sooner he completed the trial and delivered sentence, the sooner he might quit this swamphole and return to Charles Town.

"Very well," he managed to say. "If I am able, I'll hear Mr. Garrick at two o'clock."

"Wonderful!" Bidwell almost clapped his hands with joy; his obvious disregard for the magistrate's condition earned him a dagger of a glance from Dr. Shields, but he paid no heed. "I'll make certain Elias is at the gaol promptly on the hour."

Shortly afterward, the servant girl returned to the room with the pan of cool water, a cloth, and a cup of rum. When Dr. Shields saw that nearly four ounces of blood had dripped into the bowl, he said, "Mrs. Nettles, help me sit him up, please." Together they got the magistrate up to a sitting position. "Lean your head forward," Shields instructed him, and he immersed the cloth into the water and pressed it tightly against the incisions. "I have a brown jar in my case," he told the servant girl. "Fetch it out and open it." Shields scooped out some of the thick amber-colored ointment—a mixture of honey, pine oil, and hogsfat—and smeared it over the wounds. He repeated the process, and in so doing sealed together the edges of the cuts.

Woodward was light-headed. He felt sick to his stomach, but his breathing was so relieved that he didn't care. "Drink this down," Shields said, holding the rum cup to the magistrate's lips, and Woodward finished it off with three gulps. His throat flared again as the liquor scorched it, but after the rum was consumed he did feel so much the better.

"You should sleep now," Shields said. "I'll go directly and

make up the liniment." He gave the bleeding bowl to the servant girl. "Dispose of this and return the bowl here when you're done." She accepted it, but held it at arm's length. Shields returned the lancet to the leather sheath. "We will have to bleed you again tonight," he said to Woodward, "lest the condition recur." Woodward nodded, his eyes glazed over and his mouth numb. Shields turned his attention to Bidwell. "He should be looked in upon every hour. I'll return at ten o'clock to apply the liniment."

"Thank you, Ben," Bidwell said. "You're a true friend."

"I do what has to be done," Shields replied, returning his implements and medicines to the carrying case. "I trust you will do likewise?"

"You may rely on me."

"Magistrate, lie down and keep this cloth pressed against the incisions, as there may be some leakage."

"Mrs. Nettles," Bidwell said, "will you see the doctor out?"

"No need." Shields closed his case and picked it up. Behind his spectacles, his eyes were dead. "I know the way."

"Thank you for your help, doctor," Woodward whispered. "I do think I can sleep awhile." He heard the first cock crow outside.

Shields left the room and went downstairs. At the bottom of the staircase he was stopped by the servant girl who had attended him. She said, "Doctor, suh? Will you be needin' this?"

"Yes," he replied, "I think I shall," and he took from her the jug of rum she had uncorked. Then he continued on his way, out into the somber gray light and chilly drizzling rain.

BEFORE HANNIBAL GREEN arrived at the gaol with the prisoners' breakfast of biscuits and eggs, Matthew and Rachel received another visitor.

The door, its broken chain yet unmended by the blacksmith, was opened and there entered a slim black-suited figure, carrying a lantern with which to illume the murky confines.

"Who is that?" Matthew asked sharply, as the person's stealthy approach alarmed him. He'd awakened to a ragged chorus of rooster crows a short time previously, and had just finished relieving his bladder in his waste bucket. He was still in a bleary state, which caused him to fear for a few seconds that Satan himself had come to visit Rachel.

"Quiet, clerk!" came the stern reply. "'Tis not thee I have business with." Exodus Jerusalem, his prune of a face painted ruddy gold by the candlelight, wore his tricorn hat pulled low over his forehead. He passed by Matthew's cage and aimed the light toward Rachel. She was washing her face from her water bucket, her ebony hair wet and slicked back.

"Good morning to thee," the preacher said. She continued as if no one had spoken. "Well, thou canst be mute if thee please. But thou should not play at being deaf, as I have some words of interest."

"You're not supposed to be in here," Matthew said. "Mr. Green is—"

"The entry was not locked, was it? And as a commander in the army of God, I have a right to visit the battlefield, do I not?" He cast Matthew a bone-freezing stare, and then looked again upon Rachel. "Witch Howarth?" he said, his voice silken. "I had a very enlightening dinner with Mr. Bidwell and the magistrate last night." He felt no need to reveal that he had for the most part invited himself to dinner at the mansion, and had taken his sister and nephew there with him. While he had feasted at the banquet table, his relatives had been seated at the smaller table in the kitchen where Mrs. Nettles ate. "Mr. Bidwell was a genial host," Jerusalem went on. "He entertained me with the particulars of thy offenses."

Rachel began to wash her arms. "Thou hast committed murders and vile wickedness," the preacher hissed. "So vile it dost take mine breath away."

Something about Jerusalem's voice made Matthew speak up. "You should remove yourself from here. You're neither needed nor wanted."

"Of that I am sure. As I said, clerk, I have no business with thee, but take care lest thy haughty demeanor draw down misery." Jerusalem dismissed Matthew with a slight lifting of his pointed chin. "Witch Howarth?" he implored. "Thy motives intrigue me. Wouldst thou tell me why the Devil hast embraced thee so fondly?"

"You're half crazed," Rachel said, without looking at him. "And the other half is a raving lunatic."

"I shouldn't think thee would fall to the ground and kiss my boots. But at least we have moved beyond the silence of a stone. Let me pose this question, Witch Howarth: dost thou not know the power I possess?"

"Power to do *what?* Make an ass of yourself!"

"No," he replied calmly. "The power to free thee from thy prison."

"What? And walk me to the stake?"

"The power," he said, "to banish Satan from thy soul, and therefore *save* thee from the stake."

"You're mistaking your power with that belonging to Magistrate Woodward," Matthew said.

Jerusalem ignored him. "I will tell thee a tale," he offered to Rachel. "Two years ago, in a new settlement in the Maryland colony, a young widow by the name of Eleanor Peyton found herself in the same predicament as thee. Cast into a cage, she was, on accusation of witchcraft and the murder of her neighbor's wife. The magistrate who heard her case was a right true man of God, and breached no affronts by the Devil. He sentenced Madam Peyton to be hanged by the neck. But on the night before her gallows dance, Madam Peyton confessed her sins and witchcraft to me. She sank to her knees, spoke the Lord's Prayer in a reverent voice, and begged me to oust Satan from her soul. The Evil One caused her breasts to swell and her private parts to water, and these afflictions I attacked by the laying on of hands. Her salvation, though, did not come easily. That night it was a tremendous battle. The both of us struggled mightily, until we were drenched in sweat and gasping for God's air. At last, just before the dawn, she threw her head back and released a scream, and I knew it was the sound of Satan tearing loose from the depths of her innermost being." He closed his eyes; a slight smile played across his mouth, and Matthew imagined he must be hearing that scream.

When Jerusalem's eyes opened once more, some trick of the candlelight gave them a reddish glint. "At first light," he said to Rachel, "I pronounced Madam Peyton freed of the Devil's claws, and therefore petitioned the magistrate that he should hear her confession before the torches were flamed. I said I would stand as a witness for any woman who embraced Christianity and engulfed it with such passion. The end result was that Madam Peyton was banished from the town, yet she became a crusader for God and travelled with me for some months." He paused, his head cocked to one side. "Art thou listening to my tale, Witch Howarth?"

"I think your tale exposes you," Rachel answered.

"As a man who careth deeply for the right ways of women, yes. Thy breed is so easily led astray, by all manner of evil. And thus thy breed leadeth men astray as well, and woe be to the tribe of Adam."

Rachel finished washing and pushed the bucket aside. She lifted her gaze to the preacher. "You seem to know a great deal about evil."

"I do. Both from without and within."

"I'm sure you are most interested in the ins and outs, especially concerning my breed."

"Thy mockery is well aimed, but falls short of the mark," Jerusalem said. "In my youth—indeed, for most of my life—I myself walked the dark path. I was a thief and blasphemer, I sought the company of doxies and revelled in the sinful pleasures of fornication and sodomy. Indeed, I ruined the souls of many women even as I revelled in their flesh. Oh yes, Witch Howarth, I do know a great deal about evil."

"You sound prideful of it, preacher."

"My attraction to such matters was a thing of birth. I have been told by many doxies—and good widows, too—that my member is the largest they have ever seen. Some admitted it took their breath away."

"What kind of ministry is this?" Matthew asked, his face flushed by Jerusalem's indecent claims. "I think you'd better leave, sir!"

"I shall." Jerusalem kept staring fixedly at Rachel. "I want thee to know, Witch Howarth, that my gift of persuasion is undiminished. If thou desireth, I may do the same for thee that was done for Madam Peyton. She now lives a virtuous life in Virginia, all the sin having been squeezed from her bosom. Such release may be given to thee, as well, if thou but sayeth the word."

"And I would be spared from the stake?"

"Without a doubt."

"After which you would recommend that I be banished from my land and home, and you would offer me a place alongside yourself?"

"Yes."

"I am not a witch," Rachel said forcefully. "I do not follow a dark master now, and I will not follow a dark master in the future. My word to you is: *no.*"

Jerusalem smiled. The lantern's light glinted off his teeth. "The magistrate has yet to pass sentence on thee, of course. Perhaps thou hast hopes to sway the man through this boy?" He motioned with a nod toward Matthew. Rachel just glowered at him. "Well, thou dost have some time to think upon it. I would not linger too long, though, as I expect the timber will be laid for thy fire within a few days. Wouldst be a terrible pity for thee to burn, being so young and so badly in need of a Christian sword."

He'd no sooner finished his last word when the door opened and Hannibal Green entered carrying a lantern and a steaming bucket full of the biscuit-and-eggs mush that would be their breakfast. Green stopped in his tracks when he saw the preacher. Exodus Jerusalem had made a strong impression on him yesterday afternoon. "Sir?" he said, rather meekly. "No visitors are allowed here unless Mr. Bidwell approves it. That's his rule."

"The Lord God approves it," Jerusalem said, and offered a warm smile to the giant gaol-keeper. "But as I do not wish to violate the earthly rules of Mr. Bidwell, I shall immediately with-draw."

"Thank you, sir."

On his way out, Jerusalem placed a hand upon Green's shoulder. "Thou hast done a fine job guarding the witch. A man cannot be too careful in dealing with the likes of her."

"Yes sir, I know that. And I thank you for the 'preciation."

"A thankless task, I'm sure. Thou art a good Christian fellow, I can tell." He started to move on, then paused. "Oh. I am speaking this night at seven o'clock on the subject of the witch, if thou shouldst care to attend. It shall be the first of a series of sermons. Dost thou know where I am camped? On Industry Street?"

"Yes sir."

"If thou wouldst serve God, please inform your brother and sister citizens of the time. Also, please let it be known that I live from hand to mouth on the blessings of Christ and what may find its way into my offering basket. Wouldst thou serve God in such a way?"

"Yes sir," Green said. "I would. I mean . . . I *will*."

Jerusalem turned his face toward Rachel once more. "Time is short for repentance, Witch Howarth. But redemption may still be thine, if thou dost desireth it." He touched a finger to the brim of his tricorn, and then made his departure.

seventeen

MATTHEW WAS SHOCKED at his first sight of the magistrate, just before two o'clock. Woodward, who entered the gaol supported between Hannibal Green and Nicholas Paine, wore a long gray overcoat and a rust-colored scarf wrapped about his throat. His face—which glistened with sweat and was a few shades lighter than his coat—was cast downward, mindful of his walking. He took feeble steps, as if he'd aged twenty years since Matthew had seen him yesterday afternoon.

When Green had brought the midday meal, he'd explained to Matthew that the course of the trial had been delayed because the magistrate had fallen very ill during the night, but what he heard from Paine was that Elias Garrick was scheduled to appear at two o'clock. Therefore Matthew had expected to see the magistrate under the weather, but not become a near invalid. He realized at once that Woodward should be in bed—or possibly even at Dr. Shields's infirmary.

"What are you bringing him in here for?" Matthew protested, standing at the bars. "The magistrate's not healthy enough to sit at court today!"

"I'm following Mr. Bidwell's orders," Paine replied, as he steadied Woodward while Green unlocked the cell. "He said to bring the magistrate here."

"This is an outrage! The magistrate shouldn't be forced to work when he's hardly strong enough to stand!"

"I see no one forcing him," Paine answered. Green got the door open and then helped Paine walk Woodward through. A strong, bitter medicinal odor also entered.

"I demand to see Bidwell!" Matthew had almost shouted it, his cheeks reddening as his temper rose. "Bring him here this minute!"

"Hush," the magistrate whispered. "That hurts my ears."

"Sir, why did you allow yourself to be brought here? You're in no condition to—"

"The work must be done," Woodward interrupted. "The sooner the trial is ended . . . the sooner we may leave this wretched town." He eased himself down into his chair. "Hot tea," he said to Paine, his face pinched with the effort of speech.

"Yes sir, I'll get you some directly."

"But *not* from Mrs. Vaughan," Woodward said. "I'll drink any tea but hers."

"Yes sir."

"Mr. Paine!" Matthew said as he and Green started to leave the cell. "You know the magistrate has no business being here!"

"Matthew, settle yourself," Woodward cautioned, in his raw whisper. "I may be somewhat ill . . . but I have my responsibilities. You have your own. Be seated and prepare for our witness." He glanced through the bars into the next cage. "Good afternoon, madam." Rachel nodded at him from her seat on the bench, her face grim but well composed. Paine and Green left the cell and made their way out of the gaol.

"Sit and prepare," Woodward repeated to his clerk. "Mr. Garrick will soon be here."

Matthew knew there was no point in further argument. He put the Bible in front of Woodward, then opened the desk drawer into which he'd placed the box of writing supplies and placed it atop his own desk. He sat down, lifted the boxlid, and removed the quill, inkwell, and paper, after he began to massage his right hand to warm it for the exertion that was to follow. The noise of

Woodward's husky, labored breathing was going to be a considerable distraction. In fact, he didn't know how he could concentrate at all today. He said, "Sir, tell me this: how are you going to ask questions of Mr. Garrick when you can hardly speak?"

"Mr. Garrick will do most of the speaking." Woodward paused, securing a breath. His eyes closed for a few seconds; he felt so weak he feared he might have to lay his head down upon the desk. The pungent fumes of the liniment that even now heated his chest, back, and throat rose around his face and up his swollen nostrils. He opened his eyes, his vision blurred. "I will do my task," he vowed. "Just do yours."

In a few minutes Edward Winston entered the gaol with Elias Garrick, who wore a dark brown suit that appeared two sizes too small and bore fresh patches on the elbows and knees. His gray hair had been combed back against his scalp with glistening pomade. Garrick looked fearfully into the cell at Rachel Howarth, prompting Winston to say, "She can't harm you, Elias. Come along."

Garrick was motioned toward the stool that had been positioned before Woodward's desk. He sat down upon it, his gaunt-cheeked face cast toward the floor. His sinewy hands clasped together, as if in silent supplication.

"You're going to be fine." Winston placed his hand on Garrick's shoulder. "Magistrate, you can understand that Elias is a bit nervous, with the witch in such close proximity."

"He won't be kept long," was Woodward's rasped reply.

"Uh . . . well sir, I was wondering, then." Winston raised his eyebrows. "What time should I bring Violet Adams?"

"Pardon?"

"Violet Adams," Winston said. "The child. Mr. Bidwell told me to fetch her later this afternoon. What time would be agreeable?"

"One moment!" It was all Matthew could do to keep his seat. "The magistrate's only seeing one witness today!"

"Well . . . Mr. Bidwell seems to think otherwise. On the way to get Elias, I stopped at the Adams house and informed the family that Violet was expected to testify this afternoon. It was Mr. Bidwell's wish that the trial be concluded today."

"I don't care whose wish it was! Magistrate Woodward is too ill to—"

Woodward suddenly reached out and grasped Matthew's arm, squeezing it to command silence. "Very well," he whispered. "Bring the child . . . at four o'clock."

"I shall."

Matthew looked incredulously at the magistrate, who paid him no attention.

"Thank you, Mr. Winston," Woodward said. "You may go."

"Yes sir." Winston gave Garrick a reassuring pat on the shoulder and took his leave.

Before Matthew could say anything more, Woodward picked up the Bible and offered it to Garrick. "Hold this. Matthew, swear him to truth."

Matthew obeyed. When the ritual was done and Matthew reached out to take the Good Book, Garrick pressed it against his chest. "Please? Might I keep a'hold of it?"

"You may," Woodward answered. "Go ahead and tell your story."

"You mean what I already done told you?"

"This time for the record." Woodward motioned toward Matthew, who sat with his quill freshly dipped and poised over the paper.

"Where do you want me to start?"

"From the beginning."

"All right, then." Garrick continued to stare at the floor, then licked his lips and said, "Well . . . like I done told you, my land's right next to the Howarth farm. That night I was feelin' poorly, and I waked up to go outside and spew what was makin' me ill. It was silent. Everythin' was silent, like the whole world was afeared to breathe."

"Sir?" Matthew said to the farmer. "What time would you make this to be?"

"What time? Oh . . . two or three, maybe. I don't recall." He looked at Woodward. "Want me to go on?" Woodward nodded. "Anyways, I went out. That's when I seen somebody crossin' the Howarth cornfield. Wasn't no stalks that time of year, y'see. I seen this person walkin' in the field, without no lantern. I thought it was awful strange, so I went over the fence, and I followed 'em behind the barn. That's when . . ." He stared at the floor again, a pulse beating at his temple. "That's when I seen the witch naked and on her knees, tendin' to her master."

"By 'the witch,' do you mean Rachel Howarth?" Woodward's frail whisper had just about vanished.

"Yes sir."

Woodward started to ask another question, but now his voice would not respond. He had reached the end of his questioning. He looked at Matthew, his face stricken. "Matthew?" he was able to say. "Ask?"

Matthew realized the magistrate was giving over to him the reins of this interview. He redipped his quill, a dark anger simmering in him that Bidwell had either forced or persuaded the magistrate to imperil his health in such a fashion. But now that the interview had begun, it should be finished. Matthew cleared his throat. "Mr. Garrick," he said, "what do you mean by 'master'?"

"Well . . . Satan, I reckon."

"And this figure was wearing exactly what?"

"A black cloak and a cowl, like I done told you. There was gold buttons on the front. I seen 'em shine in the moonlight."

"You couldn't see this figure's face?"

"No sir, but I seen . . . that thing the witch was suckin' on. That black cock covered with thorns. Couldn't be nobody but Satan hisself, owned somethin' like that."

"And you say Rachel Howarth was completely naked?"

"Yes sir, she was."

"What were *you* wearing?"

"Sir?" Garrick frowned.

"Your clothes," Matthew said. "What were you wearing?"

Garrick paused, thinking about it. "Well sir, I had on . . . I mean to say. I . . ." His frown deepened. "That's might odd," he said at last. "I can't recall."

"A coat, I presume?" Matthew prodded. "Since it was cold out?"

Garrick slowly blinked. "A coat," he said. "Must've had on my coat, but . . . I don't remember puttin' it on."

"And shoes? Or boots?"

"Shoes," he said. "No, wait. My boots. Yes sir, I believe I had on my boots."

"Did you get a good look at Rachel Howarth's face, there behind the barn?"

"Well . . . not her face, sir," Garrick admitted. "Just her backside. She was kneelin' away from me. But I seen her hair. And she was a dark-skinned woman. It was her, all right." He glanced uneasily at the magistrate and then back to Matthew. "It had to be her. It was Daniel's land."

Matthew nodded, scribing down what Garrick had just said. "Did you spew?" he asked suddenly.

"Sir?"

Matthew lifted his face and stared directly into Garrick's dull eyes. "Did you *spew?* You left your bed to go outside for that purpose. Did you do so?"

Again, Garrick had to think about it. "I . . . don't recall if I did," he said. "No, I think I seen that figure crossin' the Howarth cornfield, and I . . . must've forgot 'bout feelin' poorly."

"Let's go back a bit, please," Matthew instructed. "What time had you gone to bed that night?"

"Usual time. 'Bout half past eight, I reckon."

"Both you and your wife went to bed at the same time?"

"Thereabouts, yes sir."

"Were you feeling poorly when you went to bed?"

"No sir. I don't think I was." He licked his lips again, a nervous gesture. "Pardon me for askin', but . . . what's all this got to do with the witch?"

Matthew looked at the magistrate. Woodward's chin had

drooped, but his eyes were open and he gave no sign of wishing to interfere—even if that were possible—with Matthew's line of inquiry. Matthew returned his attention to Garrick. "I'm trying to clear up a point of confusion I have," he explained. "So you did not go to bed feeling ill, but you awakened perhaps six hours later sick to your stomach?"

"Yes sir."

"You got out of bed carefully, so as not to awaken your wife?"

"Yes sir, that's right."

"And then?"

"Then I went outside to spew," Garrick said.

"But before that didn't you pause to put on your coat and boots?"

"I . . . well . . . yes sir, I must've, but I can't rightly recall it."

"How many gold buttons," Matthew said, "were on the front of Satan's cloak?"

"Six," Garrick answered.

"Six? Of that number you're positive?"

"Yes sir." He nodded vigorously. "I seen 'em shine in the moonlight."

"It was a full moon, then?"

"Sir?"

"A full moon," Matthew repeated. "Was it a full moon?"

"Reckon it had to be. But I don't recall ever lookin' up at it."

"And even with this bright moonlight—which enabled you to see a figure crossing a distant field without a lantern—you were unable to see Satan's face?"

"Well sir . . . the Devil was wearin' a cowl over his head."

"That may be so, but were not the buttons on the front of his cloak? If the bright moonlight made those six gold buttons so memorable, could you not see a *portion* of his face?"

"No sir." Garrick shifted uneasily on the stool. "It weren't his face that caught my sight. It was . . . that terrible big thing the witch was suckin' on."

"Covered with thorns, I think you've already told us?"

"Yes sir, it was."

"Satan spoke to you, did he not? In fact, he called you by name?" Garrick nodded. "Did you not look at Satan's face when he spoke to you?"

"I believe I did. But . . . there weren't nothin' there but dark."

"Did Rachel Howarth ever turn her face toward you?"

"No sir, she didn't."

Matthew paused to lay aside his quill and massage his hand again. He glanced once more at Woodward, and saw that the magistrate was still motionless but his eyes were open and his breathing was steady, if very labored.

"Mr. Garrick!" Rachel suddenly said, standing at the bars. "What have I ever done to you, to cause you to make up these lies?"

"They ain't lies!" Garrick hugged the Bible for protection. "You know I seen you, out there givin' service to your master!"

"I was never behind that barn, doing such a sin! And I never consorted with such a creature! If you're not lying, your mind has invented a fantasy!"

Woodward loudly slapped his hand upon the table for order, and immediately Matthew said, "Silence, please! Madam Howarth, I speak for the magistrate when I say it's in your best interest not to disrupt the testimony."

"Her best *interest?*" Garrick sounded amazed. "Have you taken the witch's side?"

"No, Mr. Garrick, I have not. I'm only pointing out to Madam Howarth that it is your right to speak without interruption." Matthew started to pick up the quill again when Nicholas Paine entered the gaol bearing a basket.

"Pardon the intrusion, but I have your tea." Paine came into the cell, placed the basket before Woodward, and opened it. Inside was a simple white clay pot and a single cup. "Compliments of Mrs. Zeborah Crawford."

"My thanks," Woodward whispered.

"Will you be needing anything else?"

Woodward thought about it. He patted the desk in front of him. "Poppets," he said.

"The poppets? You wish to see them?"

Woodward nodded. "Now."

"They're at my house. I'll go directly and fetch them." Paine cast a quick glance in the direction of Rachel and then hurried out.

Matthew had his quill in hand once more, and a fresh sheet of paper before him. "May I continue, sir?" he asked Woodward, who was pouring himself a cup of dark brown brew, and he received a slight nod as a signal to proceed. "Mr. Garrick?" Matthew said. "Think hard on this next question, if you will. Put the image of Satan's six gold buttons in your mind, and tell me if they were fixed on the cloak six in a straight line or three side by side?"

There was a sharp clatter of crockery. Matthew looked to his left to see that Woodward had spilled his tea. The magistrate was staring at him as if the clerk had taken leave of his senses.

"It *is* a pertinent question, sir," Matthew said. "I do think it deserves an answer."

"It's foolish," Woodward whispered, his gray face stern as a rock.

"Might you reserve your opinion until after the question is answered?"

"What kind of question is it?" Garrick asked, visibly agitated. "I thought I was brung here to tell you 'bout the witch, not about buttons!"

"You were brought here to tell us whatever is necessary for the magistrate to weigh his judgment," Matthew countered. "Remember, sir, that you hold a Holy Bible, and that you've vowed to speak only the truth. Remember that God is listening to your answer." He paused a few seconds to let Garrick reflect on that pronouncement. "Now: were the six buttons arranged in a single line, or were they three side by side?"

"They were . . ." Garrick suddenly stopped. His tongue flicked out again, wetting his lips. His fingers tightened on the Bible, his knuckles whitening. "They were . . ." Again he faltered. His face seemed threatened by conflicting currents that moved beneath the skin. He took a long breath, in preparation to make his decision. "Six gold buttons," he said. "On the black cloak. I seen 'em. Shine in the moonlight."

"Yes, sir," Matthew said. "But what arrangement were they in?" Garrick frowned; his mouth worked, but no sound emerged. His right hand began to rub in small circles on the Bible. He stared blankly at nothing, his eyes glazed and the pulse beating harder at his temple. Matthew realized that Woodward had leaned slightly forward and his expression had become keen.

"It was a silent town," Garrick said, in what was almost a whisper. A glaze of sweat glistened on his forehead. "Silent. The whole world, afeared to breathe."

Matthew had been taking down every word that the man uttered. He redipped his quill and held it ready. "It's a simple question, sir. Do you not have an answer?" Garrick slowly blinked, his jaw slack. "Sir?" Matthew prompted. "An answer, please?"

"The six gold buttons were . . . they . . ." He stared into nothingness for a moment longer, and then he shook his head. "I don't know."

"They caught your attention and were clearly defined by the moonlight, yes?"

"Yes."

"But you don't recall how they were arranged on the cloak?"

"No," Garrick said, his voice thick. "I . . . can see them buttons in my head. I see 'em shinin' in the moonlight, but . . . I don't know if they was straight down or three by three."

"All right, then. Tell us what happened after Satan spoke to you."

"Yes sir." Garrick lifted a hand from the Good Book and wiped his damp forehead. "He . . . asked me if I liked what I was a'lookin' at. I didn't want to speak, but he made me say 'yes.' He *made* me. Then he laughed, and I was ashamed. He let me go. I ran home, and I got in bed beside my 'Becca. That next mornin' I went to see Mr. Paine and I told him the whole story."

"When you say he let you go, do you mean he held you spellbound?"

"Yes sir, I believe he did. I wanted to run, but I couldn't move."

"Did he release you with a word or a gesture?"

Again, Garrick frowned as he tried to assemble his thoughts. "I can't say. All I know is, he let me go."

"And your wife was still sleeping when you returned to bed?"

"Yes sir, she was. She never waked up at all. I closed my eyes tight as I could, and next thing I knew I heard the cock crow and it was mornin'."

Matthew's eyes narrowed. "You mean after that experience you had no trouble falling asleep?"

"I don't know if I did or not. The cock crowed, and I waked up."

Matthew glanced quickly at the magistrate before he posed the following question: "Mr. Garrick, sir, is it possible—just *possible*—that you were never awake at all?"

"I don't know what you mean, sir."

"I'm asking if what you thought was real may have been a dream. Is there any possibility of that?"

"No sir!" Garrick clutched the Bible tightly once more. "It all happened like I said! I woke up with stomach trouble and had to spew, and I went outside! I seen that devil and the witch there behind that barn sure as I'm lookin' at you! I swear before the Lord God I did!"

Matthew said quietly, "There's no need for such swearing. You hold the Bible and you've already vowed your story is the truth. You *are* a God-fearing man, aren't you?"

"Yes sir, I am. If I was lyin' to you, I'd be struck dead in an instant!"

"I'm sure you believe so. I have only one last question for you, and then—with the magistrate's approval, of course—you may go. My question is: how many buttons are on the coat you wore that night?"

"*Sir?*" Garrick tilted his head to one side, as if his ears hadn't quite caught the inquiry.

"You seem to be a highly observant individual," Matthew said. "Can you tell me how many buttons adorn the coat you put on before you went outside to spew?"

"Well . . . like I said, I don't recall puttin' my coat on."

"But you must know how many buttons it has. I presume you wear it quite a lot in cold weather. How many? Four? Five? Six, perhaps?"

"Five," Garrick answered. "No . . . I think one of 'em broke off. It must be four."

"Thank you," Matthew said, and he put his quill aside. "Magistrate, I would suggest that Mr. Garrick be freed to go home."

"Are you *sure?*" Woodward whispered, not without some sarcasm.

"I'm sure Mr. Garrick has told us the truth, as far as he knows the truth to be. I don't think there's any use in keeping him here."

Woodward took a drink of tea and put the cup aside. "Good day," he told the farmer. "The court thanks you."

"I'm free to go, then?" Garrick stood up. He reluctantly relinquished his grip on the Bible and laid it back before the magistrate. "May I be bold to say, sir . . . I hope I've helped send that witch to the fire. Reverend Grove was a right good man, and what I knew of Daniel he was a Christian too. But when Satan slips into a town, there ain't nothin' that follows but wickedness and tears."

"Mr. Garrick?" Matthew said as the man started to leave the cell. "In your opinion, was it Rachel Howarth or Satan who committed those murders?"

"Had to be Satan, I'd say. I seen Grove's body laid out in the church, and I seen Daniel's a'layin' in the field. A throat cut like those were . . . couldn't been a woman's hand that done it."

"In your opinion, as a God-fearing soul, would you believe that Satan could freely enter a church and murder a man of the Lord?"

"I would never have thought it. But it happened, didn't it?"

"Thank you," Matthew said. "You may go."

As soon as Garrick left the gaol Rachel said, "You understand it now, don't you? He was dreaming the whole thing!"

"That is a distinct possibility." Matthew looked at the magistrate, who was stroking his unshaven chin with his fingers. "Would you agree, sir?"

Woodward took his time in offering a reply. It seemed to him that Matthew was awfully quick in his attempts to deflect Garrick's testimony. The boy was very intelligent, yes; but it appeared to Woodward that Matthew was sharper and quicker now that he'd ever seen him to be. Of course, never before had Matthew been put into the position of commanding an interrogation, and perhaps his abilities had simply risen to the challenge, but . . . there was something a bit frightening in his desire to destroy Garrick's Bible-sworn statements.

It was a fervor, Woodward decided, that bore careful watching. He sipped the bitter tea and whispered, "This court is not yet adjourned. Let us keep our opinions in rein."

"It seems to me, sir," Matthew plowed on, "that Mr. Garrick's testimony bears all the signs of being a dream. Some things he can recall quite vividly, while others—things he ought to be able to know—are lost to his memory."

"Though my voice is weak," Woodward said, "my ears are still in order. I heard exactly what you did."

"Yes, sir." Matthew decided he should retreat on this subject. "Pardon my manners."

"Pardon accepted. Now be quiet." Matthew took the time to clean his quill. Woodward poured himself a fresh cup and Rachel paced back and forth in her cage.

Nicholas Paine returned carrying a bundle wrapped with white cloth. Instantly Rachel stopped her pacing and came to the bars to watch. Paine placed the bundle on the desk before Wood-ward and started to open the cloth.

"A moment," Matthew said. "Was that how you originally found the objects?"

"The cloth is original, yes."

"It was not bound up?"

"It was just as you see it. And here are the poppets, just as they were." He opened the cloth and there were four small figures formed of straw, sticks, and what appeared to be red clay. The poppets were human-shaped, but bore no attempt at facial fea-tures; the red clay of their heads was smooth and unmarked. Two of the figures, however, had thin black ribbons tied around the sticks that would represent the human throat. On closer inspec-tion, Woodward saw that the stick-throats had been gashed with a blade.

"I assume those two were meant to be Reverend Grove and Daniel Howarth," Paine said. "The others must have been victims of enchantment, or maybe people who would've been murdered had we not captured the witch." Rachel made a sound of disgust, but was wise enough to hold her tongue.

"You can deny it all you please!" Paine turned toward her. "But I myself found these under a floorboard in your kitchen, madam! Under the very boards that your husband walked upon! Why did you murder him? Because he found you doing witch-craft? Or did he catch you servicing your master?"

"If they were hidden in my house, someone else put them there!" Rachel replied, with considerable heat. "Maybe *you* did! Maybe you murdered my husband, too!"

"I'm sure he had nothing I wanted!"

"But he did!" she said. "He had *me.*"

Paine's face froze with the last vestige of a mocking smile on his mouth.

"I *can* think of a reason you might have fashioned those pop-pets and hidden them in my house," Rachel went on, her face pressed against the bars and her eyes afire. "Do you not think I noticed the way you looked at me, when you thought Daniel didn't see? Do you not think I felt you devouring me? Well, Daniel saw it too! He told me, less than a week before he was murdered, to beware of you because you had a hungry stare and you were not to be trusted! Daniel may have been a stern and quiet man, but he was a very good judge of character!"

"Obviously he was," Paine said. "He married a witch."

"Look at the magistrate," Rachel commanded, "and tell him about your affair with Lucretia Vaughan! Oh, everyone in Fount Royal knows it but Mr. Vaughan, and he knows it too in his heart but he's too much a mouse to make a squeak! Tell him about your affair with Blessed Pearson, and your dalliance with Mary Summers! Go on, look him in the face and admit it like the man you wish to be!"

Paine did not look at the magistrate. He continued to stare at Rachel even as he let out a laugh that—to Matthew's ears— sounded a bit strangled. "You're not only a damnable witch," he said, "but you're raving insane as well!"

"Tell us all why a handsome, healthy man like yourself has never married! Isn't it because you're only pleased to possess what belongs to other men?"

"Now I *know* you're insane! I've never married because I've spent my life in travelling! I also prize freedom, and a man's freedom is destroyed when he gives it up to a wife!"

"And while you have no wife, you are free to turn wives into wenches!" Rachel said. "Mary Summers was a respectable woman before you got your hands on her, and now where is she? After you killed her husband in that duel, she perished of sorrow within a month!"

"That duel," he answered coldly, "concerned a point of honor. Quentin Summers splashed wine in my face at the tavern and called me a card cheat. I had no choice but to call him out."

"He knew you were having your way with his wife, but he couldn't catch you! He was a farmer, not a duellist!"

"Farmer or not, he was given the first shot. He missed. If you'll recall, I only wounded him in the shoulder."

"A bullet wound in this town is a death sentence! He just took longer to die than if you'd shot him through the heart!"

"The subject of my visit here, I believe, is to display the poppets." Paine turned his gaze toward the magistrate. "Which I have done. Do you wish to keep them, sir?"

Even if Woodward's voice hadn't been so diminished, it would have been altogether stolen by the accusations and statements that had just flown like wild birds in a storm. It was going to take him a while to absorb all of this, but one thing stood out in clear relief in his mind.

He remembered Dr. Shields saying in regards to Paine: *He was married, when he was a younger man. His wife perished from an illness that caused her to suffer fits until she died.* Why, then, did Paine contend he had never been married?

"Magistrate? Do you wish to keep the poppets?" Paine repeated.

"Oh! Uh . . . yes, I do," Woodward answered, in his tortured whisper. "They shall become the court's property."

"Very well, then." He fired a look at Rachel that, were it a cannonshot, might have cleaved through the hull of a warship. "I'd beware that one and her nasty tongue, sir! She holds such a grudge against me I'm surprised my murder wasn't on her list of crimes!"

"Face the magistrate and deny that what I've said is the truth!" Rachel all but shouted.

Woodward had endured enough of this discord. For want of a better instrument, he picked up the Bible and slapped it down against the desk's edge. "Hush!" he said, as loudly as he could; instantly he paid the price in pain, and tears welled up.

"Madam Howarth?" Matthew said. "I think it wise to be silent."

Paine added, "I think it wise to begin cutting the stake for her execution!"

This sarcastic remark bruised Matthew's sense of propriety, especially following on the heels of such heated wranglings. His voice tightened. "Mr. Paine, it would interest me to know if what Madam Howarth claims about you is true."

"Would it, now?" Paine put his hands on his hips. "You're overstepping your bounds, aren't you, clerk?"

"May I speak for you, sir?" Matthew asked Woodward, and the magistrate didn't hesitate to nod his assent. "There, Mr. Paine. My bounds are more clearly defined. Now: are these claims true or false?"

"I didn't know I was to be a witness today. I might've worn a better suit."

"Your delay in answering," Matthew said, "delays the outcome of this trial. Shall you be instructed to sit down and swear truth on the Bible?"

"You might instruct it, but I doubt you could enforce it."

"Yes, I'm sure you're correct. I'm no duellist, either."

Paine's face had taken on a reddish cast. "Listen to me! I didn't want to fight that man, and if he'd insulted me in private I would have let it go! But he had to test me in public, right there at Van Gundy's! What could I do but call him out? He had the choice of weapons, and the fool chose pistols instead of blades! I would've given him a single cut and called it done!" He shook his head, his expression taking on a hint of regret. "But no, Summers wanted heart's blood. Well, his pistol misfired and the ball hardly rolled out of the muzzle! Still, that was his shot. Then it was mine. I aimed for the meat of his shoulder, which I squarely hit. How would I know he was such a bleeder?"

"You might have fired at the earth," Matthew said. "Isn't that acceptable when the first shot misfires?"

"Not by my rules," came the chill reply. "If a man aims a weapon at me, whether it's a pistol or a dagger, he must account for it. I've been stabbed between the ribs before and shot through my leg; so I hold no sympathy for anyone who tries to do me harm! No matter if he *is* a farmer!"

"You suffered these wounds during your career at sea?" Matthew asked.

"The stab, yes. The shot . . . was a later incident." He stared at the clerk with fresh interest. "What do you know of my career at sea?"

"Just that you were a seaman aboard a brigantine. Mr. Bidwell told me. A brigantine is a fast ship, isn't it? In fact, brigantines are the vessels of choice by pirates, are they not?"

"They are. And they are also the vessels of choice by those who would *hunt* pirates in service of the trading companies."

"That was your profession, then?"

"Hardly a profession. I was sixteen years old, hot-tempered and eager to fight. I served one year and four months on a coastal patrol before a black-flagger's rapier laid me low. That was the end of my saltwater adventures."

"Oh," Matthew said quietly. "I see."

"What? Did you think *me* a pirate?"

"I wondered." Now that the subject had been opened, he had to ask the next question as well: "Might I inquire . . . who taught you to roll your tobacco in the Spanish fashion?"

"A Spaniard, of course," Paine said. "A prisoner aboard ship. He had no teeth, but he dearly loved his cigars. I think he was hanged with one in his mouth."

"Oh," Matthew repeated. His suspicions concerning the Spanish spy had just fallen to pieces like shattered mirrorglass, and he felt an utter fool.

"All right, I admit it! " Paine lifted his hands. "Yes, I have done the things the witch claims, but they were not all my doing! Lucretia Vaughan came after me like a shewolf! I couldn't walk the street without being near attacked by her! A match can only bear so much friction before it flames, and a single hot blaze is all I gave her! You know how such things happen!"

"Um . . ." Matthew inspected the tip of his quill. "Well . . . yes, such things do happen."

"And perhaps—*perhaps*—my eye does wander. I did, at one point, feel an attraction to the witch. *Before* she was a witch, I mean. You must admit, she's a handsome piece. Is she not?"

"My opinion is of no consequence." Matthew blushed so furiously that his face hurt.

"You do admit it. You'd have to be blind if you did not. Well,

I may have looked in her direction once or twice, but I never laid a hand on her. I had respect for her husband."

"I'd be amazed if you had respect for *anyone!*" Rachel said sharply.

Paine started to fire off another volley at her, but he checked himself. After a pause in which he stared at the floor, he answered in what was almost a saddened tone, "You don't know me very well, madam, even though you imagine you do. I am not the beast you make me out to be. It is my nature to respect only those who respect themselves. As for the others, from them I feel free to take what is offered. Whether that makes me good or bad, I can't say, but that is how I am." He looked at the magistrate and lifted his chin high. "I did not put those poppets in the witch's house. I found them, according to a dream related to me by Cara Grunewald. It seems she had a vision—God-sent, if you want my opinion—in which a shining figure told her there was something of importance hidden beneath the floor of Rachel Howarth's kitchen. We knew not what we were searching for. But there the poppets were, beneath a loosened board."

"This was how long after Madam Howarth had been removed from her house?" Matthew asked.

"Two weeks, I believe. Not any longer."

"I presume her house wasn't guarded or watched in any way?"

"No. Why should it have been?"

"No reason. But two weeks was time enough for someone else to form the poppets and hide them under the floor, don't you think?"

Paine surprised Matthew by giving a short, sharp laugh. "You're jesting, of course!"

"Two weeks," Matthew repeated. "An empty, unguarded house. The poppets are made of common materials. Anyone might have placed them there."

"Have you lost your senses, clerk? No one put them there but the witch herself! You're forgetting that Madam Grunewald had a divine vision that directed us where to look!"

"I know nothing of divine visions. I only know two weeks passed and the house was open to all who might want to enter."

"*No one* wanted to enter," Paine argued. "The only reason I and the others who were with me entered is that we had a task to perform. When it was done, we didn't linger there!"

"Who discovered the loosened board? You or someone else?"

"I did, and if you like I'll vow on the Bible that I hadn't set foot in that house since the morning the witch was taken out of it!"

Matthew glanced at the magistrate. Woodward, who was looking dourly at him, shook his head. Matthew felt he'd come to the end of this particular road. He believed Paine. Why should the man have made the poppets and placed them there? Perhaps it *had* been a divine vision sent from God to Cara Grunewald; but then again, if he followed that track, he must come to the conclusion that Rachel was indeed performing witchcraft. He sighed heavily and said, "It's not necessary that you swear on the Bible, sir. Thank you for your candor in this matter. I believe you may go, if the magistrate desires it."

"Go," Woodward said.

Paine hesitated. "Are you thinking," he said to Matthew, "that someone other than the prisoner might have murdered Reverend Grove and Daniel Howarth? If so, you'd best take care the witch is not casting a spell on your mind this very minute! She did those crimes, and she did the other sins she's been accused of too. Her ultimate purpose was the destruction of this town, which she nearly did—and still might do, if she's not soon ashes! Why should it be anyone else's purpose?"

To this question, Matthew had no answer. "Good afternoon, sir," Paine said, addressing the magistrate, and then he turned away and stalked out of the gaol.

Woodward watched through hooded eyes as the militia captain left. The magistrate had recalled something else Dr. Shields had said concerning the subject of Paine's deceased wife: *It was a long time ago, and I'm sure Paine wouldn't care to speak about it. In fact, I know he would not.* Had it been such a terrible experience that

Paine had decided to deny to the people of Fount Royal that he ever had a wife? And if so, why had he confided it to Dr. Shields? It was a small thing, to be sure . . . but still, a point of interest.

On Matthew's mind was the imminent arrival of the final witness, the child Violet Adams. He cleaned his quill and prepared a fresh sheet of paper. Rachel returned to her bench and sat down, her head lowered. Woodward closely inspected one of the black-ribboned poppets, after which he closed his eyes and took the opportunity to rest.

In a short while the gaol's door was opened, and Violet Adams had arrived.

eighteen

E DWARD WINSTON ENTERED FIRST through the door, fol-lowed by a thin brown-haired man of about thirty years who wore a dark green suit and tan stockings. Close behind him—up under his arm, it would be more accurate to say—was the child, of eleven or twelve years. She, too, was slender. Her light brown hair was pulled severely back from her forehead under the constriction of a stiff white bonnet. She wore a smoke-gray cassock from throat to ankles, and sturdy black shoes that had recently been buffed. Her right hand gripped the left of her father's, while in the crook of her own left arm she held a battered Bible. Her blue eyes, set rather far apart on her long, sallow face, were wide with fear.

"Magistrate, this is Violet Adams and her father, Martin," Winston said as he led them in. The child balked at the entrance to the cell, but her father spoke quietly and firmly to her and she reluctantly came along.

"Hello," Woodward whispered to the little girl; the sound of his raw voice seemed to alarm her further, as she stepped back a pace and might have fled had not Martin Adams put his arm around her. "I'm having trouble speaking," Woodward explained. "Therefore my clerk will speak for me."

"Tell her to quit a'lookin' at us!" Adams said, his bony face damp with sweat. "She's castin' the evil eye!"

Matthew saw that Rachel was indeed staring at them. "Madam, in the interests of keeping everyone calm, would you refrain from looking at this father and child?"

She aimed her gaze at the floor. "Ain't good 'nuff!" Adams protested. "Cain't you put her somewheres else?"

"I'm sorry, sir, but that's impossible."

"Make her turn 'round, then! Make her put her back to us!" At this Matthew looked to the magistrate for help, but all Woodward could do was give a dismissive shrug.

Adams said, "We ain't stayin' here if she don't turn 'round! I didn't want to bring Violet to this place anyways!"

"Martin, please!" Winston held up a hand to quiet him. "It's very important that Violet tell the magistrate what she knows."

Violet suddenly jumped and her eyes looked about to burst from her skull. Rachel had risen to her feet. She pulled the bench away from the wall and then sat down upon it again, this time with her back toward them.

"There," Matthew said, much relieved. "Is that agreeable?"

Adams chewed his lower lip. "For now," he decided. "But if she looks at us again, I'll take my child out of here."

"Very well, then." Matthew smoothed out the fresh sheet of paper before him. "Mr. Winston, you may remove yourself." Winston's departure made the father and daughter even more nervous; now both of them looked liable to bolt at any instant. "Violet, would you care to sit down?" Matthew motioned toward the stool, but the little girl quickly and emphatically shook her head. "We shall have to swear you to truth on the Bible."

"What's the need for that?" Adams spoke up, in what was becoming an irritant to Matthew's ears. "Violet don't lie. She ain't never lied."

"It is a formality of the court, sir. You may use your own Good Book, if you please."

With sullen hesitation, the man agreed and Matthew administered the oath to his daughter, who made hardly a sound in her acceptance to tell only the truth in the sight of God. "All right,"

Matthew said after that hurdle had been cleared, "what is it that you have to offer in this case?"

"This thing she's 'bout to tell you happent near three week ago," came back that aural irritation. "It were of an afternoon. Violet was kept late to school, so when she was comin' home she was by herself."

"School? You mean she's a *student?*" Matthew had never heard of such a thing.

"She was. I never wanted her to go, myself. Readin' is a fool's way to waste time."

Now the knave had well and truly endeared himself to Matthew. He examined the child's face. Violet was not a particularly handsome little girl, but neither was she homely; she was simply ordinary, not being remarkable in any way except perhaps the wide spacing of her eyes and a slight tic of her upper lip that was becoming a bit more pronounced as it became time for her to speak. Still, the child carried herself with grace and seemed of a sturdy nature; Matthew knew it had taken quite a lot of courage to enter this gaol.

"My name is Matthew," he began. "May I call you Violet?"

She looked to her father for aid. "That'll do," Adams agreed.

"Violet, it's important that *you* answer my questions instead of your father. All right?"

"She will," Adams said.

Matthew dipped his quill in the inkwell, not because it needed ink but because he required a moment to compose himself. Then he tried it again, first offering Violet a smile. "Your bonnet is pretty. Did your mother sew it?"

"What's that got to do with the witch?" Adams asked. "She's here to tell her tale, not talk 'bout a bonnet!"

Matthew wished for a jolt of rum. He glanced at the magistrate, who had cupped his hand to his mouth to hide what was a half-smile, half-grimace. "Very well," Matthew said. "Violet, tell your tale."

The little girl's gaze slid over toward Rachel, registering that the accused still remained sitting with her face to the wall. Then Violet lowered her head, her father's hand on her shoulder, and said in a small, frightened voice, "I seen the Devil and his imp. Sittin' there. The Devil told me the witch was to be set loose. Said if the witch was kept in the gaol everybody in Fount Royal would pay for it." Again her eyes darted to mark if Rachel had moved or responded, but the prisoner had not.

Matthew said quietly, "May I ask where this sighting occurred?"

Of course Adams spoke up. "It were in the Hamilton house. Where the Hamiltons used to live 'fore they took up and went. On Industry Street, 'bout three houses shy of our'n."

"All right. I presume the Hamiltons had left before this sighting took place?"

"They was gone right after the witch murdered Dan'l. Abby Hamilton knowed it was that woman's doin'. She told my Constance that a dark woman's got dark in her."

"Hm," Matthew said, for want of any better response. "Violet, how come you to be in that house?"

She didn't answer. Her father nudged her. "Go on and tell it, child. It's the right thing to do."

Violet began in what was almost an inaudible voice, her face angled toward the floor. "I . . . was walkin' home. From the schoolhouse. I was goin' by where the Hamiltons used to live . . . and . . . I heared somebody." She paused once more and Matthew thought he would have to urge her on, but then she said, "Somebody was callin' me. Said . . . 'Violet, come here.' Low and quiet, it was. 'Violet, come here.' I looked . . . and the door was open."

"The door to the Hamilton house," Matthew said.

"Yes sir. I knowed it was empty. But I heared it again. 'Violet, come here.' It sounded like . . . my papa was callin' me. That's why I went in."

"Had you ever been inside that house before?"

"No sir."

Matthew redipped his quill. "Please go on."

"I went in," Violet said. "There wasn't nary a noise. It was silent, like . . . it was just me breathin', and that was the only sound. I near turned to run out . . . and then . . . I heared 'Violet, look at me.' At first . . . 'cause it was so dark, I couldn't see nothin'. Then a candle was lit, and I seen 'em sittin' there in that room." Both Matthew and Woodward could see that her face, though turned downward, was agonized with the recollection. She trembled, and her father patted her shoulder for comfort. "I seen 'em," she repeated. "The Devil was sittin' in a chair . . . and the imp was on his knee. The imp . . . was holdin' the candle . . . and he was grinnin' at me." She made a soft, wounded gasp down in her throat and then was quiet.

"I know this is difficult," Matthew told her, as gently as he could, "but it has to be spoken. Please continue."

She said, "Yes sir," but offered nothing more for a space of time. Obviously the recounting of this incident was a terrible ordeal. Finally she took a long breath and let it go. "The Devil said, 'Tell them to free my Rachel.' He said, 'Let her out of the gaol, or Fount Royal is cursed.' After that . . . he asked me if I could remember what he'd said. I nodded. Then the imp blowed out the candle, and it come dark again. I run home." She looked up at Matthew, her eyes shocked and wet. "Can I go now?"

"Soon," he said. His heart had begun beating harder. "I'm going to have to ask you some questions, and I want you to think carefully before you answer to make sure that—"

"She'll answer 'em," Adams interrupted. "She's a truthful child."

"Thank you, sir," Matthew said. "Violet? Can you tell me what the Devil looked like?"

"Yes sir. He . . . had on a black cloak . . . and a hood over his head, so I couldn't see no face. I remember . . . on his cloak . . . was gold buttons. They was shinin' in the candlelight. "

"Gold buttons." Matthew's mouth had gone dry; his tongue felt like a piece of iron. "May I ask . . . if you know how many there were?"

"Yes sir," she said. "Six."

"What's this fool question for?" Adams demanded. "Six buttons or sixty, what does it matter?"

Matthew ignored him. He stared intently into the child's eyes. "Violet, please think about this: can you tell me how the buttons were arranged on the cloak? Were they six straight up and down, or were they three side by side?"

"Pah!" The man made a disgusted face. "She seen the Devil, and you're askin' 'bout his *buttons?*"

"I can answer, Papa," Violet said. "They was six straight up and down. I seen 'em shinin'."

"Straight up and down?" Matthew pressed. "You're absolutely certain of it?"

"Yes sir, I am."

Matthew had been leaning forward over his paper; now he sat back in his chair, and ink dripped upon the previous lines he'd quilled.

"Child?" Woodward whispered. He managed a frail smile. "You're doing very well. Might I ask you to describe the imp?"

Again Violet looked to her father, and he said, "Go on, tell the magistrate."

"The imp . . . was sittin' on the Devil's knee. It had white hair, looked like spider webs. It wasn't wearing no clothes, and . . . its skin was all gray and wrinkled up, like a dried apple. 'Cept for its face." She hesitated, her expression tormented; in that instant Woodward thought she more resembled a life-burned woman than an innocent child. "Its face . . . was a little boy," she went on. "And . . . while the Devil was talkin' to me . . . the imp stuck out its tongue . . . and made it wiggle 'round and 'round." She shuddered at the memory of it, and a single tear streaked down her left cheek.

Matthew couldn't speak. He realized that Violet Adams had just described perfectly one of the three grotesques that Jeremiah Buckner claimed he saw in the orchard, having unholy sexual relations with Rachel.

Add to that the child's description of Satan as seen by Elias

Garrick, right down to the black cloak and six gold buttons, and— *Dear God,* Matthew thought. *It couldn't be true!*

Could it?

"Violet?" He had to strain to keep his voice steady. "Have you heard anything of the other tales concerning the Devil and this imp that may have been told around town? What I mean to say is—"

"No sir, she ain't makin' up a lie!" Adams clenched his teeth at the very suggestion of it. "I done told you, she's a truthful child! And yes, them tales are spoken here and yon, and most like Violet's heard 'em from other children, but by God you didn't see her pale as milk when she come home that day! You didn't hear her sobbin' and wailin', near scairt to death! No sir, it ain't a lie!"

Violet had downcast her face again. When her father had ceased his ranting, she lifted it to look fully at Matthew. "Sir?" she said timorously. "It happened as I told it. I heared the voice and went in the house, and I seen the Devil and the imp. The Devil said them things to me, and then I run home quick as I could."

"You're positive—absolutely positive—that the figure in the black cloak said . . ." Matthew found the appropriate lines on the paper. "'Tell them to free my Rachel'?"

"Yes sir. I am."

"The candle. In which hand did the imp hold it?"

She frowned. "The right."

"Did the Devil have on shoes or boots?"

"I don't know, sir. I didn't see."

"Upon which knee did the imp sit? The left or right?"

Again, Violet frowned as she called up the memory. "The . . . left, I think. Yes sir. The left knee."

"Did you see anyone else on the street before you went inside?"

"No sir. I don't recall."

"And afterward? Was there anyone on the street when you came out?"

She shook her head. "I don't know, sir. I was cryin'. All I cared to do was get home."

"How come you to stay late at school?"

"It was 'cause of my readin', sir. I need help at it, and Master Johnstone had me stay late to do some extra work."

"You were the only student asked to stay late?"

"That day, yes sir. But Master Johnstone has somebody stay late most every day."

"What made you notice those gold buttons?" Matthew lifted his eyebrows. "How, with the Devil and the imp sitting there before you, did you have the presence of mind to count them?"

"I don't recall countin' 'em, exactly. They just caught my eye. I collect buttons, sir. I have a jar of 'em at home, and ever when I find one I put it up."

"When you left the schoolhouse, did you happen to speak to anyone on the—"

"*Matthew.*" Though it had been only a whisper, Woodward had delivered it with stern authority. "That's enough." He glowered at his clerk, his eyes bleary and red-rimmed. "This child has spoken what she knows."

"Yes, sir, but—"

"*Enough.*" There was no denying the magistrate's will; particularly not in this instance, since Matthew had for all intents and purposes run out of questions. All Matthew could do was nod his head and stare blankly at what he'd scribed on the paper before him. He had come to the conclusion that, of the three witnesses who'd testified, this child's story sounded the most chillingly real. She knew what details she ought to know. What she couldn't recall was forgivable, due to the stress and quickness of the incident.

Tell them to free my Rachel, the Devil had said. That single statement, coupled with the poppets, was powerful enough to burn her even if there had been no other witnesses.

"I assume," Matthew said, his own voice somewhat diminished, "that the schoolmaster has heard this story?"

"He has. I told him myself the very next mornin'," Adams said.

"And he remembers asking Violet to stay late that afternoon?"

"He does."

"Well, then." Matthew licked his dry lips and resisted turning his head to look at Rachel. He could think of nothing more to say but the same again: "Well, then."

"You are very courageous," Woodward offered the child. "Very courageous, to come in here and tell us this. My compliments and gratitude." Though in pain, he summoned up a smile albeit a tight one. "You may go home now."

"Yes sir, thank you sir." Violet bowed her head and gave the magistrate a clumsy but well-meant curtsey. Before she left the cell, though, she glanced uneasily at the prisoner, who still sat backwards upon the bench. "She won't hurt me, will she?"

"No," Woodward said. "God will protect you."

"Well . . . sir, there's somethin' else I have to tell."

Matthew roused himself from his dismayed stupor. "What is it?"

"The Devil and that imp . . . they wasn't alone in the house."

"You saw another creature, then?"

"No sir." She hesitated, hugging her Bible. "I heared a man's voice. Singin'."

"Singing?" Matthew frowned. "But you saw no other creature?"

"No sir, I didn't. The singin' . . . it was comin' from back of the house, seemed like. Another room, back there in the dark. I heared it just 'fore the candle went out."

"It was a man's voice, you say?" Matthew had put his quill aside. Now he picked it up again and began to record the testimony once more. "Loud or soft?"

"Soft. I could just hardly hear it. But it was a man's voice, yes sir."

"Had you ever heard that voice before?"

"I don't know, sir. I'm not sure if I had or hadn't."

Matthew rubbed his chin and inadvertently smeared black ink across it. "Could you make out anything of the song?"

"Well . . . sometimes I feel I'm near 'bout to know what song it is, that maybe I heared it before . . . but then it goes away. Sometimes it makes my head hurt thinkin' of it." She looked from Matthew to the magistrate and back again. "It's not the Devil cursin' me, is it, sir?"

"No, I think not." He stared at the lines on the paper, his mind working. If there was a third demonic creature in that house, why didn't it show itself to the child? After all, the idea had been to scare an alarm into her, hadn't it? What was the point of a demon singing in the dark, if the song and the voice were not loud enough to be fearful? "Violet, this may be difficult for you," he said, "but might you try to remember what the voice was singing?"

"What does it matter?" Adams had held his peace long enough. "She done told you 'bout the Devil and the imp!"

"My own curiosity, Mr. Adams," Matthew explained. "And it seems to me that the memory of this voice troubles your daughter, or she would not have brought it to light. Don't you agree?"

"Well . . ." The man made a sour face. "Mayhaps I do."

"Is there anything further?" Matthew asked the girl, and she shook her head. "All right, then. The court thanks you for your testimony." Violet and her father withdrew from the cell. Just before they left the gaol, the child looked back fearfully at Rachel, who was sitting slumped over with a hand pressed to her forehead.

When the two were gone, Woodward began to wrap the poppets back up in the white cloth. "I presume," he whispered, "that all other witnesses have fled town. Therefore . . ." He paused to try to clear his throat, which was a difficult and torturous task. "Therefore our trial is ended."

"Wait!" Rachel stood up. "What about *my* say? Don't I get a chance to speak?"

Woodward regarded her coldly. "It *is* her right, sir," Matthew reminded him.

The magistrate continued wrapping the poppets. "Yes, yes," he said. "Of course it is. Go on, then.

"You've made your decision, have you not?" She came to the bars and gripped them.

"No. I shall first read over the transcript, when I am able."

"But that's only a formality, isn't it? What can I possibly say to convince you I am not guilty of these lies?"

"Bear in mind," Matthew said to her, "that the witnesses did swear on the Bible. I would be wary in calling them liars. However . . ." He paused.

"However *what?*" Woodward rasped.

"I think there are some omissions of detail in the testimonies of Mr. Buckner and Mr. Garrick that ought to be taken into account. For instance—"

Woodward lifted a hand. "Spare me. I shall not discuss this today."

"But you do agree, don't you, sir?"

"I am going to bed." With the bundle tucked under his arm, Woodward pushed the chair back and stood up. His bones ached and his head grew dizzy, and he stood grasping the desk's edge until the dizziness abated.

Instantly Matthew was on his feet too, alert to preventing the magistrate from falling. "Is someone coming to help you?"

"I trust there's a carriage waiting."

"Shall I go out and see?"

"No. Mind you, you're still a prisoner." Woodward felt so drained of strength he had to close his eyes for a few seconds, his head bowed.

"I demand my right to speak," Rachel insisted. "No matter if you *have* decided."

"Speak, then." Woodward feared his throat was closing up again, and his nostrils seemed all but sealed.

"It is a wicked conspiracy," she began, "to contend that I

murdered anyone, or that I have made spells and poppets and committed such sins as I am accused of. Yes, I know the witnesses swore truth on the Bible. I can't understand why or how they could create such stories, but if you'll give *me* the Bible I'll swear truth on it too!"

To Matthew's surprise, Woodward picked up the Holy Book, walked unsteadily to the bars, and passed the volume through into her hands.

Rachel clasped it to her bosom. "I swear upon this Bible and every word in it that I have done no murders and I am not a witch!" Her eyes gleamed with a mixture of trepidation and triumph. "There! You see? Did I burst into flame? Did I scream because my hands were scorched? If you put such value on Bible-sworn truth, then will you not also value my denial?"

"Madam," the magistrate whispered wearily, "do not further profane yourself. Your power to confuse is very strong, I grant you."

"I am *holding* the Bible! I have just sworn on it! Would you have me *kiss* it?"

"No. I would have you return it." He held out his hand. Matthew saw the bright fire of anger leap into Rachel's eyes, and for an instant he feared for the magistrate's safety. But then Rachel stepped back from the bars, opened the Holy Book, and began to methodically rip the parchment pages from it, her expression all but dead.

"Rachel!" Matthew cried out, before he could think better of it. "Don't!"

The torn pages of God's Writ drifted to the straw around her feet. She stared into the magistrate's eyes as she did her blasphemous damage, as if daring him to prevent her.

Woodward held her gaze, a muscle clenching in his jaw. "Now," he whispered, "I see you clearly."

She yanked out another page, let it fall, and then shoved the Bible between the bars. Woodward made no move to capture the mutilated Book, which dropped to the floor. "You see *nothing,*" Rachel said, her voice trembling with emotion though her face was held under tight control. "Why did God not strike me dead just now?"

"Because, madam, He has given me that task."

"If I were truly a witch, God would never have allowed such an act!"

"Only a vile sinner would have committed it," Woodward said, showing admirable composure. He leaned down and retrieved the volume, the back of which had been broken.

Matthew said, "She's distraught, sir! She doesn't know what she's doing!"

At that, Woodward turned toward his clerk and managed to say heatedly, "She *knows!* Dear God, Matthew! Has she blinded you?"

"No, sir. But I think this action should be excused on the grounds of extreme mental hardship."

Woodward's mouth fell agape, his gray face slack. He seemed to feel the entire world wheel around him as he realized that, indeed, this woman had beguiled the very fear of God out of his clerk.

The magistrate's shocked expression was not lost on Matthew. "Sir, she *is* under difficult circumstances. I hope you'll weigh that in your consideration of this incident."

There was only one response Woodward could make to this plea. "Get your papers. You're leaving."

Now it was Matthew's turn to be shocked. "But . . . I have one more night on my sentence."

"I'll pardon you! Come along!"

Matthew saw that Rachel had moved back into the shadows of her cage. He was torn between the desire to rid himself of this dirty hovel and the realization that once he left the gaol he would most likely not see Rachel again until the morning of her death. There were still so many questions to be asked and answered! He couldn't let it go like this, or he feared he might be haunted for the rest of his days. "I'll stay here and finish my sentence," he said.

"*What?*"

"I'll stay here," Matthew repeated calmly. "One more night will be of no consequence."

"You forget yourself!" Woodward felt near collapse. "I demand you obey!"

Even though this demand had been delivered in such a frail voice, it still carried enough power to offend Matthew's sense of independence. "I am your servant," he answered, "but I am not your slave. I elect to stay here and finish my sentence. I will take my lashes in the morning, and that will be the end of it."

"You've lost your reason!"

"No, sir, I have not. My being pardoned would only cause further problems."

Woodward started to argue the point, but neither his voice nor his spirit had the strength. He stood at the cell's threshold, holding the violated Bible and the bundled poppets. A glance at Rachel Howarth showed him that she'd retreated to the far wall of her cage, but he knew that as soon as he left she would begin to work her mind-corrupting spells on the boy again. This was like leaving a lamb to the teeth of a bitch wolf. He tried once more: "Matthew . . . I beg you to come with me."

"There's no need. I can stand one more night."

"Yes, and fall for eternity," Woodward whispered.

Woodward laid the Holy Book down atop the desk. Even so desecrated, the volume might serve as a shield if Matthew called upon it. That is, if Matthew's clouded vision would allow him to recognize its power. He damned himself for letting the boy be put in this place; he might have known the witch would leap at the opportunity to entrance Matthew's mind. It occurred to Woodward that the court records were in jeopardy as well. There was no telling what might befall them during this last night they'd be within the witch's reach. "I will take the papers," he said. "Box them, please."

This was not an unreasonable request, as Matthew assumed the magistrate would want to begin his reading. He immediately obeyed.

When it was done, Woodward put the box under one arm.

There was nothing more he could do for Matthew except offer a prayer. He cast a baleful glare upon Rachel Howarth. "Beware your acts, madam. You're not yet in the fire."

"Is there any doubt I shall be?" she asked.

He ignored the question, turning his eyes toward Matthew. "Your lashing . . ." It seemed his throat was doubly swollen now, and speaking took a maximum of effort. ". . . will be at six o'clock. I shall be here . . . early as possible. Be alert to her tricks, Matthew." Matthew nodded but offered no opinion on the validity of the statement.

The magistrate walked out of the cell, leaving the door wide open. He steeled himself not to look back, as the sight of Matthew voluntarily caged and in mortal danger of witchcraft might tear his heart asunder.

Outside the gaol, in the dim gray light and with a mist hanging in the air, Woodward was relieved to see that indeed Goode had brought the carriage for him. He pulled himself up into one of the passenger seats and set the bundled poppets at his side. As soon as Woodward was settled, Goode flicked the reins and the horses started off.

Shortly after the magistrate had departed, Green came to the gaol to deliver the evening meal, which was corn soup. He locked Matthew's cell and said, "I trust you sleep well, boy. Tomorrow your hide belongs to *me.*" Matthew didn't care for the way Green laughed; then the gaol-keeper removed the lantern, as was his nightly custom, and left the prisoners in darkness.

Matthew sat on his bench and tipped the foodbowl to his mouth. He heard a rat squeaking in the wall behind him, but their numbers had dwindled dramatically in the wake of the ratcatcher's visit and they seemed not nearly so bold as before.

Rachel's voice came from the dark. "Why did you stay?"

He swallowed the soup that was in his mouth. "I intend to serve out my sentence."

"I know that, but the magistrate offered you a pardon. Why didn't you take it?"

"Magistrate Woodward is ill and confused right now."

"That doesn't answer my question. You elected to stay. Why?"

Matthew busied himself in eating. At last he said, "I have other questions to ask of you."

"Such as?"

"Such as where were you when your husband was murdered? And why is it that someone other than you found the body?"

"I remember Daniel getting out of bed that night," Rachel said. "Or perhaps it was early morning. I don't know. But he often rose in the dark and by candlelight figured in his ledger. There was nothing odd in his rising. I simply turned over, pulled the blanket up, and went back to sleep as I always did."

"Did you know that he'd gone outside?"

"No, I didn't."

"Was that usual also? That he should go out in the cold at such an early hour?"

"He might go out to feed the livestock, depending on how near it was to sunrise."

"You say your husband kept a ledger? Containing what?"

"Daniel kept account of every shilling he had. Also how much money was invested in the farm, and how much was spent on day-to-day matters such as candles, soap, and the like."

"Was money owed to him by anyone in town, or did he owe money?"

"No," Rachel said. "Daniel prided himself that he was his own master."

"Admirable, but quite unusual in these times." Matthew took another swallow of soup. "How did your husband's body come to be found?"

"Jess Maynard found it. *Him,* I mean. Lying in the field, with his throat . . . you know." She paused. "The Maynards lived on the other side of us. Jess had come out to feed his chickens at first light when he saw . . . the crows circling. He came over and that's when he found Daniel."

"Did you see the body?"

Again, there was a hesitation. Then she said quietly. "I did."

"I understand it was the throat wound that killed him, but were there not other wounds on his body? Bidwell described them, I recall, as claw or teeth marks to the face and arms."

"Yes, there were those."

"Forgive my indelicacy," Matthew said, "but is that how you would describe them? As teeth or claw marks?"

"I . . . remember . . . how terrible was the wound to his throat. I did see what appeared to be claw marks on his face, but . . . I didn't care at the moment to inspect them. The sight of my husband lying dead, his eyes and mouth open as they were . . . I remember that I cried out and fell to my knees beside him. I don't recall much after that, except that Ellen Maynard took me to her house to rest."

"Are the Maynards still living there?"

"No. They moved away after . . ." She gave a sigh of resignation. "After the stories about me began to fly."

"And who began these stories? Do you know of any one person?"

"I would be the last to know," Rachel said dryly.

"Yes," Matthew agreed. "Of course. People being as they are, I'm sure the stories were spread about and more and more embellished. But tell me this: the accusations against you did not begin until your husband was murdered, is that correct? You were not suspected in the murder of Reverend Grove?"

"No, I was not. After I was brought here, Bidwell came in to see me. He said he had witnesses to my practise of witchcraft and that he knew I—or my 'master,' as he put it—was responsible for the calamities that had struck Fount Royal. He asked me why I had decided to consort with Satan, and what was my purpose in destroying the town. At that point he asked if I had murdered the reverend. Of course I thought he'd lost his mind. He said I was to cease all associations with demons and confess myself to be a witch, and that he would arrange for me to be immediately banished. The alternative, he said, was death."

Matthew finished his soup and set the bowl aside. "Tell me," he said, "why you didn't agree to banishment. Your husband was dead, and you faced execution. Why didn't you leave?"

"Because," she answered, "I am not guilty. Daniel bought our farm from Bidwell and we had both worked hard at making it a success. Why should I give it up, admit to killing two men and being a witch, and be sent out into the wilds with nothing? I would have surely died out there. Here, at least, I felt that when a magistrate arrived to hear the case I might have a chance." She was silent for a while, and then she said, "I never thought it would take so long. The magistrate was supposed to be here over a month ago. By the day you and Woodward arrived, I had suffered Bidwell's slings and arrows many times over. I had almost lost all hope. In fact, you both looked so . . . well, *unofficial* . . . that I at first thought Bidwell had brought in two hirelings to goad a confession out of me."

"I understand," Matthew said. "But was there no effort to discover who had murdered the reverend?"

"There was, as I recall, but after Lenora Grove left, the interest faded over time, as there were no suspects and no apparent motive. But the reverend's murder was the first incident that caused people to start leaving Fount Royal. It was a grim Winter."

"I can imagine it was." Matthew listened to the increasing sound of rain on the roof. "A grim Spring, as well. I doubt if Fount Royal could survive another one as bad."

"Probably not. But I won't be here to know, will I?"

Matthew didn't answer. What could he say? Rachel's voice was very tight when she spoke again. "In your opinion, how long do I have to live?"

She was asking to be told the truth. Matthew said, "The magistrate will read thoroughly over the records. He will deliberate, according to past witchcraft cases of which he has knowledge." Matthew folded his hands together in his lap. "He may give his decision as early as Wednesday. On Thursday he might ask for your confession, and on that day as well he might require me to write, date, and sign the order of sentencing. I expect . . .

the preparations would be made on Friday. He would not wish to carry out the sentence on either the day before the Sabbath or the Sabbath itself. Therefore—"

"Therefore I burn on Monday," Rachel finished for him.

"Yes," Matthew said. A long silence stretched. Though he wished to ease her sorrow, Matthew knew of no consolation he could offer that would not sound blatantly foolish.

"Well," she said at last, her voice carrying a mixture of courage and pain, and that was all.

Matthew lay down in his accustomed place in the straw and folded himself up for warmth. Rain drummed harder on the roof. He listened to its muffled roar and thought how simple life had seemed when he was a child and all he had to fear was the pile of pig dung. Life was so complicated now, so filled with strange twists and turns like a road that wandered across a wilderness no man could completely tame, much less understand.

He was deeply concerned for the magistrate's failing health. On the one hand, the sooner they got away from Fount Royal and returned to the city, the better; but on the other hand he was deeply concerned as well for the life of the woman in the next cell.

And it was not simply because he did think her beautiful to look upon. Paine had been correct, of course. Rachel was indeed—as he had crudely put it—a "handsome piece." Matthew could understand how Paine—how any man, really—could be drawn to her. Rachel's intelligence and inner fire were also appealing to Matthew, as he'd never met a woman of such nature before. Or, at least, he'd never met a woman before who had allowed those characteristics of intelligence and fire to be seen in public. It was profoundly troubling to believe that just possibly Rachel's beauty and independent nature were two reasons she'd been singled out by public opinion as a witch. It seemed to him, in his observations, that if one could not catch and conquer an object of desire, it often served the same to destroy it.

The question must be answered in his own mind: was she a witch or not? Before the testimony of Violet Adams, he would have said the so-called eyewitness accounts were fabrications or fantasies, even though both men had sworn on the Bible. But the child's testimony had been tight and convincing. Frighteningly convincing, in fact. This was not a situation where the child had gone to bed and awakened thinking that a dream had been reality; this had happened when she was wide awake, and her grasp of details seemed about right considering the stress of the moment. The child's testimony—especially concerning the black cloak, the six gold buttons, and the white-haired dwarf, or "imp," as she'd called it—gave further believability to what both Buckner and Garrick had seen. What, then, to make of it?

And there were the poppets, of course. Yes, anyone might have made them and hidden them under the floorboards. But why would anyone have done so? And what to make of Cara Grunewald's "vision" telling the searchers where to look?

Had Rachel indulged in witchcraft, or not? Had she murdered or wished the murders of Reverend Grove and her husband, the actual killings having been committed by some demonic creature summoned from the bullypit of Hell?

Another thought came to him while he was on this awful track: if Rachel was a witch, might she or her terrible accomplices have worked a spell on the magistrate's health to prevent him from delivering sentence?

Matthew had to admit that, even though there were puzzling lapses of detail in the accounts of Buckner and Garrick, all the evidence taken together served to light the torch for Rachel's death. He knew the magistrate would read the court documents carefully and ponder them with a fair mind, but there was no question the decree would be *guilty as charged.*

So: was she a witch, or not?

Even having read and digested the scholarly volumes that explained witchcraft as insanity, ignorance, or downright malicious accusations, he honestly couldn't say, which frightened him far more than any of the testimony he'd heard.

But she was so beautiful, he thought. So beautiful and so

alone. If she was indeed a servant of Satan, how could the Devil himself let a woman so beautiful be destroyed by the hands of men?

Thunder spoke over Fount Royal. Rain began to drip from the gaol's roof at a dozen weak joints. Matthew lay in the dark, huddled up against the chill, his mind struggling with a question inside a mystery within an enigma.

nineteen

JUST BEFORE THE STORM had broken, Mrs. Nettles had answered the front door bell to admit Schoolmaster Johnstone, who inquired if the magistrate was able to see him. She took his black coat and tricorn and hung them near the door, then escorted him into the parlor, where Woodward—still bundled up in coat and scarf as he'd been at the gaol—sat in a chair that had been pulled up close to the fireplace. A tray across Woodward's knees held a bowl of steaming, milky pap that was near the same grayish hue as the color of his face, and Woodward had been stirring his dinner with a spoon to cool it.

"Pardon me. For not rising," Woodward whispered.

"No pardon necessary between Oxford brothers, sir."

"Mr. Bidwell is in his study with Mr. Winston," Mrs. Nettles said. "Shall I fetch 'im?"

"No, I won't disturb their work," Johnstone said, leaning on his cane. Woodward noted he was wigless this evening, his light brown hair shorn close to the scalp. "I have business with the magistrate."

"Very well, sir." She bowed her head in a gesture of respect and left the parlor.

Johnstone watched the magistrate stirring his pap. "That doesn't look very appetizing."

"Doctor's orders. All I can swallow."

"Yes, I had a talk with Dr. Shields this morning and he told me you'd been suffering. I'm sorry you're in such a condition. He bled you, I understand."

Woodward nodded. "More bleeding. Yet to be done."

"Well, it is helpful to drain the corrupted fluids. Might I sit down?" He motioned toward a nearby chair, and Woodward whispered, "Yes, please do." Johnstone, with the aid of his cane, eased himself into the chair and stretched his legs out toward the crackling fire. Rain began to beat at the shuttered windows. Woodward took a taste of the pap and found it just the same as what he'd eaten at midday: entirely tasteless, since his nostrils were so clogged he could not smell even the smoke from the burning pinewood.

"I won't take much of your time," Johnstone said. "I did wish to ask how the trial was coming."

"Over. The last witness has been heard."

"Then I presume your decision will be forthcoming? Tomorrow, perhaps?"

"Not tomorrow. I must review the testimony."

"I see. But your decision will be made by the end of the week?" Johnstone waited for Woodward to nod his assent. "You have a responsibility I do not envy," he continued. "Sentencing a woman to death by fire is not a kind job."

"It is not," Woodward answered between swallows of pap, "a kind world."

"Granted. We have come a long way from Oxford, the both of us. I imagine we began our careers as shining lamps. It is unfortunate that life has a way of dirtying the glass. But tell me this, Magistrate: can you in good conscience sentence Rachel Howarth to death without yourself seeing evidence of her supposed witchcraft?"

Woodward paused in bringing another spoonful of pap to his mouth. "I can. As did the magistrates of Salem."

"Ah, yes. Infamous Salem. But you're aware, of course, that since the incident in Salem there has been much written concerning questions of guilt and innocence." His right hand settled on the misshapen knee and began to massage it. "There are some who believe the incident in Salem resulted in the execution of persons who were either mentally unbalanced or falsely accused."

"And some who believe," Woodward hesitated to get a breath, "Christ was served and Satan vanquished."

"Oh, Satan is never vanquished. You know that as well as anyone. In fact, one might say that if a single innocent person died at Salem, the Devil's work was well and truly done, for the souls of the magistrates themselves were corrupted." Johnstone stared into the flames. "I have to confess something," he said at length. "I consider myself a man of the here-and-now, not a man whose opinions are rooted in the beliefs and judgments of the past. I believe in God's power and I trust in the wisdom of Christ . . . but I have difficulty with this question of witchcraft, sir. It seems to me a highly doubtful thing."

"Doubtful?" Woodward asked. "You doubt the witnesses, then?"

"I don't know." The schoolmaster shook his head. "I can't understand why such elaborate lies should be produced against Madam Howarth—whom I always thought to be, by the way, a very dignified and intelligent woman. Of course she did—and does—have her enemies here. A beautiful, strong-spirited woman as she is could not fail to have enemies. Constance Adams is one of them. Granny Lawry was another who spoke with a vehement tongue, but she passed away in late March. A number of citizens were outraged when Madam Howarth attended church, she being Portuguese and of such dark coloring. They wanted her to go worship in the slave quarters."

"The slaves have a church?"

"A shed that serves the purpose. Anyway, since the day Madam Howarth set foot in church, she was the object of bitter resentment. The citizens were looking for a reason to openly despise her. The nature of her heritage—and the fact that she'd married a much older and reasonably wealthy man—had made her a target of scorn since she and Daniel arrived here."

"Howarth was wealthy?" Woodward asked, his pap-loaded spoon poised near his mouth.

"Yes. Though not in the sense of Bidwell's wealth, of course. The Howarth land is larger than most of the other farms. He did have some money, as I understand."

"Money from what source?"

"He was a wine merchant in Virginia. From what I heard, he'd suffered some bad luck. A shipment was lost at sea, another shipment was delivered foul, and evidently there was a continuing problem with a tax collector. As I understand, Daniel simply sickened of laboring beneath the threat of losing his business. He was married to another woman at that point, but I don't know if she died or returned to England. Some women can't stand the New World, you know."

"Your own wife being an example?" Woodward whispered before he slid the spoon of pap into his mouth.

"Yes, my own Margaret." Johnstone offered a thin smile. "Ben told me you'd been asking questions. He said that somehow—he couldn't quite recall—you had wandered onto that field where Margaret lies buried. Figuratively speaking, of course. No, Margaret lives with her family now, south of London." He shrugged. "I suppose she does, if they haven't locked her up in Bedlam yet. She was—to be kind—mentally unstable, a condition that the rigors of life in Fount Royal made only worse. Unfortunately, she sought balance in the rum barrel." Johnstone was silent, the firelight and shadows moving on his thin-nosed, aristocratic face. "I expect Ben—knowing Ben as I do—has told you also of Margaret's . . . um . . . indiscretions?"

"Yes."

"The one in particular, with that Noles bastard, was the worst. The man is an animal, and for Margaret—who when I married her was a virgin and comported herself as a proper lady—to have fallen to his level was the final insult to me. Well, she had made no secret of hating Fount Royal and everyone in it. It was for the best that I took her where she belonged." He looked at Woodward with a pained expression. "Some people change, no matter how hard one tries to deny it. Do you understand what I mean?"

"Yes," Woodward answered, in his fragile voice. His own face had taken on some pain. He stared into the fire. "I do understand."

The schoolmaster continued to rub his deformed knee. Sparks popped from one of the logs. Outside, the sound of rain had become a dull roar. "This weather," Johnstone said, "plays hell with my knee. Too much damp and I can hardly walk. You know, that preacher must be getting his feet wet. He's camped up on Industry Street. Last night he gave a sermon that I understand sent a few people into spasms and separated them from their coins as well. Of course, the subject of his speech was Rachel Howarth, and how her evil has contaminated the whole of Fount Royal. He mentioned you by name as one of those so afflicted, as well as your clerk, Nicholas Paine, and myself."

"I'm not surprised."

"At the risk of verifying the preacher's opinion of me," Johnstone said, "I suppose I'm here to plead for Madam Howarth. It just makes no sense to me that she would commit two murders, much less take up witchcraft. I'm aware that the witnesses are all reliable and of good character, but . . . something about this is very wrong, sir. If I were you, I'd be wary of rushing to pass sentence no matter how much pressure Bidwell puts upon you."

"I am not *rushing*," Woodward replied stiffly. "I set my own pace."

"Surely you do, and forgive me for stating otherwise. But it *appears* there is some pressure being put upon you. I understand how Bidwell feels Fount Royal is so endangered, and it's certainly true that the town is being vacated at an alarming rate. These fires we've been suffering don't help matters. Someone is trying to paint Madam Howarth as having the power of destruction beyond the gaol's walls."

"Your opinion."

"Yes, my opinion. I'm aware that you have more experience in these matters than do I, but does it not seem very strange to you that the Devil should so openly reveal himself about town? And it seems to me quite peculiar that a woman who can burn down houses at a distance can't free herself from a rusty lock."

"The nature of evil," Woodward said as he ate another spoonful of the tasteless mush, "is never fully understood."

"Agreed. But I would think Satan would be more cunning than illogical. It appears to me that the Devil went to great pains to make certain everyone in town knew there was a witch among us, and that her name was Rachel Howarth."

After a moment of contemplation, Woodward said, "Perhaps it *is* strange. Still, we have the witnesses."

"Yes, the witnesses." Johnstone frowned, his gaze fixed upon the fire. "A puzzle, it seems. Unless . . . one considers the *possibility* that—as much as I might wish to deny it—Satan is indeed at work in Fount Royal, and has given Madam Howarth's face to the true witch. Or warlock, as the case might be."

Woodward had been about to eat the last swallow of his pap, but he paused in lifting the spoon. This idea advanced by Johnstone had never occurred to him. Still, it *was* only an idea, and the witnesses had sworn on the Bible. But what if the witnesses had been themselves entranced, without knowing it? What if they had been led to believe they were viewing Madam Howarth, when indeed it was not? And when Satan had spoken Madam Howarth's name to Violet Adams, was he simply attempting to shield the identity of the true witch?

No! There was the evidence of the poppets found in Madam Howarth's house! But, as Matthew had pointed out, the house was empty for such a period of time that someone else might have secreted them there. Afterward, Satan might have slipped the vision into Madam Grunewald's dreams, and thereby the poppets were discovered.

Was it possible—only by the slimmest possibility—that the wrong person was behind bars, and the *real* witch still free?

"I don't wish to cloud your thinking," Johnstone said in response to the magistrate's silence, "but only to point out what damage a rush to execute Madam Howarth might do. Now, that being said, I have to ask if you have progressed any in your search for the thief."

"The thief?" It took Woodward a few seconds to shift his thoughts to the missing gold coin. "Oh. No progress."

"Well, Ben also informed me that you and your clerk had questions about my knee, and if I was able to climb the staircase or not. I suppose I could, if I had to. But I'm flattered that you would consider I could move as quickly as the thief evidently did." The schoolmaster leaned forward and unbuttoned his breeches leg at the knee. "I wish you to judge for yourself."

"Uh . . . it isn't necessary," Woodward whispered.

"Oh, but it is! I want you to see." He pulled the breeches leg back and then rolled his stocking down. A bandage had been secured around the knee, and this Johnstone began to slowly unwrap. When he was finished, he turned his leg so as to offer Woodward a clear view of the deformity by the firelight. "There," Johnstone said grimly. "My pride."

Woodward saw that a leather brace was buckled around Johnstone's knee, but the kneecap itself was fully exposed. It was the size of a knotty fist, gray-colored and glistening with some kind of oil. The bone itself appeared terribly misshapen, bulging up in a ghastly ridge along the top of the kneecap and then forming a concavity at the knee's center. Woodward found himself recoiling from the sight.

"Alan! We heard the bell, but why didn't you announce yourself?" Bidwell had just entered the parlor, with Winston a few steps behind him.

"I had business with the magistrate. I wished to show him my knee. Would you care to look?"

"No, thank you," Bidwell said, as politely as possible.

But Winston came forward and craned his neck. He wrinkled up his nose as he reached the fireside. "My Lord, what's that smell?"

"The hogsfat ointment Ben sells me," Johnstone explained. "As the weather is so damp, I've had to apply it rather liberally tonight. I apologize for the odor." Woodward, because his nostrils were blocked, could smell nothing. Winston came a couple of steps closer to view the knee but then he retreated with as much decorum as he could manage.

"I realize it's not a pretty sight." Johnstone extended his index finger and moved it along the bony ridge and down into the concavity, an exploration that made the magistrate's spine crawl. Woodward had to look away, choosing to stare into the fire. "Unfortunately, it is part of my heritage. I understand my great-grandfather—Linus by name—was born with a similar defect. In good weather it has decent manners, but in such weather as we've been enduring lately it behaves rather badly. Would you care for a closer inspection?"

"No," Woodward said. Johnstone gave his knee an affectionate pat and wrapped the bandage around it once more.

"Is there a point to this, Alan?" Bidwell asked.

"I am answering the magistrate's inquiry as to whether my condition would allow me to take your staircase at any speed."

"Oh, that." Bidwell came over to the fireplace and offered his palms to the heat, as the schoolmaster pulled his stocking back up and rebuttoned the breeches leg. "Yes, the magistrate's clerk advanced one of his rather dubious theories concerning your knee. He said—"

"—that he wondered if my knee was really deformed, or if I were only shamming," Johnstone interrupted. "Ben told me. An interesting theory, but somewhat flawed. Robert, I've been in Fount Royal for—what?—three years or thereabouts? Have you ever seen me walk without the aid of my cane?"

"Never," Bidwell said.

"If I were shamming, what would be the reason for it?" Johnstone was addressing this question to Woodward. "By God's grace, I wish I *could* run down a staircase! I wish I could walk without putting my weight on a stick!" Heat had crept into the schoolmaster's voice. "I cut a fine figure at Oxford, as you can imagine! There the prizes always belonged to the young and the quick, and I was forced to carry myself like a doddering old man! But I proved myself in the classroom, that's what I did! I could not throw myself down the playing field, but I did throw myself into my studies, and thereafter I became president of my social club!"

"The Hellfires, I presume?" Woodward asked.

"No, not the Hellfires. The Ruskins. We emulated the Hellfires in some things, but we were rather more studious. Quite a bit more timid, to be truthful." Johnstone seemed to realize he had displayed some bitterness at his condition, and his voice was again under firm control. "Forgive my outburst," he said. "I am not a self-pitier and I wish no pity from anyone else. I enjoy my profession and I feel I am very good at what I do."

"Hear, hear!" Winston said. "Magistrate, Alan has shown himself to be an excellent schoolmaster. Before he came, school was held in a barn and our teacher was an older man who didn't have near Alan's qualifications."

"That's right," Bidwell added. "Upon Alan's arrival here, he insisted a schoolhouse be built and regular lessons begun in the basics of reading, writing, and arithmetic. He's taught many of the farmers and their children how to write their own names. I must say, though, that Alan's opening of the schoolhouse to the female children is a bit too liberal for my tastes!"

"That *is* liberal," Woodward remarked. "Some might even say misguided."

"Females are becoming more educated in Europe," Johnstone said, with the slightly wearied sound of someone who has defended a position time and again. "I believe at least one member of every family should be able to read. If that is a wife or a female child, then so be it."

"Yes, but Alan's had to pry some of these children away from their families," Winston said. "Like Violet Adams, for one. Education goes against the grain of these rustics."

"Violet approached me wanting to learn to read the Bible, as neither of her parents were able. How could I refuse her? Oh, Martin and Constance at first were set against it, but I convinced them that reading is not a dishonorable exercise, and thereby Violet would please the Lord. After the child's experience, however, she was forbidden to attend school again. A pity, too, because Violet is a bright child. Well . . . enough of this horn blowing." The schoolmaster braced himself with his cane and stood up from the chair. "I should be on my way now, ere this weather gets any worse. It was a pleasure speaking with you, Magistrate. I hope you're soon feeling better."

"Oh, he shall!" Bidwell spoke up. "Ben's coming by tonight to tend to him. It won't be long before Isaac is as fit as a racehorse!"

Woodward summoned a frail smile. Never in his life had he been a racehorse. A workhorse, yes, but never a racehorse. And now he was *Isaac* to the master of Fount Royal, since the trial had ended and sentencing was imminent.

Bidwell walked with Johnstone to get his coat and tricorn before he braved the rain. Winston came forward to stand before the fire. The flames reflected off the glass of his spectacles. "A chill wind in May!" he said. "I thought I'd left such a thing behind in London! But it's not so bad when one has a house as grand as this in which to bask, is it?" Woodward didn't know whether to nod or shake his head, so he did neither.

Winston rubbed his hands together. "Unfortunately, my own hearth smokes and my roof will be leaking tonight like an oarboat. But I shall endure it. Yes, I shall. Just as Mr. Bidwell has said at times of business crisis: whatever tribulations may come, they mold the character of the man."

"What say, Edward?" Bidwell had entered the parlor again after seeing Johnstone off.

"Nothing, sir," Winston replied. "I was thinking aloud, that's all." He turned from the fire. "I was about to point out to the magistrate that our sorry weather is one more evidence of the witch's spellcraft against us, as we've never been struck with such damp misery before."

"I think Isaac is already well aware of Witch Howarth's abilities. But we won't have to endure her but a day or two longer, will we, Isaac?"

Bidwell was waiting for a response, his mouth cracked by a

smile but his eyes hard as granite. Woodward, in order to keep the peace and thereby get to his bed without an uproar, whispered, "No, we won't." Instantly he felt shamed by it, because indeed he was dancing to Bidwell's tune. But at the moment he was too sick and tired to give a damn.

Winston soon said good night, and Bidwell summoned Mrs. Nettles and a servant girl to help the magistrate upstairs. Woodward, ill as he was, protested against the girl's efforts to disrobe him and insisted on preparing himself for bed. He had been under the sheet for only a few minutes when he heard the doorbell ring. Presently Mrs. Nettles knocked at his door, announcing the arrival of Dr. Shields, and the doctor came in armed with his bag of potions and implements.

The bleeding bowl was readied. The hot lancet bit true and deep through the crusted wounds of the morning's bloodletting. As Woodward lay with his head over the edge of the bed and the sound of his corrupted fluids pattering into the bowl, he stared up at the ceiling where Dr. Shields's shadow was thrown by the yellow lamplight.

"Not to fear," the doctor said, as his fingers worked the cuts to keep the blood running. "We'll banish this sickness."

Woodward closed his eyes. He felt cold. His stomach had clenched—not because of the pain he was suffering, but because he'd thought of the three lashes that would soon be inflicted upon Matthew. At least, though, after the lashing was done Matthew would be free to go from that filthy gaol; and thankfully he would be free also from Rachel Howarth's influence.

The blood continued to flow. Woodward felt—or imagined he felt—that his hands and feet were freezing. His throat, however, remained fiery hot.

He entertained himself for the moment with musings on how wrong Matthew had been in his theory concerning the Spanish spy. If indeed there was such a spy, Alan Johnstone was not the man. Or, at least, Johnstone was not the thief who'd taken Matthew's coin. Matthew was so cocksure of his theories that sometimes the boy became insufferable, and this was a good opportunity to remind him that he made mistakes just like the rest of mankind.

"My throat," he whispered to Dr. Shields. "It pains me."

"Yes, we'll tend it again after I've finished here."

It was bad fortune to become so ill without benefit of a real hospital, Woodward thought. A city hospital, that is. Well, the task here would be soon finished. Of course he didn't look forward with great relish to that trip back to Charles Town, but neither would he care to remain in this swamphole more than another week.

He hoped Matthew could bear the lashes. The first one would be a shock; the second would likely tear the flesh. Woodward had seen hardened criminals break into tears and cry for their mothers after the whip had thrice bitten their backs. But soon the ordeal would be over. Soon they could both take leave of this place, and Satan could fight the mosquitoes for its ruins as far as he cared.

Does it not seem very strange to you, Johnstone had said, *that the Devil should so openly reveal himself about town?* Woodward squeezed his eyes shut more tightly. . . . *consider the possibility that Satan is indeed at work in Fount Royal, and has given Madam Howarth's face to the true witch. Or warlock, as the case might be.*

No! Woodward thought. No! There were the witnesses, who had sworn truth on the Bible, and the poppets that were even now sitting atop the dresser! To consider that there was some other witch would not only delay his decision in regards to the prisoner but would also result in the complete abandonment of Fount Royal. *No,* Woodward told himself. It was sheer folly to march down that road!

"Pardon?" Dr. Shields said. "Did you say something, Isaac?"

Woodward shook his head. "Forgive me, I thought you did. A bit more in the bowl and we'll be done."

"Good," Woodward said. He could sleep now, if his throat were not so raw. The sound of his blood dripping into the bowl was nearly a strange kind of lullaby. But before he gave himself up to sleep he would pray for God to endow strength to

Matthew, both to resist that woman's wiles and to endure the whip with the grace of a gentleman. Then he would add a prayer to keep his own mind clear in this time of tribulation, so that he might do what was right and proper in the framework of the law.

But he was sick and he was troubled, and he had also begun to realize that he was afraid: of sinking into deeper illness, of Rachel Howarth's influence over Matthew, of making a mistake. Afraid on a level he hadn't known since his last year in London, when his whole world had been torn asunder like a piece of rotten cloth.

He feared the future. Not just the turn of the century, and what a new age might bring to this strife-burnt earth, but tomorrow and the next day and the day after that. He feared all the demons of the unknown tomorrows, for they were creatures who destroyed the shape and structure of yesterday for the sake of a merry fire.

"A little more, a little more," Dr. Shields said, as the blood continued to drip from the lancet cuts.

WHILE WOODWARD WAS BEING SO ATTENDED, Matthew lay in the dark on his pallet of straw and grappled with his own fears. It would not be seemly if tomorrow morning, at the delivering of the lashes, he should lose control and disgrace himself before the magistrate. He had seen criminals whipped before, and knew that sometimes they couldn't hold their bodily functions, so great was the pain. He could stand three lashes; he knew he could. Rather, he *hoped* he could. If that giant Mr. Green put his strength into the blows . . . well, it was best not to think about that right now, or he'd convince himself that his back would be split open like a ripe melon.

Distant thunder sounded. The gaol had taken on a chill. He wished for a coat to cover himself, but of course there was nothing but these clothes that were—from the smell and stiffness of them—fit to be boiled in a kettle and cut into rags. Instantly he thought how petty were his own discomforts, as Rachel's sackcloth robe was surely torment to her flesh by now and the punishment she faced was far more terrible—and more final—than a trio of whipstrikes.

So much was whirling through his mind that it seemed hot as a hearth, though his body was cold. He might wish for sleep, but he was his own hardest taskmaster and such relief was withheld. He sat up, folding his arms around himself, and stared into the dark as if he might see some answer there to the questions that plagued him.

The poppets. The testimony of Violet Adams. The three Devil's familiars who could not have sprung from the rather simple mind of Jeremiah Buckner. And how to explain the dwarf-creature—the "imp"—that both Buckner and Violet Adams had seen at different times and locales? What also of the cloak with six buttons? And the Devil's commandment to the child to "tell them to free my Rachel"? Could there be any more damning a decree?

But another thing kept bothering Matthew: what the child had said about hearing a man's voice, singing in the darkness of another room at that house. Was it a fragment of nothing? Or was it a shadow of great importance?

"You're awake." It had been a statement, not a question.

"Yes," Matthew said.

"I can't sleep either."

"Little wonder." He listened to the noise of rain dripping from the roof. Again there came the dull rumble of thunder.

"I have remembered something," Rachel said. "I don't know how important it is, but at the time I thought it was unusual."

"What is it?" He looked toward her shape in the darkness.

"The night before Daniel was murdered . . . he asked me if I loved him."

"This was an unusual question?"

"Yes. For him, I mean. Daniel was a good man, but he was never one to *speak* of his feelings . . . at least not where love was concerned."

"Might I ask what was your reply?"

"I told him I did love him," she answered. "And then he said that I had made him very happy in the six years of our marriage. He said . . . it made no matter to him that I had never borne a child, that I was his joy in life and no man could change that fact."

"Those were his exact words, as best you recall?"

"Yes."

"You say he was not normally so concerned with emotions? Had anything occurred in the previous few days that might have made him wish to express such feelings? A quarrel, perhaps?"

"I recall no quarrel. Not to say that we didn't have them, but they were never allowed to linger."

Matthew nodded, though he realized she couldn't see it. He laced his fingers around his knees. "You were both well matched, would you say? Even though there was such a difference in ages?"

"We both desired the same things," Rachel said. "Peace at home, and success for our farm. As for the difference in our ages, it mattered some at the beginning but not so much as the years passed."

"Then he had no reason to doubt that you loved him? Why would he ask such a question, if it was against his usual nature?"

"I don't know. Do you think it means anything?"

"I can't say. There's so much about this that begs questions. Things that should fit don't, and things that shouldn't fit do. Well, when I get out of here I plan on trying to find out why."

"What?" She sounded surprised. "Even after the child's testimony?"

"Yes. Her testimony was—pardon my bluntness—the worst blow that could have been dealt to you. Of course you didn't help your case by violating the Holy Book. But still . . . there are questions that need answers. I can't close my eyes to them."

"But Magistrate Woodward can?"

"I don't think he's able to see them as I do," Matthew said. "Because I'm a clerk and not a jurist, my opinions on witchcraft have not been formed by court records and the articles of demonology."

"Meaning," she said, "that you don't believe in witches?"

"I certainly do believe in the power of the Devil to do wickedness through men—and women. But as for your being a witch and having murdered Reverend Grove and your husband . . ." He hesitated, knowing that he was about to throw himself into the flames of commitment. "I don't believe it," he said.

Rachel said something, very quietly, that gave him a twinge deep in his stomach. "You could be wrong. I could be casting a spell on you this moment."

Matthew considered this point carefully before he answered. "Yes, I could be wrong. But if Satan is your master, he has lost his grip on logic. He wishes you released from the gaol, when he personally went to great lengths to put you here. And if his aim is to destroy Fount Royal, why doesn't he just burn the whole town in one night instead of an empty house here and there? I don't think Satan would care if a house was empty before it burned, do you? And what are these tricks of bringing the three demons out to parade them as if in a stageplay? Why would you appear to Jeremiah Buckner and invite him to view a scene that would certainly send you to the stake?" He waited for a response but there was none. "Buckner may have sworn truth on the Bible, yes. He may *believe* that what he saw was the truth. But my question is: what is it that two men—and a little girl—may see that appears to be true but is in reality a cunning fiction? It must be more than a dream, because certainly Violet Adams was not dreaming when she walked into that house in the afternoon. Who would create such a fiction, and how could it possibly be disguised as the truth?"

"I can't see how any man could do it," Rachel said.

"I can't either, but I believe it has somehow been done. My task is to find out first of all *how*. Then to find out the *why* of it. I hope from those two answers will come the third: *who*."

"And if you can't find them? What then?"

"Then . . ." Matthew paused, knowing the reply but unwilling to give it, "that bridge is best crossed when it is reached."

Rachel was silent. Even the few rats that had returned to the walls after Linch's massacre had stilled themselves. Matthew lay down again, trying to get his thoughts in order. The sound of thunder was louder; its power seemed to shake the very earth to its deepest foundations.

"Matthew?" Rachel said.

"Yes?"

"Would you . . . would you hold my hand?"

"Pardon?" He wasn't sure he'd heard her correctly.

"Would you hold my hand?" she asked again. "Just for a moment. I don't like the thunder."

"Oh." His heart was beating harder. Though he knew full well that the magistrate would look askance on such a thing, it seemed wrong to deny her a small comfort. "All right," he said, and he stood up. When he went to the bars that separated them, he couldn't find her.

"I'm here." She was sitting on the floor.

Matthew sat down as well. Her hand slipped between the bars, groping, and touched his shoulder. He said, "Here," and grasped her hand with his. At the intertwining of their fingers, Matthew felt a shock of heat that was first intense and then softened as it seemed to course slowly up his forearm. His heart was drumming; he was surprised she couldn't hear it, as surely a military march was being played next to her ear. It had occurred to him that his might be the last hand ever offered her.

The thunder again announced itself, and again the earth gave a tremble. Matthew felt Rachel's grip tighten. He couldn't help but think that in seven days she would be dead. She would be bones and ashes, nothing left of her voice or her touch or her compelling presence. Her beautiful tawny eyes would be burnt blind, her ebony hair sheared by the flames.

In seven days.

"Would you lie with me?" Rachel asked.

"What?"

"Would you lie down with me?" Her voice sounded very weary, as if now that the trial had ended her strength of spirit had been all but overwhelmed by the evidence arrayed against her. "I think I might sleep, if you were to hold my hand."

"Yes," he answered, and he eased down onto his back with his hand still gripping hers. She also reclined alongside the bars, so near to him that he felt the heat of her body even through the coarse and dirty sackcloth.

The thunder spoke, closer still and more powerful. Rachel's hand squeezed his, almost to the point of pain. He said nothing, as the sound of his heartbeat made speech impossible.

For a while the thunder was a raging young bully above Fount Royal, but at last it began to move away toward the sea and became aged and muttering in its decrease. The hands of the two prisoners remained bound together, even as sleep took them in different paths. Matthew awakened once, and listened in the quiet dark. His mind was groggy, but he thought he'd heard a sound that might have been a hushed sobbing.

If the sound had been real or not, it was not repeated. He squeezed Rachel's hand. She gave an answering pressure.

That was all.

twenty

MATTHEW EMERGED FROM SLEEP before the first rooster crowed. He found his hand still embracing Rachel's. When Matthew gently tried to work his hand free, Rachel's eyes opened and she sat up in the gray gloom with bits of straw in her hair.

The morning of mixed blessings had arrived; his lashing and his freedom were both soon to be delivered. Rachel made no statement to him, but retreated to the other side of her cage for an illusion of privacy with her waste bucket. Matthew moved to the far side of his own cell and spent a moment splashing cold water upon his face, then he too reached for the necessary bucket. Such an arrangement had horrified him when he'd first entered the gaol, but now it was something to be done and over with as quickly as possible.

He ate a piece of stale bread that he'd saved from last night, and then he sat on his bench, his head lowered, waiting for the sound of the door opening.

It wasn't a long wait. Hannibal Green entered the gaol carrying a lantern. Behind him was the magistrate, bundled in coat and scarf, the bitter reek of liniment around him and his face more chalky now than gray, with dark purplish hollows beneath his swollen eyes. Woodward's ghastly appearance frightened

Matthew more than the expectation of the lashes, and the magistrate moved with a slow, painful step.

"It's time." Green unlocked Matthew's cell. "Out with you." Matthew stood up. He was afraid, but there was no use in delay. He walked out of the cell.

"Matthew?" Rachel was standing at the bars. He gave her his full attention. "No matter what happens to me," she said quietly, the lantern's light reflecting in her amber eyes, "I wish to thank you for listening." He nodded. Green gave him a prod in the ribs to move him along. "Have courage," she said.

"And you," he replied. He wanted to remember her in that moment; she was beautiful and proud, and there was nothing in her face that betrayed the fact she faced a hideous death. She lingered, staring into his eyes, and then she turned away and went back to her bench, where she eased down and shrouded herself in the sackcloth gown once more.

"Move on!" Green rumbled.

Woodward grasped Matthew's shoulder, in almost a paternal gesture, and led him out of the gaol. At the doorway, Matthew resisted the desire to look back again at Rachel, for even though he felt he was abandoning her, he knew as well that, once free, he could better work for her benefit.

It occurred to him, as he walked out into the misty, meager light of morning, that he had accepted—to the best of his ability—the unfamiliar role of champion.

Green closed the gaol's door. "Over there," he said, and he took hold of Matthew's left arm and pulled him rather roughly away from Woodward, directing him toward the pillory that stood in front of the gaolhouse.

"Is there need for that, sir?" Woodward's voice, though still weak, was somewhat more able than the previous day.

Green didn't bother to answer. As he was being led to be pilloried, Matthew saw that the novelty of a lashing had brought a dozen or so citizens out of their homes to be entertained. Among them were Seth Hazelton, whose grinning face was still swaddled by a dirty bandage, and Lucretia Vaughan, who had brought along a basket of breads and teacakes that she was in the process of selling to the assembly. Sitting in his carriage nearby was the master of Fount Royal himself, come to make sure justice was done, while Goode sat up front slowly whittling on a piece of wood.

"Tear his back open, Green!" Hazelton urged. "Split it like he done split my face!"

Green used a key from his ring to unlatch the top half of the pillory, which he then lifted up. "Take your shirt off," he told Matthew. As Matthew did Green's bidding, he saw with a sick jolt to his stomach that coiled around a hitching-post to his right was a braided leather whip perhaps two feet in length. It certainly was not as formidable as a bullwhip or a cat-o'-nine, but the braid could do considerable damage if delivered with any sort of strength—and Green, at the moment, resembled nothing less than a fearsome, red-bearded Goliath.

"In the pillory with you," the giant said. Matthew put his arms into the depressions meant for them and then laid his neck against the damp wood. Green closed the pillory and locked it, trapping Matthew's head and arms. Matthew now was bent into a crouch, his naked back offered to the whip. He couldn't move his head to follow Green, but he heard the noise of the braid as it slithered off the hitching-post.

The whip cracked as Green tested it. Matthew flinched, the skin crawling across his spine. "Give it to 'im good!" Hazelton yelled. Matthew was unable to either lift or lower his head to any great degree. A feeling of dreadful helplessness swept over him. He clenched his hands into fists and squeezed his eyes shut.

"One!" Green said, and by that Matthew knew the first strike was about to be made. Standing close by, the magistrate had to turn away and stare at the ground. He felt he might have to spew at any second.

Matthew waited. Then he sensed rather than heard Green drawing back. The onlookers were silent. Matthew realized the whip was up and about to—

Crack!

—across his shoulders, a hot pain that grew hotter, a flame, an inferno that scorched his flesh and brought tears to his sealed eyes. He heard himself gasp with the shock of it, but he had enough presence of mind to open his mouth lest he bite into his tongue. After the whip had been withdrawn, the strip of skin it had bitten continued to burn hotter and hotter; it was the worst physical pain Matthew had ever experienced—and the second and third strikes were yet to fall.

"Damn it, Green!" Hazelton bawled. "Show us some blood!"

"Shut your mouth!" Green hollered back. "This ain't no ha'-penny circus!"

Again, Matthew waited with his eyes tightly closed. Again he sensed Green drawing back the whip, sensed the man putting his strength into the lash as it hissed down through the sodden air. "Two!" Green shouted.

Crack! it came once more, exactly upon the same strip of blistered flesh.

For an instant Matthew saw bright crimson and deepest ebony swirling in his mind like the colors of war flags, and then the truest, keenest, most savage pain under the sky of God gnawed into him. As this pain bloomed down his back and up his neck to the very top of his skull, he heard himself give an animalish groan but he was able to restrain the cry that fairly leapt from his throat.

"Three!" Green announced.

Here came the whip's hiss. Matthew felt tears on his cheeks. Oh God, he thought. Oh God oh God oh—

Crack! This time the braid had struck a few inches lower than the first two lashes, but its bite was no less agonizing. Matthew trembled, his knees about to give way. So fierce was the pain that he feared his bladder might also empty itself, so he concentrated solely on damming the flow. Thankfully, it did not. He opened his eyes. And then he heard Green say something that he would remember with joy the rest of his life: "Done, Mr. Bidwell!"

"*No!*" It was Hazelton's angry snarl. "You held back, damn you! I seen you hold back!"

"Watch that tongue, Seth, or by God I'll blister it!"

"Gentlemen, gentlemen!" Bidwell had stepped down from his carriage, and made his way to the pillory. "I think we've had violence enough for this morning." He leaned down to peer into Matthew's sweat-slick face. "Have you learned your lesson, clerk?"

"Green held back!" the blacksmith insisted. "It ain't fair to go so easy on that boy, when he done scarred me for life!"

"We agreed on the punishment, Mr. Hazelton," Bidwell reminded him. "I believe Mr. Green applied the lash with proper consideration. Wouldn't you say, Magistrate?"

Woodward had seen the red welts that had risen across Matthew's shoulders. "I would."

"I pronounce the punishment correctly administered and the young man free to go. Release him, Mr. Green."

But Hazelton was so enraged he was nearly dancing a jig. "I ain't satisfied! You didn't draw no blood!"

"I could remedy that," Green warned, as he coiled the braid and then went about unlocking the pillory.

Hazelton took two strides forward and thrust his ugly face at Matthew. "You set foot on my land again, and I'll strop your hide myself! I won't hold back, neither!" He drew himself up again and cast a baleful stare at Bidwell. "Mark this as a black day for justice!" he said, and with that he stalked away in the direction of his home.

The latch was opened. Matthew stood up from the pillory's embrace and had to bite his lip as a fresh wave of pain coursed through his shoulders. If Green had indeed held back, Matthew would have hated to be on the receiving end of a whip that the giant put his full power behind. He felt light-headed and stood for a moment with one hand grasping the pillory.

"Are you all right?" Woodward was standing beside him.

"Yes, sir. I shall be, I mean."

"Come along!" Bidwell was wearing a smirk that was not very much disguised. "You look in need of some breakfast!"

Matthew followed Bidwell to the carriage, with the magistrate walking at his side. The onlookers were going away to their daily business, the small excitement over. Suddenly a woman stepped in front of Matthew and said brightly, "My compliments!"

It took Matthew a few seconds to register that Lucretia Vaughan was offering him a teacake from her basket. "Please take one!" she said. "They're freshly baked!" He felt numbed of mind and scorched of shoulders, but he didn't wish to offend her so he did accept a teacake.

"The lashing wasn't so bad, was it?" she asked.

"I'm gratified it's over."

"Madam, we have breakfast to attend to!" Bidwell had already secured his seat in the carriage. "Would you let him pass, please?"

She kept her eyes locked on Matthew's. "You *will* come to dinner on Thursday evening, will you not? I have made plans for it."

"Dinner?" He frowned.

"My mistake," Woodward said to the woman. "I neglected to inform him."

"Oh? Then I shall make the invitation myself. Would you come to dinner on Thursday evening? At six o'clock?" She gave Woodward a brief, rather tight smile. "I would invite you also, Magistrate, but seeing as how you are so feeble I fear an evening out might only worsen your health." She turned her rapacious attention upon Matthew once more. He thought that the shine of her blue eyes was glassy enough to indicate fever. "May I count on your arrival?"

"Well . . . I thank you," he said, "but I—"

"You will find my home very hospitable," she plowed on. "I do know how to set a table, and you might ask anyone as to the quality of my kitchen." She leaned her head forward, as if offering to share a secret. "Mr. Green is quite fond of my onion bread. He told me that the loaf I presented to him yesterday afternoon was the finest he'd ever set eyes on. The thing about onion bread," and here she lowered her voice so that Bidwell might not hear, "is that it is a great persuader. A meal of it, and mercy follows."

What the woman was saying wasn't lost on Matthew. If indeed Green *had* held back in his delivery of the whip—which Matthew, in severe pain, found difficult to believe—it was likely due to Madam Vaughan's influence on his behalf. "I see," he said, though his view was not entirely clear.

"Come along!" Bidwell said impatiently. "Madam, good day!"

"Might you favor my home with your presence on Thursday evening?" Madam Vaughan was obviously not one to buckle before pressure, though she certainly knew how to apply it. "I can promise you will find it of interest."

He surely didn't feel in need of dinner company at the moment, but by Thursday he knew the pain would be a bad memory. Besides that, the woman's manipulations intrigued him. Why had she desired to intercede in his punishment? He nodded. "Yes, I'll be there."

"Excellent! Six o'clock, then. I shall send my husband to fetch you." She gave a quick curtsey and withdrew, after which Matthew pulled himself up into the carriage.

Bidwell watched Matthew try to keep his shoulders from rubbing the seatback as the carriage creaked along Peace Street. Try as he might, Bidwell couldn't wipe the smirk of satisfaction off his face. "I hope you're cured of your malady!"

Matthew had to bite at the offered hook. "What malady might that be?"

"The sickness of sticking your nose in places it doesn't belong. You got off very lightly."

"I suppose I did."

"I *know* you did! I've seen Green whip a man before. He did hold back. If he hadn't, you'd be bleeding and blubbering right now." He shrugged. "But Green doesn't care much for Hazelton, so there you have it. Magistrate, might I hope you'll pass sentence today?"

"Not today," came the hoarse reply. "I must study the records."

Bidwell scowled. "I don't for the life of me see what you have to *study!*"

"It's a matter of being fair," Woodward said.

"Being *fair?*" Bidwell gave a harsh laugh. "Yes, this is why the world's in its current shape!"

Matthew couldn't remain quiet. "Meaning what, sir?"

"Meaning that some men mistake hesitation for fairness, and thus the Devil runs rampant over the heads of good Christians!" Bidwell's eyes had a rapier glint and dared Matthew to disagree. "This world will be burnt to a cinder in another fifty years, the way Evil is allowed to prosper! We'll be barricading our doors and windows against Satan's soldiers! But we'll be *fair* about it, won't we, and therefore we'll leave a battering ram on our doorsteps!"

Matthew said, "You must have attended one of Preacher Jerusalem's speeches."

"Pah!" Bidwell waved a hand at him in disgust. "What do you know of the world? Much less than you think! Well, here's a laugh on you, clerk: your theory about Alan Johnstone is just as crippled as he is! He came to the house last night and showed us his knee!"

"He *did?*" Matthew looked to Woodward for confirmation.

The magistrate nodded and scratched a fresh mosquito bite on his gray-grizzled chin. "I saw the knee at close quarters. It would be impossible for Johnstone to be the man who stole your gold coin."

"Oh." Matthew's brow knitted. His pride had taken a blow, especially following Nicholas Paine's reasonable explanation of his career as a pirate-hunter and how he came to roll his tobacco in the Spanish fashion. Now Matthew felt himself adrift at sea. He said, "Well . . ." but then he stopped, because there was nothing to be said.

"If I were half as smart as you think yourself to be," Bidwell said, "I could build ships in my sleep!"

Matthew didn't respond to this taunt, preferring instead to concentrate on keeping his injured shoulders from making contact with the seatback. At last Goode drew the carriage up in front of the mansion and Matthew was the first to step down. He then aided the magistrate, and in doing so discovered that Woodward was warm and clammy with fever. He also for the first time caught sight of the crusted wounds behind Woodward's left ear. "You've been bled."

"Twice. My throat is still pained, but my breathing is somewhat better."

"Ben's due to bleed him a third time this evening," Bidwell said as he descended from the carriage. "Before then, might I suggest that the magistrate attend to his studying?"

"I plan on it," Woodward said. "Matthew, Dr. Shields would have something to ease your discomfort. Do you wish to see him?"

"Uh . . . beg pardon, suh," Goode spoke up from the driver's seat. "I have an ointment to cool the sting some, if he cares to use it."

"That would be helpful." Matthew reasoned that a slave would indeed have an able remedy for a whip burn. "Thank you."

"Yes suh. I'll fetch it to the house directly I barn the carriage. Or if you please you can ride along with me."

"Goode, he doesn't care to visit the slave quarters!" Bidwell said sharply. "He'll wait for you in the house!"

"One moment." Matthew's hackles had risen at the idea of Bidwell telling him what he cared to do or not to do. "I'll come along."

"You don't want to go down there, boy! The place *smells!*"

"I am not so fragrant myself," Matthew reminded him, and then he climbed back up into the carriage. "I would like a warm bath after breakfast. Is that possible?"

"I'll arrange it for you," Bidwell agreed. "Do what you please, but if you go down there you'll regret it."

"Thank you for your consideration. Magistrate, might I suggest you return to bed as soon as convenient? You do need your rest. All right, Goode, I'm ready."

"Yes suh." Goode flicked the reins, said a quiet, "Giddup," and the team started off again.

Peace Street continued past Bidwell's mansion to the stable and the slave quarters, which occupied the plot of land between

Fount Royal and the tidewater swamp. It interested Matthew that Bidwell had referred to the quarters as being "down there" but in fact the street never varied in its elevation. The stable itself was of handsome construction and had been freshly whitewashed, but in contrast the ramshackle, unpainted houses of the servants had an impermanent quality.

Peace Street passed through the village of shacks and ended, Matthew saw, in a sandy path that led across a belt of pines and moss-draped oaks to the watchman's tower. Up at the tower's summit, a man sat under a thatched roof facing out to sea, his feet resting on the railing. A more boring task, Matthew could not imagine. Yet in these times of pirate raids and with the Spanish territory so close, he understood the need for caution. Beyond the tower, the bit of land that Matthew was able to see—if indeed it could be called something so solid—looked to be waist-high grass that surely hid a morass of mud and swamp ponds.

Smoke hung low over the house chimneys. A strutting rooster, his hens in close attendance, flapped out of the carriage's way as Goode steered the team toward the stable, beside which was a split-rail fence that served as a corral for a half-dozen fine-looking horses. Presently Goode reined the team in at a water trough and dismounted. Matthew followed. "My house be there, suh," Goode said, as he aimed a finger at a structure that was neither better nor worse than the other shacks around it, but might have fit within Bidwell's banquet room with space to spare.

On the short walk, Matthew noted several small plots of cornstalks, beans, and turnips between the houses. A Negro a few years younger than Goode was busy chopping firewood, and he paused in his labor to stare as Goode led Matthew past. A lean woman with a blue scarf wrapped around her head had emerged from her house to scatter some dried corn for her chickens, and she too stared in open amazement.

"They got to looksee," Goode said, with a slight smile. "You doan' come here so much."

By *you* Matthew realized he meant the English, or possibly the larger meaning of white skins in general. From around a corner peeked a young girl, whom Matthew recognized as one of the house servants. As soon as their eyes met, she pulled herself out of view again. Goode stopped in front of his own door. "Suh, you can wait here as you please. I'll fetch the balm." He lifted the latch. "But you can step in, as you please." He pushed the door open and called into the house, "Visitah, May!" He started across the threshold but then paused; his ebony, fathomless eyes stared into Matthew's face, and Matthew could tell the old man was trying to make a decision of sorts.

"What is it?" Matthew asked.

Goode seemed to have made up his mind; Matthew saw it, in a tightening of the jaw. "Suh? Would you favor me by steppin' inside?"

"Is something wrong?"

"No suh." He offered no further explanation, but stood waiting for Matthew to enter. Matthew decided there was more to this than hospitality. Therefore he walked into the house, and Goode entered behind him and shut the door.

"Who is that?" asked the heavyset woman who stood at the hearth. She had been stirring the contents of a cooking-pot that was placed in the hot ashes, but now the revolutions of the wooden spoon had ceased. Her eyes were deep-set and wary, her face crisscrossed with lines, under a coarse brown cloth scalp-wrapping.

"This be Mastuh Matthew Corbett," Goode said. "Mastuh Corbett, this be my wife May."

"Pleased to meet you," Matthew said, but the old woman didn't respond. She looked him head to toe, made a little windy sound with her lips, and returned to her labors at the pot.

"Ain't got on no shirt," she announced.

"Mastuh Corbett got hisself three lashes today. You 'member, I told you they was gon' whip him."

"Hm," May said, at the pittance of three whipstrikes.

"Will you set y'self here, suh?" Goode motioned toward a short bench that stood before a roughly constructed table, and Matthew accepted the invitation. Then, as Goode went to a shelf that held a number of wooden jars, Matthew took the opportunity to examine his surroundings. The examination did not take long, as the house only had the single room. A pallet with a thin mattress served as the bed, and apart from the bench and table the only other furnishings were a highbacked chair (which looked as if it had once been regal but was now sadly battered), a clay washbasin, a crate in which was folded some clothing, and a pair of lanterns. Matthew noted a large tortoise shell displayed on the wall above the hearth, and a burlap-wrapped object (the violin, of course) had its own shelf near the bed. Another shelf held a few wooden cups and platters. That seemed to be the end of the inventory of Goode's belongings.

Goode took one of the jars, opened it, and came around behind Matthew. "Suh, do you mind my fingers?"

"No."

"This'll sting some." Matthew winced as a cool liquid was applied to his stripes. The stinging sensation was quite bearable, considering what he'd just endured. Within a few seconds the stinging went away and he had the feeling that the potion was deadening his raw flesh. "Ain't too bad," Goode remarked. "Seen terrible worse."

"I appreciate this. It does soothe the pain."

"*Pain,*" the woman said, as she stirred the pot. It had been spoken with an edge of mockery. "Ain't no pain in three lashes. Pain don't start 'til they gets to thirty."

"Now, now, keep that tongue still," Goode said. He finished painting the stripes and corked the jar. "Ought to do you, suh. Doubt you'll sleep so well tonight, though, 'cause whipburns get hotter 'fore they start to healin'." He walked back to the shelf and returned the jar to its proper place. "Pardon my speakin'," he said, "but Mastuh Bidwell don't care for you, do he?"

"No, he doesn't. The feeling, I have to say, is mutual."

"He thinks you're standin' up for Mistress Howarth, don't he?" Goode carefully lowered the burlap-wrapped violin from the shelf and began to unwind the cloth. "Pardon my speakin', but *be* you standin' up for her?"

"I have some questions concerning her."

"Questions?" Goode laid the wrapping aside. In the smoky yellow lanternlight, the violin took on a soft, buttery sheen. He spent a moment running his slim fingers up and down the neck. "Suh, can I ask a question of my own?"

"Yes."

"Well, it 'pears to me that Mistress Howarth's near bein' burnt. I don't know her so good, but one mornin' she picked up a bucket and helped Ginger carry water when Ginger 'as child-heavy."

"He don't know who Ginger be!" May said. "What're you goin' on for?"

"Ginger be May's sister," Goode explained. "Live right 'cross the way. Anyhows, it was a kind thing. You see, it's peculiar." Goode plucked a note, listened, and made an adjustment by tightening the string. "Why ain't no slaves heard nor seen nothin'." He plucked another string, listened and adjusted. "No, only them English seen things. An' y'know, that's kinda peculiar too."

"Peculiar? In what way?"

"Well suh, when this first start up we had us a good many tongues bein' spoke in Fount Royal. Had them Germans, had them Dutchmen too. They all gots scairt and gone, but nary a one of 'em seen or heard nothin' to mark Mistress Howarth. No suh, just them English." A third string was plucked, but he found this one satisfactory. He looked into Matthew's face. "See what I'm sayin', suh? My question be: how come Satan don't talk German nor Dutch and he don't talk to us darks neither?"

"I don't know," Matthew said, but it was a point worth consideration.

"Thought Satan knew ever' tongue there was," Goode went on. "Just peculiar, that's all." He finished tuning the violin and his fingers plucked a quick succession of notes. "Mastuh Bidwell don't care for you," he said, "'cause you askin' such questions. Mastuh Bidwell want to burn Mistress Howarth quick and be done with it, so's he can keep Fount Royal from dyin'. Pardon my spielin'."

"That's all right," Matthew said. He dared to try to put his shirt back on, but his shoulders were still too tender. "I know your master has ambitious plans."

"Yes suh, he do. Heard him talk 'bout bringin' in more darks to drain that swamp. Hard job to be done. All them skeeters and bitin' things, got gators and snakes out there too. Only darks can do that job, y'see. You English—pardon my speakin'—ain't got the backs for it. Used to I did, but I got old." Again, he played a fast flurry of notes. May poured some water from a bucket into the cooking-pot, and then she turned her efforts to a smaller pot that was brewing near the firewall. "Sure never thought I'd live to see such a world as this," Goode said quietly, as he caressed the strings. "Sixteen hundred and ninety-nine, and the cent'ry 'bout to turn!"

"Ain't got long," May offered. "World's gone be 'stroyed in fire come directly."

Goode smiled. "Maybe so, and maybe not. Could be 'stroyed in fire, could be a cent'ry of wonders."

"Fire," May said sharply. Matthew had the thought that this difference of opinion was a bone of contention between them. "Everythin' burnt and made new 'gain. That's the Lord's vow."

"'Spect it is," he agreed gently, displaying his gift of diplomacy. "'Spect it is."

Matthew decided it was time to be on his way. "Thank you again for the help." He stood up. "I do feel much—"

"Oh, not to be leavin' just yet!" Goode insisted. "Please favor me, suh! I brung you here to show you somethin' I think you might find a' interest." He put aside the violin and went once more to the shelf that held the wooden jars. When he chose the one next to the jar that had held the potion, May said with alarm in her voice, "What're you *doin'*, John Goode?"

"Showin' him. I want him to see." This jar had a lid instead of a cork and Goode lifted it.

"No! They ain't to be seen!" On May's wrinkled face was an expression that Matthew could only define as terror. "Have you lost your *mine?*"

"It's all right," Goode said, calmly but firmly. "I done decided it." He looked at Matthew. "Suh, I believe you be a decent man. I been wantin' to let somebody see this, but . . . well, I was feared to." He peered into the jar, and then lifted his gaze back to Matthew. "Would you promise me, suh, that you will not speak to anyone about what I'm gon' show you?"

"I don't know that I can make such a promise," Matthew said. "What is it?"

"See? See?" May was wringing her hands. "All he's gon' do is steal 'em!"

"Hush!" Goode said. "He ain't gone steal 'em! Just calm y'-self, now!"

"Whatever they are, I do promise not to steal them." Matthew had spoken this directly to May, and now he sat back down on the bench again.

"He *say!*" May appeared close to tears.

"It's all right." Goode put his hand on his wife's shoulder. "I want him to see, 'cause it's a thing needs answerin' and I figure he would care to know, 'specially since he got thieved hisself." Goode came to the table and upended the jar in front of Matthew. As the items inside tumbled out, Matthew caught his breath. On the table before him were four objects: a broken shard of light blue pottery, a small and delicate silver spoon, a silver coin, and . . .

Matthew's hand went to the fourth item. He picked it up and held it for close examination.

It was a gold coin. At its center was a cross that separated the figures of two lions and two castles. The letters *Charles II* and *Dei Grat* were clearly visible around the rim.

At first he thought it was the coin that had been stolen from his room, but it took only a brief inspection to tell him that—though it certainly was Spanish gold—it was not the same coin. The stamping on this piece was in much fresher condition, and on the other side was an ornately engraved *E* and a faint but discernible date: 1675.

Matthew picked up the silver coin, which was obviously old and so worn that most of the stamping had been wiped clean. Still, there was the barest impression of a *Dei Grat*.

He looked up at Goode, who stood over him. "Where did these come from?"

"Turtle bellies," Goode said.

"Pardon?"

"Yes suh." Goode nodded. "They come from turtle bellies. The spoon and silver piece came out of one I caught last year. The blue clay came out of one I got . . . oh . . . must'a been two month ago."

"And the gold coin?"

"The first night you and the magistrate was here," Goode explained, "Mastuh Bidwell asked me to catch a turtle for your supper the next night. Well, I caught a big one. There's his shell hangin'. And that gold piece was in his belly when I cut it open."

"Hm," Matthew grunted. He turned the gold coin between his fingers. "You caught these turtles out of the spring?"

"The fount. Yes suh. Them turtles like to be eatin' the reeds, y'see."

Matthew put the coins down upon the table and picked up the silver spoon. It was tarnished dark brown and the stem was bent, but it seemed remarkably preserved to have spent any length of time in a turtle's stomach. "Very strange, isn't it?" he said.

"I thought so too, suh. When I found that gold piece, and hearin' that yours was thieved a few days after'ard . . . well, I didn't know what to think."

"I can understand." Matthew looked again at the gold coin's date, and then studied the fragment of blue pottery before he replaced it and the other items in the wooden jar. He noted that May appeared very much relieved. "And I *do* promise not to tell anyone. As far as I'm concerned, it's no one's business."

"Thank you, suh," she said gratefully.

Matthew stood up. "I have no idea why turtles should have such things in their bellies, but it *is* a question that begs an answer. Goode, if you catch a turtle and happen to find anything else, will you let me know?"

"I will, suh."

"All right. I'd best return to the house. No need taking the carriage up, I'll be glad to walk." He watched as Goode put the lid back on the jar and returned it to the shelf.

"Let me ask you a question now, and please answer truthfully: do you think Rachel Howarth is a witch?"

He responded without hesitation. "No suh, I don't."

"Then how do you account for the witnesses?"

"I can't, suh."

"That's my problem," Matthew confided. "Neither can I."

"I'll walk you out," Goode said. Matthew offered a goodbye to May, and then he and the old man left the house. On the walk back toward the stable, Goode shoved his hands into the pockets of his brown breeches and said quietly, "May's got it in her mind we're gon' run to the Florida country. Take them gold and silver pieces and light out some night. I let her think it, 'cause it eases her. But we're long done past our runnin' days." He looked at the muddy earth beneath his shoes. "Naw, I come over when I was a boy. First mastuh was Mastuh Cullough, in V'ginia. Seen eight children sold. Seen my brother whipped to death for kickin' a white man's dog. I seen my little daughter's back branded, and her beggin' me to make 'em stop. That's why I play that fiddle Mastuh Bidwell give me; it be the only sound keep me from hearin' her voice."

"I'm sorry," Matthew said.

"Why? Did you brand her? I ain't askin' nobody to be sorry. All I'm sayin' is, my wife needs to dream 'bout the Florida country, just like I need to play my music. Just like anybody needs anythin' to give 'em a reason to live. That's all. Suh," he added, remembering his place.

They had reached the stable. Matthew noticed that Goode's pace had slowed. It seemed to him that there was something else the slave wanted to express, but he was taking his time in constructing it. Then Goode cleared his throat and said in a low, wary voice, "I don't believe Mistress Howarth is a witch, suh, but that ain't to say not some strange goin's-on here'bouts."

"I would certainly agree."

"You may not know the half of it, suh." Goode stopped walking, and Matthew did the same. "I'm speakin' of the man who goes out to the swamp now and again, after it's long past dark."

Matthew recalled the figure he'd seen here in the slave quarters that night the lightning had been so fierce. "A man? Who is it?"

"Couldn't see his face. I heard the horses cuttin' up one night and come out here to ease 'em. On the way back, I seen a man walkin' out to the swamp. He was carryin' a lantern, but it weren't lit. Walkin' quick, he was, like he had somewheres to go in a hurry. Well, I was spelt by it so I followed him. He slip past the watchman there and go on out through them woods." Goode motioned toward the pines with a tilt of his head. "The man that Mastuh Bidwell has watchin' at night does poorly. I've had call to wake him up m'self come dawn."

"The man who went out to the swamp," Matthew said, much intrigued. "Did you find out what his business was?"

"Well suh, nobody with right business to do would go out there, seein' as how that's where the privy wagon gets carted to and dumped. And it's a dangerous place, too, full a' mucks and mires. But this man, he just kept on goin'. I did follow him a ways, though, but it's hard travel. I had to turn 'round and come on home 'fore I seen what he was up to."

"When was this?"

"Oh . . . three, four month past. But I seen him again, near two week ago."

"He walked out to the swamp again?"

"I seen him on his way back. Both Earlyboy and me seen him, 'bout run right into him as we come 'round a corner. Bullhead—he's Ginger's man—has got some cards. We was over at his house, playin' most the night, and that's why it was such a small hour. We seen the man walkin', but he didn't see us. This time he was carryin' a dark lantern and a bucket."

"A bucket," Matthew repeated.

"Yes suh. Must'a been sealed, though. It was swingin' back and forth, but nothing was spillin' out."

Matthew nodded. He'd remembered that he had also seen something in the man's possession that might have been a bucket.

"Earlyboy was scairt," Goode said. "Still is. He asked me if we'd seen the Devil, but I told him I thought it was just a man." He lifted his thick white eyebrows. "Was I right, suh?"

Matthew paused to consider it. Then he said thoughtfully, "Yes, I think you were. Though it might have been a man with some Devil *in* him."

"That could be any man under the sun of creation," Goode observed. "I swear I can't figure why anybody would go out to that swamp, particular at night. Ain't nothin' out there a'tall."

"There must be something of value. Whatever it is, it can be carried in a bucket." Matthew looked back toward the watchtower for a moment; the watchman still had his feet up on the railing, and even now appeared to be sleeping. He doubted that anyone who wanted to get past at night would have much difficulty, especially if they weren't showing a light. Well, he felt in dire need of breakfast and a hot bath to wash off the gaol's filth. "Thank you again for the liniment," he told Goode.

"Yes suh, my pleasure. Luck to you."

"And you." Matthew turned away and walked along Peace Street, leaving the slave quarters behind. He had more things to think about now, and less time to sort them all out if indeed they could be sorted. He felt that someone—perhaps more than one person—had woven a tangled web of murder and deceits in this struggling, rough-hewn town, and had gone to great and inexplicable lengths to paint Rachel as the servant of Satan. But for what purpose? Why would anyone go to such labors to manufacture a case of witchcraft against her? It made no sense.

But then again, it must make sense—somehow, to someone.

And it was up to him to use his mind and instincts to uncover the sense of it, because if he did not—and very soon—then he could bid Rachel farewell at the burning pyre.

Who was the man who ventured at night into the swamp, carrying a dark lantern and a bucket? Why was a coin of Spanish gold in the belly of a turtle? And Goode's question: *How come Satan don't talk German nor Dutch and he don't talk to us darks neither?*

Mysteries within mysteries, Matthew thought. Unravelling them would be a task fit for a far greater champion than he—but he was all Rachel had. If he did not answer these questions, then who would? The answer to that was simple: no one.

twenty-one

T HE WARM BATH—taken in a tub room beside the kitchen—had turned out to be chilly and his shaving razor had nicked his chin, but otherwise Matthew found himself to be invigorated as he dressed in clean clothes. He had consumed a breakfast of eggs, sausage, and salted ham, put away two cups of tea and a jolt of rum, and so was eager to get out and about as the morning progressed.

His knock on the magistrate's door was not answered, but the door was unlatched. When he looked in, he saw Woodward asleep with the box of court papers beside him on the bed. The magistrate had obviously begun reading through them, as there were some papers lying in disarray near his right hand, but his illness had stolen him away. Matthew quietly entered the room and stood at the bedside, staring at Woodward's pallid yellow-tinged face.

The magistrate's mouth was open. Even in sleep he suffered, for his breathing was a harsh, painful wheeze. Matthew saw the brown stains on the pillowcase under his left ear. The room had a thick, sickly smell, an odor of dried blood and wet pus and . . . *death?* Matthew thought.

Instantly his mind recoiled. Such a thought should not be allowed. No, no, neither allowed nor dwelt upon! He looked down at the scuffed floorboards for a moment, listening to the magistrate's struggle with the very air.

At the orphanage, Matthew had seen boys grow sick and wither away in such a fashion. He suspected Woodward's illness might have begun with the cold rain that had pelted them on their flight from Shawcombe's tavern, the thought of which made him again damn that murderous villain to the innermost fires of Hell. And now Matthew was tormented by worry, because the magistrate's condition was only likely to worsen if he was not soon gotten back to Charles Town; he presumed Dr. Shields knew what he was doing—he *presumed*—but by the doctor's own admission the town of Fount Royal and its cemetery were becoming one and the same. Also, Matthew kept thinking about something the magistrate had said concerning Dr. Shields: *What prompted him to leave what was probably a well-established urban practise for a task of extreme hardship in a frontier village?*

What, indeed?

Woodward made a noise, a combination of a whisper and a groan. *"Ann,"* he said.

Matthew lifted his gaze to the man's face, which appeared fragile as bone china in the light of the room's single lamp.

"Ann," Woodward spoke again. His head pressed back against the pillow. "Ohhhhhh." It was an exclamation of heart-wrenching agony. ". . . hurting . . . he's hurting, Ann . . . hurting . . ." The magistrate's voice dwindled away, and his body relaxed once again as he fell into a deeper and more merciful realm of sleep.

Carefully Matthew came around the bed and straightened the papers into a neat stack, which he left within reach of Woodward's right hand.

"Sir? Are ye in need of anythin'?" Matthew looked toward the door. Mrs. Nettles stood on the threshold, and had spoken quietly so as not to disturb the sleeper. He shook his head.

"Very well, sir." She started to withdraw, but Matthew said, "A moment, please," and followed her out into the hallway after closing the door behind him.

"Let me say I did not mean to accuse you of stealing my coin," he told her. "I was only pointing out that a woman might have done the job as equally as a man."

"You mean, a woman a' my size, do ye not?" Mrs. Nettles's ebony eyes bored holes through him.

"Yes, that's exactly right."

"Well, I did nae steal it, so think what ye please. Now, if you'll pardon me, I ha' work to do." She turned away and walked toward the stairs.

"As do I," Matthew said. "The work of proving Rachel Howarth innocent."

Mrs. Nettles halted in her advance. She looked back at him, her face mirroring a confusion of amazement and suspicion.

"That's right," Matthew assured her. "I believe Madam Howarth to be innocent and I plan on proving it so."

"Provin' it? How?"

"It would be improper for me to say, but I thought you might like to know my intentions. Might I now ask you a question?" She made no response, but neither did she walk away. "I doubt much goes on here that escapes your attention," he said. "I'm speaking of Fount Royal as well as this house. You certainly heard the tales concerning Madam Howarth's supposed witchcraft. Why is it, then, that you so adamantly refused to believe her to be a witch, when the majority of the citizens are convinced she is?"

Mrs. Nettles glanced toward the stairs, marking that no one was close enough to overhear, before she offered a guarded reply. "I ha' seen the evil done by misguided men, sir. I saw it takin' shape here, long ere Mistress Howarth was accused. Oh yes sir, it was a thing waitin' to happen. After the rev'rend was laid low, it was bound an' sealed."

"You mean that a scapegoat was found for the murder?"

"Aye. Had to be Mistress Howarth, y'see. Had to be someone *different*—someone who was nae welcomed here. The fact that she's dark-skinned and near a Spaniard . . . it jus' had to be her accused of such crimes. And whoever murdered the rev'rend killed Mr. Howarth, too, and hid those poppets in the house to make sure Mistress Howarth fell to blame. I nae care what Cara Grunewald said about visions from God and th' like. She was ha' crazy and the other ha' dumb. How the tricks were done, I canna' say, but there's a true fox in our coop. Do y'see, sir?"

"I do," Matthew said, "but I'd still like to know why you believe Rachel to be innocent."

The woman's mouth was set in a tight, grim line. Again, she checked the staircase before she spoke. "I had an elder sister by the name a' Jane. She married a man named Merritt and come over here, settled in the town a' Hampton, in the Massachusetts colony. Jane was a wonderful spinner. She could sit at the wheel and spin most anythin'. She could read the weather by the clouds, and foretold storms by the birds. She took to bein' a midwife, as well, after Mr. Merritt died of fever. Well, they hanged her in 1680 up there in Hampton, for bein' a witch an' spellin' a woman to give birth to a Devil's baby. So they said. Jane's own son—my nephew—was accused of evils and sent to prison in Boston, and he passed away there a year later. I've tried to find their graves, but no one knows where they're lyin'. No one *cares* where they're lyin'. You know what my sister's great sin was, sir?" Matthew said nothing, but simply waited.

"She was *different,* do y'see?" Mrs. Nettles said. "Her readin' of the clouds, her spinnin', and her midwifery made her different. In Hampton they put her neck in a noose for it, and when our father read the letters and found out how she'd died, he fell sick too. Our mother and me worked the farm, best we could. He got better, and he lived another four year, but I canna' say I ever saw him smile ag'in, 'cause Jane's hangin' was always there in that house. It was always there that she had been killed as a witch, when we all knew she had a sweet, Christian soul. But who was there to defend her, sir? Who was there to be her champion of justice?" She shook her head, a bitter smile pinching her mouth.

"Nae, not a single man nor woman stood up for her, for they must'a feared the same thing as we fear in this town: anyone who speaks up in defense must be also bewitched and fit for the hangin' tree. Yes sir, *he* knows that, too." Mrs. Nettles again stared through Matthew with fierce intensity. "The fox, I mean. He knows what happened in Salem, and in a dozen other towns. No one's gonna speak out for Mistress Howarth, for fear of their own necks. They'd rather quit this town and drag a guilty shadow. *I'd* quit it m'self, if I had the courage to turn my back on Mr. Bidwell's coin . . . but I do not, and so there you have it."

"The witnesses insist that what they've seen is neither dream nor phantasm," Matthew said. "How would you account for that?"

"If I *could* account for it—and could prove it—I would make sure it was brought to Mr. Bidwell's attention."

"Exactly what I'm trying to do. I understand that Rachel was not well liked here, and was forced away from the church, but can you think of anyone who might have held such a grudge against her that they would wish to paint her as a witch?"

"No sir, I canna'. As I say, there were plenty who disliked her for bein' dark and near Spaniard. Disliked her for bein' a handsome woman, too. But no one I can think of who had that much hate in 'em."

"What about Mr. Howarth?" Matthew asked. "Did he have enemies?"

"A few, but as far as I know they've all either died or left town."

"And Reverend Grove? Did anyone display ill feelings toward him?"

"No one," Mrs. Nettles said flatly. "The rev'rend and his wife were fine people. He was a smart man, too. If he was still alive, he'd be the first to defend Mistress Howarth and that's the truth."

"I wish he *were* alive. I'd much rather Reverend Grove calm the crowd than Exodus Jerusalem work them into a frenzy."

"Yes sir, he's a right loose cannon," Mrs. Nettles agreed. "May I ask if I should set a plate for you at the midday meal?"

"No, it's not necessary. I have some places to go. But would you please look in on the magistrate from time to time?"

"Yes sir." She glanced quickly toward the closed door. "I'm feared he's doin' poorly."

"I know. All I can hope is that Dr. Shields tends him adequately until we can return to Charles Town, and that he doesn't grow any worse."

"I ha' seen this sickness before, sir," she said, after which she was silent but Matthew grasped what was left unspoken.

"I'll return in the afternoon," he told her, and then he walked by Mrs. Nettles and descended the stairs.

The day continued gloomy, befitting Matthew's state of mind. He trudged past the spring on his way to the conjunction of streets, where he turned west onto Industry. A sharp eye had to be kept ready for the blacksmith, but Matthew put Hazelton's property behind him without incident. He did, however, receive a generous spattering of mud from the wheels of a wagon that creaked past, freighted with the belongings of a family—father, mother, three small children—who evidently had chosen this as the day to abandon Fount Royal.

Indeed, the town under this murky gray sky appeared all but deserted, with only a few citizens in evidence. Matthew saw on both sides of Industry Street the fallow fields and forlorn dwellings that were the results of wretched weather, ill fate, and the fear of witchcraft. It seemed to him that the further he ventured along Industry, in the direction of the orchards and farmland that should have been the pride of Fount Royal, the worse became the sense of desolation and futility. Piles of animal manure littered the street, among them more than a few nuggets of human waste as well. Matthew saw the wagon and campsite of Exodus Jerusalem but the preacher was not in view. When Matthew came upon the carcass of a pig, its bulk having been gnawed open and the innards being ravaged by a couple of desperate-looking mongrels, he thought that the days of Fount Royal were numbered—no matter what Bidwell did to save the place—simply because the lethargy of the doomed had settled here like a funeral shroud.

He did spy an elderly man who was outside his barn lathering a saddle, and from him he inquired as to the home of Martin Adams. "House is up the way. Got blue shutters," the aged gent answered. Then, "Seen you take the lash this mornin'. You done good not to holler. When's that witch gonna burn?"

"The magistrate is debating," Matthew said, starting to move along.

"Hope it's in a day or two. I'll be there, you can mark it!"

Matthew kept going. The very next house—whitewashed but losing its paint in large, ugly splotches—looked to be long vacant and its front door was partway open but all the shutters sealed. Matthew suspected this was the Hamilton place, where Violet had experienced her encounter. Three more houses, and there stood the one with blue shutters. He walked to the door and knocked.

When the door was opened, Violet herself stood before him. Her eyes widened and she started to retreat but Matthew said, "Hello, Violet. May I speak with you?"

"No sir," she said, obviously overcome by his presence and the memory it stirred. "I have to go, sir." She made a motion to close the door in his face.

"Please." Matthew put his hand against the door. "Just one moment."

"Who is that?" came a woman's rather shrill voice from within. "Violet, who's there?"

"The man who asked me questions, Mama!" Almost at once Violet was pulled aside none too gently and a woman who was as thin and rawboned as her husband stepped upon the threshold. Constance Adams wore a drab brown dress and white bonnet, a stained and frayed apron, and held a broom. She was older than her husband, possibly in her late thirties, and might have been a handsome woman but for the length of her pointed chin and the unrestrained anger in her pale blue eyes.

"What do you want?" she snapped, as if biting off a piece of beef jerky.

"Pardon my intrusion," he said. "I wanted to ask your daughter another question pertaining to—"

"No," she interrupted. "Violet's answered enough questions.

That woman is a curse and a plague on us, and I wish her dead. Now go away!"

Matthew kept his hand on the door. *"One* question," he said firmly. He saw the little girl standing behind her mother, about to bolt like a scared deer. "Violet told me that in the Hamilton house she heard the voice of a man singing. I asked her to think about it further, and try to remember what she heard."

"You're painin' her, don't you see that? All these questions are like to make her head split open, she's hurtin' so bad!"

"Mama?" Violet said, close to tears. "Don't yell, Mama!"

"Hush!" The woman laid the broom's handle against Matthew's chest. "Violet can't sleep at night, her head aches so! Dr. Shields can't even help her! All this thinkin' and rememberin' of such evil things is drivin' us all to madness!"

"I can understand your difficulty, but I have to—"

"You don't have to do nothin' but turn around and *go!*" she said, all but shouting. "If the witch had been put to death three month past, this town would be all right, but look at it now! She's near killed it, just like she killed the reverend and her own husband! Just like she's killed Sarah Davis and James Lathrop, Giles Geddy and Dorcas Chester and all the rest of 'em laid down in them graves! And now she's tryin' to kill my Violet by a knife to the brains!" Spittle had spewed from the woman's mouth and glistened on her chin. The expression in her eyes, wild to begin with, now had taken on a frightening fever. "I told 'em she was no good! I told 'em all along, but they didn't care to hear me! No, they let her walk in that church, just walk in and her a black nigger from Hell!"

"Mama! Mama!" Violet was crying, and had clasped her hands to her ears.

"She will damn us all before she's done!" Constance Adams continued to rave, her voice now risen to a dreadful, piercing pitch. "I've begged him to leave! By Christ I've begged him, but he says we ain't runnin'! She's tainted his mind, too, and she'll have him dead a'fore long!"

Matthew presumed she meant her husband. It was obvious

that the woman was in danger of losing her last tattered rag of sanity. And obvious as well that no good was being done here. He backed away from the door as the distraught wretch went on jabbering, "She killed Phillip Beale! Choked him on blood in his sleep! I told 'em to run her out of this town! I told 'em she was evil, and Abby Hamilton knew it too! Lord God protect and save us! Burn her, for the love of Almighty God, burn her!" The door slammed shut, and from beyond it Matthew heard Constance Adams wailing like an injured, terrified animal caught in a cage.

He turned around and walked away from the house, going eastward along Industry Street. His heart was pounding, his stomach seemingly twisted into a knot by his encounter with the madwoman. He understood, though, the power of fear to distort and destroy. Perhaps Constance Adams had been long balanced on a precarious edge, and this situation had pushed her over. In any case, he could expect no further help from woman or child. This he found extremely unfortunate, because the matter of a man's singing voice in the demon-inhabited Hamilton house was so strange that he felt it might have great bearing on the truth.

In a few moments he came once again to the house itself. There was nothing particularly forbidding about it, other than the fact that it had the air of abandonment, but Matthew thought that on this grim day it was like an ugly fist clenched around a secret. It was made of the same pine timbers as the other houses and was the same small size—two or three rooms, at the most—yet this house was indeed different for it had been chosen, if one believed the child, as the site of Satan's warning against the citizens of Fount Royal.

He decided to see the interior for himself, and particularly find the back room from whence the man's voice had come. The door was already open wide enough to admit him, and Matthew recalled Violet saying that the door was open when she entered as well. He doubted that anyone had set foot here since the child's experience, and so he thought there might be some evidence of interest. Possibly the imp's candle, or the chair upon which Satan had been sitting?

Matthew approached the door, not without some trepidation. Because all the shutters were closed, the interior was as dark as the gaol at midnight. He was greeted at the threshold by a damp, putrid, altogether unsavory odor. He called on the sternest stuff he had and entered the house.

His first task was to make his way to the nearest window and open the shutters wide, which he did. Now, with the aid of feeble though welcome light, his courage grew. He went to the other window and opened those shutters also, allowing God's illumination into the refuge of Satan.

When he turned to survey the room in which he stood, there were three things he noted in rapid succession: the Hamiltons had evidently carried everything away in a wagon, for there was not a stick of furniture remaining; the floor was littered with what appeared to be dog droppings, some of them relatively fresh; and a skeleton lay in the corner.

The skeleton, of course, secured his attention. Matthew approached it for a closer inspection.

It had been at one time a medium-sized dog, obviously aged because its teeth were so worn down. The skeleton lay on its right side on a mat of its own grayish-brown hair, its bones picked clean by the flies that even now buzzed around the fresher mounds of excrement. The smell in this corner of the room was not pleasant, as the boards beneath the dead animal had been stained by the liquids of decay. Matthew wondered how long this carcass had been lying here, being whittled down to its foundations by scavenging insects.

He remembered what Martin Adams had said before Violet had related her story: *This thing she is 'bout to tell you happent near three week ago.*

Surely, to have been so completely consumed, the dead dog had been lying in this room for at least that long, he thought. The smell must have been sickening. It must have struck a person in the face as soon as that threshold was crossed, and indeed must have been quite apparent even before the entry was reached. Yet it had not stopped Violet Adams from entering the house, and indeed she'd not noticed it even when she was well within.

One might say the Devil had masked the odor, or that Violet had been too entranced to let it wrinkle her nose, but still . . . Of course, the dog could have died here two weeks ago rather than three. *But still . . .*

Matthew turned his mind to the fact that there were no furnishings in the room. No chair, no bench, nothing upon which the Devil might have been sitting with the imp upon his knee. Of course Satan might have conjured a chair from thin air, but still . . .

He heard a noise from the rear of the house.

It was a slight sound, just a whisper of a noise, but it was enough to make the small hairs stir on the back of his neck. He stood very still, his mouth gone dry. He stared into the darkness that held reign back there, beyond the spill of meager light.

The sound—whatever it was—was not repeated. Matthew thought it had been the creaking of a board, or the slow shifting of something that would not be seen. He waited, his hands clenched into fists at his sides, his eyes trying to pierce the gloom. A fly landed on his forehead, and he quickly brushed it away.

The room back there. From where the child had said she'd heard a man's voice, singing.

Matthew was terrified by the thought of what might be lurking just beyond his range of vision. Or, indeed, lying in wait for him. But, God help him, he had come to this house to ascertain the truth and therefore he must go back into that dark room, for who would go if he would not?

Still, his feet had grown roots. He looked around for a weapon of some kind—of any kind—but found nothing. No, that was not quite correct: amid the ashes of the hearth he saw two items that had been left by the Hamiltons—a broken clay tankard and a small iron cooking pot. He picked up the pot, which had been so used its bottom was burned black, and again faced the gathered dark.

Matthew would have traded two teeth for a sword and a lantern, but a cooking pot was at least substantial enough to strike a blow with, if need be. He sincerely hoped there would be no need. And now came the test of his own mettle. To go or not to go, that was the question. If he slinked out, would it not be an admittance that the Devil really might be back in that room awaiting him? And had he heard a noise, or had it been only his fevered imagination?

It could have been a rat, of course. Yes, a rat. That was all.

He took one step toward the dark and stopped, listening. There was no sound other than the pounding of his heartbeat in his ears. One more step, and then another. He could now make out an open doorway, beyond which might have been a bottomless pit.

Slowly, slowly, Matthew approached the room and winced as his weight made a board groan. He peered inside, all his senses alert for any hint of motion or threat of attack from a spectral fiend. He saw the barest crack of daylight back there: the seam of closed shutters.

Again his courage faltered. To have a view of the room meant he must cross it and unlatch the shutters. A cold hand might grip the back of his neck before he could get there.

No, it was ridiculous! he thought. His very reticence here was giving weight to the notion—absurd, in his belief—that indeed Satan had visited this house and might still be a presence in its darkness. The longer he tarried on the threshold, the more claws and teeth Satan bared. There was nothing to do but enter the room, go straight to the shutters, and throw them open.

And, of course, while doing so keep a tight grip on the iron pot.

Matthew took as much of a deep breath as he could stand, as the smell was less than fragrant. Then he gritted his teeth and walked into the room.

He felt the darkness take him. His spine crawling, he went the ten feet or so to the opposite wall, found the shutter latch, and lifted it with a quick—one might say frantic—motion. As he opened the shutters the blessed gray light rushed in, and never had he been so glad to see a skyful of ugly clouds.

At the instant of Matthew's relief, a groan came from behind him that rose in volume and power and quite near sent him hurtling through the window. This sound of a vengeful demon all but lifted Matthew out of his shoes. He twisted around with his face frozen into a terrified rictus and the iron pot lifted to strike a blow against a horned skull.

It was difficult to say who was more frightened, the wild-eyed young man or the wild-eyed brown mongrel that cowered in a corner. But it was definitely Matthew's fear that passed first, as directly he saw on the floor the six pups that had been suckling at their mother's swollen teats. He gave a reflexive, strangled laugh, though his testicles were yet to descend from the height they had risen.

The bitch was trembling, but now she began to show her teeth and mutter a growl, therefore Matthew felt it prudent to take his leave. He had a look around the room, which was quite bare except for the animals, their excrement, and a couple of tattered chicken carcasses. He lowered the cooking pot and backed out, and was on his way to the door when the master of the house suddenly arrived.

It was one of the dogs that had been pulling the entrails from the dead pig in the street. It came in bloody-mouthed, carrying between its jaws a hunk of something dark red and dripping. As soon as its glinting eyes took sight of Matthew, the animal dropped its gory prize and crouched down in an attitude of attack, its husky growl indicating that Matthew had intruded upon a territory off-limits to the humans of Fount Royal. The beast was about to jump for Matthew's throat, that much was dangerously clear. Matthew wasted no time in making his decision; he flung the pot to the floor in front of the dog, causing it to leap backward and issue a fusillade of indignant barks, and then he immediately turned to the nearest window, climbed up over the sill, and jumped out.

Up on his feet again, he made haste in an easterly direction.

He glanced back, but the dog did not follow. Matthew kept his pace brisk until he'd left the Hamilton house well in his wake, and then he stopped to take account of a scraped right shin and a number of splinters in the palm of his right hand. Otherwise, he was none the worse for his venture.

As he continued to walk toward the conjunction of streets, he reflected on the meaning of this experience. Possibly the dogs had belonged to the Hamiltons and had been left behind months ago, or possibly they were curs abandoned by some other fleeing family. The question was: how long had the dogs been living there? More or less than three weeks? Was it reasonable to assume they had been there when Violet Adams had entered the house?

If she had entered the house. There had been no chair. No candle or candlestick. Bidwell and Exodus Jerusalem would say that those items had been spectral and of course had vanished with the demons, but Matthew needed to see them to believe they had been there at all. And what of the dog's skeleton? The decaying carcass would have filled that room with a repulsive odor, yet Violet had not noticed it nor been hesitant in entering the house. Matthew doubted very much if he would have gone into a deserted house that had the smell of death wafting from its front door, no matter who'd been calling to him. Therefore, what to make of the child's testimony?

Had she really been in there, or not? The strangest thing about this was that, as far as he could tell, Violet—like Buckner and Garrick—was not lying. She fervently—and fearfully—believed in the truth of what she'd witnessed. It was *her* truth, perhaps, just as what had happened to Buckner and Garrick were truths to them . . . but was it the whole and actual truth?

But what kind of truth was it, that might be both true and false at the same time?

He felt he was venturing onto philosophical ground, worthy of intense thought and debate yet not very helpful to Rachel's cause. He'd been planning on asking directions to Dr. Shields's infirmary, in order to more thoroughly understand the magistrate's illness, but somehow he did not approach the next person he saw, which was a man mending a wagon's wheel, nor did he approach the next two men who were standing together smoking pipes and conversing. Perhaps he didn't wish to answer questions concerning the magistrate's health or the fate of the witch, but in any case he kept walking from Industry Street onto Truth Street and therefore in the direction of where he knew he'd been heading all along: the gaol.

The door was still left unsecured. The sight of the pillory standing beside the gaol did nothing for his fond memories of this morning, yet he realized—and would be loath to admit it to anyone, especially Bidwell or the magistrate—that he missed Rachel's presence. And why was that? He asked himself that question, as he stood just outside the door.

Because she needed him. That was it, in an acorn's shell.

He went inside. A lantern burned and the roof's hatch had been opened, courtesy of Mr. Green, therefore the gloom had been somewhat conquered. Upon seeing who her visitor was, Rachel stood up from the bench and pushed the hood of her coarse cloak back from her face. She allowed as much of a smile as she was able to muster—so feeble it was hardly worth the effort—and she came to the bars to meet him.

He approached her cell. He didn't know what to say, didn't know how to explain his return. So he was relieved when Rachel spoke first, "I heard the whip strike. Are you all right?"

"I am."

"It sounded painful."

He felt suddenly very shy in her company. He didn't know whether to look at the floor or into Rachel's eyes, which caught the yellow lamplight and gleamed like gold coins. Though her smile had been weak, her eyes still held remarkable strength, and Matthew had the sensation that she could see through his frame of flesh and bones, into the depths of his guarded soul. He shifted uncomfortably from one foot to the other. What she might see there, he knew, was his own desire to be needed, which had always been true in his relationship with the magistrate but was now a bright, hot bonfire. It was that he had

seen her naked, he thought: not the moment of her being physically unclothed, but the moment in which she had exposed her
own need and reached for his hand through the bars to seek
comfort.

He'd realized he was all the hope she had left in the world.
Whatever aid and comfort would be given to her for the rest of
her short days, it would come from him. How could he banish
her from his mind and soul? Woodward was in dire need as well,
but he had the care of Dr. Shields. This woman—this beautiful,
tragic woman standing before him—had no one on earth to care
for her but himself.

"Has Green brought your meal yet?" he asked.

"I've just now finished it."

"Do you need fresh water? I could go fetch you some."

"No," she said. "I have enough water. But thank you."

Matthew looked around at the dirty hovel. "This place should
be swept out and fresh straw laid down. It's abysmal that you
should have to endure such filth."

"I imagine it's a late hour for that," she replied. "May I ask
how goes the magistrate's deliberations?"

"He has issued no word yet."

"I know there can be no other decree but that of guilty," she
said. "The evidence against me is too strong, particularly after
what the child said. I know also I didn't help myself by violating
the Bible, but I lost my senses. So . . . Bidwell will have his witch-
burning before long." There was pain in her face, but she lifted
her chin. "When the time comes, I shall be ready. I will have
made my preparations. When I am led out of this place I will be
glad, because I know that though I am banished from earth I
shall be received in Heaven."

Matthew started to protest her surrender, but words failed
him.

"I am very, very tired," Rachel said quietly. She pressed the
fingers of her right hand to her forehead and closed her eyes for
a few seconds. "I will be ready to fly this cage," she said. "I did
love my husband. But I have so long felt alone . . . that death

must be better." Her eyes opened, and she lowered her hand. "Will you attend it?"

Matthew realized what she meant. "No," he said.

"Will I be buried near my husband? Or somewhere else?"

There was no use in telling her anything but the truth. "Probably outside the town."

"I thought as much. They won't behead me, will they? I mean . . . after I'm burned, will my body be violated?"

"No." He would make sure not even a fingerbone was cleaved off to be shown for two pence at Van Gundy's tavern. Of course, what some graverobber did to her skeleton after he and Woodward had departed was beyond his control and beyond his wish to think about.

Rachel's expression of concern told Matthew this thought had entered her mind as well, but she didn't give it voice. She said, "I'll have only one regret: that whoever murdered Daniel and Reverend Grove will never be brought to justice. That's not fair, is it?"

"No, it certainly is not."

"But by then I won't care, will I?" She looked up at the clouded sky through the roof hatch. "I thought—I *hoped*—I would die of old age, in bed in my own home. I never dreamed my life would end like this, and that I'd not even be allowed to lie beside my husband! That's not fair either, is it?" She breathed in and let go a long sigh, and finally she lowered her gaze, her mouth drawn into a tight line.

The gaol's door opened, and instantly upon seeing who had arrived Rachel stepped back from the bars.

"Ah ha!" Exodus Jerusalem tilted his head to one side, smiling slyly. "What doth go on here?"

Matthew turned to confront him. "May I ask what your business is?"

"Whatever I do, wherever I goeth, 'tis the business of my Lord God." Jerusalem, clad in his black tricorn and black suit, came forward within an arm's length of Matthew. "I should wager thy business doth not be so holy."

"Your presence is not wanted here, sir."

"Oh, I am sure of that. But I hath come to speak to the witch, not to her cock-a-doodler."

Matthew felt the blood burn in his cheeks. "I don't think Madam Howarth has anything to say to you."

"She might, as without my influence her tongue should be forever silent." The preacher directed his next statement to Rachel: "Witch Howarth, thy hourglass is near empty. I have heard it said the tree hath been selected from which thy stake shall be cut. Even now, the axes are being sharpened. I sincerely hope thou hast given some thought to the offer I made thee on my last visit."

"What, the offer to be your travelling doxy?" Rachel asked sharply.

"To be my travelling *disciple*," he answered, his voice a smooth adagio, so leisurely that Matthew felt sure Jerusalem had proposed this arrangement so many times it was second nature. Or perhaps first nature. "And companion in study and prayer," Jerusalem added.

"The study of sin and prayer that you find another woman whom you can pluck from a gaol?" On Rachel's face was an expression of sheer disgust that might have curdled a pail of milk. "I would rather kiss the flames."

"Thy wish shall become reality," Jerusalem said. "And thy dark beauty shall be burnt from thy skull and crushed beneath the foot of God, and where thou dost lie the beasts shall come and tear thy very bones asunder."

The anger was rising up in Matthew like a floodtide. "I wish you to leave."

"Boy, this a public place, and I have just as much right to enter it as thyself." His eyes narrowed. "At least I entered here to bring salvation to the witch, not to receive her vile blessings."

"Madam Howarth and I are both aware of your purpose."

"Oh, thou and the witch are coupled now, is that it? Yes, I knew it was only a matter of time." He lifted his right hand and inspected his fingernails. "I hath seen witches at work before. I hath seen them promise all manner of pleasures to young boys. Tell me this, then: how did she propose thou should ride her? From the north or the south?"

Matthew swung at him. It was so fast he hardly knew what he was doing, but the blood roared in his ears and his right fist came up and cracked across the preacher's prominent jaw. Jerusalem staggered back two steps but found his balance; he blinked, touched his lower lip, and then regarded the smear of crimson on his fingertips. Instead of offering a wounded and angry countenance, as Matthew had thought he would, the preacher only smiled, but there was some wicked triumph in it. "Thou nicked me, boy. Yet I think I drew first blood."

"I should apologize, but I will not." Matthew rubbed his stinging knuckles.

"Oh, don't apologize! This action speaks for itself, and therefore should be reported to thy master."

"As you please. The magistrate trusts my judgment."

"Really?" Jerusalem's smile broadened. He licked his injured lip. "What shall Woodward say, upon report that his clerk was caught in intimate conversation with the witch, and that his clerk is so bewildered in the mind that he hath struck a proper man of God? And look here! 'Tis the damage to prove it!"

"Tell what you like, then." Matthew feigned indifference, but he knew this would not go over very well with the magistrate.

"When a right Christian boy is entranced by a witch, who knoweth where such actions may lead? Thou may find thyself sharing the fire with her, and thereafter thou may fornicate in Hell to thy eternal delight."

Matthew shouted, "Get out! By God, I'll strike you again!"

"And blasphemous as well!" Jerusalem crowed. "This is a sorry day for thee, that I can promise!" His gaze slid toward Rachel. "Then burn, witch!" His voice, at the fullest of its power, seemed to shake the walls. "I offered thee salvation, and thou hast spurned the last hope of a Godly life! Yes, burn, and call upon me with thy last tortured breath but thou—"

Rachel reached to the floor. "Move!" she told Matthew, who

saw what she had picked up and so dodged the oncoming deluge.

"—shall call in vain, for Exodus Jerusalem shall not ans— *ohhhhh!*" he bellowed, as Rachel threw the contents of her waste bucket through the bars at him, and he danced backward to avoid as much as possible a meeting between the sacred and the profane. For the most part he was lucky, but his shoes received a washing.

Matthew couldn't help it; he burst out laughing at the preacher's whirligigging, and thus called upon himself Jerusalem's blackest regards.

"You'll be damned too, you young bastard!" It was amazing how a bucket of pee could knock the *thees* and *thous* out of a man. "I'll call the wrath of Heaven down on both your heads!"

"Call away, then!" Rachel said. "But do it somewhere else!"

Matthew was still grinning. Then he saw a fleeting look in Jerusalem's eyes that should only be described as terror; in that moment he realized that ridicule was the sharpest sword that could pierce the preacher's swollen pride, and thereafter Jerusalem spun around and fled the gaol like a cat with a burning tail.

Rachel threw the emptied bucket aside and viewed the wet floor. "Mr. Green will have a few choice words to say about this, I'm sure."

Matthew's grin faded away, as did the hilarity that had for a brief time lightened his soul. "I'll tell the magistrate what happened."

"Jerusalem will be there before you." She sank down on her bench. "You will have some explaining to do."

"I'll take care of it."

"The magistrate won't understand why you came here. I don't fully understand why, either."

"I wished to see you," he said, before he could ponder his choice of words.

"Why? Your business is finished here, is it not?"

"Magistrate Woodward's business is finished," he corrected. "I intend to continue working at this puzzle."

"I see. Is that what I've become, then? A puzzle to be worked at?"

"Not entirely."

Rachel looked at him, but said nothing for a stretch of time. Then she spoke in a quiet voice, "Are you becoming interested in me?"

"Yes." He had to pause to swallow. "In your situation, I mean to say."

"I'm not speaking of my situation, Matthew. I mean: are you interested in *me?*" He didn't know what to say, therefore he did not answer.

Rachel sighed and stared at the floor. "I am flattered," she said. "Honestly. You are a bright and kind young man. But . . . though you're twenty and I am twenty-six, I am fifty years older than you. My heart is used up, Matthew. Can you understand that?"

Again, words failed him. He had never in his life felt so confused, timid, and utterly strange, as if his powers of self-control had melted away like a lump of butter set on a forge. He might have preferred three more lashes than wearing this simpleton's suit.

"As I said, I will be ready to die when the time comes," Rachel continued. "It will come soon, I know. I thank you for your help and care . . . but please don't make my death any more difficult than it has to be." She sat for a moment, her hands clasped together in her lap, and then she lifted her head. "How is the magistrate's health?"

Matthew forced himself to speak. "Not well. I was on my way to see Dr. Shields. Where is the infirmary from here?"

"On Harmony Street, toward the gate."

Matthew knew it was time to go. His presence seemed to be sinking Rachel into deeper gloom. "I won't give up," he vowed.

"Give what up?"

"Trying to find an answer. To the puzzle. I won't give up, because . . ." He shrugged. *"I can't."*

"Thank you," she replied. "I think—if you ever do find an

answer—it will come much too late to save my life, but I thank you just the same."

He went to the door, where he felt the need to look back at Rachel once again. He saw her lift her hood over her head and face, as if to block out everything possible of this treacherous world.

"Goodbye," he said. There was no response.

He left the gaol, but he had the most compelling sensation that part of himself did not follow.

twenty-two

MRS. NETTLES CAUGHT MATTHEW at the staircase when he returned to the mansion after his visit with Dr. Shields. "The magistrate asked that you see him directly ye arrived. I ha' to tell you that the preacher's been here, and he was might loud."

"I expected it. Thank you." He braced himself for what was ahead and started up the stairs.

"Oh, sir!" Mrs. Nettles said before he'd gotten more than halfway up. "I recalled somethin' I thought you might find of interest. About Rev'rend Grove."

"Go on," Matthew urged.

"Well, sir . . . you asked if the rev'rend had any enemies, and I said he had none I knew of. But I was thinkin' over it some, and I recall a strange thing happened—oh, I'd say it was three or four days 'fore he was killed."

"What was it?"

"He'd come for dinner," she said. "Had some business 'bout the church to talk over with Mr. Bidwell and Mr. Winston, so his wife had stayed home. I remember they were talkin' there in the parlor, with the fire goin'." She nodded toward that room. "Mr. Bidwell had walked with Mr. Winston out to the carriage. I had come in to ask the rev'rend if I could refresh his cup, and he said no, that he was fine as he was. I turned my back and started to leave, and he says, 'Mrs. Nettles? What would you do if you knew a thing, and tellin' it might be right but it would serve no good purpose?' That's what he said."

"Did you ask what he meant?"

"No sir, that would not have been proper. I told him I was nae one to be givin' advice to a man a' God, but that it depended on what it was he knew."

"And what was the reverend's response?"

"He just sat there, lookin' at the fire. I started out again, on my way to the kitchen, and then I heard him say, 'No Latin.' That was all, and he'd said it so quiet I hardly heard it. But I said, 'Sir?' 'cause I didn't know what he meant. He didn't answer; he was just sittin' there, lookin' at the fire and thinkin'."

"Hm," Matthew grunted. "You're sure he spoke those words, and not something else?"

"I heard him say, 'No Latin.' At least, it sounded like that to me. Then Mr. Bidwell came back in, and I went about my business."

"And you say Reverend Grove was killed three or four days afterward?"

"Yes sir, he was. His wife found him, lyin' there on the church floor." She frowned. "What do ye think he meant?"

"I have no idea," Matthew said, "but his question to you may mean that someone of physical rather than spectral nature had cause to wish him harm. I'd very much like to find out what it might have been he knew. May I ask why you've not brought this up before?"

"I'd forgot it, 'til this mornin'. Bein' who he was, the rev'rend knew a lot of things about a lot of people," she said. "But like I told ye, he had no enemies."

"Obviously he did," Matthew corrected. "Only it was someone who might have worn the disguise of being a friend."

"Yes sir, I suppose so."

"Thank you for telling me this." Matthew decided to store this information away and pursue it at a later date. Right now there was the magistrate to deal with. "I'd better go up." He ascended the stairs, his face grim.

He had spoken to Dr. Shields at length concerning the magistrate's condition, and had been informed that though the sickness appeared serious it was well under control. The doctor said more bleeding would have to be done and there would be times when the magistrate would feel both better and then worse before he improved. But, said Dr. Shields, the road to recovery was never easy, especially from a malady such as this coastal fever. The magistrate was a strong specimen and otherwise in good health, Dr. Shields had said, therefore there was no reason he shouldn't respond to the bleeding and put this sickness behind him within a week or two.

Matthew reached the magistrate's door and tentatively knocked. "Who is it?" came his voice: a weary but serviceable croaking.

"It's me, sir."

There was a pointed silence. Then, "Come in." Matthew entered. Woodward was still in bed, propped up by two pillows. The box of documents lay beside him, a sheaf of the papers on the blanket that covered his lap. Three candles burned on the bedside table. He didn't look up from his reading. "Please close the door," he said, and Matthew obeyed. Woodward let his clerk stand there for a while; his throat was agonizing him again, his nostrils were swollen, his head ached, and he had a hellish mixture of chills and fever, so when Exodus Jerusalem had told him what Matthew had done it did no good to his nerves or temper. But Woodward kept himself calm and continued reading, unwilling yet to display one iota of anger.

"Sir?" Matthew said. "I know you had a visit from—"

"I'm involved at the moment," Woodward interrupted. "Allow me to finish this page."

"Yes, sir." He stared at the floor, his hands clasped behind him. Finally, he heard the magistrate put aside the documents and clear his throat with what sounded to be painful difficulty.

"As usual," Woodward began, "you have done an admirable job. The papers are excellent."

"Thank you."

"I should finish reading them tonight. Tomorrow morning at the latest. Oh, I'll be glad to get out of this place!" He lifted a hand and massaged his tender throat; his shaving mirror had told him how bad he appeared—pasty-faced, dark hollows under the eyes, and a sheen of fever sweat on his cheeks and forehead. He was extremely tired as well, weakened by both the ravages of his illness and the bleeding lancet, and all he really cared to do was lie back in this bed and sleep. "I'm sure you shall be glad too, won't you?"

A trick, Matthew thought. So obvious it was hardly worth dodging. "I'll be glad when justice is done, sir."

"Well, justice is about to be done. I shall deliver my decree tomorrow."

"Pardon me," Matthew said, "but usually you spend at least two days reviewing the documents."

"Is it etched in stone? No, I hardly need to read these papers."

"Does it matter at all that I feel—very strongly—that Rachel Howarth is neither a murderess nor a witch?"

"Evidence, Matthew." Woodward tapped the sheaf of papers. "The evidence is right here. You heard it, and you recorded it. There are the poppets on the dresser over there. Tell me what evidence refutes the testimony?" Matthew remained silent. "None," Woodward said. "Your opinion, and your opinion only."

"But do you agree that some of the testimony is questionable?"

"I find the witnesses to be credible. How do you explain that all their stories have overlapping elements?"

"I can't."

Woodward swallowed and winced at the pain. He had to speak, though, while his voice had at least a minimum of strength. "You know what will be best for this town, just as I do. I don't relish it. But it has to be done."

"Will you not allow me time to ask some more questions, sir? I believe that Violet Adams may—"

"*No,*" came the firm answer. "Leave that child alone. And I want you to stay away from the gaol, from this minute on."

Matthew took a deep breath. He said, "I believe I should be able to go where I please, sir." He saw the fire jump into Woodward's eyes, even as sick as the magistrate was. "If you are basing your restrictions on what Exodus Jerusalem told you, I might inform you that the preacher has filthy designs on Madam Howarth. He wants her to confess and throw herself at your mercy, whereupon he will step in and vouch for her newfound Christian soul. His aim is to recruit her as his travelling doxy."

Woodward started to speak, but his voice cracked and so he had to pause until he regained it. When he was able, he said, "I don't give a damn about Exodus Jerusalem! Of course he's a scoundrel. I knew that the minute I saw him. My concern is your soul."

"My soul is well protected," Matthew answered.

"Is it? Really?" Woodward stared up at the ceiling for a time, composing his thoughts. "Matthew," he said, "I fear for you. That woman . . . she can do you some harm, if she pleases."

"I can take care of myself."

At that Woodward had to laugh, though it fiercely pained him. "The famous last words of a million sons to their fathers!"

"I am not your son," Matthew said, a muscle clenching in his jaw. "You are not my father. We have a professional relationship, sir, and that is all."

Woodward didn't reply, but simply closed his eyes and rested his head on the pillows. His breathing was slow and steady, if somewhat ragged-sounding. He opened his eyes and looked directly at Matthew. "The time has come," he said.

"Sir?"

"The time," Woodward repeated, "has come. To tell you things . . . that perhaps should already have been told. Sit down, if you like." He nodded toward the chair that was placed close beside the bed, and Matthew sat down upon it.

"Where to begin?" It was a question the magistrate had posed to himself. "The beginning, of course. When I was a prosperous attorney, I lived in London with my wife, Ann. We had a very fine house. A garden in the back, with a fountain. Oxford had prepared me well." He gave Matthew a slight, sad smile, and then it went away. "We had been wed two years when we had a son, whom we named Thomas, after my father."

"A son?" This was an amazement to Matthew.

"Yes. A good boy he was. Very intelligent, very . . . serious, I suppose. He loved for me to read to him, and he loved to hear his mother sing." Woodward heard in his mind the woman's sweet soprano and saw shadows on the green Italian tiles that graced the fountain. "Those were the finest days of my life," he said as softly as his tortured voice would allow. "On our fifth anniversary, I presented Ann with a silver music box, and she gave me the gold-striped waistcoat. I remember the moment I opened the wrapping. I recall thinking . . . that no man on earth had ever been so fortunate. So privileged to be alive. There I was, with my loved ones before me, my house, my possessions, my career. I had tasted the full fruit of life and I was a rich man. Rich in so many ways."

Matthew said nothing, but now he more fully understood the magistrate's anguish at leaving the treasured garment in Shawcombe's hands.

"Four years later," Woodward continued after a painful swallow, "Ann and my partners encouraged me to pursue the robe. I passed the necessary examinations . . . became a jurist apprentice. In time I was informed I would advance when the next appointments were made." He drew a long, suffering breath and let it go. "I didn't have long to wait. That summer the plague came. Many openings were created."

Woodward lapsed into silence as the memories came up around him like so many whispering ghosts. "The plague," he said, his gaze fixed on nothing. "Summer ended. A wet and nasty autumn, and the plague remained. It was a visitation of blisters on the flesh, followed by fits and terrible agonies until death. I saw my closest friend die that September. He withered from a sturdy athlete into a weeping skeleton in the space of two weeks. And then . . . one morning in October . . . the maidservant screamed in Thomas's bedchamber. I rushed in. Knowing already. And fearing what I would find."

His voice had dwindled to a mere whisper and his throat was a burning hellpit, yet he felt the necessity to go on. "Thomas was twelve years old. The plague cared not for age, nor social position, nor riches nor . . . anything. It set in on Thomas . . . as if determined to destroy not only him, but his mother and myself. The best the doctors could do was sedate him with opium. It was not enough to make him stop hurting. Not nearly enough."

He had to halt once more to swallow, and felt the scum of infection ooze down his throat.

"May I get you something to drink?" Matthew asked, standing up.

"No. Sit down. I must speak while I can." He waited for Matthew to settle himself again. "Thomas fought it," he said. "But of course . . . he could not win. His skin was so raw he couldn't turn over in bed. Once . . . when a fit struck him, he thrashed so much that the flesh . . . peeled from his back like wet bark from a rotten tree. And everything was blood and pestilence and that smell . . . that smell . . . that death-reeking, hideous smell."

"Sir," Matthew said, "you don't have to—"

Woodward lifted a hand. "Please hear me out. Thomas lived for ten days after he was afflicted. No, *lived* is not the correct word. *Survived.* The days and nights were of indistinguishable damnation for us all. He vomited torrents of blood. His eyes were swollen closed from crying, and he lay in filth because we had no help and . . . we could not wash the sheets fast enough. On the last day . . . he was seized by uncontrollable fits. So strong he grasped hold of the iron bedstead, and the bowing of his body . . . made the entire bed jump up and down . . . like some demonic toy. I remember his face, in that final hour. His face." Woodward squeezed his eyes shut, sweat glistening on his cheeks, and

Matthew could barely look at him, so awful was the sight of his soul-caged grief.

"Oh, my God, his face," the magistrate rasped. His eyes opened, and Matthew saw they had gone red with the memory of such torment. "The pox . . . had consumed most of his face. At the end, he . . . hardly appeared human. As he was dying . . . being racked by those fits . . . he gripped the bedstead with all his remaining strength. I saw his fingers tighten . . . tighten . . . and he looked at me." Woodward nodded, marking the moment. "He couldn't speak, but I saw him ask a question of me, as if I had been God Almighty. He asked me: *Why?* And to that question— that unknown, unfathomable question—I was mute. Hardly ten minutes later . . . he let loose a groan, and at last he left us. I had such plans for him. Such plans. And I loved him, more than I had even known.

"His death . . . the way he died . . . could not help but taint the rest of our days," Woodward said. "Ann had always been frag- ile . . . now her mind was blighted. Her spirit grew dark, as did mine. She turned against me. She could no longer bear to live in that house, and she began to suffer violent rages. I think . . . she was so frustrated . . . so angry against God . . . that she was re- duced to the impulses of an animal." He paused and swallowed. "Took to drink. Took to being seen in unsavory places . . . with unsavory people. I reached out for her, tried to get her into church, but that made things worse. I believe . . . she needed someone to hate on this earth as much as she hated the Lord. Fi- nally, she left the house. I was told that Ann had been seen drunk in a certain neighborhood, in the company of a man of ill repute. My career began to suffer. It was rumored that I was a drunk as well—which was sometimes true—and that I was open to bribes. Which was never true. A convenient lie for some persons who wished me harm. My debts came due, as debts will when a man is down. I sold most of what I owned. The house . . . the garden, the fountain, the bed upon which Thomas had died . . . all of it was repugnant to me, anyway."

"But you kept the waistcoat," Matthew said.

"Yes. Because . . . I don't know why. Or perhaps I do. It was one item of my past . . . that remained clean and unblemished. It was . . . a breath of yesterday, when all the world was fragrant."

"I'm sorry," Matthew said. "I had no idea."

"Well, why would you? Over time . . . the cases I heard grew fewer. I must say much of my disgrace was my fault, as I allowed Brother Rum to accompany me to the bench. I decided . . . as my future appeared to be dim in London, I might try my torch in the colonies. But before I left . . . I tried to find Ann. I heard she'd fallen in with other women of her class who had . . . experienced the deaths of their husbands by the plague, and who had become . . . rumpots and flesh merchants by necessity. By this time, she was completely gone to me. Gone to herself, as well." He gave a labored sigh. "I think that's what she wished. To lose her identity, and thus the past." He stared past Matthew, into the incalculable distance. "I believe I saw her. In a crowd at the harbor. I wasn't sure. I didn't care to be sure. I walked away. Later I boarded a ship . . . and hence to a new world."

Woodward lay his head back and closed his eyes again. He swallowed pus and tried to clear his throat, to no avail. His voice was all but gone now, yet he forced himself on because he feared so for Matthew's soul and wished him to understand these things. "Imagine my surprise . . . to find that Manhattan was not paved with gold. I found that the New World . . . is no different from the Old. There are the same passions and crimes. The same sins and scoundrels. Only here . . . there's so much more *opportunity* to sin . . . and so much more space in which to do it. God only knows what the next century will bring."

"I spoke with Goode about that," Matthew said, offering a trace of a smile. "His wife believes the world will be destroyed by fire, while he believes it might be—as he put it—a 'century of wonders.'"

Woodward opened his bloodshot eyes. "I don't know . . . but I do believe it will be a wonder if Fount Royal reaches the new century. This town will surely die if Rachel Howarth is not executed."

Matthew's smile vanished. "Is the future of this settlement your basis for putting a woman to death, sir?"

"Of course not. Not entirely, I mean. But the evidence is there . . . the witnesses . . . the poppets . . . her own blasphemous demeanor. Not to mention her grip on *you.*"

"What grip? I fail to see how my interest in the truth can be construed as—"

"Cease and desist," Woodward said. "Please. The more you go on, the less you convince anyone . . . least of all me. I daresay it is not only Jerusalem who has designs on the woman . . . though I believe it's actually *she* who has designs on *you.*"

Matthew shook his head. "You're absolutely wrong."

"I have heard enough cases. To know how blinding is the fire of temptation. And how hot it burns." Woodward massaged his throat once more. "My voice is near its end, but this I have to tell you," he whispered. "There was once a merchant. An eager, industrious young man. His business . . . required him to rise early and thus to bed early. But one evening . . . he stayed awake past his usual hour . . . and in so doing he heard the wondrous singing of something he'd never heard before: a nightbird. The next night, he managed to stay awake later . . . to hear more of the bird's song. And the following night. He became so . . . so intoxicated with the nightbird's voice that he thought only of it during the day. Came the time when he spent all the night listening to that song. Could not carry out his business during the sunlit hours. Soon he turned his back altogether on the day, and gave himself over to the nightbird's beautiful voice . . . much to the sad end of his career, his health . . . eventually his life."

"A fine parable," Matthew said curtly. "Is there a point to it?"

"You know its point. A parable, yes, but there's great truth and warning in it." He gave Matthew a piercing stare. "It is not enough to love the nightbird's song. One must also love the nightbird. And . . . one must eventually fall in love with the night itself."

"You mistake my motives. I am simply interested in—"

"*Helping* her," Woodward interrupted. "Finding the truth. Being of service. However you choose to phrase it . . . Rachel Howarth is your nightbird, Matthew. I'd be no guardian if I saw you in danger of being consumed by the darkness and failed to warn you."

"Consumed by the darkness?" Matthew raised his eyebrows. "I think that's an overstatement, sir."

"I think it's an *under*statement." Woodward gazed up at the ceiling, his strength almost expired. He felt as if his body were a cumbersome clay jar being baked over a fire, his true self trapped within it and yearning for a breath of clean, cool air. "That woman has entranced you, for her own purposes. She wants nothing more of you . . . than to help her escape the stake . . . which would be a sin that would forever mark you in the eyes of God."

Matthew stood up, unwilling to listen to such nonsense. It occurred to him to stalk out of the room, but he did not because he knew the magistrate was sincere and also that he would regret such rashness. "Sir? May I ask you a question, and request that you think hard on it before you answer?"

A nod gave him permission.

"Do you honestly—with all your heart and soul—believe that Rachel is a witch?"

"Your question . . . is weighted on the side of emotion," Woodward answered. "I have responsibility to uphold and carry out the law. The evidence tells me she *is* a witch . . . therefore I must apply the law in its strictest measure."

"Put aside the robe for one moment, and then reply."

"I am satisfied," came the firm response. "Yes, there are missing details. Yes, there are questions I would have answered, and more witnesses interviewed. But . . . I must proceed on what I have. And what I have . . . obvious to both of us . . . is testimony and physical evidence any judge would rule sufficient to burn her. She knows it. She must find a way to escape . . . and that involves *you.*"

"I'd think Satan would free her, if she were really his servant."

"Servants are cheap," Woodward said. "I think . . . it suits Satan's purpose to stand aside and let his nightbird speak."

Matthew started to parry the thrust, but he realized it was no use. They had come to an impasse, and beyond it they could not travel together.

"I will continue to read through the documents," the magistrate offered. "I would not wish to present my decree with any undue haste."

"May I read what you've already gone through?"

"As you wish." Woodward picked up the sheaf of papers and put them into his clerk's hands. "Beware, though . . . no further words on this matter. Do you hear me?"

"Yes, sir," Matthew said, though the agreement had a bitter taste.

"And you'll not return to see Madam Howarth?"

This was a more difficult point. Matthew didn't have to ponder it. "I'm sorry, but I can't promise that."

The magistrate pursed his lips and released a forlorn exhalation. He too, however, had realized the limits of Matthew's obedience. "Your choice," he whispered. "I pray to God it is a wise one." Then he motioned toward the door. "Go. I need my rest."

"Yes, sir." Matthew stared at Woodward for a moment, studying the angles and planes of the man's face.

"What is it?" Woodward asked.

"I have to ask this, sir. Did you come to the almshouse in search of a clerk, or a replacement for your son?"

"My son . . . could never be replaced."

"I'm aware of that. But you and I both know you might have secured an experienced clerk through a legal office. I had to ask, that's all." He turned and went to the door.

"Matthew?" Woodward pushed himself up on his pillows, his face bleached with pain. "I don't know . . . if I came looking for a son or not. Perhaps I did. But I do know I wanted to shape someone. I wanted to . . . protect someone . . . to keep him clean, from this filthy world. Do you understand?"

"I do," Matthew replied. "And I wish to thank you for your

concern on my behalf. If you hadn't removed me from that place, I dread to think what might have become of me."

Woodward eased himself back down. "The whole world is before you. You have a bright future. Please . . . beware those who would destroy it, I beg you."

Matthew left the room with the sheaf of papers under his arm, and in his own room he lit a candle, washed his face with cool water, and then opened the shutters. The light was almost gone, but he looked out across the slaves' quarters toward the watchman's tower and the swamp beyond. It seemed to him now that one might wander into a morass at any time, anywhere, without warning. There were no easy answers to any question in this world, and it seemed that year after year the questions grew more complicated.

He did believe that the magistrate had entered the almshouse searching for a son. How it must agonize Woodward now, to think he might lose another one to the corruption of circumstance. But as much as Matthew felt for the magistrate, he would not—*could* not—turn away from Rachel. He might be a substitute for a son, yes . . . but he was also a man, and he must do what he thought to be the correct thing.

Which meant fighting to prove her innocence, right up to the moment of her execution.

Nightbird or not, she had indeed spoken to him. He heard her even now, suffering in the darkness of her cage. What was he going to do tomorrow, when the magistrate asked him to prepare the decree of death and sign it as a witness beneath Woodward's seal?

He set the candle down and reclined on his bed—carefully, as the stripes on his back were hot. Then he began reading the court documents in the hope that something in them would lead him to a fact that had been overlooked, and that single fact might be the key to Rachel's freedom.

But he feared it would not be there.

Time was very short now. If Satan indeed dwelled in Fount Royal, Matthew presumed he must be grinning. Or if not Satan . . .

then the grin belonged to someone else. A true fox, as Mrs. Nettles had said.

But even the most crafty fox left a trace of its passage, Matthew believed. It was up to him to find it, with all the blood-hound instincts in his possession. If they failed him, Rachel was lost, and he himself was damned to a fate he considered worse than the flames of Hell: the struggle with unanswerable questions that would haunt him to his grave.

twenty-three

S ATAN SAID, "I have a gift for thee."

Matthew could not speak or move; his mouth was frozen shut, his body rigid. He saw, however, in the leaping crimson firelight that Satan indeed wore a black cloak with six gold buttons arranged three by three. A hood covered the fiend's head, and where his face should have been was only deeper darkness.

"A gift," Satan repeated, in a voice that sounded much like that of Exodus Jerusalem. He opened his cloak with long-fingered, bloodless hands, exposing the gold-striped waistcoat he wore beneath it. Then from the confines of his waistcoat he produced a wet and dripping turtle, squirming in its dark green shell, which he held out toward Matthew.

Satan's hands gripped opposite edges of the shell and with no apparent effort tore the reptile open. The carapace cracked like a musket shot. The slow and horrid twisting of those infernal hands ripped the turtle's exposed body in two, and Matthew saw the creature's mouth gape wide with agony. Then its gory internals oozed and slithered out, their colors the red, white, and blue of the British flag.

Gold and silver coins began to fall from the mass of ruined vitals, like money spilling from the bottom of a razor-sliced purse. Satan winnowed his left hand into the guts and showed Matthew his bloody palm: in it was a single gold piece, fouled with car-nage.

"This one belongs to thee," Satan said. He drifted forward, his left arm outstretched and the coin between forefinger and thumb. Matthew was unable to retreat, as if his legs and arms were bound. Then Satan was upon him like a dark bird of prey, and placed the coin's edge against Matthew's lips.

Slowly, inexorably, the gold piece was pushed into Matthew's mouth. He felt his eyes widen and tasted bitter blood. It was then that he saw what was aflame, just behind the master of Pandemo-nium: a burning stake, and lashed to it was a fire-consumed fig-ure that writhed in untold damnations of the flesh.

Matthew heard himself moan. The coin was in his throat. He was choking on it. And then from within the hood Satan's face began to emerge, within inches of Matthew's own. Bared fangs came out, set in a jaw of exposed bone. A skeletal muzzle fol-lowed, and empty canine eyesockets. The dog's skull pressed against Matthew's face and exhaled a hot breath that carried all the mephitic abomination of the charnel house.

He awakened with a further moan. A few heartbeats passed before he realized where he was, and that his audience with the Devil had been an exceptionally vivid dream. He thought he could still taste the blood, but then he recognized it as the strongly peppered sausage Bidwell had offered him at dinner. In fact, the sausage was most likely responsible for the entire pro-duction. His heartbeat was still rapid, and beads of sweat had col-lected on his face and chest. The first order of business was banishing this darkness. He found the matchholder and flint on his bedside table, struck a flame—a match never flared on the first strike when one really needed it—and lit the lantern he'd ex-tinguished upon retiring. Then he got out of bed and went to the dresser, where he poured himself a cup from the water pitcher and drank it down, followed by a second.

"Whew!" Matthew said, in an exclamation of relief. Still, he felt his senses were yet affected by the nightmare, as the walls of his room seemed to be closing in on him. He crossed to the win-

dow, opened the shutters wide, and drew a long, deep breath to clear his head of the confusion.

But for the distant barking of a single dog, the night was quiet. No lanterns burned in the slave quarters. Matthew saw a flash of lightning over the sea, though the storm looked to be very far away. And then he saw something that gladdened his soul: a glimpse of stars through the slow-moving clouds. Dare he hope that the grim weather was taking its leave? This strange May with its chills and swelters had been enough to drain the energy of the strongest man, and perhaps with the coming of sustained sunlight June might be a kinder month for Fount Royal.

Then again, what did it matter to him? He and the magistrate would very soon be departing this town, never to return. And good riddance to it and Bidwell, Matthew thought. At dinner, the man had been contentious in his remarks concerning Rachel, such as—between bites of that hellish sausage—"Clerk, if you're growing so fond of the witch, I'm sure it might be arranged for you to hold her hand while she burns!"

Matthew had answered that and other goads with silence, and after a while Bidwell had ceased his needling and concentrated on stuffing his face. Matthew would rather have taken his dinner upstairs with the magistrate, who forced down his distressed throat a bowlful of pap and some hot tea. Then Dr. Shields had arrived again, and the lancet and bleeding bowl had seen more work. Matthew had left Woodward's room halfway through the grisly procedure, his stomach in knots, and he reckoned that sight of the dripping crimson fluid had also counted toward his nightmare.

He watched the stars disappear and then reappear again, as the clouds continued their advance. He had read Buckner's testimony in the documents Woodward had already finished, but had found nothing there that might lead him toward his fox; tomorrow he would read the testimonies of Garrick and Violet Adams after the magistrate was done, but by then Woodward would be close to dictating his decree.

The particulars of his nightmare haunted him: Satan in the black cloak with six gold buttons . . . nothing but darkness where the face should have been . . . the fresh-caught turtle . . . the sinewy hands breaking open the green shell, and bloody coins spilling out . . .

The coins, Matthew thought. Gold and silver pieces. He saw in his mind's eye the contents of the turtle bellies that Goode had shown him. Spanish coins swallowed by turtles. Where had they come from? How was it that an Indian and turtles shared possession of such lucre?

His theory about the Spanish spy was still alive, even though it had been severely wounded by Paine's revelations. However, the fact remained that Shawcombe *had* gotten the gold piece from a redskin, and that the Indian must've received it from a Spaniard. But what Spaniard had fed gold and silver coins to turtles?

Matthew had taken his fill of the night air, though he was in no hurry to return to bed. He watched the dance of the stars for a moment longer, and then he grasped hold of one of the shutters in preparation of closing it.

Before he did, he saw an orange glare of light that reminded him much too uncomfortably of the burning stake in his dream. It was not a light whose source was visible, but rather the reflection of light originating from a westerly direction. Perhaps ten seconds passed, and then there came a man's distant shout affirming what Matthew had already suspected: *"Fire! Fire!"*

The call was picked up and echoed by a second man. Directly Matthew heard a door slam open and knew it must be Bidwell, roused from sleep. The alarm bells began to ring, more people were shouting, and the dogs of Fount Royal were barking up a fury. Matthew hurriedly dressed in the clothes he'd worn yesterday, took the lantern to illume his way down the stairs, and went outside. There he saw the red and orange flames attacking a structure on Truth Street, terribly near to the gaol.

In fact, the fire was so close to the gaol that Matthew was

420 • Robert McCammon

struck with dread like a blow to the belly. If the gaol was aflame, and Rachel was trapped in her cell . . .

He started running toward Truth Street, his face tight with fear. He passed the spring, where one horse-drawn wagon was pulling away with a load of water barrels while a second had just arrived. "What's burnin'?" a woman yelled at him as he went by a house, but he dared not answer. A score of citizens were converging onto the scene, some of them still wearing their nightclothes. He beat the water-wagon to its destination, and was keenly gratified to find that the fire was not burning down the gaol but was instead destroying the schoolhouse.

It was a hot conflagration and was working with great speed. There was Bidwell, wearing a powdered wig but clad in a blue silk night-robe and slippers, hollering at the onlookers to make way for the approaching wagon. The horses got through, and the six firemen aboard the wagon jumped down and began to haul the barrels off. One of them scooped a bucket into the water and ran forward to dash the flames, but—as in the case of the previous fire Matthew had witnessed—it was clear to all that the schoolhouse was doomed.

"Get that fire out! Hurry, all of you!" came a shout that was part command and part plea. Matthew saw the schoolmaster, bareheaded and wearing a long dark green robe with yellow trim. Johnstone was standing perilously close to the roaring blaze, leaning on his cane with one hand and motioning the firemen on with the other, sparks flying around him like red wasps and his face contorted with urgency. "Hurry, I beg of you, hurry!"

"Alan, stand back!" Bidwell told him. "You're in danger there!" A man grasped Johnstone's arm and attempted to pull him away from the flames, but the schoolmaster's mouth twisted with anger and he wrenched his arm free.

"Damn it!" Johnstone bellowed at the firemen, who were obviously doing their best to throw their buckets of water but were being hindered by the sheer cruelty of the heat. "Put that fire out, you idiots! Can't you move any quicker?"

Unfortunately they could not, and all but the schoolmaster seemed to realize the futility of the battle. Even Bidwell simply stood with his hands on his hips and made no effort to bully the firefighters to a frenzied pace.

As the schoolhouse was a small structure and the fire was so eager, Matthew doubted that sixty firemen with sixty buckets could have saved it. The second wagon arrived, bringing three additional men. Several more stalwarts from the crowd stepped forward to help, but it was a matter not of enough hands and hearts but of enough buckets and time.

"Damn it!" Johnstone had ceased his pleading now, and had become visibly enraged. He hobbled back and forth, occasionally aiming a shout of disgust or derision at the ineffective firemen, then cursing the blaze itself. Fire had begun to chew through the schoolhouse's roof. In another few moments Johnstone's raving stopped; he seemed to accept that the fight was truly lost—lost, even, before it had begun—and so he retreated from the flames and smoke. The firemen continued to work, but at this point it was more to justify their presence than anything else. Matthew watched Johnstone, who in turn watched the fire with glazed eyes, his shoulders slumped in an attitude of defeat.

And then Matthew happened to turn his head a few more degrees to the right and his heart rose to his throat. There not ten feet away stood Seth Hazelton. The blacksmith, who still wore a bandage bound to his injured face, was attentive to the spectacle of the flames and thus hadn't seen his antagonist. Matthew doubted if Hazelton was aware of very much anyway, as the man held a brown clay jug at his side and took a long swig from it as Matthew observed him. Hazelton's slow blink and slack-jawed countenance spoke as to the contents of that jug, and his dirty shirt and breeches proclaimed that Hazelton was definitely more interested in wine than water.

Matthew carefully stepped backward a few paces, putting two other onlookers between them just in case the blacksmith might glance around. The thought—an evil thought, but compelling just the same—came to him that now would be an excellent time to search Hazelton's barn. What with the man here at the fire, and weak from strong drink as well . . .

No, no! Matthew told himself. That barn—and whatever was hidden in it—had caused him trouble enough! Hang it, and let it go!

But Matthew knew his own nature. He knew he might present every reason in the world not to go to the blacksmith's barn and search for the elusive burlap sack, up to and including further lashings. However, his single-minded desire to know—the quality that made him, in the magistrate's opinion, "drunk beyond all reason"—was already at work in him. He had a lamp and the opportunity. If ever he was to find that well-guarded bag, now was the moment. Dare he try it? Or should he listen to that small voice of warning and chalk his back-stripes up as a lesson learned?

Matthew turned and walked briskly away from the fire. One backward glance showed him that Hazelton had never noted his presence, but was again indulging in a taste from the jug. Matthew's jury was still in deliberation concerning his future actions. He knew what Woodward would say, and he knew what Bidwell would say. Then again, neither of them doubted Rachel's guilt. If whatever Hazelton was hiding had something to do with her case . . .

He was aware that this was the same reasoning that had lured him into trying to open the grainsack to begin with. Yet it *was* a valid reasoning, in light of the circumstances. So what was the decision to be?

As he reached the conjunction of streets, his scale swung in the direction that Matthew had known it would. He looked over his shoulder, making sure that the blacksmith was not coming up from behind, and then he held the lantern before him and broke into a run toward Hazelton's barn.

When Matthew reached the barn, he lifted the locking timber and pulled the door open just enough for him to squeeze through. The two horses within rumbled uneasily at his presence as he followed the glow of his lantern. He went directly to the area where he remembered finding the sack, put the lamp down on the ground, and then started searching through the straw. Nothing there but straw and more straw. Of course Hazelton had moved the sack, had dragged it to some other location either inside the barn or perhaps inside his house. Matthew stood up, went to another pile of straw on his right, and searched there, but again there was nothing. He continued his explorations to the very back of the barn, where the straw was piled up in copious mounds along with an ample supply of horse apples. Matthew thrust his hands into the malodorous piles, his fingers questing for the rough burlap without success.

At last he realized it was time to go, as he'd already been here longer than was sensible. The sack, if indeed it remained in the straw, was not to be found this night. So much for his opportunity of discovery!

He stood up from his knees, picked up the lantern, and started for the door. As he reached it, something—an instinct of caution perhaps, or a stirring of the hairs on the back of his neck—made him pause to blow down the lantern's chimney and extinguish the candle since he no longer needed the incriminating light.

Which turned out to be a blessing of fortune, because as Matthew prepared to leave the barn he saw a staggering figure approaching, so close he feared Hazelton would see him, roar with rage, and attack him with the jug. Matthew hung in the doorway, not knowing whether to run for it or retreat. He had only a few seconds to make his decision. Hazelton was coming right at him, the blacksmith's head lowered and his legs loose at the knees.

Matthew retreated. He went all the way to the rear of the barn, where he sprawled flat and frantically dug both himself and the lantern into a mound of straw. But before he could do half a good job, the door was pulled open wider and there entered Hazelton's hulking dark figure.

"Who's in here?" Hazelton growled drunkenly. "Damn your eyes, I'll *kill* you!" Matthew stopped his digging and lay very still, the breath catching in his lungs. "I know you're in here! I closed that damn door!" Matthew dared not move, though a piece of straw was fiercely tickling his upper lip.

"I closed it!" Hazelton said. "I know I did!" He lifted the jug and Matthew heard him gulp a swallow. Then he wiped his mouth with his sleeve and said, "I *did* close it, didn't I, Lucy?"

Matthew realized he was addressing one of the horses. "I *think* I did. John Shitass, I think I'm drunk too!" He gave a harsh laugh. "Drunk as a damned lord, that's what I am! What d'ya think of *that,* Lucy?" He staggered toward one of the horses in the dark, and Matthew heard him patting the animal's hindquarters.

"My sweet girl. Love you, yes I do."

The noise of Hazelton's hand on horseflesh ceased. The blacksmith was silent, possibly listening for any sound of an intruder hiding in the barn. "Anybody in here?" he asked, but the tone of his voice was uncertain. "If you're here, you'd best get out 'fore I take a fuckin' axe to you!" Hazelton staggered back into Matthew's field of vision and stood at the center of the barn, his head cocked to one side and the jug hanging loosely. "I'll let you go!" he announced. "Go on, get out!"

Matthew was tempted, but he feared that even drunk and unsteady the blacksmith would seize him before he reached the door. Better to just lie right here and wait for the man to leave.

Hazelton said nothing and did not move for what seemed a full minute. Finally the blacksmith lifted the jug to his lips and drank, and then upon reaching the bottom he reared back and flung the jug against the wall nearly square above Matthew's head. The jug whacked into the boards and fell, broken into five or six pieces, and the startled horses whinnied and jumped in their stalls.

"The hell with it!" Hazelton shouted. He turned around and made his way out of the barn, leaving the door open.

Now Matthew was faced with a dangerous choice: should he get out while he could, risking the fact that Hazelton might be waiting for him out there just beyond the doorway, or should he lie just as he was? He decided it was best to remain in his prone position for a while longer, and indeed he took the opportunity to bury himself more completely in the straw.

Within a minute or two, Hazelton returned carrying a lighted lantern, though the glass was so dirty it hardly counted as illumination. The lantern was not so fearsome to Matthew as the short-handled hatchet Hazelton gripped in his right hand.

Matthew took a deep breath and let it out, trying to flatten himself even further under his covering of straw and horse apples. Hazelton started staggering around the barn, probing with the dim light, the hatchet held ready for a brain-cleaving blow. He gave the nearest strawpile a kick that might have broken Matthew's ribs. Then, muttering and cursing, Hazelton stomped the straw for good measure. He paused and lifted the lantern. Through the mask of hay that covered his face, Matthew saw the blacksmith's eyes glitter in the foul light and knew Hazelton was looking directly at his hiding place.

Don't move! Matthew cautioned himself. For God's sake, be still!

And the sake of his own skull, he might have added.

Hazelton came toward Matthew's refuge, his heavy boots crushing down. Matthew realized with a start of terror that the man was going to step on him momentarily, and he braced himself to burst out of the straw. If he came up hollering and shrieking, he reasoned he might scare Hazelton into a retreat or at least might cause him to miss with the first swing of the hatchet.

He was ready. Two more steps, and the blacksmith would be upon him.

Then: *crack!*

Hazelton stopped his advance, the straw up around his knees. He reached down with his free hand, searching. Matthew knew what the noise had been. The lantern's glass had broken, the lantern lying perhaps eight inches from the fingertips of Matthew's right hand. Reflexively, Matthew closed his hand into a fist.

The blacksmith discovered what he'd stepped on. He held the lamp by its handle, lifting it up for inspection. There was a long, dreadful silence. Matthew clenched his teeth and waited, his endurance stretched to its boundary.

At last Hazelton grunted. "Lucy, I found that damn lantern!" he said. "Was a good one, too! Hell's sufferin' bells!" He tossed it aside with a contemptuous gesture, and Matthew realized the man thought in his tipsied state that it was a lamp he had previously misplaced. If he'd been coherent enough to touch the pieces of broken glass, Hazelton might have found they were still warm. But the blacksmith thereafter turned and crunched back through the straw to the barn's bare earth, leaving Matthew to contemplate how near he'd come to disaster.

But—as was said—a miss was as good as a mile. Matthew began breathing easier, though he would not take a full breath until Hazelton had gone. Then another thought struck him, and it might well have been a hatchet to the head: if Hazelton went out and locked the door, he'd be trapped in here. It might be sunrise or later before Hazelton came to the barn again, and then Matthew would be forced to face him anyway! Better run for it while he was able, Matthew decided. But there was the problem of the straw. That which protected him would also hinder his flight.

Now, however, his attention was drawn to the blacksmith once more. Hazelton had hung the lantern up on a wallpeg beside the far stall, and he was speaking to the horse he seemed to favor. "My fine Lucy!" he said, his voice slurred. "My fine, beautiful girl! You love me, don't you? Yes, I know you do!" The blacksmith began to murmur and whisper to his horse, and though Matthew couldn't hear the words he was beginning to think this affection was rather more than that of a man for his mount.

Hazelton came back into sight. He thunked the hatchet's blade into the wall next to the door, and then he pulled the door shut. When he turned again, moisture glistened on his face; and his eyes—directed toward Lucy—seemed to have sunken into dark purple hollows.

"My good lady," Hazelton said, with a smile that could only

be described as lecherous. A cold chill crept up Matthew's spine. He had an inkling now of what the blacksmith intended to do.

Hazelton went into Lucy's stall. "Good Lucy," he said. "My good and lovely Lucy. Come on! Easy, easy!"

Carefully, Matthew lifted his head to follow the blacksmith's movements. The light was dim and his view was restricted, but he could make out Hazelton turning the horse around in her stall so her hindquarters faced the door. Then Hazelton, still speaking quietly though drunkenly to Lucy, eased her forward and guided her head and neck into a wooden collar-like apparatus that was meant to hold horses still as they were being shod. He latched the collar shut, and thus the horse was securely held. "Good girl," he said. "That's my lovely lady!" He went to a corner of the stall and began to dig into a pile of hay provided for Lucy to eat. Matthew saw him reach down for something and pull it out. Whether it was the grainsack or not, Matthew couldn't tell, but he presumed it was at least what might have been secreted *inside* the sack.

Hazelton came out of the stall carrying what appeared to be an elaborate harness made out of smoothed cow's hide. The blacksmith staggered and almost fell under its bulk, but it seemed that his fevered intent had given him strength. The harness had iron rings attached to both ends: the two circles Matthew had felt through the burlap. Hazelton fixed one of the rings around a peg on the wall, and the second ring was fixed to a peg on a nearby beam so that the harness was stretched to its full width at the entrance to Lucy's stall.

Matthew realized what Hazelton had devised. He recalled Gwinett Linch saying about the smithy: *He's an inventor, once he puts his mind to a task.* It was not Hazelton's mind, however, that was about to be put to work.

At the center of the harness-like creation was a seat formed of leather lattice. The pegs had been placed so the iron rings could stretch the harness and lift the seat up until whoever sat in it would be several feet off the ground and positioned just under Lucy's tail.

"Good Lucy," Hazelton crooned, as he dropped his breeches and pulled them off over his boots. "My good and beautiful girl." His bum naked and his spike raised, Hazelton brought over a small barrel that appeared to be empty, from the ease with which he handled it. He stepped up onto the barrel, swung his behind into the leather seat and lifted the horse's tail, which had begun flopping back and forth in what might have been eager anticipation.

"Ahhhhh!" Hazelton had eased his member into Lucy's channel. "There's a sweet girl!" His fleshy hips began to buck back and forth, his eyes closed and his face florid.

Matthew remembered something Mrs. Nettles had said, concerning the blacksmith's deceased wife: *I happ'n to know that he treated Sophie like a three-legged horse 'fore she died.* It was very clear, from the noises of passion he was making, that Hazelton much preferred horses of the four-legged variety.

Matthew also knew now why Hazelton had so desired this apparatus of strange pleasure not to be discovered. In most of the colonies the sodomizing of animals was punishable by hanging; in a few, it was punishable by being drawn and quartered. It was a rare crime, but quite morally heinous. In fact, two years ago Woodward had sentenced to hanging a laborer who had committed buggery with a chicken, a pig, and a mare. By law, the animals were also put to death and buried in the same grave with their human offender.

Matthew ceased watching this loathsome spectacle and stared instead at the ground beneath him. He could not, however, voluntarily cease from hearing Hazelton's exhortations of passion for his equine paramour.

At last—an interminable time—the barnyard lothario groaned and shuddered, indicating the climax of his copulation. Lucy, too, gave a snort but hers seemed to be more relief that her stud was done. Hazelton lay forward against the horse's hind and began to speak to Lucy with such lover's familiarity that Matthew blushed to the roots of his hair. Such speech would be indecent between a man and his maid, but was absolutely shameless between a man and his mare. Obviously, the blacksmith had banged one too many horseshoes over a red-hot forge.

Hazelton didn't try to remove himself from the harness. His voice was becoming quieter and more slurred. Shortly thereafter, he stopped speaking entirely and began to offer a snore and whistle to his object of affection.

Just as Matthew had recognized an opportunity to enter the barn, now he recognized an opportunity to depart it. He began to slowly push himself out of the straw, mindful that he not suffer a cut from the lantern's broken glass. Hazelton's snoring continued at its regularity and volume, and Lucy seemed content to stand there with her master in repose against her hindquarters. Matthew eased up to a crouch, and then to a standing position. It occurred to him that even if Hazelton awakened and saw him, he couldn't free himself at once from the harness and would be quite reluctant to give chase. But Matthew wasn't above giving Hazelton something to think about, so he picked up the man's dirty breeches and took them with him when he walked unhurriedly to the door, pushed it open, and left the site of such immoral crime. In this case, he pitied not Hazelton but poor Lucy.

Matthew saw that the flames over on Truth Street had died down. He reckoned he'd entered the barn an hour or so ago, and thus most of the schoolhouse had by now been consumed. There would be much conjecture tomorrow about Satan's fiery hand. Matthew didn't doubt that daylight would see another wagon or two leaving Fount Royal.

He laid Hazelton's breeches out in the middle of Industry Street, after which he was glad to rinse his hands in a nearby horse trough. Then he set off on the walk to Bidwell's mansion, his curiosity concerning the hidden grainsack well and truly quenched.

As the hour was so late and the excitement of the fire worn off, the streets were deserted. Matthew saw a couple of houses where the lanterns were still lit—probably illuminating talk between husband and wife of when to quit the Satan-burnt town—but otherwise Fount Royal had settled again to sleep. He saw one elderly man sitting on a doorstep smoking a long clay pipe, a white dog sprawled beside him, and as Matthew neared him the old man said simply, "Weather's breakin'."

"Yes, sir," Matthew answered, keeping his stride. He looked up at the vast expanse of sky and saw now that the clouds had further dwindled, exposing a multitude of sparkling stars. The scythe of a pumpkin-colored moon had appeared. The air was still damp and cool, but the soft breeze carried the odor of pinewoods rather than stagnant swamp. Matthew thought that if the weather broke and held, the magistrate's health would surely benefit.

He'd decided not to inform Woodward of the blacksmith's activities. It might be his duty to report such a crime—which would surely lead to Hazelton's dance on the gallows—but the magistrate didn't need any further complications. Besides, the loss of a blacksmith would be a hard blow to Fount Royal. Matthew thought that sooner or later someone might discover Hazelton's bizarre interest and make an issue of it, but for his part he would keep his mouth shut.

Before he proceeded to the mansion and therefore to bed, Matthew approached the spring and stood beside an oak tree on its grassy bank. A chorus of frogs thrummed in the darkness, and a number of somethings—turtles, he presumed—plopped into the water off to his right. He saw the reflection of stars and moon on the surface, over which spread slow ripples.

How was it that turtles had Spanish gold and silver coins—as well as silverware and pottery shards—in their bellies? Matthew sat down on his haunches, plucked up some grass, and stared out across the ebon pond.

I have a gift for thee, Satan had said in his dream.

He thought of the coins spilling from the turtle's guts. He thought of Goode showing him what he'd found, and saying, *It's a thing needs answerin'.*

It surely is, Matthew told himself. From where might the turtles have gotten such coins? They'd swallowed them, of course. Most likely the limit of their world was this spring, and so . . .

Oh, Matthew thought. *Oh!*

The suspicion went off like a cannon blast inside his head. He realized he should have heard such a blast as soon as Goode had shown him the coins, but there had been too many other questions crowding his mind. Now, though, here in the quiet dark, the idea was thunderous in its impact.

Goode had found Spanish gold and silver coins within the bellies of turtles that lived in the spring . . . because there were Spanish gold and silver coins within the spring.

Abruptly, Matthew stood up. He placed a hand on the trunk of the oak tree beside him, if only to steady his thoughts. This suspicion—like the tearing open of a turtle in his dream—was full of glittering possibilities.

One gold and one silver piece, one pottery shard, and one silver spoon did not make a treasure hoard . . . but who might say what was lying down in the mud at the very bottom of Fount Royal's center of existence?

He recalled with a jolt of the senses something that Nicholas Paine had said, back at Shawcombe's tavern, upon viewing the original gold piece: *No black-flagger in his right mind would bury his loot in redskin wilderness. They hide their gold where they can easily get to it, but it would be a poor pirate whose winnings could be found and unearthed by savages.*

Unearthed? But what about sunken to the bottom of a freshwater spring?

His brain had caught fire. Bidwell had decided to build Fount Royal around the spring, as it would be—among other considerations—convenient as a source of fresh water for merchant ships arriving from the Indies.

But what was fresh water for merchants was also fresh water for those flying a blacker flag, was it not? And was it not possible that the spring had been discovered and used for such a purpose long before Bidwell had even set eyes on it? If that were true, the spring would make an excellent vault in which to deposit—as Paine had put it—"winnings."

This was all, however, the wildest possible conjecture. Still . . . how else to explain the coins in the turtles' bellies? The turtles, searching for food down at the bottom of the spring, may have scooped up the coins from the mud or else been attracted by their shine. The same might be true of the spoon and the pottery shard. The question remained: what else could be down there, secreted away for safekeeping?

But how to explain an Indian's possession of Spanish gold? If indeed there had been pirate treasure in the spring, had the Indians found and raised it before Fount Royal was born? If so, they'd missed a few trinkets. He would have to sleep on these questions, and pursue them—quietly—in the morning. Bidwell might know something, but he would have to be carefully approached.

Matthew paused a little longer, staring out at the pond that seemed now to contain a further enigma. Nothing could be answered tonight, so it was time to get to bed though sleep might be nigh impossible.

He continued on his way along Peace Street toward the mansion, which was dark. He had no idea what the hour was, though it must be long past midnight. And with the next step he took he suddenly stopped and froze, looking straight ahead.

A figure in a tricorn hat and dark cloak was striding briskly past the mansion, in the direction of the slaves' quarters. It took no more than five or six seconds for the figure to disappear from view. Matthew hadn't seen if the man was carrying an unlit lantern or not, but he knew who it was. The fox was on the prowl, he thought. Going to what destination, and for what purpose?

This indeed was a night of opportunities, though this one Matthew realized might be far more treacherous than the blacksmith's hatchet.

His mouth was dry, his blood racing. He looked around but saw no other person out on the street. The embers of the schoolhouse still glowed a faint red, and the breeze blew a whirl of sparks into the sky.

He would have to go. He knew it. But he would have to hurry, to find the fox before he got away into the swamp. The fox would be wary around the watchman's tower, and so too would Matthew have to be because he couldn't depend on the fact that the watchman was asleep.

A little dagger of fear stabbed Matthew in the chest. Whoever that midnight prowler was, he was likely to be dangerous if he realized he was being followed. There was the chance that, out in the swamp, anything could happen, and all of it bad.

But there was no time for dawdling. Fear would have to be conquered. The fox was moving fast, and so must Matthew.

twenty-four

MATTHEW COULD HEAR the tempestuous sound of the sea. Breakers were hitting islands or exposed sandbars some distance away from the swamp that he was now negotiating with great difficulty. Ahead of him and almost at the limit of his perception was the midnight traveller—a dark, moving blotch within further darkness—who would have been totally lost to him had it not been for the faint orange moonlight, and even that meager illumination was jealously guarded by the streams of moving clouds.

The man had come this way before, that was a certainty. And more than once. His pace was swift and sure-footed, even without benefit of a lantern. Matthew was up to the task of following through the waist-high grasses and across the muck that pulled at his shoes, but it was a tough and laborious journey.

They had left Fount Royal far behind. Matthew estimated the distance at least a quarter mile from the watchman's tower, which had been easily circumvented by cutting through the pinewoods. If the watchman had been awake—and this Matthew seriously doubted—he'd been looking out to sea. Who would expect anyone in their right mind to venture out into this morass in the dead of night?

The midnight traveller had a definite purpose, one that gave speed to his step. Matthew heard something rustle off in the grass to his right; it sounded large and quite sinister, therefore he found a little extra speed himself. He discovered in the next moment, however, that his worst enemy was the swamp itself, as he walked into a shallow pond that closed about his knees and almost sent him sprawling. The mud at the pond's bottom seized his shoes and it was only with extreme tenacity that Matthew worked his way to freedom. Once out of the water he realized he could no longer detect his quarry's movement. He scanned from right to left and back again, but the darkness had truly dropped its curtain.

Still, he knew the man must be going in this general direction. He started off again, more mindful of where he was stepping. The swamp was indeed a treacherous place. The midnight traveller must surely have come out here many times to be able to navigate these dangers. Indeed, Matthew thought the man may have made a map of his route and consigned it to memory.

After three or four minutes, Matthew was yet unable to spy any movement in the darkness. He glanced back and saw that his course had taken him around a headland. A black line of pines and swamp oaks stood between his current position and the watchman's tower, which was probably the greater part of a mile behind. Beyond him was only more swamp. He debated whether to turn back or forge on. Everything out here was only greater and lesser shades of dark, so what was the point? He did continue on a few paces, though, and again paused to scan the horizon. Mosquitoes hummed about his ears, hungry for blood. Frogs croaked in the rushes. Of another human, however, there was not a sign.

What was there to bring a person out here? This was wild desolation, hardly a civilized soul standing between his footprints and the city of Charles Town. So what did the midnight traveller seek to accomplish?

Matthew looked up at the banners of stars. The sky was so huge and the horizon so wide that it was fearsome. The sea, too, was a dark continent. Standing on this coast with the unknown world at his back, he felt more than a little distress, as if his equilibrium and very place on earth were challenged by such immensity. He understood at that moment the need for men to build towns and cities and surround them with walls—not only to keep out the threat of Indians and wild beasts, but to maintain the illusion of control in a world that was too large to be tamed.

His contemplation was suddenly broken. Out at sea, two lights blinked in quick succession.

Matthew had been about to turn his face toward Fount Royal again, but now he stood motionless. A few seconds went by. Then, once again, the two lights blinked.

What followed next gave his heart a jolt. Not fifty yards from where Matthew was standing, a lighted lantern appeared and was uplifted. The lantern swung back and forth, and then disappeared—concealed, Matthew suspected, by the midnight traveller's cloak. The man must have either crouched down to strike a match and flame the candle, or done it within the cloak's folds. Whatever and however, a signal had been answered.

Matthew lowered himself into the protection of the marsh grass, so that just his eyes were above it. He desired a closer view, and began to move quietly and carefully toward where the lantern had been revealed. It came to mind that if he stepped on a venomous reptile in his present posture, its fangs would strike a most valuable area. He got to within thirty feet of the dark-cloaked man and was forced to stop when the cover of the high grass ended. The man was standing on a stretch of hard-packed sand, just a few yards short of the Atlantic's foamy waves. He was waiting, his face aimed toward the ocean and his lantern hidden in the cloak.

Matthew also waited. Presently, after the passage of perhaps ten minutes during which the man paced back and forth but never left his station, Matthew was aware of a shape emerging from the darkness of the sea. Only when it was about to make landfall did Matthew make out an oarboat, painted either black or dark blue. There were three men aboard, all of whom also wore night-hued clothing. Two of the men jumped out into the surf and pulled the oarboat to shore.

Matthew realized the boat must have come from a larger vessel some distance away. His thought was: *I have found the Spanish spy.*

"Greetin's!" the man who had remained in the oarboat called, his accent as far from being Spanish as Gravesend was from Valencia. He stepped down onto the sand. "How goes it?"

The midnight traveller answered, but his voice was so low Matthew heard only a murmur.

"Seven this trip," the oarboater said. "That oughta do you. Get 'em out!" He had delivered this command to the other two men, who began to unload what appeared to be wooden buckets. "Same place?" he asked the midnight traveller, who answered with a nod. "You're a man of habit, ain't you?"

The midnight traveller raised his lantern from the folds of his cloak and by its yellow glow Matthew saw his face in profile. "A man of *good* habit," Edward Winston said sternly. "Cease this prattle, bury them, and be done with it!" He dropped the lantern, which had been used to show the other man that he was in no mood for dawdling.

"All right, all right!" The oarboater reached into the bottom of his craft and brought up two shovels, and then he walked up the beach to the edge of the high grass. His path brought him within fifteen feet of Matthew's concealment. He stopped at a thatch of spiny palmettos. "This where you want 'em?"

"It will do," Winston said, following.

"Bring 'em on!" the man ordered his crew. "Hurry it, we ain't got all night!" The buckets, which appeared to be sealed, were carried to the designated place. The oarboater handed the two shovels to the other men, who began to dig into the sand.

"You know where a third shovel is," Winston said. "You might employ it, Mr. Rawlings."

"I ain't no damn Injun!" Rawlings replied tartly. "I'm a chief!"

"I beg to differ. You *are* an Indian, and your chief is Mr. Danforth. I suggest you earn the coin he's paying you."

"Very *little* coin, sir! Very *little,* for this night work!"

"The faster they're buried, the sooner you may go."

"Well, why bury 'em anyway? Who the hell's comin' out here to find 'em?"

"Safe is better than sorry. Just lay one bucket aside and put the others under with no further argument."

Muttering beneath his breath, Rawlings reached carefully into the palmettos and pulled out a short-handled shovel that had been hidden there. Matthew watched as Rawlings fell to digging at rhythm with his companions. "What of the witch?" he asked Winston as he worked. "When's she gonna hang?"

"Not hang. She'll be burned at the stake. I expect it shall be within the next few days."

"You'll be cooked too then, won't you? You and Danforth both!"

"Just concern yourself with your digging," Winston said tersely. "You needn't put them deep, but make sure they're well covered."

"All right! Work on, my lads! We don't want to tarry long in this Satan's country, do we?"

Winston grunted. "Here or there, it's *all* Satan's country, isn't it?" He gave the left side of his neck a sound slap, executing some bloodsucking beastie.

It took only a few moments for a hole to be opened, six buckets secreted within it, and the sand shovelled over them. Rawlings was a master at appearing to work hard, with all the necessary facial contortions and exertions of breath, but his shovel might have been a spoon, for all the sand it moved. When the buckets were laid under, Rawlings stepped back, wiped his brow with his forearm, and said, "Well done, well done!" as if he were congratulating himself. He returned the implement to its hiding place amid the palmettos and grinned broadly at Winston, who stood nearby watching in silence. "I expect this'll be the last trip, then!"

"I think we should continue one more month," Winston said.

Rawlings's grin collapsed. "What need will you have of any more, if she's to be burned?"

"I'll make a need. Tell Mr. Danforth I shall be here at the hour."

"As you please, your majesty!" Rawlings gave Winston an exaggerated comical bow and the two other men laughed. "Any other communications to the realm?"

"Our business is concluded." Winston said coldly. He picked up by its wire handle the seventh bucket that had been laid aside, and then he abruptly turned toward Matthew—who instantly ducked down and pressed himself against the earth—and began to walk through the grass.

"I've never seen a burnin' before!" Rawlings called after him. "Make sure you take it all in, so's you can describe it to me!" Winston didn't respond, but kept on walking. His course, Matthew was relieved to see, took him along a diagonal line perhaps ten or twelve feet to Matthew's west. Then Winston had gone past, holding the lantern low under his cloak to shed some light on where he was stepping. Matthew presumed he would extinguish the candle long before he got within view of the watchman's tower.

"That tight-assed prig! I could lay him out with my little finger!" Rawlings boasted to his companions after Winston had departed.

"You could lay him out with your bloody *breath!*" one of the others said, and the third man guffawed.

"Right you are, at that! Come on, let's cast off this damned shingle! Thank Christ we've got a fair wind for a change tonight!"

Matthew lifted his head and watched as the men returned to their oarboat. They pushed it off the beach, Rawlings clambered over the side first and then the other men, the oars were taken up—though not by the big chief—and the vessel moved out through the lathery surf. It was quickly taken by the darkness.

Matthew knew that if he waited long enough and kept a

sharp enough eye he might see some evidence of a larger craft at anchor out there—possibly the flare of a match lighting a pipe, or a stain of mooncolor on a billowing sail. He did not, however, have the time or the inclination. Suffice it to know that an oarboat was not a vessel suitable for a sea voyage.

He looked in the direction Winston had gone, back toward Fount Royal. Satisfied that he was alone, Matthew got up from his defensive posture and immediately went on the offensive. He found the disturbed area beside the palmettos where the buckets had been buried, and—two painful palmetto-spike stabs later—gripped his hand on the concealed shovel.

As Winston had specified, the buckets were not buried very deeply. All Matthew desired was one. The bucket he chose was of common construction, its lid sealed with a coating of dried tar, and of weight Matthew estimated between seven and eight pounds. He used the shovel again to fill the cavity, then returned it to the palmettos and set off for Fount Royal with the bucket in his possession.

The way back was no less difficult than his previous journey. It came to him that he was most likely locked out of Bidwell's mansion and would have to ring the bell to gain entrance; did he wish to let anyone in the household see him with this bucket in hand? Whatever game Winston was up to, Matthew didn't want to tip the man that his table had been overturned. He trusted Mrs. Nettles to a point, but in his opinion the jury was still out on everyone in the damned town. So: what to do with the bucket?

He had an idea, but it would mean trusting one person implicitly. Two persons, if Goode's wife should be counted. He was eager to learn the bucket's contents, and most likely Goode would have an implement to force it open.

With a great degree of thankfulness Matthew put the swamp at his back, negotiated the pinewoods to avoid the watchtower, and shortly thereafter stood before John Goode's door. Upon it he rapped as quietly as he thought possible, though the sound to his ears was alarmingly loud and must have awakened every slave in the quarters. To his chagrin, he had to knock a second time—and harder—before a light blotched the window's covering of stretched oilskin cloth.

The door opened. A candle was pushed out, and above it was Goode's sleepy-eyed face. He'd been prepared to be less than courteous to whoever had come knocking at such an hour, but when he saw first the white skin and then who wore it he put himself together. "Oh . . . yes suh?"

"I have something that needs looking at." Matthew held up the bucket. "May I enter?"

Of course he was not to be denied. "What is it?" May asked from their pallet of a bed as Goode brought Matthew in and closed the door. "Nothin' that concerns you, woman," he said as he lit a second candle from the first. "Go back to sleep, now." She rolled over, pulling a threadbare covering up to her neck.

Goode put the two candles on the table and Matthew set the bucket down between them. "I followed a certain gentleman out to the swamp just a while ago," Matthew explained. "I won't go into the particulars, but he has more of these buried out there. I want to see what's in it."

Goode ran his fingers around the tar-sealed lid. He picked up the bucket and turned it so its bottom was in the light. There, burnt by a brand into the wood, was the letter K and beneath that the letters CT. "Maker's mark," he said. "From a cooper in Charles Town, 'pears to be." He looked around for a tool and put his hand on a stout knife. Then he began chipping the tar away as Matthew watched in eager anticipation. When enough of the seal had been broken, Goode slid the blade under the lid and worked it up. In another moment the lid came loose, and Goode lifted it off.

Before sight was made of what the bucket concealed, smell gave its testimony. "Whoo!" Goode said, wrinkling his nose. Matthew put the sharp odor as being of a brimstone quality, with interminglings of pine oil and freshly cooked tar. Indeed, what the bucket held looked to be thick black paint.

"Might I borrow your blade?" Matthew asked, and with it he stirred the foul-smelling concoction. As he did, yellow streaks of sulphur appeared. He was beginning to fathom what he might be confronted with, and it was not a pretty picture. "Do you have a pan we might put some of this in? A spoon, as well?"

Goode, true to his name, supplied an iron pan and a wooden ladle. Matthew put a single dip of the stuff into the pan, just enough to cover its bottom. "All right," Matthew said. "Let us see what we have." He picked up one of the candles and lowered its flame into the pan.

As soon as the wick made contact, the substance caught fire. It was a blue-tinged flame, and burned so hot both Matthew and Goode had to draw back. There were small pops and cracklings as more flammable additives in the mixture ignited. Matthew picked up the pan and took it to the hearth so that the fumes might be drawn upward. Even with so little an amount, the heat on his hand was considerable.

"That's the Devil's own brew, ain't it?" Goode said.

"No, it's made by men," Matthew answered. "Diabolical chemists, perhaps. It's called 'infernal fire,' and it has a long history of being used in classical naval warfare. The Greeks made bombs from it and shot them from catapults."

"The Greeks? What're you goin' on about? Uh . . . beggin' your pardon, suh."

"Oh, it's all right. I think the use of this material is very clear. Our swamp-travelling gentleman has a zest for fire."

"Suh?"

"Our gentleman," Matthew said, watching the flames continue to burn brightly in the pan, "likes to see houses alight. With this chemical, he is sure of setting fire to even damp wood. I expect he might paint it on the walls and floor with a brush. Then the stuff is touched off at several strategic places . . . and the firemen will inevitably be too late."

"You mean . . ." The truth of the matter was dawning on Goode. "The man's been usin' this to burn down houses?"

"Exactly. His last strike was against the schoolhouse." Matthew set the pan down in the fireplace's ashes. "Why he would wish to do so, I have no idea. But the fact that this bucket was fashioned in Charles Town and was brought by sea bodes ill for his loyalty."

"Brought by sea?" He stared long and hard at Matthew. "You know who the man be, don't you?"

"I do, but I'm unprepared to speak the name." Matthew returned to the table and pushed the lid down firmly on the bucket once more. "I have a request to make. Will you hold this in safekeeping for a short time?"

Goode regarded the bucket with trepidation. "It won't blow us up, will it?"

"No, it needs a flame to ignite. Just keep it closed and away from fire. You might wrap it up and treat it with the same care you treat your violin."

"Yes suh," he said uncertainly. "Only thing be, I don't believe nobody ever got blowed up from fiddle music."

At the door, Matthew cautioned, "Not a word to anyone about this. As far as you should be concerned, I was never here."

Goode had picked up both candles to remove them from the immediate vicinity of such destructive power. "Yes suh. Uh . . . you'll be comin' back to *get* this here thing, won't you?"

"I will. I expect I'll need it very soon." But not until he determined exactly why Edward Winston was burning down his employer's town, he might have added.

"The sooner I'll like it," Goode said, already looking for a piece of burlap with which to wrap the offensive visitor.

Matthew left Goode's house and walked to the mansion, which was a relatively short distance but a world away from the slave quarters. He knew he should get to sleep quickly, as there was much to do at daylight. But he knew also that sleep was going to be difficult in the few hours of dark that remained, because his mind would twist this new revelation into every possible shape in an attempt to understand it. Banished now from his thoughts was the equine lust of Seth Hazelton; the crimes of Edward Winston loomed far larger, for the man had set those fires and willingly ascribed them—as did Bidwell and everyone else— to Rachel's pact with the Devil.

Matthew had every intention of going to the door and ringing the bell to gain entry if necessary, but between intention and deed he shifted his course a few degrees and soon found himself standing again on the grassy bank of the spring. He sat down, pulled his knees up to his chin, and stared out across the smooth water, his mind turbulent with questions of what was and what might be.

Presently he decided to stretch out, and lying on his back in the grass he looked up at the streams of stars that showed between the moving clouds. His last conscious thought before he drifted to sleep was of Rachel in the darkness of her cage; of Rachel, whose life depended on his actions in the hours that remained.

Of Rachel.

twenty-five

A CHORUS OF ROOSTERS CROWED like triumphant horns. Matthew opened his eyes to a rose-colored light. Above him, the sky was pale pink and dappled with purple-edged clouds. He sat up, drawing in the sweet air of what seemed the first true morning of May.

Someone began ringing a bell, and then a second higher-toned bell added its voice. Matthew got to his feet. He heard a man's joyous shout from further along Harmony Street, and then Matthew saw perhaps the most beautiful sight of his life: the sun, a golden fireball, was rising over the sea. This was the sun of creation, and its mere touch had the force to waken the earth. Matthew lifted his face toward the light as a third bell chimed. Two birds began to chirp in one of the oaks that stood around the spring. Tendrils of low-lying mist still clung to the ground, but they were pitiful and short-fated relatives to the massive thunderclouds that had so long held dominion. Matthew stood breathing the air as if he'd forgotten what springtime smelled like, as indeed he had: not the wet, foul stagnance of a swamp, but the clean soft breeze that brought the promise of new beginnings.

If ever there had been a morning to put Satan to flight, this was the one. Matthew stretched his arms up toward the sky to loosen the tight muscles in his back, though it could certainly be said that sleeping outdoors in the grass was preferable to grappling with Somnus in the gaol. He watched the sunlight strengthening across the roofs, yards, and fields of Fount Royal, the mist in full retreat. Of course the clear weather might only last one day before the rain returned, but he dared think nature's pendulum had swung in Bidwell's favor.

He had business this morning with the master of Fount Royal. He left the spring and walked to the mansion, the shutters of which had already been opened to the air. He found the entrance unlatched, and as he considered himself somewhat more than a visitor he opened it without ringing the bell and proceeded up the stairs to look in on the magistrate.

Woodward was still asleep, though either Mrs. Nettles or one of the other servants had already entered to crack the shutters of his room. Matthew approached the bed and stood beside it, looking at the magistrate. Woodward's mouth was partway open, the sound of his breathing like the faint scraping together of rusted iron wheels in a mechanism that was near failure. Brown bloodstains on the pillow behind his head marked the administrations of Dr. Shields's lancet last night, a task that was becoming a nocturnal ritual. A plaster medicated with some kind of nose-searing ointment bad been pressed upon Woodward's bare chest, and grease glistened on the magistrate's upper lip and around his green-crusted nostrils. On the bedside table, three candles that had burned down to stubs indicated that Woodward had attempted more reading of the documents last night, and the documents themselves had spilled off the bed and lay now on the floor.

Matthew set about picking up the papers, carefully arranging them in proper sequence, and when he was done he returned them to the wooden box. The portion that Matthew had taken to his room and read yesterday evening had not delivered any further insights, much to his disappointment. He stared at Woodward's face, at the way the yellow-tinged flesh stretched over the skull, at the pale purple eyelids through which could be seen the protrusions of the orbs. A spiderwork of tiny red blood vessels had appeared on either side of Woodward's nose. The man seemed to have become thinner since Matthew last saw him, though this was due possibly to the change of light. He appeared much older too, the lines upon his face cut deeper by suffering. The blotches on his scalp had darkened as the flesh paled. There was a terrible fragility about him now, something breakable as a clay cup. Looking upon the magistrate in this condition frightened Matthew, yet he was compelled to observe.

He had seen the mask of Death before. He knew it was now before him, clasping on to the magistrate's face. The skin was being shrunken, the skull sharpened for its imminent emergence. A dagger of panic pierced him and twisted in his guts. He wished to shake Woodward awake, to pull him to his feet and make him walk, talk, dance . . . anything to banish this sickness. But, no . . . the magistrate needed his rest. He needed to sleep long and hard, with the benefit of the ointments and the bloodletting. And now there was good reason to hope for the best, with the freshened air and the sun's appearance! Yes, it was best to let the magistrate sleep until he awakened on his own, no matter how long, and let nature work its medicine.

Matthew reached out and gently touched Woodward's right hand. Instantly he drew back, because even though the magistrate's flesh was hot there was yet a moist waxy sensation to it that greatly disturbed him. Woodward made a soft moaning sound, and his eyelids fluttered but he didn't awaken. Matthew backed to the door, the panic dagger still jabbing at his stomach, and then he went quietly out into the hallway.

Downstairs, he followed the noise of cutlery scraping a plate and found Bidwell at the feasting table attacking a breakfast of corncakes, fried potatoes, and hambone marrow. "Ah, here is the clerk this fine, God-lit morning!" Bidwell said before he stuffed his mouth. He wore a peacock-blue suit, a lace-ruffled shirt, and one of his most elaborately combed and curled wigs.

He washed the food down with a drink of apple beer and nodded toward the place that had been set for Matthew. "Sit down and feed yourself!"

Matthew accepted the invitation. Bidwell shoved a platter of corncakes in his direction and Matthew speared two of them with his knife. The marrow platter followed.

"Mrs. Nettles told me you weren't in your room when she knocked." Bidwell continued to eat as he talked, which resulted in half-chewed food spilling from his mouth. "Where were you?"

"Out," Matthew answered.

"*Out*," Bidwell said, with a note of sarcasm. "Yes, I know you were out. But out where, and doing what?"

"I went outside when I saw the schoolhouse on fire. I stayed out the rest of the night."

"Oh, that's why you look so poorly then!" He started to stab a fried potato with his knife, but paused in mid-thrust. "Wait a moment." His eyes narrowed. "What mischief have you been up to?"

"Mischief? You presume the worst, I think."

"You may think, but I *know*. Whose barn have you been poking around in this time?"

Matthew looked him in the eyes. "I went back to the blacksmith's barn, of course."

There was a deadly quiet. Then Bidwell laughed. His knife came down into the potato; he claimed it from the platter and shoved the rest of the charred tubers toward Matthew. "Oh, you're full of spite today, aren't you? Well, I know you may be a young fool but you are not fool enough to go back to Hazelton's place! No sirrah! That man would put a pole to your backside!"

"Not unless I was a mare," Matthew said quietly, taking a bite of a corncake.

"What?"

"I said . . . I would do well to beware. Hazelton, I mean."

"Yes, and that's the smartest thing I've heard leave your lips!" Bidwell spent a moment eating again, as if food would be outlawed by the King on the morrow, before he spoke. "Your back. How is it?"

"A little painful. Otherwise, all right."

"Well, eat up. A full belly dulls all pain. That's what my father used to tell me, when I was your age. Of course, by the time I was your age I was working on the docks fourteen hours a day, and if I could steal a pear I was as happy as a lord." He paused to quaff from his tankard. "Have you ever worked a whole day in your life?"

"Physical work, you mean?"

"What other kind of work is there for a young man? Yes, I mean physical! Have you ever sweated to move a pile of heavy crates twenty feet because the bastard in charge says you'll do it or else? Have you ever pulled a rope until your hands bled, your shoulders cracked, and you cried like a baby but you knew you had to keep pulling? Have you ever gotten on your knees and scrubbed the deck of a ship with a brush, and then gotten down and scrubbed it again when that bastard in charge spat on it? Well? Have you?"

"No," Matthew said.

"Ha!" Bidwell nodded, grinning. "I have. Many times! And I'm damned proud of it, too! You know why? Because it made me a man. And you know who that bastard in charge was? My father. Yes, my father, rest his soul." He stabbed a chunk of potato with a force that Matthew thought might send the knife through the plate and table both. When Bidwell chewed it, his teeth ground together.

"Your father sounds like a hard taskmaster," Matthew said.

"My father," Bidwell replied, "came up from London's dirt, just as I did. My first memory of him was the smell of the river. And he knew those docks and those ships. He started out as a cargo handler, but he had a gift for working wood and he could lay a hull patch with the best who ever lived. That's how the yard started. One ship here, another there. Then more and more, and soon he had his own drydock. Yes, he was a hard taskmaster, but just as hard on himself as on anyone else."

"You inherited your business from him, then?"

"*Inherited?*" Bidwell cast a scornful glance. "I inherited nothing from him but misery! My father was inspecting a hulk for salvage—something he'd done dozens of times before—when a section of rotten planks gave way and he fell through. His knees were shattered. Gangrene set in and to save his life the surgeon took both his legs. I was nineteen years old, and suddenly I was responsible for my invalid father, my mother, and two younger sisters, one of whom was sickly to the point of emaciation. Well, it quickly became clear to me that though my father was a hard taskmaster he was a sorry bookkeeper. The records of income and debts were abysmal, if they existed at all. And here came the creditors, who presumed the yard would be sold now that my father was confined to his bed."

"But you didn't sell it?" Matthew asked.

"Oh, I sold it all right. To the highest bidder. I had no choice, the records being as they were. My father raged like a tiger. He called me a fool and a weakling, and vowed he would hate me to his grave and beyond for destroying his business." Bidwell paused to swig from the tankard. "But I paid off the debtors and settled all accounts. I put food on our table and bought medicine for my sister, and I found I had a small amount of money left. There was a small marine carpentry shop that advertised for investors, as they were expanding their workplace. I decided to put every last shilling I had into it, so I might have some influence over the decisions. My family name was already known, of course. The greatest problem I first faced was in raising more money to put into the business, which I did by laboring at other jobs and also by some bluffing at the gaming tables. Then there were the small-thinkers to be gotten rid of, those men who let caution be their rulers and so never dared to win for fear of losing."

Bidwell chewed on bone marrow, his eyes hooded. "One of those men, unfortunately, had his name above the workplace door. He was too concerned with inches, while I thought in terms of leagues. He saw marine carpentry, while I saw shipbuilding.

Thus—though he was thirty years older than me, and had built the shop from its beginnings—I knew the pasture belonged to him, but the future was mine. I set out to procure business that I knew he would not condone. I prepared profit statements and cost predictions, down to the last timber and nail, which I then presented to a meeting of the craftsmen. My question to them was: did they wish to take a risk of a great future under my guidance, or did they wish to continue their current plodding path under Mr. Kellingsworth? Two of them voted to throw me out the door. The other four—including the master draftsman— voted to take on the new work."

"And Mr. Kellingsworth?" Matthew raised his eyebrows. "I'm sure he had something to say?"

"At first he was mute with anger. Then . . . I think he was relieved, because he didn't want the mantle of responsibility. He wanted a quiet life far removed from the specter of failure that haunted his successes." Bidwell nodded. "Yes, I think he'd been searching for a way to that pasture for a long time, but he needed a push. I gave it to him, along with a very decent buyout settlement and a percentage of future income . . . to decrease with the passage of time, of course. But my name was on the placard above the door. My name and my name only. That was the starting of it."

"I expect your father was proud of you."

Bidwell was silent, staring at nothing though his eyes were fierce. "One of the first things I purchased with my profits was a pair of wooden legs," he said. "The finest wooden legs that could be made in all of England. I took them to him. He looked at them. I said I would help him learn to walk. I said I would hire a specialist to teach him." Bidwell's tongue emerged, and he slowly licked his upper lip. "He said . . . he would not wear them if I had bought him a pair of real legs and could bind them solid again. He said I could take them to the Devil, because that is where a traitor was destined to burn." Bidwell pulled in a long breath and let it go. "And those were the final words he ever spoke to me."

Though he didn't particularly care for Bidwell, Matthew couldn't help but feel little sad for him. "I'm sorry."

"*Sorry?*" Bidwell snapped. "Why?" He thrust his food-streaked chin forward. "Sorry because I'm a success? A self-made man? Sorry because I am rich, that I have built this house and this town and there is more building yet to be done? Because Fount Royal will become a center of maritime trade? Or because at long last the weather has cleared and the spirits of my citizens will rise accordingly?" He jabbed another piece of potato with his knife and pushed it into his mouth. "I think," he said as he chewed, "that the only thing you're sorry for is the impending execution of that damned witch, because you won't be able to get up her skirt!" A wicked thought struck him and made his eyes glint. "Ah ha! Perhaps *that's* where you were all night! Were you in the gaol with her? I wouldn't doubt it! Preacher Jerusalem told me about you striking him yesterday!" He gave a dark grin. "What, did a blow upon the preacher earn you a blow from the witch?"

Matthew slowly put down his knife and spoon. Flames were burning behind his face, but he said coldly, "Preacher Jerusalem has his own intents toward Rachel. You may think as you please, but be aware that he has put a ring through your nose."

"Oh yes, of course he has! And she hasn't put a ring through *yours,* I suppose? Or perhaps she has put her kiss of approval on your balls, is that it? I can see her now, on her knees, and you up close against those bars! Oh, that's a precious sight!"

"I had a precious sight of my own last night!" Matthew said, the flames beginning to burn through his self-control. "When I went out to the—" He stopped himself before the words could flow. He'd been on the verge of telling Bidwell about Winston's escapade and the buckets of infernal fire, but he was not going to be goaded to spill his knowledge before he was ready. He stared down at his plate, a muscle working in his jaw.

"I never met a young man so full of pepper and manure as you," Bidwell went on, calmer now but oblivious to what Matthew had been about to say. "If it were up to you, my town would be a witch's haven, wouldn't it? You'd even defy your own poor, sick master to save that woman's flesh from the fire! I think you ought to get to a monastery up there in Charles Town and become a monk to save your soul. Either that, or go to a bawdy-house and fuck the doxies 'til your eyeballs blow out."

"Mr. Rawlings," Matthew said, his voice strained.

"*Who?*"

"Mr. Rawlings," he repeated, realizing he had set one foot into the morass. "Do you know that name?"

"No. Why should I?"

"Mr. Danforth," Matthew said. "Do you know *that* name?"

Bidwell scratched his chin. "Yes, I do. Oliver Danforth is the harbormaster in Charles Town. I have had some trouble with him, in getting supplies through. What of him?"

"Someone mentioned the name," Matthew explained. "I hadn't met anyone by that name, so I wondered who he might be."

"Who mentioned him?"

Matthew saw ahead of him a maze taking shape, and he must quickly negotiate out of it. "Mr. Paine," he said. "It was before I went into the gaol."

"Nicholas, eh?" Bidwell frowned. "That's odd."

"Is it?" Matthew's heart gave a thump.

"Yes. Nicholas can't stand the sight of Oliver Danforth. They've had some arguments over the supply situation, therefore I've been sending Edward to deal with him. Nicholas goes along too, to protect Edward from harm on the road, but Edward is far better a diplomat. I don't understand why Nicholas should be talking about Danforth to *you*."

"It wasn't to me, exactly. It was a name I overheard."

"Oh, you have big ears too, is that it?" Bidwell grunted and finished off his drink. "I should have guessed!"

"Mr. Winston seems a valuable and loyal man," Matthew ventured. "Has he been with you very long?"

"Eight years. Now what're all these questions about?"

"My curiosity, that's all."

"Well for Christ's sake, rein it in! I've had enough of it!" He pushed himself up from his seat in preparation to leave.

"Please indulge me just a minute longer," Matthew said, also standing up. "I swear before God I won't bother you with any further questions if you'll just answer a few more."

"Why? What is you wish to know about Edward?"

"Not about Mr. Winston. About the spring."

Bidwell looked as if he wasn't sure whether to laugh or cry. "The *spring?* Have you lost your senses altogether?"

"The spring," Matthew repeated firmly. "I'd like to know how it came to be found, and when."

"You're serious, aren't you? Lord, you really are!" Bidwell started to blast at Matthew, but all the air seemed to leave him before he could gather himself. "You have worn me out," he admitted. "You have absolutely tattered my rag."

"Humor me, as it is such a beautiful morning," Matthew said steadfastly. "I repeat my promise not to plague you again, if you'll tell me how you came to find the spring."

Bidwell laughed quietly and shook his head. "All right, then. You must know that, in addition to royally funded explorers, there are men for hire who will carry out private explorations for individuals or companies. It was one of these that I contracted to find a settlement area with a fresh water source at least forty miles south of Charles Town. I stressed the fact that access to the sea was needed, yet a direct seafront was not necessary. I could drain a marsh, therefore the presence of such was tolerable. I also needed an abundance of hardwood and an area defensible from pirates and Indian raiders. When the proper place was found— *this* place—I presented the findings and my plans to the royal court, whereupon I waited two months for a grant to purchase the land."

"It was given readily?" Matthew asked. "Or did anyone attempt to block the grant?"

"Word had gotten to Charles Town. A coalition of their paid magpies swooped in and tried to dissuade the transaction, but I was already ahead of them. I had greased so many palms I could be called an oil pot, and I even added free giltwork to the yacht of the colonial administrator so he might turn heads on his jaunts up and down the Thames."

"But you hadn't visited this area before you made the purchase?"

"No, I trusted Aronzel Hearn. The man I'd hired." Bidwell took his snuffbox from his coat pocket, opened it, and noisily sniffed a pinch. "I saw a map, of course. It suited my needs, that's all I had to know."

"What of the spring?"

"*What of it,* boy?" Bidwell's patience was fraying like a rope rubbing splintered wood.

"I know the land was mapped," Matthew said, "but what of the spring? Did Hearn take a sounding of it? How deep is it, and from where does the water come?"

"It comes from . . . I don't know. Somewhere." Bidwell took another sniff. "I do know there are other smaller springs out in the wilderness. Solomon Stiles has seen them, and drunk from them, on his hunting trips. I suppose they're all connected underground. As far as the depth is concerned . . ." He stopped, with his snuff-pinched fingers poised near his nostrils. "Now that's strange," he said.

"What is?"

"Speaking of the spring like this. I remember someone else asking me similar questions."

At once Matthew's bloodhound sense came to full alert. "Who was it?"

"It was . . . a surveyor who came to town. Perhaps a year or so after we began building. He was mapping the road between Charles Town and here, and wished to map Fount Royal as well. I recall he was interested in the depth of the spring."

"So he took a sounding?"

"Yes, he did. He'd been set upon by Indians several miles from our gate. The savages had stolen all his instruments, therefore I had Hazelton fashion him a rope with a sounding weight tied at the end. I also had a raft built for him, that he might take his measurements from various areas of the fount."

"Ah," Matthew said quietly, his mouth dry. "A surveyor without instruments. Do you know if he discovered the spring's depth?"

"As I remember, the deepest point was found to be some forty feet."

"Was this surveyor travelling alone?"

"He was alone. On horseback. I recall he told me he had left the savages playing with his bag, and he felt lucky to escape with his hair. He had a full beard too, so I expect they might have sheared his face off to get it."

"A beard," Matthew said. "Was he young or old? Tall or short? Fat or thin?"

Bidwell stared blankly at him. "Your mind is as addled as a cockroach, isn't it? What the bloody hell does it matter?"

"I would really like to know," Matthew persisted. "What was his height?"

"Well . . . taller than me, I suppose. I don't remember much about him but the beard."

"What color was it?"

"I think . . . dark brown. There might have been some gray in it." He scowled. "You don't expect me to fully remember a man who passed through here four years ago, do you? And what's the point of these foolish questions?"

"Where did he stay?" Matthew asked, oblivious to Bidwell's rising ire. "Here in the house?"

"I offered him a room. As I recall, he refused and asked for the loan of a tent. He spent two or possibly three nights sleeping outside. I believe it was early September, and certainly warm enough."

"Let me guess where the tent was pitched," Matthew said. "Was it beside the spring?"

"I think it might have been. What of it?" Bidwell cocked his head to one side, flakes of snuff around his nostrils.

"I am working on a theory," Matthew answered.

Bidwell giggled; it sounded like a woman's laugh, it was so quick and high-pitched, and Bidwell instantly put his hand to his mouth and flushed crimson. "A theory," he said, about to laugh again; in fact, he was straining so hard to hold back his merriment that his jowls and corncake-stuffed belly quivered. "By God, we must have our daily theories, mustn't we?"

"Laugh if you like, but answer this: for whom was the surveyor working?"

"For whom? Why . . . one moment, I have a *theory!*" Bidwell widened his eyes in mockery. "I believe he must have been working for the Council of Lands and Plantations! There *is* such an administrative body, you know!"

"He told you he was working for this council, then?"

"Damn it, boy!" Bidwell shouted, the mighty schooner of his patience smashing out its belly on the rocks. "I've had enough of this!" He stalked past Matthew and out of the banquet room.

Matthew instantly followed him. "Please, sir!" he said as Bidwell walked to the staircase. "It's important! Did this surveyor tell you his name?"

"Pah!" Bidwell replied, starting up the steps. "You're as crazy as a loon!"

"His name! Can you recall it?"

Bidwell stopped, realizing he could not shake the flea that gave him such a maddening itch. He looked back at Matthew, his eyes ablaze. "No, I do not! Winston walked him about the town! Go ask him and leave me be! I swear, you could set Satan himself running for sanctuary!" He jabbed a finger toward the younger man. "But you won't ruin this glorious day for me, no sirrah you won't! The sun is out, praise God, and as soon as that damned witch is ashes this town will grow again! So go march to the gaol and tell her that Robert Bidwell has never failed, *never,* and will never *be* a failure!"

A figure suddenly appeared at the top of the stairs. Matthew saw him first, of course, and Matthew's astonished expression made Bidwell jerk his head around.

Woodward braced himself against the wall, his flesh near the same hue as his pap-stained cotton nightgown. A sheen of sweat glistened on his sallow face, and his eyes were red-rimmed and weak with pain.

"Magistrate!" Bidwell climbed the risers to lend a supporting arm. "I thought you were sleeping!"

"I *was*," he said hoarsely, though speaking with any volume caused his throat grievous suffering. "Who can sleep . . . during a duel of cannons?"

"I apologize, sir. Your clerk has roused my bad manners yet again."

The magistrate stared down into Matthew's face, and at once Matthew knew what had been important enough to force him from his bed.

"My deliberations are done," Woodward said. "Come prepare a quill and paper."

"You mean . . . you mean . . ." Bidwell could hardly contain himself. "You have reached your decision?"

"Come up, Matthew," Woodward repeated, and then to Bidwell, "Will you help me to my bed, please?"

Bidwell might have bodily lifted the magistrate and carried him, but decorum prevailed. Matthew ascended the stairs, and together he and the master of Fount Royal took Woodward along the hallway to his room. Once settled in bed again and propped up on the blood-spotted pillow, Woodward said, "Thank you, Mr. Bidwell. You may depart."

"If you don't mind, I would like to stay and hear the decree." Bidwell had already closed the door and claimed a position next to the bed.

"I *do* mind, sir. Until the decree is read to the accused"— Woodward paused to gasp a breath—"it is the court's business. It would not be seemly otherwise."

"Yes but—"

"Depart," Woodward said. "Your presence delays our work." He glanced irritably at Matthew, who stood at the foot of the bed. "The quill and paper! *Now!*" Matthew turned away to get the document box that also held sheets of clean paper, the quill, and the inkjar.

Bidwell went to the door, but before he left he had to try once again. "Tell me this, then: should I have the stake cut and planted?"

Woodward squeezed his eyes shut at Bidwell's dogged disregard for propriety. Then he opened them and said tersely, "Sir . . . you may accompany Matthew to read my decree to the accused. Now please . . . leave us."

"All right, then. I'm going."

"And . . . Mr. Bidwell . . . please refrain from dawdling in the hall."

"My word on it as a gentleman. I shall be waiting downstairs." Bidwell left the room and closed the door.

Woodward stared out the window at the gold-tinged sun-illumed morning. It was going to be beautiful today, he thought. A more lovely morning than he'd seen in the better part of a month. "Date the decree," he told Matthew, though it was hardly necessary.

Matthew sat upon the stool beside the bed, using the document box as a makeshift writing table propped on his knees. He dipped the quill into the ink and wrote at the top of the paper *May Seventeenth, Sixteen-Ninety-Nine.*

"Ready it," Woodward prodded, his eyes fixed on the outside world.

Matthew scribed the preface, which he had done enough times in enough different circumstances to know the correct wording. It took him a few moments and a few dips of the quill: *By Decree of the Right Honorable King's Appointed Magistrate Isaac Temple Woodward on This Day in the Settlement of Fount Royal, Carolina Colony, Concerning the Accusations of Murder and Witchcraft to Be Detailed As Follows Against the Defendant, a Woman Citizen Known Hereby As Rachel Howarth . . .*

He had to stop to work out a kink in his writing hand. "Go on," Woodward said. "It must be done."

Matthew had an ashen taste in his mouth. He dipped the

quill again, and this time he spoke the words aloud as he wrote them: "On the Charge of the Murder of the Reverend Burlton Grove, I Find the Aforesaid Defendant—" He paused once more, his quill poised to record the magistrate's decree. The flesh of his face seemed to have drawn tight beyond endurance, and a heat burned in his skull.

Suddenly Woodward snapped his fingers. Matthew looked at him quizzically, and when the magistrate put a finger to his lips and then motioned toward the door Matthew realized what he was trying to communicate. Matthew quietly put aside his writing materials and the document box, got up from the stool, went to the door, and quickly opened it.

Bidwell was down on one knee in the hallway, busily buffing his right shoe with his peacock-blue sleeve. He turned his head and looked at Matthew, lifting his eyebrows as if to ask why the clerk had emerged so stealthily from the magistrate's room.

"Gentleman, my ass!" Woodward hissed under his breath.

"I thought you were going downstairs to wait," Matthew reminded the man, who now ferociously buffed his shoetop and then heaved himself up to his feet with an air of indignance.

"Did I say I would *race* there? I saw a blemish on my shoe!"

"The blemish is on your vow, sir!" Woodward said, with a measure of fire that belied his watery constitution.

"Very well, then! I'm going." Bidwell reached up and adjusted his wig, which had become somewhat tilted during his ascent from the floor. "Can you blame me for wanting to know? I've waited so long for it!"

"You can wait a little longer, then." Woodward motioned him away. "Matthew, close the door." Matthew resettled himself, with the box on his knees and the writing materials and paper before him.

"Read it again," Woodward said.

"Yes, sir." Matthew took a deep breath. "On the Charge of the Murder of the Reverend Burlton Grove, I Find the Aforesaid Defendant—"

"Guilty," came the whispered answer. "With a stipulation. That the defendant did not actually commit the murder . . . but caused it to be committed by her words, deeds, or associations."

"Sir!" Matthew said, his heart pounding. "Please! There's absolutely no evidence to—"

"*Silence!*" Woodward lifted himself up on his elbows, his face contorted with a mixture of anger, frustration, and pain. "I'll have no more of your second opinions, do you hear me?" He locked his gaze with Matthew's. "Scribe the next charge."

Matthew might have thrown down the quill and upset the inkjar, but he did not. He knew his duties, whether or not he agreed with the magistrate's decision. Therefore he swallowed the bitter gall in his throat, redipped the quill—that bastard weapon of blind destruction—and spoke again as he wrote: "On the Charge of the Murder of Daniel Howarth, I Find the Aforesaid Defendant—"

"Guilty, with a stipulation. The same as above." Woodward glared at him when Matthew's hand failed to make the entry. "I should like to finish this sometime today."

Matthew had no choice but to write down the decree. The heat of shame flared in his cheeks. Now, of course, he knew what the next decision must be. "On the Charge of Witchcraft . . . I Find the Aforesaid Defendant—"

"Guilty," Woodward said quickly. He closed his eyes and rested his head back down on the stained pillow, his breathing harsh. Matthew heard a rattling sound deep in the magistrate's lungs. "Scribe the preface to sentencing."

Matthew wrote it as if in a trance. *By Virtue of the Power Ascribed to Me As Colonial Magistrate, I Hereby Sentence the Aforesaid Defendant Rachel Howarth to . . .* He lifted his quill from the paper and waited.

Woodward opened his eyes and stared up at the ceiling. A moment passed, during which could be heard the singing of birds in the springtime sunlight. "Burning at the stake, as warranted by the King's law," Woodward said. "The sentence to be carried out on Monday, the twenty-second of May, sixteen-ninety-nine.

In case of inclement weather . . . the earliest necessary date following." His gaze ticked toward Matthew, who had not moved. "Enter it."

Again, he was simply the unwitting flesh behind the instrument. Somehow the lines were quilled on the paper.

"Give it here." Woodward held out his hand and took the document. He squinted, reading it by the light that streamed through the window, and then he nodded with satisfaction. "The quill, please." Matthew had the presence of mind—or rather the dignity of his job—to dip the quill in the inkjar and blot the excess before he handed it over.

Woodward signed his full name and, below it, the title *Colonial Magistrate*. Ordinarily an official wax seal would be added, but the seal had been lost to that blackhearted Will Shawcombe. He then returned the paper and the quill to Matthew, who knew what was expected of him. Still moving as if enveloped in a gray haze, Matthew signed his name beneath Woodward's, along with the title *Magistrate's Clerk*.

And it was done.

"You may read it to the defendant," Woodward said, avoiding looking at his clerk's face because he knew what he would see there. "Take Bidwell with you, as he should also hear it."

Matthew realized there was no use in delaying the inevitable. He slowly stood up, his mind yet fogged, and walked to the door with the decree in hand.

"Matthew?" Woodward said, "For whatever this is worth . . . I know you must think me heartless and cruel." He hesitated, swallowing thick pus. "But the proper sentence has been given. The witch must be burned . . . for the good of everyone."

"She is innocent," Matthew managed to say, his gaze cast to the floor. "I can't prove anything yet, but I intend to keep—"

"You delude yourself . . . and it is time for delusions to cease."

Matthew turned toward the man, his eyes coldly furious. "You are *wrong*, sir," he added. "Rachel is not a witch, she's a pawn. Oh yes, all the conditions for a burning at the stake have been met, and all is in order with the law, sir, but I am damned if

I'll let someone I know to be innocent lose her life on hearsay and fantasy!"

Woodward rasped, "Your task is to read the decree! No more and no less!"

"I'll read it." Matthew nodded. "Then I'll drink rum to wash my mouth out, but I will not surrender! If she burns on Monday, I have five days to prove her innocent, and by God that's what I intend to do!"

Woodward started to answer with some vinegar, but his strength failed him. "Do what you must," he said. "I can't . . . protect you from your nightbird, can I?"

"The only thing I fear is that Rachel is burned before I can prove who murdered her husband and Reverend Grove. If that happens, I don't know how I can live with myself."

"Oh, my Christ." It had been spoken as nearly a moan. Woodward closed his eyes, feeling faint. "She has you so deeply . . . and you don't even realize it."

"She has my trust, if that's what you infer."

"She has your *soul.*" His eyes opened; in an instant they had become sunken and bloodshot. "I long for the moment we shall leave this place. Return to Charles Town . . . civilization and sanity. When I am cured and in good health again, we'll put all this behind us. And then . . . when you can see clearly . . . you'll understand what danger tempted you."

Matthew had to get out, because the magistrate had been reduced to babbling. He couldn't bear to see the man—so proud, so regal, and so correct—on the verge of becoming a fever-dulled imbecile. He said, "I'm going," but he still hesitated before he left the bedchamber. His tone had softened; there was no point now in harshness. "Can I get anything for you?"

Woodward drew in a suffering breath and released it. "I want . . ." he began, but his agonized throat felt in jeopardy of closing and he had to start again. "I want . . . things to be as they were . . . between us. Before we came to this wretched place. I want us to return to Charles Town . . . and go on, as if none of this ever happened." He looked hopefully at Matthew. "All right?"

Matthew stood at the window, staring out at the sunlit town. The sky was turning bright blue, though the way he felt it might have been a dismal downpour out there. He knew what the magistrate wanted him to say. He knew it would ease him, but it would be a lie. He said quietly, "I wish it might be so, sir. But you and I both know it will not be. I may be your clerk . . . I may be under your watchcare, and live in your house . . . but I am a man, sir. If I fail to fight for the truth as I see it, then what kind of man am I? Surely not the kind you have taught me to be. So . . . you ask for something I am unable to give you, Isaac."

There was a long, torturous silence. Then the magistrate spoke in his dry husk of a voice: "Leave me."

Matthew walked out, taking the hateful decree downstairs to where Bidwell was waiting.

twenty-six

"THE MAGISTRATE HAS MADE HIS DECREE," Matthew said.
Rachel, who was sitting on her bench with the coarse
robe around her and the cowl shielding her face, hadn't moved
when Matthew and Bidwell entered the gaol. Now she simply
gave a brief nod, signifying her acknowledgment of the document that was about to be read.

"Go on, let's hear it!" Bidwell had been in such a hurry that
he'd demanded they walk instead of waiting for the horses and
carriage to be readied, and now he was truly champing at his bit.

Matthew stood beneath the roof hatch, which was open. He
unrolled the document and began to read the preface in a calm,
emotionless voice. Behind him, Bidwell paced back and forth.
The master of Fount Royal abruptly stopped when Matthew
reached the portion that began: "On the Charge of the Murder of
the Reverend Burlton Grove . . ." Matthew could hear the man's
wolfish breathing at his back. "I Find the Aforesaid Defendant
Guilty."

There was a *smack* as Bidwell struck his palm with his fist in a
gesture of triumph. Matthew flinched, but kept his attention focused on Rachel. She showed no reaction whatsoever. "With a
Stipulation," Matthew continued. "That the Defendant Did Not

Actually Commit the Murder, But Caused It to be Committed by Her Words, Deeds, or Associations."

"Yes, but it's all the same, isn't it?" Bidwell crowed. "She might as well have done it with her own hands!"

Matthew kept going by sheer force of will. "On the Charge of the Murder of Daniel Howarth, I Find the Aforesaid Defendant Guilty, With a Stipulation." At the word *guilty,* this time Rachel had given a soft cry and lowered her head. "That the Defendant Did Not Actually Commit the Murder, But Caused It to be Committed by Her Words, Deeds, or Associations."

"Excellent, excellent!" Bidwell gleefully clapped his hands together.

Matthew looked fiercely into the man's grinning face. "Would you please restrain yourself? This is not a five-pence play requiring comments from the idiots' gallery!"

Bidwell's grin only broadened. "Oh, say what you like! Just keep reading that blessed decree!"

Matthew's task—performed so many times at the magistrate's behest over criminals common and extraordinary—had become a test of endurance. He had to go on.

"On the Charge of Witchcraft," he read to Rachel, "I Find the Aforesaid Defendant . . ." and here his throat almost clenched shut to prevent him from speaking, but the horrible word had to be uttered, ". . . Guilty."

"Ah, sweet deliverance!" Bidwell all but shouted.

Rachel made no sound, but she put a trembling hand to her cowl-shrouded face as if the word—which she had known would be delivered—had been a physical blow.

"By Virtue of the Power Ascribed to Me As Colonial Magistrate," Matthew read, "I Hereby Sentence the Aforesaid Defendant Rachel Howarth to Burning at the Stake As Warranted by the King's Law. The Sentence to be Carried Out on Monday, the Twenty-Second of May, Sixteen-Ninety-Nine." When the distasteful chore was finished, he dropped the document down by his side.

"Your hours are numbered!" Bidwell said, standing behind

Matthew. "Your master may have torched the schoolhouse last night, but we'll build it back!"

"I think you should leave," Matthew told him, though he was too drained to raise his voice.

"You may go to your reward knowing that all your work to destroy my town was for nothing!" Bidwell raved on. "Once you're dead, Fount Royal shall rise to fame and glory!"

Rachel gave no response to these cutting comments, if indeed she felt them through her sphere of misery.

Still Bidwell wasn't done. "This is truly the day that God made!" He couldn't help it; he had to reach out and clap Matthew on the back. "A fine job you and the magistrate have done! And an excellent decision! Now . . . I must go start the preparations! There's a stake to be cut, and by Christ's blood it'll be the best stake any damned witch was ever burned on!" He glared at Rachel through the bars. "Your master may send every demon in his barn to cause us woe between now and Monday morn, but we'll weather it! You may rely on that, witch! So tell your black-cocked dog that Robert Bidwell never failed at anything in his life and Fount Royal will be no exception! Do you hear me?" He was no longer speaking directly to Rachel now but was looking around the gaol, his voice thunderous and haughty as if he were sending a warning to the very ears of the Devil. "We shall live and thrive here, no matter what treacheries you send against us!"

His chest-beating complete, Bidwell stalked to the door but stopped when he realized Matthew had not followed. "Come along! I want you to read that decree in the streets!"

"I take my commands from the magistrate, sir. If he requires me to read it for the public, I shall, but not until he so orders it."

"I've neither the time nor inclination to wrangle with you!" Bidwell's mouth had taken on an ugly sneer. "Ohhhh . . . yes, I see why you wish to dawdle! You intend to console her! If Woodward could see this lovely scene, it would send him two steps nearer his death!"

Matthew's initial impulse was to advance upon Bidwell and

strike his face so hard that what served as the man's brains might dribble from his ears, but the ensuing duel that would likely follow would provide no good purpose save work for the gravedigger and a probable misspelling of his own name on the marker. Therefore he reined in his inclination and simply glowered daggers at the man.

Bidwell laughed, which acted as a bellows to further heat Matthew's banked fires. "A tender, touching moment between the witch and her latest conquest! I swear, you'd be better off lying in the lap of Mrs. Nettles! But do as you please!" He aimed his next jibe at Rachel. "Demons, old men, or babes in the woods: it doesn't matter what flavor your suckets! Well, take your rapture, as you shall be paying dearly for it come Monday!" He turned and made his leave like the strutting bird whose gaudy blue colored his suit.

In the aftermath of Bidwell's departure, Matthew realized that words were not potent enough instruments with which to communicate his sorrow. He rolled up the document, as it would have to be placed on official file in Charles Town.

Rachel spoke, her face still shielded. "You have done what you could. For that I thank you." Her voice, though weakened and listless, yet held a full measure of dignity.

"Listen to me!" Matthew stepped forward and grasped one of the bars with his free hand. "Monday is still a distance off—"

"A small distance," she interrupted.

"A *distance,* nevertheless. The magistrate may have issued his decree, but I don't intend to stop my inquiries."

"You might as well." She stood up and pushed the cowl back from her face. "It is finished, whether you accept it or not."

"I *don't* accept it!" he shouted. "I never shall accept it!" He shut his mouth, shamed by his loss of control; he stared down at the dirty floor, searching within himself for any semblance of an articulate response. "To accept such a thing . . . means I agree with it and that is impossible. I can never, as long as I live, agree with this . . . this wrongful execution of an innocent victim."

"Matthew?" she said softly, and he looked at her. They stared at each other for a moment. Rachel approached him but stopped well short of the bars.

She said, "Go on about your life."

He found no answer.

"I am dead," Rachel told him. "Dead. When I am taken on Monday to be burned, my body will be there for the flames . . . but the woman I used to be before Daniel was murdered is no longer here. Since I was brought to this gaol, I have slipped away. I did have hope, at one point, but I hardly remember what it felt like."

"You mustn't give up hope," Matthew insisted. "If there is one more day, there is always—"

"Stop," she said firmly. "Please . . . just stop. You think you are doing the right thing, by encouraging my spirit . . . but you are not. The time has come to embrace reality, and to put aside these . . . fantasies of my life being spared. Whoever committed these murders is too smart, Matthew. Too . . . demonic. Against such a power, I have no hope and I wish to cease this pretending. It does not prepare me for the stake, and that above all else is what I must do."

"I am close to learning something," Matthew said. "Something important, though I'm not sure yet how it relates to you. I think it *does,* though. I think I have uncovered the first strands that form a rope, and the rope will lead me to—"

"I am begging you," she whispered, and now there were tears in her eyes though her face displayed no other betrayal of emotion, "to cease this playing with Fate. You can't free me. Neither can you save my life. Do you not understand that an end has been reached?"

"An end has *not* been reached! I'm telling you, I have found—"

"You have found something that may mean something," Rachel said. "And you might study it until a year from Monday, but I can't wish for freedom any longer, Matthew. I am going to be burned, and I must—I *must*—spend the time I have left in prayer and preparation." She looked up at the sunlight that streamed through the hatch, and at the cloudless azure sky beyond. "When they come for me . . . I'll be afraid, but I can't let them see it. Not Green, not Paine . . . especially not Bidwell. I can't allow myself to cry, or to scream and thrash. I don't want them sitting in Van Gundy's tavern, boasting over how they broke me. Laughing and drinking and saying how at the end I begged for mercy. I will not. If there is a God in Heaven, He will seal my mouth on that morning. They may cage me and strip me, dirty me and call me witch . . . but they will not make me into a shrieking animal. Not even on the stake." Her eyes met Matthew's again. "I have a single wish. Will you grant it?"

"If it's possible."

"It is. I wish you to walk out of here and not return."

Matthew hadn't known what to expect, but this request was as painful—and as startling—as a slap across the face.

Rachel watched him intently. When he failed to respond, she said, "It is more than a wish, it is a demand. I want you to put this place behind you. As I said before: go on about your life." Still he couldn't summon an answer. Rachel came forward two more paces and touched his hand that gripped the bar. "Thank you for your belief in me," she said, her face close to his. "Thank you for *listening*. But it's over now. Please understand that, and accept it."

Matthew found his voice, though it was near perished. "How can I go on about my life, knowing such injustice was done?"

She gave him a faint, wry smile. "Injustice is done somewhere every day. It is a fact of living. If you don't already know that to be true, you are much less worldly than I thought." She sighed, and let her hand fall away from his. "Go away, Matthew. You've done your best."

"No, I haven't."

"You *have*. If you need me to release you from some imagined obligation to me . . . there." Rachel waved her hand past his face. "You are released."

"I cannot just walk out of here like that," he said.

"You have no choice." Again, she levelled her gaze at him.

"Go on, now. Leave me alone." She turned away and went back to her bench.

"I will not give up," Matthew said. *"You* may . . . but *I* swear I won't."

Rachel sat down and leaned over toward her waterbowl. She cupped her hand into it and brought water to her mouth.

"I won't," he repeated. "Do you hear me?" She pulled her hood over her head, shrouding her face once more, and withdrew into her mansion of solitude.

Matthew realized he might stand here as long as he pleased, but Rachel had removed herself to a sanctum that only she could inhabit. He suspected it was the place of reflection—perhaps of the memories of happier times—that had kept her mind from cracking during the long hours of her imprisonment. He realized also, with a twist of anguish, that he was no longer welcome in her company. She did not wish to be distracted from her inner dialogue with Death.

It was indeed time to leave her. Still he lingered, watching her immobile figure. He hoped she might say something again to him, but she was silent. After a few moments he went to the door. There was no movement or response from Rachel. He started to speak once more, but he knew not what to say. *Goodbye* seemed the only proper word, yet he was loath to utter it. He walked out into the cruel sunlight.

Shortly the smell of charred wood drifted to his nostrils, and he paused at the pile of blackened ruins. There was hardly anything left to attest that it had ever been a schoolhouse. All four walls were gone, and the roof had fallen in. He wondered if somewhere in the debris might be the wire handle of what had been a bucket.

Matthew had almost told Rachel about his findings of last night, but he'd decided not to for the same reason he'd decided to withhold the information from Bidwell: for the moment, the secret was best kept locked in his own vault. He needed an answer to the question of *why* Winston was spiriting infernal fire from

Charles Town and using it to set flame to Bidwell's dream. He also needed from Winston further details—if the man could supply them—of the so-called surveyor who'd come to Fount Royal. Therefore his mission this morning was clear: to find Edward Winston.

He inquired from the first person he saw—a pipe-smoking farmer carrying a flasket of yellow grain—as to the location of Winston's house, and was informed that the dwelling stood on Harmony Street just shy of the cemetery. Matthew started off to his destination, walking at a brisk pace.

The house did stand within a stone's toss of the first row of grave markers. Matthew noted that the shutters were sealed, indicating that Winston must be out. It was by no means a large dwelling, and probably only held two or three rooms. The house had been painted white at some point in the past but the white-wash had worn off, leaving a mottled appearance to the walls. It occurred to Matthew that—unlike Bidwell's mansion and some of the sturdier farmhouses—Winston's abode had an air of shoddy impermanence akin to that found in the slave quarters. Matthew continued up the walk, which was made of packed sand and hammer-crushed oyster shells, and knocked soundly at the door.

There was but a short wait. "Who is it?" came Winston's voice—rough-edged and perhaps a bit slurred—from within the house.

"Matthew Corbett. May I please speak with you?"

"Concerning what?" This time he was making an obvious effort to disguise what might be termed an unbalanced condition. "The witch?"

"No, sir. Concerning a surveyor who came to Fount Royal four years ago." Silence fell. "Mr. Bidwell has told me you walked the man around," Matthew pressed on. "I'd like to know what you might recall of him."

"I . . . have no recollection of such a man. If you'll forgive me now . . . I have some ledger business to attend to."

Matthew doubted that Winston had any business other than

drinking and plotting more conflagrations. "I do have some information pertaining to Rachel Howarth. Might you want to see the magistrate's decision? I've just come from reading it to her."

Almost at once there was the sound of a latch being undone. The door opened a few inches, enough for a slice of sunlight to enter the house and fall upon Winston's haggard, unshaven face. "The decision?" he said, squinting in the glare. "You have it with you?"

"I do." Matthew held up the rolled document. "May I come in?"

Winston hesitated, but Matthew knew the die had been cast. The door was opened wide enough to admit Matthew and then closed again at his back.

Within the small front room, two candles burned on a wicker table. Beside the candles, and set before the bench that Winston had been occupying, was a squat blue bottle and a wooden tankard. Up until this moment Matthew had thought Winston to be—judging from his usual neatness of appearance and his precise manners—a paradigm of efficiency, but Matthew's opinion suddenly suffered a sharp reversal.

The room might have sickened a pig. On the floor lay scattered shirts, stockings, and breeches that Winston had not bothered to pick up. The smell of damp and musty cloth—coupled with body odor from some of the gamier articles—was somewhat less than appealing. Also littering the floor were crumpled balls of paper, spilled tobacco, a broken clay pipe here and there, a few books whose bindings had come unstitched, and sundry other items that had outlived their use but not been consigned to a proper garbage pit. Even the narrow little hearth was near choked with cold ashes and bits of trash. In fact, it might be within bounds to say that the entire room resembled a garbage pit, and Matthew shuddered to think what Winston's bedchamber might conceal. A bucket of sulphurous chemicals might be the least noxious of it.

Nearby stood the desk that Winston had recovered from the gaol. Now Matthew understood why it had been so thoroughly cleaned out when Winston had it carted over, as its surface was a jumbled mess of more crumpled and ink-splattered papers, a number of candles melted down to stubs, and a disorderly pile of ledger books. Matthew was surprised that Winston had been able to lay his hands on a clean sheaf of paper and an unspilled inkjar in this rat's nest. It occurred to him, in his brief but telling inspection, that all Winston's business with Bidwell was done at the mansion because Winston wished not to reveal his living conditions—and possibly the condition of his mental affairs—to his employer.

Winston was pouring liquid from the blue bottle into his tankard. He wore a long gray nightshirt that bore evidence of many poor repatchings, as well as several small scorched holes that told Matthew the man's control of fire did not extend to power over a spilled pipe. "So," Winston said. "The decree's been made, eh?" He downed some of his pleasure, which Matthew assumed was either hard cider or rum. "Bring it over here and spread it out."

Matthew did, but he kept a hand on the document, as it was his charge. Winston leaned over and read the ornate handwriting. "No surprises there, I see. She's to be burned on Monday, then?"

"Yes."

"High time. She should've gone to the stake a month ago; we'd all be the better for it."

Matthew rolled the decree up again. He cast a disdainful eye about his surroundings. "Do you always live in this fashion?"

Winston had been about to drink again, but the tankard's ascent paused. "No," he said with sarcasm. "My servants have been called away. Ordinarily I have a footman, a parlor wench, and a chamberpot scrubber." The tankard went to his mouth and he wiped his lips with the back of his hand. "You may go now, Sir Reverence."

Matthew smiled slightly, but his face was tight. *Sir Reverence* was gutter slang for human excrement. "You must have had a late night," he said.

"A late night?" Winston's eyebrows went up. "Meaning what?"

"Meaning . . . a late night. I had assumed you were an early riser, and therefore must have been working into the small hours."

"Working." He nodded. "Yes. I'm always working." He motioned toward the ledger-laden desk. "See there? Managing his money. His pence and guineas and dog dollars. His ins and outs. That's what I do."

"You don't sound particularly proud of your accomplishments for Mr. Bidwell," Matthew ventured. "He must rely on your services quite a lot, doesn't he?"

Winston stared at Matthew, his bloodshot eyes wary. "You may go now," he repeated, with a more ominous inflection.

"I shall. But Mr. Bidwell himself suggested I find you and ask about the surveyor. As you were the one who escorted the man around, I hoped that—"

"A *surveyor?* I hardly remember the man!" Again Winston quaffed from the tankard, and this time the gleaming residue trickled down his chin. "What was it? Four years ago?"

"Or thereabouts."

"Go on, get out!" Winston sneered. "I don't have time for your foolishness!"

Matthew took a deep breath. "Yes, you do," he answered.

"What? By God, will I have to throw you out of here?"

Matthew said quietly, "I know about your nocturnal activities."

The hand of God might have come down to stop time and still all sounds.

Matthew went on, taking advantage of the moment. "In addition, I have one of the six buckets that Mr. Rawlings and the others buried. Therefore it's no use to go out tonight and move them. The seventh bucket you took away is hidden here somewhere, I presume?"

The hand of God was a mighty instrument. It had turned Edward Winston into a gape-mouthed statue. In another few seconds, however, the tankard slipped from Winston's grasp and crashed to the floor.

"I presume it is," Matthew said. "You used a brush to paint the chemicals on the walls of the houses you set afire, am I correct? It does seem to be a potent concoction."

Winston did not move, did not speak, and hardly appeared to be breathing. The color of his face and the somber *grisard* of his nightshirt were one and the same.

Matthew spent a moment looking around the littered room before he spoke again. "This is what I believe," he said. "That on one of your supply trips to Charles Town with Nicholas Paine, you approached someone of authority there. Possibly Mr. Danforth, the harbormaster, but possibly someone with more interest in seeing that Fount Royal never grows to Bidwell's ambition. I suspect you might have sent Mr. Paine on some errand or another while you made this contact. He doesn't know, does he?"

Matthew hadn't expected Winston to reply, therefore he was not disappointed. "I don't think he knows," Matthew said. "I think this is your intrigue alone. You volunteered to take advantage of Rachel Howarth's plight and set numerous fires to empty houses, thus speeding along the process of emptying more. Am I so far correct?" Winston slowly sank down upon his bench, his mouth still open.

"The problem was that you needed an incendiary to ignite in wet weather." Matthew prodded some discarded clothes with the toe of his right shoe. "The buckets of chemicals had to be mixed in Charles Town and secreted here by ship. The crew must have had some rough voyages, I'd suspect. But Mr. Rawlings must be making a profit for his risk. I would think *you* are making a profit for your risk as well. Or perhaps you've been promised a position in Charles Town after Fount Royal fails?"

Winston lifted a hand and put it to his forehead, his eyes glassy with shock.

"It is to your credit that you don't mar your dignity with denials," Matthew offered. "I *am* curious, though. Bidwell tells me you've been in his employ for eight years. Why did you turn against him?"

Now both hands were pressed to Winston's face. He breathed raggedly, his shoulders slumped.

"I have seen enough of human nature to have an idea." Matthew went to the cluttered desk and opened one of the ledger books. He flipped through the pages as he spoke. "You know more than anyone else how much Bidwell is worth. You see his wealth on display, you see his plans for the future, and you see . . . your own existence, which according to the way you live is at a low flux. So I would venture to say this revolves around your own perceived misery. Did they promise you a mansion in Charles Town? A statue in your honor? What exactly *did* they promise, Mr. Winston?"

Winston reached with a feeble hand for the blue bottle, brought it to his mouth, and took a long swallow of courage. When he lowered the bottle, he blinked away tears and said, "Money."

"Considerably more than Bidwell was paying you, yes?"

"More than . . . I could hope to earn in two lifetimes." Again he drank copiously from the bottle. "You don't know what it's like, working for him. Being around him . . . and all that he has. He spends on wigs alone every year an amount I might live on as a prince. And the clothes and food! If you knew the numbers, you would understand and be sickened as I am by the man's philosophy: not a shilling more for a servant's needs, but spare no expense for the master's desires!"

"I won't defend him, but I will say that such is the right of a master."

"It is the right of *no* man!" Winston said heatedly. "I have an education, I am literate, and I consider myself reasonably bright! But I might as well be a slave, as far as he's concerned! I might even be the better for it!" He laughed harshly. "At least Bidwell cares enough about Goode to have bought him a fiddle!"

"The difference is that Goode is a slave and you're a free man. You can choose your employer. Then again . . ." Matthew nodded. "I suppose you *have*."

"Oh, be as smug as you please!" Winston turned upon Matthew an expression of the deepest disgust. "Look at my house, and look at his! Then look in the ledgers and see who directs the course of his monies! *I* do! He pretends to be such a sterling businessman, but in fact he is skilled at two things: intimidation and bluster. I ought to be a partner in his enterprises, for what I've encouraged! But it has been clearly and plainly shown to me by his actions that Bidwell takes good opinions and presents them as his own."

He held up a finger to mark his point. "Now, failed ventures . . . that's a different cart. Failure is always the fault of someone else . . . someone who invariably deserves to be banished from the kingdom. I have seen it happen. When Fount Royal fails—and it will, regardless of how many houses I flamed and how long the witch roasts on her stake—he will begin to fire his cannons of blame at every possible target. Including this one." He thumped his chest with his fist. "Do you think I should sit at his beck and call and await a further slide into poverty? *No.* For your information—and whatever you choose to do with it—I did not do the approaching. They approached *me,* when Paine and I were on separate tasks in Charles Town. At first I refused . . . but they sweetened their offer with a house and a position on the Shipping Council. It was my idea to set the fires."

"And a clever idea it was," Matthew said. "You hid behind Rachel Howarth's skirts and the Devil's shadow. Did it not trouble you in the least that these fires were ascribed to her?"

"No," he answered without hesitation. "If you'll read that document you hold, you'll find there's no charge there concerning the setting of fires. She fashioned the poppets, committed the murders, and consorted with Satan of her own accord. I simply used the situation to my benefit."

"*Simply?*" Matthew echoed. "I don't think there's anything simpleminded about you, Mr. Winston. I think *coldly* might be a better word."

"As you please." Winston offered a bitter smile. "I have

learned from Bidwell that one fights fire with fire and ice with ice." His eyes narrowed. "So. You have a bucket. I presume you were hiding out there?" He waited for Matthew to nod. "Who else knows?"

"If you are considering violence as a solution, you might think otherwise. Someone else *does* know, but your secret is in no current danger."

Winston frowned. "What, then? Aren't you going to go running to Bidwell and tell him?"

"No, I'm not. As you've pointed out, the fires were incidental in the charges against Madam Howarth. I am hunting a smarter—and colder—fox than you."

"Pardon my dulled wits, but what are you talking about?"

"Your grievance against Bidwell is not my concern. Whatever you choose to do from this point is not of interest to me, either. As long as there are no future conflagrations, I might add."

Winston let go a sigh of relief. "Sir," he said, "I bow gratefully before your mercy."

"My mercy has a price. I wish to know about the surveyor."

"The surveyor," Winston repeated. He rubbed his temples with both hands. "I tell you . . . I can hardly recall the man. Why do you care to know about him, anyway?"

"My interest is a personal matter. Do you remember his name?"

"No. Wait . . . give me a moment . . ." He closed his eyes, obviously trying his best to concentrate. "I think . . . it was Spencer . . . Spicer . . . something similar to that, at least." His eyes opened.

"The man was bearded?"

"Yes . . . a heavy beard. And he wore a hat."

"A tricorn?"

"No. It was . . . a loose-brimmed shade hat. Much like any farmer or traveller might wear. I remember . . . his clothing was rustic, as well."

"You took him walking around Fount Royal. How much time would you say you spent with him?"

Winston shrugged. "The better part of an afternoon, I suppose."

"Do you recall his description?"

"A beard and a hat," Winston said. "That's all I can remember."

"And probably all you were meant to remember."

Winston gave him a questioning look. "What does this concern?"

"It concerns the manipulation of memory," Matthew answered. "Something I think my fox knows a great deal about."

"If you are making sense, I am unable to follow it."

"I believe I have information enough. Thank you for your time." Matthew started toward the door, and Winston stood up.

"Please!" Winston's voice held a note of urgency. "If you were in my position . . . what would you do? Remain here—and await the end—or go to Charles Town and try to salvage what I can of a future?"

"A difficult question," Matthew said after a short consideration. "I would agree that your present is precarious, and since you have neither love nor loyalty for Bidwell you might as well seek your fortune elsewhere. However . . . as much a dog you think Bidwell to be, your masters in Charles Town are probably mongrels of similar breed. You might have known that, judging from the voracity with which they have eaten your soul. So . . . flip a coin, and good luck to you."

Matthew turned his back and left Edward Winston standing forlorn and alone in the midst of his self-made chaos.

twenty-seven

HIS THOUGHTS STILL CLOUDED by Winston's betrayal, Matthew was ascending the stairs to look in upon the magistrate when he almost collided with Mrs. Nettles, who was descending with a tray upon which sat a bowl of pap.

"How is he?" Matthew asked.

"Not verra well," she said, her voice low. "He's havin' some trouble even swallowin' the mush."

Matthew nodded grimly. "I have my doubts about whether the bloodletting is doing any good."

"I've seen it do wonders, though. That afflicted blood's got to be rid of."

"I hope you're right. I'm not sure his condition isn't being hastened by all this bleeding." He started to slide past her up the stairs, which was a precarious maneuver due to her formidable size and the lack of a railing.

"Just a moment, sir!" she said. "You have a visitor."

"A *visitor?* Who?"

"The child," she said. "Violet Adams. She's in the library, waitin' for you."

"Oh?" Matthew instantly went back down the stairs and entered the library. His quick entrance startled the little girl, who was standing before the open window studying a bishop she had picked up from the chessboard. She jumped and backed away from him like a cornered deer.

"Forgive me," Matthew said in a calming tone. He showed one palm in a non-threatening gesture, while he held the rolled-up decree at his side. "I should have announced myself."

She just stared at him, her body rigid as if she might either decide to flee past him or leap through the window. On this occasion she definitely was not groomed for a court appearance. Her light brown hair was loose about her shoulders and in need of washing, her tan-and-red-checked shift was held together with patches, and her shoes were near worn through.

"You've been waiting for me?" Matthew asked. She nodded. "I presume this is not an errand on behalf of your father and mother?"

"No sir," she answered. "They sent me to fetch some water."

Matthew looked down and saw two empty buckets on the floor. "I see. But you decided to come here first?"

"Yes sir."

"For what reason?"

Violet carefully placed the chesspiece back in its proper place on the board. "What are these, sir? Are they toys?"

"It's a game called chess. The pieces have different patterns of movement across the board."

"Ohhhh." She seemed much impressed. "Like knuckles 'n' stones, 'ceptin' you play that in the dirt."

"I imagine so, yes."

"They're pretty," she said. "Did Mr. Bidwell carve 'em?"

"I doubt it."

She continued staring at the chessboard. The tic of her upper lip had returned. "Last night," she said, "a rat got in my bed." Matthew didn't quite know how to respond to this matter-of-fact statement, so he said nothing.

"It got all tangled up in the beddin's," she went on. "It couldn't get out, and I could feel it down at my feet, thrashin'. I couldn't get loose, neither. Both of us were tryin' to get out. Then my papa come in and I was scared I was gonna get bit so I was screamin'. So he grabbed it up in the sheet and hit it with a candlestick, and then my mama started screamin' 'cause there was blood everywhere and that sheet was ruined."

"I'm sorry," Matthew said. "It must have been traumatic." Especially for a child of her sensitive nature, he might have added.

"Trau—*what,* sir?"

"I meant it must have been a fearsome experience."

"Yes sir." She nodded, and now she picked up a pawn and studied it in the sunlight. "The thing about it, though . . . is that . . . near mornin', I started rememberin' somethin'. About that man's voice I heard singin' in the Hamilton house."

Matthew's heart suddenly lodged in his throat. "Remembering what?"

"Whose voice it was." She put down the pawn and lifted her eyes to his. "It's still a fog . . . and thinkin' about it makes my head hurt somethin' awful, but . . . I recollected what he was singin'." She took a breath and began to softly sing, in a sweet and clear timbre: "*Come out, come out, my dames and dandies. Come out, come out, and taste my candies . . .*"

"The ratcatcher," Matthew said. In his mind he heard Linch singing that same macabre song during the massacre of rats at the gaol.

"Yes sir. It was Mr. Linch's voice I heard, from that room back there."

Matthew stared intensely into the child's eyes. "Tell me this, Violet: how did you know it was Linch's voice? Had you ever heard that song before?"

"One time he come to kill a nest of rats my papa found. They were all big ones, and black as night. Mr. Linch came and brought his potions and his sticker, and that was what he was singin' when he was waitin' for the rats to get drunk."

"Did you tell anyone else about this? Your mother and father?"

"No sir. They don't like for me to talk of it."

"Then you shouldn't tell them you've been here to see me, either."

"No sir, I wouldn't dare. I'd get a terrible whippin'."

"You ought to get your water and go home, then," Matthew said. "But one more thing: when you entered the Hamilton house, do you remember *smelling* anything? Like a very bad odor?" He was thinking of the decaying carcass. "Or did you see or hear a dog?"

Violet shook her head. "No sir, none of that. Why?"

"Well . . ." Matthew reached down to the chessboard and traded positions between the king's knight and the king's bishop. "If you were to describe this board and the pieces upon it to someone not in this room, how would you do so?"

She shrugged. "I suppose . . . that it's a wooden board with light and dark squares and some pieces in position on it."

"Would you say the game is ready to be played?"

"I don't know, sir. I would say . . . it is, but then again I don't know the particulars."

"Yes." He smiled slightly. "And it is the *particulars* that make all the difference. I want to thank you for coming to tell me what you've remembered. I know this has been very difficult for you."

"Yes sir. But my mama says when the witch is burnt up my head won't pain me no more." She picked up the two buckets. "May I ask you somethin' now, sir?"

"You may."

"Why do you suppose Mr. Linch was back there in the dark, singin' like that?"

"I don't know," he answered.

"I thought on it all this mornin'." She stared out the window, the yellow sunlight coloring her face. "It made my head ache so bad I almost cried, but it seemed like somethin' I had to keep thinkin' on." Violet didn't speak for a moment, but Matthew could tell from the set of her jaw that she had come to an important conclusion. "I think . . . Mr. Linch must be a friend of Satan's. That's what I think."

"You might possibly be right. Do you know where I might find Mr. Linch?"

An expression of alarm tightened her face. "You're not going to *tell* him, are you?"

"No. I promise it. I would just like to know where he lives."

She hesitated for a few seconds, but she knew he would find out anyway. "At the end of Industry Street. He lives in the very last house."

"Thank you."

"I don't know if I was right to come here," she said, frowning. "I mean to say . . . if Mr. Linch is a friend of the Devil, shouldn't he be called to account for it?"

"He'll be called for an accounting," Matthew said. "You may depend on that." He touched her shoulder. "You *were* right to come. Go ahead, now. Get your water."

"Yes sir." Violet left the library with her buckets in tow, and a moment later Matthew stood at the window watching her walk to the spring. Then, his mind aflame with this new information, he hurried upstairs to look in on the magistrate.

He found Woodward sleeping again, which was probably for the best. The magistrate's face sparkled with sweat, and when Matthew approached the bed he could feel the man's fever long before he placed his fingers to Woodward's hot forehead.

The magistrate stirred. His mouth opened, yet his eyes remained sealed. *"Hurting,"* he said, in that tormented whisper. *"Ann . . . he's hurting . . ."*

Matthew drew his hand back. The tips of his fingers felt as if he had held them over a forge. Matthew placed the rolled-up decree atop the dresser and then picked up the box that held the remainder of the court documents so that he might continue reading through them tonight. For now, though, he had other things to do. He went to his room, put the document box on the table beside his bed, splashed water in his face from his shaving bowl to revive his flagging energies, and then was again out the door.

It had become a truly magnificent day. The sky was bright blue and cloudless and the sun was gorgeously warm. A light breeze was blowing from the west, and in it Matthew could detect the fragrances of wild honeysuckle, pine sap, and the rich aroma of fulsome earth. He might have sat down upon the bank of the spring to enjoy the warmth, as he saw several citizens doing, but he had a task ahead of him that granted no freedom of time for simple pleasures.

On his way along Industry Street—which he was beginning to know quite well—he passed Exodus Jerusalem's camp. Actually, he heard the bluster of Jerusalem's preaching before he got there and he marvelled that the breeze didn't become a hot and malodorous tempest in this quarter of Fount Royal. Jerusalem's sister—and by that term Matthew didn't know whether the preacher meant by blood or by indecent patronage—was scrubbing clothes in a washpot next to the wagon, while the young nephew—and here it was best to make no mental comment—was lying on a quilt in the shade nearby, picking the petals off a yellow flower and tossing them idly aside. The black-garbed master of ceremonies, however, was hard at work; he stood upon an overturned crate, orating and gesticulating for a somber crowd of two men and a woman.

Matthew stared straight ahead, hoping to invoke invisibility as he slipped past Jerusalem's field of view, but he knew it was not to be. "Ah!" came the sky-ripping shout. "Ah, there walketh a sinner! Right there! Look, everyone! Look how he doth scurry like a thief in broad daylight!"

What Jerusalem called scurrying Matthew called picking up his pace. He dared not pause to deflect Jerusalem's hook, for then he would be nattered to holes by this pseudo-holy imbecile. Therefore he kept a constant course, even though the preacher began to rant and rave in a fashion that made Matthew's blood start to boil: "Yes, look at him and thy looketh upon the pride of a witch's bed! Oh, did thou not all know the vile truth? Well, it is as plain as the writ of God across the soul of a righteous man! That sinner yonder hath actually struck me—*struck* me, I sayeth!—in defense of that wanton sorceress he so dearly yearneth to protect! And not just protect! Gentle flock, if thou but kneweth the cravings in that sinner's mind concerning the dark woman, thou might falleth to thy knees in the frenzy of madness! He wisheth the flesh of her body be gripped in his hands, her mouth open to his abominable needs, her every orifice a receptacle of his goatly lusts! And there he goeth, the blind wretched beast, scurrying away from the word of God lest it scorcheth some light into his eyes and maketh him see the path to Damnation upon which he rusheth to travel!"

The only path upon which Matthew rusheth was the one leading away from Exodus Jerusalem. It occurred to him, as he gladly left the preacher's caterwaulings behind, that the gentle flock would probably cough up some coins to hear more on the subject of orifices, receptacles, and goatly lusts, which was probably at the heart of it the whole reason for their attendance today. Matthew had to admit that Jerusalem had a talent at painting horny pictures. For now, though—until, dreadfully, he had to come back this way—his attention was focused on finding the ratcatcher's domicile.

He passed the Hamilton house and Violet's home, and continued by a large weed-choked field where a split-rail fence had fallen to disrepair. Further on, what appeared to be an attempt at an apple orchard was stubbled with dwarfed and twisted trees that seemed to be begging for the mercy of an axe. On the opposite side of Industry Street, the feeble trees of another unfortunate planting drooped in apparent pain, their few remaining leaves blotched with brown and ochre sores. In this area of Fount Royal, the sun might be shining but there was definitely no rejoicing of nature.

Matthew saw that Bidwell's orchards had suffered greatly during the long period of storms. The coarse, sandy earth had been washed away to such an extent that some trees seemed more exposed roots than branches, and what branches there were had shrivelled and malformed in their piteous reach for sunlight. Here and there some kind of knobby-looking thing had sprouted, but it was more green mold than edible product. This display of blighted agriculture seemed to stretch on and on like a preview of the harvests of Hell, and Matthew could readily understand how Bidwell and the citizens might ascribe the devastation not to natural causes but to a demonic purpose.

As Matthew continued walking between the miserable fields he reflected on the possibility that, in addition to the havoc wreaked by the deluge, this climate and soil might not be suited to sustain the types of crops that Bidwell was trying to grow. Of course Bidwell was trying to produce something that would earn him money and attention from the home country, but it might be that apples, for instance, were doomed in this swamp air. Likewise doomed was whatever those green molded things were. It might be, then, that a suitable cash crop for Fount Royal was yet to be planted, and Bidwell could benefit from the advice of a professional botanist. Yet a botanist would command a sizeable fee, and Matthew thought that if Winston was correct about Bidwell's combination of stinginess and swollen self-worth—and there was no reason to doubt it—then the master of Fount Royal was apt to consider himself as much an expert on growing crops as in building ships.

Presently Matthew came to the last dwelling on Industry Street, beyond which stood the fortress wall.

If the ratcatcher desired to live apart from other human beings, he could only have created a more suitable abode by digging a hole in the earth and covering it with a mudcaked roof. The house—if it might be distinguished by such a term—made Winston's shack appear the brother of Bidwell's mansion. Brush had been allowed to grow up around it, all but obscuring it from view. Vines gripped the gray clapboards and ivy grew abundant on the roof. The house's four windows were sealed by unpainted and badly weathered shutters, and Matthew thought it was a wonder the rains hadn't broken the poor place down to the ground entirely.

Matthew made his way to the door over a bare yard still treacherous with mud. Over the door Linch had hung three large rat skeletons from leather cords, as if to announce his trade to the world—whatever portion of the world cared to come to this place, that is. But then again, perhaps those three rats had given him such a fight Linch felt the need to mount them as trophies. Matthew swallowed his disgust, balled up his fist, and knocked at the door.

He waited, but there was no response. Matthew knocked again, and this time called, "Mr. Linch? May I speak with you, please?" Still there was no answer. The ratcatcher was out, probably pursuing some long-tailed dame or dandy.

Matthew had come a distance to see the man, and he despised the thought of making a second trip. He might wait for Linch, he decided, though there was no telling when the ratcatcher would return. He knocked a third time, just to know he had, and then he put his hand on the door's crude latch. He paused, weighing his sense of morality as concerning entering a man's home unbidden.

Pulling his hand back, he stepped away from the door and stood looking at the latch with his hands on his hips. What was the right thing to do? He glanced up Industry Street the way he'd come. There was no sign of a living soul. Of course, the *right* thing was to leave and return at a later time. The *necessary* thing . . . now that was a horse pulling a different cart.

But he wasn't sure he *wanted* to enter Linch's sanctum. If a place ever smelled like dead rats, he was sure this one did. And those skeletons did not speak well of what else might be on display in there. Matthew looked again down Industry Street. Still no sign of anyone. If he wanted a chance to explore the ratcatcher's quarters, this was definitely the moment.

He took a deep breath. Trespassing upon a house was far different than intruding upon a barn . . . or was it? He didn't care to debate the distinction.

He quickly lifted the latch, before he could think better of it, and pushed the door open. It went smoothly, on oiled hinges. And by the sunlight that entered the house Matthew saw a very strange thing.

He stood at the threshold, peering in and wondering if he had lost his senses. Or at least his sense of order. This revelation took him inside. He looked around, his curiosity now well and truly piqued.

There was a desk and a sleeping pallet, a hearth and a shelf of cooking utensils. There was a chair and beside it a table on which sat a lantern. Nearby were a half-dozen candles wrapped up in oiled paper. A chamberpot was placed at the foot of the pallet. Two pairs of dirty shoes were lined up side-by-side next to the hearth, which was perfectly devoid of ashes. A broom leaned against the wall, ready for work.

And this was what so completely astounded Matthew: Linch's dwelling was the absolute picture of neatness.

The pallet had been made, its bedding tight and precise. The chamberpot was spotless. So too were the cooking pots and utensils. The lantern's glass bore not a trace of candlesoot. The floor and walls had been recently scrubbed, and the house still smelled of pinetar soap. Matthew thought he might have eaten off that floor and not tasted a grain of dirt. Everything was so orderly that it put a scare into Matthew even more than the terrible chaos of Winston's home, for the single reason that— like Winston had been—the ratcatcher was not who he appeared to be.

"Well," Matthew said, and his voice trembled. He looked once more toward town, but thankfully Industry Street was still empty. Then he continued his examination of this place that seemed to be a hovel from without but within was the epitome of . . . might the word Matthew was searching for be *control?*

This was one of the damnedest things he'd ever seen. The only bad note in the house was the foursome of dirty shoes, and Matthew thought those were part of Linch's ratcatching costume. He decided to add a pound to his penny of intrusion and therefore opened a trunk, finding within it more clothes—shirts, breeches, and stockings, all of them clean and perfectly folded.

Beside the lantern and the candles was a small ivory box. Matthew opened it and discovered matches and a flint, the matches all lined up like obedient soldiers. In a larger box that occupied a corner Matthew discovered a supply of salted beef, ears of corn, a pot of flour and a pot of grain, a bottle of rum and a bottle of wine, and various other foodstuffs. Upon the desk was a clay pipe and a carefully wrapped packet of tobacco. There was also an inkpot, a quill, and some papers ready to be written upon. He slid open the desk's top drawer, and found a second inkpot and a stack of paper, a leather wallet and . . . wonder of wonders . . . a book.

It was a thin volume, but a well-read and well-travelled tome, from the wear and tear of the binding. Matthew gently opened it to the title page—which threatened to fall out between his fingers—and received another puzzlement. The book's title, faded as it was, read *A Pharaoh's Life, or Concerning Fanciful Events in Ancient Egypt.*

Matthew knew that Egyptian culture, known through the travails of Moses in the Holy Bible, was a source of great fascination to a certain segment of the English and European populace—mainly, those gentry who had the time and inclination to indulge in theories and discourse on what that mysterious civilization might have been like. He could have expected a book of this nature to adorn Bidwell's library, simply for the show of it, but never touched; it was absolutely incredible that the ratcatcher might have an interest in the life of a pharaoh, however fancifully described. Matthew would have paged through the book to get an idea of its contents, but as the leaves were so fragile he decided to forgo that particular exploration. It was enough for now to know that Gwinett Linch was not the man he presented himself to be.

But if not . . . then who *was* he?

Matthew closed the book and made sure it was exactly in the position it had been when he'd touched it, as he had the feeling that Linch would know if it had been moved a hair's width. He picked up the wallet, unfolded it, and found inside a small object wrapped in brown cotton cloth and secured with knotted twine. Matthew's interest was further sharpened. The problem, however, was not the undoing of the twine but in the redoing of it. Was it worth the time and effort?

He decided it was.

He carefully untied the cord, noting the structure of the knot. Then he opened the cloth.

It was a piece of jewelry: a circular gold brooch, but missing its clasping pin. Picking up the item, he held it into the sunlight . . . and stared with amazement into the blazing dark blue depths of a sapphire that was near the size of his thumbnail.

The hairs stood up on the back of his neck. He twisted his head around, his eyes widening, but the doorway was empty.

Linch—or the man who called himself Linch—was not there. From where he stood, Matthew could see no one approaching. But he was certain that if Linch found him with this fabulous jewel in his hand, his life would be as short as that of a belly-gashed rat on the bloody blade of that sticker.

Time to go. Time to get out, while he could.

First, though, to wrap the brooch up once more, return it to the wallet and replace the wallet exactly—*exactly*—as it had been. His hands were shaking, as precision was a demanding taskmaster. When the wallet was correctly positioned, Matthew slid the drawer shut and stepped back, wiping his moist palms on his hips.

There were other drawers he might have wished to go through, and he might have desired to inspect the underside of Linch's pallet and further explore the house, but it would be daring Fate. He retreated to the door and was about to shut it when he realized with a shock that he had smeared across the otherwise-pristine floor a small amount of mud from the sodden yard.

He bent down, attempting to get the debris up with his hand. He succeeded somewhat but there was still a telltale streak. No doubt of it: Linch was going to know his sanctum had been violated.

A bell began ringing in the distance. Matthew, still working at removing the stain of his presence by spittle and elbow-grease, realized it was the watchman at the gate signaling an arrival. He had done the best he could do. A little grime on the floor would pall before the gore that would flow if Linch found him here. He stood up, went out, pulled the door shut, and dropped its latch.

As Matthew started walking back along Industry Street, the signal bell ceased. He assumed that the new arrival had been allowed into Fount Royal. Would that it was a doctor whose method was more medicine and less bloodletting!

The sun warmed his face and the breeze blew softly at his back. Yet Matthew had never felt as if he walked a darker or colder path. The sapphire in that brooch had to be worth a small fortune, therefore why was Linch stabbing rats for a living? And why did he go to such effort to disguise his true nature, which appeared to be a preference for order and control, behind a facade of filthiness? It seemed to Matthew that Linch even wished his house to look absolutely decrepit from the outside and had gone to some lengths to make it so.

This pit of deceit was deeper than he'd expected. But what did it have to do with Rachel? Linch was obviously a learned, intelligent man who could write with a quill and read books of theoretical substance; he was also quite well off financially, judging from the sapphire brooch. Why in the world was he acting such a wretched part?

And then there was the singing to consider. Had Violet gone into the Hamilton house or not? If she had, why didn't she notice the disagreeable odor of that dead dog? And if she had not gone in, then what strange power had made her believe she *had?* No, no; it was confusing to even his disciplined mind. The most troubling things about Violet's supposed entrance into the house were her sighting of the white-haired imp and her memory of the six gold buttons on Satan's cloak. Those details she shared with Buckner and Garrick were damnable evidence against Rachel. But what about the ratcatcher singing in that dark room where Matthew had found the bitch and her pups? One might say Violet had imagined it, but then could one not infer that she'd imagined the whole incident? But she could not imagine details that had already been supplied by Buckner and Garrick!

So: if Violet *had* entered the house, why was the ratcatcher singing back there in the dark? And if she had *not* entered the house, why—and how—did she fervently believe she had, and from where did those details of the white-haired imp and the six gold buttons come?

He was thinking so furiously on these questions that he failed to gird his wits for his return engagement with Exodus Jerusalem, but he found that the preacher's tongue had ceased its salivation over orifices. Indeed, Jerusalem, the trio of audience, and the so-called sister and the so-called nephew had departed and were nowhere to be seen. Matthew was soon aware, however, of a *balhaloo* in progress on Harmony Street. He saw four covered wagons and fifteen or twenty townspeople thronged about them. A lean gray-bearded man wearing a green tricorn sat at the reins of the first wagon's team and was engaged in conversation with Bidwell. Matthew also saw Winston standing behind his master; the cur had gone to some effort to shave and dress in clean clothes to make a presentable picture, and he was speaking to a young blond-haired man who appeared to be a companion to the wagon driver.

Matthew approached a farmer standing nearby. "May I ask what's going on?"

"The maskers have come," the man, who had perhaps three teeth in his head, answered.

"Maskers? You mean *actors?*"

"That's right. They come every year and show a play. Weren't expected 'til midsummer, though."

Matthew was amazed at the tenacity of a travelling actors' troupe to negotiate the bone-jarring road between here and Charles Town. He recalled a book on the English theater he'd seen in Bidwell's library, and realized Bidwell had engineered a yearly entertainment—a midsummer festival, so to speak—for his citizenry.

"Now we'll have a fine time!" the farmer said, grinning that cavernous mouth. "A witch-burnin' in the morn and a play in the eve!"

Matthew did not reply. He observed that the gray-bearded man, who appeared to be the troupe's leader, seemed to be asking instructions or directions from Bidwell. The master of Fount Royal conferred for a moment with Winston, whose outward mannerisms gave no inkling that he was anything but a loyal servant. Then, the conference done, Bidwell spoke again to the bearded man and motioned westward along Industry Street. Matthew realized Bidwell must be telling the man where the actors might set up their camp. He would have paid an admission fee to hear the thoughts of Exodus Jerusalem when the preacher learned his neighbors would be thespians. Then again, Jerusalem might make some extra coins by giving the players acting lessons.

Matthew went on his way, avoiding contact with Bidwell and the scoundrel in his shadow. He paused for a short while at the spring, watching the golden sunlight ripple on the water's surface. It entered his mind to go to the gaol and look in on Rachel; in fact, he felt an urgent need to see her, but with a considerable effort of willpower he declined. She had made it clear she did not want his presence there, and as much as it pained him, he must respect her wishes.

He returned to the house, found Mrs. Nettles, and asked if he might have some lunch. After a quick repast of corn soup and buttered bread, he ascended the stairs to his room and settled in a chair by the open window to contemplate his findings and to finish reading through the documents.

He could not shake the feeling, as he read the answers to the questions he had posed, that a revelation was close at hand. He only dimly heard the singing of birds and sensed the warmth of the sun, as all his attention was focused on these responses. There had to be something in here—something small, something overlooked—that might be a key to prove Rachel's innocence. As he read, however, he was distracted by two things: first, the bellringing and braying voice of a public crier announcing the magistrate's decree even in the slave quarters; and second, the sound of an axe chopping timber in the woods between the mansion and the tidewater swamp.

Matthew reached the end of the documents. He had found nothing. He realized he was looking for a shadow that may or may not exist, and to find it—if it was discoverable—he must concentrate on reading between the lines. He ran a weary hand over his face, and began once more from the beginning.

twenty-eight

LANTERNS GLOWED across Fount Royal, and the stars shone down.

Isaac Woodward inhabited a realm that lay somewhere between twilight and Tartarus. The agony of his swollen throat had spread now through his every nerve and fiber, and the act of breathing seemed itself a defiance toward the will of God. His flesh was slick with sweat and sore with fever. Sleep would fall upon him like a heavy shroud, bearing him into blessed insensibility, but while he was awake his vision was as blurred as a candle behind soot-filmed glass. In spite of all these torments, however, the worst was that he was keenly aware of his condition. The deterioration of his body had not yet reached his mind, and thus he had sense enough to realize he was perilously close to the grave's edge.

"Will you help me turn him over?" Dr. Shields asked Matthew and Mrs. Nettles.

Matthew hesitated, his own face pallid in the light from a double candleholder to which was fixed a circle of reflective mirror. "What are you going to do?"

Dr. Shields pushed his spectacles up on the bridge of his nose. "The afflicted blood is pooling in his body," he answered. "It must be moved. Stirred up from its stagnant ponds, if you will."

"Stirred up? How? By more bleeding?"

"No. I think at this point the lancet will not perform its necessary function."

"How, then?" Matthew insisted.

"Mrs. Nettles," the doctor said curtly, "if you'll please assist me?"

"Yes sir." She took hold of Woodward's arm and leg on one side and Shields took the opposite side.

"All right, then. Turn him toward me," Shields instructed. "Magistrate, can you help us at all?"

"I shall try," Woodward whispered.

Together, the doctor and Mrs. Nettles repositioned Woodward so he lay on his stomach. Matthew was torn about whether to give a hand, for he feared what Dr. Shields had decided to do. The magistrate gave a single groan during the procedure, but otherwise bore the pain and indignity like a gentleman.

"Very well." Dr. Shields looked across the bed at Mrs. Nettles. "I shall have to lift his gown up, as his back must be bared."

"What procedure is this?" Matthew asked. "I demand to know!"

"For your information, young man, it is a time-tested procedure to move the blood within the body. It involves heat and a vacuum effect. Mrs. Nettles, would you remove yourself, please? For the sake of decorum?"

"Shall I wait outside?"

"No, that won't be necessary. I shall call if you're needed." He paused while Mrs. Nettles left the room, and when the door was again closed he said to Woodward, "I am going to pull your gown up to your shoulders, Isaac. Whatever help you may give me is much appreciated."

"Yes," came the muffled reply. "Do what is needed."

The doctor went about the business of exposing Woodward's buttocks and back. Matthew saw that at the base of the magistrate's spine was a bed sore about two inches in diameter, bright red at its center and outlined with yellow infection. A second, smaller, but no less malignant sore had opened on the back of Woodward's right thigh.

Dr. Shields opened his bag, brought out a pair of supple deer-skin gloves, and began to put them on. "If your stomach is weak," he said quietly to Matthew, "you should follow Mrs. Nettles. I need no further complications."

"My stomach is fine," Matthew lied. "What . . . is the procedure?"

The doctor reached into the bag again and brought out a small glass sphere, its surface marred only by a circular opening with a pronounced curved rim. The rim, Matthew saw with sickened fascination, had been discolored dark brown by the application of fire. "As I said before . . . heat and vacuum." From the pocket of his tan waistcoat he produced the fragrant piece of sassafras root, which he deftly pushed to the magistrate's lips. "Isaac, there will be some pain involved, and we wish your tongue not to be injured." Woodward accepted the tongue-guard and sank his teeth into the accustomed grooves. "Young man, will you hold the candles, please?"

Matthew picked up the double candlestick from the table beside Woodward's bed. Dr. Shields leaned forward and stroked the sphere's rim from one flame to the other in a circular motion, all the time staring into Matthew's eyes in order to gauge his nerves. As he continued to heat the rim, Shields said, "Magistrate, I am going to apply a blister cup to your back. The first of six. I regret the sensation, but the afflicted blood will be caused to rise to the surface from the internal organs and that is our purpose. Are you ready, sir?"

Woodward nodded, his eyes squeezed tightly shut. Shields held the cup's opening directly over the flames for perhaps five seconds. Then, rapidly and without hesitation, he pressed the hot glass rim down upon Woodward's white flesh a few inches upward from the virulent bedsore.

There was a small noise—a snake's hiss, perhaps—and the cup clamped tightly as the heated air within compressed itself. An instant after the hideous contact was made, Woodward cried out around the sassafras root and his body shivered in a spasm of pure, animal pain.

"Steady," Shields said, speaking to both the magistrate and his clerk. "Let nature do its work."

Matthew could see that already the flesh caught within the blister cup was swelling and reddening. Dr. Shields had brought a second cup from his bag, and again let the flames lick its cruel rim. After the procedure of heating the air inside the cup, the glass was pressed to Woodward's back with predictable and—at least to Matthew—spine-crawling result.

By the time the third cup was affixed, the flesh within the first had gone through the stages of red to scarlet and now was blood-gorged and turning brown like a maliferous poison mushroom.

Shields had the fourth cup in his gloved hand. He offered it to the candle flames. "We shall see a play directly, I understand," he said, his voice divorced from his actions. "The citizens do enjoy the maskers every year."

Matthew didn't answer. He was watching the first brown mushroom of flesh becoming still darker, and the other two following the path of swollen discoloration.

"Usually," the doctor went on, "they don't arrive until the middle of July or so. I understand from Mr. Brightman—he's the leader of the company—that two towns they customarily play in were decimated by sickness, and a third had vanished altogether. That accounts for their early arrival this year. It's a thing to be thankful for, though, because we need a pleasant diversion." He pressed the fourth blister cup onto Woodward's back, and the magistrate trembled but held back a moan. "My wife and I used to enjoy the theater in Boston," Shields said as he prepared the fifth implement. "A play in the afternoon . . . a beaker of wine . . . a concert on the Commons." He smiled faintly. "Those were wonderful times."

Matthew had recovered his composure enough to ask the question that at this point naturally presented itself. "Why did you leave Boston?"

The doctor waited until the fifth cup was attached before he replied. "Well . . . let us say I needed a challenge. Or perhaps . . . there was something I wished to accomplish."

"And have you? Accomplished it, I mean?"

Shields stared at the rim of the sixth cup as he moved it between the flames, and Matthew saw the fire reflected in his spectacles. "No," he said. "Not yet."

"This involves Fount Royal, I presume? And your infirmary?"

"It involves . . . what it involves." Shields glanced quickly into Matthew's eyes and then away again. "You *do* have a fetish for questions, don't you?"

If this remark was designed to seal Matthew's mouth and turn aside his curiosity, it had the opposite effect. "Only for questions that go unanswered."

"Touché," the doctor said, and he pressed the sixth blister cup firmly onto Woodward's back. Again the magistrate trembled with pain but was steadfastly silent. "All right, then: I left Boston because my practise was failing there. The city has a glut of doctors, as well as lawyers and ministers. There must be a dozen physicians alone, not to mention the herbalists and faith-healers! So I decided that for a space of time I would leave Boston—and my wife, whose sewing enterprise is actually doing quite well—and offer my services elsewhere."

"Fount Royal is a long distance from Boston," Matthew said.

"Oh, I didn't come directly here. I lived for a month in New York, spent a summer in Philadelphia, and lived in other smaller places. I always seemed to be heading southward." He began peeling off his deerskin gloves. "You may put the candles down now."

Matthew returned the double candlestick to the table. He had seen—though he certainly didn't let his eyes linger on the sight, or his imagination linger on what the sensation must be—that the flesh gripped by the first two cups had become hideous, blood-swollen ebony blisters. The others were following the gruesome pattern.

"We shall let the blood rise for a time." Dr. Shields put the gloves into his bag. "This procedure breaks up the stagnant pools within his body, you see."

Matthew saw nothing but grotesque swellings. He dared not dwell on what pressures were inflicted within the magistrate's suffering bones. To keep his mind from wandering in that painful direction, he asked, "Do you plan on staying in Fount Royal very much longer?"

"No, I don't think so. Bidwell pays me a fee, and he has certainly built a fine infirmary for my use, but . . . I do miss my wife. And Boston, too. So as soon as the town is progressing again, the population healthy and growing, I shall seek to find a replacement for myself."

"And what then would be the accomplishment you crave, sir?"

Dr. Shields cocked his head to one side, a hint of a smile on his mouth but his owlish eyes stony. "You're a regular goat amid a briar patch, aren't you?"

"I pride myself on being persistent, if that's your meaning."

"No, that is *not* my meaning, but I'll answer that rather meddlesome question in spite of my reluctance to add pine knots to your fire. My accomplishment—my *hoped-for* accomplishment, that is—would be twofold: one, to aid in the construction of a settlement that would grow into a city; and two, to have my name forevermore on the title of Fount Royal's infirmary. I plan on remaining here long enough to see both those things come to pass." He reached out and gently grasped the first blister cup between thumb and forefinger, checking its suction. "The influence of Rachel Howarth," he said, "was an unfortunate interruption in the forward motion of Fount Royal. But as soon as her ashes are buried—or scattered or whatever Bidwell's going to do with them—we shall put an end to our calamities. As the weather has turned for the better, the swamp vapors have been banished. Soon we shall see an increase in the population, both by people coming in from elsewhere and by healthy babies being born. Within a year, I think Fount Royal will be back to where it was before this ugly incident ever happened. I shall do my best to aid that growth, leave my mark and name for posterity, and return to Boston and my wife. *And,* of course, the comfort and culture of the city."

"Admirable aims," Matthew said. "I expect having your name on the mast of an infirmary would help your standing in Boston, as well."

"It would. A letter from Bidwell stating that fact and his appreciation for my services could secure me a place in a medical partnership that ordinarily I might be denied."

Matthew was about to ask if Bidwell knew what the doctor intended when there was a knock at the door. Shields said, "Who is it, please?"

"Nicholas," came the reply. "I wanted to look in on the magistrate."

Instantly Matthew sensed a change in Dr. Shields's demeanor. It was nothing radical, but remarkable nevertheless. The doctor's face seemed to tighten; indeed, his entire body went taut as if an unseen hand had gripped him around the back of his neck. When Shields answered, even his voice had sharpened. "The magistrate is indisposed at the moment."

"Oh . . . well, then. I'll return later."

"Wait!" Woodward had removed the sassafras root from his mouth, and was whispering in Matthew's direction. "Ask Mr. Paine to come in, please."

Matthew went to the door and stopped Paine before he reached the stairs. When Paine entered the room, Matthew watched the doctor's face and saw that Shields refused to even cast a glance at his fellow citizen.

"How is he?" Paine inquired, standing at the door.

"As I said, indisposed," Shields replied, with a distinct chill. "You can see for yourself."

Paine flinched a little at the sight of the six glass cups and the ebony blisters they had drawn, but he came around to Matthew's side of the bed for a view of the magistrate's face. "Good evening," he said, with as much of a smile as he could summon. "I see . . . Dr. Shields is taking care of you. How are you feeling?"

"I have felt . . . much superior," Woodward said.

"I'm sure." Paine's smile faltered. "I wanted to tell you . . . that I approve heartily of your decree, sir. Also that your efforts—and the efforts of your clerk, of course—have been nothing short of commendable."

"My thanks," Woodward replied, his eyes heavy-lidded.

"Might I get you anything?"

"You might *leave,*" Shields said. "You're taxing him."

"Oh. I'm sorry. I don't wish to do any harm."

"No harm." Woodward gasped for a breath, a green crust around his nostrils. "I appreciate . . . your taking . . . time and effort . . . to come and see me."

"I also wanted to tell you, sir, that the stake has been cut. I understand Mr. Bidwell hasn't yet decided where the execution shall take place, but the likelihood is in one of the unused fields on Industry Street."

"Yes." Woodward swallowed thickly. "That would do."

Shields grasped the first blister cup and popped it free. Woodward winced and bit his lower lip. "I think you should depart now," the doctor said to Paine. "Unless you'd like to give a hand in this procedure?"

"Uh . . . yes, I'd best be going." Paine, for all his manly experiences, appeared to Matthew to be a little green around the gills. "Magistrate, I'll look in on you at a later time." He glanced at Matthew with a pained expression of commiseration and took a step toward the door.

"Mr. Paine?" Woodward whispered. "Please . . . may I ask you something?"

"Yes, surely." Paine returned to the bedside and stood close, leaning toward the magistrate, the better to hear him clearly.

Shields removed the second blister cup. Again Woodward winced, and now his eyes were wet. He said, "We share . . . a commonality."

"We do, sir?"

"Your wife. Died of fits, I understand. I wanted you to

know . . . my son . . . perished of fits . . . suffered by the plague. Was your wife . . . also plague-stricken?"

Dr. Shields's hand had seized the third blister cup, but had not yet removed it.

Nicholas Paine stared into Woodward's face. Matthew saw a pulse beating at Paine's temple. "I fear you're mistaken, sir," Paine said, in a strangely hollow voice. "I have never been married."

"Dr. Shields told me," Woodward went on, with an effort. "I know . . . such things are difficult to speak of. Believe me, I do know."

"Dr. Shields," Paine repeated, "told you."

"Yes. That she suffered fits until she died. And that . . . possibly it was the plague."

Shields removed the third cup and placed it almost noiselessly into his bag.

Paine licked his lower lip. "I'm sorry," he said, "but I fear Dr. Shields is just as mistaken as—" He chose that instant to look into the doctor's face, and Matthew was a witness to what next occurred.

Something passed between Paine and Shields. It was something intangible, yet absolutely horrific. For the briefest of seconds Matthew saw the doctor's eyes blaze with a hatred that defied all reason and logic, and Paine actually drew back as if from a threatening physical presence. Matthew also realized that he'd witnessed very little direct communication between Dr. Shields and Paine. It dawned on Matthew that it was the doctor who preferred to keep his distance from Paine, yet the feeling had been so well disguised that Paine might not even have been aware of a void between them.

However, now an ugly animosity was clearly revealed if only for that fleeting second. Paine perhaps recognized it for the first time, and his mouth opened as if he might exclaim or protest against it. Yet in the next heartbeat Paine's face froze as tightly as the doctor's and whatever he might have said remained unborn.

Shields held the dark bond between them for only a second or two longer, and then he very calmly returned his attention to his patient. He removed the fourth blister cup, and into the bag it went.

Matthew looked questioningly at Paine, but the other man had blanched and would not meet his gaze. Matthew realized a piece of information had been delivered from Dr. Shields to Paine in that brief hateful glare, and whatever it was had almost buckled Paine's knees.

"My wife," Paine's voice was choked with emotion. "My wife."

"My son . . . died," Woodward said, oblivious to the drama. "Fits. From the plague. Pardon my asking you . . . but I wished you to know . . . you were not alone in your grief."

"Grief," Paine repeated. Shadows lay in his eye sockets, and his face appeared to have become more gaunt and aged by five years in as many seconds. "Yes," he said quietly. "Grief."

Dr. Shields pulled the fifth blister cup free, none too gently, and Woodward winced.

"I should . . . tell you about my wife," Paine offered, his face turned toward the window. "She did perish from fits. But not caused by the plague. No." He shook his head. "Hunger was the killer. Hunger . . . and crushing despair. We were very young, you see. Very poor. We had a baby girl who was sick, as well. And I was sick in the mind . . . and very desperate."

No one spoke. Even the magistrate, in his cloudy realm on the edge of delirium, realized Paine had dropped his mask of sturdy self-control and was revealing heart's blood and fractured bones.

"I think I understand this," Paine said, though that strange remark itself was a puzzle to Matthew. "I am . . . quite overcome . . . but I must tell you . . . all of you . . . that I never intended . . . the result of what happened. As I said, I was young . . . I was brash, and I was frightened. My wife and my child needed food and medicine. I had nothing . . . but an ability I had learned from hunting cruel and violent men." He was silent for a time, during which Dr. Shields stared intently at the sixth blister cup but made no attempt at removing it.

"I did not fire the first shot," Paine went on, his voice tired and heavy. "I was first struck myself. In the leg. But you must know that already. Something I had been taught by the older men . . . during my career at sea . . . was that once a weapon— pistol or rapier—was aimed at you, you fired or slashed back with grievous intent. That was our creed, and it served to keep us— most of us—among the living. It was a natural reaction, learned by watching other men die wallowing in their own blood. That was why I could not—*could* not—spare Quentin Summers in our duel. How can a man be taught the ways of a wolf and then live among sheep? Especially . . . when there is hunger and need involved . . . and the specter of death knocking at the door."

Matthew's curiosity had ignited from a flame to a bonfire and he yearned to ask Paine exactly what he was talking about, but something of the moment seemed almost sacred in its self-revelation, in its picture of a proud man giving up his pride to the overwhelming desire for confession and—perhaps—sanctuary from past misdeeds. Therefore he felt it small of himself to speak and break this spell of soul-broaching.

Paine walked to the window and looked out over the lantern-spangled town. On Industry Street, two fires some distance apart marked the camps of Exodus Jerusalem and the newly arrived maskers. Through the warm night wafted the faint sound of laughter and the trilling of a recorder from Van Gundy's tavern. "My compliments," Paine said, his face still averted. "I presume my wound left a trail. Is that what you followed?"

Dr. Shields at last freed the ebony flesh under the sixth blister cup. He put the implement into his bag, followed by the sassafras root. Then, slowly and methodically, he began to close the bag by its buttons and loops.

"Are you not going to answer me?" Paine asked. "Or is this a torture by silence?"

"I think," the doctor said with grit in his voice, "that the time has come for you to depart."

"Depart? What game are you playing at?"

"No game. I assure you . . . no game." Shields pressed a finger to one of the six horrid black swellings that protruded from Woodward's back. "Ah, yes. Quite firm now. We have drawn the stagnant blood upward from the organs, you see?" He glanced at Matthew, then away. "This procedure has a cleansing effect, and we should see some improvement in the magistrate's condition by morning."

"And if not?" Matthew had to ask.

"If not . . . then there is the next step."

"Which is?"

"Again applying the cups," Shields said, "and then bleeding the blisters." Matthew instantly regretted his inquiry. The thought of those swellings being burst by a lancet was almost too much to consider.

Shields lowered the magistrate's gown. "You should endeavor to sleep on your stomach tonight, Isaac. I know your position is less than comfortable, but I'm afraid it's necessary."

"I shall endure it," Woodward rasped, drifting even now toward sleep again.

"Good. I'll have Mrs. Nettles send a servant with a cold compress for your fever. In the morning we shall—"

"Shields, what do you want of me?" Paine interrupted, this time daring to face the other man. Moisture glistened on Paine's forehead and cheeks.

The doctor lifted his eyebrows. "I've already told you, sir. I wish you to *depart.*"

"Are you going to hold this over my head for the rest of my life?"

Shields did not answer, but stared fixedly through his spectacle lenses at his antagonist. So damning was this wordless accusation that Paine was forced at length to drop his gaze to the floorboards. Then, abruptly, Paine turned toward the door and slinked out in the manner of the wolf he had proclaimed himself to be—yet, however, a wolf whose tail had been shorn off by an unexpected blade.

In the wake of Paine's departure, Dr. Shields let free a breath he'd been hoarding. "Well," he said, and behind the lenses his magnified eyes appeared stunned by the rapid turn of events. He blinked slowly several times, as if clearing his mind as well as his vision. "What was I saying? Oh . . . in the morning we shall administer a colonic and apply fresh plasters. Then we shall proceed as necessary." He took a handkerchief from inside his jacket and mopped his brow. "Is it hot in here to you?"

"No, sir," Matthew said. "The temperature seems very regular." He now saw his opportunity. "May I ask what your exchange with Mr. Paine concerned?"

"I will have Mrs. Nettles look in on the magistrate from time to time tonight," the doctor said. "You might keep yourself aware, also. I will be ready to come if any emergency presents itself." He placed a reassuring hand on Woodward's shoulder. "I'm going to leave now, Isaac. Just rest and be of good spirits. Tomorrow we might have you up and walking for some exercise." From the magistrate there was no reply, because he had already fallen asleep.

"Good night," Shields said to Matthew and, taking his bag with him, he left the bedchamber.

Matthew was after him like a shot. "One moment, sir!" he called in the hallway, but to be such a small-framed man Dr. Shields suddenly had the stride of a racehorse. Just before the doctor reached the stairs, Matthew said, "If you refuse to tell me, I shall find out on my own."

This statement caused an immediate reaction. Dr. Shields halted in his tracks, spun around with furious speed, and advanced on Matthew as if to strike the clerk a blow. By the Mars-orange glow of the hallway's lantern, Shields's face was a hellish, sweating rictus with bared and clenched teeth, his eyes drawn into narrow slits that made him appear a stranger to the man Matthew had seen only seconds before. To compound this transformation, Shields gripped the front of Matthew's shirt with one hand and forced his back solidly and painfully into the wall.

"You *listen!*" Shields hissed. His hand tightened, twisting the fabric it clenched. "You do not—I repeat, do *not*—have the right to interfere in my business. What transpired between Paine and myself tonight will remain just that: between him and me. No one else. Certainly not *you*. Do you understand me, boy?" Shields gave Matthew a violent shake to underscore his vehemence. *"Answer!"*

In spite of the fact that he towered over the doctor, Matthew was stricken with fright. "Yes, sir," Matthew said. "I do understand."

"You'd better, or by God you'll wish you had!" Shields held Matthew pressed up against the wall for a few seconds longer— an eternity to Matthew—and then the doctor's hand left his shirt. Without a further word, Shields walked away and descended the stairs.

Matthew was left severely confused and no less severely scared. The doctor might have been a brother to Will Shawcombe, for all that rough treatment. As he straightened his shirt and tried to steady his nerves, Matthew realized something truly treacherous was going on between Shields and Paine; indeed, the violence induced from Shields spoke volumes about the doctor's mental state. What had all that been, about wounds and weapons and Paine's deceased wife? *I presume my wound left a trail,* Paine had said. *Is that what you followed?*

Whatever the problem was, it had to do with Paine's past— which seemed more infamous now than ever. But Matthew was faced with so many puzzles to untangle concerning Rachel's plight—and such a short time to untangle them—that this new situation seemed more of a sideshow than a compelling attraction. He didn't believe the strife between the two men had anything to do with Rachel, whereas, for instance, Gwinett Linch's voice singing in the darkness of the Hamilton house while Satan laid an ultimatum at the feet of Violet Adams most certainly did.

Therefore, though he might fervently desire to know more about the relationship he'd witnessed tonight, he felt pressed by time to keep his focus on proving Rachel's innocence and let old griefs fall by the wayside. For now, at least.

He looked in once more on the magistrate and waited for the servant girl to come with the cold compress. Matthew thanked her, bade her go, and himself applied the compress—a water-soaked cotton cloth, to be accurate—to the sleeping man's face and on the back of his neck where the fever seemed most heated. Afterward, Matthew went downstairs and found Mrs. Nettles closing the shutters for the night. He asked if he might have a pot of tea and some biscuits, and was soon thereafter in possession of a tray with both. He took the moment to inquire of Mrs. Nettles what she knew about the ratcatcher, but she could supply nothing other than the facts that Linch kept to himself, and though he was sorely needed he was something of a pariah because of the nature of his craft. Matthew also asked—in a most casual way—if Mrs. Nettles had ever detected a tension between Dr. Shields and Nicholas Paine, or knew of anything that might be a cause of trouble in their dealings with each other.

Mrs. Nettles answered that she knew of no trouble, but that she was aware of a certain chill emanating from the good doctor regarding Mr. Paine. By contrast, she said, Dr. Shields acted warmly toward Mr. Winston and Mr. Bidwell, but it was apparent to her that the doctor would rather not share the same room in which Mr. Paine was present. It was nothing so dramatic that anyone else might notice, but in her opinion Dr. Shields had a marked distaste for the man.

"Thank you," Matthew said. "Oh . . . one more thing. Who arrived first in Fount Royal? Mr. Paine or the doctor?"

"Mr. Paine did," she replied. "It was . . . oh, more'n a month or two a'fore Dr. Shields came." She knew there must be a valid reason for these questions. "Does this concern Rachel Howarth?"

"No, I don't believe so. It's only an observation I needed verified."

"Oh, I swan it's more'n that!" She offered him a sly smile. "You canna' leave a thread undone, can ya?"

"I might find employment as a weaver of rugs, if that's what you mean."

"Ha!" She gave a rough bark of a laugh. "Yes, I 'spect you

might!" However, her smile vanished and her countenance darkened until she had reached her customary grim composure. "It's all up for Madam Howarth then, is that the basket?"

"The lid has not yet been closed," Matthew said.

"Meanin' what?"

"Meaning that the execution flame has not yet been lighted . . . and that I have some reading to do. Excuse me and good night." Matthew took his tray of tea and biscuits upstairs to his room, where he poured himself a cup and sat down next to the open window, his lantern burning on its sill. For the third time he took the documents from their protective box and began reading through them, starting at the beginning.

By now he might have recited the testimony by heart. Still he felt—or, rather, ardently *hoped*—that something in the thicket of words might leap out at him like a directional signpost, signaling the next step in his exploration. He drank from his cup of tea and chewed on a biscuit. Bidwell had taken his own repast at Van Gundy's tavern, as Matthew had discovered from Dr. Shields, who had earlier seen Bidwell hoisting a tankard with Winston and several other men in a general air of merry celebration.

He finished—for the third time—Jeremiah Buckner's account and paused to rub his eyes. He felt in need of a tankard himself, yet strong drink would weaken his resolve and blur his sight. Oh, for a night of pure sleep untouched by the thought of Rachel afire on the stake!

Or even a night untouched by the thought of Rachel. Period.

He recalled what the magistrate had said: *Helping her. Finding the truth. Being of service. Whatever and however you choose to phrase it . . . Rachel Howarth is your nightbird, Matthew.* Perhaps the magistrate was right, but not in the sinister way he had meant it.

Matthew closed his eyes for a moment to rest them. Then he opened them, drank some more tea to fortify himself, and continued his reading. Now he was venturing into the testimony of Elias Garrick, and the man's recollection of the night he had awakened and— *Wait,* he thought. *That was odd.*

He read again over the section he had just digested. *That night I was feelin' poorly, and I waked up to go outside and spew what was makin' me ill. It was silent. Everythin' was silent, like the whole world was afeared to breathe.*

Matthew sat up from his slouched position in the chair. He reached out and pulled the lantern nearer. Then he turned back through the pages until he found the beginning of Jeremiah Buckner's testimony.

And there it was.

Me and Patience went to bed just like usual that night. She put out the lamp. Then . . . I don't know how long it was later . . . I heard my name spoke. I opened my eyes. Everythin' was dark, and silent. I waited, a'listenin'. Just silent, like there was nothin' else in the whole world makin' a sound but my breathin'. Then . . . I heard my name spoke again, and I looked at the foot of the bed and seen her.

With an eager hand, Matthew turned to the beginning of Violet Adams's testimony, as she recounted entering the Hamilton house. He put a finger on the line of importance, his heart starting to slam hard in his chest.

There wasn't nary a noise. It was silent, like . . . it was just me breathin' and that was the only sound.

Three witnesses.

Three testimonies.

But the same word: *silent.*

And that about breathing being the only sound . . . what possible coincidence could that be? Also the repeated phrase *whole world* by both Buckner and Garrick . . . it defied reason to think both men would speak the exact same words.

Unless . . . without knowing it . . . all three of the witnesses had been told what to say.

Matthew felt a chill skitter up his spine. The hairs on the back of his neck moved. He realized he had just had a glimpse of the shadow he sought.

It was a terrifying realization. Because the shadow was larger and darker and more strangely powerful than he had dared believe. The shadow had been standing behind Jeremiah Buckner,

Elias Garrick, and Violet Adams there in the gaol, all the time they'd been giving their accounts.

"My God," Matthew whispered, his eyes wide. Because he had realized the shadow was in their minds, directing their words, emotions, and counterfeit memories. The three witnesses were no more than flesh-and-blood poppets, constructed by the hand of an evil beyond Matthew's imagining.

One hand. The same hand. A hand that sewed six gold buttons on a Satanic cloak. That created a white-haired imp, a leathery lizard-like manbeast, and a bizarre creature that had a male penis and female breasts. The same hand had created these scenes of sickening depravity, had painted them on the very air to display to Buckner, Garrick, Violet, and probably other citizens, who had fled for their sanity. For that's what the scenes were: air-paintings. Or, rather, paintings that came to life inside the minds that were spelled to accept them as truth.

That was why Buckner could not recall where he'd put his cane, which he was unable to get around without, or whether he had worn a coat outside in the cold February air, or whether he had taken his shoes off when he'd climbed back into bed.

That was why Garrick could not recall what clothes he had worn outside to go spew, or whether he had put on shoes or boots, or what pattern the six gold buttons were arranged in though he clearly noted their number.

That was why Violet Adams had not noticed the reek of a decaying dog's carcass, or the fact that the Hamilton house was overrun by canines.

Not one of the three witnesses had actually witnessed anything but these mental paintings, constructed by a shadowy hand that had emphasized some details for the purpose of shock and disgust—the kind of details that would make for damning court testimony—but had omitted other details of a more commonplace nature.

Except for the pattern of gold buttons on the cloak, Matthew thought. That was where the shadowy hand had been . . . the only word Matthew could think of was *precious*.

The hand had made the oversight of not detailing the arrangement of buttons for Buckner or Garrick, but had attempted to make up for it by providing that detail to Violet, who collected buttons and therefore might be more observant as to their pattern.

It occurred to Matthew that the shadowy hand might have placed the poppets under the floor of Rachel's house, and then painted the dream by which Cara Grunewald had seen an item of importance hidden there. He would have liked to have spoken to Madam Grunewald, to learn if, when she'd gone to sleep that night, everything was silent, as if the whole world was feared to breathe.

Matthew turned through the pages to another point he recalled of Garrick's account. It was when he had challenged Garrick concerning the arrangement of the six gold buttons, and had pressed his question to the man's obviously confused agitation.

Garrick's response had been a whispered *It was a silent town. Silent. The whole world, afeared to breathe.*

Matthew realized that what he had heard was Garrick repeating a phrase supplied to him by the owner of the shadowy hand. Garrick had been unable to answer the question, and had unwittingly fixed on that somnambulistic phrase in a moment of great stress because it was one of the clearest things he *did* remember.

And now there was the question of Linch's voice, singing in the dark at the Hamilton house. If Violet had not actually set foot in the house, how could she have heard the ratcatcher singing his grotesque ditty from the back room?

Matthew put aside the documents and finished his cup of tea, staring out the window toward the slaves' quarters and the darkness beyond. He might have decided that Violet had been dreaming the involvement of Linch as well as the rest of it, but his own exploration of Linch's dwelling told Matthew the ratcatcher had concealed the secrets of his identity behind a cleverly constructed front.

Linch was literate and obviously cunning. Was it possible his was the shadowy hand that had guided the three witnesses?

But *why?* And *how?* By what form of sorcery had Linch—or whomever—caused three individuals to see similar apparitions and believe without a doubt they had been viewing reality? It had to be black magic, of a sort. Not the kind popularly associated with Satan, but the kind that evolves from a corrupt and twisted human mentality. But also a mentality that was well ordered and precise, as Linch's must be.

Matthew couldn't understand how Linch, or anyone else, might have done it.

Such a thing—the guiding of three minds toward a common fiction—seemed to be absolutely impossible. Nevertheless, Matthew was certain that was exactly what had occurred.

And what of the question of motive? Why go to such lengths—and such incredible risk—to paint Rachel as being a servant of the Devil? It had to be much more than simply covering the tracks that led away from the murders of Reverend Grove and Daniel Howarth. In fact, those killings seemed to Matthew to have been committed to add weight of suspicion upon Rachel.

So the point was to create a witch, Matthew thought. Rachel was already disliked by many of the citizens before Grove was murdered. Her dark beauty could not have aided her popularity among the other women, and her Portuguese heritage reminded the men of how close the Spanish territory lay to their farmland. She had a tongue, a willful spirit, and courage that ruffled the feathers of the church-guarding hens. Therefore Rachel was from the beginning a perfect candidate.

Matthew chewed on another biscuit. He looked at the stars that glittered above the ocean, and at the candle that burned within the lantern's glass. The light of understanding was what he sought, yet it was a difficult illumination to unveil.

Why create a witch? What possible reason was there for it? To hurt Bidwell? Was all this engineered by the jealous ravens of Charles Town to destroy Fount Royal before it could grow to rivalry?

If that were so, wouldn't Winston have known Rachel was innocent? Or had the Charles Town elders planted another traitor or two within Fount Royal's midst and for the sake of security not informed Winston?

And then there was the question of the mysterious surveyor, and what might lie in the mud at the fount's bottom. It struck him that tomorrow night—very late, after the last lantern had gone out and the final celebrants swept from Van Gundy's tavern—he might try his strength at some underwater swimming.

Though the tea was certainly sturdy enough, Matthew still felt weariness pulling at him. It was his mind that needed rest just as much—if not more so—than his body. He needed to climb into bed, sleep until dawn, and awaken ready for a fresh appraisal of what he suspected, what he knew, and what he had yet to learn.

Matthew relieved himself at the chamberpot, then undressed and lay down upon the bed. He left the lantern burning, as his realization of the shadowy hand's strange and compelling power had made him somewhat less than easy with the dark.

He tossed and turned in the first bout of what would be a nightlong grappling with the hot gearwheels of his brain. At last, though, he relaxed enough to sleep for a time, and except for the occasional barking of a mongrel the town was ruled by silence.

twenty-nine

UPON AWAKENING AT FIRST LIGHT and the rooster chorale, Matthew hurriedly pulled on his breeches and crossed the hall to look in on the magistrate.

Woodward was still sleeping on his stomach, his breathing harsh but steady. Matthew was curious as to the state of the blisters on Woodward's back, and so carefully lifted the gown to view them.

Instantly he wished he had not. The blisters had flattened into ugly ebony bruises surrounded by circles of mottled flesh. Streaks of red ran underneath the skin, attesting to the pressures that the magistrate's body had endured. It occurred to Matthew that this procedure of heat and blister cups was more suited for the torture chamber than the sickbed. He lowered Woodward's gown again, then dipped a cloth into the bowl of water that sat atop the dresser and spent a moment wiping away the green crust that had accumulated around the magistrate's nostrils. The magistrate's face was damp and swollen, the fever radiating from him like the calidity from a bellows-coaxed blaze.

"What . . ." Woodward whispered, his eyelids fluttering. "What is the day?"

"Thursday, sir."

"I must . . . get up . . . and about. Can you help me?"

"I don't think it's wise to get up quite yet, sir. Possibly later in the day."

"Nonsense. I . . . shall miss court . . . if I don't get up." Matthew felt something as keen as an icy dagger pierce his guts. "They . . . already think me . . . lax in my duties," Woodward continued. "They think . . . I am more fond . . . of the rumpot . . . than the gavel. Yes, I saw Mendenhall yesterday. That peacock. Laughing at me . . . behind his hand. What day is it, did you say?"

"Thursday." Matthew's voice was hushed.

"I . . . have a larceny trial to hear. This morning. Where are my boots?"

"Sir?" Matthew said. "I fear . . . that court has been postponed for the day."

Woodward was quiet. Then, "Postponed?"

"Yes, sir. The weather being so bad." Even as he spoke it, he could hear birds singing in the trees around the spring.

"Ahhhhh, the weather," Woodward whispered. His eyes had never fully opened, but remained hidden behind the fever-inflamed lids. "Then I shall stay indoors today," he said. "Shall light a fire . . . drink a hot rum."

"Yes, sir, I think that would be best."

Woodward said something that was more gibberish than language, as if he were losing control over even his speech, but then he spoke clearly enough for Matthew to make out the words, "My back. Pains me."

"It will be well soon. You must lie still and rest."

"A bottle," Woodward said, drowsing off once more. "Will you . . . bring me a bottle?"

"I shall, yes, sir." It seemed a small but helpful untruth. The magistrate's eyelids had ceased their war against gravity and he lay quiet again, his breathing returned to its accustomed rasp like that of a rusted hinge being slowly worked back and forth.

Matthew finished his task of carefully cleaning Woodward's nostrils. When he left the room, he was stricken in the middle of the hallway by what might have been a crushing weight suddenly applied to his shoulders. At the same time, the icy dagger that had entered his entrails seemed to twist toward his heart. He stood short of his own door, one hand clasped to his mouth and above it his eyes wide and brimming with tears.

He was trembling, and wished to make it cease but could not. A sensation of utter powerlessness had come upon him, a sensation of being a leaf stripped from a tree in a high wind and blown through a terrifying altitude of lightning and rain.

He had realized that every day—every *hour*—brought the magistrate closer to death. It was not now a question of whether the magistrate *might* die, but *when*. Matthew was sure this bleeding-and-blistering treatment was not sufficient; indeed, he doubted the ability of Dr. Shields to heal a man who was only half as ill as the magistrate. If Woodward could be gotten to Charles Town, to the attentions of the urban doctors who commanded fully equipped infirmaries and a benefit of medicines, then there was a chance—be it however diminished—that he might be cured of this savage malady.

Yet Matthew knew that no one here would volunteer to carry Woodward the long distance to Charles Town, especially if it meant denigrating the abilities of their own doctor. If he undertook to convey Woodward there, he would lose at the very least two vital days from his investigation, and by the time he returned here Rachel would likely be a black smudge on a charred stake. Woodward might not be his father, it was true, but the man had served in as near that capacity as was humanly possible, saving him from the drear almshouse and setting him on a path of purpose. Did he not, then, owe the magistrate at least *something?*

He might persuade Winston to take Woodward to Charles Town, under threat of revealing the incriminating bucket, but should such a disloyal dog be trusted with a man's life? Winston could as well leave his charge on the side of the road for the animals to eat, and never return.

No, not Winston. But . . . would Nicholas Paine be willing to do the job?

It was a spark, but it might kindle a flame. Matthew pulled himself together, wiped his eyes clear with the back of his hand,

and continued into his room. There he shaved, cleaned his teeth, and finished dressing. Downstairs, he found Bidwell clad in a lime-green suit at the bountiful breakfast table, the foxtail of his wig tied with an emerald-hued ribbon.

"Sit down, sit down!" Bidwell offered, his mood jovial because the day promised to be as sunwarmed and beautiful as the one before. "Come have breakfast, but please let us announce a truce on the subject of theories."

"I haven't time for breakfast," Matthew said. "I am on my way to—"

"Oh, of *course* you have time! Come sit down and at least eat a blood sausage!" Bidwell indicated the platter heaped with sausages, but their color was so similar to the ebon collapsed blisters on the magistrate's back that Matthew couldn't have swallowed one if it had been shot into his throat from a pistol. "Or, here, have a pickled melon!"

"No, thank you. I am on my way to see Mr. Paine. Can you tell me where he lives?"

"To see Nicholas? Why?" Bidwell speared a segment of pickled melon with his knife and slid it into his mouth.

"Some business I wish to discuss."

"What business?" Bidwell now was truly suspicious. "Any business you have with him is also business with me."

"All right, then!" Matthew had reached his zenith of frustration. "I wish to ask him to take the magistrate to Charles Town! I want him placed in an infirmary there!"

Bidwell cut a blood sausage in two and chewed thoughtfully on half of it. "So you don't trust Dr. Shields's method of treatment? Is that what you're saying?"

"It is."

"I'll have you know," and here Bidwell aimed his knife at Matthew, "that Ben is just as good a doctor as any of those quacks in Charles Town." He frowned, knowing that hadn't come out as he'd intended. "I mean to say, he's an *able* practitioner. Without his treatment, I'll grant you that the magistrate would have been deceased days ago!"

"It's the days hence I'm concerned about. The magistrate is showing no improvement at all. Just now he was speaking to me in delirium!"

Bidwell pushed his knife into the second half of sausage and guided the greasy black thing into his mouth. "You should by all means be on your way, then," he said as he chewed. "Not to see Nicholas, but to visit the witch."

"Why should I wish to do that?"

"Well, isn't it *obvious?* One day after the decree is delivered, and the magistrate lies at death's door? Your skirt has placed a curse on him, boy!"

"That's nonsense!" Matthew said. "The magistrate's condition has worsened because of this excessive bloodletting! And also because he was required to sit in that cold gaol for hours when he should have been in bed resting!"

"Oh, ho! His sickness is now *my* fault, is that it? You cast about for blame from everyone except that to whom it rightly belongs! Besides . . . if *you* hadn't pulled your stunt with Seth Hazelton, the witch's case would have been heard in the public meetinghouse—which has a very comfortable hearth, I might add. So if you wish to blame anyone, go speak to a mirror!"

"All I wish to do is find the house of Nicholas Paine," Matthew said, his cheeks flushed and his teeth gritted. "I don't care to argue with you, for that is like trying to outbray a jackass. Will you direct me to his house, or not?"

Bidwell busied himself by stirring the scrambled eggs on his plate. "I am Nicholas's employer, and I direct his comings and goings," he said. "Nicholas will not go to Charles Town. He is needed here to help with the preparations."

"By God!" Matthew shouted, with such force that Bidwell jumped in his chair. "Would you deny the magistrate a chance at *living?*"

"Calm your vigor," Bidwell warned. A servant girl peeked in from the kitchen and then quickly drew her head back. "I will not be shouted at in my own house. If you wish to spend time hollering down the walls at the gaol, I might arrange it for you."

"Isaac needs better medical attention than what he's getting," Matthew insisted. "He needs to be taken to Charles Town *immediately*. This morning, if possible."

"And I say you're wrong. I'd also say that the trip to Charles Town might well kill the poor wretch. But . . . if you're so willing to gallop in that direction, you should load him on a wagon and take him yourself. I will even make you a loan of a wagon and two horses, if you will sign a note of agreement."

Matthew had stood listening to this with his face downcast, staring at the floor. Now he drew in a deep breath, his cheeks mottled with red, and he walked purposefully to the end of the table. Something in his pace or demeanor alerted Bidwell to danger, because the man started to push his chair back and rise to his feet—but before he could, Matthew had reached Bidwell's side and with one sweep of his arm sent the breakfast platters off the table to the floor in a horrendous echoing crash.

As Bidwell struggled to stand up, his distended belly jiggling and his face dark with rage, Matthew clamped a hand on his right shoulder and bore down with all his weight, at the same time thrusting his face into Bidwell's.

"That man you call a *wretch*," Matthew said, in what was barely more than an ominous whisper, "has served you with all of his heart and soul." Matthew's eyes blazed with a fire that promised to scorch Bidwell to a cinder, and the master of Fount Royal was for the moment transfixed. "That man you call a *wretch* lies dying because he has served you so well. And you, sir, for all of your wealth, fine clothes, and pufferies, are not worthy to clean the magistrate's boots with your dung-dripping tongue."

Bidwell suddenly laughed, which made Matthew draw back.

"Is *that* the worst insult you can construct?" Bidwell lifted his eyebrows. "Boy, you are a rank amateur! On the matter of the boots, however, I'll have you recollect that they are *not* the magistrate's. Indeed, every item of your own clothing was supplied by me. You came to this town near-naked, the both of you. So remember that I clothed you, fed you, and housed you, while you are flinging insults in my face." He noted the presence of Mrs.

Nettles from the corner of his eye, and he turned his head toward her and said, "All's well, Mrs. Nettles. Our young guest has shown his tail, that's—"

The noise of the front door bursting open interrupted him. "What the bloody *hell?*" he said, and now he brushed Matthew's hand aside and hoisted himself to his feet.

Edward Winston came into the dining room. But it was a different Winston than Matthew had seen; this one was breathing hard, as if he'd been running, and his face was drawn and pale in the aftermath of what seemed a terrible shock.

"What's the matter?" Bidwell asked. "You look as if you've—"

"It's Nicholas!" Winston put a hand up to his forehead and appeared to be fighting a faint.

"What about him? Talk *sense,* man!"

"Nicholas . . . is dead," Winston answered. His mouth gaped, trying to form the words. "He has been murdered."

Bidwell staggered as if from a physical blow. But instantly he righted himself and his sense of control came to the forefront. "Not a word about this!" he told Mrs. Nettles. "Not to a single servant, not to *anyone!* Do you hear me?"

"Yes sir, I do." She appeared just as stunned as her master.

"Where is he?" Bidwell asked Winston. "The body, I mean?"

"His house. I just came from there."

"You're *sure* of this?"

Winston managed a grim, sickened half-smile. "Go look for yourself. I promise you won't soon forget such a sight."

"Take me there. Clerk, you come too. Remember, Mrs. Nettles: not a word about this to a single soul!"

During the walk in the early sunlight, Bidwell maintained his pace at a quick clip for a man of his size. Several citizens called a morning greeting, which Bidwell had the presence of mind to answer in as carefree a voice as he could manage. It was only when one farmer tried to stop him to talk about the forthcoming execution that Bidwell snapped at the man like a dog at a worrisome flea. Then Bidwell, Winston, and Matthew reached the whitewashed dwelling of Nicholas Paine, which stood on Harmony Street four houses northward of Winston's shuttered pigsty.

Paine's house was also shuttered. Winston's pace slowed as they neared the closed door, and finally he stopped altogether.

"Come along!" Bidwell said. "What's wrong with you?"

"I . . . would rather stay out here."

"Come along, I said!"

"*No,*" Winston answered defiantly. "By God, I'm not going in there again!"

Bidwell stared at him openmouthed, thunderstruck by this show of impudence. Matthew walked past both men, lifted the door's latch, and pushed the door open. As he did, Winston turned his face and walked away a few strides.

Matthew's first impression was of the copious reek of blood. Secondly, he was aware of the buzzing of flies at work. Thirdly, he saw the body in the slanting rays of vermilion light that entered between the shutter slats.

Fourthly, his gorge rose and if he had eaten any breakfast he surely would have expelled it.

"Oh . . . my Jesus," Bidwell said softly, behind him. Then Bidwell was overcome by the picture. He hurried outside and around the house to vomit up his blood sausage and pickled melon where he would not be seen by any passing citizen.

Matthew stepped across the threshold and closed the door to block this sight from view of the street. He stood with his back against the door, the fresh sunlight reflecting off the huge pool of blood that surrounded the chair in which Paine was sitting. Indeed, it appeared that every drop had flowed from the man's veins onto the floor, and the corpse had taken on a waxy sallow color. Matthew saw that Paine had been tied in an upright position, ropes binding his arms behind him and his ankles to the chair legs. His shoes and stockings had been removed, and his ankles and feet slashed to sever the arteries. Likewise slashed were the insides of both arms beginning at the elbows. Matthew shifted his position to see that the deep, vein-slicing cuts continued down the forearms to the wrists. He moved a little closer to the corpse, careful that he not step into the crimson sea of gore.

Paine's head was tilted backward. In his mouth was stuffed a yellow cloth, possibly a pair of stockings. His eyes, mercifully, were closed. Around his neck was knotted a noose. On the right side of his forehead there was a vicious black bruise, and blood had flowed from both nostrils down the white of his shirt. A dozen or more flies crawled over the gashes in Paine's corpse and supped from the bloody banquet at his feet.

The door opened and Bidwell dared enter. He held a hand-kerchief pressed to his mouth, his face gleaming with beads of sweat. Quickly, he closed the door at his back and stood staring numbly at all the carnage.

"Don't be sick again," Matthew warned him. "If you are, I shall be as well and it will not add to this prettiness."

"I'm all right," Bidwell croaked. "I . . . oh dear God . . . oh Christ . . . who could have done such a murder as this?"

"One man's murder is another man's execution. That's what this is. You see the hangman's noose?"

"Yes." Bidwell rapidly averted his eyes. "He . . . he's been drained of blood, hasn't he?"

"It appears his arteries have been opened, yes." Matthew walked around to the back of the body, getting as close as possible without sinking his shoes into the quagmire. He saw a red clump of blood and tissue near the crown of Paine's head. "Who-ever killed him beat him first into insensibility with a blunt object," Matthew said. "He was struck on the head by someone standing behind and above him. I think that would be a require-ment because otherwise Paine would be a formidable opponent."

"This is the Devil's work!" Bidwell said, his eyes glassy. "Satan himself must have done it!"

"If that is so, Satan has a clinical eye as to the flow of blood. You'll notice that Paine's throat was not slashed, as I understand was done to Reverend Grove and Daniel Howarth. Whoever murdered Paine wished him to bleed to death slowly and in ex-cruciating fashion. I venture Paine might have regained consciousness during the procedure, and then was struck again on the forehead. If he was able to return to sensibility after that, by that time he would have been too weak to struggle."

"Ohhhh . . . my stomach. Dear God . . . I'm going to be sick again."

"Go outside, then," Matthew directed, but Bidwell lowered his head and tried to ward off the flood. Matthew looked around the room, which showed no other signs of tumult, and fixed his attention on a nearby desk. Its chair was missing, and probably was the chair in which Paine had died. On a blotter atop the desk was a sheet of paper with several lines written upon it. An inkpot was open, and on the floor lay the quill pen. A melted stub in a candlestick attested to his source of light. Matthew saw drops and smears of blood on the floor between the desk and where the chair was positioned. He walked to the desk and read the paper.

"*I, Nicholas Paine,*" he recited, "*being of sound mind and of my own free will do hereby on this date of May eighteenth, sixteen hundred and ninety-nine, confess to the murder of . . .*" And here the writing ended in a blotch of ink. "Written sometime after midnight, it seems," Matthew said. "Or close enough that Paine scribed today's date." He saw something else in the room that warranted his attention: on the bedpallet was an open trunk that had been partly packed with clothing. "He was about to leave Fount Royal, I think."

Bidwell stared with dread fascination at the corpse. "What . . . murder was he confessing?"

"An old one, I believe. Paine had some sins in his past. I think one of them caught up with him." Matthew walked to the bed to inspect the contents of the trunk. The clothes had been thrown in, evidence of intention of a hurried departure.

"You don't think the Devil had anything to do with this? Or the witch?"

"I do not. The murders of the reverend and Daniel Howarth were—as I understand their description—meant to kill quickly. This was meant to linger. Also, you'll note there are no claw marks, as in the other killings. This was done with a very sharp blade by a hand that was both vengeful and . . . shall we say . . . experienced in the craft of cutting."

"Oh my God . . . what shall we *do?*" Bidwell lifted a trembling hand to his forehead, his wig tilted to one side on his pate. "If the citizens find out about this . . . that we have another murderer among us . . . we won't have a soul in Fount Royal by the end of the day!"

"That," Matthew said, "is true. It will do no good to advertise this crime. Therefore, don't expose it."

"What do you suggest? Hiding the corpse?"

"The details, I'm sure, are better left to you. But yes, I propose wrapping the corpse in a bedsheet and disposing of it at a later date. The later, of course, the more . . . disagreeable the task will be."

"We cannot just pretend Paine has left Fount Royal! He has friends here! And he at least deserves a Christian burial!"

Matthew aimed his stare at Bidwell. "It is your choice, sir. And your responsibility. After all, you *are* his employer and you direct his comings and goings." He walked around the body again and approached the door, which Bidwell stood against. "If you'll excuse me?"

"Where are you going?" A flare of panic leaped in Bidwell's eyes. "You can't leave!"

"Yes, I can. Don't concern yourself with my speaking about this to anyone, for I vow I shall not." Except for one person, he might have added. The person he now intended to confront.

"Please . . . I need your help."

"By that, if you mean you need a pair of hands to strip the pallet, roll Paine up in the sheet, and scrub the floor with ashes and tar soap . . . then I must deny your noble request. Winston might help you, but I doubt if any amount of coercion or threat will make him cross that threshold again." Matthew smiled tightly. "Therefore . . . speaking to a man who so abhors failure . . . I sincerely hope you are successful at your present challenge. Good day to you, sir." Matthew thought he was going to have to bodily pry Bidwell away from the door, which might have been a labor fit for Hercules, but at last the master of Fount Royal moved aside.

As Matthew started to open the door, Bidwell said in a small voice, "You say . . . ashes and tar soap, then?"

"Some sand, too," Matthew advised. "Isn't that how they scrub blood off the deck of a ship?" Bidwell didn't answer, but stood looking at the corpse with his handkerchief pressed against his mouth.

Outside, the air had never smelled sweeter. Matthew closed the door again, his stomach still roiling and what felt like cold sweat down the valley of his spine. He approached Winston, who stood in the shadow of an oak tree a few yards away.

"How did you come to find him?" Matthew asked.

Winston still appeared dazed, his color not yet returned. "I . . . intended . . . to ask Nicholas to escort me to Charles Town. On the pretense of negotiating for supplies."

"After which, you intended not to return here?"

"Yes. I planned on leaving Nicholas while I went to see Danforth. Then . . . I would simply lose myself in Charles Town."

"Well, half of your intent has come to fruition," Matthew said. "You are indeed lost. Good day." He turned away from Winston and walked back along Harmony Street in the direction they'd come, as he had seen the infirmary in passing.

Presently Matthew stood before the door and pulled the bell-cord. There was no response to the first pull, nor to the fifth. Matthew tried the door, found it unlatched from within, and entered the doctor's domain.

The parlor held two canaries in a gilded cage, both singing happily toward the shafts of light that filtered through the white shutters. Matthew saw another door and knocked at it, but again there was no reply. He opened it and ventured into a hallway. Ahead there were three rooms, the doors of the first two ajar. In the initial room stood the barber's chair and leather razor-sharpening strop; in the second room there was a trio of beds, all of which were neatly made and unoccupied. Matthew continued down the hallway to the third door, where he knocked once more.

When there was no response he pushed the door open and faced what appeared to be the doctor's chemistry study, judging from all the arcane bottles and beakers. The chamber held a single shuttered window through which the rays of bright sunlight streamed, though hazed by a pall of blue-tinged smoke.

Benjamin Shields sat in a chair with his back against the wall, holding a small object in a clamplike instrument in his right hand. The object was smoldering, emitting a thin smoke plume. Matthew thought the clouded air smelled of a combination of burnt peanuts and a rope that had been set afire.

The doctor's face was veiled by shadow, though stripes of contaminated light lay across the right shoulder and arm of his tan-colored suit. His spectacles had been placed atop a stack of two leatherbound books that sat on the desk to his right. His legs were crossed at the ankles, in a most casual pose. Matthew didn't speak. He watched as the doctor lifted the burning object—some kind of wrapped tobacco stick, it appeared—to his lips and pulled in a long, slow draw.

"Paine has been found," Matthew said. Just as slowly as he had drawn the smoke, the doctor released it from his mouth. It floated in a shimmering cloud through the angled sunrays.

"I thought your creed was to save lives, not take them," Matthew went on. Again, Shields drew from the stick, held it, then let the smoke dribble out.

Matthew looked around at the vessels of the doctor's craft, the glass bottles and vials and beakers. "Sir," he said, "you are as transparent as these implements. For what earthly reason did you commit such an atrocity?"

Still there was no reply.

Matthew felt as if he'd entered a tiger's den, and the tiger was playing with him like a housecat before it bared its fangs and claws and sprang at him. He kept firmly in mind the position of the door behind him. The savagery of Paine's death was undeniable, and therefore the ability of savagery lay within the man who sat not ten feet away. "May I offer a possible scenario?" Matthew asked, and continued anyway when the doctor refused to speak. "Paine committed some terrible offense against you—or your family—some years ago. Did he murder a family member? A son or a daughter?" A pause did not coax a reaction, except for a further cloud of smoke.

"Evidently he did," Matthew said. "By a gunshot wound, it seems. But Paine was wounded first, therefore I'm inclined to believe his victim was male. Paine must have had cause to find a doctor to treat his injury. Is that how you followed his trail? You searched for the doctor who treated him, and tracked Paine from that point? How many months did it take? Longer than that? *Years?*" Matthew nodded. "Yes, I'd suspect several years. Many seasons of festering hatred. It must have taken that long, for a man of healing to give himself over so completely to the urge for destruction."

Shields regarded the burning tip of his tobacco stick.

"You learned the circumstances of the death of Paine's wife," Matthew said. "But Paine, in wishing to put the past behind him, had never told anyone in Fount Royal that he'd ever been married. He must have been astounded when he realized you knew his history . . . and, Paine being an intelligent man, he also realized *why* you knew. So you went to his house sometime around midnight, is that correct? I presume you had all the ropes and blades you needed in your bag, but you probably left that outside. Did you offer to keep your silence if Paine would write a confession and immediately leave Fount Royal?"

Smoke drifted slowly through the light.

"Paine never dreamt you'd gone there to kill him. He assumed you were interested in unmasking him before Bidwell and the town, and that the confession was the whole point of it. So you let Paine sit down and begin writing, and you took the opportunity to bash him in the head with a blunt instrument. Was it something you had hidden on you or something already there?"

No response was forthcoming.

"And then came the moment you relished," Matthew said.

"You *must* have relished it, to have performed it so artfully. Did you taunt him as you opened his veins? His mouth was gagged, his head near cracked, and his blood running out in streams. He must have been too weak to overturn the chair, but what would it have mattered? He probably *did* hear you taunting him as he died, though. Does that knowledge give you a feeling of great joy, sir?" Matthew raised his eyebrows. "Is this one of the happiest mornings of your life, now that the man you've sought so long and steadfastly is a blood-drained husk?"

Shields took another draw from the stick, released the smoke, and then leaned forward. Light touched his moist, perspiring face, and revealed the dark violet hollows of near-madness beneath his eyes.

"Young man," the doctor said calmly, his voice thick with constrained emotion, "I should like to tell you . . . that these baseless accusations are *extremely* ill advised. My attention should rightly be directed to the magistrate's health . . . rather than any other mental pressure. Therefore . . . if you desire the magistrate to live beyond this evening . . . what you ought to do is . . ." He paused to suck once more from the dwindling stick. ". . . is make absolutely certain I am free to treat him." He leaned back again, and the shadows claimed his countenance. "But you have already decided that, have you not? Otherwise you never would have come here alone."

Matthew watched the smoke move slowly across the room. "Yes," he said, feeling that his soul had less foundation than those miniature clouds. "I have already decided."

"An excellent . . . *splendid* decision. How goes his health this morning?"

"Badly." Matthew stared at the floor. "He's been delirious."

"Well . . . that may wax and wane. The fever, you see. I do believe the blistering will show a benefit, though. I intend to apply a colonic today, and that should aid in his recovery."

"His *recovery?*" Matthew had spoken it with a shade of mockery. "Do you honestly believe he's going to recover?"

"I honestly believe he has a chance," came the reply. "A

small chance, it is true . . . but I have seen patients come back from such an adverse condition. So . . . the best we can do is continue treatment and pray that Isaac will respond."

It was insane, Matthew thought. Here he was, talking about the healing arts with a half-crazed butcher! And talking about *prayer*, to add another level of lunacy! But what choice did he have? Matthew remembered what Bidwell had said, and it had rung very true though he'd made a show of temper over it: *The trip to Charles Town might well kill the poor wretch.*

Springtime or not, the open air and the swamp humours it carried were dangerous to Woodward's remaining strength. The wagon trip over that road would be torture to him, no matter how firmly he was swaddled. In spite of how much he wished to the contrary, Matthew sincerely doubted that the magistrate would reach Charles Town alive.

So he was forced to trust this man. This doctor. This murderer. He had noted a mortar and pestle on the shelf, and he said, "Can't you mix some medicine for him? Something that would break his fever?"

"Fever does not respond to medicine as much as it responds to the movement of blood," Shields said. "And as a matter of record, the supply of medicine through Charles Town has become so pinched as to be withered. But I do have some vinegar, liverwort, and limonum. I could mix that with a cup of rum and opium and have him drink it . . . say . . . thrice daily. It might heat the blood enough to destroy the afflictions."

"At this point, anything is worth trying . . . as long as it doesn't poison him."

"I do know my chemicals, young man. You may rest assured of that."

"I won't rest," Matthew said. "And I am not assured."

"As you please." Shields continued smoking what was now only a stub. The blue clouds swirled around his face, obscuring it from scrutiny even the more.

Matthew released a long, heavy sigh. "I don't doubt you had sufficient reason to kill Paine, but you certainly seemed to enjoy the process. The hangman's noose was a bit much, don't you think?"

Shields said, "Our discussion of Isaac's treatment has ended. You may go."

"Yes, I'll go. But all that you told me of leaving Boston because your practise was suffering . . . of wanting to aid in the construction of a settlement and having your name forever emblazoned upon this infirmary . . . those were all lies, weren't they?" Matthew waited, but he knew there would be no reply. "The one true accomplishment you sought was the death of Nicholas Paine." This had not been phrased as a question, because Matthew needed no answer to what he knew to be fact.

"You will pardon me," Shields said quietly, "if I do not rise to show you out."

There was nothing more to be said, and certainly nothing more to be gained. Matthew retreated from the doctor's study, closed the door, and walked back along the hallway in a mind-numbed daze. The burning-rope smell of that tobacco stick had leeched into his nostrils. When he got outside, the first thing he did was lift his face to the sunlight and draw in a great draught of air. Then he trudged the distance to Bidwell's mansion, his head yet clouded on this clear and perfect day.

thirty

T HERE WAS A KNOCK at Matthew's door. "Young sir?" asked Mrs. Nettles. "Mr. Vaughan has come for ye."

"Mr. Vaughan?" He got up from his chair, where he'd been drowsing in the twilight of early evening, and opened the door. "What does he want?"

Mrs. Nettles pursed her lips, as if in a silent scold for his deficient memory. "He says he's come to escort you to his home for dinner, and that it shall be a'table at six o'clock."

"Oh, I did forget! What time is it now?"

"Near ha' past five, by the mantel clock."

"If there was ever an evening I didn't care to go out to dinner, this is it," Matthew said, rubbing his bleary eyes.

"That may be so," Mrs. Nettles said curtly, "but as much as I do nae care for Lucretia Vaughan, I am also sure some effort has been made to show you hospitality. Ye ought nae to disappoint 'em."

Matthew nodded, though he couldn't erase his frown. "Yes, you're right. Very well, then: please tell Mr. Vaughan I'll be downstairs in a few minutes."

"I shall. Oh . . . have ye seen Mr. Bidwell since mornin'?"

"No, I haven't."

536 • Robert McCammon

"He always tells me if he's gonna attend dinner. I'm driftin' without a sea-chain, nae knowin' what he cares ta do."

"Mr. Bidwell . . . likely is wrapped up in the sorry engagement involving Mr. Paine," Matthew said. "You of all people must know how buried he becomes in his work."

"Oh, yes sir, 'tis true! But y'know, we're havin' a festival of sorts here tomorra eve. Mr. Bidwell's hostin' a dinner for some of the maskers. Even though we've suffered such a tragedy, I do need ta know what he desires a'table."

"I'm sure he'll be around sooner or later tonight."

"Mayhaps. I've told no one about the murder, sir. Just as he wished. But do you have any idea who mi' ha' done it?"

"*Not* Rachel, the Devil, or any imagined demon, if that's what you're asking. This was a man's work." He dared go no further. "Excuse me, I'd best get ready."

"Yes sir, I'll tell Mr. Vaughan."

As he hurriedly scraped a razor across the day's growth and then washed his face, Matthew steeled himself for companionship though he fervently wished only to be left alone. He had spent the day attending to the magistrate, and observing Dr. Shields as the excruciating colonic was applied. A fresh plaster had been pressed to the pine oil dressing on Woodward's chest, and the pine oil liniment had also been rubbed around his nostrils. The doctor on his first visit this morning had brought a murky amber liquid that the magistrate swallowed with great difficulty, and had administered a second dose of the potion around four o'clock. Matthew could not help but watch Dr. Shields's hands and envision their grisly work of the previous midnight.

If Matthew had been expecting rapid results, he was disappointed; for most of the day Woodward had remained in a stupor, his fever merciless; but at least the magistrate once asked Matthew if preparations for Madam Howarth's execution were proceeding, therefore he seemed to have returned from his bout with delirium.

Matthew put on a fresh shirt and buttoned it up to the neck, then left his room and went downstairs. Waiting for him was a slim, small-statured man in a gray suit, white stockings, and polished square-toed black shoes. On his head was a brown tricorn and he was holding a lantern that bore double candles. It took only a few seconds of observation for Matthew to detect the darned patches at the man's knees and the fact that his suit jacket was perhaps two sizes too large, indicating either a borrow or a barter.

"Ah, Mr. Corbett!" The man exhibited a smile that was strong enough, but something about his deep-set pale blue eyes, in a face that had a rather gaunt and skeletal appearance, suggested a watery constitution. "I am Stewart Vaughan, sir. Pleased to make your acquaintance."

Matthew shook his hand, meeting a grip that had little substance. "Good evening to you, sir. And I thank you for your invitation to dinner."

"Our gratitude that you might grace us. The ladies are waiting. Shall we go?"

Matthew followed the man, who walked with a pronounced bowlegged gait. Over the roofs of Fount Royal the sky was crimson to the west and violet to the east, the first stars gleaming in the ruddy orange directly above. The breeze was soft and warm, and crickets chirruped in the grass around the spring.

"A lovely evening, is it not?" Vaughan asked as they left Peace Street and walked along Harmony. "I feared we would all drown ere we saw Good Sol again."

"Yes, it *was* a difficult time. Thanks be to God the clouds have passed for a time."

"Thanks be to God that the witch will soon be dead! She had a hand in that deluge, I'll swear to it!"

Matthew answered with a grunt. He realized it was going to be a very long evening, and he was still measuring that phrase Vaughan had used: *The ladies are waiting.*

They passed Van Gundy's tavern, which—from the racket of its customers and the caterwauls of two aspiring musicians playing a gittern and a drum—seemed to be a place of high and potent spirits. Matthew thought that Vaughan aimed a wistful eye at the establishment as they continued on. In another moment they walked by the house of the recently deceased Nicholas Paine, and Matthew noted with interest that candlelight could be seen through the shutter slats. He envisioned Bidwell on his knees, scrubbing blood off the floor with tar soap, ashes, and sand, and cursing cruel Fate while Paine's corpse was wrapped up in a sheet and stowed beneath the pallet for future disposal. He was sure Winston had invented some reason to tell Bidwell why he'd gone to see Paine so early in the morning. If nothing else, Winston was an agile liar.

"There is the house," Vaughan said, indicating a well-lit dwelling two houses northward and across Harmony Street from Paine's. Matthew had remembered Paine's admission of having carnal relations with Lucretia Vaughan, and he could see her approaching his house with a basket of hot buns and he returning the favor by knocking at her entry with a pistol in his pocket.

Matthew saw a small sign above the door that read *Breads & Pies Baked Daily.* Then Vaughan opened the door with the announcement, "I've brought our guest!" and Matthew entered the abode.

The house smelled absolutely delicious. A fragrant bread or pie had only just been baked, but also in the house were the commingled aromas of past delights. Matthew saw that the lady Vaughan possessed an extremely neat and painstaking hand, as the floor had been swept spotless, the white-washed walls free of any trace of hearth soot or smoke, and even the wood surfaces of the furniture smoothed and polished. Around the large stone fireplace stood a well-organized battery of skillets and cooking pots, the genteel fire burning under a pot on a jackhook. Even the cooking implements appeared to have been scrubbed clean. Adding to the pleasant, welcoming air of the house were several sprays of wildflowers set about in hammered-tin containers, and the remarkable extravagance of perhaps a dozen candles casting golden light. The supper table, which was covered with a snowy linen cloth and displayed four places readied, stood in the corner of the room opposite the hearth.

The hostess made her entrance from another door at the rear of the house, where the bedchamber likely was. "Mr. Corbett!" she said, showing a toothy smile that might have shamed the sun's glow. "How *wonderful* to have you in our home!"

"Thank you. As I told your husband, I appreciate the invitation."

"Oh, our pleasure, I assure you!" Lucretia Vaughan, in this wealth of candlelight, was indeed a handsome woman, her fine figure clad in a rose-hued gown with a lace-trimmed bodice, her light brown curls showing copper and aureate glints. Matthew could readily see how Paine could be spelled by her; to be fixed in the sights of her penetrating blue eyes was akin to the application of heat. Indeed, Matthew felt a sensation of melting before her leonine presence.

As perhaps she sensed this, she seemed to increase the power of her personality. She approached him nearer, her eyes locked with his. He caught the scent of a peach-inspired perfume. "I *know* you have many other offers to attend dinner," she said. "It is not often that we find such a sophisticated gentleman in our midst. *Stewart, leave your jacket on.* We are so very pleased you have chosen to grace our humble table with your presence." Her instruction to her husband had been like the swift stroke of a razor, not even requiring her to glance at him. Matthew was aware of Stewart standing to his left, shrugging again into the garment the man had nearly gotten out of. "Your hat is removed," Lucretia said. Stewart's hand instantly obeyed, revealing a thin thatch of blond hair.

"'Sophistication is what we yearn for in this rustic town." It seemed to Matthew that the woman had come even closer to him, though he hadn't seen her move. "I note you have buttoned your shirt to your throat. Is that the current fashion in Charles Town?"

"'Uh . . . no, I simply did it on the moment."

"Ah!" she said brightly. "Well, I'm sure it shall be fashionable in the *future*." She turned her head toward the rear doorway. "Cherise? Dearest? Our guest wishes to meet you!"

There was no response. Lucretia's smile appeared a shade frayed. Her voice rose to a higher, sharper pitch: "Cherise? You are *expected!*"

"Obviously," Stewart ventured meekly, "she's not yet ready."

The wife speared her husband with a single glance. "I shall help her *prepare*. If you'll pardon me, Mr. Corbett? Stewart, offer our guest some wine." She was through the door and gone before she'd completed her last direction.

"Wine," Stewart said. "Yes, wine! Would you care for a taste, Mr. Corbett?" He proceeded to a round table on which was placed a rather ostentatious green glass decanter and three cuplike glasses of the same *emeraude*. Before Matthew had answered "Yes," the decanter was unstoppered and the pouring begun. Stewart passed a glass to Matthew and set in on his own with the gusto of a salt-throated sailor.

Matthew had no sooner taken his first sip of what was rather a bitter vintage when from the rear doorway two feminine voices, determined to overpower each other, rose in volume, tangled like the shrieks of harpies, and then fell to abrupt silence as if those winged horrors had dashed themselves upon jagged rocks.

Stewart cleared his throat. "I myself have never been whipped," he said. "I imagine it is a less than pleasant experience?"

"Less than pleasant," Matthew agreed, glancing now and again at the doorway as at a portal beyond which an infernal struggle raged. "But more than instructive."

"Oh yes! I would think so! You committed an injury to the blacksmith, I understand? Well, I'm sure you must have had a reason. Did you see him treating a horse with less than affection?"

"Um . . ." Matthew took a sturdier drink of wine. "No, I believe Mr. Hazelton has a strong affection for horses. It was . . . let us say . . . a matter best kept stabled."

"Yes, of course! I've no wish to pry." Stewart drank again, and after a pause of three or four interminable seconds he laughed. "Oh! *Stabled!* I get your jest!"

Lucretia emerged once more, her radiance undiminished by the wrangling that had just occurred. "My apologies," she said, still smiling. "Cherise is . . . having some difficulty with her hair. She wishes to make a good presentation, you see. She is a perfectionist, and so magnifies even small blemishes."

"Her mother's daughter," Stewart muttered, before he slid his lips into the glass.

"But what would this world be without its perfectionists?" Lucretia was addressing Matthew, and deigned not to respond to her husband's comment. "I shall tell you: it would be all dust, dirt, and utter confusion. Isn't that right, Mr. Corbett?"

"I'm sure it would be disastrous," Matthew replied, and this was enough to put a religious shine in the woman's eyes.

She made a sweeping gesture toward the table. "As Cherise may be some moments yet, we should adjourn to dinner," she announced. "Mr. Corbett, if you will sit at the place that has a pewter plate?"

There was indeed a pewter plate on the table, one of the few that Matthew had ever seen. The other plates were of the common wooden variety, which indicated to Matthew the importance the Vaughans gave to his visit. Indeed, he felt as if they must consider him royalty. He sat in the appointed chair, with Stewart seated to his left. Lucretia quickly donned an apron and went about spooning and ladling food from the cooking pots into white clay serving bowls. Presently the bowls were arranged on the table, containing green stringbeans with hogsfat, chicken stew with boiled potatoes and bacon, corncakes baked in cream, and stewed tomatoes. Along with a golden loaf of fresh fennel-seed bread, it was truly a king's feast. Matthew's glass was topped with wine, after which Lucretia took off her apron and seated herself at the head of the table, facing their guest, where by all rights of marriage and household the husband ought to be.

"I shall lead us in our thanks," Lucretia said, another affront to the duties of her husband. Matthew closed his eyes and bowed his head. The woman gave a prayer of thanksgiving that included Matthew's name and mentioned her hope that the wretched soul of Rachel Howarth find an angry God standing ready to smite her spectral skull from her shoulders after the execution stake had done its work. Then the fervent "Amen" was spoken and Matthew opened his eyes to find Cherise Vaughan standing beside him.

"Here is our lovely daughter!" Lucretia exclaimed. "Cherise, take your place."

The girl, in a white linen gown with a lace bodice and sleeves, continued to stand where she was and stare down at Matthew. She was indeed an attractive girl, perhaps sixteen or seventeen, her waves of blonde hair held fixed by a series of small wooden combs. Matthew imagined she must closely resemble her mother at that age, though her chin was longer and somewhat more square and her eyes almost as pale blue as her father's. In these eyes, however, there was no suggestion of a watery constitution; there was instead a haughty chill that Matthew instantly dropped his gaze from, lest he shiver from a December wind on this May night.

"Cherise?" Lucretia repeated, gently but firmly. "Take. Your. Place. Please."

The girl sat down—slowly, at her own command—on Matthew's right. She wasted no time in reaching out and spooning chicken stew onto her plate.

"Are you not even going to say hello to Mr. Corbett?"

"Hello," she answered, pushing the first bite of food into her cupid's-bow mouth.

"Cherise helped prepare the stew," Lucretia said. "She has been desirous to make certain it was to your liking."

"I'm sure it's excellent," Matthew answered. He spooned some of the stew onto his plate and found it as good as it appeared, then he tore off a hunk of bread and sopped it in the thick, delicious liquid.

"Mr. Corbett is a fascinating young man." This was spoken to Cherise, though Lucretia continued to gaze upon him. "Not only is he a sophisticated gentleman and a judicial apprentice from Charles Town, but he fought off that mob of killers and thieves who attacked the magistrate. Armed only with a rapier, I understand?"

Matthew accepted a helping of stewed tomatoes. He could feel three pairs of eyes upon him. Now was the moment to explain that the 'mob' consisted of one ruffian, an old crone, and an infirm geezer . . . but instead his mouth opened and what came out was, "No . . . I . . . had not even a rapier. Would you pass the corncakes, please?"

"My Lord, what a night that must have been!" Stewart was profoundly impressed. "Did you not have a weapon at *all?*"

"I . . . uh . . . used a boot to good advantage. This is an absolutely *wonderful* stew! Mr. Bidwell's cook ought to have this recipe."

"Well, our Cherise is a wonderful cook herself," Lucretia assured him. "I am currently teaching her the secrets of successful pie baking. Not an easy subject to command, I must say."

"I'm sure it's not." Matthew offered a smile to the girl, but she was having none of it. She simply ate her food and stared straight ahead with no trace of expression except, perhaps, absolute boredom.

"And now . . . about the treasure chest full of gold coins you found." Lucretia laid her spoon and knife delicately across her plate. "You had it sent back to Charles Town, I understand?"

Here he had to draw the line. "I fear there was no treasure chest. Only a single coin."

"Yes, yes . . . of course. Only a single coin. Very well, then, I can see you are a canny guardian of information. But what can you tell us of the witch? Does she weep and wail at the prospect of burning?"

The stew he was about to swallow had suddenly sprouted thorns and lodged in his throat. "Mrs. Vaughan," he said, as politely as possible, "if you don't mind . . . I would prefer not to talk about Rachel Howarth."

Suddenly Cherise looked at him and grinned, her blue eyes

gleaming. "Oh, *that* is a subject I find of interest!" Her voice was pleasingly melodic, but there was a wickedly sharp edge to it as well. *"Do* tell us about the witch, sir! Is it true she shits toad-frogs?"

"Cherise!" Lucretia had hissed the name, her teeth gritted and her eyes wide with alarm. Instantly her composure altered with the speed of a chameleon's color change; her smile returned, though fractured, and she looked down the table at Matthew. "Our daughter has . . . an earthy sense of humor, Mr. Corbett. You know, it is said that some of the finest, most gracious ladies have earthy senses of humor. One must not be *too* stiff and rigid in these strange times, must one?"

"Stiff and rigid," the girl said, as she pushed a tomato into her mouth and gave a gurgling little laugh. Matthew saw that Lucretia had chosen to continue eating, but red whorls had risen in her cheeks. Stewart drank down his glass of wine and reached for the decanter.

No one spoke for a time. It was then that Matthew was aware of a faint humming sound, but he couldn't place where it was coming from. "I might tell you, as a point of information," he said, to break the wintry silence, "that I am not yet a judicial apprentice. I am a magistrate's clerk, that's all."

"Ah, but you *shall* be a judicial apprentice in the near future, will you not?" Lucretia asked, beaming again. "You are young, you have a fine mind and a desire to serve. Why should you not enter the legal profession?"

"Well . . . I probably shall, at some point. But I do need much more education and experience."

"A *humble* soul!" She spoke it as if she had found the Grail itself. "Do you hear that, Cherise? The young man stands on the precipice of such political power and wealth, and he remains humble!"

"The problem with standing on a precipice," he said, "is that one might fall from a great height."

"And a *wit* as well!" Lucretia seemed near swooning with delight. "You know how wit charms you, Cherise!"

Cherise stared again into Matthew's eyes. "I desire to know more about the witch. I have heard tell she took the cock of a black goat into her mouth and sucked on it."

"Umph!" A rivulet of wine had streamed down Stewart's chin and marred his gray jacket. He had paled as his wife had reddened.

Lucretia was about to either hiss or shriek, but before she could, Matthew met the girl's stare with equal force and said calmly, "You have heard a lie, and whoever told you such a thing is not only a liar but a soul in need of a mouth-soaping."

"Billy Reed told me such a thing. Shall I find him tomorrow and tell him you're going to soap his mouth?"

"That thug's name shall not be uttered in this *house!*" The veins were standing out in Lucretia's neck. "I forbid it!"

"I *will* find Billy Reed tomorrow," Cherise went on, defiantly. "Where shall I tell him you will meet him with your soap?"

"I beg your pardon, Mr. Corbett! I beg a *thousand* pardons!" In her agitation, the woman had spilled a spoonful of corncake and cream on the front of her gown, and now she was blotting the stain with a portion of the tablecloth. "That thug is James Reed's miscreant son! He's near an imbecile, he has the ambition of a sloth . . . *and* he has wicked designs on my daughter!"

Cherise grinned—or, rather, leered—into Matthew's face. "Billy is teaching me how to milk. In the afternoons, at their barn, he shows me how to hold the member. How to slide my hand up and down . . . up and down . . . up and down . . ." She displayed the motion for him, much to his discomfort and her mother's choked gasp. "Until the cream spurts forth. And a wonderful hot cream it is, too."

Matthew didn't respond. It did occur to him that—absolutely, positively—he'd lately been hiding in the wrong barn.

"I think," Stewart said, rising unsteadily to his feet, "that the rum bottle should be unstoppered."

"For God's sake, stay away from that rum!" Lucretia hollered, oblivious now to their honored guest. "That's the cause of all our troubles! That, and your poor excuse for a carpentry shop!"

Matthew's glance at Cherise showed him she was eating her dinner with a smirk of satisfaction upon her face, which was now not nearly so lovely. He put his own spoon and knife down, his appetite having fled. Stewart was fumbling in a cupboard and Lucretia was attacking her food with a vengeance, her eyes dazed and her face as red as the stewed tomatoes. In the silence that fell, Matthew heard the strange humming sound again. He looked up.

And received a jolt.

On the ceiling directly above the table was a wasp's nest the size of Mr. Green's fist. The thing was black with wasps, all crowded together, their wings folded back along their stingers. As Matthew watched, unbelieving, he saw a minor disturbance ripple across the insects and several of them commenced that angry humming noise.

"Uh . . . Mrs. Vaughan," he said thickly. "You have . . ." He pointed upward.

"Yes, wasps. What of it?" Her manners—along with her composure, her family, and the evening—had greatly deteriorated.

Matthew realized why the nest must be there. He'd heard of such a thing, but he'd never before seen it. As he understood, a potion could be bought or made that, once applied to an indoor ceiling, enraptured wasps to build their nests on the spot.

"Insect control, I assume?" he asked.

"Of course," Lucretia said, as if any fool on earth knew that. "Wasps are jealous creatures. We suffer no mosquitoes in this house."

"None that will bite *her,* anyway," Stewart added, and then he continued suckling from the bottle.

This evening, Matthew thought, might have been termed a farce had there not been such obvious suffering from all persons involved. The mother ate her dinner as if in a stunned trance, while the daughter now set about consuming her food more with fingers than proper utensils, succeeding in smearing her mouth and chin with gleaming hogsfat. Matthew finished his wine and a last bite of the excellent stew, and then he thought he should make his exit before the girl decided he might look more appealing crowned with a serving-bowl.

"I . . . uh . . . presume I'd best go," he said. Lucretia spoke not a word, as if her inner fire had been swamped by her daughter's wanton behavior. Matthew pushed his chair back and stood up. "I wish to thank you for the dinner and the wine. Uh . . . no need to walk me back to the mansion, Mr. Vaughan."

"I wasn't plannin' on it," the man said, clutching the rum bottle to his chest.

"Mrs. Vaughan? May I . . . uh . . . take some of that delicious bread with me?"

"All you wish," she murmured, staring into space. "The rest of it, if you like."

Matthew accepted what was perhaps half a loaf. "My appreciation."

Lucretia looked up at him. Her vision cleared, as she seemed to realize that he actually was leaving. A weak smile flickered across her mouth. "Oh . . . Mr. Corbett . . . where are my manners? I thought . . . hoped . . . that after dinner . . . we might all play at *lanctie loo*."

"I fear I am without talent at card games."

"But . . . there are so *many* things I wished to converse with you about. The magistrate's condition being one. The state of affairs in Charles Town. The gardens . . . and the balls."

"I'm sorry," Matthew said. "I don't have much experience with either gardens or balls. As to the state of affairs in Charles Town, I would call them . . . somewhat less interesting than those in Fount Royal. The magistrate is still very ill, but Dr. Shields is administering a new medicine he's concocted."

"You know, of course," she said grimly, "that the witch has cursed your magistrate. For the guilty decree. I doubt he shall survive with such a curse laid on him."

Matthew felt his face tighten. "I believe differently, madam."

"Oh . . . I . . . I am being so *insensitive.* I am only repeating what I overhead Preacher Jerusalem saying this afternoon. Please forgive me, it's just that—"

"That she has a knife for a tongue," Cherise interrupted, still eating with graceless fingers. "She only apologizes when it cuts herself."

Lucretia leaned her head toward her daughter, much in the manner of a snake preparing to strike. "You may leave the table and our presence," she said coldly. "Inasmuch as you have disgraced yourself and all of us, I do hope you are happy."

"I *am* happy. I am also still hungry." She refused to budge from her place. "You know that you were brought here to *save* me, do you not?" A quick glance was darted at Matthew, as she licked her greasy fingers. "To rescue me from Fount Royal and the witless rustics my mother despises? Oh, if you are so sophisticated you must have known that already!"

"Stop her, Stewart!" Lucretia implored, her voice rising. "Make her hush!"

The man, however, tilted the bottle to his mouth and then began peeling off his suit jacket.

"Yes, it's true," Cherise said. "My mother sells them breads and pies and wishes them to choke on the crumbs. You should hear her talk about them behind their backs!"

Matthew stared down into the girl's face. *Her mother's daughter,* Stewart had said. Matthew might have recognized the streak of viciousness. The pity, he mused, was that Cherise Vaughan seemed to be highly intelligent. She had recognized, for instance, that speaking of Rachel Howarth had caused him great discomfort of a personal nature.

"I will show myself out," Matthew said to Mrs. Vaughan. "Again, thank you for the dinner." He started toward the door, carrying the half-loaf of fennel-seed bread with him.

"Mr. Corbett? Wait, please!" Lucretia stood up, a large cream stain on the front of her gown. Again she appeared dazed, as if these verbal encounters with her daughter sapped the very life from her. "Please . . . I have a question for you."

"Yes?"

"The witch's hair," she said. "What is to become of it?"

"Her . . . *hair?* I'm sorry, I don't understand your meaning."

"The witch has such . . . shall I say . . . *attractive* hair. One might say *beautiful,* even. It is a sadness that such thick and lovely hair should be burnt up." Matthew could not have replied even if he'd wished to, so stunned was he by this direction of thinking.

But the woman continued on. "If the witch's hair should be washed . . . and then shorn off, on the morning of her execution . . . there are *many,* I would venture—who might pay for a lock of it. Think of it: the witch's hair advertised and sold as a charm of good fortune." Her countenance seemed to brighten at the very idea of it. "It might be heralded as firm evidence of God's destruction of Evil. You see my meaning now?"

Still Matthew's tongue was frozen solid.

"Yes, and I would grant you a portion of the earnings as well," she said, mistaking his amazed expression as approval. "But I think it best if you washed and cut the hair yourself, on some pretext or another, as we wouldn't wish too many fingers in our pie."

He just stood there, feeling sick. "Well?" she urged. "Can we consider ourselves in company?"

Somehow, he turned from her and got out the door. As he walked away along Harmony Street, a cold sheen of moisture on his face, he heard the woman calling him from her doorway: "Mr. Corbett? Mr. Corbett?"

And louder and more shrill: *"Mr. Corbett?"*

thirty-one

PAST THE HOUSE of deceased Nicholas Paine he went, past Van Gundy's tavern where the revelers made merry, past Dr. Shields's infirmary and the squalid house of Edward Winston. Matthew walked on, his head bowed and the half-loaf of fennel-seed bread in his hand, the night sky above him a field of stars and, in his mind, darkness heavy and unyielding.

He turned left onto Truth Street. Further along, the black-ened ruins of Johnstone's schoolhouse secured his attention. It was a testament to the power of the infernal fire as well as a testa-ment to the power of infernal men. He recalled how Johnstone had raged in helpless anguish that night, as the flames had burned unchecked. The schoolmaster might be bizarre—with his white face powder and his deformed knee—but it was a surety that the man had felt his teaching was a vital calling, and that the loss of the schoolhouse was a terrible tragedy. Matthew might have had his suspicions about Johnstone, but the fact that the man believed Rachel not to be a witch—and, indeed, that the en-tire assertion of witchcraft was built on shaky ground—gave Matthew hope for the future of education.

He went on, nearer to where he had known he was going.

And there the gaolhouse stood. He didn't hesitate, but qui-etly entered the darkened structure.

Though he endeavored to be quiet, his opening of the door nevertheless startled Rachel. He heard her move on her pallet of straw, as if drawing herself more tightly into a posture of self-protection. It occurred to him that, with the door still unchained, anyone might enter to taunt and jeer at her, though most persons would certainly be afeared to do so. One who would not be afeared, however, would be Preacher Jerusalem, and he imagined the snake must have made an appearance or two when no other witnesses were present.

"Rachel, it's me," he said. Before she could answer or protest his presence, he said, "I know you've wished me not to come, and I do respect your wishes . . . but I wanted to tell you I am still working on your . . . um . . . your situation. I can't yet tell you what I've found, but I believe I have made some progress." He approached her cell a few more paces before he stopped again. "That is not to say I've come to any kind of solution, or have proof of such, but I wished you to know I have you always in mind and that I won't give up. Oh . . . and I've also brought you some very excellent fennel-seed bread."

Matthew went the rest of the way and pushed the bread through the bars. In the absolute dark, he was aware only of her vague shape coming to meet him, like a figure just glimpsed in some partially remembered dream.

Without a word, Rachel took the bread. Then her other hand grasped Matthew's and she clutched it firmly against her cheek. He felt the warm wetness of tears. She made a choked sound, as if she were trying mightily to restrain a sob.

He didn't know what to say. But at this revelation of unexpected emotion his heart bled and his own eyes became damp.

"I . . . shall keep working," Matthew promised, his voice husky. "Day and night. If an answer is to be found . . . I swear I will find it."

Her response was to press her lips against the back of his hand, and then she held it once more to her tear-stained cheek. They stood in that posture. Rachel clutched to him as if she wanted nothing else in the world at that moment but the warmth—the care—of another human being. He wished to take his other hand and touch her face, but instead he curled his fingers around one of the iron bars between them.

"Thank you," she whispered. And then, perhaps overcoming with an effort of will her momentary weakness, she let go of his hand and took the bread with her back to her place in the straw.

To stay longer would be hurtful both to himself and her, for in his case it would make leaving all the more painful. He had wished her to know she was not forgotten, and that had certainly been accomplished. So he took his leave and presently was walking westward along Truth Street, his face downcast and his brow freighted with thought.

Love.

It came to him not as a stunning blow, but as a soft shadow.

Love. What was it, really? The desire to possess someone, or the desire to free them?

Matthew didn't believe he had ever been in love before. In fact, he knew he had not been. Therefore, since he had no experience, he was at a loss to clearly examine the emotion within him. It was an emotion, perhaps, that defied examination and could not be shaped to fit into any foursquare box of reason. Because of that, there was something frightening about it . . . something wild and uncontrollable, something that would not be constrained by logic.

He felt, though, that if love was the desire to possess someone, it was in reality the poor substance of self-love. It seemed to him that a greater, truer love was the desire to open a cage—be it made of iron bars or the bones of tormented injustice—and set the nightbird free.

He wasn't sure what he was thinking, or why he was thinking it. On the subjects of the Latin and French languages, English history, and legal precedents he was comfortable with his accumulated knowledge, but on this strange subject of love he was a total imbecile. And, he was sure the magistrate would say, also a misguided youth in danger of God's displeasure.

Matthew was here. So was Rachel. Satan had made a recent

fictitious appearance and certainly dwelled in both the lust of Exodus Jerusalem and the depraved soul of the man who worked the poppet strings.

But where was God, in all this?

If God intended to show displeasure, it seemed to Matthew that He ought to take a little responsibility first.

Matthew was aware that these thoughts might spear his head with lightning on a cloudless night, but the paradox of Man was the fact that one might have been made in the image of God, yet it was often the most devilish of ideas that gave action and purpose to the human breed.

He returned to Bidwell's mansion, where he learned from Mrs. Nettles that the master had not yet returned from his present task. However, Dr. Shields had just left after giving Woodward a third dose of the medicine, and currently the magistrate was soundly asleep. Matthew chose a book from the library—the tome on English plays and dramatists, so that he might better acquaint himself with the craft of the maskers—and went upstairs. After looking in on Woodward to verify that he was indeed sleeping but breathing regularly, Matthew then retired to his bedchamber to rest, read, think, and await the passage of time.

In spite of what had been a very trying day, and the fact that the image of Paine's butchered corpse was still gruesomely fresh in his mind, Matthew was able to find short periods of sleep. At an hour he judged to be past midnight, he relit the lantern he had blown out upon lying down and took it with him into the hallway.

Though it was certainly late, there was still activity in the house. Bidwell's voice could be heard—muffled but insistent—coming from the upstairs study. Matthew paused outside the door, to hear who was in there with him, and caught Winston's strained reply. Paine's name was mentioned. Matthew thought it best he not be a party to the burial plans, even through the thickness of a door, and so he went on his way down the stairs, descending quietly.

A check of the mantel clock in the parlor showed the time to be thirty-eight minutes after midnight. He entered the library and unlatched the shutters so that if the door was later locked from the inside he might still gain admittance without ringing for Mrs. Nettles. Then he set off for the spring, the lantern held low at his side.

On the eastern bank, Matthew set the lamp on the ground next to a large water oak and removed his shoes, stockings, and shirt. The night was warm, but a foot slid into the water gave him a cold shock. It was going to take a sturdy measure of fortitude just to enter that pond, much less go swimming about underwater in the dark.

But that was what he had come to do, and so be it. If he could find even a portion of what he suspected might be hidden down there, he would have made great progress in solving the riddle of the surveyor's visit.

He eased into the shallows, the cold water stealing his breath. A touch of that fount's kindness upon his groin, and his stones became as true rocks. He stood in water up to his waist for a moment, his feet in the soft mud below, as he steeled himself for further immersion. Presently, though, he did become acclimated to the water and he reasoned that if turtles and frogs could accept it, then so could he. The next challenge was going ahead and sliding the rest of the way down, which he did with clenched teeth.

He moved away from the bank. Instantly he felt the bottom angling away under his feet. Three more strides, and he was up to his neck. Then two more . . . and suddenly he was treading water. Well, he thought. The time had come.

He drew a breath, held it, and submerged.

In the darkness he felt his way along the sloping bottom, his fingers gripping into the mud. As he went deeper, he was aware of the thump of his own heartbeat and the gurgle of bubbles leaving his mouth. Still the bottom continued to slope downward at perhaps an angle of thirty degrees. His hands found the edges of rocks protruding from the mud, and the soft matting of moss-like grass. Then his lungs became insistent, and he had to return to the surface to fill them.

Again he dove under. Deeper he went this time, his arms and legs propelling his progress. A pressure clamped hold of his face and began to increase as he groped his way down. On this descent he was aware of a current pulling at him from what seemed to be the northwestern quadrant of the fount. He had time to close his fists in the mud, and then he had to rise once more.

When he reached the surface, he trod water and squeezed the mud between his fingers. There was nothing but finely grained *terra liquum*. He took another breath, held it, and went down a third time.

As Matthew descended what he estimated to be more than twenty feet, he again felt the insistent pull of a definite current, stronger as he swam deeper. He reached into the sloping mud. His fingers found a flat rock—which suddenly came to life and shot away underneath him, the surprise bringing a burst of bubbles from his mouth and causing him to instantly rise.

On the surface he had to pause to steady his nerves before he dove again, though he should have expected to disturb turtles. A fourth descent allowed him to gather up two more fistfuls of mud, but in the muck was not a trace of gold or silver coinage.

He resolved on the fifth dive to stay down and search through the mud as long as possible. He filled his lungs and descended, his body beginning to protest such exertion and his mind beginning to recoil from the secrets of the dark. But he did grip several handfuls and sift through them, again without success.

After the eighth dive, Matthew came to the conclusion that he was simply muddying the water. His lungs were burning and his head felt dangerously clouded. If indeed there was a bounty of gold and silver coins down there, they existed only in a realm known by the turtles. Of course, Matthew had realized that a pirate's treasure vault would be no vault at all if just anyone—particularly a land creature like himself—could swim down and retrieve it. He had never entertained the illusion that he could—

556 • Robert McCammon

or *cared* to—reach the fount's deepest point, which he recalled Bidwell saying was some forty feet, but he'd hoped he might find an errant coin. He imagined the retrieval process would involve several skilled divers, the kind of men who were useful at scraping mollusks from the bottoms of ships while still at sea. The process might also demand the use of hooks and chains, a dense netting and a lever device, depending on how much treasure was hidden.

He had surfaced from this final dive near the center of the spring, and so he began the swim back to the shallows. He was intrigued by the current he'd felt below the level of fifteen feet or thereabouts. It had strengthened as he'd gone deeper, and Matthew wondered at the ferocity of its embrace at the forty-foot depth. Water was definitely flowing down there at the command of some unknown natural mechanism.

In another moment his feet found the mud, and he was able to stand. He waded toward the bank and the tree beside which he'd left his clothes and the lantern.

And that was when he realized his lamp was no longer there.

Instantly a bell of alarm clanged in his mind. He stood in the waist-deep water, scanning the bank for any sign of an intruder.

Then a figure stepped out from behind the tree. In each hand was a lantern, but they were held low so Matthew couldn't see the face.

"Who's there?" Matthew said, trying mightily to keep his speech from shivering as much as his body was beginning to.

The figure had a voice: "Would you care to tell me what you're up to?"

"I am swimming, Mr. Winston." Matthew continued wading toward the bank. "Is that not apparent?"

"Yes, it's apparent. My question remains valid, however."

Matthew had only a few seconds to construct a reply, so he gave it his best dash of pepper. "If you knew anything of health," he said, "which obviously you do not, because of your living habits, you would appreciate the benefit to the heart of a nocturnal swim."

"Oh, of course! Shall I fetch a wagon to help load this manure?"

"I'm sure Dr. Shields would be glad to inform you of the benefit." Matthew left the water and, dripping, approached Winston. He took the lantern that Winston offered. "I often swim at night in Charles Town," he plowed on, deepening the furrow.

"Do tell."

"I *am* telling." Matthew leaned down to pick up his shirt and blot the moisture from his face. He closed his eyes in so doing. When he opened them he realized that one of his shoes—which had both been on the ground when he'd picked up the shirt— was now missing. At the same instant he registered that Winston had taken a position behind him.

"Mr. Winston?" Matthew said, quietly but clearly. "You don't really wish to do what you're considering." From Winston there was no word or sound.

Matthew suspected that if a blow from the stout wooden heel was going to come, it would be delivered to his skull as he turned toward the other man. "Your disloyalty to your master need not deform itself into murder." Matthew blotted water from his chest and shoulders with a casual air, but inwardly he was an arrow choosing his direction of flight. "The residents might find a victim of drowning on the morrow . . . but you will know what you've done. I don't believe you to be capable of such an act." He swallowed, his heart pounding through his chest, and took the risk of looking at Winston. No blow fell. "I am not the reason for your predicament," Matthew said. "May I please have my shoe?"

Winston sighed heavily, his head lowered, and held out his hand with the shoe in it. Matthew noted that it was offered heel-first. "You are not a killer, sir," Matthew said, after he'd accepted the shoe. "If you'd really wished to bash my head in, you never would have signalled your presence by moving the lantern. May I ask how come you to be here?"

"I . . . just left a meeting with Bidwell. He wants me to take care of disposing of Paine's corpse."

"So you came to consider the fount? I wouldn't. You might

weigh the corpse down well enough, but the water supply would surely be contaminated. Unless . . . that's what you intend." Matthew had put on his shirt and was buttoning it.

"No, that's not my intention, though I *had* considered the fount for that purpose. I might wish the *town* to die, but I don't wish to cause the deaths of any citizens."

"A correction," Matthew said. "You wish not to bear the *blame* for the death of Fount Royal. Also, you wish to improve your financial and business standing with Mr. Bidwell. Yes?"

"Yes, that's right."

"Well, you're aware then that you have Mr. Bidwell stretched over a very large barrel now, don't you?"

Winston frowned. "What?"

"You and he share important knowledge he would rather not have revealed to his citizens. If I were in your position, I would make the most of it. You're adept at drawing up contracts, are you not?"

"I am."

"Then simply contract between yourself and Mr. Bidwell the task of corpse disposal. Write into it whatever you please and negotiate, realizing of course that you will most likely not get everything you feel you deserve. But I'd venture your style of living would find some improvement. And with Bidwell's signature on a contract of such . . . *delicate* nature, you need never fear losing your position with his company. In fact, you might find yourself promoted. Where is the body now? Still at the house?"

"Yes. Hidden under the pallet. Bidwell wept and moaned such that I . . . had to help him place it there."

"That was your first opportunity to negotiate terms. I hope you won't miss the next one." Matthew sat down in the grass to put on his stockings.

"Bidwell will never sign any contract that implicates him in hiding evidence of a murder!"

"Not gladly, no. But he *will* sign, Mr. Winston. Particularly if he understands that you—his trusted business manager—will take care of the problem without bringing anyone else into it.

That's his greatest concern. He'll also sign when you make him understand—firmly but diplomatically, I hope—that the task will not and cannot be done without your doing it. You might emphasize that the contract with his signature upon it is a formality for your legal protection."

"Yes, that would make sense. But he'll know I might use the contract as future leverage against him!"

"Of course he will. As I said, I doubt if you'll find yourself without a position at Bidwell's firm anytime soon. He might even send you back to England on one of his ships, if that's what you want." The job of putting on his stockings and shoes done, Matthew stood up. "What *do* you want, Mr. Winston?"

"More money," Winston said. He took a moment to think. "And a fair shake. I should be rewarded for my good work. *And* I ought to get credit for the business decisions I've made that have helped pad Bidwell's pockets."

"What?" Matthew raised his eyebrows. "No mansion or statue?"

"I am a realistic man, sir. I might only push Bidwell so far."

"Oh, I think you should at least try for the mansion. If you'll excuse me now?"

"Wait!" Winston said when Matthew started to walk away. "What do you suggest I do with Paine's corpse?"

"Actually, I have no suggestion and I don't care to know what you do," Matthew replied. "My only thought is . . . the dirt beneath Paine's floor is the same dirt that fills the cemetery graves. I know you have a Bible and consider yourself a Christian."

"Yes, that is right. Oh . . . one more thing," Winston added before Matthew could turn to leave. "How are we to explain Paine's disappearance? And what shall we do to find his killer?"

"The explanation is your decision. About finding his killer . . . from what I understand, Paine dabbled with other men's wives. I'd think he had more than his share of enemies. But I am not a magistrate, sir. It is Mr. Bidwell's responsibility, as the mayor of this town, to file the case. Until then . . ." Matthew shrugged. "Good night."

"Good night," Winston said as Matthew departed. "And good swimming to you."

Matthew went directly to Bidwell's house, to the library shutters he'd unlatched, opened them, and put the lantern on the sill. Then he carefully pulled himself up through the window, taking care not to overturn the chess set on his entry. Matthew took the lantern and went upstairs to bed, disappointed that no evidence of a pirate's hoard had been found but hopeful that tomorrow—or later today, as the fact was—might show him some path through the maze of questions that confronted him.

When the rooster choir of Friday's sunrise sounded, Matthew awakened with the fading impression of a dream but one very clear image remaining in his memory: that of John Goode, talking about the coins he'd discovered and saying *May's got it in her mind we're gon' run to the Florida country.*

He rose from bed and looked out the window at the red sun on the eastern horizon. A few clouds had appeared, but they were neither dark nor pregnant with rain. They moved like stately galleons across the purple sky.

The Florida country, he thought. A Spanish realm, the link to the great—though English-despised—cities of Madrid and Barcelona. The link, also, to Rachel's Portuguese homeland.

He recalled Shawcombe's voice saying *You know them Spaniards are sittin' down there in the Florida country, not seventy leagues from here. They got spies all in the colonies, spreadin' the word that any black crow who flies from his master and gets to the Florida country can be a free man. You ever heard such a thing? Them Spaniards are promisin' the same thing to criminals, murderers, every like of John Badseed.*

Seventy leagues, Matthew thought. Roughly two hundred miles. And not simply a two-hundred-mile *jaunt,* either. What of wild animals and wild Indians? Water would be no hardship, but what of food? What of shelter, if the heavens opened their floodgates again? Such a journey would make his and the magistrate's muddy trek from Shawcombe's tavern seem an afternoon's idyll.

But evidently others had made the journey and survived, and from much greater distances than two hundred miles. May was an elderly woman, and she had no qualms about going. Then again, it was her last hope of freedom.

Her last hope.

Matthew turned away from the window, walked to the basin of water atop his dresser, and liberally splashed his face. He wasn't sure what he'd been thinking, but—whatever it may have been—it was the most illogical, insane thought he'd ever had. He was surely no outdoorsman or leatherstocking, and also he was proud to be a British subject. So he might dismiss from his mind all traces of such errant and unwise consideration.

He shaved, put on his clothes, and crossed the hallway to look in on the magistrate. Dr. Shields's latest potion was evidently quite powerful, as Woodward still dwelled in the land of Nod. A touch of the magistrate's bare arm, however, gave Matthew reason for great joy: sometime during the night, Woodward's fever had broken.

At breakfast Matthew sat alone. He ate a dish of stirred eggs and ham, washed down with a strong cup of tea. Then he was out the door on a mission of resolve: to confront the ratcatcher in his well-ordered nest.

The morning was pleasantly warm and sunny, though a number of white-bellied clouds paraded across the sky. On Industry Street, Matthew hurried past Exodus Jerusalem's camp but neither the preacher nor his relations were in evidence. He soon came to the field where the maskers had made their camp, near the Hamilton house. Several of the thespians were sitting around a fire over which a trio of cooking pots hung. Matthew saw a burly, Falstaffian fellow smoking a churchwarden pipe while conversing with emphatic gestures to two other colleagues. A woman of equal if not greater girth was busy with needle and thread, darning a red-feathered hat, and a more slender female was at work polishing boots. Matthew knew little about the craft of acting, though he did know that all thespians were male and therefore the two women must be wives who travelled with the troupe.

"Good day, young man!" one of the actors called to him, with a lift of the hand.

"Good day to you!" Matthew answered, nodding.

In another few minutes Matthew entered the somber area of deformed orchards. It was fitting, then, that this was the locale chosen for Rachel's burning, as the justice such a travesty represented was surely misshapen. He looked at a barren brown field upon which had been erected the freshly axed execution stake. At its base, ringed by rocks, was a large firemound of pinewood timbers and pineknots. About twenty yards away from it stood another pile of wood. The field had been chosen to accommodate the festive citizens and to be certain no errant sparks could reach a roof.

At first light on Monday morning Rachel would be brought here by wagon and secured to the stake. Some kind of repugnant ceremony would take place, with Bidwell as its host. Then, after the crowd's flame had been sufficiently bellowed, torches would be laid to the firemound. More fuel would be brought over from the woodpile, to keep the temperature at a searing degree. Matthew had never witnessed an execution by burning, but he reasoned it must be a slow, messy, and excruciating business. Rachel's hair and clothes might be set aflame and her flesh roasted, but if the temperature wasn't infernal enough the real burning would take hours. It would be an all-day thing, anyway, for Matthew suspected that even a raging fire had difficulty gnawing a human body to the bones.

At what point Rachel would lose consciousness, he didn't know. Even though she wished to die with dignity and might have readied herself for the ordeal as much as humanly possible, her screams would be heard from one wall of Fount Royal to the other. It was likely Rachel would perish of asphyxiation before the fire cooked her. If she had her senses about her, she might hurry death by breathing in the flames and copious smoke. But who at that agonizing moment could do anything but wail in torment and thrash at their bonds?

Matthew assumed the fire would be kept burning throughout the night, and the citizens encouraged to witness as the witch shrank away to a grisly shade of her former self. The execution stake would dwindle too, but would be kept watered to delay its disappearance. On Tuesday morning, when there was nothing left but ashes and blackened bones, someone—Seth Hazelton, possibly—might come with a mallet to smash the skull and break the burnt skeleton into smaller fragments. It was then that Matthew could envision the swooping down of Lucretia Vaughan—armed with as many buckets, bottles, and containers as she might load upon a wagon—eager to scoop up ashes and bits of bone to sell as charms against evil. It occurred to him that her intelligence and rapacity might encourage her to enter an unholy alliance with Bidwell and Preacher Jerusalem, the former to finance and package this abomination and the latter to hawk it in towns and villages up and down the seaboard.

He had to banish such thoughts, ere they sapped the strength of his belief that an answer could be found before that awful Monday dawn.

He continued westward along Industry. Presently he saw a wisp of white smoke curling from the chimney of Linch's house. The lord of rodents was cooking his breakfast.

The shutters were wide open. Obviously Linch wasn't expecting any visitors. Matthew walked to the door, under the hanging rat skeletons, and knocked without hesitation.

A few seconds passed. Then, suddenly, the shutters of the window nearest the door were drawn closed—not hastily or loudly, but rather with quiet purpose. Matthew knocked again, with a sterner fist.

"Who is it?" came Linch's wary voice.

Matthew smiled thinly, realizing that Linch might just as easily have looked out the window to see. "Matthew Corbett. May I speak with you?"

"I'm eatin' my breakfast. Don't care for no mornin' chat."

"It should just take a minute."

"Ain't got a minute. Go 'way."

"Mr. Linch," Matthew said, "I do need to speak with you. If not now, then I'll have to persist."

"Persist all you please. I don't give a damn." There was the sound of footsteps walking away from the door. The shutters of a second window were pulled closed, followed by the shutters of a third. Then the final window was sealed with a contemptuous *thump*.

Matthew knew there was one sure way to make Linch open the door, though it was also surely a risk. He decided to take it.

"Mr. Linch?" Matthew said, standing close to the door. "What interests you so much about the Egyptian culture?"

A pot clattered to the floor within.

Matthew stepped away from the door several paces. He waited, his hands clasped behind his back. A latch was thrown with violent force. But the door was not fairly ripped from its hinges in being opened, as Matthew had expected. Instead, there was a pause.

Control, Matthew thought. *Control is Linch's religion, and he's praying to his god.* The door was opened. Slowly.

But just a crack. "Egyptian culture? What're you blatherin' about, boy?"

"You know what I mean. The book in your desk."

Again, a pause. Something about it this time was ominous.

"Ohhhhh, it was *you* come in my house and gone through my things, eh?" Now the door opened wider, and Linch's clean but unshaven face peered out. His pale, icy gray eyes were aimed at Matthew with the power of weapons, his teeth bared in a grin. "I found your shoemud on my floor. You didn't shut my trunk firm enough, either. Have to be blind not to see it was open a quarter-inch."

"You're very observant, aren't you? Does that come from catching rats?"

"It does. I see, though, I let a whorin' mother's two-legged rat creep in and nibble my cheese."

"Interesting cheese, too," Matthew said, maintaining his distance from the door. "I would never have imagined you . . . how shall I say this? . . . lived in such virtuous order, from the wreck you've allowed the exterior of your house to become. I also would never have imagined you to be a scholar of ancient Egypt."

"There is a law," Linch said, his grin still fixed and his eyes still aimed, "against enterin' a man's house without bein' invited. I believe in this town it's ten lashes. You care to tell Bidwell, or you want me to?"

"Ten lashes." Matthew frowned and shook his head. "I would surely hate to suffer ten lashes, Mr. Linch."

"Fifteen, if I can prove you thieved anythin'. And you know what? I might just be missin' a . . ."

"Sapphire brooch?" Matthew interrupted. "No, that's in the drawer where I left it." He offered Linch a tight smile.

The ratcatcher's expression did not change, though there might have been a slight narrowing of the eyes. "You're a cocksure bastard, ain't you? But you're good. I'll grant you that. You knotted the twine back well enough to fool me . . . and I ain't fooled very often."

"Oh, I think it's you who does the fooling, Mr. Linch. What is this masquerade about?"

"Masquerade? You're talkin' riddles, boy!"

"Now you just said an interesting word, Mr. Linch. You yourself are a riddle, and one I mean to solve. Why is it that you present yourself to the town as being . . . and let us be plainspoken here . . . a roughhewn and filthy dolt, when you actually are a man of literacy and good order? *Meticulous* order, I might say. And need I add the point of your obvious financial status, if indeed that brooch belongs to you?"

From Linch there was not a word nor a trace of reaction but Matthew could tell from the glint of his extraordinary eyes that the man's mind was working, grinding these words into a fine dust to be weighed and measured.

"I suspect that even your harborfront accent is shammed," Matthew went on. "Is it?"

Linch gave a low, quiet laugh. "Boy, your brainpan has been dented. If I were you, I'd either go get drunk or ask the town quack for a cup of opium."

"You are not who you pretend to be," Matthew said, defying the man's cutting stare. "Therefore . . . who are you?"

Linch paused, thinking about it. Then he licked his lower lip and said, "Come on in and we'll have us a talk."

"No, thank you. I do enjoy the sun's warmth. Oh . . . I also spoke to one of the maskers as I passed their camp. If I were to . . . suffer an accident, say . . . I'm sure the man would recall I'd been walking in this direction."

"Suffer an *accident?* What foolishness are you prattlin'? No, come on in and I'll spell you what you care to know. Come on." Linch hooked a finger at him.

"You may spell me what I care to know right here as well as in there."

"No, I can't. 'Sides, my breakfast is coolin'. Tell you what: I'll open all the shutters and leave the door wide. That suit you?"

"Not really. I *have* noticed a dearth of neighbors in this vicinity."

"Well, either come in or not, 'cause I'm done with this chattin'." He opened the door to its widest possible degree and walked away. Soon afterward, the nearest window was opened, the shutters pushed as far as their hinges would allow. Then the next window was opened, and afterward the third and fourth.

Matthew could see Linch, wearing tan-colored breeches and a loose-fitting gray shirt, busying himself around the hearth. The interior of the house appeared just as painstakingly neat as Matthew had previously seen it. He realized that he'd begun a duel of nerves with the ratcatcher, and this challenge to come into the house was the riposte to his own first slash concerning Linch's interest in Egyptian culture.

Linch stirred something in a skillet and added what might have been spices from a jar. Then, seemingly unconcerned with Matthew, he fetched a wooden plate and spooned food onto it.

Matthew watched as Linch sat down at his desk, placed the plate before him, and began to eat with a display of mannered restraint. Matthew knew nothing was to be gained by standing out here, yet he feared entering the ratcatcher's house even with the door and every window open wide. Still . . . the challenge had been given, and must be accepted.

Slowly and cautiously, he advanced first to the doorway, where he paused to gauge Linch's reaction. The ratcatcher kept eating what looked to be a mixture of eggs, sausage, and potatoes all cooked together. Then, even more cautiously, Matthew walked into the house but stopped with the threshold less than an arm's length behind him.

Linch continued to eat, using a brown napkin to occasionally wipe his mouth. "You have the manners of a gentleman," Matthew said.

"My mother raised me right," came the reply. "You won't find me stealin' into private houses and goin' through people's belongin's."

"I presume you have an explanation for the book? And the brooch as well?"

"I do." Linch looked out the window that his desk stood before. "But why should I explain anythin' to you? It's *my* business."

"That's true enough. On the other hand, can't you understand how . . . uh . . . *strange* this appears?"

"*Strange* is one of them things in the eye of the beholder now, ain't it?" He put his spoon and knife down and turned his chair a few inches so that he was facing Matthew more directly. The movement made Matthew back away apace. Linch grinned. "I scare you, do I?"

"Yes, you do."

"Well, why should you be scared of me? What have I ever done to *you*, 'cept save your ass from bein' et up by rats there in the gaol?"

"You've done nothing to me," Matthew admitted. He was ready to deliver the next slash. "I just wonder what you may have done to Violet Adams."

To his credit—and his iron nerves—Linch only exhibited a slight frown. "Who?"

"Violet Adams. Surely you know the child and her family."

"I do. They live up the street. Cleaned some rats out for 'em not too long ago. Now what am I supposed to have done to that little girl? Pulled her dress up and poked her twat?"

"No, nothing so crude . . . or so obvious," Matthew said. "But I have reason to believe that you may have—"

Linch suddenly stood up and Matthew almost jumped out the door.

"Don't piss your breeches," Linch said, picking up his empty plate. "I'm gettin' another helpin'. You'll pardon me if I don't offer you none?"

Linch went to the hearth, spooned some more of the breakfast onto his plate, and came back to his chair. When he sat down, he turned the chair a few more inches toward Matthew so that now they almost directly faced each other. A stream of sunlight lay across Linch's chest. "Go on," he said as he ate, the plate in his lap. "You were sayin'?"

"Uh . . . yes. I was saying . . . I have reason to believe you may have defiled Violet Adams in a way other than physical."

"What other way is there?"

"Mental defilement," Matthew answered. Linch stopped chewing. Only for a space of perhaps two heartbeats, however. Then Linch was eating once more, staring at the pattern of sunlight on the floorboards between them.

Matthew's sword was aimed. It was time to strike for the heart, and see what color blood spurted out. "I believe you created a fiction in the child's mind that she had an audience with Satan in the Hamilton house. I believe you've had a hand in creating such a fiction in many people hereabouts, including Jeremiah Buckner and Elias Garrick. *And* that you planted the poppets under Rachel

Howarth's floor and caused Cara Grunewald to have a 'vision' that led to their discovery."

Linch continued to eat his breakfast without haste, as if these damning words had never been uttered. When he spoke, however, his voice was . . . somehow changed, though Matthew couldn't quite explain its difference other than a subtle shift to a lower pitch.

"And just how am I supposed to have done such a thing?"

"I have no idea," Matthew said. "Unless you're a warlock, and you've learned sorcery at the Devil's knee."

Linch laughed heartily and put his plate aside. "Oh, that's rich indeed! Me a warlock! Oh, yes! Shall I shoot a fireball up your arse for you?"

"That's not necessary. If you wish to begin refuting my theory by explaining your masquerade, you may proceed."

Linch's smile faded. "And if I don't, you'll have me burnin' at the stake in place of your wench? Listen to me, boy: when you go see Dr. Shields, ask for a whole *keg* of opium."

"I'm sure Mr. Bidwell's curiosity about you will be fired just as mine was," Matthew said calmly. "Particularly after I tell him about the book and the brooch."

"You mean you haven't *already?*" Linch gave a faint, sinister smile.

"No. Mind you, the maskers saw me pass their camp."

"The *maskers!*" Linch laughed again. "Maskers have less sense than rats, boy! They pay attention to no details but lookin' at their own damned faces in mirrors!"

This had been said with contemptuous ferocity . . . and suddenly Matthew knew.

"Ahhhhh," he said. "Of course. *You* are a professional actor, aren't you?"

"I've already told you I spent some time with a circus," Linch said smoothly. "My act with trained rats. I had some dealin's with actors, much to my sorrow. I say to Hell with the whole lyin', stealin' breed. But look here." He opened the drawer and brought out the Egyptian tome and the wallet that hid the sapphire brooch. Linch placed both objects on the desktop, then removed the twine-tied brown cotton cloth from the wallet and began to untie it with nimble fingers. "I expect I *should* give you some kind of explanation, such as it is."

"It would be much appreciated." And very intriguing to see what Linch came up with, Matthew thought.

"The truth is . . . that I *am* more learned than I let on. But I ain't shammin' the accent. I was born on the breast of the Thames, and I'm proud of it." Linch had undone the twine, and now he opened the cloth and picked up the sapphire brooch between the thumb and forefinger of his right hand. He held it in the stream of sunlight, inspecting it with his pale, intense eyes. "This belonged to my mother, God rest her lovin' soul. Yes, it's worth a good piece of coin but I'd never part with it. Never. It's the only thing I've got to remember her by." He turned the brooch slightly, and light glinted from its golden edge into Matthew's face. "It's a thing of beauty, ain't it? So beautiful. Like she was. So, so beautiful." Again, the brooch was turned and again a glint of light struck Matthew's eyes.

Linch's voice had almost imperceptibly softened. "I'd never part with it. Not for any amount of money. So beautiful. So very, very beautiful."

The brooch turned . . . the light glinted . . .

"Never. For any amount of money. You see how it shines? So, so beautiful. Like she was. So, so beautiful."

The brooch . . . the light . . . the brooch . . . the light . . .

Matthew stared at the golden glint. Linch had begun to angle the brooch slowly in and out of the sun's stream, in a regular—and transfixing—pattern.

"Yes," Matthew said. "Beautiful." With a surprising amount of difficulty, he pulled his gaze away from the brooch. "I want to know about the book."

"Ahhhh, the book!" Linch slowly raised the index finger of his left hand, which again secured Matthew's attention. Linch made a small circle in the air with that finger, then slid it down to the brooch. Matthew's eyes followed its smooth descent, and suddenly he was staring once more at the light . . . the brooch . . . the light . . . the brooch . . .

"The book," Linch repeated softly. "The book, the book, the book."

"Yes, the *book,*" Matthew said, and just as he attempted to pull his gaze again from the brooch Linch held it motionless in the light for perhaps three seconds. The lack of movement now seemed as strangely compelling as the motion. Linch then began to move the brooch in and out of the light in a slow clockwise direction.

"The book." This was peculiar, Matthew thought. His voice sounded hollow, as if he were hearing himself speak from the distance of another room. "Why . . ." The brooch . . . the light . . . the brooch . . . the light. "Why Egyptian culture?"

"Fascinating," Linch said. "I find the Egyptian culture fascinating."

The brooch . . . the light . . .

"Fascinating," Linch said again, and now he too seemed to be speaking from a distance. "How they . . . forged an empire . . . from shifting sand. Shifting sand . . . all about . . . shifting sand . . . flowing . . . softly, softly . . ."

"*What?*" Matthew whispered. The brooch . . . the light . . . the brooch . . .

"Shifting . . . shifting sand," Linch said.

. . . the light . . .

"Listen, Matthew. Listen."

Matthew was listening. It seemed to him that the room around him had become darkened, and the only glint of illumination came from that brooch in Linch's hand. He could hear no sound but Linch's low, sonorous voice, and he found himself waiting for the next word to be spoken.

"Listen . . . Matthew . . . the shifting sand . . . shifting . . . so so beautiful . . ."

The voice seemed to be whispering right in his ear. No, no: Linch was closer than that. Closer . . .

. . . the brooch . . . the light . . . the brooch . . .

Closer.

"Listen," came the hushed command, in a voice that Matthew now hardly recognized. "Listen . . . to the silence."

. . . the light . . . the shifting shifting sand . . . the brooch . . . the so so beautiful light . . .

"Listen, Matthew. To the silence. Every. Thing. Silent. Every. Thing. So so beautiful. The shifting shifting sand. Silent, silent. The town . . . silent. As if . . . the whole world . . . holds its breath . . ."

"Uh!" Matthew said; it was the panicked sound of a drowning swimmer, searching for air. His mouth opened wider . . . he heard himself gasp . . . a terrible noise . . .

"Silent, silent," Linch was saying, in a hushed, slow singsong voice. "Every. Thing. Silent. Every. Till—"

"No!" Matthew took a backward step and collided with the doorframe. He jerked his eyes away from the glinting brooch, though Linch continued to turn it in and out of the sunlight. "No! You're not . . . going to . . ."

"What, Matthew?" Linch smiled, his eyes piercing through Matthew's skull to his very mind. "Not going to what?" He stood up from his chair . . . slowly . . . smoothly . . . like shifting shifting sand . . .

Matthew felt terror bloom within him unlike anything he'd ever experienced. His legs seemed weighted in iron boots. Linch was coming toward him, reaching out to grasp his arm in what seemed a strange slow-motion travesty of time. Matthew could not look away from Linch's eyes; they were the center of the whole world, and everything else was silent . . . silent . . .

He was aware that Linch's fingers were about to take hold of his sleeve.

With all the effort of will he could summon, Matthew shouted, *"No!"* into Linch's face. Linch blinked. His hand faltered, for perhaps a fraction of a second.

It was enough.

Matthew turned and fled from the house. Fled, though his

eyes felt bloodshot and swollen. Fled though his legs were heavy and his throat as dry as shifting sand. Fled with silence thundering in his ears, and his lungs gasping for breath that had seemed stolen away from him only a few seconds before.

He fled along Industry Street, the warm sunlight thawing the freeze that had tightened his muscles and bones. He dared not look back. Dared not look back. Dared not.

But as he ran, putting precious distance between himself and that soft trap he had nearly been snared by, he realized the enormity and strange power of the force that Linch wielded. Such a thing was unnatural . . . monstrous . . . such a thing was *shifting sand . . . shifting* . . . sorcery and must be *silent silent* of the very Devil himself.

It was in his head. He couldn't get it out, and that further terrified him because the contamination of his mind—his most dependable resource—was utterly unthinkable.

He ran and ran, sweat on his face, and his lungs heaving.

thirty-two

MATTHEW SAT, shivering in the sunlight, in the grass beside the spring.

It had been a half hour since he'd fled Linch's house, and still he suffered the effects of their encounter. He felt tired and sluggish, yet frightened to the very core of his being. Matthew thought—and thinking seemed more of an effort than ever in his life—that Linch had done to his mind what *he* had done to Linch's dwelling: entered it without permission, poked about, and left a little smear of mud to betray his presence.

Linch had without a doubt been the winner of their duel.

But—also without a doubt—Matthew now knew Linch was the owner of the shadowy hand that could reach into the human mind and create whatever fiction it pleased. Matthew considered himself intelligent and alert; if *he* had been so affected by the rat-catcher's trancing ability, how simple a task it must have been to overwhelm the more rustic and less mentally agile Buckner, Garrick, and the other targets. And indeed Matthew suspected that the persons in whose minds Linch had planted the scenes of depravity had been carefully chosen because of their receptivity to such manipulation. Linch had obviously had a great deal of experience at this bizarre craft, and most surely he could recognize certain signals that indicated whether a person was a likely candidate for manipulation. Matthew thought that in his own case, Linch had been probing his line of mental defense and had been unsuccessful in breaking the barrier. Linch would probably have never even attempted such a thing if the man hadn't been desperate.

Matthew offered his face to the sun, trying to burn out the last vestiges of shifting sand from the storehouse of memory.

Linch, Matthew believed, had underestimated Violet Adams. The child was more intelligent than her timidity let her appear. Matthew believed that the house in which she described seeing Satan and the white-haired imp was not the Hamilton house, but the house of her own mind. And back there in the dark room was the memory of Linch trancing her. Surely the man had not actually sung that song as he'd done the work, but perhaps the recollection of the event had been locked away from her and so the song—which Violet had heard when Linch had come ratcatching at her house—was an alternate key.

The question was: where and when had Violet been entranced? Matthew thought that if Buckner and Garrick could remember correctly, they might supply the fact that Linch had also come ratcatching—or simply spreading poisoned bait as a "precaution"—to their own houses. Matthew could envision Linch asking either man to step out to the barn to look at evidence of rodent infestation, and then—once away from the sight of wives or other relatives—turning upon them the full power of this strange weapon that both erased reality and constructed a lifelike fiction. What was particularly amazing to Matthew was the fact that the effects of this power might be delayed some length of time; that is, Linch had given some mental command that the fiction not be immediately recollected, but instead recalled several nights later. And the memory of being entranced was erased from the mind altogether . . . except in the case of Violet Adams, whose mind had begun to sing to her in Linch's voice.

It was the damnedest thing he'd ever heard of. Surely it was some form of sorcery! But it was real and it was here and it was the reason Rachel was going to be burned on Monday morning.

And what could he do about it?

Nothing, it seemed. Oh, he could go to Bidwell and plead his case, but he knew what the result of that would be. Bidwell might arrange shackles for him and put him in a cushioned room where he would be no danger to others or himself. Matthew would fear even mentioning such a theory to the magistrate; even if Woodward were able to hear and respond, he would believe Matthew to be so severely bewitched that the stress might sink him into his grave.

The ratcatcher, it seemed, had done much more than winning a duel. Linch had demonstrated that the war was over and declared himself its absolute and cunning victor.

Matthew drew his knees up to his chin and stared out over the blue water. He had to ask the question that seemed to him the most basic query in existence yet also the most complex: *Why?*

For what reason would Linch put forth such an effort to paint Rachel as a witch? And why, indeed, was a man of his vile nature even *in* Fount Royal? Had he murdered Reverend Grove and Daniel Howarth? If Rachel was only a pawn in this strange game—if, for the sake of conjecture, Bidwell was the real target—then why go to such extremes to destroy Fount Royal? Was it possible Linch had been sent from Charles Town to do these dark deeds?

It seemed to Matthew that the jealous watchdogs in Charles Town might encourage the burning of a few empty houses, but they wouldn't stoop so low as to subsidize murder. Then again, who could say what reigned in a man's heart? It would not be the first time that gold coins were spent on a spill of crimson blood.

Matthew narrowed his eyes slightly, watching the surface of the spring ripple with a passing breeze.

Gold coins. Yes. Gold coins. Gold and silver, that is. Of the Spanish stamp.

Taking shape in Matthew's mind was a theory worth chewing on.

Say that, even though he'd found nothing last night, there

was indeed a fortune of pirate coins down at the bottom of the fount. Say that somehow Linch—whoever he really was—had learned of its presence, possibly months or even years before he'd arrived on the scene. When Linch got here, he discovered a town surrounding the treasure vault. What, then, could he do to get the coins for himself and himself alone?

The answer: he could create a witch and cause Fount Royal to wither and die.

Perhaps Linch had gone swimming on more than one occasion, late at night, and discovered . . . *Oh,* Matthew thought, and the realization was like a punch . . . discovered not only gold and silver coins . . . but a sapphire brooch.

What if there was not just coinage in that treasure vault, but also jewelry? Or loose gemstones? If indeed Linch had brought that brooch up from the depths, then the ratcatcher was aware of how necessary it was to clear the town away before a real attempt at salvage could be undertaken.

Yes, Matthew thought. Yes. It was definitely a reason to kill two men and create a witch. But wait . . . Was it not in Linch's best interest that Rachel *not* be burned? With the removal of the "witch," Fount Royal would likely start to grow healthy again. So what was he going to do to make sure the town's decline continued? Create a second witch? That seemed to Matthew to be a task requiring a great deal of risk and months of planning. No, Rachel had been the perfect "witch," and the more reasonable action would be to somehow capitalize on her death.

Perhaps . . . with another murder? And who might find himself throat-slashed by the vengeance of "Satan" in a dimly lit room or hallway some evening hence?

Matthew suspected that this time Linch would go for Fount Royal's jugular. Would it be Dr. Shields lying in a pool of blood? Schoolmaster Johnstone? Edward Winston? No. Those three men, though vital, were replaceable in the future of Fount Royal.

The next victim would be Bidwell himself.

Matthew stood up, his flesh in chillbumps. Near him a woman was dipping two buckets while conversing with a man who was filling a keg. Their faces, though lined by their lives of difficult labor, were free from concern; in them was the statement that all was right with Fount Royal . . . or soon to be right, with the execution of the witch.

Little did they know, Matthew thought. Little did anyone know, except Linch. Especially little did Bidwell know, for as Rachel died writhing in the flames the plan would be set in motion to cut his throat in the same manner as the other victims.

And what could be done about it?

Matthew needed evidence. One sapphire brooch would not do; besides, Matthew was certain Linch would now hide it in a place even a rat couldn't discover. To expose the coins that Goode had found would be beneficial, but would also be a betrayal of Goode's trust. Obviously Linch was the thief who had entered Bidwell's house that night and taken the gold coin from Matthew's room, probably in an effort to ascertain if it was part of the treasure and where it might have come from. That was another question, however: how had an Indian gotten hold of a Spanish coin?

Matthew was feeling more like himself now. He wouldn't return to Linch's house alone for a barrel full of gold coins. But if he could find some piece of evidence that might implicate Linch . . . some hard proof to show Bidwell . . .

"There you are! I was just on my way to see you!" That voice, high-pitched and waspish, struck him with fresh dread.

He turned to face Lucretia Vaughan. She was smiling brightly, her hair contained under a stiff white bonnet, and she wore a lilac-colored dress. In her arms was a small basket. "I hoped to find you in good spirits this day!"

"Uh . . . yes. Good spirits." He was already edging away from her.

"Mr. Corbett, please allow me to present you with a gift! I know . . . well, I know our dinner last night was difficult for you, and I wished to—"

"It's all right," Matthew said. "No gift is necessary."

"Oh, but it is! I realized how much you enjoyed your food—

in spite of my daughter's display of willful misbehavior—therefore I wished to bake you a pie. I trust you like sweet yams?" She lifted the golden-crusted pie from the basket to show him. It was held in a pie dish of white clay decorated with small red hearts.

"It . . . truly looks wonderful," Matthew told her. "But I can't accept it."

"Nonsense! Of course you can! And you may return the dish the next time you come to dinner. Say . . . Tuesday evening at six o'clock?"

He looked into her eyes and saw there a rather sad combination of voracity and fear. As gently as possible, he said, "Mrs. Vaughan, I can't accept the pie. And I can't accept your invitation to dinner, either."

She just stared at him, her mouth partway open and the pie dish still offered. "It is not in my power to help your daughter," Matthew continued. "She seems to have her own mind about things, just as you do, and there lies the collision. I regret you have a problem in your household, but I can't solve it for you."

The woman's mouth had opened a little wider.

"Again, thank you for the dinner. I truly did enjoy it, and the company. Now, if you'll excuse—"

"You . . . ungrateful . . . young . . . *bastard!*" she suddenly hissed, her cheeks flaming red and her eyes half-crazed with anger. "'Do you *realize* what *effort* was expended to please you?"

"Uh . . . well . . . I'm sorry, but—"

"You're *sorry,*" she mimicked bitterly. *"Sorry!* Do you know how much money and time I spent on Cherise's gown? Do you know how I worked over that hearth and cleaned that house for your pleasure? Are you sorry about that, too?"

Matthew noticed that several citizens who'd come to the spring for water were watching. If Lucretia noticed, it made no difference to her because she kept firing cannonades at him. "Oh, but you came in our house and ate your fill, didn't you? You sat there like a lord at feast! You even took bread away with you! And now you're *sorry!*" Tears of rage —misguided rage, Matthew thought—wet her eyes. "I thought you were a gentleman! Well, you're a right *sorry* gentleman, aren't you?"

"Mrs. Vaughan," Matthew said firmly, "I cannot save your daughter from what you perceive as—"

"Who asked you to save *anybody,* you self-righteous prig? How dare you speak to me as if I'm a milkmaid! I am a person of esteem in this town! Do you hear me? *Esteem!*"

She was shouting in his face. Matthew said quietly, "Yes, I hear you."

"If I were a man you wouldn't speak to me with such disrespect! Well, damn you! Damn you and Charles Town and damn all you who think you're better than other people!"

"Pardon me," he said, and began walking toward the mansion.

"Yes, go on and *run!*" she hollered. "Run back to Charles Town, where your kind belongs! You city dog!" Something in her voice broke, but she forced it back. "Playing in your ludicrous gardens and dancing at your sinful balls! Go on and run!"

Matthew didn't run, but his walking pace was brisk enough. He saw that the window of Bidwell's upstairs study had opened and there was the master himself, looking out upon this unfortunate scene. Bidwell was grinning, and when he realized Matthew had seen him he put his hand to his mouth to hide it.

"Wait, wait!" the brazen woman shouted. "Here, take your pie!"

Matthew looked back in time to see Lucretia Vaughan hurl the pie—dish and all—into the spring. Then she fired a glare at him that might have scorched iron, turned on her heel, and stalked away, her chin lifted high as if she had put the Charles Town draggletail in his fly-blown place.

Matthew entered the mansion and went directly up the stairs to the magistrate's room. Woodward's shutters were closed, but Matthew thought the woman's enraged vocals must have frightened birds back in the swamp. The magistrate, however, still slept on, though he did shift his position to the side as Matthew stood next to his bed.

"Sir?" Matthew said, touching his shoulder. "Sir?"

Woodward's sleep-swollen eyes opened to slits. He struggled to focus. "Matthew?" he whispered.

"Yes, sir."

"Oh . . . I thought it was you. I had a dream. A crow . . . shrieking. Gone now."

"Can I get you anything?"

"No. Just . . . tired . . . very tired. Dr. Shields was here."

"He was? This morning?"

"Yes. Told me . . . it was Friday. My days and nights . . . they run together."

"I can imagine so. You've been very ill."

Woodward swallowed thickly. "That potion . . . Dr. Shields gives me. It has . . . a very disagreeable taste. I told him I should . . . wish some sugar in it on the next drinking."

Here was a reason for hope, Matthew thought. The magistrate was lucid and his senses were returning. "I think the potion is doing you some good, sir."

"My throat still pains me." He put a hand to it. "But I do feel . . . somewhat lighter. Tell me . . . did I dream this, or . . . did Dr. Shields apply a funnel to my bottom?"

"You had a colonic," Matthew said. He would long remember the aftermath of that particularly repugnant but necessary procedure. So too would the servant who had to wash out the two chamberpots filled with black, tar-like *refusal.*

"Ah. Yes . . . that would explain it. My apologies . . . to all involved."

"No apologies are necessary, sir. You've comported yourself with extreme grace for the . . . uh . . . unpleasantness of your situation." Matthew went to the dresser and got the bowl of fresh water that had been placed there and one of several clean cotton cloths.

"Always . . . the diplomat," Woodward whispered. "This potion . . . does tire me. Matthew . . . what was done . . . to my back?"

"The doctor used blister cups." Matthew dipped the cloth into the water bowl.

"Blister cups," Woodward repeated. "Oh. Yes . . . I do remember now. Quite painful." He managed a grim smile. "I must have been . . . knocking at death's door."

"Not nearly so close as that." Matthew wrang out the wet cloth and then began to gently apply the cool cotton to Woodward's still-pallid face. "Let us just say you were on a precarious street. But you're better now, and you're going to continue improving. Of that I'm positive."

"I trust . . . you are right."

"I am not only right, I am *correct,*" Matthew said. "The worst part of your illness has been vanquished."

"Tell that . . . to my throat . . . and my aching bones. Oh, what a sin it is . . . to be old."

"Your age has nothing to do with your condition, sir." Matthew pressed the cloth to Woodward's forehead. "You have youth in you yet."

"No . . . I have too much past behind me." He stared at nothing, his eyes slightly glazed in appearance, as Matthew continued to dampen his face. "I would . . . give . . . so much . . . to be you, son." Matthew's hand may have been interrupted in its motions for only a few fleeting seconds.

"To be you," Woodward repeated. "And where you are. With the world . . . ahead of you . . . and the luxury of time."

"You have much time ahead of you too, sir."

"My arrow . . . has been shot," he whispered. "And . . . where it fell . . . I do not know. But you . . . you . . . are just now drawing back your bow." He released a long, strengthless sigh. "My advice to you . . . is to aim at a worthy target."

"You will have much further opportunity to help me identify such a target, sir."

Woodward laughed softly, though the act seemed to pain his throat because it ended in a grimace. "I doubt . . . I can help you . . . with much anymore, Matthew. It has come . . . to my attention on this trip . . . that you have a very able mind of your own. You . . . are a man, now . . . with all that manhood entails. The bitter . . . and the sweet. You have made a good start . . . at manhood . . . by standing up for your convictions . . . even against *me*."

"You don't begrudge my opinions?"

"I would feel . . . an utter failure . . . if you had none," he answered.

"Thank you, sir," Matthew said. He finished his application of the cloth and returned it to the water bowl, which he placed atop the dresser again.

"That is *not* to say," Woodward added, in as loud and clear a voice as he could summon, "that . . . we are in agreement. I still say . . . the woman is your nightbird . . . intent on delivering you to the dark. But . . . every man hears a nightbird . . . of some form or fashion. It is the . . . struggle to overcome its call that either . . . creates or destroys a man's soul. You will understand what I mean. Later . . . after the witch is long silenced."

Matthew stood beside the dresser, his head lowered. He said, "Sir? I need to tell you that—" And then he stopped himself. What was the use of it? The magistrate would never understand. Never. He hardly understood it himself, and he'd experienced Linch's power. No, putting these things into words might rob the magistrate of his improving health, and no good could come of it.

"Tell me what?" Woodward asked.

"That Mr. Bidwell is hosting a dinner tonight," was the first thing that entered his mind. "The maskers have arrived early, and evidently there's to be a reception to honor them. I . . . wanted to tell you, in case you heard voices raised in festivity and wished to know why."

"Ah. This Satan-besieged town . . . could benefit . . . from voices raised in festivity." Woodward let his eyes close again. "Oh . . . I am so tired. Come visit me later . . . and we shall talk about . . . our trip home. A journey . . . I sincerely look forward to."

"Yes, sir. Sleep well." Matthew left the room.

In his own bedchamber, Matthew settled down in the chair by the window to continue reading the book on English plays. It was not that he was compelled to do so by the subject matter, but because he wished to give his mind a rest from its constant maze-crawl. It was his belief, also, that one might see a large picture only by stepping back from the frame. He'd been reading perhaps ten minutes when there came a knock at his door.

"Young sir?" It was Mrs. Nettles. "I ha' somethin' sent from Mr. Bidwell."

Matthew opened the door and found that the woman had brought a silver tray on which rested a single, beautifully blown glass goblet filled with amber liquid.

"What's this?"

"Mr. Bidwell asked that I open a verra old bottle of rum. He said ta tell you that you deserved a taste of such, after such a foul taste as ye had just recently." She looked at him questioningly. "Bein' a servant, I did nae ask what he meant."

"He's being kind. Thank you." Matthew took the goblet and smelled its contents. From the heady aroma, the liquor promised to send him to the same peaceful Elysium that the magistrate currently inhabited. Though it was quite early for drinking so numbing a friend, Matthew decided to allow himself at least two good swallows.

"I ha' another direction from Mr. Bidwell," Mrs. Nettles said. "He asks that you take dinner in your room, the kitchen, or at Van Gundy's this eve. He asks me to inform you that your bill at Van Gundy's would be his pleasure."

Matthew realized it was Bidwell's way of telling him he was not invited to the maskers' dinner. Bidwell had no more use for the services of either the magistrate or Matthew, thus out of sight and out of mind. Matthew also suspected that Bidwell was a little wary of allowing him to roam loose at a gathering. "I'll eat at the tavern," he said.

"Yes sir. May I get you anythin' else?"

"No." As soon as he said it, he reversed his course. "Uh . . . yes." The unthinkable thing had entered his mind once more, as if bound to determine how strong was his fortress wall between common sense and insanity. "Would you come in for a moment, please?" She entered and he shut the door.

He drank his first swallow of the rum, which lit a conflagration down his throat. Then he walked to the window and stood looking over the slave quarters in the direction of the tidewater swamp.

"I ha' things ta tend," Mrs. Nettles said.

"Yes. Forgive me for drifting, but . . . what I need to ask you is . . ." He paused again, knowing that in the next few seconds he would be walking a thin and highly dangerous rope. "First of all," he decided to say, "I passed by the field this morning. Where the execution will take place. I saw the stake . . . the firemound . . . everything in preparation."

"Yes sir," she answered, with no emotion whatsoever.

"I know that Rachel Howarth is innocent." Matthew looked directly into Mrs. Nettles's dark, flesh-hooded eyes. "Do you hear me? I *know* it. I also know who is responsible for the two murders and Rachel's predicament . . . but I am absolutely unable to prove any of it."

"Are you free to name this person?"

"No. And please understand that my decision is not because I don't trust you, but because telling you would only compound your agony in this situation, as it has mine. Also, there are . . . circumstances I don't fathom, therefore it's best to speak no names."

"As you wish, sir," she said, but it was spoken with a broad hint of aggravation.

"Rachel will burn on Monday morning. There is no doubt about that. Unless some extraordinary event occurs between now and then to overturn the magistrate's decree, or some revealing proof comes to light. You may be assured I will continue to shake the bushes for such proof."

"That is all well and good, sir, but what does this ha' to do with *me?*"

"For you I have a question," he said. He took his second swallow of rum, and then waited for his eyes to cease watering. Now he had come to the end of the rope, and beyond it lay . . . what?

He took a deep breath and exhaled it. "Do you know anything of the Florida country?"

Mrs. Nettles gave no visible reaction. "The Florida country," she repeated.

"That's right. You may be aware that it's Spanish territory? Perhaps two hundred miles from—"

"I do know your meanin'. And yes, for sure I know them Spaniards are down there. I keep up with my currents."

Matthew gazed out the window again, toward the swamp and the sea. "Do you also then know, or have you heard, that the Spanish offer sanctuary to escaped English criminals and English-owned slaves?"

Mrs. Nettles was a moment in replying. "Yes sir, I've heard. From Mr. Bidwell, talkin' at table one eve with Mr. Winston and Mr. Johnstone. A young slave by the name of Morganthus Crispin took flight last year. He and his woman. Mr. Bidwell believed they was goin' to the Florida country."

"Did Mr. Bidwell try to recapture the slaves?"

"He did. Solomon Stiles and two or three others went."

"Were they successful?"

"Successful," she said, "in findin' the corpses. What was left of 'em. Mr. Bidwell told John Goode somethin' had et 'em, jus' tore 'em up terrible. Likely a *burr,* is what he said."

"Mr. Bidwell told this to John Goode?" Matthew lifted his eyebrows. "Why? To discourage any of the other slaves from running?"

"Yes sir, I 'spect so."

"Were the corpses brought back? Did you see them?"

"No sir, neither one. They left 'em out there, since there wasn't a value to 'em na' more."

"A value." Matthew said, and grunted. "But tell me this, then: was it possible that the slaves were indeed *not* killed? Was it possible they were never found, and Bidwell had to invent such a story?"

"I wouldn't know, sir. Of that Mr. Bidwell would nae confide in me."

Matthew nodded. He took a third drink. "Rachel is going to die for crimes she did not commit, because she fits someone's twisted need. And I can't save her. As much as I wish to . . . as much as I know she is innocent . . . *I can't.*" Before he could think about it, a fourth swallow of rum had burned down his hatch. "Do you remember saying to me that she needed a champion?"

"I do."

"Well . . . she needs one now more than ever. Tell me this: have any other slaves but Crispin and his wife fled south? Have any tried to reach the Florida country, been caught and returned?"

Her mouth slowly opened. "My Lord," she said softly. "You . . . want to know what the land's like 'tween here and there, don't ye?"

"I said nothing about that. I simply asked if any other—"

"What you asked and what you *meant,*" Mrs. Nettles said, "are two different horses. I'm gettin' your drift, sir, and I can't believe what I'm hearin'."

"Exactly what are you hearing, then?"

"You know. That you'd be willin' ta take her out of that gaol and down ta th' Florida country."

"I said nothing of the sort! And please keep your voice lowered!"

"Did you *have* to speak it?" she asked pointedly. "All these questions, like ta run out my ears!" She advanced a step toward him, looking in her severe black dress like a dark-painted wall in motion. "Listen to me, young man, and I trust ye listen *well.* For your further warrant, it is my understandin' that the Florida country lies near a hundred and fifty miles from Fount Royal, nae two hundred . . . but you would nae make *five* miles a'fore you 'n Madam Howarth both were either et by wild animals or scalped by wild Indians!"

"You forget that the magistrate and I arrived here on foot. We walked considerably more than five miles, through mud and in a pouring rain."

"Yes sir," she said, "and look at the magistrate now. Laid low, he is, 'cause of that walk. If you don't believe that had somethin' to do with at least wearin' him out, you're sadly mistook!" Matthew might have become angered, but Mrs. Nettles was only voicing what he already knew to be true.

"The likes of this I've never heard!" She crossed her arms over her massive bosom in a scolding posture, the silver tray gripped in her right hand. "This is a damn dangerous land! I've seen grown men—men with a mite more meat on their bones than *you*—chopped ta their knees by it! What would you do, then? Jus' parade her from the gaol, mount y'selves two horses and ride out th' gate? Ohhhhh, I think nae!"

Matthew finished the glass of rum and hardly felt the fire. "And even if ye *did* fetch her out," the woman continued, "and *did* by some God-awe miracle get her down ta th' Florida country, what then? You think it's a matter of givin' her over ta th' Spanish and then comin' back? No, again you're sadly mistook! There would be *no* comin' back. *Ever.* You'd be livin' the rest of your life out with them *conquista-* . . . them *con-* . . . them squid-eaters!"

"So long as they wouldn't mix it with blood sausage," Matthew muttered.

"What?"

"Nothing. Just . . . thinking aloud." He licked the goblet's rim and then held the glass out. Mrs. Nettles reverted to the role of servant and put the silver tray up to receive the empty goblet.

"Thank you for the information and the candor," Matthew said. Instead of luffing his sails, the rum had stolen his wind. He felt light-headed but heavy at heart. He went to the window and stood beside it with his hand braced against the wall and his head drooping.

"Yes sir. Is there anythin' else?" She walked to the door, where she paused before leaving.

"One thing," Matthew said. "If someone had taken your sister to the Florida country, after she was accused and convicted of witchcraft, she would still be alive today. Wouldn't you have wanted that?"

"Of course, sir. But I wouldn't ask a body to give up his life ta do it."

"Mrs. Nettles, my life will be given up when Rachel is burned on that stake Monday morning. Knowing what I do . . . and unable to save her through the proper legal channels . . . it's going to be more than I can bear. And I fear also that this is a burden that will never disappear, but only grow heavier with the passage of time."

"If that's the case, I regret ever askin' you ta take an interest in her."

"It *is* the case," he replied, with some heat in it. "And you did ask me to take an interest, and I have . . . and here we are."

"Oh, my," Mrs. Nettles said quietly, her eyes widening. "*Oh . . . my.*"

"Is there a meaning behind that? If so, I'd like to hear it."

"You . . . have a *feelin'* for her, do you nae?"

"A feeling? Yes, I care whether she lives or dies!"

"Nae only that," Mrs. Nettles said. "You know of what I'm speakin'. Oh, my. Who'd ha' *thought* such a thing?"

"You may go now." He turned his back to her, directing his attention out the window at some passing figment.

"Does she know? She ought ta. It mi' ease her—"

"Please *go,*" he said, through clenched teeth.

"Yes sir," she answered, rather meekly, and she closed the door behind her.

Matthew eased himself down in the chair again and put his hands to his face. What had he ever done to deserve such torment as this? Of course it was nothing compared to the anguish Rachel would be subjected to in less than seventy-two hours.

He couldn't bear it. He couldn't. For he knew that wherever he ran on Monday morning . . . wherever he hid . . . he would hear Rachel's screams and smell her flesh burning.

He was near drunk from the goblet of fiery rum, but in truth he could have easily swallowed down the bottle. He had come to the end of the road. There was nothing more he could do, say, or discover. Linch had won. When Bidwell was found murdered a week or so hence—after Matthew and the magistrate had left, of course—the tales of Satan's vengeance would spread through Fount Royal and in one month, if that long, the town would be deserted. Linch might even move into the mansion and lord over an estate of ghosts while he plundered the fount.

Matthew's mind was beleaguered. The room's walls had begun to slowly spin, and if he hadn't put down the Sir Richard he might have feared Linch was still trampling through his head.

There were details . . . details that did not fit.

The surveyor, for instance. Who had he been? Perhaps just a surveyor, after all? The gold coin possessed by Shawcombe. From where had the Indian gotten it? The disappearance of Shawcombe and that nasty brood. Where had they gone, leaving their valuables behind?

And the murder of Reverend Grove.

He could understand why Linch had killed Daniel Howarth. But why the reverend? To emphasize that the Devil had no use for a man of God? To remove what the citizens would feel was a source of protection from evil? Or was it another reason altogether, something that Matthew was missing?

He couldn't think anymore. The walls were spinning too fast. He was going to have to stand up and try to reach the bed, if he could. Ready . . . one . . . two . . . three!

He staggered to the bed, barely reaching it before the room's rotation lamed him. Then he lay down on his back, his arms outflung on either side, and with a heaving sigh he gave himself up from this world of tribulations.

thirty-three

A T HALF-PAST SEVEN, Van Gundy's tavern was doing a brisk business. On any given Friday night the lamplit, smoky emporium of potables and edibles would have a half-dozen customers, mostly farmers who wished to socialize with their brethren away from the ears of wives and children. On *this* Friday night, with its celebratory air due to the fine weather and the imminent end of Rachel Howarth, fifteen men had assembled to talk, or holler as the case might be, to chew on the tavern's salted beef and drink draught after draught of wine, rum, and apple beer. For the truly adventurous there was available a tavern-brewed corn liquor guaranteed to elevate the earth to the level of one's nose.

Van Gundy—a husky, florid-faced man with a trimmed gray goatee and a few sprouts of peppery hair that stood upright on his scalp—was inspired by this activity to perform. Taking up his gittern, he planted himself amid the revelers and began to howl bawdy songs that involved succulent young wives, chastity belts, duplicate keys, and travelling merchants. This *cattawago* proved so ennobling to the crowd that more orders for strong drink thundered forth and the thin, rather sour-looking woman who tended to the serving was gazed upon by bleary eyes as if she were a veritable Helen of Troy.

"Here is a song!" Van Gundy bellowed, his wind puffing the blue pipe smoke that wafted about him. "I made this up myself, just today!" He struck a chord that would've made a cat swoon and began:

"Hi hi ho, here's a tale I know,
'tis a sad sad tale I am sure,
Concerns the witch of Fount Royal,
and her devilish crew,
To call her vile is calling shit mannnnure!"

Much laughter and tankard-lifting greeted this, of course, but Van Gundy was a fool for music.

"Hi hi ho, here's a tale I know,
'tis a sorry sorry tale I know well,
For when the witch of Fount Royal.
has been burnt to cold gray ash,
She'll still be suckin' Satan's cock way down in Helllllll!"

Matthew thought the roof might be hurled off the tavern by the hurricane of noise generated by this ode. He had chosen his table wisely, sitting at the back of the room as far as possible from the center of activity, but not even the two cups of wine and the cup of apple beer he'd consumed could dull the sickened pain produced by Van Gundy's rape of the ear. These fools were insufferable! Their laughing and gruesome attempts at jokes turned Matthew's stomach. He had the feeling that if he remained much longer in this town he would become an accomplished drunkard and sink to a nadir known only by the worms that thrived in dog dates.

Now Van Gundy turned his talents to tunes concocted on the spot. He pointed at a gent nearby and then walloped a chord:

"Let me sing 'bout old Dick Cushing,
Wore out his wife from his constant pushin'

She called for an ointment to ease her down there,
But all the stuff did was burn off her hair!"

Laughter, hilarity, drinking, and rousting aplenty followed. Another customer was singled out:

"Woe to all who cross Hiram Abercrombie,
For he's got a temper would sting a bee,
He can drink any ten men under a table,
And plow their wives' furrows when they are unable!"

Oh, this was torture! Matthew pushed aside the plate of chicken and beans that had served as a not very appetizing dinner. His appetite had been further killed by that unfortunate filth flung at Rachel, who might have silenced this haven of jesters with a single regal glance.

He finished the last swallow of the apple beer and stood up from his bench. At that moment Van Gundy launched into a new tuneless tune:

"Allow us to welcome fine Solomon Stiles,
Whose talent in life lies in walking for miles,
Through Indian woods and beast-haunted glen,
Searchin' for a squaw to put his prick in!"

Matthew looked toward the door and saw that a man had just entered. As a reply to the laughter and shouts directed at him, this new arrival took off his leather tricorn and gave a mocking bow to the assembled idiots. Then he proceeded to a table and sat down as Van Gundy turned his graceless wit upon the next grinning victim, by name Jethro Sudrucker.

Matthew again seated himself. He'd realized that an interesting opportunity lay before him, if he handled it correctly. Was not this the Solomon Stiles who Bidwell had told him was a hunter, and who had gone out with a party of men in search of the escaped slaves? He watched as Stiles—a lean, rawboned man of perhaps fifty years—summoned the serving-woman over, and then he stood up and went to the table.

Just before Matthew was about to make his introduction, Van Gundy strummed his gittern and bellowed forth:

"We should all feel pity for young Matthew Corbett,
I heard beside the spring he was savagely bit.
By that venomous serpent whose passion is pies,
And whose daughter bakes loaves between her hot thighs!"

Matthew blushed red even before the wave of laughter struck him, and redder yet after it had rolled past. He saw that Solomon Stiles was offering only a bemused smile, the man's square-jawed face weathered and sharp-chiselled as tombstone granite. Stiles had closely trimmed black hair, gray at the temples. From his left eyebrow up across his forehead was the jagged scar of a dagger or rapier slash. His nose was the shape of an Indian tomahawk, his eyes dark brown and meticulous in their inspection of the young man who stood before him. Stiles was dressed simply, in black breeches and a plain white shirt.

"Mr. Stiles?" Matthew said, his face still flushed. Van Gundy had gone on to skewer another citizen on his gittern spike. "My name is—"

"I'm aware of your name, Mr. Corbett. You are famous."

"Oh. Yes. Well . . . that incident today was regrettable."

"I meant your scuffle with Seth Hazelton. I attended your whipping."

"I see." He paused, but Stiles did not offer him a seat. "May I join you?"

Stiles motioned toward the opposite bench, and Matthew sat down. "How's the magistrate's health?" Stiles asked. "Still poorly?"

"No, actually he's much improved. I have hopes he'll be on his feet soon."

"In time for the execution, possibly?"

"Possibly," Matthew said.

"It seems only fitting he should witness it and have the satisfaction of seeing justice done. You know, *I* selected the tree from which the stake was cut."

"Oh." Matthew busied himself by flicking some imaginary dust from his sleeve. "No, I didn't know that."

"Hannibal Green, I, and two others hauled it and planted it. Have you been out to take a look?"

"I've seen it, yes."

"What do you think? Does it look sufficient for the purpose?"

"I believe it does."

Stiles took a tobacco pouch, a small ebony pipe, and an ivory matchbox from his pocket. He set about filling the pipe. "I inherited the task from Nicholas. That rascal must have gotten down on bended knee to Bidwell."

"Sir?"

"Nicholas Paine. Winston told me that Bidwell sent him to Charles Town this morning. A supply trip, up the coast to Virginia. What that rascal will do to avoid a little honest labor!" He fired a match with the flame of the table's lantern and then set his tobacco alight.

Matthew assumed Winston had performed trickery upon the morning watchman to advance this fiction of Paine's departure. Obviously an agreement had been reached that would benefit Winston's pockets and status.

Stiles blew out a whorl of smoke. "He's dead."

Matthew's throat clutched. "Sir?"

"Dead," Stiles repeated. "In *my* book, at least. The times I've helped him when he asked me, and then he runs when there's sweating to be done! Well, he's a proper fool to go out on that road alone, I'll tell you. He knows better than that. Bidwell must have some intrigue in the works, as usual." Stiles cocked his head to one side, smoke leaking between his teeth. "*You* don't know what it might be, do you?"

Matthew folded his hands together. He spent a few seconds in thought. "Well," he said. "I might. It *is* interesting what one overhears in that house. Not necessarily meaning to, of course."

"Of course."

"I'm sure both Mr. Bidwell and Mr. Winston would deny it," Matthew said, leaning his head forward in a conspiratorial gesture, "but I might have . . . or might *not* have, you understand . . . overheard the mention of muskets."

"Muskets," Stiles repeated. He took another draw from his pipe.

"Yes sir. Could it be a shipment of muskets? And that might be what Mr. Paine has gone to negotiate?"

Stiles grunted and puffed his pipe. The serving-woman came with a steaming bowl of chicken stew, a spoon, and a rum cup. Matthew asked for another cup of apple beer.

"I was wondering," Matthew said after a space of time during which Stiles put aside his pipe and began eating the stew, "if Mr. Bidwell might fear an Indian attack."

"No, not that. He would have told me if he feared the redskins were wearing paint."

"There are Indians near Fount Royal, I presume?"

"Near. Far. Somewhere out there. I've seen their signs, but I've never seen a redskin."

"They're not of a warlike nature, then?"

"Hard to say what kind of nature they are." Stiles paused to take a drink of rum. "If you mean, do I think they'd attack us? No. If you mean, would I go in with a band of men and attack *them?* No. Not even if I knew where they were, which I don't."

"But they do know where *we* are?"

Stiles laughed. "Ha! That's a good one, young man! As I said, I've never seen a redskin in these woods, but I *have* seen them before, further north. They walk on leaves as birds fly on air. They disappear into the earth while you're looking in their direction, and come up again at your back. Oh yes. They know everything about us. They watch us with great interest, I'm sure, but we would never see them unless they wanted to be seen. And they definitely do *not.*"

"Then in your opinion a traveller, say, need not fear being scalped by them?"

"I myself don't fear it," Stiles said. He spooned stew into his mouth. "Then again, I always carry a musket and a knife and I always know what direction to run. Neither would I go out there alone. It's not the redskins I would fear most, but the wild beasts."

Matthew's apple beer was delivered. He drank some and waited a time before he made his next move. "If not Indians, then," he said thoughtfully, "there might be another reason for a possible shipment of muskets."

"And what would that be?"

"Well . . . Mrs. Nettles and I were engaged in conversation, and she made mention of a slave who escaped last year. He and his woman. Morganthus Crispin, I think the name was."

"Yes. Crispin. I recall that incident."

"They tried to reach the Florida country, I understand?"

"Yes. And were killed and half-eaten before they got two leagues from town."

"Hm," Matthew said. So it was true, after all. "Well," he went on, "I wonder if possibly . . . just possibly, mind you . . . Mr. Bidwell might be concerned that other slaves could follow Crispin's example, and that he wishes the muskets as a show of . . . shall we say . . . keeping his valuables in their place. Especially when he brings in younger and stronger slaves to drain the swamp." He took a stiff drink and then set the cup down. "I'm curious about this, Mr. Stiles. In your opinion, could anyone . . . a slave, I mean . . . actually reach the Florida country?"

"Two of them almost did," Stiles answered, and Matthew sat very still. "It was during Fount Royal's first year. Two slaves—a brother and sister—escaped, and I was sent after them with three other men. We tracked them to near a half-dozen leagues of the Spanish territory. I suppose the only reason we found them is that they lit a signal fire. The brother had fallen in a gully and broken his ankle."

"And they were brought back here?"

"Yes. Bidwell held them in irons and immediately arranged for them to be shipped north and sold. It wouldn't do for any slave to be able to describe the territory or draw a map." Stiles relit his pipe with a second match from the ivory matchbox. "Tell me this, if you are able," he said as he drew flame into the pipe's bowl. "When Mrs. Nettles mentioned this to you, in what context was it? I mean to ask, have you seen any indication that Bidwell is concerned about the slaves?"

Matthew again took a few seconds to formulate a reply. "Mr. Bidwell did express some concern that I not go down into the quarters. The impression I got was that he felt it might be . . . uh . . . detrimental to my health."

"I wouldn't care to go down there in any case," Stiles said, his eyes narrowing. "But it seems to me he might be in fear of an uprising. Such a thing has happened before, in other towns. Little wonder he'd wish to keep such fears a secret! Coming on the heels of the witch, an uprising would surely destroy Fount Royal!"

"My thoughts exactly," Matthew agreed. "Which is why it's best not spoken to anyone."

"Of course not! I wouldn't care to be blamed for starting a panic."

"And neither would I. My curiosity again, sir . . . and pardon me for not knowing these things an experienced hunter as yourself knows . . . but I would think you might lose your way on such a long journey as from here to the Florida country. How far exactly *is* it?"

"I judge it to be a hundred and forty-seven miles, by the most direct route."

"The most direct route?" Matthew asked. He took another drink. "I am still amazed, though, sir. You must have an uncanny sense of direction."

"I pride myself on my woods craft." Stiles pulled from the pipe, leaned his head slightly back, and blew smoke toward the ceiling. "But I must admit I did have the benefit of a map."

"Oh," Matthew said. "Your map."

"Not *my* map. Bidwell's. He bought it from a dealer in Charles Town. It's marked in French by the original explorer—that's how old it is—but I've found it to be accurate."

"It so happens I read and speak French. If you have need of a translation, I'd be glad to be of service."

"You might ask Bidwell. He has the map."

"Ah," Matthew said.

"Van Gundy, you old goat!" Stiles shouted toward the tavern-keeper, not without affection. "Let's have some more rum over here! A cup for the young man, too!"

"Oh, not for me, thank you. I think I've had my fill." Matthew stood up. "I must be on my way."

"Nonsense! Stay and enjoy the evening. Van Gundy's going to be playing his gittern again shortly."

"I hate to miss such an experience, but I have some reading to be done."

"That's what's wrong with you legalists!" Stiles said, but he was smiling. "You think too much!"

Matthew returned the smile. "Thank you for the company. I hope to see you again."

"My pleasure, sir. Oh . . . and thank *you* for the information. You can be sure I'll keep it to myself."

"I have no doubt," Matthew said, and he made his way out of the smoke-filled place before that deadly gittern could be again unsheathed.

On his walk back to the mansion, Matthew sifted what he'd learned like a handful of rough diamonds. Indeed, with luck and fortitude, it was possible to reach the Florida country. Planning the trip—taking along enough food, matches, and the like— would be essential, and so too would be finding and studying that map. He doubted it would be in the library. Most likely Bidwell kept the map somewhere in his upstairs study.

But what was he *considering?* Giving up his rights as an Eng-lishman? Venturing off to live in a foreign land? He might know French and Latin, but Spanish was not a point of strength. Even if he got Rachel out of the gaol—the first problem—and out of the town—the second problem—and down to the Florida country— the third and most mind-boggling problem—then was he truly prepared never to set foot again on English earth?

Or never to see the magistrate again?

Now here was another obstacle. If indeed he surmounted the first two problems and set off with Rachel, then the realization of what Matthew had done could well lay the magistrate in his grave. He might be setting his nightbird free at the cost of killing the man who had opened his own cage from a life of grim despair.

That's what's wrong with you legalists. You think too much.

Candles and lamps were ablaze at the mansion. Obviously the festivity was still under way. Matthew entered the house and heard voices from the parlor. He was intent on unobtrusively walking past the room on his way to the stairs when someone said, "Mr. Corbett! Please join us!"

Alan Johnstone had just emerged on his cane from the dining room, along with the gray-bearded man that Matthew had assumed was the acting troupe's leader. Both men were well dressed—Johnstone certainly more so than the masker—and held goblets of wine. The schoolmaster had adorned his face with a dusting of white powder, just as he'd done the night of Matthew's and the magistrate's arrival. The men appeared fed and satisfied, indicating that dinner had just recently adjourned.

"This young man is Matthew Corbett, the magistrate's clerk," Johnstone explained to his companion. "Mr. Corbett, this is Mr. Phillip Brightman, the founder and principal actor of the Red Bull Players."

"A pleasure!" Brightman boomed, displaying a basso voice powerful enough to wake cemetery sleepers. He shook Matthew's hand with a grip that might have tested the blacksmith's strength, but he was in fact a slim and rather unassuming-looking fellow though he did have that commanding, theatrical air about him.

"Very good to meet you." Matthew withdrew his hand, thinking that Brightman's power had been seasoned by a life of turning a gruelling wheel between the poles of the maskers' art and the necessity of food on the table. "I understand your troupe has arrived somewhat early."

"Early, yes. Our standing engagements in two other communities were . . . um . . . unfortunately cancelled. But now we're glad to be here among such treasured friends!"

"Mr. Corbett!" Winston strolled out of the parlor, wineglass in hand. He was clean, close-shaven, relaxed and smiling, and dressed in a spotless dark blue suit. "Do join us and meet Mr. Smythe!"

Bidwell suddenly appeared behind Winston to toss in his two pence. "I'm sure Mr. Corbett has matters to attend to upstairs. We shouldn't keep him. Isn't that right, Mr. Corbett?"

"Oh, I believe he should at least step in and say hello," Winston insisted. "Perhaps have a glass of wine."

Bidwell glowered at Matthew, but he said with no trace of rancor, "As you please, Edward," and returned to the parlor.

"Come along," Johnstone urged, as he limped on his cane past Matthew. "A glass of wine for your digestion."

"I'm full up with apple beer. But may I ask who Mr. Smythe is?"

"The Red Bull's new stage manager," Brightman supplied. "Newly arrived from England, where he performed excellent service to the Saturn Cross Company and before that to James Prue's Players. I wish to hear firsthand about the witch, too. Come, come!" Before Matthew could make an excuse to leave— since he *did* have a matter to attend to upstairs concerning a certain French-drawn map—Brightman grasped him by the upper arm and guided him into the parlor.

"Mr. David Smythe, Mr. Matthew Corbett," Winston said, with a gesture toward each individual in turn. "The magistrate's clerk, Mr. Smythe. He delivered the guilty decree to the witch."

"Really? Fascinating. And rather fearful too, was it not?" Smythe was the young blond-haired man Matthew had seen sitting beside Brightman on the driver's plank of the lead wagon. He had an open, friendly face, his smile revealing that he'd been blessed with a mouthful of sturdy white teeth. Matthew judged him to be around twenty-five.

"Not so fearful," Matthew replied. "I did have the benefit of iron bars between us. And Mr. Bidwell was at my side."

"Fat lot of good I might have done!" Bidwell said mirthfully, also in an effort to take control of this conversation. "One snap from that damned woman and I would've left my boots standing empty!"

Brightman boomed a laugh. Smythe laughed also, and so did Bidwell at his own wit, but Winston and the schoolmaster merely offered polite smiles.

Matthew was stone-faced. "Gentlemen, I remain unconvinced that—" He felt a tension suddenly rise in the room, and Bidwell's laugh abruptly ended. "—that Mr. Bidwell would have been anything less than courageous," Matthew finished, and the sigh of relief from the master of Fount Royal was almost audible.

"I neither recall meeting the woman nor her husband last year," Brightman said. "Did they not attend our play, I wonder?"

"Likely not." Bidwell crossed the parlor to a decanter of wine and filled his own glass. "He was a rather quiet . . . one might say reclusive . . . sort, and she was surely busy fashioning her own acting skills. Uh . . . *not* to infer that your craft has anything whatsoever to do with the infernal realm."

Brightman laughed again, though not nearly so heartily. "Some would disagree with you, Mr. Bidwell! Particularly a reverend hereabouts. You know we had occasion to oust a certain Bible-thumper from our camp this afternoon."

"Yes, I heard. Reverend Jerusalem possesses a fire that unfortunately sears the righteous as well as the wicked. Not to fear, though: as soon as he applies the rite of sanctimony to the witch's ashes, he'll be booted out of our Garden of Eden."

Oh, the wit overflowed tonight! Matthew thought. "The rite of sanctimony?" He recalled hearing Jerusalem use that phrase when the preacher had first come to the gaol to confront his "enemy mine." "What kind of nonsense is *that?*"

"Nothing you would understand," Bidwell said, with a warning glance.

"I'm sure he would," Johnstone countered. "The preacher plans to administer some kind of ridiculous rite over Madam

Howarth's ashes to keep her spirit, phantasm, or whatever from returning to haunt Fount Royal. If you ask me, I think Jerusalem has studied Marlowe and Shakespeare at least as much as he's studied Adam and Moses!"

"Oh, you speak the names of our gods, sir!" Brightman said, with a huge smile. His smile, however, quickly faded as a more serious subject came to mind. "I do heavily regret the passing of *another* reverend, though. Reverend Grove was a man who saw a noble place for theatrical endeavors. I do miss seeing him this trip. David, you would have liked the man. He was of good humor, good faith, and certainly good reason. Mr. Bidwell, I'm sure your community is diminished by his absence."

"It most certainly is. But after the witch is dead—and thank God it will be soon—and our town back on an even keel, we shall endeavor to find a man of similar sterling qualities."

"I doubt you shall find a reverend who was a better player at chess!" Brightman said, smiling again. "Grove trounced me soundly on two occasions!"

"He trounced us all," Johnstone said, with a sip of his wine. "It got to the point I refused to play him."

"He once beat me in a game that took all of five minutes," Winston added. "Of course, with him calling out all his moves in Latin and me being a dunce at that language, I was befuddled from the opening pawn."

"Well," Brightman said, and he lifted his wineglass. "Let me propose a toast to the memory of Reverend Grove. And also the memory of so many others who have departed your town, whether by choice or circumstance."

All but Matthew, who had no glass, participated in the toast. "I do miss seeing others I recall," Brightman continued, sadness in his voice. "A stroll around town told me how much the witch has hurt you. There weren't nearly so many empty houses, were there? Or burned ones?"

"No, there were not," Winston said, with either admirable pluck or stunning gall.

"Demonic doings, I gather?" Brightman asked Bidwell, who nodded. Then the thespian turned his attention to Johnstone. "And the schoolhouse burned too?"

"Yes." The schoolmaster's voice held an angry edge. "Burned to the ground before my eyes. The sorriest sight of my life. If our fire fighters had been at all trained and a great deal less lazy, the schoolhouse might have been saved."

"Let us not delve into that again, Alan." It was obvious to Matthew that Bidwell was trying to soothe a terribly sore point. "We must let it go."

"*I'll* not let it go!" Johnstone snapped, his eyes darting toward Bidwell. "It was a damned crime that those so-called firemen stood there and allowed that schoolhouse—*my schoolhouse*—to burn! After all that work put into it!"

"Yes, Alan, it was a crime," Bidwell agreed. He stared into his glass. "But all the work was done by others, so why should you be so angry? The schoolhouse can be—and shall be—rebuilt." Brightman nervously cleared his throat, because again a tension had entered the room.

"What you mean to say, Robert, is that due to my deformity I simply stood aside while others did the labor?" Johnstone's anger was turning colder. "Is that your meaning?"

"I said . . . and meant . . . nothing of the sort."

"Gentlemen, gentlemen!" Brightman's smile was intended to return warmth to the gathering. "Let us not forget that Fount Royal faces the morning of a wondrous new day! I have no doubt the schoolhouse and all the rest of the structures shall be returned to their former glory, and that those houses vacated by past friends shall be soon inhabited by new ones." Still the chilly air lingered between Bidwell and Johnstone. Brightman looked to Smythe. "David, what was that you were telling me this afternoon? You recall, before that preacher stormed in? Mr. Bidwell, you might find this of interest!"

"Yes?" Bidwell raised his eyebrows, while Johnstone hobbled away to refill his glass.

"Oh . . . about the man," Smythe said. "Yes, this was peculiar.

A man came to the camp today. He was looking about. I know it sounds very odd, but . . . I found something familiar about him. His walk . . . his bearing . . . something."

"And you know who it was?" Brightman asked Bidwell. "Of all people, your ratcatcher!" At the mere mention of the man, Matthew's throat seemed to clutch.

"Linch?" Bidwell frowned. "Was he over there bothering you?"

"No, not that," Smythe said. "He seemed to be just . . . inspecting us, I suppose. We'd had several visitors who just strolled around the camp. But this man . . . well, it *does* sound very strange, but . . . I watched him for a moment or two, and then I approached him from behind. He had picked up a blue glass lantern that is used in one of our morality scenes. The way his fingers moved over the glass . . . the way he turned the lantern this way and that . . . I thought I had *seen* such movements before. And I also thought I knew who the man was, yet . . . he was dressed in filthy clothes, and he was so very changed from the last time I'd seen him, when I was perhaps . . . oh . . . sixteen or seventeen years old."

"Pardon me," Matthew said, his throat still tight. "But who did you think Mr. Linch might have been?"

"Well, I spoke the name. I'm sure I sounded incredulous. I said: 'Mr. Lancaster?' and he turned around." Smythe put a finger to his mouth, as if determining whether to continue this tale or not.

"Yes?" Matthew prodded. "What then?"

"I . . . know this is absolutely ridiculous . . . but then again, Mr. Lancaster *did* have an act in the circus that involved trained rats, so when Mr. Brightman explained to me that the man was Fount Royal's ratcatcher, then . . . it's all very puzzling."

"Puzzling?" Johnstone had returned with his fresh glass of wine. "How so?"

"I could swear the man *was* Jonathan Lancaster," Smythe said. "In fact, I *would* swear it. He turned toward me and looked me right in the face . . . and I saw his eyes. Such eyes . . . pale as ice . . . and piercing to the soul. I have seen them before. The man *is* Jonathan Lancaster, but . . ." He shook his head, his blond brows knit. "I . . . had not planned on mentioning this to anyone but Mr. Brightman. I intended first to locate Mr. Lancaster— your ratcatcher, I mean—and find out for myself, in private, why he has . . . um . . . sunken to such a low profession."

"My pardon, please!" Brightman said. "I didn't realize this was a personal matter!"

"Oh, that's all right." He gave Brightman a rather vexed glance. "Once a cat is out of a bag, sir, it is very difficult to put it back in again."

"The same might be said of a fox," Matthew offered. "But tell me: did Linch—or Lancaster—speak to you? Did he seem to recognize you as well?"

"No, I saw no recognition on his part. As soon as I spoke his name, he hurried away. I was going to follow him, but . . . I decided he might be ashamed to be seen dressed in rags. I wished not to intrude on his privacy until I had considered if I was mistaken or not."

"Gwinett Linch has *always* been Gwinett Linch, from what I know," Bidwell contended. "Who *is* this Jonathan Lancaster?"

"Mr. Lancaster was employed at the circus at the same time my father was its manager," Smythe said. "I had the run of the place, and I helped where my father directed me. As I said, Mr. Lancaster had an act that involved trained rats, but he also—"

The door's bell rang with such ferocity that it must have been near pulled off its hinge. Before two seconds had passed, the door burst open and the visitor announced himself with a soul-withering shout: "How *dare* ye! How *dare* ye do me such an injury!"

"Oh my Lord!" Brightman said, his eyes wide. "The storm returns!"

Indeed the black-clad, black-tricorned whirlwind entered the room, his gaunt and wrinkled face florid with rage and the cords standing out in his neck. "I demand to know!" Exodus Jerusalem hollered, aiming his mouth at Bidwell. "Why was I not invited to thy preparations?"

"What preparations?" Bidwell fired back, his own temper in danger of explosion. "And how dare *you* enter my house with such rudeness!"

"If thee wisheth to speak of rudeness, we might speak of the rudeness thou hast not only shown to me, but also shown to thy God Almighty!" The last two words had been brayed so loudly the walls seemed to tremble. "It was not enough for thee to allow such sinful filth as *play-actors* into thy town, but then thou forceth me to abide within nostril's reach of them on the same *street!* God warrant it, I should have given thy town up as lost to Hell's fires that very instant! And I still wouldst, if not for the rite of just layment!"

"The rite of *just layment?*" Bidwell now exhibited a suspicious scowl. "Hold a moment, preacher! I thought you said it was the rite of sanctimony!"

"Oh . . . yes, it *is* also called such!" Jerusalem's voice had faltered, but already it was gathering hot wind again for another bellow. "Wouldst thou believe that so important a rite wouldst only have *one* name? Even God Himself is also called Jehovah! Lord above, deliver thy servant from such blind pride as we vieweth aplenty in this room!"

Matthew was not so blind as to fail to realize that Jerusalem, as was his nature, had taken center stage in the prideful parlor. Brightman and Smythe had retreated for the safety of their ears, Bidwell had backed up several paces, and even the stalwart schoolmaster had staggered back, the knuckles of his cane-gripping hand white with pressure.

Winston, however, had stood his ground. "What's the meaning of bursting in on Mr. Bidwell's private affairs?"

"Sir, in God's great kingdom there are *no* private affairs!" Jerusalem snapped. "It is only Satan who craveth secrecy! That is why I am so amazed and confounded by the fact that thou wouldst hide this meeting with the play-actors from mine eyes!"

"I did *not* hide anything from you!" Bidwell said. "Anyway, how the hell . . . I mean . . . how on earth did you find out the actors were even *here?*"

"I wouldst have remained unenlightened had I not ventured to the play-actors' camp—as a man who loveth peace and brotherhood—to speak with their leader. And *then* I learneth from some fat thespian whose saint must surely be gluttony that Mr. Brightman is here with thee! And I kneweth exactly what must be transpiring!"

"And exactly what *is* transpiring?" Winston asked.

"The planning, as thou well knoweth!" It was spoken with dripping sarcasm. "To cut me out of the execution day!"

"*What?*" Bidwell saw that Mrs. Nettles and two serving-girls had come to peer into the room, perhaps fearing violence from the wall-shaking volume. He waved them away. "Preacher, I fail to understand what you're—"

"I went to see thee, brother Brightman," Jerusalem interrupted, addressing the other man, "for the purpose of creating an agreement. I understand that thou planneth a play after the witch hath been burned. That evening, as I hear. I mineself have intentions that very eve to deliver a message to the citizens upon the burning battleground. As an observer of debased human nature, I fully realize there are more misguided sinners who wouldst attend a pig-and-bear show than hear the word of God Almighty, no matter how compelling the speaker. Therefore I wished—as a peaceful, brotherly man—to offer up mine services to enricheth your performance. Say . . . a message delivered to the crowd between each scene, building to a finale that will hopefully enricheth us *all?*"

A stunned quiet reigned. Brightman broke it, with thunder. "This is *outrageous!* I don't know from where you hear your faulty information, but we're planning no play on the night of the witch's burning! Our plans are to exhibit morality scenes several nights afterward!"

"And from where *do* you get this information, preacher?" Winston challenged.

"From a fine woman of thy town. Madam Lucretia Vaughan came to speak with me earlier this evening. She wisheth to afford the crowd with her breads and pies, a sample of which she was most delighted to give." Matthew had to wonder if that was the only sample the woman had given the lecherous rogue.

"In fact," Jerusalem went on, "Madam Vaughan hath created a special bread to be offered at the burning. She calleth it 'Witch Riddance Loaf.'"

"For God's justice!" Matthew said, unable to hold his silence an instant longer. "Get this fool out of here!"

"Spoken as a true demon in training!" Jerusalem retorted, with a sneering grin. "If thy magistrate knew anything of God's justice, he would have a second stake prepared for *thee!*"

"His magistrate . . . *does* know God's justice, sir," came a weak but determined voice from the parlor's doorway.

Every man turned toward the sound.

And there—miraculously!—stood Isaac Temple Woodward, returned from the land of the near-dead.

"Magistrate!" Matthew exclaimed. "You shouldn't be out of bed!" He rushed to his side to offer him support, but Woodward held out a hand to ward him off while he gripped the wall with his other.

"I am sufficiently able . . . to be out, up, and about. Please . . . allow me room in which to draw a breath."

Not only had Woodward climbed out of bed and negotiated the staircase, he had also dressed in a pair of tan breeches and a fresh white shirt. His thin calves were bare, however, and he wore no shoes. His face was yet very pallid, which made the dark purple hollows beneath his eyes darker still; his scalp was also milk-pale, the age-spots upon his head a deep red in contrast. Gray grizzle covered his cheeks and chin.

"Please! Sit down, sit down!" Bidwell recovered from his shock and motioned to the chair nearest Woodward.

"Yes . . . I think I shall. The stairs have winded me." Woodward, with Matthew's aid, eased to the chair and sank down onto it. Matthew felt no trace of fever from the magistrate, but there was still emanating from him the sweetish-sour odor of the sickbed.

"Well, this is quite amazing!" Johnstone said. "The doctor's potion must have gotten him up!"

"I believe . . . you are correct, sir. A dose of that elixir . . . thrice a day . . . would surely awaken Lazarus."

"Thank God for it!" Matthew pressed his hand to Woodward's shoulder. "I would never have let you get out of bed, if I'd known you were able, but . . . this is wonderful!"

The magistrate put his hand on Matthew's. "My throat still pains me. My chest as well. But . . . any improvement is welcome." He squinted, trying to make out the faces of two men he didn't know. "I'm sorry. Have we met?"

Bidwell made the introductions. Neither Brightman nor Smythe stepped forward to shake hands; in fact, Matthew noted, they stayed well on the other side of the room.

"Some wine, Magistrate?" Bidwell pushed a glass into Woodward's hand, whether he wanted it or not. "We are so very glad you've come out the other side of your ordeal!"

"No one more glad than I," Woodward rasped. He sipped the wine, but couldn't taste a hint of it. Then his gaze went to the preacher, sharpening as it travelled. "In reply to your comment concerning God's justice, sir . . . I must say that I believe God to be the most lenient judge . . . in all of creation . . . and merciful beyond all imaginings. Because if He were not . . . you would have found yourself called to His courtroom on a lightning bolt by now."

Jerusalem braced himself to make some cutting reply, but he seemed to think better of it. He bowed his head. "I humbly apologize for any remark that might have caused thee distress, sir. It is not mine wish to offend the law."

"Why not?" Woodward asked, taking another tasteless drink. "You've offended . . . everyone else hereabouts, it seems."

"Uh . . . pardon, please," Brightman spoke up, a little nervously. "David and I ought to be going. I mean no offense either, Magistrate. We both wish to hear about your experience with the witch, but . . . as you might well understand . . . the ability of a thespian to project lies in the throat. If we should . . . um . . . find difficulty, in that area, then—"

"Oh, I didn't think!" Woodward said. "Please forgive me. Of course . . . you don't wish to risk any health complications!"

"Exactly, sir. David, shall we go? Mr. Bidwell, thank you for a wonderful dinner and a gracious evening." Brightman was obviously in a hurry to leave, fearing that any throat affliction might doom his play-acting. Matthew was eager to know more about Linch or Lancaster or whatever his name was, but now was not the time. He decided that first thing in the morning he would seek out Smythe for the rest of the story.

"I shall join thee!" Jerusalem announced to the two men, and both of them looked further stricken. "It seems we have much to talk over and plan, does it not? Now . . . concerning these morality scenes. How long are they to be? I ask because I wish to keep a certain . . . shall we say . . . rhythm to the pace of my message!"

"Ahhhh, how magnificent it is . . . to be free from that bed!" Woodward said, as Bidwell showed his guests and the pest out. "How goes it, Mr. Winston?"

"Fine, sir. I can't tell you how gratified I am to see you doing so much better."

"Thank you. Dr. Shields should be here soon . . . for my third dose of the day. The stuff has . . . burned my tongue to a cinder, but thank God I can breathe."

"I have to say, you seemed at a dangerous point." Johnstone finished his wine and set the glass aside. "Far *past* a dangerous point, to be more truthful. I'm sure you had no way of knowing this, but there are some—many—who feel Madam Howarth cursed you for handing down the decree."

Bidwell entered again, and had heard the last of what Johnstone had said. "Alan, I don't think it's proper to mention such a thing!"

"No, no, it's all right." Woodward waved a reassuring hand. "I would be surprised if . . . people did *not* say such a thing. If I *was* cursed, it was not by the witch . . . but by the bad weather and my own . . . weak blood. But I'm going to be fine now. In a few days . . . I shall be as fit as I ever was."

"Hear, hear!" Winston said, and raised his glass.

"And fit to travel, too," Woodward added. He lifted his hand and rubbed his eyes, which were still bloodshot and bleary. "This is an . . . incident I wish to put far behind me. What say you, Matthew?"

"The same, sir."

Johnstone cleared his throat. "I should be going myself, now. Robert, thank you for the evening. We shall . . . um . . . have to discuss the future of the schoolhouse at a later date."

"That brings something to mind!" Woodward said. "Alan . . . you should find this of interest. In my delirium . . . I had a dream of Oxford."

"Really, sir?" Johnstone wore a faint smile. "I should say many former students suffer deliriums of Oxford."

"Oh, I was *there!* Right there, on the sward! I was . . . a young man. I had places to go . . . and much to accomplish."

"You heard the tolling of Great Tom, I presume?"

"Certainly I did! One who hears that bell . . . never forgets it!" Woodward looked up at Matthew and gave him a weak smile that nevertheless had the power to rend the clerk's heart. "I shall take you to Oxford one day. I shall show you . . . the halls . . . the great rooms of learning . . . the wonderful *smell* of the place. Do you recall that, Alan?"

"The most singular aroma of my experience was that of the bitter ale at the Chequers Inn, sir. That and the dry aroma of an empty pocket, I fear."

"Yes, that too." Woodward smiled dreamily. "I smelled the *grass.* The chalk. The oaks . . . that stand along the Cherwell. I was there . . . I swear it. I was there as much as . . . any flesh and blood can be. I even found myself at the door of my social fraternity. The old door . . . of the Carleton Society. And there . . . right there before me . . . was the ram's head bellpull . . . and the brass plaque with its motto. *Ius omni est ius omnibus.* Oh, how I recall that door . . . that bellpull, and the plaque." He closed his eyes for a few seconds, taking in the wondrous memory. Then he opened them again and Matthew saw that Woodward's eyes had grown moist. "Alan . . . your society was . . . what did you say it was?"

"The Ruskins, sir. An education fraternity."

"Ah. Do you recall your motto?"

"Certainly I do. It was . . ." He paused, gathering it from the mist. *The greatest sin is ignorance.*"

"There's a fitting motto for an educator . . . is it not?" Woodward asked. "As a jurist, I might . . . disagree with it . . . but then again, we were all young and yet to be schooled . . . at the university of life, were we not?"

"Oxford was difficult," Johnstone said. "But the university of life is well nigh impossible."

"Yes. It does . . . grade rather harshly." The magistrate gave a long sigh, his newfound strength now almost spent. "Pardon me . . . for my rambling. It seems that when one is ill . . . and so near death . . . the past becomes paramount . . . to ease the dwindling of one's future."

"You need never ask apology of me to reflect on Oxford, Magistrate," Johnstone said with what seemed to Matthew an admirable grace. "I too still walk those halls in my memory. Now . . . if you'll please forgive me . . . my knee also has a memory, and it is calling for liniment. Good night to you all."

"I'll walk with you, Alan," Winston offered, and Johnstone accepted with a nod. "Good night, Mr. Bidwell. Magistrate. Mr. Corbett."

"Yes, good night," Bidwell replied.

Winston followed as Johnstone limped out of the room, leaning even more than usual on his cane. Then Bidwell poured himself the last few swallows of wine from the decanter and went upstairs to avoid any discourse or possible friction with Matthew. As Woodward half-dozed in the chair, Matthew awaited the arrival of Dr. Shields.

The question of Linch/Lancaster was uppermost in Matthew's mind. Here, at last, might be some hope to cling to. If Smythe could positively identify Linch as this other man, it would be a starting point to convince Bidwell that a fiction had been created around Rachel. Was it too much to hope for that all this might be accomplished on the morrow?

thirty-four

A PASSING THUNDERSHOWER had wet the earth just before dawn, but Saturday's sun shone through the dissipating clouds, and the blue sky again reappeared before the hour of eight. By then Matthew had finished his breakfast and was on his way to the maskers' camp.

He discovered—by sense of hearing before sense of sight—Phillip Brightman in discourse with two other thespians, all of them sitting in chairs behind a canvas screen, reading over and reciting pages from one of their morality scenes. When Matthew asked where he might find David Smythe, Brightman directed him to a yellow awning set up to protect a number of trunks, lanterns, and sundry other prop items. Beneath it Matthew found Smythe inspecting some brightly hued costumes that one of the troupe's women was adorning with rather used-looking peacock feathers.

"Good morning, Mr. Smythe," Matthew said. "May I have a word with you?"

"Oh . . . good morning, Mr. Corbett. What may I help you with?"

Matthew glanced quickly at the seamstress. "May we speak in private, please?"

"Certainly. Mrs. Prater, these are coming along very well. I'll speak with you again when the work is further advanced. Mr. Corbett, we might go over there if you like." Smythe motioned toward a stand of oak trees about sixty feet behind the encampment.

As they walked, Smythe slid his thumbs into the pockets of his dark brown breeches. "I think an apology is in order for our behavior last night. We left so abruptly . . . and for such an obvious reason. At least we might have tempered it with a more diplomatic excuse."

"No apology is necessary. Everyone understood the reason. And better the truth than a false excuse, no matter how diplomatic."

"Thank you, sir. I appreciate your candor."

"The reason I wished to speak to you," Matthew said as they reached the oak trees' shade, "concerns Gwinett Linch. The man you believe to be Jonathan Lancaster."

"If I may correct you, not *believe* to be. As I said last night, I would swear to it. But he appears . . . so different. So changed. The man I knew would not be . . . well, would not be caught *dead* in such dirty rags. In fact, I recall he had a marked affinity for cleanliness."

"And order?" Matthew asked. "Would you say he had an affinity for that as well?"

"He kept his wagon neat enough. I remember one day he complained to my father about not having a supply of wheel grease on hand to silence a squeak."

"Hm," Matthew said. He leaned against the trunk of an oak and crossed his arms. "Exactly who was . . . I mean, who is . . . Jonathan Lancaster?"

"Well, I mentioned he had an act that involved trained rats. He had them jump through hoops and run races and such. The children loved it. Our circus travelled through most of England, and we did play London on several occasions but we found ourselves restricted to a very bad part of the city. So we mostly travelled from village to village. My father was the manager, my mother sold tickets, and I did whatever needed doing."

"Lancaster," Matthew said, guiding Smythe back to the subject. "He made his living with this trained rat show?"

"Yes, he did. None of us were exactly wealthy, but . . . we all pulled together." Smythe frowned, and Matthew could tell he was forming his next statement. "Mr. Lancaster . . . was a puzzling man."

"How so? Because he worked with rats?"

"Not only that," Smythe said. "But because of the other act he performed. The one that was done . . . well . . . that was done only behind closed curtains, for a small audience of adults—no children allowed—who wished to pay an extra coin to see it."

"And what was that?"

"His display of animal magnetism."

"Animal magnetism?" Now it was Matthew's turn to frown. "What is *that?*"

"The art of magnetic manipulation. Have you not heard of such a thing?"

"I've heard of the process of magnetism, but never *animal* magnetism. Is this some theatrical whimsy?"

"It's been more popular in Europe than in England, I understand. Particularly in Germany, according to what my father told me. Mr. Lancaster was once a leading light of the cult of magnetism in Germany, though he was English-born. This is also according to my father, who if nothing else has a fortune of friends in the craft of public entertainment. That was, however, in Mr. Lancaster's younger years. An incident occurred that caused him to flee Germany."

"An incident? Do you know what it was?"

"I know what my father told me, and wished me to keep secret."

"You are no longer in England and no longer under your father's jurisdiction," Matthew said. "It is *vital* that you tell me everything you know about Jonathan Lancaster. *Particularly* the secrets."

Smythe paused and cocked his head to one side. "May I ask why this is so important to you?"

It was a fair question. Matthew said, "I'm going to trust you, as I hope you will trust me. Obviously Lancaster has hidden his true identity from Mr. Bidwell and everyone else in this town. I wish to know why. Also . . . I have reason to believe that Lancaster may be involved with the current situation in which this town finds itself."

"What? You mean the *witch?*" Symthe offered a nervous smile. "You're joking!"

"I am not," Matthew said firmly.

"Oh, that can't be! Mr. Lancaster may have been strange, but he wasn't *demonic*. I'd venture that his closed-curtain talent *appeared* to some to be witchcraft, but it was evidently based on principles of science."

"Ah." Matthew nodded, his heartbeat quickening. "Now we approach the light, Mr. Smythe. What exactly was his closed-curtain talent?"

"Manipulation of the mind," Smythe answered, and Matthew had to struggle to suppress a victorious grin. "By the application of magnetic force, Mr. Lancaster could deliver mental commands to some members of his audience, and cause them to do, believe, and say things that . . . um . . . would probably not suit the eyes and ears of children. I have to admit; I sneaked behind the curtains and watched on more than a few occasions, because it *was* a fascinating show. I recall he would cause some to believe day was night, and that they were getting ready for their beds. One woman he caused to believe was freezing in a snowstorm in the midst of July. A particular scene I remember was a man he caused to believe had stepped into a nest of biting ants, and how that man jumped and hollered was nothing short of ludicrous. The other members of the audience laughed uproariously, but that man never heard a giggle of it until Mr. Lancaster awakened him."

"Awakened him? These people were put to sleep in some way?"

"It was a sleep-like state, yet they were still responsive. Mr. Lancaster used various objects to soothe them into this state, such as a lantern, a candle, or a coin. Anything that served to secure their attention. Then he would further soothe and command them with his voice . . . and once you heard his voice, it was unforgettable. I myself would have fallen under his magnetism, if I hadn't known beforehand what he was doing."

"Yes," Matthew said, staring past Smythe in the direction of Fount Royal. "I can well understand that." He directed his gaze back to the man. "But what is this about *magnetism?*"

"I don't quite fathom it, but it has to do with the fact that all bodies and objects hold iron. Therefore a skilled practitioner can use other objects as tools of manipulation, since the human body, blood, and brain also contain iron. The attraction and manipulation is called magnetism. That, at least, is how my father explained it when I asked him." Symthe shrugged. "Evidently it was a process first discovered by the ancient Egyptians and used by their court magicians."

Matthew was thinking *I have you now, Sir Fox.*

"This must be very important to you indeed," Smythe said, dappled sunlight falling through the oak branches and leaves onto his face.

"It is. As I said, vital."

"Well . . . as you also said, I am no longer in England or under my father's jurisdiction. If it's so vital that you know . . . the secret my father asked me to keep concerns Mr. Lancaster's career before he joined the circus. In his younger years he was known as a healer of sorts. A faith-healer, I suppose, in that he could use magnetism to deliver people from illnesses. Apparently he travelled to Europe to practise this art, and drew the attention of a German nobleman who wished Mr. Lancaster to teach him and his son how to be magnetizers themselves. Now . . . be aware that all this I recall my father telling me, and I might have garbled it in the retelling."

"I shall," Matthew said. "But please continue."

"Mr. Lancaster did not speak German, though his host spoke a little English. There was a translation problem. Whether that had anything to do with the results, I don't know, but my father told me Mr. Lancaster had fled Germany because the nobleman and his son were adversely affected by their studies. The latter killed himself with a poisoned dagger, and the former went half-mad. Which I suppose testifies to the power of magnetism falling into the wrong hands. In any case, a bounty was offered on Mr. Lancaster's head and so he returned to England. But he obviously was a changed man, too, and he sank to the level of trained rats and a few magnetist's tricks behind closed curtains."

"Possibly he wished to keep a low profile," Matthew said, "for fear that someone would seek him out and claim the bounty." He nodded. "Yes, that explains a lot. As, for instance, why Goode told me no Dutchmen or Germans had seen the Devil. It was because Lancaster feared Germans and likely is limited to only the English tongue."

"Goode?" Smythe asked, looking perplexed. "I'm sorry, I'm not following you."

"My apologies. My thoughts became words." Matthew, his nervous energy at high flux, began to pace back and forth. "Tell me this, if you will: what caused Lancaster to leave the circus, and when was this?"

"I don't know. My family and I left before Mr. Lancaster did."

"Oh. Then you haven't seen Lancaster since?"

"No. Certainly we didn't wish to return to that circus."

Matthew caught a hint of bitterness. "Why? Was your father discharged?"

"Not that. It was my father's wish to leave. He didn't care for the way Mr. Cedarholm—the man who owned the circus—had decided to run things. My father is a very decent man, God love him, and he bridled about bringing in the freaks."

Matthew suddenly stopped his pacing. "Freaks?"

"Yes. Three of them, to begin with."

"*Three,*" Matthew repeated. "May I . . . ask what they were?"

"The first was a black-skinned lizard, as big as a ram. The thing had come from some South Sea island, and it near made my mother faint to look upon it."

"The second," Matthew said, his mouth dry. "Might it have

been an imp of some kind? A dwarf, possibly, with a childlike face and long white hair?"

"Yes. Exactly that. How did . . ." Now Smythe truly appeared confounded. "How did you *know?*"

"The third," Matthew prompted. "Was it . . . an unspeakable thing?"

"The third one was what made my father pack our bags. It was a hermaphrodite with the breasts of a woman and . . . the tools of a man. My father said even Satan would shrink to look upon such a blasphemy."

"Your father might be interested, Mr. Smythe, to know that all three of those creatures have lately found work in Fount Royal, with Satan's blessing. Oh, I have him now! I have him!" Matthew couldn't restrain himself from smacking his palm with his fist, his eyes bright with the fire of the hunt. He immediately reined in his enthusiasm, as he noted that Smythe took a backward step and appeared concerned that he might be dealing with a lunatic. "I have a request. Again, a very important one. I happen to know where Lancaster lives. It's not very far from here, at the end of this street. Would you go there with me—this moment—and look upon him face-to-face and tell me you positively know he's the man you claim him to be?"

"I've already told you. I saw his eyes, which are as unforgettable as his voice. It *is* him."

"Yes, but nevertheless I require you to identify him in my presence." Matthew also wanted Lancaster to know before another hour had passed that a blade had been thrust into his repugnant, inhuman plans, and twisted for good measure.

"I . . . do have some work to get done. Perhaps later this afternoon?"

"No," Matthew said. "Now." He correctly read the reticence in Smythe's eyes. "As an officer of the court, I must tell you this is official business. Also that I am empowered by Magistrate Woodward to compel you to accompany me." It was an outright falsehood, but Matthew had no time for dawdling.

Smythe, who obviously had well learned the lessons of decency from his esteemed father, said, "No compelling is necessary, sir. If this has to do with a matter of law, I should be glad to go."

Matthew and Smythe proceeded along Industry Street—the former in expectant haste and the latter more understandably moderate in his willingness to advance—toward the house of the formerly known Gwinett Linch. Smythe's pace slowed as they reached the execution field, and he regarded the stake and pyre with dread fascination. An oxcart had been pulled up beside the woodpile, and two men—one of them the giant Mr. Green, Matthew saw—were at work unloading another cargo of witch-burning fuel.

Yes, build it up! Matthew thought. Waste your muscles and your minutes, for when this day is done one less nightbird shall be confined in a cage and one more vulture there in her place!

Further on stood the house. "My God!" Smythe said, aghast. "Mr. Lancaster lives *there?*"

"Lancaster lives within," Matthew replied, his pace yet quickening. "The ratcatcher has groomed the exterior."

He felt a gnaw of disappointment. No smoke rose from the chimney, though indeed the breakfast hour was long past. But all the shutters were closed, indicating that Lancaster was out. Matthew inwardly muttered a curse, for he'd wished to have this identification promptly done and then escort Smythe directly to see Bidwell. It dawned on him that if Lancaster was indeed in there, closed up from the sunlight like a night-faring roach, he might turn violent, and they had no weapon of defense. Perhaps it would be best to go fetch Mr. Green as a precaution. But then another thought hit Matthew, and this one had terrible implications.

What if Lancaster, upon knowing he'd been recognized, had fled Fount Royal? He would have had ample time last night. But what was the procedure for getting out the gate after sunset? Surely such a thing was unheard of. Would the watchman have allowed him to leave without informing Bidwell? But what if Lancaster had saddled a horse and gone yesterday afternoon while it was still light?

"You're near running!" Smythe said, trying to keep up. Without Lancaster, Rachel's fate was still in doubt. Damned right Matthew was nearly running, and he did break into a run the final twenty yards.

He slammed his fist on the door. He had expected no answer, and therefore was immediately prepared to do what he next did: open the door and enter.

Before he could cross the threshold, Matthew was struck in the face.

Not by any physical fist, but rather by the overwhelming smell of blood. He instinctively recoiled, his mouth coming open in a gasp.

These were the things he saw, in a torrent of hideous impressions: light, streaming between the shutter slats and glistening off the dark red blood that had pooled on the floorboards and made large brown blotches on the pallet's sheet; Lancaster's corpse, lying on its right side on the floor, the left hand gripping at the sheet as if to pull itself up, the mouth and icy gray eyes horribly open in a slashed and clawed face, and the throat cut like a red-lipped grin from ear to ear; the formerly meticulous household ravaged as if by a whirlwind, clothes pulled from the trunk and strewn about; desk drawers wrenched out and upturned, cooking implements thrown hither and yon; hearth ashes scooped up and tossed to settle over the corpse like grave dust.

Smythe had also seen. He gave a choked moan and staggered back, and then off he ran along Industry Street in the direction of his companions, his face bone-white and his mouth trailing the shattering cry, "Murder! Murder!"

The shout might have alarmed everyone else who heard it, but it served to steady Matthew's nerves because he knew he had only a short time to inspect this gruesome scene before being intruded upon. He realized as well that the sight of Lancaster lying dead and so brutally disfigured must have been the same sight viewed by Reverend Grove's wife and by Jess Maynard, who had discovered Daniel Howarth's body. Little wonder, then, that Mrs. Grove and the Maynards had fled town.

The cut throat. The face savaged by demonic claws. And, it appeared, the shoulders, arms, and chest also slashed through the bloody ribbons of the man's shirt.

Yes, Matthew thought. A true Satan had been at work here.

He felt sick to his stomach and scared out of his wits, but he had time for neither debility. He looked about the wreckage. The desk's drawers, all the papers and everything else dumped out, the inkwell smashed. He wished to find two items before Mr. Green surely arrived: the sapphire brooch and the book on ancient Egypt. But even as he knelt down to negotiate this mess of blood, ink, and blood-inked papers he knew with a sinking certainty that those two items, above all else, would not be found.

He spent a moment or two in search, but when he suffered the smear of blood on his hands he gave up the quest as both impossible and unreasonable. He was fast weakening in this charnel house, and the desire for fresh air and untainted sunlight was a powerful call. It occurred to him that Smythe had been correct: Lancaster would indeed not be caught dead in his ratcatcher's rags, as he wore what had once been a white shirt and a pair of dark gray breeches.

And now the need to get out was too much to withstand. Matthew stood up and, as he turned to the door—which had not opened to its full extent, but rather just enough to allow his entry—he saw what was scrawled there on its inner surface in the clotted ink of Lancaster's veins.

My Rachel
Is Not
Alone

In the space of a hammered heartbeat Matthew's flesh prickled and the hairs rose at the back of his neck. The first words that came to his mind were *Oh . . . shit.*

He was still staring numbly at that damning declaration a moment later when Hannibal Green came through the door, followed by the other rustic with whom he'd been working. At once

Green stopped in his tracks, his red-bearded face twisted with horror. "Christ's Mercy!" he said, stunned to the soles of his fourteen-inch boots. *"Linch?"* He looked at Matthew, who nodded, and then Green saw the clerk's gore-stained hands and hollered, "Randall! Go fetch Mr. Bidwell! *Now!*"

In the time that ensued, Green would have thought Matthew a bloody-handed murderer had not David Smythe, pallid but resolute, returned to the scene and explained they'd both been together when the corpse was discovered. Matthew took the opportunity to wipe his hands on one of the clean shirts that had been so rudely torn from the trunk. Then Green had his own hands full trying to keep people who'd been alerted by Smythe's cry—among them Martin and Constance Adams—out of the house.

"Is that Lancaster?" Matthew asked Smythe, who stood to one side staring down at the corpse.

Smythe swallowed. "His face is . . . so . . . swollen, but . . . I know the eyes. Unforgettable. Yes. This man . . . was Jonathan Lancaster."

"Move back!" Green told the onlookers. "Move back, I said!" Then he had no choice but to close the door in the gawkers' faces, and thereupon he saw the bloody scrawl.

Matthew thought Green might go down, for he staggered as if from a mighty blow. When he turned his head to look at Matthew, his eyes seemed to have shrunken and retreated in his face. He spoke in a very small voice, "I shall . . . I shall guard the door from the *outside."* So saying, he was gone like a shot.

Smythe had also seen the bloody writing. His mouth opened, but he made not a sound. Then he lowered his head and followed Green out the door with similar haste.

Now the die was well and truly cast. Alone in the house with the deadly departed, Matthew knew this was the funeral bell for Fount Royal. Once word got out about that declaration on the door—and it was probably beginning its circuit of tongues right now, starting with Green—the town wouldn't be worth a cup of cold drool.

He avoided looking at Lancaster's face, which had not only been severely clawed but had become misshapen from such injury. He knelt down and continued his search for the brooch and book, this time using a cloth to move aside blood-spattered wreckage. Presently a wooden box caught his attention, and he lifted its lid to find within the tools of the ratcatcher's trade: the odious long brown seedbag that had served to hold rodent carcasses, the stained deerskin gloves, the cowhide bag, and various wooden jars and vials of—presumably—rat bait. Also in the box was the single blade—wiped clean and shining—that had been secured to the end of the ratcatcher's sticker.

Matthew lifted his gaze from the box and looked around the room. Where was the sticker itself? And—most importantly—where was that fearsome appliance with the five curved blades that Hazelton had fashioned?

Nowhere to be seen.

Matthew opened the cowhide bag, and in doing so noted two drops and a smear of dried blood near its already-loosened draw-string. The bag was empty.

To be such a cleanliness fanatic, why would Lancaster have not wiped the rodent blood from the side of this bag before putting it back into the wooden box? And why was the five-bladed appliance—that "useful device" as Lancaster had called it—not here with the other utensils?

Now Matthew did force himself to look at Lancaster's face, and the claw marks upon it. With a mind detached from his revulsion he studied the vicious slashings on the corpse's shoulders, arms, and chest.

He knew.

In perhaps another fifteen minutes, during which Matthew searched without success for the appliance, the door opened again—tentatively, this time—and the master of Fount Royal peered in with eyes the size of teacup saucers. "What . . . what has happened here?" he gasped.

"Mr. Smythe and I found this scene. Lancaster has left us," Matthew said.

"You mean . . . Linch."

"No. He was never truly Gwinett Linch. His name is—was—Jonathan Lancaster. Please come in."

"Must I?"

"I think you should. And please close the door."

Bidwell entered, wearing his bright blue suit. The look of sickness contorted his face. He did close the door, but he remained pressed firmly against it.

"You ought to see what you're pressing against," Matthew said.

Bidwell looked at the door, and like Green he staggered and almost fell. His jerking away from it made him step into the bloody mess on the floor and for a dangerous instant he balanced on the precipice of falling alongside the corpse. His fight against gravity was amazing for a man of his size, and with sheer power of determination—and more than a little abject, breeches-wetting terror—he righted himself.

"Oh my Jesus," he said, and he took off both his bright blue tricorn and his gray curled wig and mopped his sandy pate with a handkerchief. "Oh dear God . . . we're doomed now, aren't we?"

"Steady yourself," Matthew instructed. "This was done by a human hand, not a spectral one."

"A human hand? Are you out of your mind? Only Satan himself could have done this!" He pushed the handkerchief to his nose to filter the blood smell. "It's the same as was done to the reverend and Daniel Howarth! Exactly the same!"

"Which should tell you the same man committed all three murders. In this case, though, I think there was a falling out of compatriots."

"What are you running off at the lips about *now?*" Bidwell's sickness had receded and anger was beginning to flood into its mold. "Look at that on the door! That's a message from the damned Devil! Good Christ, my town will be dust and maggots before sunset! *Oh!*" It was a wounded, terrible cry, and his eyes appeared near bursting out. "If the witch is not alone . . . then *who* might the other witches and warlocks be?"

"Shut up that yammering and listen to me!" Matthew advanced upon Bidwell until they stood face to sweating face. "You'll do yourself and Fount Royal no good to fall to pieces! If your town needs anything now, it's a true leader, not a bullier or a weeper!"

"How . . . how *dare* you . . ."

"Put aside your bruised dignity, sir. Just stand there and listen. I am as confounded about this as you, because I thought Linch—Lancaster—was alone in his crimes. Obviously—and stupidly—I was wrong. Lancaster and his killer were working together to paint Rachel as a witch and destroy your town."

"Boy, your love for that witch will put you burning at her side!" Bidwell shouted, his face bright red and the veins pulsing at his temples. He looked to be courting an explosion that would blow off the top of his head. "If you wish to go to Hell with her, I can arrange it!"

"This was written on the door," Matthew said coldly, "by a human hand determined to finish Fount Royal at one fell swoop. The same hand that cut Lancaster's throat and—when he was dead or dying—used the ratcatcher's own five-bladed device to strike him repeatedly, thereby giving the impression of a beast's claws. That device was also used to inflict similar wounds on Reverend Grove and Daniel Howarth."

"Yes, yes, yes! It's all as you say, isn't it? *Everything* is as you say!"

"Most everything," Matthew answered.

"Well, you didn't even see those other bodies, so how can you *know?* And what nonsense is this about some kind of five-bladed device?"

"You've never seen it? Then again, I doubt you would have. Seth Hazelton forged it for the use—he thought—of killing rats. Actually, it was probably planned for its current use all along."

"You're mad! Absolutely roaring mad!"

"I am neither mad," Matthew said, "nor roaring, as you are. To prove my sanity, I will ask Mr. Smythe to go to your house and explain to you Lancaster's true identity as he explained it to me. I think you'll find it worth your while."

"Really?" Bidwell sneered. "If that's the case, you'd best go find him! When my carriage passed their camp, the actors were packing their wagons!"

Now a true spear of terror pierced Matthew's heart. *"What?"*

"That's right! They were in a fever to do it, too, and now I know why! I'm sure there's nothing like finding a Satan-mauled corpse and a bloody message from Hell to put one in mind for a merry play!"

"No! They can't leave yet!" Matthew was out the door faster even than Green's pistol-ball exit. Straightaway his progress was blocked by the seven or eight persons who stood just outside, including Green himself. Then he had to negotiate a half-dozen more citizens who dawdled between the house and Industry Street. He saw Goode sitting in the driver's seat of Bidwell's carriage, but the horses faced west and getting them turned east would take too long. He set off toward the maskers' camp, running so fast he lost his left shoe and had to forfeit precious time putting it back on.

Matthew let loose a breath of relief when he reached the campsite and saw that, though the actors were indeed packing their trunks, costumes, featherboxes, and all the rest of their theatrical belongings, none of the horses had yet been hitched to a wagon. There was activity aplenty, however, and it was obvious to Matthew that Smythe's tale of what was discovered had put the fear of Hell's wrath into these people.

"Mr. Brightman!" Matthew called, seeing the man helping another thespian lift a trunk onto a wagon. He rushed over. "It's urgent I speak with Mr. Smythe!"

"I'm sorry, Mr. Corbett. David is not to be spoken with." Brightman looked past Matthew. "Franklin! Help Charles fold up that tent!"

"I *must*," Matthew insisted.

"That's impossible, sir." Brightman stalked off toward another area of the camp, and Matthew walked at his side. "If you'll pardon me, I have much work to do. We plan on leaving as soon as we're packed."

"You needn't leave. None of your troupe is in danger."

"Mr. Corbett, when we discovered your . . . um . . . situation with the witch from a source in Charles Town, I myself was reluctant—extremely reluctant—to come here. But to be perfectly honest we had nowhere else to go. Mr. Bidwell is a very generous friend, therefore I was talked into making the trip." Brightman stopped walking and turned to face Matthew. "I regret my decision, young man. When David told me what had happened . . . and what he saw in that house . . . I immediately gave the order to break camp. I am not going to risk the lives of my troupe for any amount that Mr. Bidwell might put on our table. End of pronouncement." He began walking once more and boomed, "Thomas! Make sure all the boots are in that box!"

"Mr. Brightman, please!" Matthew caught up with him again. "I understand your decision to leave, but . . . please . . . it is absolutely urgent that I speak to Mr. Smythe. I need for him to tell Mr. Bidwell about—"

"Young man," Brightman said with an exasperated air as he halted abruptly. "I am trying to be as pleasant as possible under the circumstances. We must—I repeat *must*—get on the road within the hour. We'll not reach Charles Town before dark, but I wish to get there before midnight."

"Would it not be better to stay the night here, and leave in the morning?" Matthew asked. "I can assure you that—"

"I think neither you nor Mr. Bidwell can assure us of *anything*. Including the assurance that we'll all be alive in the morning. No. I thought you had only one witch here, and that was bad enough; but to have an unknown number, and the rest of them lurking about ready and eager to commit murder for their master . . . no, I can't risk such a thing."

"All right, then," Matthew said. "But can't I request that Mr. Smythe speak to Mr. Bidwell? It would only take a few minutes, and it would—"

"David cannot speak to anyone, young man," Brightman said firmly. "Did you hear me? I said can *not*."

"Well, where is he? If I can have a moment with him—"

"You are not listening to me, Mr. Corbett." Brightman took a step toward him and grasped his shoulder with one of those vise-like hands. "David is in one of the wagons. Even if I allowed you to see him, it would do no good. I am being truthful when I say that David cannot speak. After he told me what he'd seen—and particularly about the writing—he broke into a fit of shivering and weeping and thereafter was silent. What you don't know about David is that he is a very sensitive young man. Precariously sensitive, I might say."

Brightman paused, staring intently into Matthew's eyes. "He has had some nervous difficulties in the past. For that reason, he lost his positions with both the Saturn Cross Company and James Prue's Players. His father is an old friend of mine, and so when he asked me to take his son on as a favor—and watch over him—I agreed. I think the sight of that murdered man has sent him to the edge of . . . well, it's best not to say. He has been given a cup of rum and a pair of day-blinders. Therefore I certainly will not let you see him, as he must rest and be quiet for any hope of a prompt recovery."

"Can't I . . . just . . . for one . . ."

"*No,*" Brightman said, his voice like the tolling of a bass-tuned bell. He released his grip on Matthew's shoulder. "I'm sorry, but whatever it is you want with David cannot be granted. Now: it was a pleasure to meet you, and I hope all goes well with this witchcraft situation. I hope you sleep with a Bible in your bed and a candle by your hand tonight. Perhaps also a pistol under your pillow. Good luck to you, and goodbye." He stood with his arms crossed, waiting for Matthew to move away from the camp.

Matthew had to give it one more try. "Sir, I'm begging you. A woman's life lies in the balance."

"What woman?"

He started to speak the name, but he knew it wouldn't help. Brightman regarded him with a stony stare.

"I don't know what intrigues are in progress here," Bright-man said, "and neither do I wish to know. It is my experience that the Devil has a long arm." He scanned the vista of Fount Royal, his eyes saddened. "It pains me to say it, but I doubt we shall have need to come this way next summer. Many fine people lived here, and they were very kind to us. But . . . such are the tides of life. Now please pardon me, as I have work to do."

Matthew could say nothing more. He watched as Brightman walked away to join a group of men who were taking down the yellow awning. Horses were being hitched to one of the wagons, and the other horses were being readied. It occurred to him that he might assert his rights and go to each wagon in turn until Smythe was found, but what then? If Smythe was too anguished to speak, what good would it do? But no, he couldn't let Smythe just ride out of here without telling Bidwell who the ratcatcher really was! It was inconceivable!

And it was equally inconceivable to grab an ailing person with a nervous disorder by the scruff of the neck and shake him like a dog until he talked.

Matthew staggered, light-headed, to the other side of Industry Street and sat down at the edge of a cornfield. He watched the camp dwindling as the wagons were further packed. Every few minutes he vowed he would stand, march defiantly over there and find Smythe for himself. But he remained seated, even when a whip cracked and the cry "Get up!" rang out and the first wagon creaked away.

Once the departure of wagons had begun, the others soon followed. Brightman, however, remained with the final wagon and helped the Falstaffian-girthed thespian lift a last trunk and two smaller boxes. Before the work was completed, Bidwell's carriage came into view. Bidwell bade Goode halt, and Matthew watched as the master of Fount Royal climbed down and went to speak with Brightman.

The discussion lasted only three or four minutes. Bidwell did a lot of listening and nodding. It ended with the two men shaking hands, and then Brightman got up onto the driver's plank of his wagon, which the Falstaffian gentleman already occupied. A whip popped, Brightman boomed, "Go on there, go on!" and the horses began their labor.

Matthew felt tears of bitter frustration burn his eyes. He bit his lower lip until it nearly bled. Brightman's wagon trundled away. Matthew stared at the ground until he saw a shadow approaching, and even then he kept his head bowed.

"I have assigned James Reed to guard the house," Bidwell said. His voice was wan and listless. "James is a good, dependable man."

Matthew looked up into Bidwell's face. The man had donned both his wig and tricorn again, but they sat at crooked angles. Bidwell's face appeared swollen and the color of yellow chalk, his eyes like those of a shot-stunned animal. "James will keep them out," he said, and then he frowned. "What shall we do for a rat-catcher?"

"I don't know," was all Matthew could say.

"A ratcatcher," Bidwell repeated. "Every town must have one. Every town that wishes to grow, I mean." He looked around sharply as another wagon—this one open-topped and carrying the hurriedly packed belongings of Martin and Constance Adams—passed along Industry Street on its way out. Martin was at the reins, his face set with grim resolve. His wife stared straight ahead also, as if terrified to even glance back at the house they were fleeing. The child, Violet, was pressed between them, all but smothered.

"Essential for a town," Bidwell went on, in a strangely calm tone. "That rats be controlled. I shall . . . I shall put Edward on the problem. He will give me sound advice."

Matthew clasped his fingers to his temples and then released the pressure. "Mr. Bidwell," he said. "We are dealing with a human being, not Satan. *One* human being. A cunning fox of which I have never before seen the like."

"They'll be frightened at first," Bidwell replied. "Yes, of course they will be. They were so looking forward to the maskers."

"Lancaster was murdered because his killer knew he was about to be exposed. Either Lancaster told that man—or a very strong and ruthless woman—about Smythe identifying him . . . or the killer was in your house last night when Smythe related it to me."

"I think . . . some of them will leave. I can't blame them. But they'll come to their senses, especially with the burning so near."

"Please, Mr. Bidwell," Matthew said. "Try to hear what I'm saying." He lowered his head again, his mind almost overwhelmed by what he was thinking. "I don't believe Mr. Winston to be capable of murder. Therefore . . . if indeed the killer was someone in your house last night . . . that narrows the field to Mrs. Nettles and Schoolmaster Johnstone." Bidwell was silent, but Matthew heard his rough breathing.

"Mrs. Nettles . . . could have overheard, from outside the parlor. There may be . . . may be a fact I've missed about her. I recall . . . she said something important to me, concerning Reverend Grove . . . but I can't draw it up. The schoolmaster . . . are you absolutely *certain* his knee is—"

Bidwell began to laugh.

It was possibly the most terrible sound Matthew had ever heard. It was a laugh, yes, but also in the depths of it was something akin to a strangled shriek.

Matthew raised his eyes to Bidwell and received another shock. Bidwell's mouth was laughing, but his eyes were holes of horror and tears had streaked down his cheeks. He began to back away as the laughter spiralled up and up. He lifted his arm and aimed his index finger at Matthew, his hand trembling.

The crazed laughter abruptly stopped. *"You,"* he rasped. And now not only was he weeping, but his nose had begun to run. "You're one of them, aren't you? Sent to ruin my town and drive me mad. But I'll beat you yet! I'll beat all of you! I've never failed and I shall *not* fail! Do you hear me? Never failed! And I shall not . . . shall not . . . shall—"

"Mr. Bidwell, suh?" Goode had stepped beside the man and gently taken hold of his arm. Though it was such an improper gesture between slave and master, Bidwell made no attempt to pull away. "We ought best be goin'."

Bidwell continued to stare at Matthew, his eyes seeing only a prince of destruction. "Suh?" Goode prompted quietly. "Ought be goin'." He gave Bidwell's arm just the slightest tug.

Bidwell shivered, though the sun was bright and warm. He lowered his gaze and wiped the tearstreaks from his face with the back of his free hand. "Oh," he said; it was more the exhalation of breath than speech. "I'm tired. Near . . . worn out."

"Yes suh. You do needs a rest."

"A rest." He nodded. "I'll feel better after a rest. Help me to the carriage, will you?"

"Yes suh, I will." Goode looked at Matthew and put a finger to his lips, warning Matthew to make no further utterances. Then Goode steadied Bidwell, and the slave and master walked together to the carriage.

Matthew remained where he was. He watched Goode help his master into a seat, and then Goode got up behind the horses, flicked the reins, and the horses started off at an ambling pace.

When the carriage had departed from sight, Matthew stared blankly at the empty field where the maskers had been and thought he might weep himself.

His hopes of freeing Rachel were wrecked. He had not a shred of evidence to prove any of the things he knew to be true. Without Lancaster—and without Smythe to lend credence to the tale—the theory of how Fount Royal had been seduced by mental manipulation was a madman's folly. Finding the sapphire brooch and the book on ancient Egypt would have helped, but the killer had already known their value—and must have been well aware of their presence—and so had stolen them away as efficiently as he had murdered Lancaster. He—or she, God forbid—had even torn up the house so no one would know the ratcatcher's true living habits.

So. What now?

He had come through this maze to find himself at a dead end. Which only meant, he believed, that he must retrace his steps and search for the proper passage. But the time was almost gone.

Almost gone.

He knew he was grasping at straws by accusing either the schoolmaster or Mrs. Nettles. Lancaster might have told his killer yesterday that he'd been recognized, and the cunning fox had waited until long after dark to visit the wretched-looking house. Just because Smythe had revealed his recognition to Matthew in Bidwell's parlor didn't mean the killer had been there to overhear it.

He trusted Mrs. Nettles, and did not *want* to believe she had a hand in this. But what if everything the woman had said was a lie? What if she had been manipulating him all along? It might not have been Lancaster who took the coin, but Mrs. Nettles. She certainly could have laid the magistrate out cold if she'd chosen to.

And the schoolmaster. An Oxford man, yes. A highly educated man. The magistrate had seen Johnstone's deformed knee, it was true, but still . . .

There was the question of the bearded surveyor and his interest in the fount. It was important. Matthew knew it was, but he could not prove it.

Neither could he prove the fount was a pirate's treasure vault, nor indeed that it held a single coin or jewel.

Neither could he prove that any of the witnesses had not actually seen what they believed to see, and that Rachel hadn't made those damning poppets and hidden them in her house.

Neither could he prove that Rachel had been chosen as the perfect candidate to paint as a witch by two persons—possibly more?—who both were masters of disguise.

Certainly he couldn't prove that Linch was Lancaster and Lancaster had been murdered by his accomplice, and that Satan himself didn't scrawl that message on the door.

Now Matthew truly felt close to weeping. He knew everything—or almost everything—of how it had been done, and he felt sure he knew why it had been done, and he knew the name of one of the persons who'd done it . . .

But without proof he was a beggar in the house of justice, and could expect not a single scrap.

Another wagon passed along Industry Street, carrying a family and their meager belongings away from this accursed town. The last days of Fount Royal had come.

And Matthew was keenly aware that Rachel's last hours were passing away, and that on Monday morning she would surely burn and for the rest of his life—the rest of his miserable, frost-souled life—only he would know the truth.

No, that was wrong. There would be one other, who would grin as the flames roared and the ashes flew, as the houses emptied and the dream perished. Who would grin as the thought came clear: *All the silver, gold, and jewels . . . all mine now . . . and those fools never even knew.*

Only one fool knew. And he was powerless to stop either the flow of time or the flow of citizens fleeing Fount Royal.

thirty-five

A ND NOW THE WHOLE WORLD was silent.
Or at least it seemed so, to Matthew's ears. In fact, the world was so silent that the sound of his feet creeping on the hallway's floorboards sounded to him like barely muffled cannonades, and the errant squeak of a loose timber like a high-pitched human shriek.

He had a lantern in hand. He was dressed in his bedclothes, as he had retired to sleep several hours ago. In reality, though, he had retired to ponder and wait. The time had arrived, and he was on a journey to Bidwell's upstairs study.

It was now the Sabbath morning. He reasoned it was sometime between midnight and two o'clock. The previous day had truly been nightmarish, and this current day promised to be no less an ordeal.

Matthew had himself seen eight more wagons departing Fount Royal. The gate had been opened and closed with a regularity that would have been comical had it not been so tragic. Bidwell had remained in his bedchamber all day. Winston had gone in to see him, as had Dr. Shields, and once Matthew had heard Bidwell's voice raving and raging with a frightful intensity that made one believe all the demons of Hell had ringed his bed to pay their ghastly respects. Perhaps in Bidwell's tortured mind they had.

During the course of the day Matthew had sat at the magistrate's bedside for several hours, reading the book on English plays and attempting to keep his mind from wandering to the Florida country. He was also there to guard against the magistrate finding out what had occurred this morning, as it might cause Woodward deep grief that would sink him again into sickness. The magistrate, though certainly able to communicate more clearly and feeling positive about his chances of improvement, was yet weak and in need of further rest. Dr. Shields had administered three more doses of the powerful medicine, but had been wise enough during his visits not to mention anything that could harm his patient's outlook. The medicine did what it was meant to do: it sent Woodward to the dreamer's land, where he could not know what tumult was taking place in reality.

Fortunately, the magistrate had been asleep—or, rather, drugged—when Bidwell had carried out his raging. In the evening, as darkness called upon Fount Royal and many fewer lamps answered than the night before, Matthew had asked Mrs. Nettles for a deck of cards and played a dozen or so games of five and forty with the magistrate, who was delighted at the chance to challenge his sluggish mind. As they played, Matthew made mention of Woodward's dream of Oxford, and how Johnstone had also seemed to enjoy the recollections.

"Yes," Woodward had said, studying his cards. "Once an Oxford man . . . always so."

"Hm." Matthew had decided to let another hand go by before he mentioned the schoolmaster again. "It *is* a shame about Mr. Johnstone's knee. Being so deformed. But he does get around well, doesn't he?"

A slight smile had crept across the magistrate's mouth. "Matthew, Matthew," he'd said. "Do you never quit?"

"I'm sorry, sir?"

"Please. I am not . . . so ill and . . . weak-minded that I can't see through you. What is this now . . . about his knee?"

"Nothing, sir. I was just making mention of it, in passing. You *did* say you saw it, did you not?"

"I did."

"At close quarters?"

"Close enough. I could smell nothing . . . because of my condition . . . but I recall that Mr. Winston was . . . quite repelled . . . by the odor of Mr. Johnstone's hogsfat liniment."

"But you did clearly view the deformity?"

"Yes," Woodward had said. "Clearly, and . . . it was a viewing . . . I would not care to repeat. Now . . . may we return to our game?"

Not long after that, Dr. Shields had arrived with the magistrate's third dose of the day, and Woodward had been sleeping calmly ever since.

Matthew had, in the afternoon, taken the opportunity for a quick look into Bidwell's study, so now in the middle of the night he had no problem getting inside. He closed the door behind him and crossed the gold-and-red Persian rug to the large mahogany desk that commanded the room. He sat down in the desk's chair and quietly pulled open the topmost drawer. He found no map there, so he went on to the next drawer. A careful search through papers, wax seals with the scrolled letter *B,* official-looking documents and the like revealed no map. Neither did the third drawer, nor the fourth and final one.

Matthew stood up, taking his lantern to the study's bookshelves. On the way, the squeal of a loose pinewood floorboard made his flesh crawl. Then he began to methodically move all the leatherbound books one from another, thinking that perhaps the map might be folded up and stored between two of them. Of course, the map might also be folded up *inside* one of the books, which was going to necessitate a longer search than he'd anticipated.

He was perhaps near midway in his route through the

bookshelves when he heard the sound of footsteps on the stairs. He hesitated, listening more intently. The footsteps reached the top of the stairs and also hesitated. There was a space of time in which neither Matthew nor the person in the hallway moved. Then he heard the footsteps approaching and he saw lantern light in the space between door and floorboards.

Quickly he opened the glass of his own lamp and blew out the flame. He retreated to the protection of the desk and crouched down on the floor.

The door opened. Someone entered, paused for a few seconds, and then the door was closed again. Matthew could see the ruddy glow of the person's lantern upon the walls as it moved from side to side. And then the voice came, but cast low so as not to leave the room: "Mr. Corbett, I know ye just blew out a candle. I can smell it. If you'd show y'self, please?"

He stood up and Mrs. Nettles centered her lamplight on him. "Ye mi' care to know that my own quarters are 'neath this room," she said. "I heard someone walkin' and 'sumed it must be Mr. Bidwell, as this is his private study."

"Pardon me, I didn't mean to wake you."

"I'm sure you didn't, but I was already waked. I was plannin' on comin' up and lookin' in on 'im, since he was in such an awful bad way." She approached him and set the lantern down on the desktop. She wore a somber gray nightcap and a nightgown of similar hue, and on her face was a smoothing of ghastly green-tinted skin cream. Matthew had to believe that if Bidwell saw Mrs. Nettles in this state, he might think a froggish phantasm had crawled from its Hellish swamp. "Your intrusion in this room," she said sternly, "canna' be excused. What're you *doin'* in here?"

There was nothing to be done but tell the truth. "I understand from Solomon Stiles that Bidwell has a map of the Florida country, drawn by a French explorer. I thought it might be hidden in this room, either in his desk or on the bookshelves."

Mrs. Nettles made no reply, but simply stared holes through

him. "I am not saying I've decided," Matthew continued. "I'm only saying I wish to see the map, to gain some idea of what the terrain is like."

"It would kill you," she said. "And the lady too. Does she know what you're wantin'?"

"No."

"Don't ye think askin' her oughta be the first thing, a'fore ye start the plannin'?"

"I'm not planning. I'm only looking."

"Plannin', lookin' . . . whate'er. Mi' be she doesn't care ta perish in the jaws of a wild beast."

"What, then? She'd rather perish by burning? I think not!"

"Keep your voice reined," she warned. "Mr. Bidwell mi' be mind-sick, but he's nae ear-deef."

"All right. But . . . if I were to continue my search for this map . . . would you leave the room and forget you saw me here? This is my business and my business alone."

"Nae, you're wrong. It's *my* business too, for it was my urgin' brought you into this. If I'd kept my tongue still, then—"

"Pardon," Matthew interrupted, "but I must disagree. Your urging, as you put it, simply alerted me to consider that not all was as it seemed in this town. Which, whether you realize it or not, was a grand understatement. I would have had serious doubts as to Rachel's being a witch even if you had been one of the witnesses against her."

"Well then, if her innocence is all so clear to you, why canna' the magistrate see it?"

"A complicated question," he said. "The answer involves age and life experience . . . both of which, in this case, seem to be liabilities to clear thinking. Or rather, I should say, liabilities to thinking beyond the straight furrow in a crooked field, which you so elegantly pointed out on our first meeting. Now: Will you allow me to search for the map?"

"Nae," she answered. "If you're so all-fired to find it, I'll point it out." She picked up the lantern and directed its glow to the wall behind the desk. "There it hangs."

Matthew looked. Indeed on the wall hung a brown parchment map, stretched by a wooden frame. It was about fifteen inches or so across and ten inches deep, and it was positioned between an oil portrait of a sailing ship and a charcoal drawing of what appeared to be the London dockside. "Oh," he said sheepishly. "Well . . . my thanks."

"Best make sure it's what you're needin'. I know it's French, but I've never paid much mind to it." She offered him the lantern.

Matthew found in another moment that it was indeed what he was needing. It actually appeared to be part of a larger map, and displayed the country from perhaps thirty miles north of Fount Royal to the area identified, in faded quill pen, as *Le Terre Florida*. Between Fount Royal and the Spanish territory the ancient quill had drawn a representation of vast forest, broken here and there by clearings, the meandering of rivers, and a number of lakes. It was a fanciful map, however, as one lake displayed a kraken-like creature and was named by the mapmaker *Le Lac de Poisson Monstre*. The swamp—identified with symbols of grass and water instead of tree symbols—that stretched along the coastline all the way from Fount Royal to the Florida country was titled *Marais Perfide*. And there was an area of swamp in the midst of the forest, some fifty or sixty miles southwest of Fount Royal, that was named *Le Terre de Brutalitie*.

"Is it he'pful to ye?" Mrs. Nettles asked.

"More daunting than helpful," Matthew said. "But yes, it does do *some* good." He had seen what looked to be a clearing in the wilderness ten or twelve miles southwest of Fount Royal that stretched for what might have been—by the strange and skewed dimensions of this map—four miles in length. Another clearing of several miles lay to the south of the first, and in this one was a lake. A third, the largest of the three, was reachable to the southwest. They were like the footprints of some primordial giant, and Matthew thought that if indeed those cleared areas—or at least areas where the wilderness was not so *perfide*—existed, then they constituted the route of least resistance to the Florida country. Perhaps this was also the "most direct route" Solomon Stiles had mentioned. In any case, it appeared somewhat less tasking than day after day of negotiating unbroken woodland. Matthew also noted the small scratchings of *Indien?* at three widely separate locations, the nearest being twenty miles or so southwest of Fount Royal. He assumed the question mark indicated a possible sighting of either a live Indian, the discovery of an artifact, or even the sound of tribal drums.

It was not going to be easy. In fact, it would be woefully hard.

Could the Florida country be reached? Yes, it could. By the directions of southwest, south, southwest and the linking together of those less-wooded giant's footprints. But, as he had previously considered, he was certainly no leatherstocking and the merest miscalculation of the sun's angle might lead him and Rachel into the *Terre Brutalitie.*

Then again, all of it was *terre brutalitie,* was it not?

It was insane! he thought as the frustration of reality hit him. Absolutely insane! How could he have ever imagined doing such a thing? To be lost in those terrible forests would be death a thousand times over!

He handed the lantern back to Mrs. Nettles. "Thank you," he said, and he heard the defeated resignation in his voice.

"Aye," she said as she took the lamp, "it does seem a beast."

"More than a beast. It seems impossible."

"You're puttin' it out of mind, then?"

He ran a hand across his brow. "What am I to do, Mrs. Nettles? Can you possibly tell me?"

She shook her head, looking at him with saddened compassion. "I'm sorry, but I canna'."

"No one can," he said wearily. "No one, except myself. The saying may be that no man is an island . . . but I feel very much like at least a solitary dominion. Rachel will be led to the stake within thirty hours. I know she is innocent, yet I can do nothing to free her. Therefore . . . what *am* I to do, except devise outlandish schemes to reach the Florida country?"

"You are ta forget her," Mrs. Nettles said. "You are ta go on about your own life, and let the dead be dead."

"That is the sensible response. But part of me will die on Monday morning too. The part that believes in justice. When that dies, Mrs. Nettles, I shall never be worth a damn again."

"You'll recover. Ever'one goes on, as they must."

"Everyone goes on," he repeated, with a taint of bitter mockery. "Oh, yes. They go on. With crippled spirits and broken ideals, they do go on. And with the passage of years they forget what crippled and broke them. They accept it grandly as they grow older, as if crippling and breaking were gifts from a king. Then those same hopeful spirits and large ideals in younger souls are viewed as stupid, and petty . . . and things to be crippled and broken, because everyone does go on." He looked into the woman's eyes. "Tell me. What is the point of life, if truth is not worth standing up for? If justice is a hollow shell? If beauty and grace are burnt to ashes, and evil rejoices in the flames? Shall I weep on that day, and lose my mind, or join the rejoicing and lose my soul? Shall I sit in my room? Should I go for a long walk, but where might I go so as not to smell the smoke? Should I just go on, Mrs. Nettles, like everyone else?"

"I think," she said grimly, "that you do nae have a choice." He had no response for this, which by its iron truth crushed him.

Mrs. Nettles sighed, her face downcast and her shadow thrown huge by the lamplight. "Go ta bed, sir," she said. "There's nae any more can be done."

He nodded, retrieved his dark lantern, and took the first two steps to the door, then hesitated. "You know . . . I really thought, for a brief while at least, that I might be able to do it. That I might be able, if I dared hard enough."

"Ta do what, sir?"

"To be Rachel's champion," he said wistfully. "And when Solomon Stiles told me about the two slaves who'd escaped—the brother and sister—and that they'd nearly reached the Florida country . . . I thought . . . it *is* possible. But it's not, is it? And it never was. Well. I do need to get to bed, don't I?" He felt as if he could sleep for a year, and awaken bearded and forgetful of time. "Good night. Or rather . . . good morning."

"The brother and sister?" Mrs. Nettles said, with a perplexed expression. "You mean . . . the two slaves who ran away . . . oh, I s'pose it must'a been the verra first year."

"That's right. Stiles told me it was the first year."

"Those two got near ta the Florida country? Mr. Corbett, they were but *children!*"

"Children?"

"Yes sir. Oakley Reeves and his sister, Dulcine. I recall they ran away after their mother died. She was a cook. The boy was all of thirteen, sir, and the girl no older'n twelve."

"What? But . . . Stiles told me they were put in irons. I assumed they were adults!"

"Oh, they *were* held in irons, even though the boy was lamed. They were both put on a wagon and taken away. I knew they'd run a piece, but I had nae an idea they'd gotten so *far.*"

"Children," Matthew repeated. He blinked, stunned by this revelation. "My God. If two children could make it that distance . . ." He took the lantern from her hand and again studied the French explorer's map, this time with a silent intensity that spoke volumes.

"They were desperate," Mrs. Nettles said.

"No more so than I."

"They cared nae if they lived or died."

"I care that Rachel lives. And myself as well."

"I'm sure they had someone helpin' 'em. An older slave, gatherin' what they needed."

"Yes," Matthew said. "They probably did." He turned toward her, his eyes glittering with fierce resolve. "Would you perform such a function for *me,* Mrs. Nettles?"

"Nae, I wouldn't!" she answered. "I'm dead set against it!"

"All right, then. Would you betray me if I myself gathered the necessary items? Some of them would be matches and a flint, a knife, clothing and shoes both for myself and Rachel, and a supply of food. I would have to take those items from the household."

Mrs. Nettles did not reply. She scowled, her froggishly green face nothing short of fearsome.

"I ask only of you what you once asked of me," he said.

"The Lord my witness, I canna' bear ta see ye go on such a folly and lose your young life. And what of the magistrate? Would you abandon him?"

"I thank the same Lord who is your witness that Magistrate Woodward is on the path to recovery. There is nothing I can do to speed his progress."

"But leavin' him like this can ruin it. Have you thought on that?"

"I have. It is a bitter choice to have to make, between the magistrate and Rachel. But that's where I find myself. I intend on writing a letter to him, explaining everything. I must hope that he reads that letter and fully understands my reasoning. If not . . . then not. But I hope—I believe—the magistrate will."

"Your time. It's awful wee."

"Everything would have to be gathered and readied within twenty-four hours. I want to get her out of there and be gone long before sunrise."

"This is daft!" she said. "How do ye plan on gettin' that key from Green? He won't likely open up the door and let you march in and out!"

"I'll have to give that some thought."

"And how will you go, then? Right through the front gate?"

"No," Matthew said. "Through the swamp, the same as the slaves."

"Ha! If ye make five miles, you'll have the luck of Angus Mc-Coody!"

"I have no idea who that might be, but I presume it's some personage of fortune in your native land. If it's a blessing, I accept it." He had put his own darkened lantern on the desk and was measuring with the fingers of his free hand the distances involved. "I must have a compass," he decided. "I'll never find the way without one." A thought came to him. "I would wager Paine owned a compass. I don't think he would mind if I searched his house. Alas, Mrs. Nettles, I shall also have to free this map from its prison."

"Don't tell me such a thing. I don't care ta know."

"Well, I'll leave it alone for the time being. There's no point in advertising my intentions."

"They'll be after you," she said. "Most likely Mr. Stiles, leadin' the way. They'll hunt ye down quick enough."

"Why should they? Rachel and I have no value to Bidwell. In fact, he may be more pleased to see the last of me than of her. I think he'll send Stiles out to make a quick search, but it will be only rudimentary."

"I say you're mistaken. Mr. Bidwell wants ever'one here ta see her burn."

"I doubt there will be many remaining to watch the display." Matthew removed the candle from his lantern and lit it with hers. Then he returned the lamp to her hand. "After I get Rachel there—to a place of safety, a town or fort or some such—and come back, I'll explain everything to him."

"Hold." Mrs. Nettles regarded him now as if his bell was severely cracked. "What're you *sayin'*? Come *back?*"

"That's correct. I'm taking Rachel to the Florida country, but I don't intend to stay. If I can follow the map and compass there, I can follow them back."

"You young fool! They won't *let* you come back! No, sirrah! Once those Spaniards get their claws on you—an English citizen—they'll ship you right quick ta their own damned land! Oh, they'll treat Rachel fair enough, her bein' a Portuguese, but you they'll parade through their streets like a dancin' monkey!"

"Not if they don't *get* their claws—as you put it—on me. I said I would take Rachel to some town or fort, but I didn't say I myself would enter it. Oh . . . one more thing I need to find: a stick, line, and hook I might use for fishing."

"You're a city boy," she said, shaking her head. "What do ye know of *fishin'*? Well, that wilderness will cure your insanity soon enough. God help you and that poor woman, and bless your bones when they're a-layin' in a beast's lair chewed ta the marra!"

"A delightful image to sleep upon, Mrs. Nettles. And now I must leave your company, as my day will surely be full." He took his lantern and went to the door, treading lightly.

"A moment," she said. She stared at the floor, a muscle working in her jaw. "If ye haven't yet considered this . . . you mi' think to fetch some clothes and the like from her house. All her belongin's are still in there, I believe. If you're wantin' an extra pair a' boots . . . I mi' can he'p you with that."

"Any help would be greatly appreciated."

She looked up sharply at him. "Sleep on this, and think on it again with a clear mind. Hear me?"

"I do. And thank you."

"You ought ta curse me, and thank me only if I put a pan ta the side of your head!"

"That makes me think of breakfast. Would you awaken me promptly at six o'clock? And grant me an extra helping of bacon?"

"Yes," she said glumly. "Sir."

Matthew left the room and went to his own. He got into bed, extinguished the lantern, and lay on his back in the dark. He heard Mrs. Nettles go along the hallway to Bidwell's room and quietly open the door. There was a period of quiet, during which Matthew could envision the woman lifting her light to check on her sleeping—and near-mad—master. Then he heard her walk back along the hall and descend the stairs, after which all was silent again.

He had less than four hours to sleep, so he ought to get to it. There was indeed much to do on the morrow, most of it not only duplicitous but highly dangerous.

How was that key to be gotten from Green? Possibly something would come to him. He hoped. It was vital to find a compass. And clothes and proper shoes for Rachel, as well. Then food must be procured; preferably dried beef, though if it was heavily salted the need for water would increase. He had to write a letter to the magistrate, and that might be the most difficult task of all.

"My God," he whispered. "What am I about to do?"

At *least* a hundred and forty miles. On foot. Through a land cruel and treacherous, following a path of least resistance mapped out by a long-dead hand. Down to the Florida country, where he would set his nightbird free. And then *back* again, alone?

Mrs. Nettles was right. He didn't know a damn thing about fishing.

But he had once survived by his wits for four months at the harbor of Manhattan. He had fought for crumbs, stolen, and scavenged in that urban wilderness. He had endured all manner of hardships, because he had to. The same was true of his trek with the magistrate through the wet woods and across the sodden earth from Shawcombe's tavern. He had kept the magistrate going, when Woodward had wanted to quit and sit down in the muck. And Matthew had done that because he had to.

Two children had nearly made the Florida country. And might have, had not the eldest broken his ankle.

It was possible. It *had* to be possible. There was no other answer.

But the question remained in his mind, and it disturbed him so much that sleep became more elusive: *What am I about to do?*

He turned over on his side, curling up like an infant about to be expelled from a womb into the hard reality of life. He was afraid to the very marrow of those bones that Mrs. Nettles predicted would be chewed in a beast's lair. He was afraid, and hot tears born of that fear burned his eyes but he wiped them away before they spilled. He was no champion, no leatherstocking, and no fisherman.

But, by God, he was a survivor, and he intended for Rachel to survive as well.

It was possible. It was.

It was. It was. It was.

He would say that to himself a hundred times, but at the rising of the sun and the first cock's crow he would be no less afraid than he was in this merciless dark.

thirty-six

"ARE YOU WELL? Truthfully, now."

Matthew had been staring out the open window in the magistrate's room, out over the sun-washed roofs and the fount's sparkling blue water. It was mid-afternoon, and he was watching yet another wagon pass through the distant gate. This morning he'd been aware of an almost-continual departure of wagons and oxcarts, their rumbling wheels and thudding animal hooves kicking up a haze of yellow dust that blotted the air around the gate like a perpetual stain. A sad sight had been that of Robert Bidwell, his wig dusty and his shirttail hanging out, as he stood on Harmony Street pleading with his citizens to remain in their homes. At last Winston and Johnstone had led him away to Van Gundy's tavern, even though it was the Sabbath. Van Gundy himself had loaded his belongings—included that wretched gittern—and quit Fount Royal. Matthew assumed that a few bottles still stocked the tavern, and in them Bidwell was seeking to lessen the agony of his perceived failure.

Matthew would have been surprised if any less than sixty persons had departed Fount Royal since dawn. Of course the threat of meeting nightfall between here and Charles Town had choked off the flow as the day progressed, but obviously there were those who preferred to risk the night journey rather than spend another eve in a witch-haunted town. Matthew predicted a similar flight at tomorrow's sunrise, notwithstanding the fact that it was Rachel's execution morn, since by the declaration so cleverly written in Lancaster's house, every neighbor might be a servant of Satan.

Today the church had been empty, but Exodus Jerusalem's camp had been full of terrified citizens. Matthew mused that Jerusalem must have thought he'd truly found himself a gold-pot. The preacher's braying voice had risen and fallen like the waves of a storm-whipped sea, and also rising and falling in accord had been the frenzied cries and shrieks of his fear-drowned audience.

"Matthew? Are you well?" Woodward asked again, from his bed.

"I was just thinking," Matthew said. "That . . . even though the sun shines brightly, and the sky is clear and blue . . . it is a very ugly day." So saying, he closed the shutters, which he had only opened a minute or two before. Then he returned to his chair at the magistrate's bedside and sat down.

"Has something . . ." Woodward paused, as his voice was still frail. His throat was again in considerable pain and his bones ached, but he wished not to mention such worrisome things to Matthew on the eve of the witch's death. "Has something happened? My ears seem stopped up, but . . . I think I have heard wagon wheels . . . and much commotion."

"A few citizens have decided to leave town," Matthew explained, deliberately keeping his tone casual. "I suspect it has something to do with the burning. There was an unfortunate scene in the street, when Mr. Bidwell stationed himself to try to dissuade their departure."

"Was he successful?"

"No, sir."

"Ah. That poor soul. I feel for him, Matthew." Woodward leaned his head back on his pillow. "He has done his best . . . and the Devil has done his worst."

"Yes, sir, I agree."

Woodward turned his face so he had a good view of his clerk. "I know we have not been in agreement . . . on very much of late. I regret that any harsh words were spoken."

"As do I."

"I know also . . . how you must be feeling. The despondence and despair. Because you still believe her to be innocent. Am I correct?"

"You are, sir."

"Is there nothing . . . I can say or do to change your mind?"

Matthew offered him a slight smile. "Is there nothing I can say or do to change *yours?*"

"No," Woodward said firmly. "And I suspect that . . . we might never come to common ground on this." He sighed, his expression pained. "You will disagree, of course . . . but I appeal to you . . . to lay aside your obvious emotion and consider the facts as I did. I made my decree . . . based on those facts, and those facts alone. *Not* based on the accused's physical beauty . . . or her prowess at twisting words . . . or her misused intelligence. The facts, Matthew. I had no choice . . . but to pronounce her guilty, and to sentence her to such a death. Can you not understand?"

Matthew didn't reply, but instead stared at his folded hands.

"No one ever told me," Woodward said softly, "that . . . being a judge would be *easy*. In fact . . . I was promised . . . by my own mentor that it would be an iron cloak . . . once put on, impossible to remove. I have found it doubly true. But . . . I have tried to be fair, and I have tried to be correct. What more can I do?"

"Nothing more," Matthew said.

"Ah. Then perhaps . . . we might return to common ground after all. You will understand these things so much better . . . after *you* wear the iron cloak yourself."

"I don't believe I ever shall," came Matthew's answer, before he could guard his speech.

"You say that now . . . but it is your youth and despair speaking. Your affronted sense of . . . what is right and wrong. You are looking at the dark side of the moon, Matthew. The execution of a prisoner . . . is never a happy occasion, no matter the crime." He closed his eyes, his strength draining away. "But what joy . . . what relief . . . when you are able to discover the truth . . . and set an innocent person free. That alone . . . justifies the iron cloak. You will see . . . all in God's time."

A tap at the door announced a visitor. Matthew said, "Who is it?"

The door opened. Dr. Shields stood on the threshold, holding his medical bag. Matthew had noted that since the murder of Nicholas Paine, the doctor's countenance had remained gaunt and hollow-eyed, much as Matthew had found him at the infirmary. In truth, the doctor appeared to Matthew to be laboring under an iron cloak of his own, as Shields's moist face was milk-pale, his eyes watery and red-rimmed beneath the magnifying lenses of his spectacles. "Pardon my intrusion," he said. "I've brought the magistrate's afternoon dose."

"Come in, doctor, come in!" Woodward pulled himself up to a sitting position, eager for a taste of that healing tonic.

Matthew got up from his chair and moved away so Dr. Shields might administer the dose. The doctor had already this morning been cautioned again—as yesterday—not to mention the events transpiring in Fount Royal, which he had the good sense not to do even if he hadn't been cautioned. He agreed with Matthew that, though the magistrate appeared to be gaining strength, it was yet wise not to pressure his health with the disastrous news.

When the dose had been swallowed and Woodward settled again to await the oncoming of precious sleep, Matthew followed Dr. Shields out into the hallway and closed the magistrate's door.

"Tell me," Matthew said in a guarded tone. "Your best and honest opinion: When will the magistrate be able to travel?"

"He does improve daily." Shields's spectacles had slipped down his beak, and he pushed them up again. "I am very pleased with his response to the tonic. If all goes well . . . I would say two weeks."

"What do you mean, 'if all goes well'? He's out of danger, isn't he?"

"His condition was very serious. Life-threatening, as you well know. To say he's out of danger is an oversimplification."

"I thought you were so pleased with his response to the tonic."

"I am," Shields said forcefully. "But I must tell you something about that tonic. I created it myself from what I had at hand. I purposefully strengthened it as much as I dared, to encourage the body to increase its blood flow and thereby—"

"Yes, yes," Matthew interrupted. "I know all that about the stagnant blood. What of the tonic?"

"It is . . . how shall I say this . . . an extreme experiment. I've never before administered that exact mixture, in so powerful a dosage."

Matthew had an inkling now of what the doctor was getting at. He said, "Go on."

"The tonic was mixed strong enough to make him feel better. To lessen his pain. To . . . reawaken his natural healing processes."

"In other words," Matthew said, "it's a powerful narcotic that gives him the *illusion* of well-being?"

"The word *powerful* is . . . uh . . . an understatement, I fear. The correct term might be *Herculean.*"

"Then without this tonic he would regress to the state he was in before?"

"I can't say. I do know for certain that his fever is much reduced and his breathing greatly freed. The condition of his throat has also improved. So: I have done what you required of me, young man. I have brought the magistrate back from death's door . . . at the penalty of his being dependent on the tonic."

"Which means," Matthew said grimly, "that the magistrate is also dependent on the tonic's *maker.* Just in case I might wish to pursue you in the future for the murder of Nicholas Paine."

Shields flinched at this, and pressed a finger to his mouth to request that Matthew regulate his volume. "No, you're wrong," he said. "I swear it. That had nothing to do with my mixing the tonic. As I said, I used what was at hand, in a strength I judged sufficient for the task. And as for Paine . . . if you'd please not mention him again to me? In fact, I demand you do not."

Matthew had seen what might have been a blade-twist of agony in the doctor's eyes, a fleeting thing that had been pushed down as quickly as it had appeared. "All right, then," he said. "What's to be done?"

"I am planning, after the execution, to begin watering the dosage. There will still be three cups a day, but one of them will be half strength. Then, if all goes well, we shall cut a second cup to half strength. Isaac is a strong man, with a strong constitution. I am hopeful his body will continue to improve by its own processes."

"You're not going back to the lancet and blister cups, are you?"

"No, we have crossed those bridges."

"What about taking him to Charles Town? Could he stand the trip?"

"Possibly. Possibly not. I can't say."

"Nothing more can be done for him?"

"Nothing," Shields said. "It is up to him . . . and to God. But he does feel better and he does breathe easier. He can communicate, and he is comfortable. These days . . . with the medicines I have on hand . . . I would say that is a miracle of sorts."

"Yes," Matthew said. "I agree, of course. I . . . didn't wish to sound ungrateful for what you've done. I believe that under the circumstances you've performed with admirable skill."

"Thank you, sir. Perhaps in this case there was more luck involved than skill . . . but I have done my best."

Matthew nodded. "Oh . . . have you finished your examination of Linch's body?"

"I have. I calculate from the thickness of blood that he had been dead some five to seven hours before discovery. His throat wound was the most glaring, but he was also stabbed twice in the back. It was a downward thrust, both stabs piercing his lung on the right side."

"So he was stabbed by someone standing behind and over him?"

"It would appear so. Then I believe his head was pulled backward and the throat wound administered."

"He must have been sitting at his desk," Matthew said. "Talking to whoever killed him. Then, when he lay dying on the floor, the slash marks were applied."

"Yes, by Satan's claws. Or by the claws of some unknown demon."

Matthew was not going to argue the matter with Dr. Shields. Instead, he changed the subject. "And what of Mr. Bidwell? Has he recovered?"

"Sadly, no. He sits at the tavern with Winston as we speak, getting drunker than I've ever seen him. I can't blame him. Everything is crumbling around him, and with more witches yet to be identified . . . the town will soon be empty. I slept last night—the little I *did* sleep—with a Bible at both ends of my bed and a dagger in my hand."

Matthew's thought was that Shields could use a lancet with far deadlier effect than a dagger. "You needn't fear. The damage has been done, and there's no need for the fox now to do anything but wait."

"The fox? Satan, you mean?"

"I mean what I said. Pardon me, doctor. I have some things to tend to."

"Certainly. I shall see you later this evening."

Matthew retired to his room. He drank a cup of water and picked up the ebony-wood compass he'd found in Paine's house early this morning. It was a splendid instrument, the size of his palm, with a blued steel needle on a printed paper card indicating the degrees of direction. He'd realized the compass was a prime example of the process of magnetism, the needle having been magnetized—by a method he didn't fully understand—so as to point north.

Matthew had made other discoveries in Paine's bloodless

house, not including the body-sized area of floorboards that had been pulled up and then hastily laid down again underneath the pallet. A brown cotton bag with a shoulder strap served to hold his other finds: a knife with a seven-inch-long blade and an ivory handle; a buckskin bladesheath and waistbelt; and a pair of knee-high boots that could be made useable by an inch of padding at the toes. He also found Paine's pistol and the wheel-lock spanner, but as he knew absolutely nothing about loading, preparing, and firing the temperamental weapon, its use would probably result in his shooting himself in the head.

Matthew had much to do, now that he'd decided.

Near midday, his decision—which up until that point had been wavering—was made solid. He had walked to the execution field and actually gone right up to the pyre and the stake. He'd stood there imagining the horror of it, yet his imagination was not so deranged as to permit him a full and complete picture. He could not save Fount Royal, but at least he might cheat the fox of Rachel's life.

It was possible, and he was going to do it.

He had been on his way to the gaol, to inform Rachel, when his steps had slowed. Of course she needed to know beforehand . . . or did she? If his resolve failed tonight, should she be waiting in the dark for a champion who never arrived? If he tried with all his intelligence and might and could not get the key from Green, should Rachel be waiting, hopeful of freedom?

No. He would spare her that torment. He had turned away from the gaol, long before he'd reached its door.

Now, in his room, Matthew sat down in his chair with the document box. He opened it and arranged before him three clean sheets of paper, a quill, and the inkpot.

He spent a moment arranging his thoughts as well. Then he began writing.

Dear Isaac:

> *By now you have discovered that I have taken Rachel from the gaol. I regret any distress this action may cause you, but I*

have done such because I know her to be innocent yet I cannot offer proof.

It is my knowledge that Rachel has been the pawn in a scheme designed to destroy Fount Royal. This was done by a manipulation of the mind called "animal magnetism" which I understand will be as much of a puzzle to you as it was to me. Fount Royal's ratcatcher was not who he appeared to be, but indeed was a master at this process of manipulation. He had the ability to paint pictures in the air, as it were. Pictures that would seem to be true to life, except for the lack of several important details such as I have pointed out in our conversations. Alas, I have no proof of this. I learned Linch's true identity from Mr. David Smythe, of the Red Bull Players, who knew him from a—

Matthew stopped. This sounded like utter madness! What was the magistrate going to think when he read these ramblings! Go on he told himself. Just go on.

—circus in England several years ago; I do not wish to ramble any further and alarm you. Suffice it to say I was devastated when Mr. Smythe and the players left town, as he was my last hope at proving Rachel guiltless.

I have a great concern for the safety of Mr. Bidwell. The person who murdered Linch did so before that true identity could be revealed. That same person has been behind the scheme to destroy Fount Royal all along. I believe I know the reason, but as I have no proof it matters not. Now about Mr. Bidwell's safety: if Fount Royal is not soon totally abandoned, Mr. Bidwell's life may be in jeopardy. To save himself, he may have to leave his creation. I am sorry to pass this news on, but it is vital that Mr. Winston remain at Mr. Bidwell's side day and night. I do trust Mr. Winston.

Please believe me, sir, when I tell you I am neither out of my mind nor bewitched. However, I cannot and will not bear to see justice so brutally raped. I am taking Rachel to the Florida country, where she might proclaim herself a runaway slave or English captive and thereby receive sanctuary by the Spanish.

Yes, I can hear your bellow, sir. Please calm yourself and let me explain. I plan on returning. When, I do not know. What will happen to me when I do return, I do not know either. It will be your judgment, and I bow before your mercy. At the same time, I would hope that Mr. Smythe might be found and encouraged to speak, as he will make everything clear to you. And, sir, this is very important: make certain you ask Mr. Smythe to explain why his family left the circus. You will understand much.

As I said, I do plan on returning. I am an English subject, and I do not wish to give up that privilege.

Matthew paused. He had to think about the next part.

Sir, if by some chance or the decision of God that I should not return, I wish to here and now thank you for your intercession in my life. I wish to thank you for your lessons, your labors, and—

Go on, he told himself.

—your love. Perhaps you did not come to the almshouse that day in search of a son. Nevertheless, you found one.

Or, more accurately, sir, you crafted one. I would like to think that I made as good a son as Thomas might have been. You see, sir, you have been a magnificent success at crafting a human being, if I may speak so grandly of myself. You have given me what I consider to be the greatest gifts: that of self-worth and a knowledge of the worth of others.

It is because I understand such worth that I choose to free Rachel from her prison and her unjust fate. No one has made this decision but myself. When I go to the gaol tonight to free her, she will be unaware of my intentions.

There is no way you could have known that Rachel was not guilty. You have steadfastly followed the rules and tenets of law as outlined for cases of this nature. Therefore you came to the only conclusion available to you, and performed the necessary action. In doing what I have done this night, I have put on my own iron cloak and performed the only action available to me.

I suppose that is everything I need to say. I will close by saying that I wish you good health, a long life, and excellent fortunes, sir. I intend to see you again, at some future date. Again, please attend to Mr. Bidwell's safety.

I remain Sincerely Your Servant, Matthew—

He was about to sign his last name, but instead he made one final dot.

Matthew.

Folding the pages carefully, he slid them into an envelope he'd taken from the desk in Bidwell's study. He wrote on the front of the envelope *To Magistrate Woodward,* then he lit a candle and sealed the letter with a few drops of white wax.

It was done.

The evening crept up, as evenings will. In the fading purple twilight, with the last bold artist's stroke of red sun painting the bellies of clouds across the western horizon, Matthew took a lantern and went walking.

Though his pace was leisurely, he had a purpose other than taking in a sunset view of the dying town. He had at dinner inquired of Mrs. Nettles where Hannibal Green lived, and had been directed to it by a single clipped and disapproving sentence. The small whitewashed house stood on Industry Street, very near the intersection and the fount. Thankfully it wasn't as far down the street as Jerusalem's firelit camp, from which hollering and shrill lamentations issued forth to hold back the devils of night. To the right of Green's house was a neatly arranged garden of flowers and herbs, indicating either that the giant gaol-keeper was a man of varied interests or he was graced with a wife who had—yes, it was true—a green thumb.

The shutters were cracked open only a few inches. Yellow lamplight could be seen within. Matthew had noticed that the shutters of most of the still-occupied houses were closed, presumably on this warm evening to guard against the invasion of those same demons Reverend Jerusalem currently flailed. The streets were all but deserted, save for a few wandering dogs and the occasional figure hurrying from here to there. Matthew also couldn't fail to note the alarming number of wagons that were packed with furniture, household goods, baskets, and the like, in preparation for a sunrise departure. He wondered how many families would lie on bare floors tonight, restless until the dawn.

Matthew stood in the middle of Industry Street and looked from Green's house toward Bidwell's mansion, studying the windows that could be seen from this perspective. Then, satisfied with his findings, he walked back the way he'd come.

Winston and Bidwell were in the parlor when he arrived, the former reading over figures in a ledgerbook while the latter slumped gray-faced in a chair, his eyes closed and an empty bottle on the floor beside him. Matthew approached with the intention to ask how Bidwell was feeling but Winston lifted a hand in warning, his expression telling Matthew that the master of Fount Royal would not be pleased to awaken and set eyes upon him. Matthew retreated and quietly climbed the stairs.

When he entered his room, he found on his dresser a package wrapped in white waxed paper. Opening it he discovered a loaf of dense dark bread, a fist-sized chunk of dried beef, a dozen slices of salted ham, and four sausages. Matthew saw also that on his bed lay three candles, a package of matches and a flint, a corked glass bottle filled with water, and—lo and behold—a coil of cat-gut line with a small lead ballweight and a hook already tied, a small bit of cork pressed onto the sharp point. Mrs. Nettles had done all she could; it was up to him to find the stick.

Later that night, Dr. Shields arrived to give the magistrate his third dose. Matthew remained in his room, lying on the bed with his gaze directed to the ceiling. Perhaps an hour after that, the sound of Bidwell's intoxicated raging came up the stairs along with the sound of his footsteps and those of the person—two persons, it sounded to be—assisting him. Matthew heard Rachel's name hurled like a curse, and God's name taken in vain. Bidwell's voice gradually quieted, until at last it faded to nothing.

The house slept, fitfully, on this execution eve.

Matthew waited. Finally, when there were no more noises for a long while and his inner clock sensed the midnight hour had been passed, Matthew drew a breath, exhaled it, and stood up.

He was terrified, but he was ready.

He struck a match, lit his lantern, and put it on the dresser, then he soaped his face and shaved. It had occurred to him that his next opportunity to do so would be several weeks in the future. He used the chamberpot, and then he washed his hands and put on a clean pair of brown stockings, sand-colored breeches, and a fresh white shirt. He tore up another pair of stockings and padded the boot toes. He worked his feet into the boots and pulled them up snugly around his calves. In his bag, grown necessarily heavy with the food and other items, he packed the soap-cake and a change of clothes. He placed the explanatory letter on his bed, where it would be seen. Then he slipped the bag's strap over his shoulder, picked up the lantern, and quietly opened the door.

A feeling of panic struck him. *I can yet change my mind,* he thought. *I can step back two paces, shut the door and—Forget?*

No.

Matthew shut the door behind him when he entered the hallway. He went into the magistrate's room and lit the double-candled lantern he had earlier brought there from downstairs. Opening the shutters, he set the lantern on the windowsill.

The magistrate made a muffled noise. Not of pain, simply some statement in the justice hall of sleep. Matthew stood beside the bed, looking down at Woodward's face and seeing not the magistrate but the man who had come to that almshouse and delivered him to a life he never would have imagined.

He almost touched Woodward's shoulder with a fond embrace, but he stayed his hand. Woodward was breathing well, if rather harshly, his mouth partway open. Matthew gave a quick and silent prayer that God would protect the good man's health and fortunes, and then there was no more time for lingering.

In Bidwell's study, that damned floorboard squealed again and almost sent Matthew out of his stolen boots. He lifted the map from its nail on the wall, carefully removed it from its frame and then folded it and put it down into his bag.

Downstairs—after an agonizingly slow descent meant to avoid any telltale thumps and squeaks that might bring Bidwell staggering out into the hallway—Matthew paused in the parlor to shine his lantern on the face of the mantel clock. It was near quarter to one.

He left the mansion, closed the door, and without a backward glance set off under a million stars. He kept the lantern low at his side, and shielded by his body in case the gate watchman—if indeed there remained in town anyone brave or foolish enough to sit up there all night—might happen to spy the moving flame and set off a bell-ringing alarm.

At the intersection he turned onto Truth Street and proceeded directly to the Howarth house. It was wretched in its abandonment, and made even more fearsome by the fact that Daniel Howarth had been found brutally murdered nearby. As Matthew opened the door and crossed the threshold, shining the lantern before him, he couldn't help but wonder that a ghost with a torn throat should be wandering within, forever searching for Rachel.

Ghosts there were none, but the rats had moved in. The gleam of red eyes and rodent teeth glittering under twitching whiskers greeted him, though he was certainly not a welcome guest. The rats scurried for their holes, and though Matthew had seen only five or six it sounded as if a duke's army of them festered the walls. He searched for and found the floorboard that had been lifted up to display the hidden poppets, and then he followed the lantern's glow into another room that held a bed. Its sheets and blanket were still crumpled and lying half on the floor from the March morning when Rachel was taken away.

Matthew found a pair of trunks, one containing Daniel's clothing and the other for Rachel's. He chose two dresses for her, both with long hems and full sleeves, as that was both the fashion and her favor. One dress was of a cream-colored, light material that he thought would be suitable for travelling in warm weather, and the other a stiffer dark blue printed material that impressed him as being of sturdy all-purpose use. At the bottom of the trunk were two pairs of Rachel's no-nonsense black shoes. Matthew put a pair of the shoes into his bag, the garments over his arm, and gladly left the sad, broken house to its current inhabitants.

His next destination was the gaol. He didn't go inside yet, however. There was still a major obstacle to deal with, and its name was Hannibal Green. Pinpricks of sweat had formed on his cheeks and forehead, and his insides had jellied at the thought of what could go wrong with his plan.

He left the garments and the shoulderbag in the knee-high grass beside the gaol. If all went as he hoped, he wouldn't be gone long enough for any rodent to find and investigate the package of food. Then he set his mind to the task ahead and began walking to Green's house.

As he went west on Truth Street he glanced quickly around and behind, just as a matter of reassurance—and suddenly he stopped in his tracks, his heart giving a vicious kick. He stood staring behind him, toward the gaol.

A light. Not there now, but he thought he'd seen a very brief glow there on the right side of the street, perhaps seventy or eighty feet away.

He paused, waiting, his heart slamming so hard he feared Bidwell might hear it and think a night-travelling drum corps had come to town.

If a light had indeed been displayed, it was gone. Or hidden when someone carrying it had dodged behind the protection of a hedge or wall, he thought grimly.

And another thought came to him, this one with dark consequences: had a citizen seen the flame of his lantern and emerged from a house to follow him? He realized someone might think he was either Satan incarnate or a lesser demon, prowling Fount Royal for another victim here in the dead of night. A single pistol shot would end his plans and possibly his life, but a single shout would have the same effect.

He waited. The urge to blow out his lamp was upon him, but that might truly be an admittance of foul deeds in progress. He scanned the dark. No further light appeared, if it had been there at all.

Time was passing. He had to continue his task. Matthew went on, from time to time casting a backward glance but seeing no evidence that he was being tracked. Presently he found himself in front of Green's house.

Now was the moment of truth. If he failed in the next few moments, everything would be ended.

He swallowed down a lump of fear and approached the door. Then, before he could lose his nerve, he balled up his fist and knocked.

thirty-seven

W HO . . . WHO'S *THERE?*"
Matthew was taken aback. Green actually sounded
frightened. Such was the double power of murder and fear, to
imprison persons inside their own homes.

"It's Matthew Corbett, sir," he said, emboldened by the
tremor in Green's voice. "I have to speak with you."

"Corbett? My Lord, boy! Do you know the hour?"

"Yes, sir, I do." And here was the beginning of the necessary
lie. "I've been sent by Magistrate Woodward." Amazing, how
such a falsehood could roll off a desperate tongue!

A woman's voice spoke within, the sound muffled, and Green
answered her with, "It's that magistrate's clerk! I'll have to open
it!" A latch was thrown and the door cracked. Green looked out,
his red mane wild and his beard a fright. When he saw that it was
only Matthew standing there and not an eight-foot-tall demon he
opened the door wider. "What's the need, boy?"

Matthew saw a rotund but not unpleasant-looking woman
standing in the room behind him. She was holding a lantern in
one hand and the other arm cradled a wide-eyed, red-haired child
two or three years of age. "The magistrate wishes to have Madam
Howarth brought before him."

"What? Now?"

"Yes, now." Matthew glanced around; no other lights had appeared in the houses surrounding Green's, which was either a testament to fear or the fact that they had been abandoned.

"She'll be led to the stake in three or four hours!"

"That's why he wishes to see her now, to offer her a last chance for confession. It's a necessary part of the law." Again, an able-tongued lie. "He's waiting for her." Matthew motioned toward Bidwell's mansion.

Green scowled, but he took the bait. He emerged from his house, wearing a long gray nightshirt. He looked in the direction of the mansion and saw the light in the upstairs window.

"He would have preferred to go to the gaol, but he's too ill," Matthew explained. "Therefore I'm to accompany you to the gaol to remove the prisoner, and from there we shall escort her to the magistrate."

Green was obviously dismayed at this request, but since he was the gaol-keeper and this was official business he could not refuse. "All right, then," he said. "Give me a minute to dress."

"A question for you, please," Matthew said before Green could enter the house again. "Can you tell me if the watchtowers are manned tonight?"

Green snorted. "Would *you* sit up there tonight, alone, so somethin' might swoop in and get you like Linch was got? Every man, woman and child in Fount Royal—*left* in Fount Royal, I mean to say—are huddled in their houses behind latched doors and closed shutters!"

"I thought as much," Matthew said. "It's a shame, then, that you should have to leave your wife and child alone. Undefended, I mean. But then again, it *is* an official request."

Green looked stricken. He rumbled, "Yes, it is. So there's no use jawin' about it."

"Well . . . I might make a suggestion," Matthew offered. "This is a very precarious time, I know. Therefore you might give me the key, and I'll take Madam Howarth to the magistrate. She'll probably not need to be returned to her cell before the execution hour. Of course, I wouldn't care to face her without a pistol or sword. Do you have either?"

Green stared him in the face. "Hold a minute," he said. "I've heard talk you were sweet on the witch."

"You have? Well . . . yes, it was true. *Was* true. She blinded me to her true nature while I was imprisoned with her. But I've since realized—with the magistrate's help—the depth of her powers."

"There are some who say *you* might be turned to a demon," Green said. "Lucretia Vaughan spoke such at the reverend's camp on the Sabbath."

"Oh . . . did she?" That damned woman!

"Yes, and that you might be in league with the witch. And Reverend Jerusalem said he knew you to be desirous of her body."

It was very difficult for Matthew to maintain a calm expression, when inside he was raging. "Mr. Green," he said, "it was I who delivered the execution decree to the witch. If I were truly a demon, I would have entranced the magistrate to prevent him from finding her guilty. I had every opportunity to do so."

"The reverend said it could'a been you made Woodward sick, hopin' he'd die 'fore he could speak the decree."

"Was I the central subject of the reverend's rantings? If so, I should at least ask for a percentage of the coin he made off my name!"

"The central subject was the Devil," Green said. "And how we're to get out of this town still wearin' our skins."

"After the reverend is done, you'll still have your skins, but your wallets will be missing." He was wandering from the point of his mission, and doing himself no good. "But please . . . there is the magistrate's request to consider. As I said, if you'll give me the key, I might—"

"No," Green interrupted. "Much as I despise to leave my home, the prisoner's my charge, and no hand shall unlock her cage but my own. Then I'll escort the both of you to the magistrate."

"Well . . . Mr. Green . . . I think that, in light of the reason to stay and defend your—" But Matthew was left talking to the air, as the giant gaol-keeper turned and entered his house.

His plan, tenuous at best, had already begun unravelling. Obviously Green was wary of Matthew's intentions. Also, the red-bearded monolith was faithful to duty even to the point of leaving his wife and child on this Satan-haunted eve. The man was to be commended, if Matthew wasn't so busy cursing him.

In a few moments Green emerged again, wearing his night-shirt over his breeches and heavy-soled boots on his feet. Around his neck was the leather cord and two keys. He carried a lantern in his left hand and his right paw brandished, to Matthew's great discomfort, a sword that might be used to be-head an ox. "Remember," he said to his wife, "keep this door latched! And if anyone even tries to get in, let out the loudest holler your lungs ever birthed!" He closed the door, she latched it, and he said to Matthew, "All right, off with you! You walk ahead!"

It was time, Matthew thought, for his second plan.

The only problem was that there was no second plan. He led Green toward the gaol. He didn't look but, from the way the flesh on the back of his neck crawled, he assumed Green kept the sword's point aimed at it. The barking of a dog further up on Harmony Street caused a second canine to reply from Industry, which Matthew knew would be no soothing melody to Green's nerves.

"Why wasn't I told about this?" Green asked, as they approached the gaol. "If it is such a necessary part of the law. Couldn't it have been done in daylight?"

"The law states the accused in a witchcraft trial shall be afforded the opportunity for confession no more than six hours and no less than two hours before execution. It is called the law of . . . um . . . *confessiato.*" If Jerusalem could get away with his rite of sanctimony, Matthew figured he might employ a similar strata-gem. "Usually the magistrate would visit the accused's cell in the company of a clergyman, but in this case it is impossible."

"Yes, that makes sense," Green admitted. "But still . . . why wasn't I told to expect it?"

"Mr. Bidwell was supposed to inform you. Didn't he?"

"No. He's been ill."

"Well," Matthew said with a shrug, "there you have it."

They entered the gaol, Matthew still leading. Rachel spoke to the lights instead of the persons carrying them, her voice wan and resigned to her fate. "Is it time?"

"Almost, madam," Matthew said stiffly. "The magistrate wishes to see you, to allow you opportunity for confession."

"For *confession?*" She stood up. "Matthew, what's this about?"

"I suggest you be silent, witch, for your own good. Mr. Green, open the cell." He stepped aside, feverishly trying to think of what he was going to do when the key had turned.

"You step over there, away from me," Green instructed, and Matthew did.

Rachel came to the bars, her face and hair dirty, her amber eyes piercing him. "I asked you a question. What is this about?"

"It is about your life *after* you leave this place, witch. Your afterlife, in a faraway realm. Now please hold your tongue."

Green slid the key into its lock, turned it, and opened the cage's door. "All right. Come out." Rachel hesitated, gripping the bars. "It's the law of *confessiassho!* Come on, the magistrate's waitin'!"

Matthew's mind was racing. He saw the two buckets in Rachel's cell, one for drinking water and the other for bodily functions. Well, it wasn't much but it was all he could think of. "By God!" he said, "I think the witch wants to *defy* us, Mr. Green! I think she refuses to come out!" He stabbed an urgent finger at her, motioning toward the rear of the cell. "Will you come out, witch, or shall we drag you?"

"I don't . . ."

"By *God,* Mr. Green! She's defying the magistrate, even at this final hour! Will you come out, or will you *make things difficult?*" He added the emphasis on the last three words, and he saw that Rachel was still puzzled but she'd realized what he wanted her to do. She retreated from the bars, stopping only when her back met the wall.

"Matthew?" she said. "What game is this?"

"A game you will regret, madam! And don't think speaking so familiarly to me shall prevent Mr. Green from going in there and dragging you out! Mr. Green, have at it!"

Green didn't budge. He leaned on his sword. "I ain't goin' in there and risk gettin' my eyeballs scratched out. Or worse. You want her so bloody bad, *you* go get her."

Matthew felt the wind leave his sails. This was becoming a farce worthy of a drunken playwright's most fevered scribblings. "Very well then, sir." He clenched his teeth and held out his hand. "Your sword, please?"

Green's eyes narrowed. "I'll go in and drag her out," Matthew pressed on, "but you don't expect me to enter a tiger's den without a weapon, do you? Where's your Christian mercy?"

Green said nothing, and did not move. "Matthew?" Rachel said. "What's this—"

"Hush, witch!" Matthew answered, his gaze locked with the giant's.

"Ohhhhh, no." A half-smile slipped across Green's mouth. "No, sirrah. I ain't givin' up my sword. You must think me a proper fool, if you'd believe I'd let it out of my hand."

"Well, *someone* has got to go in there and pull her out! It seems to me it should be the man with the *sword!*" By now Matthew was a human sweatpond. Still Green hesitated. Matthew said, with an exasperated air, "Shall I go to the magistrate and tell him the execution will be postponed because the law of confessiato cannot be applied?"

"She doesn't care to confess!" Green said. "The magistrate can't force her to!"

"That's not the point. The law says . . ." Think, think! ". . . the accused must be afforded an opportunity, in the *presence* of a magistrate, whether they want to confess or not. Go on, please! We're wasting time!"

"That's a damn ridiculous law," Green muttered. "Sounds

just like somethin' from a bunch of highwigs." He aimed his sword at Rachel. "All right, witch! If you won't move on your own will, you'll move at a prick on your arse!" Sweat glistening on his face, he entered the cell.

"Look how she steps back!" Quickly, Matthew set his lantern on the floor and entered directly behind him. "Look how she hugs the wall! Defiant to a fault!"

"Come on!" Green stopped, motioning with the sword. "Out with you, damn it!"

"Don't let her make a fool of you!" Matthew insisted. He looked down at the buckets and made the choice of the one that was about half-full of water. "Go on!"

"Don't rush me, boy!" Green snapped. Rachel had slid away from him along the wall toward the bars of the cell Matthew had occupied during his incarceration. Green went after her, but cautiously, the lantern in his left hand and the sword in his right.

Matthew picked up the water bucket. *Oh God,* he thought. Now or never!

"I don't want to draw blood," Green warned Rachel as he neared her, "but if I have to I'll—"

Matthew said sharply, "Look here, Mr. Green!"

The giant gaol-keeper whipped his head around. Matthew was already moving. He took two steps and flung the water into Green's face.

It hit the behemoth directly, blinding him for an instant but an instant of blindness was all Matthew had wanted. He followed the water by swinging the empty bucket at Green's head. *Wham!* went the sound of the blow, wood against skull, and skull won. The sturdy bucket fairly burst to pieces on impact, leaving Matthew gripping the length of rope that had served as its handle.

Green staggered backward, past Rachel as she scrambled aside. He dropped the lantern and collided with the bars with a force that made the breath whoosh from his lungs. His eyes had rolled back in his head. The sword slipped from his fingers.

Then Green toppled to his knees in the straw, the floor trembling as he hit.

"Have you . . . have you gone *mad?*" was all Rachel could think to say.

"I'm getting you out of here." Matthew bent, picked up the sword—a heavy beast—and pushed it between the bars into the next cell.

"Getting me . . . out? What're you—?"

"I'm not going to let you burn," he said, turning to face her. "I have clothes for you, and supplies. I'm taking you to the Florida country."

"The . . . Florida . . ." She stepped back, and Matthew thought she might fall as Green had. "You . . . *must* be mad!"

"The Spanish will give you sanctuary there, if you pass yourself as a runaway slave or English captive. Now, I really don't think we have time to debate this, as I have crossed my own personal point of no return."

"But . . . why are you—"

She was interrupted by a groan from the awakening gaol-keeper, who was still on his knees. Matthew looked at Green in alarm and saw his eyes fluttering. Then, suddenly, Green's blood-shot eyes opened wide. They darted from Matthew to Rachel and back again—and then Green's mouth opened to deliver a yell that would awaken not only Fount Royal but the sleepers in Charles Town.

In a heartbeat, Matthew grabbed up a double-handful of straw and jammed it deeply into Green's mouth even as the yell began its exit. Perhaps a syllable escaped before the straw did its work. Green began to gag and choke, and Matthew followed the act with a blow to the gaol-keeper's face that seemed to do not a whit of damage except to Matthew's knuckles. Then, still dazed and his voice unavailable, Green grasped the front of Matthew's shirt and his left forearm, lifted him off the floor like one of the demonic poppets, and flung him against the wall.

Now it was Matthew's turn to lose his breath as he crashed against the timbers. He slid down to the floor, his ribs near caved in, and saw through a haze of pain that Green was reaching through the bars to grasp the sword's handle, bits of straw flying around his face as he tried to cough the stuff out. Green's fingers closed on the weapon, and he began drawing it toward himself.

Matthew looked at Rachel, who was still too stunned at this turn of events to react. Then he saw the wooden bench beside her, and he hauled himself up.

Green almost had the sword pulled through. His large hand, clasping the sword's grip, had lodged between the bars. He gave a mighty heave, near tearing the flesh from his paw, and suddenly the sword was again his protector.

But not for long, if Matthew had his way. Matthew had picked up the bench, and now he slammed it down across Green's head and shoulders with all his strength. The bench went the way of the bucket, exploding upon impact. Green shuddered and made a muffled groan, his throat still clogged, and again the sword fell from his spasming fingers.

Matthew reached down to get that damned blade and do away with it once more—and Green's hands, the right one bruised and blackening from its contest with the bars, seized his throat.

Green's face was mottled crimson, the eyes wild with rage and terror, a stream of blood running from the top of his head down to his eyebrows and straw clenched between his teeth. He stood up to his full height, lifting Matthew by the throat, and began to strangle him as surely as if Matthew had been dangling from a gallows-tree. Matthew's legs kicked and he pushed against Green's bearded chin with both hands, but the giant's grasp was killing him.

Rachel now saw that she must act or Matthew would die. She saw the sword, but her wish was not to kill to save. Instead she launched herself at Green's back like a wildcat, scratching and pummelling at his face. He turned and with a motion that was almost casual flung her off, after which he continued his single-minded execution as Matthew thrashed ineffectually.

A shimmering red haze was starting to envelope Matthew's

head. He cocked back his right fist, judging where he should strike to inflict the most pain. It hardly mattered. Green gave the threatening fist a quick glance and a straw-lipped sneer and his crushing hands tightened even more.

The blow was delivered, with a sound like an axe striking hardwood. Green's head snapped back, his mouth opened, and a tooth flew out, followed by a spatter of blood.

Instantly the giant's hands loosened. Matthew dropped to the floor. He clutched at his throat, his lungs heaving.

Green turned in a dazed circle, as if he were dancing a reel with an invisible partner. He coughed once, then again, and straw burst from his throat. His eyes showing only red-tinged whites, he fell like a hammer-knocked steer and lay stretched out on the floor.

It had been one hell of a blow.

However, it had been delivered before Matthew's own puny offering. Mrs. Nettles spat on her knuckles and wrung her hand. "Ow," she said. "I've nae hit a harder head!"

Matthew croaked, *"You?"*

"Me," she answered. "I heard you up 'n' about in Mr. Bidwell's study. I thought I'd tag along, keep a watch o'er ye. Near saw my lantern, 'fore I dowsed it." She looked at Rachel, and then cast a disapproving eye around the cell. "Lord, what a filthpot!"

Rachel was so amazed at all this, when she'd been preparing herself for the final morn, that she felt she must be in some strange dream even though she'd not slept since early afternoon.

"Here, c'mon." Mrs. Nettles reached down, grasped Matthew's hand, and hauled him up. "You'd best be off. I'll make sure Mr. Green keeps his silence."

"You're not going to hurt him, are you? I mean . . . any more than you already have?"

"No, but I'm gonna strip him naked and bind his wrists and ankles. His mouth, too. That nightshirt ought ta give up some ropes. But it wouldn't do for him ta ever know I was here. Go on now, the both of you!"

Rachel shook her head, still unbelieving. "I thought . . . I was to burn today."

"You shall *yet* burn, and the young man too, if you do'nae go." Mrs. Nettles was already pulling the nightshirt off Green's slumbering body.

"We have to hurry." Still rubbing his bruised throat, Matthew took Rachel's hand and guided her toward the threshold. "I have clothes and shoes for you outside."

"Why are *you* doing this?" Rachel asked Mrs. Nettles. "You're Bidwell's woman!"

"Nae, lass," came the reply. "I am employed by Mr. Bidwell, but I am my *own* woman. And I am doin' this 'cause I never thought you guilty, no matter what was claimed. Also . . . I am rightin' an old wrong. Off with ye!"

Matthew picked up his lantern. "Thank you, Mrs. Nettles!" he said. "You saved my life!"

"No, sir." She continued her methodical stripping of Green, her back turned to Matthew. "I just sentenced you both ta . . . whatever's out there."

Outside, Rachel staggered and held out her arms as if to embrace the night and the stars, her face streaked with tears. Matthew grasped hold of her hand again, and hurried her to where he'd left the shoulderbag, garments, and shoes. "You can change clothes after we get out," he said, slipping the bag's strap over his shoulder. "Will you carry these?" He gave her the garments. "I thought the light one would be best for travelling."

She gave a soft gasp as she took the dresses, and she caressed the cream-colored garment as if it were the returning to her of a wonderful treasure. Which it was. "Matthew . . . you've brought my wedding dress!"

If he'd had the time to spare, he might have laughed or he might have cried, but which one he was never to know. "Your shoes," he said, giving them to her. "Put them on, we're going through rough country."

They started off, Matthew leading the way toward Bidwell's house and the slave quarters. He had considered going out the front gate, as there was no watchman, but the gate's locking timber was too heavy for one man, and certainly for one man who had nearly been rib-busted and choked to death.

He looked up at the lantern in Isaac's window and wished the man might truly know what he meant to Matthew. Alas, a note was a poor goodbye but the only one available to him.

Through the slave quarters, Matthew and Rachel moved as if they were dark, flying shadows. Perhaps the door of John Goode's house cracked open a few inches, or perhaps not.

Freedom awaited, but first there was the swamp.

thirty-eight

THE LAND WAS GOD and Devil both.

Matthew had this thought during the third hour of daylight, as he and Rachel paused at a stream to refill the water bottle. Rachel dipped the hem of her bride's dress into the water and pressed the cool cloth—once white on her wedding day, but faded by the Carolina humidity to its current cream hue—against her face. She scooped up a handful of water, which gurgled over flat stones and moved quietly through reeds and high grasses, and wet her thick ebony hair back from her forehead. Matthew glanced at her as he went about uncorking and filling the bottle, thinking of Lucretia Vaughan's repugnant idea concerning Rachel's locks.

Rachel took off her shoes and slid her sore feet into the sun-warmed stream. "Ahhhhh," she said, her eyes closed. "Ahhhhhh, that feels better."

"We can't tarry here very long." Matthew was already looking back through the woods in the direction they'd come. His face was red-streaked from an unfortunate encounter with a thorn thicket before the sun had appeared, and patches of sweat blotched his shirt. This certainly wasn't horse country, though, and therefore Solomon Stiles and whoever else might be with him would also be travelling on foot. It was rough going, no matter how experienced the leatherstocking. Still, he knew better than to underestimate Stiles's tracking skills, if indeed Bidwell had sent men in pursuit.

"I'm tired." Rachel lowered her head. "So tired. I could lie in the grass and sleep."

"I could, as well. That's why we have to keep moving."

She opened her eyes and looked at him, a pattern of leaf-shadow and morning sun on her face. "Don't you know you've given up everything?"

Matthew didn't respond. She'd asked him this question earlier, at the violet-blushed dawn, and neither had he answered then.

"You have," she said. "For what? Me?"

"For the truth." He removed the bottle from the stream and pushed its cork back in.

"The truth was worth so much?"

"Yes." He returned the bottle to his shoulderbag, and then he sat down in the wiry grass because—though his spirit was willing—his aching legs were not yet ready to travel again. "I believe I know who killed Reverend Grove and your husband. Also this person was responsible for the ratcatcher's murder."

"*Linch* was murdered?"

"Yes, but don't trouble yourself over him. He was as vile as his killer. Almost. But I believe I know the motive, and how these so-called witnesses were turned against you. They really did think they saw you . . . um . . . in unholy relations, so they were not lying." He cupped some water from the stream and wet his face. "Or, at least, they didn't realize they were."

"You *know* who killed Daniel?" Her eyes had taken on a hint of fury. "Who was it?"

"If I spoke the name, your response would be incredulity. Then, after I'd explained the reasoning, it would be anger. Armed with what you know, you would wish to go back to Fount Royal and bring the killer to justice . . . but I fear that is impossible."

"Why? If you *know* the name?"

"Because the cunning fox has erased all evidence," Matthew

said. "Murdered it, so to speak. There is no proof whatsoever. So I would say a name to you, and you would be forever anguished that nothing can be done, just as I shall be." He shook his head. "It's best that only one of us drinks from that poisoned cup."

She pondered this for a moment, watching the flowing stream, and then she said, "Yes. I *would* want to go back."

"You may as well forget Fount Royal. I think the final hand has been dealt to Bidwell's folly, anyway." He roused himself and, considering that he wanted to put at least ten more miles at their backs before sundown, he stood up. He took a moment to study the map and align himself with the compass, during which Rachel put her shoes back on. Then Rachel pulled herself up too, wincing at the stiffness of her legs.

She looked around at the green-leafed trees, then up at the azure sky. After so long being confined, she was still half-dazed with the pine-perfumed breeze of freedom. "I feel so small," she said. "Hardly worth the sacrifice of a young man's life."

"If the young man has anything to do with it," he said, "it will not be a sacrifice. Are you ready?"

"I am."

They set off again, crossing the stream and heading once more into the dense forest. Matthew might not be a leatherstocking, but he was doing all right. Even very well, he thought. He had gone so far as to cinch the buckskin knife in its sheath around his waist in the best Indian-scout tradition, so the blade's handle was within easy reach.

Of Indians they'd seen not a footprint nor a feather. The wild beasts they'd encountered, not counting the chirping birds in the trees, consisted of a profusion of squirrels and a black snake coiled on a sun-splashed rock. The most difficult part of the journey so far had been the two miles of tidewater swamp they'd negotiated upon leaving Fount Royal.

But the land was God and Devil both, Matthew mused, because it was so beautiful and frighteningly vast in the sunny hours—but in the night, he knew, the demons of the unknown would creep to their pinestick fire and whisper of terrors beyond the circle of light. He had never ventured into a territory where there were no paths at all, just massive oaks, elms, and huge pines with cones the size of cannonballs, a carpet of leaf decay and pine needles in some places ankle deep, and the feeling that one would survive or perish here almost at the whim of Fate. Thank God for the map and the compass, or he would have already misplaced his sense of direction.

The land rose, forcing them up a slight but rugged incline. At its top, a crust of red rocks afforded a view of more unbroken wilderness stretching beyond the power of the eye. God spoke to Matthew and told him of a country almost too grand to imagine; the Devil spoke in his other ear, and told him such tremendous, fearful expanse and space would be seeded by the bones of some future generation.

They descended, Rachel walking a few paces behind Matthew as he cleaved a path through waist-high grass. Her wedding dress made a rustling sound, and small thorny pods stung her legs and clung to her hem.

As the sun continued its climb, the day warmed. Matthew and Rachel walked through a forest of gigantic, primeval trees where the hot sun was bright one second, streaming between the limbs seventy feet above, and the next second the shadows were dark green and as cool as caverns. Here they saw their first true wilderness creatures: four grazing does and a huge, watchful buck with a spread of antlers easily five feet across. The does lifted their heads to stare at the two humans, the buck gave a snort and bounded between his charges and the intruders, and then suddenly all the animals turned and vanished into the green curtains.

Not very further on, Matthew and Rachel again stopped at the edge of light and shadows. "What are those?" Rachel asked, her voice tensing.

Matthew approached the nearest oak. It was a Goliath of a tree that must've stood a hundred feet tall and had a trunk thirty feet around, but it was by no means the largest in these ancient woods. Lichens and moss had been pulled away from the trunk.

Carved into the bark were man-shaped pictograms, swirling symbols, and sharp-edged things that might have been the representations of arrowheads. Matthew saw that it was indeed not the only trunk so adorned; a dozen more trees had been carved upon, displaying the figures of more humans, deer, what might have been the sun or moon, and waved lines that possibly stood for wind or water, among a variety of other symbols.

"They're Indian signs," Rachel said, answering her own question, as Matthew ran his fingers over a head-high symbol that seemed to either be a frightfully large man or a bear. "We must be in their territory."

"Yes, we must." Ahead of them, in that vast shadowy forest, were a few more carved trunks beyond the main line of decorated trees, and then beyond those the oaks were unadorned. Matthew consulted his map and compass once again.

"Perhaps we should change our route," Rachel suggested.

"I don't think changing our route would suffice. According to the compass, we're moving in the proper direction. I also think it would be difficult to say what was Indian territory and what was not." Uneasily, he looked around. A breeze stirred the leaves far overhead, making the shadows and sunlight shift. "The sooner we get through here, the better," he said, and he started walking again.

In an hour of rigorous travel, during which they saw thirty or forty more grazing deer, they emerged from the green forest into a wide clearing and in so doing were greeted with an amazing sight. Nearby a hundred wild turkeys the size of sheep were pecking in the grass and brush, and the intrusion of humans startled them to ungainly flight. The wind of their wings fanned the clearing and made a sound like the onrush of a hurricane.

"Oh!" Rachel cried out. "Look there!" She pointed, and Matthew's sight followed the line of her finger to a small lake whose still water reflected blue sky and golden Sol. "I'm going to rest here," she told him, her eyes weary. "I'm going to take a bath and wash the gaol smell off me."

"We should keep moving."

"Can we not make our camp here for the night?"

"We could," Matthew said, judging the sun's progress, "but there's still plenty of light. I didn't intend to camp until night-fall."

"I'm sorry, but I *must* rest," she insisted. "I can hardly feel my legs anymore. And I must bathe, too."

Matthew scratched his forehead. He, as well, was just about worn to a nubbin. "All right. I think we might stay here for an hour or so." He slipped the bag's strap off his chafed shoulder and retrieved the soapcake, offering it to her further amazement. "Never let it be said I did not bring civilization to the wilderness."

At this point in their relationship, which seemed more intimate than the wedded state, it was nonsense for Matthew to walk into the dark line of woods and afford Rachel privacy. Neither did she expect it. On the edge of the lake, as Matthew reclined on his back and stared up at the sky, Rachel took off her shoes and the faded bridal dress and waded naked into the water to her waist. She turned her back to the shore and soaped her private area, then her stomach and breasts. Matthew glanced once . . . then again . . . a third time, more than a glance . . . at her brown body, made lean by gaolhouse soup. He might have counted her ribs, if he'd chosen. Her body was womanly, yes, but there was a hardness of purpose to it as well, a purity of the will to survive. He watched as she walked deeper into the water, chillbumps rippling across her taut skin even as the sun soothed her. She leaned over and wet her hair, then soaped a lather into it.

Matthew sat up and pulled his knees to his chin. His thorn-cut face had blushed at the image in his mind: that of his own hands, moving over the curves and hollows of Rachel's body as if they too were explorers in a new territory. A winged insect of some kind buzzed his head, which helped to distract him from that line of thought.

After her hair was washed and she was feeling clean, Rachel's attention returned again to Matthew. Also returned was her sense of modesty, as if the gaol's grime had clothed her from view and now she was truly naked. She knelt down in the water, up to her neck, and approached the shore.

Matthew was eating half of a slice of ham from the food package, and had set aside the other half for Rachel. He saw she intended to emerge from the water, so he turned his back. She came out of the lake, dripping, and stood for a moment to dry herself, her face offered to the sun.

"I fear you'll have to invent a falsehood when you enter a Spanish town or stockade," Matthew said, painfully aware of how near she stood. "I doubt even the Spanish would care to grant sanctuary to an accused witch." He finished the ham and licked his fingers, watching her shadow on the ground. "You should claim yourself to be an escaped household servant, or simply a wife who sickened of British rule. Once they know your country of birth, you should have no troubles." Again that insect—no, two of them—buzzed around him, and he waved them away.

"Wait," she said, picking up her wedding dress. "You're speaking only of me. What about *you?*"

"I am helping you reach the Florida country . . . but I'm not going to stay there with you." Rachel let this revelation sink in as she put her dress back on.

He had seen her shadow don the garment, so he turned toward her again. Her beauty—the thick, wet black hair, the lovely proud face and intense amber eyes—was enough to quicken his heart. The nightbird was even more compelling by day. He sighed and chose to stare at the ground once more. "I'm an Englishman," he said. "Bound by the conventions and laws of English life, whether I like them or not. I couldn't survive in a foreign land." Matthew managed a brief, halfhearted smile. "I should be too longing for boiled potatoes and roast beef. Besides . . . Spanish is not my tongue."

"I don't understand you," she said. "What kind of man are you, who does what you've done and expects nothing in return?"

"Oh, I do expect something, make no mistake. I expect to be able to go on living with myself. I expect you will return to

Portugal, or Spain, and rebuild your life. I expect to see Magistrate Woodward again and plead my case before him."

"I expect you'll find yourself behind stronger bars than held me," Rachel said.

"A possibility," he admitted. "A *likelihood*. But I won't stay there long. Here, do you want this?" He held up the portion of ham for her.

She accepted it. "How can I tell you how much this means to me, Matthew?"

"What? One half slice of ham? If it means so much, you can have a whole—"

"You know what I'm saying," she interrupted. "What you've done. The incredible risk." Her face was grim and set, but tears glistened in her eyes. "My God, Matthew. I was ready to die. I had given up my spirit. How can I ever repay such a debt?"

"It is I who owe the debt. I came to Fount Royal a boy. I left it as something more," Matthew said. "You should sit down and rest."

She did sit down, and pressed her body against his as if they sat crushed by a crowd of a thousand people, instead of just alone in this God-made, Devil-touched land. He started to move away, discomforted by his own reaction to her closeness, but she gently grasped his chin with her left hand.

"Listen to me," Rachel said, in what was nearly a whisper. Her eyes stared into his own, their faces only parted by a few inches of inconsequential air. "I loved my husband very much," she said. "I gave him my heart and my soul. Even so, I think . . . I could love you the same . . . if you would allow it."

The few inches of air shrank. Matthew did not know who had first leaned toward the other, but did it really matter? One leaned and one met, and that was both the geometry and poetry of their kiss.

Though Matthew had never before done this, it seemed a natural act. What was most alarming was the speed of his heart, which if it had been a horse might have reached Boston by first star. Something inside him seemed molten, like blue-flamed glass being changed and reshaped by the power of a breath. It was both strengthening and weakening, thrilling and frightening—again that conjunction of God and Devil that seemed to be at the essence of all things.

It was a moment he would remember the rest of his life.

Their lips remained sealed together, melded by bloodheat and heartbeat. Who drew away first was also unknown to Matthew, as time had slipped its boundaries like rain and river.

Matthew looked into Rachel's eyes. The need to speak was as strong as a force of nature. He knew what he would say. He opened his mouth. "I—"

A winged insect suddenly landed on the shoulder of Rachel's wedding dress. His attention was drawn to it, and away from the moment. He saw it was a honeybee. The insect hummed its wings and took flight, and then Matthew was aware of several more of them circling round and round.

"I—" Matthew said again, and suddenly he was not sure at all what he was going to say. She waited for him to speak, but he was speechless.

He stared into her eyes once more. Was it the desire to love him he saw there, or the desire to thank him for the gift of her life? Did she even know which emotion reigned in her heart? Matthew didn't think so.

Even as they travelled together, they were moving in opposite directions. It was a bitter realization, but a true one. Rachel was bound for a place he could not live, and he must live in a place where she could not be bound.

He dropped his gaze from her. She, too, had realized that there could be no future for two such as them, and that Daniel was still as close to her as the dress she had worn on the day of their joining. She drew away from Matthew, and then noticed the circling insects.

"Honeybees." Matthew scanned the clearing, his eyes searching. And there it was!

A stand of two dead oaks—probably lightning-struck, he thought—stood apart from the main line of forest, fifty yards from the lake's edge. Near the top of one of them was a large knothole. Around it the air was alive with a dark, shifting mass. Sunlight made a stream of liquid down the tree's trunk shine gold.

"Where there are honeybees," Matthew said, "there is honey." He took the bottle from the bag, emptied its water—since fresh water was an abundant resource at this distance from the seacoast and swamp—and stood up. "I'll see if I can obtain us some."

"I'll help." She started to stand, but Matthew put his hand on her shoulder.

"Rest while you can," he advised. "We're going to have to move on very soon."

Rachel nodded and relaxed again. In truth, she would have to summon the energy for their continued journey, and a walk to a dead tree fifty yards there and back—even for the sweet delicacy of honey—strained her imagination.

Matthew, however, was intent on it, particularly after their kiss and the jarring return to reality that had followed. As Matthew started toward the tree, Rachel warned, "Take care you're not stung! The honey wouldn't be worth it!"

"Agreed." But he'd seen the spill of golden nectar down the trunk from what appeared a very copious comb, and he felt sure he might at least get a bottleful without incurring rage.

The bees had been highly productive. The honey had streamed down from forty feet above all the way to the ground, where a sticky puddle had accumulated. Matthew drew the knife from its sheath, uncorked the bottle, and held it into the flow, at the same time pushing the thick elixir—a natural medicine good for all ills, Dr. Shields would have said—in with his blade. A few bees hummed around, but they did not strike and seemed mostly curious. He could hear the steady, more ominous tone of the large dark mass of them as they went about their business tending the comb.

As he worked, Matthew's mind went to the magistrate. The letter would have been long read by now. Whether it had been digested or not was more difficult to say. Matthew listened to the singing of birds in the forest beyond, and wondered whether the magistrate might be able to hear such song at this very moment, or be able to see the sun on this cloudless day. What must Isaac be thinking? Matthew fervently hoped that he'd written the missive coherently—and eloquently—enough so that Isaac would know he was in his right mind, and adamant about Smythe being located. If that man would agree to talk, then much could be—

Matthew paused in his work, the bottle near halfway filled. Something had changed, he thought.

Something.

He listened. He could still hear the drone of the working bees. But . . . the birdsong. Where was the birdsong? Matthew looked toward the shadowed line of forest.

The birds had ceased their singing.

A movement to the left caught his eye. Three crows burst from the foliage, cawing loudly as they shot across the clearing.

Beside the lake, Rachel lay on her back, drowsing. The voices of the crows came to her, and she opened her eyes in time to watch the birds pass overhead.

Matthew stood motionless, staring at the impenetrable area from which the crows had come.

Another movement seized his attention. Far up in the sky, a single vulture was slowly wheeling around and around.

All the saliva had left his mouth and become cold sweat on his face. The sensation of danger stabbed him like a knife in the neck.

He felt certain something in the woods was watching him.

Moving with careful deliberation though his nerves shrieked to turn and run, Matthew pushed the cork back into the bottle. His right fist tightened around the knife's handle. He began to retreat from the honey-flowing tree, one step at the time, his eyes darting back and forth across the treacherous woods.

"Rachel?" he called. His voice cracked. He tried again. "Rachel?!" This time he looked over his shoulder to see if she'd heard.

A heavy form suddenly exploded from its place of concealment at the forest's edge. Rachel was the first to see it, by only a
second, and she let go a scream that savaged her throat.

Then Matthew faced it too. His feet seemed rooted to the
earth, his eyes wide and his mouth open in a soundless cry of
terror.

The monstrous bear that was racing toward him was an old
warrior and fully gray. Patches of ashy malignant mange infected
its shoulders and legs. Its jaws were stretched to receive human
flesh, streams of drool flying back past its head. Matthew had just
an instant to register that the bear's left eye socket was puckered
and empty, and he knew.

He was about to be embraced by Jack One Eye.

Maude . . . at Shawcombe's tavern . . . *Jack One Eye hain't jus'
a burr. Ever'thin' dark 'bout this land . . . ever'thin' cruel, and wicked.*

"Rachel!" he screamed, twisting toward her and running for
his life. "Get in the water!"

There was nothing she could do to help him except pray to
God he made the lake. She ran toward the water and leaped into
it, swimming in her bridal dress toward deep water.

Matthew dared not look behind. His legs were pumping furiously, his face distorted by fear, his heart on the verge of bursting.
He heard the thunderous impact of paws behind him, gaining
ground, and he knew with awful certainty that he would never
reach the lake.

He clenched his teeth and threw himself to the left—the
bear's blind side—at the same time letting out a shriek that he
hoped might startle the beast enough to give him extra time.
Jack One Eye hurtled past him, its rear claws digging up furrows
of earth. A front claw swung and made the air between them
shimmer.

Then Matthew was running for the lake again, dodging and
swerving with every step. Again the earth trembled at his heels.
The bear was bigger than the biggest horse he'd ever seen, and it
could crush every bone in his body just with its forward progress
alone.

Matthew leaped to the left in a maneuver that nearly snapped his knees. He almost lost his balance as the bear went past, its massive mange-riddled head thrusting in search of him. The jaws came together with a noise like a musket shot. He smelled the reeking bestial stink of the thing, and was close enough to see the broken shafts of four arrows in its side. Then he was running again, and he prayed that God grant him the speed of a crow.

Again Jack One Eye was almost upon him. Again Matthew lunged to the left—but this time he had misjudged both the geometry and the flexibility of his knees. The angle was too sharp and his feet skidded out from beneath him. He went down on his right side in the grass. He was only vaguely aware of Rachel's screams through the thunder in his head. The gray wall of Jack One Eye rose before him. He staggered up, fighting for balance.

Something hit him.

He had the impression of the world turned upside down. A searing pain filled his left shoulder. He knew he was tumbling head over heels, but could do nothing about it. Then he landed hard on his back, the breath bursting from his lungs. He tried to scramble away, as again that gray wall came upon him. Something was wrong with his left arm.

Matthew was struck in the ribs on the left side by a red-hot cannonball that picked him up and flung him like a grainsack. Something grazed by his forehead while he was tumbling—a musket ball, he thought it must be, here on this field of battle—and a red film descended over his eyes. Blood, he thought. Blood. He hit the ground, was dragged and tossed again. His teeth snapped together. I'm going to die, he thought. Right here. This sunny, clear day. I am going to die.

His left arm was already dead. His lungs hitched and gurgled. The mangy gray wall was there in his face again, there with an arrow shaft stuck in it.

He decided, almost calmly, that he would do his own sticking.

"Hey!" he hollered, in a voice that surprised him with its

desperate power. "Hey!" He brought the knife up and stabbed and twisted and wrenched and stabbed and twisted and wrenched, and the beast grunted roared roared breath hot as Hades smelling of decayed meat and rotten teeth *stabbed and twisted and wrenched* blood red on the gray streaming down a glorious sight *die you bastard you bastard you!*

Jack One Eye might be huge, but it had not grown to such a ripe old age by being stupid. The stickings had an effect, and the bear backed away from the mosquito.

Matthew was on his knees. In his right hand, the blade was covered with blood. He heard a dripping, pattering sound, and he looked down at the gore falling into the red-stained grass from the twitching fingers of his left hand. He seemed to be burning up from within, yet the fiery pain of shoulder and ribs and forehead was not what made him sob. He had peed in his breeches, and he had brought no other pair.

Jack One Eye circled him to the left. Matthew turned with the beast, dark waves beginning to fill his head. He heard, as if from another world, the sound of a woman—Rachel was her name, Rachel yes Rachel—screaming his name and crying. He saw blood bubbling around the bear's nostrils, and crimson matted the gray fur at its throat. Matthew was near fainting, and he knew when that happened he was dead.

The bear suddenly stood up on its hind legs, to a height of eight feet or more. It opened its broken-toothed mouth. What emerged was a hoarse, thunderous, and soul-shaking roar that brimmed with agony and perhaps the realization of its own mortality. Two snapped arrow shafts were buried in festered flesh at the beast's belly, near a bloody-edged claw wound that must have been delivered by one of its own breed. Matthew also saw that a sizeable bite had been ripped from Jack One Eye's right shoulder, and this ugly wound was green with infection.

It occurred to him, in his haze of pain and the knowledge of his impending departure from this earth, that Jack One Eye was dying too.

The bear fell back down onto its haunches. And now Matthew pulled himself up, staggered and fell, pulled himself up again, and shouted, "Haaaaaaaaaaaa!" in the maw of the beast.

After which he fell to the ground once more, into his own blood. Jack One Eye, its nostrils dripping gore, shambled toward him with its jaws open.

Matthew wasn't ready to die yet. Come all this way, to die in a clearing under the sun and God's blue sky? No, not yet.

He came up with the sheer power of desperation and drove the blade under the bear's jaw, giving the knife a violent ripping twist. Jack One Eye gave a single grunt, snorted blood into Matthew's face, and pulled back, taking the imbedded blade with it. Matthew fell on his belly, the pain in his ribs making him curl up like a stomped worm.

Again the bear circled him to the left, shaking its head back and forth in an effort to rid itself of the stinger that had pierced its throat. Banners of blood flew in the air from its nostrils. Even on his belly, Matthew crawled to keep the beast from getting behind him. Suddenly Jack One Eye came in again, and Matthew pulled himself up, throwing his right arm up over his face to protect what was left of his skull.

The movement made the bear turn aside. Jack One Eye backed away, its single orb blinking and glazed. The bear lost its equilibrium for a second and staggered on the edge of falling. It caught itself, then stood less than fifteen feet from Matthew, staring at him with its head lowered and its arrow-stubbled sides heaving. Its gray tongue emerged, licking at the bleeding nostrils.

Matthew pulled himself up to his knees, his right hand clutching his ribs on the left side. It seemed the most important thing in the world to him, to keep his hand pressed there so that his entrails would not stream out.

The world, red-tainted and savage, had dwindled to the single space of distance between man and animal. They stared at each other, measuring pain, blood, life, and death each by their own calculations.

Jack One Eye made no sound. But the ancient, wounded warrior had reached a decision.

It abruptly turned away from Matthew. It began half-loping, half-staggering across the clearing the way it had come, shaking its head back and forth in a vain effort to dislodge the blade. In another moment the beast entered its wilderness again.

And Jack One Eye was gone.

Matthew fell forward onto the bloody battleground, his eyes closed. In his realm of drifting, he thought he heard a high-pitched and piercing cry: *Hiyiiiiiii! Hiyiiiiiii! Hiyiiiiiii!* The vulture's voice, he thought. The vulture, swooping down upon him.

Tired. So . . . very . . . very . . . tired. Rachel. What . . . is to . . . become . . . of . . .

The vulture, swooping down.

Screaming *Hiyiiiiiii! Hiyiiiiiii! Hiyeeeeee!*

Matthew felt himself fall away from the earth, toward that distant territory so many explorers had gone to journey through, and from which return was impossible.

thirty-nine

MATTHEW'S FIRST REALIZATION of his descent to Hell was the odor.

It was as strong as demon's sweat and twice as nasty. It entered his nostrils like burning irons, penetrated to the back of his throat, and he was suddenly aware that he was being wracked by a fit of coughing though he had not heard it begin.

When the smell went away and his coughing ended, he tried to open his eyes. The lids were heavy, as if weighted by the coins due Charon for his ferry trip across the Styx. He couldn't open them. He heard now a rising and falling voice that must surely be the first of untold many souls lamenting their scorched fate. The language sounded near Latin, but Latin was God's language. This must be Greek, which was more suitably earthy.

A few more breaths, and Matthew became knowledgeable of the torment of Hell as well as its odor. A fierce, stabbing, white-hot pain had begun to throb at his left shoulder and down the arm. The ribs on that side also began an agonizing complaint. There was a pain at his forehead too, but that was mild compared to the others. Again he tried to open his eyes and again he failed.

Neither could he move, in this state of eternal damnation. He thought he was attempting to move, but he couldn't be sure.

There was so much pain, growing worse by the second, that he decided it was more reasonable to give up and conserve his energy, as surely he would need it when he walked through the brimstone valley. He heard the crackling of a fire—of course, a fire!—and felt an oppressive, terrible heat as if he were being roasted over an inferno.

But now a new feeling began to come over him: anger. It threatened to burst into full-flamed rage, which would put him right at home here.

He had considered himself a Christian and had tried his very best to follow the Godly path. To find himself cast into Hell like this, with no court to hear his case, was a damned and unreasonable sin. He wondered in his increasing fury what it was he'd done that had doomed him. Run with the orphans and young thugs on the Manhattan harbor? Flung a horse-apple at the back of a merchant's head, and stolen a few coins from the dirty pocket of a capsized drunk? Or had it been more recent wrongdoing, such as creeping into Seth Hazelton's barn and later cutting the man's face with a tin lantern. Yes, that might be it. Well, he would be here to greet that lover of mares when Hazelton arrived, and by that time Matthew hoped to have built up some seniority in this den of lawyers.

The pain was now excruciating, and Matthew clenched his teeth but he felt the cry rising up from his parched throat. He couldn't restrain it. He was going to have to scream, and what would the company of *diaboliques* then think of his fortitude?

His mouth opened, and he let loose not a scream but a dry, rattling whisper. Even so, it was enough to further drain him. He was aware that the murmuring had ceased.

A hand—so rough-fleshed it might have been covered with treebark—touched his face, the fingers starting at his chin and sliding up his right cheek. The singsong murmuring began once more, still in that undecipherable language. What felt like a thumb and finger went to his right eye, and endeavored to push the lid up.

Matthew had had enough of this blindness. He gave a soft

gasp at the effort it involved, but he forced his eyes open of his own accord.

Immediately he wished he had not. In the red, leaping light and drifting smoke of Hades, the visage of a true demon greeted him.

This creature had a narrow, long-chinned brown face with small black eyes, its flesh wrinkled and weathered like ancient wood. Blue whorls decorated the gaunt cheeks, and a third eye— daubed bright yellow as the sun—was painted in the center of the forehead. The earlobes were pierced with hooks from which dangled acorns and snail shells. The head was bald save for a top- knot of long gray hair that grew from the back of the scalp and was adorned with green leaves and the bones of small animals.

To make Matthew's induction to Hell even worse, the demon opened its mouth and displayed a set of teeth that might have served as a sawblade. "Ayo pokapa," the creature said, nodding. Or at least that was the sound Matthew heard. "Ayo pokapa," the de- mon spoke again, and lifted to its lips half of a broken clay dish in which something was densely smoking. With a quick inhalation, the creature pulled smoke into its mouth and then blew the nox- ious fumes—that nasty demon's-sweat odor—into Matthew's nostrils.

Matthew attempted to turn his head aside, and that was when he realized his skull was bound in some way to whatever hard pallet he lay upon. Avoiding the smoke was impossible.

"Yante te napha te," the creature began to murmur. "Saba yante napha te." It slowly rocked back and forth, eyes half-closed. The light from one or more hellfires glowed red through the dense pall of smoke that drifted above Matthew. What sounded like a pineknot burst, and then there came a hissing noise like a roomful of rattlesnakes from beyond the murmuring, rocking di- abolist. The acrid woodsmoke seemed to thicken, and Matthew feared that the little breath he could grasp would soon be poi- soned. "Yante te napha te, saba yante napha te," went the re- peated, rising and falling voice. Again the ritual with the broken dish and the inhalation was repeated, and again the smoke—

damn Hell, if there was such a powerful stink to be smelled for eternity!—was blown up Matthew's nostrils.

He couldn't move, and assumed that not only his head was bound down but also both wrists and ankles. He wished to be a man about this, but tears sprang to his eyes.

"Ai!" the demon said, and patted his cheek. "Mouk takani soba se ha ha." Then it was back to the steady murmuring and rocking, and another blast of smoke up the nose.

After a half-dozen draughts, Matthew was feeling no pain. The cogwheels that usually regulated the order of his mind had lost their timing, and one rocking motion by the demon stretched to the speed of the snails whose shells hung from the earlobe hooks, while the next was gone past in an eyeblink. Matthew felt as if he were floating in a red-flamed, smoky void, though he could of course sense the hard pallet at his back.

And then Matthew knew he must be truly insane, for he suddenly realized something very strange about the piece of broken dish from which the murmuring, smoke-blowing creature was inhaling.

It was white. And on it was a decoration of small red hearts.

Yes, he was insane now. Absolutely insane, and ready for Hell's Bedlam. For that was the same dish Lucretia Vaughan had thrown into the fount, only then it had been whole and contained a sweet yam pie.

"Yante te napha te," the demon crooned, "saba yante napha te."

Matthew was fading again. Losing himself to the swelling dark. Reality—such as it was in the Land of Chaos—disappeared in bits and pieces, as if the darkness were a living thing that hungered first for sound, then light, and then smell.

If it was possible to die a death in the country of the dead, then that was Matthew's accomplishment.

But he found that such a death was fleeting, and there was very little peace in it. The pain grew again, and again ebbed. He opened his eyes, saw moving, blurred figures or shadows, and closed them for fear of what had arrived to visit him. He thought he slept, or died, or suffered nightmares of Jack One Eye running him down in a bloody clearing while the ratcatcher rode the bear's back and thrust at him with the five-bladed sticker. He awakened sweating summer floods, and fell to sleep again dry as a winter leaf.

The smoke-breathing demon returned, to continue its tortures. Matthew once more saw that the broken dish was white, with small red hearts. He dared to speak to the creature, in a feeble and fearful voice, "Who are you?" The murmured chant went on.

"*What* are you?" Matthew asked. But no answer was given.

He slept and waked, slept and waked. Time had no meaning. He was tended to by two more demons, these more in the female shape with long black hair similarly adorned by leaves and bones. They lifted the mat of woven grasses, moss, feathers, and such that covered his nakedness, cleaned him when he needed to be cleaned, fed him a gray paste-like food that tasted strongly of fish, and put a wooden ladle of water to his lips.

Fire and smoke. Shifting shadows in the gloom. That murmured, singsong chanting. Yes, this was surely Hell, Matthew thought.

And then came the moment when he opened his eyes and found Rachel standing beside him in this realm of flames and fumes. "Rachel!" he whispered. "You too? Oh . . . my God . . . the bear . . ."

She said nothing, but pressed a finger to her lips. Though dead, her eyes were as bright as gold coins. Her hair cascaded in ebony waves about her shoulders, and Matthew would have been lying if he'd said the infernal light didn't make her heart-achingly beautiful. She was wearing a dark green shift decorated around the neck with intricate blue beadwork. He stared at the pulse that beat in the hollow of her throat, and saw moisture glisten on her cheeks and forehead.

It must be said, these demons did excellent work at the illusion of life.

He tried to angle his face toward her, but still his head was confined as were his arms and legs. "Rachel . . . I'm sorry," he whispered. "You shouldn't be here. Your time in Hell . . . was already served on earth."

Her finger went to his lips, to bid him be silent.

"Can you ever . . . ever forgive me?" he asked. "For bringing you to . . . such a bad end?" Smoke drifted between them, and somewhere beyond Rachel the fires crackled and seethed.

She gave him an eloquent answer. Leaning down, she pressed her lips to his own. The kiss lingered, and became needful.

His body—the illusion of a body, after all—reacted to this kiss as it would have done in the earthly sphere. Which didn't surprise Matthew, for it was a well-known fact Heaven would be full of angelic lutes and Hell full of flesh flutes. In that particular regard, perhaps it was not such a disagreeable place.

Rachel pulled back. Her face remained within his field of vision, her lips damp. Her eyes were shining, and the fire shadows licked her cheek.

She reached back and undid something. Suddenly the blue-beaded garment slipped off her and fell to the ground.

Her hands returned, lifting the woven mat from Matthew's body. Then she stepped up onto what must be a platform of some kind and slowly, gently eased her naked body down against his own, after which she pulled the grass mat over them again and kissed his mouth with longing.

He wanted to ask her if she knew what she was doing. He wanted to ask her if this was love, or passion, or if she looked at him and saw Daniel's face.

But he didn't. Instead, he surrendered to the moment; to be more accurate, the moment demanded him. He returned her kiss with a soul-deep longing of his own, and her body pressed against his with undeniable urgency.

As they kissed, Rachel's hand found the scrivener's readied instrument. Her fingers closed about him. With a slow shifting of her thighs, she eased him into her, into the moist and heated opening that relaxed to allow entry and then more firmly grasped once he was sheathed deep.

Matthew was unable to move, but Rachel was unrestricted. Her hips began a leisurely, circular motion punctuated by stronger thrusts. A groan left Matthew's mouth at the incredible, otherworldly sensation, and Rachel echoed it with her own. They kissed as if eager to merge one into the other. As the woodsmoke swirled about them and the fires burned, as their lips sought and held and Rachel's hips moved up and then down to push him still deeper, Matthew cried out with a pleasure that was verging on pain. Even this central act, he thought in his state of sweating rapture, was a cooperation of God and Devil.

Then he just stopped thinking and allowed nature to rule.

Rachel's movements were steadily strengthening. Her mouth was against his ear, her pine-scented hair in his face. She was breathing quickly and harshly. His heartbeat slammed, and hers pounded against his damp chest. She gave two more thrusts and her back arched, her head coming up and her eyes squeezed tightly shut. She shivered and her mouth opened to release a long, soft moan. An instant later, the feeling of pleasure did translate into a white flashing pain for Matthew, a fierce jolt that rippled from the top of his head down his spine. In the midst of this riot of sensations, he was aware of his burst into Rachel's clinging humidity, an explosion that brought a grimace to his face and a cry from his lips. Rachel kissed him again, so ardently as if she wished to capture that cry and keep it forever like a golden locket in the secret center of her soul.

With a strengthless sigh, Rachel settled against him yet supported herself on her elbows and knees so as not to rest all her weight. He was still inside her, and still firm. His virginity was a thing of the past and its passage left him with a delicious aching, but his flame had not yet been extinguished. And obviously neither had Rachel's, for she looked him in the face, her wondrous eyes sparkling in the firelight and her hair damp from the heat of exertion, and began to move upon him once again.

If this was indeed Hell, Matthew thought, no wonder everyone was in such a fever to make their reservations.

The second time was slower-paced, though even more intense than the first. Matthew could only lie and vainly attempt to match Rachel's motions. Even if his movements had been totally free, a weakness that affected every muscle save one had claimed his strength.

Finally, she pressed down on him and—though he'd tried to restrain it for as long as he might—he again experienced the almost-blinding combination of pleasure and pain that signalled the imminent nearing of a destination two lovers so vigorously sought to reach.

Then, in the warm wet aftermath, as they breathed and kissed and played a game of tongues, Matthew knew the coach must by necessity be retired to its barn, as the horses had gone their distance.

Presently, he closed his eyes and slumbered again. When he opened them—who knew how much later—the demon with a yellow third eye was at his side, using a white stone to crush up a foul-looking brown mixture of seeds, berries, and fetid whatnot—and the whatnot was the worst of it—in a small wooden bowl. Then the demon gave a combination grunt-and-whistle and pushed some of the stuff toward Matthew's mouth between thumb and forefinger.

Ah ha! Matthew thought. Now the true torments were to begin! The mixture being forced upon him looked like dog excrement and smelled like vomit. Matthew clamped his lips shut. The demon pushed at his mouth, grunting and whistling in obvious irritation, but Matthew steadfastly refused to accept it.

Another figure emerged from the smoke and stood beside Matthew's pallet. He looked into her face. Without speaking, she took up a pinch of the exquisite garbage and put it into her own mouth, chewing it as a display of its worth.

Matthew couldn't believe his eyes. Not because she'd voluntarily eaten it, but because she was the dark-haired, thin mute girl he'd last seen at Shawcombe's tavern. Only she was much changed, both in demeanor and dress. Her hair was clean and shining, more chestnut colored than truly dark brown, and on her head was a tiara-like toque formed of densely woven, red-dyed grass. Smudges of ruddy paint had been applied to her cheekbones. Her eyes were no longer glazed and weak but held determined purpose. Also, she wore a deerskin garment adorned with a pattern of red and purple beads down the front.

"*You!*" Matthew said. "What are *you* doing h—" The thumb and forefinger struck, getting some of that gutter porridge past his lips. Matthew's first impulse was to spit, but the demon had already clamped one hand to his mouth and was massaging his throat with the other.

Matthew had no choice but to swallow it. The stuff had a strange, oily texture, but he'd tasted cheese that was worse. In fact, it had a complexity of tastes, some sour and some sweet, that actually . . . well, that actually called for a second helping.

The girl—*Girl,* he recalled Abner saying with a laugh when Matthew had asked her name—moved away into the fire-thrown shadows before he could ask her anything else. The demon continued to feed him until the bowl was empty.

"What is this place?" Matthew asked, his tongue picking at seeds in his teeth. There was no answer. The demon took his bowl and began to also move away. "This *is* Hell, isn't it?" Matthew asked.

"Se hapna ta ami," the demon said, and then made a clucking noise.

In another moment Matthew sensed he was alone. Up above, he now could make out through the smoke haze what looked to be wooden rafters—or rather, small pinetrees with the bark still on them.

It wasn't long before his eyelids grew heavy. There was no resisting this sleep; it crashed over him like a green sea wave and took him down to depths unknown.

Dreamless. Drifting. A sleep for the ages, absolute in its peace and silence. And then, a voice.

"*Matthew?*"

Her voice.

"Can you hear me?"

"Ahhhhh," he answered: a sustained, relaxed exhalation of breath.

"Can you open your eyes?"

With only a little difficulty—and regret, really, for his rest had been so deeply satisfying—he did. There was Rachel, her face close to his. He could see her clearly by the flickering firelight. The dense smoke had gone away.

"They want you to try to stand up," she said.

"*They?*" He had a burned, ashy taste in his mouth. "Who?"

The demon, who no longer wore the third eye, came up and stood beside her. With an uplifting motion of the hands and a guttural grunting, the meaning was made plain.

Two of the females who'd attended Matthew appeared, and began to work around his head. He heard something being cut— a leather strap, he thought it might be—and suddenly his head was free to move, which immediately put a cramping pain in his neck muscles.

"I want you to know," Rachel said as the two females continued to cut Matthew free from his pinewood pallet, "that you've been terribly injured. The bear—"

"Yes, the bear," Matthew interrupted. "Killed me, and you as well."

She frowned. "What?"

"The bear. It killed—" He felt the straps give way around his left wrist, then around the right. He'd stopped speaking because he realized Rachel wore her wedding dress. On it were grass stains. He swallowed thickly. "Are we . . . not dead?"

"No, we're very much alive. *You* nearly died, though. If they hadn't come when they did, you would have bled to death. One of them bound your arm to stop the flow."

"My arm." Matthew remembered now the terrible pain in his shoulder and the blood dripping from his fingers. He couldn't move—or even feel—the fingers of his left hand. He had a sickened sensation in the pit of his stomach. Dreading to even glance at the limb, he asked, "Do I still have it?"

"You do," Rachel answered grimly, "but . . . the wound was very bad. As deep as the bone, and the bone broken."

"And what else?"

"Your left side. You took an awful blow. Two, three ribs . . . how many were broken I don't know."

Matthew lifted his right arm, unscathed save for a scabbed wound on his elbow, and gingerly touched his side. He found a large patch of clay covering the area, adhered by some sort of sticky brown substance, with a bulge underneath that to indicate something else pressed directly to the wound.

"The doctor made a poultice," Rachel said. "Herbs, and tobacco leaves, and . . . I don't know what all."

"What doctor?"

"Um." Rachel glanced toward the watchful demon. "This is their physician."

"My God!" Matthew said, dumbstruck. "I *must* be in Hell! If not, then where?"

"We have been brought," Rachel answered calmly, "to an Indian village. How far it is from Fount Royal, I can't say. We travelled over an hour from where the bear attacked you."

"An Indian village? You mean . . . I've been doctored by an *Indian?*" This was absolutely unthinkable! He would have preferred a demonic doctor to a savage one!

"Yes. And well doctored, too. They have been very kind to me, Matthew. I've had no reason to fear them."

"Pok!" the doctor said, motioning for Matthew to stand. The two women had cut the leather thongs that had secured his ankles, then had withdrawn. "Hapape pok pokati!" He reached out, picked up the woven mat that covered Matthew's torso, and threw it aside, leaving Matthew naked to the world. "Puh! Puh!" the doctor insisted, slapping his patient's legs.

Reflexively, Matthew started to cover his private area with both hands. His right hand went quickly enough, but a searing pain shot through his shoulder at the mere nerve impulse of moving the left. He gritted his teeth, fresh sweat on his face, and made himself look at the injury.

His shoulder all the way past his elbow was wrapped in clay, and presumably other so-called medicines were pressed to the wound beneath the earthen bandage. The clay also was smoothed over a wooden splint, and his elbow was immobilized in a slightly bent position. From the edge of the clay to the fingertips, the flesh was mottled with ugly black and purple bruises. It was a ghastly sight, but at least he still had the arm. He lifted his free hand to touch his forehead. He found another clay dressing, secured with the sticky paste-like material.

"Your head was gashed," Rachel said. "Do you think you can stand?"

"I might, if I don't fall to pieces." He looked at the doctor. "Clothes! Do you understand me? I need clothes!"

"Puh! Puh!" the doctor said, again slapping Matthew's legs.

Matthew directed his appeal at Rachel. "Might you please get me some clothes?"

"You have none," she told him. "Everything you wore was covered with blood. They performed some kind of ritual over them, the first night, and burned them."

What she'd said sent a spear through him. "The first night? How long have we been here?"

"This is the fifth morning."

Four whole days in the grasp of the Indians! Matthew couldn't believe it. Four whole days, and they still had their scalps! Were they waiting for him to get well enough to slaughter both him and Rachel together?

"I think we've been summoned by their mayor, or chief, or whatever he is. I've not seen him yet, but there's some special activity going on."

"Puh! Puh!" the doctor insisted. "Se hapape ta mook!"

"All right," Matthew said, choosing to face the inevitable. "I'll try to stand."

With Rachel's help, he eased down off the pallet onto a dirt floor. Modesty called him but he couldn't answer. His legs held him though they were fairly stiff. The clay dressing on his broken arm was heavy, but the way the splint crooked his elbow made it bearable. At his left side his ribs thundered with dull pain under the clay and poultice, but that too could be borne if he didn't try to breathe too deeply.

He knew he would have been instantly killed if Jack One Eye himself hadn't been so old and infirm. To meet that beast in its younger years would have meant a quick decapitation, or a long suffering death by disembowelment such as Maude's husband had endured.

The Indian doctor—who would have been naked himself but for a small buckskin garment and strap covering his groin— walked ahead, to the far side of the rectangular wooden struc- ture that housed a number of pallets. Matthew realized it was their version of an infirmary. A small fire crackled in a pit ringed with stones, but from the huge pile of ashes nearby it was evi- dent a smoky inferno had raged in here.

He leaned on Rachel for support, if just until his legs grew used to holding him up again. His mind was still hazed. It wasn't clear to him now if his amorous encounter with Rachel had been real or a fevered dream brought on by his injuries. Surely she wouldn't have crawled up on that pallet to make love to a dying man! From her there was no indication that anything had oc- curred between them.

Yet still . . . *might* it have happened?

But here was something real that he'd imagined to be a fig- ment of his dreams: on the floor, along with other clay cups and wooden bowls and carved bone pipes around the fire, was the broken half of Lucretia Vaughan's heart-decorated pie dish.

The healing savage—who would have made his compatriot Dr. Shields blanch with terror—drew aside a heavy black-furred bearskin from the infirmary's entryway.

Blinding white sunlight flooded across the floor, making Matthew squeeze his eyes shut and stagger. "I have you," Rachel said, leaning into him so he might not fall.

There was a great excited clamor from outside, complete with squeals, whoops, and giggling. Matthew was aware of a brown mass of grinning faces pressing forward. The Indian doctor began to shout in a voice whose irritated tone was universal: *Stand back, and give us space to breathe!*

Rachel led Matthew, naked and dazed, into the light.

forty

THE ASSEMBLED MULTITUDE, which numbered eighty to a hundred or thereabouts, went silent as Matthew emerged.

The foremost group of them backed away, heeding the doctor's continued shouts. As Matthew and Rachel followed the loinclothed healer, the Indians trailed in their wake and the shouting, giggling, and excited vocals began to surge loudly again.

Matthew would have never dreamed in a barrel of rum that he might have found himself naked before the world, clinging to Rachel and walking through a horde of grinning, hollering Indians. His vision was returning, though he was still overwhelmed by all this light. He saw a score of round wooden huts, some covered with dried mud and others moss-grown, with roofs upon which grass grew as thickly as from the earth. He caught sight of a lush plot of cornstalks that would have dropped the farmers of Fount Royal to their knees. Two dogs— one gray and the other dark brown—came to sniff around Matthew's legs, but a shout from the doctor sent them running. The same happened when a giggling pack of four naked brown children neared the pallid patient, and they ran away squealing and jumping.

Matthew saw that most of the men—who shared the doctor's

narrow facial structure, lean body, and topknot of hair growing from an otherwise shaved head—were nearly nude, but the women were clothed in either deerskin garments or brightly dyed shifts that appeared to be woven from cotton. Some of the females, however, had chosen to let their breasts be bared, a sight that would have made the citizens of Fount Royal swoon. Their feet were either bare or clad in deerskin slippers. Many of the men were adorned with intricate blue-dye tattoos, and also a few of the older women. These tattoos appeared not only on the face but also on the chest, arms, thighs, and presumably just about everywhere else.

The mood was festive. Men and women were childlike in their glee, and the children—of which there were many—like little scampering squirrels. Of real creatures, there were aplenty as well: pigs, chickens, and a barking battery of dogs. Then the doctor led Matthew and Rachel to a hut that seemed to be centrally located within the village, drew back a buckskin decorated with blade carvings to gain admittance, and escorted the visitors into the cool, dimly lit interior.

The light came from small flames burning in clay bowls that held pools of oil, set in a circle. Facing this circle, a man sat cross-legged on a dais supported by wooden poles about three feet off the ground, and cushioned by various animal skins.

It was the sight of this man that made Matthew stop in his tracks. His mouth opened and his teeth might have fallen out, so great was his shock.

The man—who obviously was the village's chief, governor, lord, or however the savages termed him—wore a buckskin loincloth that barely covered his genitalia. That, however, was by now a commonplace. What so shocked Matthew was that the chief had a long, white, tightly curled judicial wig on his head, and his chest was covered by . . .

I'm dreaming! Matthew thought. I *have* to be insensible to imagine *this!*

. . . Magistrate Woodward's gold-striped waistcoat.

"Pata ne." The doctor motioned Matthew and Rachel into

the circle, and then made gestures for them to sit. "Oha! Oha!"

Rachel obeyed. When Matthew started to lower himself, pain stabbed his ribs and he clutched at the clay bandage, his face tightening.

"Uh!" the chief spoke. He had the long-jawed, narrow face and wore circular blue tattoos on both cheeks, more tattoos trailing down his arms, like blue vines, and covering his hands. The tips of his fingers were dyed red. "Se na oha! Pah ke ne su na oha sau-papa!" His commanding voice instantly stirred the doctor to action, namely that of grasping Matthew's right arm and pulling him up straight. When Rachel saw, she thought the chief wanted her to rise as well, but as she began to stand she was pushed down again—rather firmly—by the doctor.

The chief stood up on his dais. His legs were tattooed from the knees to the bare feet. He put his hands on his hips, his deep-set black eyes fixed on Matthew, and his expression serious as demanded his position of authority. "Te te weya," he said. The doctor retreated, walking backward, and left the hut. The next words were directed at Matthew: "Urn ta ka pa pe ne?"

Matthew simply shook his head. He saw that the chief wore Woodward's prized waistcoat unbuttoned, and more tattoos adorned his chest. Though age was difficult to estimate among these foreign people, Matthew thought the chief was a young man, possibly only five or six years older than himself.

"Oum?" the chief asked, frowning. "Ka taynay calmet?"

Again, Matthew could only shake his head.

The chief looked down at the ground for a moment, and crossed his arms over his chest. He sighed and seemed lost in thought; deliberating, Matthew feared, how best to murder his captives.

Then the chief lifted his gaze again and said, "*Quel chapeau portez-vous?*"

Matthew now almost fell down. The Indian had spoken French. A bizarre question, yes, but French all the same. The question had been: "What hat do you wear?"

Matthew had to steady himself. That this tattooed savage

could speak a classic European language boggled the mind. It was such a jolt that Matthew even forgot for a few seconds that he was standing there totally naked. He replied, *"Je ne porte pas de chapeau."* Meaning "I don't wear a hat."

"Ah ah!" The chief offered a genuine smile that served to further light and warm the chamber. He clapped his hands together, as if equally amazed and delighted at Matthew's understanding of the language. *"Tous les hommes portent des chapeaux. Mon chapeau est Nawpawpay. Quel chapeau portez-vous?"*

Matthew now understood. The chief had said, "All men wear hats. My hat is Nawpawpay. What hat do you wear?"

"Oh," Matthew said, nodding. *"Mon chapeau est Mathieu."*

"Mathieu," Nawpawpay repeated, as if testing its weight on his tongue. *"Mathieu . . . Matthew,"* he said, still speaking French. "That is a strange hat."

"Possibly it is, but it's the hat I was given at birth."

"Ah! But you've been reborn now, and so you must be given a new hat. I myself will give it to you: Demon Slayer."

"Demon Slayer? I don't understand." He glanced down at Rachel, who—not having a grasp of French—was totally confounded at what they were saying.

"Did you not slay the demon that almost took your life? The demon that has roamed this land for . . . oh . . . only the dead souls know, my father among them. I can't say how many brothers and sisters have passed away by those claws and fangs. But we tried to slay that beast. Yes, we tried." He nodded, his expression grave again. "And when we tried, the demon worked its evil on us. For every arrow that was shot into its body, it delivered ten curses. Our male infants died, our crops withered, the fishing was poor, and our seers had dreams of the end of time. So we stopped trying, for our own lives. Then everything got better, but the beast was always hungry. You see? None of us could slay it. The forest demons look after their own kind."

"But the beast still lives," Matthew said.

"No! I was told how the hunters saw you travelling, and followed you. Then the beast struck! I was told how it attacked you, and how you stood before it and gave a mighty war cry. That must have been a sight to see! They said it was hurt. I sent some men. They found it, dead in its den."

"Oh, I see. But . . . it was old and tired. I think it was already dying."

Nawpawpay shrugged. "That may be so, Matthew, but who struck the last blow? They found your knife, still under here." He pressed beneath his own chin with a forefinger. "Ah, if it's the forest demons that concern you, you may rest knowing they only haunt our kind. Your kind frightens them."

"Of that I have no doubt," Matthew said.

Rachel could stand it no longer. "Matthew! What's he saying?"

"They found the bear dead and they believe I killed it. He's given me a new name: Demon Slayer."

"Is it French you're speaking?"

"Yes, it is. I have no idea how—"

"An interruption, my pardon," Nawpawpay said. "How is it you come to know King LaPierre's tongue?"

Matthew shifted his thinking from English back to French once more. "King LaPierre?"

"Yes, from the kingdom of Franz Europay. Are you a member of his tribe?"

"No, I'm not."

"But you've had some word from him?" It was said with eagerness. "When will he return to this land?"

"Um . . . well . . . I'm not certain," Matthew said. "When was he last here?"

"Oh, during my grandfather's father's time. He left his tongue with my family, as he said it was the tongue of kings. Do I speak it well?"

"Yes, very well."

"Ah!" Nawpawpay beamed like a little boy. "I do recite it, so as not to lose its taste. King LaPierre showed us sticks that shot fire, and he caught our faces in a pouch pond. *And* . . . he had a little moon that sang. All these are carved down on the tablet."

He frowned, perplexed. "I do wish he would return, so I might see those wonders as my grandfather's father did. I feel I'm missing something. You're not of his family? Then how do you speak the king's tongue?"

"I learned it from a member of King LaPierre's tribe," Matthew decided to say.

"I see now! Someday . . . someday . . ." He lifted a finger for emphasis. "I shall go over the water in a cloudboat to Franz Europay. I shall walk in that village and see for myself the hut of King LaPierre. It must be a grand place, with a hundred pigs!"

"Matthew!" Rachel said, about to go mad from this conversation of which she could not partake. "What is he *saying?*"

"Your woman, sad to say, is not civilized like you and I," Nawpawpay ventured. "She speaks mud words like that white fish we caught."

"White fish?" Matthew asked. He motioned for Rachel to remain quiet. "What white fish?"

"Oh, he's nothing. Less than nothing, for he's a murderer and thief. The least civilized beast I have ever had the misfortune to look upon. Now: can you tell me anything more of the village of Franz Europay?"

"I'll tell you everything I know of that place," Matthew answered, "if you'll tell me about the white fish. Did you . . . find your present clothing . . . and your headdress, at his hut?"

"These? Yes. Are they not wonderful?" He spread his arms wide, grinning, so as to better display the gold-striped waistcoat.

"May I ask what else you found there?"

"Other things. They must have some use, but I just like to look at them. And . . . of course . . . I found my woman."

"Your woman?"

"Yes, my bride. My princess." His grin now threatened to slice his face in two. "The silent and lovely one. Oh, she shall share all my treasures and give me a hut full of sons! First, though, I'll have to make her fat."

"And what of the white fish? Where is he?"

"Not far. There were two other fish—old ones—but they have gone."

"Gone? To where?"

"Everywhere," Nawpawpay said, spreading his arms wide again. "The wind, the earth, the trees, the sky. You know."

Matthew feared that he did know. "But you say the white fish is still here?"

"Yes, still here." Nawpawpay scratched his chin. "You have a nature full of questions, don't you?"

"It's just that . . . I might know him."

"Only uncivilized beasts and dung buzzards know him. He is unclean."

"Yes, I agree, but . . . why do you say he's a murderer and thief?"

"Because he is what he is!" Like a child, Nawpawpay put his hands behind himself and began to bounce up and down on his toes. "He murdered one of my people and stole a courage sun. Another of my people saw it happen. We took him. Took them all. They were all guilty. All except my princess. She is innocent. Do you know how I know that? Because she was the only one who came willingly."

"A courage sun?" Matthew realized he must mean the gold coin. "What is that?"

"That which the water spirit gives." His bouncing ceased. "Go visit the white fish, if you like. See if you know him, and ask him to tell you what crimes he's committed."

"Where can I find him?"

"This direction." Nawpawpay pointed to Matthew's left. "The hut that stands nearest the woodpile. You will know it."

"What's he pointing to, Matthew?" Rachel asked. "Does he want us to go somewhere?" She started to stand.

"Ah, no no!" Nawpawpay said quickly. "A woman doesn't stand before me in this place."

"Rachel, please stay where you are." Matthew rested his hand on her shoulder. "Evidently it's the chief's rule." Then, to Nawpawpay, "Might she go with me to see the white fish?"

"No. That hut is not a woman's territory. You go and come back."

"I'm going to go somewhere for a short time," he told her. "You'll need to stay here. All right?"

"Where are you going?" She grasped his hand.

"There's another white captive here, and I want to see him. It won't take long."

He squeezed her hand and gave her a tight but reassuring smile. Rachel nodded and reluctantly let go.

"Oh . . . one other thing," Matthew said to Nawpawpay. "Might I have some clothing?"

"Why? Are you cold on such a hot day as this?"

"Not cold. But there is a little too much air here for my comfort." He gestured toward his exposed penis and testicles.

"Ah, I see! Very well, I shall give you a gift." Nawpawpay stepped out of his own loincloth and offered it.

Matthew got the thing on with a delicate balancing act, since he was able only to use one arm. "I'll return presently," he told Rachel. Then he retreated from the hut, out into the bright sun.

The hut and the woodpile were not fifty paces from the chief's abode. A small band of chattering, giggling children clung to his shadow as he walked, and two of them ran round and round him as if to mock his slow, pained progress. When he neared the hut, however, they saw his destination, fell back, and ran away.

Nawpawpay had been correct, in saying that Matthew would know the place.

Blood had been painted on the outside walls, in strange patterns that a Christian would say was evidence of the Indians' satanic nature. Flies feasted on the gore paintings and buzzed about the entrance, which was covered with a black bearskin.

Matthew stood outside for a moment, steeling himself. This looked very bad indeed. With a trembling hand, he pulled aside the bearskin. Bitter blue smoke drifted into his face. There was only a weak red illumination within, perhaps the red embers of a past fire still glowing.

"Shawcombe?" Matthew called. There was no answer. "Shawcombe, can you hear me?"

Nothing.

Matthew could make out only vague shapes through the smoke. "Shawcombe?" he tried again, but in the silence that followed he knew he was going to have to cross the dreadful threshold.

He took a breath of the sulphuric air and entered. The bearskin closed behind him. He stood where he was for a moment, waiting for his eyes to grow used to such darkness again. The awful, suffocating heat coaxed beads of sweat from his pores. To his right he could make out a large clay pot full of seething coals from which the light and smoke emitted.

Something moved—a slow, slow shifting—there on his left.

"Shawcombe?" Matthew said, his eyes burning. He moved toward the left, as currents of smoke undulated before him.

Presently, with some straining of the vision, he could make out an object. It looked like a raw and bloody side of beef that had been strung up to dry, and in fact was hanging from cords that were supported further up in the rafters.

Matthew neared it, his heart slamming.

Whatever hung there, it was just a slab of flayed meat with neither arms nor legs. Matthew stopped, tendrils of smoke drifting past his face. He couldn't bear to go any further, because he knew.

Perhaps he made a sound. A moan, a gasp . . . something. But—as slowly as the tortures of the inner circle of Hell—the scalped and blood-caked head on that slab of meat moved. It lolled to one side, and then the chin lifted.

His eyes were there, bulging from their sockets in that hideously swollen, black-bruised, and black-bloodied face. He had no eyelids. His nose had been cleaved off, as had been his lips and ears. A thousand tiny cuts had been administered to the battered torso, the genitals had been burned away and the wound cauterized to leave a glistening ebony crust. Likewise sealed with terrible fire were the hacked-off stumps of arms and legs. The cords had been tied and knotted around those grue-somely axed ruins.

If there was a description for the utter horror that wracked Matthew, it was known only by the most profane demon and the most sacred angel.

The motion of that lifted chin was enough to cause the torso to swing slightly on its cords. Matthew heard the ropes squeak up in the rafters, like the rats that had plagued Shawcombe's tavern.

Back and forth, and back and forth.

The lipless mouth stretched open. They had spared his tongue, so that he might cry for mercy with every knife slash, hatchet blow, and kiss of flame.

He spoke, in a dry rattling whisper that was almost beyond all endurance to hear. "Papa?" The word was as mangled as his mouth. "Wasn't me killed the kitten, was Jamey done it." His chest shuddered and a wrenching sob came out. The bulging eyes stared at nothing. His was the small, crushed whine of a terrified child: "Papa please . . . don't hurt me no more . . ."

The brutalized bully began to weep.

Matthew turned—his eyes seared by smoke and sight—and fled lest his own mind be broken like Lucretia Vaughan's pie dish.

He got outside, was further blinded and disoriented by the glare. He staggered, was aware of more naked children ringing him, jumping and chattering, their grins joyful even as they danced in the shadow of the torture hut. Matthew nearly fell in his attempts to get away, and his herky-jerky flailing to retain his balance made the children scream with laughter, as if they thought he was joining in their dance. Cold sweat clung to his face, his insides heaved, and he had to bend over and throw up on the ground, which made the children laugh and leap with new energy.

He staggered on, the pack of little revelers now joined by a brown dog with one ear. A fog had descended over him, and he knew not if he was going in the right direction amid the huts. His progress attracted some older residents who put aside their seed-gathering and basket-weaving to accompany the merry throng, as if he were some potentate or nobleman whose fame rivalled the very sun. The laughter and hollering swelled as did the numbers of his followers, which only served to heighten Matthew's terror. Dogs barked at his heels and children darted underfoot. His ribs were killing him, but what was pain? In his dazed stupor he realized he had never known pain, not an ounce of it, compared to what Shawcombe had suffered. Beyond the grinning brown faces he saw sunlight glitter, and suddenly there was water before him and he fell to his knees to plunge his face into it, mindless of the agony that seized his bones.

He drank like an animal and trembled like an animal. A fit of strangulation struck him and he coughed violently, water bursting from his nostrils. Then he sat back on his haunches, his face dripping, as behind him the throng continued its jubilations.

He sat on the bank of a pond. It was half the size of Fount Royal's spring, but its water was equally blue. Matthew saw two women nearby, both filling animal-skin bags. The sunlight glittered golden off the pond's surface, putting him in mind of the day he'd seen the sun shine with equal color on Bidwell's fount.

He cupped his hand into the water and pressed it to his face, letting it stream down over his throat and chest. His mind's fever was cooling and his vision had cleared.

The Indian village, he'd realized, was a mirror image of Fount Royal. Just like Bidwell's creation, the village had probably settled here—who could say how long ago—to be so near a water supply.

Matthew was aware that the crowd's noise had quietened. A shadow fell over him, and spoke. "Na unhuh pah ke ne!"

Two men grasped Matthew, careful to avoid his injuries, and helped him to his feet. Then Matthew turned toward the speaker, but he knew already who'd given that command.

Nawpawpay stood four inches shorter than Matthew, but the height of the judicial wig gave the chief the advantage. The waistcoat's gold stripes glowed in this strong sunlight. Add to that the intricate tattoos, and Nawpawpay was an absorbing sight as well as a commanding presence. Rachel stood a few feet behind him, her eyes also the color of Spanish coins.

"Forgive my people," Nawpawpay said in the tongue of kings. He gave a shrug and a smile. "We don't often entertain visitors."

Matthew still felt faint. He blinked slowly and lifted his hand to his face. "Is . . . what you've done to . . . Shawcombe . . . the white fish . . . part of your entertainment?"

Nawpawpay looked shocked. "Oh, no! Surely not! You misunderstand, Demon Slayer! You and your woman are honored guests here, for what you've done for my people! The white fish was an unclean criminal!"

"You did such to him for murder and thievery? Couldn't you finish the task and display some mercy?"

Nawpawpay paused, thinking this over. "Mercy?" he asked. He frowned. "What is this *mercy?*"

Evidently it was a concept the French explorer who'd passed himself off as a king had failed to explain. "Mercy," Matthew said, "is knowing when . . ." He hesitated, formulating the rest of it. "When it is time to put the sufferer out of his misery."

Nawpawpay's frown deepened. "Misery? What is that?"

"How you felt when your father died," Matthew answered.

"Ah! That! You're saying then the white fish should be slit open and his innards dug out and fed to the dogs?"

"Well . . . perhaps a knife to the heart would be faster."

"Faster is not the point, Demon Slayer. The point is to punish, and let all who see know how such crimes are dealt with. Also, the children and old people so enjoyed hearing him sing at night." Nawpawpay stared at the pond, still deliberating. "This mercy. This is how things are done in Franz Europay?"

"Yes."

"Ah, then. This is something we should seek to emulate. Still . . . we'll miss him." He turned to a man standing next to him. "Se oka pa neha! Nu se caido na kay ichisi!" At the last hissed sound he made a stabbing motion . . . and, then, to Matthew's chagrin, a twist and a brutal crosscutting of the invisible blade. The man, who had a face covered with tattoos, ran off hollering and whooping, and most of the onlookers—men, women, and children alike—ran after him making similar noises.

Matthew should have felt better but he did not. He turned his mind to another and more important subject. "A courage sun," he said. "What is that?"

"What the water spirit gives," Nawpawpay answered. "Also moons and stars from the great gods."

"The water spirit?"

"Yes." Nawpawpay pointed at the pond. "The water spirit lives there."

"Matthew?" Rachel asked, coming to his side. "What's he saying?"

"I'm not sure," he told her. "I'm trying to—"

"Ah ah!" Nawpawpay wagged a finger at him. "The water spirit might be offended to hear mud words."

"My apologies. Let me ask this, if I may: how does the water spirit give you these courage suns?"

In answer, Nawpawpay walked into the water. He set off from shore, continuing as the water rose to his thighs. Then Nawpawpay stopped and, steadying the wig on his head with one hand, leaned over and searched the bottom with the other. Every so often he would bring up a handful of mud and sift through it.

"What's he looking for?" Rachel asked quietly. "Clams?"

"No, I don't think so." He was tempted to tell her about Shawcombe, if just to relieve himself of what he'd seen, but there was no point in sharing such horror. He watched as Nawpawpay waded to a new location, a little deeper, bent over, and searched again. The front of Woodward's waistcoat was drenched.

After another moment, the chief moved to a third location. Rachel slipped her hand into Matthew's. "I've never seen the like of this place. There's a wall of trees around the whole village."

Matthew grunted, watching Nawpawpay at work. The protective wall of trees, he thought, was a further link between the village and Fount Royal. He had a feeling that the two towns, untold miles apart, were also linked in a way that no one would ever have suspected.

The nearness of her and the warmth of her hand put their lovemaking in mind. As if it were ever really a stone's toss from the center of his memory. But it had all been an illusion. Hadn't it? Of course it had been. Rachel would not have climbed up on a pallet to give herself to a dying man. Not even if he *had* saved her life. Not even if she *had* thought he was not much longer for this earth.

But . . . just a speculation . . . what if by then it was known he was on the road to recovery? And what if . . . the doctor had actually *encouraged* such physical and emotional contact, as an Indian method of healing akin to . . . well . . . akin to bloodletting?

If that were so, Dr. Shields had a lot to learn.

"Rachel?" Matthew said, his fingers gently caressing her hand. "Did you . . ." He stopped, not knowing how to approach this. He decided on a roundabout method. "Have you been given any other clothes to wear? Any . . . uh . . . native clothing?"

She met his gaze. "Yes," she said. "That silent girl brought me a garment, in exchange for the blue dress that was in your bag."

Matthew paused, trying to read her eyes. If he and Rachel had actually made love, her admittance of it was not forthcoming. Neither was it readable in her countenance. And here, he thought, was the crux of the matter: she might have given her body to him, as a gesture of feeling or as some healing method devised by the doctor, who sounded to Matthew to be cut from Exodus Jerusalem's cloth; or it might have been a wishful fantasy induced by fever and drugged smoke.

Which was the truth? The truth, he thought, was that Rachel still loved her husband. Or, at least, the memory of him. He could see that, by what she would not say. If indeed there was something to be said. She might hold a feeling for him, Matthew thought, like a bouquet of pink carnations. But they were not red roses, and that made all the difference.

He might ask what color the garment was. He might describe it for her exactly. Or he might start to describe it, and she tell him he could not be more wrong.

Perhaps he didn't need to know. Or wish to know, really. Perhaps things were best left unspoken, and the boundary between reality and fantasy left to run its straight and undisturbed course.

He cleared his throat and looked toward the pond again. "I recall you told me we'd travelled an hour after the Indians came. Do you know in which direction?"

"The sun was on our left for a while. Then at our backs."

He nodded. They must have travelled an hour's distance back toward Fount Royal. Nawpawpay moved to a fourth location, and called out, "The water spirit is a trickster! Sometimes he gives them freely, other times we must search and search to find one!" Then, with a child's grin, he returned to his work.

"It's amazing!" Rachel said, shaking her head. "Absolutely amazing!"

"What is?"

"That he should speak French, and you can understand him! I wouldn't be more surprised if he should know Latin!"

"Yes, he *is* a remarkable—" He stopped abruptly, as if a wall of rough stones had crashed down upon him. "My God," he whispered. "That's it!"

"What?"

"*No Latin.*" Matthew's face had flushed with excitement. "What Reverend Grove said to Mrs. Nettles, in Bidwell's parlor. 'No Latin.' That's the key!"

"The key? To what?"

He looked at her, and now his grin was childlike too. "The key to proving you innocent! It's the proof I've been needing, Rachel! It was right there, as close as . . ." He struggled for an analogy, and touched his grizzled chin. "Whiskers! The cunning fox can't—"

"Ah!" Nawpawpay's hand lifted, muddy to the wrist. "Here is a find!" Matthew waded into the water to meet him. The chief opened his hand and displayed a single silver pearl. It wasn't much but, coupled with the fragment of pie dish, was enough.

Matthew was curious about something, and he waded on past the chief until the water neared his waist.

And there! His suspicion was confirmed; he felt a definite current swirling around his knees. "The water moves," he said.

"Ah, yes," Nawpawpay agreed. "It is the breathing of the spirit. Sometimes more, sometimes less. But always, it breathes. You find interest in the water spirit?"

"Yes, very much."

"Hm." He nodded. "I didn't know your kind was religious. I shall take you to the house of the spirits, as an honored guest."

Nawpawpay led Matthew and Rachel to another hut near the pond. This one had walls daubed with blue dye, its entrance cloaked by a fantastically woven curtain of turkey and pigeon feathers, rabbit fur, fox skins with the heads still attached, and various other animal hides. "Alas," Nawpawpay said, "your woman can't have entrance here. The spirits deign only to speak to men, and to women through men. Unless, of course, the woman was born with the spirit marks and becomes a seer."

Matthew nodded. It had occurred to him that one culture's "spirit marks" were another culture's "marks of the devil." He told Rachel that the chief's custom required her to wait while they went inside. Then he followed Nawpawpay.

The interior was very dim, only one flame burning in a small clay pot full of oil. Thankfully, though, there was no eye-searing smoke. The house of the spirits appeared empty, as far as Matthew could tell.

"We speak respectfully here," Nawpawpay said. "My father built this, many passings of seasons ago. I often come here, to ask his advice."

"And he answers?"

"Well . . . no. But then again, he does. He listens to my problem, and then his answer is always: Son, decide for yourself." Nawpawpay picked up the clay pot. "Here are the gifts the water spirit gives." He followed the flickering flame deeper into the hut, with Matthew a few paces behind.

Still, there was nothing. Except one thing. On the floor was a larger bowl full of muddy water. Nawpawpay reached into it with the same hand that held the pearl, and then his hand reappeared muddy and dripping. "We honor the water spirit in this way," he said. As Matthew watched, Nawpawpay approached a wall. It was not pinewood, as the others were, but was thickly plastered with dried brown mud from the pond.

Nawpawpay pressed his handful of mud and the pearl into the wall and smoothed it down. "I must speak to the spirit now," he said. And then, in a soft singsong chant, "Pa ne sa nehra cai ke panu. Ke na pe pe kairu." As he chanted, he moved the flame back and forth along the mud-caked wall.

There was a red glint, first. Then a blue one.

Then . . . red . . . gold . . . more gold, a dozen gold . . . and silver . . . and purple and . . .

. . . a silent explosion of colors as the light moved back and forth along the wall: emerald green, ruby crimson, sapphire blue . . . and gold, gold, a thousand times gold . . .

"*Oh,*" Matthew gasped, as the hairs stood up on the back of his neck.

Held in that wall was the treasure.

A pirate's fortune. Jewels by the hundreds—sky blue, deep green, pale amber, dazzling white—and the coins, gold and silver enough to make the king of Franz Europay gibber and drool. And the most stunning thing was that Matthew realized he was seeing only the outermost layer. The plastering of dried mud had to be at least four inches thick, six feet tall, and four feet wide.

Here it was. In this dirt wall, in this hut, in this village, in this wilderness. Matthew wasn't sure, but he thought he could hear God and the Devil joined together in common laughter.

He knew. What was put into the spring at Fount Royal was carried out by the current of an underground river. It might take time, of course. Everything took time. The entrance to that river, there somewhere in the depths of Bidwell's spring, might only be the diameter of Lucretia Vaughan's pie plate. If a pirate had taken a sounding of the fount before lowering bags of jewels and coins, he would have found a bottom at forty feet—but he would not have found the hole that eventually pulled everything into the subterranean flow. Perhaps the current drew more powerfully in a particular season, or was affected by the moon just as were the ocean's tides. In any case, the pirate—most probably a man who was only smart enough to loot vessels, but not to vessel his loot in a sturdy container—had chosen a vault that suffered the flaw of a funnel at its bottom.

Spellbound, Matthew approached the wall. "Se na caira pa pa kairu," chanted Nawpawpay, as he slowly moved the flame back and forth and the small sharp glints and explosions of reflected light continued.

Matthew saw in another moment that the dried mud also held bits of pottery, gold chains, silver spoons, and so forth. Here the gold-encrusted hilt of a knife protruded, and there was the cracked face of a pocket watch.

It made sense that Lucretia Vaughan's pie dish would go to the doctor, as some sort of enchanted implement sent from the water spirit. After all, it was decorated with a pattern that they most likely had figured out was a human organ.

"Na pe huida na pe caida," Nawpawpay said, and that seemed to finish it, as he held the flame toward Matthew.

"The courage—" Matthew's voice cracked. He tried again. "The courage suns. You say the white fish stole one?"

"Yes, and murdered the man to whom it was given."

"May I ask why it was given to this man?"

"As a reward," Nawpawpay said, "for courage. This man saved another who was gored by a wild tusked pig, and afterward killed the pig. It's a tradition my father began. But that white fish has been luring my people with his bad ways, making them sick in the mind with strong drink, and then making them work for him like common dogs. It was time for him to go."

"I see." Matthew recalled that Shawcombe had said his tavern had been built with Indian labor. And now he really did see. He saw the whole picture, and how it fit together in an intricate pattern.

"Nawpawpay," Matthew said, "my . . . uh . . . woman and I

must leave this place. Today. We have to go back from where we came. Do you know the village near the sea?"

"Of course I do. We watch it all the time." Nawpawpay wore an expression of concern. "But Demon Slayer, you can't leave *today!* You're still too weak to travel that distance. You must tell me what you know of Franz Europay, and I also have a celebration planned for you tonight. Dancing and feasting. And we have the demon's head, carved out for you to wear."

"Um . . . well . . . I—"

"In the morning you may leave, if you still desire to. Tonight we celebrate, to honor your courage and the death of that beast." He directed the light to the treasure wall again. "Here, Demon Slayer! A gift for you, as is proper. Take one thing you see that shines strong enough to guide your hand."

It was astounding, Matthew thought. Nawpawpay didn't realize—and God protect him from ever finding out—that there were those in the outside world, the civilized world, who would come through the forest to this place and raze it to the ground to obtain one square foot of dirt from that wall.

But a gift of fantastic worth had been offered, and Matthew's hand was so guided.

forty-one

AS THE SUN SETTLED and the blue shadows of evening advanced, Fount Royal slumbered in a dream of what might have been.

It was a slumbering that prefigured death. Stood the empty houses, stood the empty barns. A scarecrow drooped on its frame in a fallow field, two blackbirds perched upon its shoulders. A straw hat lay discarded on Harmony Street, and had been further destroyed by the crush of wagon wheels. The front gate was ajar, its locking timber thrown aside and left in the dirt by the last family who'd departed. Of the thirty or so persons who remained in the dying dream of Fount Royal, not one could summon the energy of spirit to put the gate in order. It seemed madness, of course, to leave the gate unlocked, for who knew what savages might burst through to scalp, maim, and pillage?

But in truth, the evil *within* Fount Royal seemed much worse, and to secure the gate was like locking oneself in a dark room with a beast whose breath stroked the back of the neck.

It was all clear now. All of it, very clear to the citizens.

The witch had escaped with the help of her demon-possessed lover. *That boy! You know the one! That clerk had fallen in with her—had fallen into the pit of Hell, I say—and he overcame Mr. Green and got her out. Then they fled. Out into the wilderness, out where Satan has his own village. Yes, he does, and I've heard tell Solomon Stiles saw it himself! You might ask him, but he's left town for good. This is the story, though, and guard your souls at the listening: Satan's built a village in the wilderness and all the houses are made of thornwood. They have fields that seethe of hellfire, and they grow crops of the most treacherous poison. You know the magistrate's fallen sick again, don't you? Yes, he has. Sick unto death. He's near given out. Now this is what I hear: someone in that mansion house is a witch or warlock themselves, and has fed that poor magistrate Satan's poisoned tea! So guard what you drink! Oh my . . . I was just thinking . . . what a horror to think on . . . mayhaps it wasn't the tea that was poisonous, but the very water. Oh my . . . if Satan had it in mind . . . to curse and poison the fount itself . . . we would all die writhing in our beds, wouldn't we? Oh my . . . oh my . . .*

A breeze moved across Fount Royal on this warm and darkening eve. It rippled the waters of the fount, and kissed the roofs of lightless houses. It moved along Industry Street, where it had been sworn that the phantasm of Gwinett Linch had been seen, hurrying along with its rat sticker and its torn throat, warning in a ghastly cry that the witches of Fount Royal were hungry for more souls . . . more souls . . .

The breeze stirred dust from Harmony Street, and whirled that dust into the cemetery where it had been sworn a dark figure was seen walking amid the markers, counting numbers on an abacus. The breeze whispered along Truth Street, past the accursed gaol and that house—that witch's house—from which sounds of infernal merriment and the scuttling of demons' claws could be heard, if one dared approach too closely.

Yes, it all was very clear now to the citizens, who had responded to this clarity of vision by fleeing for their lives. Seth Hazelton's house lay empty, the stalls of his barn bare, his forge cold. The hearth at the abandoned Vaughan house still held the perfume of baked bread, but the only movement in that forsaken domicile was the agitation of the wasps. At the infirmary, bags and boxes had been packed in preparation for departure, the glass vials and bottles nestled in cotton and waiting for . . .

Just waiting.

They were almost all gone. A few stalwarts remained, either out of loyalty to Robert Bidwell, or because their wagons had to be repaired before a trip could be undertaken, or because—the rarest cases—they had nowhere else to go and continued to delude themselves that all would be well. Exodus Jerusalem remained in his camp, a fighter to the end, and though the audience at his nightly preachings had dwindled he continued to assail Satan for the appreciation of his flock. Also, he had made the acquaintance of a certain widow woman who had not the benefit of male protection, and so after his feverish sermons were done he protected her at close quarters with his mighty sword.

But lanterns still glowed in the mansion, and light sparkled off four lifted wineglasses.

"To Fount Royal," Bidwell said. "What it was, I mean. And what it might have been." The toast was drunk without comment by Winston, Johnstone, and Shields. They stood in the parlor, in preparation to go into the dining room for the light dinner to which Bidwell had invited them.

"I deeply regret it's turned out this way, Robert," Shields said. "I know you—"

"Hush." Bidwell lifted the palm of his free hand. "We'll have no tears this evening. I have travelled my road of grief, and wish to go on to the next destination."

"What, then?" Johnstone asked. "You're going back to England?"

"Yes, I am. In a matter of weeks, after some business is finished. That's why Edward and I went to Charles Town on Tuesday, to prepare for our passage." He drank another sip of his wine and looked about the room. "My God, how shall I ever salvage such a folly as this? I must have been mad, to have dumped so much money into this swamp!"

"I myself must throw in my cards," Johnstone said, his face downcast. "There's no point in my staying any longer. I should say in the next week."

"You did a fine job, Alan," Shields offered. "Fount Royal was graced by your ideas and education."

"I did what I could, and thank you for your appreciation. As for you, Ben . . . what are *your* plans?"

Shields drank down his wine and walked to the decanter to refill his glass. "I will leave . . . when my patient departs. Until then, I will do my damnedest to make him comfortable, for that's the very least I can do."

"I fear at this point, doctor, it's the *most* you can do," Winston said.

"Yes, you're right." Shields took down half the fresh glass at a swallow. "The magistrate . . . hangs on from day to day by his fingernails. I should say he hangs on from hour to hour." Shields lifted his spectacles and scratched his nose. "I've done everything I could. I thought the potion was going to work . . . and it *did* work, for a while. But his body wouldn't accept it, and it virtually collapsed. Therefore: the question is not *if* he will pass, but *when.*" He sighed, his face strained and his eyes bloodshot. "But he *is* comfortable now, at least, and he's breathing well."

"And still he's not aware?" Winston asked.

"No. He still believes Witch Howarth burned on Monday morning, and he believes his clerk looks in on him from time to time, simply because that's what I tell him. As his mind is quite feeble, he has no recollection of the passage of days, nor of the fact that his clerk is not in the house."

"You don't intend on telling him the truth, then?" Johnstone leaned on his cane. "Isn't that rather cruel?"

"We decided . . . *I* decided . . . that it would be supremely cruel to tell him what has actually happened," Bidwell explained. "There's no need in rubbing his face in the fact that his clerk was bewitched and threw in his lot with the Devil. To tell Isaac that the witch did not burn . . . well, there's just no point to it."

"I agree," Winston said. "The man should be allowed to die with peace of mind."

"I can't understand how that young man could have bested

Green!" Johnstone swirled the wine around his glass and then finished it. "He must have been either very lucky or very desperate."

"Or possessed supernatural strength, or had the witch curse Green to sap the man's power," Bidwell said. "That's what I think."

"Pardon me, gentlemen." Mrs. Nettles had come. "Dinner's a'table."

"Ah, yes. Good. We'll be there directly, Mrs. Nettles." Bidwell waited for the woman to withdraw, and then he said quietly to the others, "I have a problem. Something of the utmost importance that I need to discuss with all of you."

"What is it?" Shields asked, frowning. "You sound not yourself."

"I am *not* myself," Bidwell answered. "As a matter of fact . . . since we returned from Charles Town and I have taken stock of my impending failure, I am changed in a way I would never have thought possible. In fact, that is what I need to discuss with all of you. Come, let's go into the library where voices don't carry as freely." He picked up a lamp and led the way.

Two candles were already burning in the library, shedding plenty of light, and four chairs had been arranged in a semicircle. Winston followed Bidwell in, then the doctor entered, and lastly Johnstone limped through the doorway.

"What's this, Robert?" Johnstone asked. "You make it sound so secretive."

"Please, sit down. All of you." When his guests were seated, Bidwell put his lantern on the sill of the open window and settled himself in his chair. "Now," he said gravely. "This problem that I grapple with . . . has to do with . . ."

"Questions and answers," came a voice from the library's entrance. Instantly Dr. Shields and Johnstone turned their heads toward the door.

"The asking of the former, and the finding of the latter," Matthew said, as he continued into the room. "And thank you, sir, for delivering the cue."

"My God!" Shields shot to his feet, his eyes wide behind his spectacles. "What are *you* doing here?"

"Actually, I've been occupying my room for the afternoon." Matthew walked to a position so that he might face all the men, his back to the wall. He wore a pair of dark blue breeches and a fresh white shirt. Mrs. Nettles had cut the left sleeve away from the clay dressing. He didn't tell them that when he'd shaved and been forced to regard his bruise-blotched face and the clay plaster on his forehead, he'd been cured of unnecessary glances in a mirror for some time to come.

"Robert?" Johnstone's voice was calm. He gripped the shaft of his cane with both hands. "What trickery is this?"

"It's not a trick, Alan. Simply a preparation in which Edward and I assisted."

"A preparation? For what, pray tell?"

"For this moment, sir," Matthew said, his face betraying no emotion. "I arrived back here—with Rachel—around two o'clock. We entered through the swamp, and as I was . . . um . . . deficient in clothing and did not wish to be seen by anyone, I asked John Goode to make my presence known to Mr. Bidwell. He did so, with admirable discretion. Then I asked Mr. Bidwell to gather you all together this evening."

"I'm lost!" Shields said, but he sat down again. "You mean to say you brought the witch back here? Where is she?"

"The *woman* is currently in Mrs. Nettles's quarters," Bidwell offered. "Probably eating her dinner."

"But . . . but . . ." Shields shook his head. "She's a *witch*, by God! It was proven so!"

"Ah, proof!" Now Matthew smiled slightly. "Yes, doctor, proof is at the crux of things, is it not?"

"It certainly is! And what you've proven to me is that you're not only bewitched, but a bewitched *fool!* And for the sake of God, what's *happened* to you? Did you fight with a demon to gain the witch's favors?"

"Yes, doctor, and I slayed it. Now: if it is proof you require, I shall be glad to satisfy your thirst." Matthew, for the fourth or fifth time, found himself absentmindedly scratching at the clay plaster that covered his broken ribs beneath the shirt. He had a small touch of fever and was sweating, but the Indian physician—through Nawpawpay—had this morning announced him fit to travel. Demon Slayer hadn't had to walk the distance, however; except for the last two miles, he'd been carried by his and Rachel's Indian guides on a ladder-like conveyance with a dais at its center. It had been quite the way to travel.

"It seems to me," Matthew said, "that we have all—being learned and God-fearing men—come to the conclusion that a witch cannot speak the Lord's Prayer. I would venture that a warlock could neither speak it. Therefore: Mr. Winston, would you please speak the Lord's Prayer?"

Winston drew a long breath. He said, "Of course. Our Father, Who art in heaven, hallowed be thy name; Thy kingdom come; Thy will be done . . ."

Matthew waited, staring into Winston's face, as the man perfectly recited the prayer. At the "Amen," Matthew said, "Thank you," and turned his attention to Bidwell.

"Sir, would you also please speak the Lord's Prayer?"

"*Me?*" Instantly some of the old accustomed indignation flared in Bidwell's eyes. "Why should *I* have to speak it?"

"Because," Matthew said, "I'm telling you to."

"*Telling* me?" Bidwell made a flatulent noise with his lips. "I won't speak such a personal thing just because someone *orders* me to!"

"Mr. Bidwell?" Matthew had clenched his teeth. This man, even as an ally, was insufferable! "It is *necessary.*"

"I agreed to this meeting, but I didn't agree to recite such a powerful prayer to my God on demand, as if it were lines from a maskers' play! No, I shall not speak it! And I'm not a warlock for it, either!"

"Well, it appears you and Rachel Howarth share stubborn natures, does it not?" Matthew raised his eyebrows, but Bidwell didn't respond further. "We shall return to you, then."

"You may return to me a hundred times, and it won't matter!"

"Dr. Shields?" Matthew said. "Would you please cooperate with me in this matter, as one of us refuses to do, and speak the Lord's Prayer?"

"Well . . . yes . . . I don't understand the point, but . . . all right." Shields ran the back of his hand across his mouth. During Winston's recitation he'd finished the rest of his drink, and now he looked into the empty glass and said, "I have no more wine. Might I get a fresh glass?"

"After the prayer is spoken. Would you proceed?"

"Yes. All right." The doctor blinked, his eyes appearing somewhat glazed in the ruddy candlelight. "All right," he said again. Then: "Our Father . . . who art in heaven . . . hallowed be Thy name; Thy kingdom come; Thy . . . will be done . . . on earth as it is . . . is in heaven." He stopped, pulled a handkerchief from the pocket of his sand-colored jacket and blotted moisture from his face. "I'm sorry. It *is* warm in here. My wine . . . I do need a cooling drink."

"Dr. Shields?" Matthew said quietly. "Please continue."

"I've spoken enough of it, haven't I? What madness is this?"

"Why can you not finish the prayer, doctor?"

"I *can* finish it! By Christ, I can!" Shields lifted his chin defiantly, but Matthew saw that his eyes were terrified. "Give us this day our daily bread; and forgive us our . . . forgive us our trespasses . . . as we forgive those who . . . who trespass . . . trespass . . ." He pressed his hand to his lips and now he appeared to be distraught, even near weeping. He made a muffled sound that might have been a moan.

"What is it, Ben?" Bidwell asked in alarm. "For God's sake, tell us!" Dr. Shields lowered his head, removed his glasses, and wiped his damp forehead with the handkerchief. "Yes," he answered in a frail voice. "Yes. I should tell it . . . for the sake of God."

"Shall I fetch you some water?" Winston offered, standing up.

"No." Shields waved him down again. "I . . . should . . . tell it, while I am able."

"Tell *what,* Ben?" Bidwell glanced up at Matthew, who had an idea what was about to be revealed. "Ben?" Bidwell prompted. "Tell what?"

"That . . . it was I . . . who murdered Nicholas Paine."

Silence fell. Bidwell's jaw might have been as heavy as an anvil.

"I murdered him," the doctor went on, his head lowered. He dabbed at his forehead, cheeks, and eyes with small, birdlike movements. "Executed him, I should say." He shook his head slowly back and forth. "No. That is a pallid excuse. I murdered him, and I deserve to answer to the law for it . . . because I can no longer answer to myself or God. And He asks me about it. Every day and night, He does. He whispers . . . Ben . . . now that it's done . . . at long last, now that it's done . . . and you have committed with your own hands the act that you most detest in this world . . . the act that makes men into beasts . . . how shall you go on living as a healer?"

"Have you . . . lost your *mind?*" Bidwell thought his friend was suffering a mental breakdown right before his eyes. "What are you saying?"

Shields lifted his face. His eyes were swollen and red, his mouth slack. Saliva had gathered in the corners. "Nicholas Paine was the highwayman who killed my elder son. Shot him . . . during a robbery on the Philadelphia Post Road, just outside Boston eight years ago. My boy lived long enough to describe the man . . . and also to say that he'd drawn a pistol and shot the highwayman through the calf of his leg." Shields gave a bitter, ghastly smile. "It was *I* who told him never to travel that road without a prepared pistol near at hand. In fact . . . it was my birthday gift to him. My boy was shot in the stomach, and . . . there was nothing to be done. But I . . . I went mad, I think. For a very long time." He picked up the wineglass, forgetting it was empty, and started to tip it to his mouth before he realized the futility of it.

Shields drew a long, shuddering breath and released it. All eyes were on him. "Robert . . . you know what the officers in these colonies are like. Slow. Untrained. Stupid. I knew the man might lose himself, and I would never have the satisfaction . . . of doing to his father what he had done to me. So I set out. First . . . to find a doctor who might have treated him. It took a search through every rumhole and whorehouse in Boston . . . but I eventually found the doctor. The so-called doctor, a drunken slug who tended to the whores. He knew the man, and where he lived. He had also . . . recently buried the man's wife and baby daughter, the first who'd died of fits, and the second who'd perished soon after."

Shields again wiped his face with the handkerchief, his hand trembling. "I had no pity for Nicholas Paine. None. I simply . . . wanted to extinguish him, as he had extinguished something in my soul. So I began to track him. From place to place. Village to town to city, and back again. Always close, but never finding. Until I learned he had traded horses in Charles Town and had told the stable master his destination. And it took me eight years." He looked into Bidwell's eyes. "Do you know what I realized, the very hour after I killed him?"

Bidwell didn't reply. He couldn't speak.

"I realized . . . I had also killed myself, eight years ago. I had given up my practise, I had turned my back on my wife and my other son . . . who both needed me, then more than ever. I had forsaken them, to kill a man who in many ways was also already dead. And now that it was done . . . I felt no pride in it. No pride in anything anymore. But he was dead. He was bled like my heart had bled. And the most terrible thing . . . the most terrible, Robert . . . was that I think . . . Nicholas was not the same man who had pulled that trigger. I wanted him to be a coldhearted killer . . . but he was not that man at all. But me . . . I was the same man I had always been. Only much, much worse."

The doctor closed his eyes and let his head roll back. "I am prepared to pay my debt," he said softly. "Whatever it may be. I am used up, Robert. All used up."

"I disagree, sir," Matthew said. "Your use is clear: to comfort Magistrate Woodward in these final hours." It hurt him like a dagger to the throat to speak such, but it was true. The magistrate's health had collapsed the very morning of Matthew's departure, and it was terribly clear that the end would be soon. "I'm sure we all appreciate your candor, and your feelings, but your duty as a doctor stands first before your obligation to the law, whatever Mr. Bidwell—as the mayor of this town—decides it to be."

"What?" Bidwell, who had paled during this confession, now appeared shocked. "You're leaving it up to *me?*"

"I'm not a judge, sir. I am—as you have reminded me so often and with such hot pepper—only a clerk."

"Well," Bidwell breathed, "I'll be damned."

"Damnation and salvation are brothers separated only by direction of travel," Matthew said. "When the time is right, I'm sure you'll know the proper road upon which to progress. Now: if we may continue?" He directed his attention to the schoolmaster. "Mr. Johnstone, would you please speak the Lord's Prayer?"

Johnstone stared intently at him. "May I ask what the purpose of this is, Matthew? Is it to suggest that one of us is a *warlock,* and that by failing to utter the prayer he is exposed as such?"

"You are on the right track, yes, sir."

"That is absolutely ridiculous! Well, if you go by that faulty reasoning, Robert has already exposed himself!"

"I said I would go back to Mr. Bidwell, and offer him a chance at redemption. I am currently asking *you* to speak the prayer."

Johnstone gave a harsh, scoffing laugh. "Matthew, you know better than this! What kind of game are you playing?"

"I assure you, it's no game. Are you refusing to speak the prayer?"

"Would that then expose *me* as a warlock? Then you'd have two warlocks in a single room?" He shook his head, as if in pity for Matthew's mental slippage. "Well, I shall relieve your burdensome worry, then." He looked into Matthew's eyes. "Our Father, who art in heaven, hallowed be Thy name; Thy kingdom come; Thy will be done on earth as it is in—"

"Oh, one moment!" Matthew held up a finger and tapped his lower lip. "In your case, Mr. Johnstone—your being an educated man of Oxford, I mean to say—you should speak the Lord's Prayer in the language of education, which would be Latin. Would you start again from the beginning, please?"

Silence.

They stared at each other, the clerk and the fox.

Matthew said, "Oh, I understand. Perhaps you've forgotten your Latin training. But surely it should be easily refreshed, since Latin was such a vital part of your studies at Oxford. You must have been well versed in Latin, as the magistrate was, if only to obtain entrance to that hallowed university. So allow me to help: *Pater noster: qui es in caelis; Sanctificetur nomen tuum; Adventiat regnum tuum*—well, you may finish what I've begun."

Silence. Utter, deadly silence.

Matthew thought, *I have you.*

He said, "You don't know Latin, do you? In fact, you neither understand nor speak a word of it. Tell me, then, how a man may attend Oxford and come away an educator without knowing Latin."

Johnstone's eyes had become very small.

"Well, I'll seek to explain what I believe to be true." Matthew swept his gaze across the other men, who were also stricken into amazed silence by this revelation. He walked to the chess set near the window and picked up a bishop. "Reverend Grove played chess, you see. This was his chess set. Mr. Bidwell, you informed me of that fact. You also said the reverend was a Latin scholar, and liked to infuriate you by calling out his moves in that language." He studied the bishop by the lamplight. "On the occasion of the fire that burned down a house that same night, Mr. Johnstone, you mentioned to me that you and Mr. Winston were in the habit of playing chess. Would it ever have happened, sir, that—this being a town of rare chess players and even more rare Latin scholars—Reverend Grove challenged *you* to a game?"

Bidwell was staring at the schoolmaster, waiting for a response, but from Johnstone there was no reply.

"Would it have happened," Matthew went on, "that Reverend Grove assumed you knew Latin, and spoke to you in that language during a game? Of course, you wouldn't have known if he was speaking to you or announcing a move. In any case, you wouldn't have been able to respond, would you?" He turned toward Johnstone. "What's wrong, sir? Does the Devil have your tongue?"

Johnstone simply stared straight ahead, his fingers gripping the cane's handle and the knuckles bleached.

"He's thinking, gentlemen," Matthew said. "Thinking, always thinking. He is a *very* smart man, no doubt of it. He might actually have become a real schoolmaster, if he'd chosen to. What exactly *are* you, Mr. Johnstone?"

Still no response or reaction.

"I do know you're a murderer." Matthew placed the bishop back on the table. "Mrs. Nettles told me she recalled Reverend Grove seemed bothered about something not long before he was killed. She told me he spoke two words, as if in reflection to himself. Those words were: *No Latin.* He was trying to reason out why an Oxford man didn't know the language. Did he ask you why, Mr. Johnstone? Was he about to point out the fact to Mr. Bidwell, and thus expose you as a fraud? And that's why Reverend Grove became the first victim?"

"Wait," the doctor said, his mind fogged. "The Devil killed Reverend Grove! Cut his throat and clawed him!"

"The Devil sits in this room, sir, and his name—if it *is* his real name—is Alan Johnstone. Of course he wasn't alone. He did have the help of the ratcatcher, who was a . . ." He stopped and smiled thinly. "Ah! Mr. Johnstone! Do you also have a background in the theater arts? You know, Mr. Bidwell, why he wears that false knee. Because he'd already visited Fount Royal in the guise of a surveyor. The beard was probably his own, as at that point he had no need for a disguise. It was only when he verified what he needed to know, and later returned, that a suitable masking was necessary. Mr. Johnstone, if indeed you were—are—an actor, did you perchance ever play the role of a schoolmaster? Therefore you fixed upon what you already knew?"

"You," Johnstone said, in a hoarse whisper, "are quite . . . raving . . . mad."

"Am I? Well, let's see your knee then! It'll only take a moment."

Instinctively, Johnstone's right hand went down to cover the misshapen bulge.

"I see," Matthew said. "You wear your brace—which I presume you purchased in Charles Town—but you didn't put on the device you displayed to the magistrate, did you? Why would you? You thought I was long gone, and I was the only one who ever questioned your knee."

"But I saw it myself!" Winston spoke up. "It was terribly deformed!"

"No, it *appeared* terribly deformed. How did you construct such a thing, Mr. Johnstone? Come now, don't be modest about your talents! You are a man of many black facets! If I myself had wished to make a false knee, I might have used . . . oh . . . clay and candle wax, I suppose. Something to cover the kneecap, build it up and make it appear deformed. You chose a time to reveal the knee when I was unfortunately otherwise occupied." He swung his gaze to Dr. Shields. "Doctor, you sell a liniment to Mr. Johnstone for the supposed pain in his knee, don't you?"

"Yes, I do. A hogsfat-based liniment."

"Does this liniment have an objectionable odor?"

"Well . . . it's not pleasant, but it can be endured."

"What if the hogsfat is allowed to sit over heat, and become rancid before application? Mr. Winston, the magistrate mentioned to me that you were repelled by the odor. Is that correct?"

"Yes. Very quickly repelled, as I recall."

"That was a safeguard, you see. To prevent anyone from either looking too closely at the false knee, or—heaven forbid—touching it. Isn't that true, Mr. Johnstone?"

Johnstone stared at the floor. He rubbed the bulge of his knee, a pulse beating at his temple.

"I'm sure that's not very comfortable. Is it intended to force a limp? You probably really *can't* climb stairs with it on, can you? Therefore you removed it to go up and look at the gold coin? Did you mean to steal that coin, or were you simply surprised at being caught in the act? Did your greedy hand clutch it in what was for you a normal reaction?"

"Wait," the doctor said. He was struggling to keep up, his own brain blasted by the rigors of his confession. "You mean to say . . . Alan was never educated at Oxford? But I myself heard him trading tales of Oxford with the magistrate! He seemed to know the place so well!"

"Seemed to is right, sir. I expect he must have played a schoolmaster's role in some play and picked up a modicum of information. He also knew that by passing himself off as having an Oxford education, the town would more readily dismiss the efforts of the man who served as the previous teacher."

"But what about Margaret? Johnstone's wife?" Winston asked. "I know her bell seemed cracked, but . . . wouldn't she have known if he wasn't really a schoolmaster?"

"He had a wife?" This was the first Matthew had heard of it. "Was he wed in Fount Royal, or did he bring her with him when he arrived?"

"He brought her," Winston said. "And she seemed to despise Fount Royal and all of us from the beginning. So much so that he was obliged to return her to her family in England." He shot Johnstone a dark glance. "At least that's what he told us."

"Ah, now you're beginning to understand that what he told you was never necessarily the truth—and rarely so. Mr. Johnstone, what about this woman? Who was she?"

Johnstone continued to stare at the floor.

"Whoever she was, I doubt she was really wed to you. But it was a clever artifice, gentlemen, and further disguised himself as a decent schoolmaster." Matthew suddenly had a thought, a flashing sun of revelation, and he smiled slightly as he regarded the fox. "So: you returned this woman to her family in England, is that correct?"

Of course there was no answer.

"Mr. Bidwell, how long was it after Johnstone came back from England that the ratcatcher arrived here?"

"It was . . . I don't know . . . a month, possibly. Three weeks. I can't recall."

"Less than three weeks," Winston said. "I remember the day Linch arrived and offered his services. We were so glad to see him, as the rats were overrunning us."

"Mr. Johnstone?" Matthew prompted. "Had you, as a thespian, ever seen John Lancaster—and that was his true name—performing his act? Had you heard about his magnetism abilities while your troupe was travelling England? Perhaps you'd already met him?" Johnstone only stared blankly at the floorboards. "In any case," Matthew continued with authority, "you didn't go to England to return that so-called wife to her family. You went to England to seek a man you thought could help carry out your scheme. You knew what it would take. By then you had probably decided who the victims were going to be—even though I think your murder of Reverend Grove had more to do with hiding your falsehood than anything else—and you needed a man with the uncommon ability to create perceived truth from wholesale illusion. And you found him, didn't you?"

"Mad." Johnstone's voice was husky and wounded. "Mad . . . goddamned mad . . ."

"Then you convinced him to join your mission," Matthew went on. "I presume you had a trinket or two to show him as proof? Did you give him the brooch? Was that one of the things you'd found during those nights you posed as a surveyor? As you declined Mr. Bidwell's offer of a bed and pitched your tent right there beside the spring, you could go swimming without being discovered. What else did you find down there?"

"I'm not . . ." Johnstone struggled to stand. "I'm not staying to hear this madman's slander!"

"Look how he remains in character!" Matthew said. "I should have known you were an actor the first night we met! I should have realized from that face powder you wore, as you wore it the night of the maskers' dinner, that an actor never feels truly comfortable before a new audience without the benefit of makeup."

"I'm leaving!" Johnstone had gained his feet. He turned his sallow, sweating face toward the door.

"Alan? I know all about John Lancaster." Johnstone had been about to hobble out; now he froze again, at the sound of Bidwell's quiet, powerful voice.

"I know all about his abilities, though I don't understand such things. I *do* understand, however, from where Lancaster took his concept of the three demons. They were freaks he'd seen, at that circus which employed David Smythe's father."

Johnstone stood motionless, staring at the door, his back to Matthew. Perhaps the fox trembled, at this recognition of being torn asunder by the hounds.

"You see, Alan," Bidwell went on, "I opened a letter that Matthew had left for the magistrate. I read that letter . . . and I began to wonder why such a demon-possessed boy would fear for my safety. *My* safety, after all the insults and taunts I hurled at him. I began to wonder . . . if I had not best take Mr. Winston and go to Charles Town to find the Red Bull Players. They were camped just to the south. I found Mr. Smythe, and asked him the questions that were directed in that letter."

Johnstone had not moved, and still did not.

"Sit down," Bidwell commanded. "Whatever your name is, you bastard."

forty-two

MATTHEW AND THE OTHERS now witnessed a transformation.

Instead of being cowed by this command, instead of slumping under the iron fist of truth, Alan Johnstone slowly straightened his spine. In seconds he seemed an inch or two taller. His shoulders appeared to widen against the fabric of his dark blue jacket, as if the man had been tightly compressing himself around his secret core.

When he turned toward Matthew again, it was with an unhurried grace. Johnstone was smiling, but the truth had delivered its blow; his face was damp, his eyes deep-sunken and shock-blasted.

"Sirs," he said, "dear sirs. I must confess . . . I never attended Oxford. Oh, this is embarrassing. Quite so. I attended a small school in Wales. I was . . . the son of a miner, and I realized at an early age . . . that some doors would be closed to my ascent, if I did not attempt to hide some . . . um . . . unfortunate and unsavory elements of my family. Therefore, I created—"

"A lie, just as you're creating now," Matthew interrupted. "Are you incapable of telling the truth?"

Johnstone's mouth, which was open to speak the next falsehood, slowly closed. His smile had vanished, his face as grim as gray stone.

"I think he's lived with lies so long they're like a suit, without which he would feel nude to the world," Matthew said. "You did learn a great deal about Oxford, though, didn't you? Did you actually go there and tour the place when you returned to England, just in case you needed the information? It never hurts to add details to your script, does it? And all that about your social club!" Matthew shook his head and clucked his tongue. "Are the Ruskins even really in existence, or is that your own true name? You know, I might have realized I had proof of your lies that very night. When the magistrate recited the motto of his own social club to you, he spoke it in Latin, believing that as a fellow Oxford brother you would need no translation. But when you recited back the motto of the Ruskins, you spoke English. Have you ever known the motto of a social fraternity to be in *English?* Tell me, did you make that motto up on the spot?"

Johnstone began to laugh. The laughter, however, was strained through his tightly clenched teeth, and therefore was less merry than murderous.

"This woman who was purported to be your wife," Matthew said. "Who was she? Some insane wretch from Charles Town? No, no, you would have had to find someone you at least imagined you could control. Was she then a doxy, to whom you could promise future wealth for her cooperation?"

The laughter faded and went away, but Johnstone continued to grin. His face, the flesh drawn over the bones and the eyeholes dwindled to burns, had taken on the appearance of a truly demonic mask.

"I presume you made quick work of the woman, as soon as you'd left sight of Charles Town," Matthew ventured. "Did she believe you were returning her to the dove roost?"

Johnstone suddenly turned and began to limp toward the door, proving that his kneebrace enforced the fiction of his deformity.

"Mr. Green?" Matthew called, in a casual tone. The doorway

was presently blocked by the red-bearded giant, who also held at his side a pistol. "That weapon has been prepared for firing, sir," Matthew said. "I don't for an instant doubt your ability to inflict deadly violence, therefore the necessary precaution against it. Would you please come back to your chair?"

Johnstone didn't respond. Green said, "I 'spect you'd best do as Mr. Corbett asks." The air had whistled through the space a front tooth used to occupy.

"Very well, then!" Johnstone turned toward his tormentor with a theatrical flourish, the death's-head grin at full force. "I shall be glad to sit down and listen to these mad ravings, as I find myself currently imprisoned! You know, you're all bewitched! Every one of you!" He stalked back to the chairs, taking a position not unlike center stage. "God help our minds, to withstand such demonic power! Don't you see it?" He pointed at Matthew, who was gratified to see that the hand trembled. "This boy is in league with the blackest evil to ever crawl from a pit! God help us, in its presence!" Now Johnstone held his hand palm-upward, in a gesture of supplication. "I throw myself before your common sense, sirs! Before your decency and love of fellow man! God knows these are the first things any demon would try to destr—"

Smack! went a book down onto Johnstone's offered palm. Johnstone staggered, and stared at the volume of English plays that Matthew had devoured, and that Mrs. Nettles had returned to the nearby bookcase.

"*Poor Tom Foolery,* I believe," Matthew said. "I think on page one-seventeen or thereabouts is a similar speech, in case you wish to be more exact."

Something moved across Johnstone's face in that instant, as he met Matthew's gaze. Something vulpine, and mean as sin. It was as if for a fleeting space of time the animal had been dragged from its den and made to show itself; then the instant passed, and the glimpse was gone. Johnstone's countenance had formed again into stone. Disdainfully, he turned his hand over and let the book fall to the floor.

"Sit down," Matthew said firmly, as Mr. Green guarded the doorway. Slowly, with as much dignity as he could cloak himself, Johnstone returned to his chair.

Matthew went to the fanciful map of Fount Royal that hung on the wall behind him. He tapped the spring with his forefinger. "This, gentleman, is the reason for such deception. At some time in the past—several years, I believe, before Mr. Bidwell sent a land scout to find him suitable property—this spring was used as a vault for pirate treasure. I don't mean just Spanish gold and silver coins, either. I mean jewels, silverware, plates . . . whatever this pirate and his crew managed to take. As the spring was likely used by this individual as a source of fresh water, he decided to employ it for a different purpose. Mr. Johnstone, do you know this individual's name?" No response. "Well, I'm assuming he was English, since he seemed to prefer attacking Spanish merchant ships. Probably he attacked a few Spanish pirates who were themselves laden with treasure. In any case, he built up a wondrous fortune . . . but of course, he was always in fear of being attacked himself, therefore he needed a secure hiding-place for his loot. Please correct me, Mr. Johnstone, if I am mistaken at any of these conjectures."

Johnstone might have burned the very air between them with his stare.

"Oh, I should tell you, sir," Matthew said, "that the vast majority of the fortune you schemed to possess is now lost. In my investigation of the pond, I found an opening to an underground flow. A small opening but, regretfully for you, an efficient one as to the movement of water. Over a period of time, most of the loot went down the hole. I don't doubt that there are a few items of value remaining—some coins or pieces of pottery—but the vault has been emptied by the one who truly owns it: Mother Nature."

He saw now a flinch of true pain on Johnstone's face, as this nerve was so deeply struck. "I suspect you found some items when you posed as the surveyor, and those financed your schoolmaster's suits. A wagon and horses, too? And clothes for your cardboard wife? Then I presume you also had items to finance your passage back to and from England, and to be able to show Lancaster what was awaiting him. Did you also show him the blade that was awaiting his throat?"

"My God!" Dr. Shields said, aghast. "I . . . always thought Alan came from a wealthy family! I saw a gold ring he owned . . . with a ruby in it! And a gold pocket watch he had, inscribed with his initials!"

"Really? I'd say the ring was something he'd found. Perhaps he purchased the pocket watch in Charles Town before he came here, and had those initials inscribed to further advance his false identity." Matthew's eyesbrows lifted. "Or was it a watch you had previously murdered someone to get, and those initials prompted your choice of a name?"

"You," Johnstone said, his mouth twisting, "are absolutely a fool."

"I have been called so, sir, but never let it be said that I am *fooled*. At least not for very long. But you *are* a smart man, sir. I swear you are. If I were to ask Mr. Green to sit in your lap, and take Mr. Bidwell and Mr. Winston for a thorough search of your house, would we find a sapphire brooch there? A book on ancient Egypt? Would we find the ratcatcher's five-bladed device? You know, that was a crowning move! The claw marks! A deception only a talented thespian could construct! And to create a *ratcatcher* out of John Lancaster . . . well, it was an inspiration. Did you know that he had experience with training rats? Had you seen his circus act? You knew Fount Royal was in need of a ratcatcher . . . therefore, instant acceptance by the town. Was it you or Lancaster who created the poppets? Those, too, were very convincing. Just rough-edged enough to appear real."

"I shall . . . lose my mind, listening to you," Johnstone said. He blinked slowly. "Lose my mind . . . altogether."

"You decided Rachel was perfect witch material. You knew, as everyone knows, what occurred at Salem. But you, with your sterling abilities to manipulate an audience, realized how such mass fear might be scripted, act upon act. The only problem is that you, sir, are a man who has the command of a crowd's mind, yet you needed a man with the command of the *individual* mind. The point being to seed this terror in Fount Royal by using selected persons, and thus to ruin the town and cause it to be abandoned. After which you—and Lancaster, or so he believed—might remove the riches."

Johnstone lifted a hand and touched his forehead. He rocked slightly back and forth in his chair.

"As to the murder of Daniel Howarth," Matthew said, "I suspect you lured him out of the house that night to a prearranged meeting? Something he would not have mentioned to Rachel? She told me that the night of his murder he asked her if she loved him. She said it was rare for him to be so . . . well . . . needful. He already had fears that Nicholas Paine was interested in Rachel. Did you fan those flames, by intimating that Rachel might also have feelings for Paine? Did you promise to meet him in a private place, to exchange information that should not be overheard? Of course he wouldn't have known what you were planning. I'm sure your power of persuasion might have directed Daniel to any place you chose, at any time. Who cut his throat, then? You or Lancaster?"

When Johnstone didn't answer, Matthew said, "You, I think. I presume you then applied the five-bladed device to Daniel's dead or dying body? I'm sure Lancaster never would have imagined he'd meet his end the same way. He panicked when he learned he'd been discovered, didn't he? Did he want to leave?" Matthew smiled grimly. "But no, you couldn't have that, could you? You couldn't let him leave, knowing what he knew. Had you always planned to murder him, after he'd helped you remove the treasure and Fount Royal was your own private fortress?"

"Damn you," Bidwell said to Johnstone, his face reddening. "Damn your eyes, and heart, and soul. Damn you to a slow death, as you would have made me a murderer too!"

"Calm yourself," Matthew advised. "He *shall* be damned, as I understand the colonial prison is one step above a hellhole and dungheap. Which is where he shall spend some days before he hangs, if I have anything to do with it."

"That," Johnstone said wanly, "may be true." Matthew sensed the man was now willing to speak. "But," Johnstone continued, "I have survived Newgate itself, and so I doubt I shall be much inconvenienced."

"Ahhhhh!" Matthew nodded. He leaned against the wall opposite the man. "A graduate not of Oxford, but of Newgate prison! How did your attendance in such a school come about?"

"Debts. Political associations. And friends," he said, staring at the floor, "with knives. My career was ruined. And I did have a good career. Oh . . . not that I was ever a major lamp, but I did have aspirations. I hoped . . . at some point . . . to have enough money to invest in a theater troupe of my own." He sighed heavily. "My candle was extinguished by jealous colleagues. But was I not . . . credible in my performance?" He lifted his sweat-slick face to Matthew, and offered a faint smile.

"You are deserving of applause. From the hangman, at least."

"I take that as a backhanded compliment. Allow me to deliver one of my own: you have a fair to middling mind. With some work, you might become a thinker."

"I shall take such into consideration."

"This beast." Johnstone put his hand on the convexity on his leg. "It does pain me. I am glad, in that regard, to get it off once and for all." He unbuttoned the breeches at the knee, rolled down the stocking, and began to unstrap the leather brace. All present could see that the kneecap was perfectly formed. "You're correct. It *was* candle wax. I spent a whole night shaping it before I was satisfied with the damn thing. Here: a trophy." He tossed the brace to the floor at Matthew's feet.

Matthew couldn't help but think it was much more palatable than the trophy of a carved-out, horrible-smelling bear's head he'd been presented with at the celebration last night. Also a much more satisfying one.

Johnstone winced as he stretched the leg out straight and briskly massaged the knee. "I was suffering a muscle cramp the other night that near put me on the floor. Had to wear a similar apparatus for a role I played . . . oh . . . ten years ago. One of my last roles, with the Paradigm Players. A comedy, actually. Unfortunately there was nothing funny about it, if you discount the humor of having the audience pelt you with tomatoes and horse-shit."

"By *God,* I ought to strangle you myself!" Bidwell raged. "I ought to save the hangman a penny rope!"

Johnstone said, "Strangle yourself while you're at it. You were the one in such a rush to burn the woman." This statement, delivered so offhandedly, was the straw that broke Bidwell's back. The master of dead Fount Royal gave a shouted oath and lunged from his chair at Johnstone, seizing the actor's throat with both hands.

They went to the floor in a tangle and crash. At once Matthew and Winston rushed forward to disengage them, as Green looked on from his position guarding the door and Shields clung to his chair. Bidwell was pulled away from Johnstone, but not before delivering two blows that bloodied the actor's nostrils.

"Sit down," Matthew told Bidwell, who angrily jerked out of his grasp. Winston righted Johnstone's chair and helped him into it, then immediately retreated to a corner of the library as if he feared contamination from having touched the man. Johnstone wiped his bleeding nose with his sleeve and picked up his cane, which had also fallen to the floor.

"I ought to kill you!" Bidwell shouted, the veins standing out in his neck. "Tear you to pieces myself, for what you've done!"

"The law will take care of him, sir," Matthew said. "Now please . . . sit down and keep your dignity."

Reluctantly, Bidwell returned to his chair and thumped down into it. He glowered straight ahead, ideas of vengeance still crackling like flames in his mind.

"Well, you should feel very pleased with yourself," Johnstone said to Matthew. He leaned his head back and sniffled. "The hero of the day, and all that. Am I your stepping-stone to the judicial robes?"

Matthew realized Johnstone the manipulator was yet at work, trying to move him into a defensive position. "The treasure," he said, ignoring the man's remark. "How come you to know about it?"

"I believe my nose is broken."

"The treasure," Matthew insisted. "Now is not the time to play games."

"Ah, the treasure! Yes, that." He closed his eyes and sniffled blood again. "Tell me, Matthew, have you ever set foot inside Newgate prison?"

"No."

"Pray to God you never do." Johnstone's eyes opened. "I was there for one year, three months, and twenty-eight days, serving restitution for my debts. The prisoners have the run of the place. There are guards, yes, but they withdraw for their own throats. Everyone—debtors, thieves, drunks and lunatics, murderers, child fuckers and mother rapers . . . they're all thrown together, like animals in a pit, and . . . believe me . . . you do what you must to survive. You know why?"

He brought his head forward and grinned at Matthew, and when he did fresh crimson oozed from both nostrils. "Because no one . . . *no one* . . . cares whether you live or die but yourself. *Yourself,*" he hissed, and again that vulpine, cruel shadow passed quickly across his face. He nodded, his tongue flicking out and tasting the blood that glistened in the candlelight. "When they come at you—three or four at a time—and hold you down, it is not because they wish you well. I have seen men killed in such a fashion, battered until they are mortally torn inside. And still they go on, as the corpse is not yet cold. Still they go on. And you must—you *must*—sink to their level and join them if you wish to live another day. You must shout and shriek and howl like a beast, and strike and thrust . . . and *want* to kill . . . for if you show any weakness at all, they will turn upon you and it will be *your* broken corpse being thrown upon the garbage pile at first light."

The fox leaned toward his captor, heedless now of his bleeding nose. "Sewage runs right along the floor there. We knew it had rained outside, and how hard, when the sewage rose to our ankles. I saw two men fight to the death over a pack of playing cards. The fight ended when one drowned the other in that indescribable filth. Wouldn't that be a lovely way to end your life, Matthew? Drowned in human shit?"

"Is there a point to this recitation, sir?"

"Oh, indeed there is!" Johnstone grinned broadly, blood on his lips and the shine of his eyes verging on madness. "No words are vile enough, nor do they carry enough weight of bestiality, to describe Newgate prison, but I wished you to know the circumstances in which I found myself. The days were sufficiently horrible . . . but then came the nights! Oh, the joyous bliss of the darkness! I can feel it even now! Listen!" he whispered. "Hear them? Starting to stir? Starting to crawl from their mattresses and stalk the night fantastic? Hear them? The creak of a bedframe here—and one over there, as well! Oh, listen . . . someone weeps! Someone calls out for God . . . but it is always the Devil who answers." Johnstone's savage grin faltered and slipped away.

"Even if it was so terrible a place," Matthew said, "you still survived it."

"Did I?" Johnstone asked, and let the question hang. He stood up, wincing as he put weight on his unbraced knee. He supported himself with his cane. "I pay for wearing that damn brace, you may be sure. Yes, I did live through Newgate prison, as I realized I might offer the assembled animals something to entertain them besides carnage. I might offer them plays. Or, rather, scenes from plays. I did all the parts, in different voices and dialects. What I didn't know I made up. They never knew the difference, nor did they care. They were particularly pleased at any scene that involved the disgrace or degradation of court officials, and as there are a pittance of those in our catalogue, I found myself concocting the scenes as I played them out. Suddenly I was a very popular man. A *celebrity,* among the rabble."

Johnstone stood with the cane on the floor and both hands on the cane, and Matthew realized he had—as was his nature—again taken center stage before his audience. "I came into the favor of a very large and very mean individual we called the Meatgrinder, as he . . . um . . . had used such a device to dispose of his wife's body. But—lo and behold!—he was a fan of the stagelamps! I was elevated to the prospect of command performances, and also found myself protected from the threat of harm."

As Matthew had known he sooner or later would, Johnstone now swivelled his body so as to have a view of the other men in the room. Or rather, so they would have a full view of the thespian's expressions. "Near the end of my term," Johnstone went on, "I came into the acquaintance of a certain man. He was my age or therebouts, but looked very much older. He was sick, too. Coughing up blood. Well, needless to say a sick man in Newgate prison is like a warm piece of liver to wolves. It's an interesting thing to behold, actually. They beat him because he was an easy target, and also because they wanted him to go ahead and die lest they fall sick themselves. I tell you, you can learn quite a lot about the human condition at Newgate; you ought to put yourself there for a night and make a study of it."

"I'm sure there are less dangerous universities," Matthew said.

"Yes, but none teaches as quickly as Newgate." Johnstone flashed a sharp smile. "And the lessons are very well learned. But: this man I was telling you about. He realized the Meatgrinder's power in our little community, yet the Meatgrinder was . . . well, he'd rather kill a man than smell his breath, shall we say. Therefore this sick and beaten individual asked me to intercede on his behalf, as a gentleman. He actually was quite educated himself. Had once been a dealer in antiques, in London. He asked me to intercede to save him further beatings or other indignities . . . in exchange for some very interesting information concerning a waterhole across the Atlantic."

"Ah," Matthew said. "He knew of the treasure."

"Not only knew, he helped place the fortune there. He was a member of the crew. Oh, he told me all about it, in fascinating detail. Told me he'd never revealed it to a soul, because he was going to go back for it someday. *Someday,* he said. And I might be his partner and share it with him, if I would protect his life. Told me that the spring was forty feet deep, told me that the treasure had been lowered in wicker baskets and burlap bags . . . told enough to put a sea voyage in the mind of a poor starving ex-thespian who had no prospects, no family, and absolutely no be-lief in that straw poppet you call God." Again, Johnstone displayed a knife-edged smile. "This man . . . this crewman . . . said there'd been a storm at sea. The ship had been wrecked. He and five or six others survived, and reached an island. Pirates being as they are, I suppose stones and coconuts did the job of knives and pistols. At last, one man survived to light a fire for a passing English frigate." Johnstone shrugged. "What did I have to lose to at least come look for myself? Oh . . . he had an in-scribed gold pocket watch hidden in his mattress that he also gave to me. You see, that man's name was Alan Johnstone."

"What's *your* name, then?" Bidwell asked.

"Julius Caesar. William Shakespeare. Lord Bott Fucking Tott. Take your pick, what does it matter?"

"And what happened to the real Alan Johnstone?" Matthew inquired, though he already had an idea. It had dawned on him, as well, that the turtles—reed-eaters by nature—had probably loved feasting on all those baskets and bags.

"The beatings ceased. I had to prove my worth to him. He survived for a time. Then he grew very, very ill. Sick unto death, really. I was able to get the coordinates of the waterhole's latitude and longitude from him . . . something I'd been trying to do for a month or more without seeming overly demanding. Then some-one told the Meatgrinder that very night . . . someone . . . a little shadow of a someone . . . that the sick man coughing up all that blood over there in the corner . . . well, it was dangerous to every-one. Such disease might wipe out our little community, and we were so fond of it. By morning, alas, my partner had set off on his final voyage, alone and unlamented."

"By Christ," Matthew said softly, his guts twisting. "Little wonder you decided to invent the witchcraft scheme. You're on regular speaking terms with Satan, aren't you?"

Johnstone—for want of a better name—laughed quietly. He threw his head back, his eyes gleaming, and laughed louder.

There was a faintly audible *click*.

And suddenly, moving with a speed that belied his stiff leg, Johnstone lunged forward. He pressed against Matthew's throat the pointed edge of a five-inch blade that had been concealed within the cane's shaft.

"Be still!" Johnstone hissed, his eyes boring into Matthew's. Bidwell had stood up, and now Winston and Dr. Shields rose to their feet. "Everyone, be still!"

Green crossed the threshold, pistol in hand. Johnstone reached out, grasped Matthew's shirt, and turned him so the thespian's back was to the wall and Matthew's back was in danger of a pistol ball should Green lose his head. "No, no!" Johnstone said, as if scolding a wayward pupil. "Green, stand where you are."

The red-bearded giant halted. The blade pressed perilously near entering the flesh. Though he was quaking inside, Matthew was able to keep a calm mask. "This will do you no good."

"It will do me less good to be sent to prison and have my neck stretched!" Johnstone's face was damp, a pulse beating rapidly at his temple. Blood still stained his nostrils and upper lip. "No, I can't bear that. Not prison." He shook his head with finality. "One season in Hell is enough for any man."

"You have no choice, sir. As I said, this will do you no—"

"Bidwell!" Johnstone snapped. "Get a wagon ready! *Now!* Green, take the pistol by the barrel. Come over here . . . slowly . . . and give it to me."

"Gentlemen," Matthew said, "I would suggest doing neither."

"I have a knife at your throat. Do you feel it?" He gave a little jab. "There? Would you like a sharper taste?"

"Mr. Green," Matthew said, staring into the wild eyes of the fox. "Take a position, please, and aim your pistol at Mr. Johnstone's head."

"Christ, boy!" Bidwell shouted. "No! Green, he's crazy!"

"No further play at heroics," Johnstone said tightly. "You've strutted your feathers, you've shown your cock, and you have blasted me with a cannon. So spare yourself, because I'm going out that door! No power on earth will ever send me back to a goddamned prison!"

"I understand your rush to avoid judgment, sir. But there are the two men with axes waiting just outside the front door."

"What two men? You're lying!"

"You see the lantern on the windowsill? Mr. Bidwell placed it there as a signal to tell the two men to take their positions."

"Name them!"

"Hiram Abercrombie is one," Bidwell answered. "Malcolm Jennings is the other."

"Well, neither of *those* fools could hit a horse in the head with an axe! Green, I said give me the pistol!"

"Stay where you are, Mr. Green," Matthew said.

"Matthew!" Winston spoke up. "Don't be foolish!"

"A pistol in this man's hand will mean someone's death." Matthew kept his eyes directed into Johnstone's. Bloodhound and fox were now locked together in a duel of wills. "One bullet, one death, I assure you."

"The pistol! I won't ask again before I start cutting!"

"Oh, is this the instrument?" Matthew asked. "The very one? Something you bought in Charles Town, I presume?"

"Damn you, you talk too fucking much!" Johnstone pushed the blade's tip into the side of Matthew's neck. The pain almost sent Matthew to his knees, and it did bring tears to his eyes and make him clench his teeth. In fact, his whole body clenched. But he was damned if he'd cry out or otherwise display agony. The blade had entered only a fraction of an inch, deep enough to cause warm blood to well out and trickle down his neck, but it had not nicked an artery. Matthew knew Johnstone was simply raising the stakes in their game.

"Would you like a little more of it?" Johnstone asked.

Bidwell had positioned himself to one side of the men, and therefore saw the blood. "For God's sake!" he brayed. "Green! Give him the pistol!"

Before Matthew could protest, he heard Green's clumping

boots behind him and the pistol's grip was offered to Johnstone. The weapon was instantly snatched into Johnstone's hand, but the blade remained exactly where it was, blood-deep and drinking.

"The wagon, Bidwell!" Johnstone demanded, now aiming the pistol at Matthew's midsection. "Get it ready!"

"Yes, do get it ready." Matthew was speaking with an effort. It wasn't every day he talked with a knife blade in his neck. "And while you're at it, fix the wheels so they'll fall off two hours or so down the road. Why don't you take a single horse, Johnstone? That way it can step into a rut in the dark, throw you, and break your neck and be done with it. Oh . . . wait! Why don't you simply go through the swamp? I know some lovely suckpits that would be glad to take your boots."

"Shut up! I want a wagon! I want a wagon, because *you're* going with me!"

"Oh *ho!*" With an even greater effort, Matthew forced himself to grin. "Sir, you're an excellent comedian after all!"

"You think this is funny?" Johnstone's face was contorted with rage. He blew spittle. "Shall you laugh harder through the slit in your throat or the hole in your gut?"

"The real question is: shall *you* laugh, when your intended hostage is on the floor and your pistol is empty?"

Johnstone's mouth opened. No sound emerged, but a silver thread of saliva broke over his lower lip and fell like the undoing of a spider's web.

Carefully, Matthew took a backward step. The blade's tip slid from his neck. "Your problem, sir," he said as he pressed his fingers to the small wound, "is that your friends and associates seem to have short spans of life. If I were to accompany you in a wagon, my own life span would be dramatically reduced. So: I dislike the idea of dying—*greatly* dislike it—but since I shall certainly die *somewhere* if I follow your wishes, it would be better to die *here*. That way, at least, the sterling gentlemen in this room may rush you and end this hopeless fantasy of escape you have seized upon. But actually, I don't think anyone would mind if you were to run for it.

Just go. Out the front door. I swear I'll be silent. Of course, Mr. Bidwell, Mr. Green—or even Mrs. Nettles, whom I see there in the doorway—might shout a warning to the axemen. Let me think." He frowned. "Two axes, versus a knife and one bullet. Yes, you might get past them. Then you could go to . . . well, where *would* you go, Mr. Johnstone? You see, that's the thorny part: where *would* you go?"

Johnstone said nothing. He still pointed both the pistol and knife, but his eyes had blurred like a frost on the fount in mid-winter.

"Oh!" Matthew nodded for emphasis. "Through the forest, why don't you? The Indians will grant you safe passage, I'm sure. But you see my condition? I unfortunately met a bear and was nearly killed. Then again, you do have a knife and a single bullet. But . . . oh . . . what shall you do for food? Well, you have the knife and bullet. Best take matches, and a lamp. Best go to your house and pack for your trip, and we'll be waiting at the gate to give you a fine farewell. Run along, now!"

Johnstone did not move.

"Oh, my," Matthew said quietly. He looked from the pistol to the blade and back again. "All dressed up, and nowhere to go."

"I'm . . . not . . ." Johnstone shook his head from side to side, in the manner of a gravely wounded animal. "I'm not . . . done. Not done."

"Hm," Matthew said. "Picture the theatre, sir. The applause has been given, the bows taken. The audience has gone home. The stagelamps are ever so slowly extinguished. They gave a beautiful dream of light, didn't they? The sets are dismantled, the costumes folded and retired. Someone comes to sweep the stage, and even yesterday's dust is carried away." He listened to the harsh rising and falling of Johnstone's chest.

"The play," Matthew said, "is over." An anxious silence reigned, and none dared challenge it.

At last Matthew decided a move had to be made. He had seen that the knife's cutting edge had small teeth, which would have severed arteries and vocal cords with one or two swift, unexpected slashes. Especially if one came up behind the victim, clasped a hand over the mouth, and pulled the head back to better offer the throat. Perhaps this wasn't the original cane Johnstone had first brought with him to Fount Royal, but one he'd had made in either Charles Town or England after he'd determined how the murders were to be done.

Matthew held out his hand, risking a blade stab. "Would you give me the pistol, please?" Johnstone's face looked soft and swollen by raging inner pressures. He seemed not to realize Matthew had spoken, but was simply staring into space.

"Sir?" Matthew prompted. "You won't be needing the pistol."

"Uh," Johnstone said. "Uh." His mouth opened, closed, and opened again. The gasping of an air-drowning fish. Then, in a heartbeat, the consciousness and fury leapt into Johnstone's eyes once more and he backed away two steps, nearly meeting the wall. Behind him was the fanciful map of Fount Royal, with its elegant streets and rows of houses, quiltwork farms, immense orchards, precise naval yard and piers, and at the town's center the life-giving spring.

Johnstone said, "No. I shall not."

"Listen to me!" Bidwell urged. "There's no point to this! Matthew's right, there's nowhere for you to go!"

"I shall not," Johnstone repeated. "Shall not. Return to prison. No. Never."

"Unfortunately," Matthew said, "you have no choice in the matter."

"Finally!" Johnstone smiled, but it was a terrible, skull-like grimace. "Finally, you speak a misstatement! So you're not as smart as you think, are you?"

"Pardon me?"

"A misstatement," he repeated, his voice thickened. "Tell me: though I . . . know my script was flawed . . . did I at least play an adequate role?"

"You did, sir. Especially the night the schoolhouse burned. I was taken with your grief."

Johnstone gave a deep, bitter chuckling that might have

briefly wandered into the territory of tears. "That was the only time I *wasn't* acting, boy! It killed my soul to see the schoolhouse burn!"

"What? It really mattered so much to you?"

"You don't know. You see . . . I actually *enjoyed* being a teacher. It was like acting, in a way. But . . . there was greater worth in it, and the audience was always appreciative. I told myself . . . if I couldn't find any more of the treasure than what I'd discovered . . . I could stay here, and I could be Alan Johnstone the schoolmaster. For the rest of my days." He stared at the pistol in his hand. "Not long after that, I brought the ruby ring up. And it set me aflame again . . . about why I was really here." He lifted his face and looked at Matthew. He stared at Winston, Dr. Shields, and Bidwell all in turn.

"Please put aside the pistol," Matthew said. "I think it's time."

"Time. Yes," Johnstone repeated, nodding. "It *is* time. I can't go back to prison. Do you understand that?"

"Sir?" Matthew now realized with a surge of alarm what the man intended. "There's no need!"

"My need." Johnstone dropped the knife to the floor and put his foot on it. "You were correct about something, Matthew: if I was given the pistol . . ." He paused, beginning to waver on his feet as if he might pass out. "Someone had to die."

Suddenly Johnstone turned the weapon toward his face, which brought a gasp of shock from Bidwell. "I do have a choice, you see," Johnstone said, the sweat glistening on his cheeks in the red-cast candlelight. "And damn you all to Hell, where I shall be waiting with eager arms.

"And now," he said, with a slight tilting forward of his head, "exit the actor."

He opened his mouth, slid the pistol's barrel into it, squeezed his eyes tightly shut, and pulled the trigger.

There was a loud metallic *clack* as the wheel-lock mechanism was engaged. A shower of sparks flew, hissing like little comets, into Johnstone's face.

The pistol, however, failed to fire.

Johnstone opened his eyes, displaying an expression of such terror that Matthew hoped never to witness its like again. He withdrew the gun from his mouth. Something inside the weapon was making a chirrupy cricket sound. Tendrils of blue smoke spun through the air around Johnstone's face, as he looked into the gun's barrel. Another spark jumped, bright as a gold coin.

Crack! went the pistol, like a mallet striking a board.

Johnstone's head rocked back. The eyes were wide open, wet, and brimming with shock. Matthew saw blood and reddish-gray clumps of matter clinging to the wall behind Johnstone's skull. The map of Bidwell's Fount Royal had in an instant become gore-drenched and brain-spattered.

Johnstone fell, his knees folding. At the end, an instant before he hit the floor, he might have been giving a final, arrogant bow.

And then his head hit the planks, and from that gruesome hole in the back of it, directly opposite the only slightly tidier hole in his forehead, streamed the physical matter of the thespian's memories, schemes, acting ability, intelligence, pride, fear of prison, desires, evil, and . . .

Yes, even his affinity for teaching. Even that, now only so much liquid.

forty-three

IN THE DISTANCE a dog barked. It was a forlorn, searching sound. Matthew looked over the darkened town from the window of the magistrate's room, thinking that even the dogs knew Fount Royal was lost.

Five hours had passed since the suicide of Alan Johnstone. Matthew had spent most of that time right here, sitting in a chair by Woodward's bed and reading the Bible in a solemn circle of lamplight. Not any particular chapter, just bits and pieces of comforting wisdom. Actually, he read most of the passages without seeing them, and had to read them again to glean their illumination. It was a sturdy book, and it felt good between his hands.

The magistrate was dying. Shields had said the man might not last until morning, so it was best that Matthew stay close. Bidwell and Winston were in the parlor, talking over the recent events like survivors of a soul-shaping battle. The doctor himself was sleeping in Matthew's room, and Mrs. Nettles was up at this midnight hour making tea, polishing silver, and doing odds and ends in the kitchen. She had told Matthew she ought to do some small labors she'd been putting off for a while, but Matthew knew she was standing the deathwatch too. Little wonder Mrs.

Nettles couldn't sleep, though, as it had been her task to mop up all the blood in the library, though Mr. Green had volunteered to put the brains and skull pieces in a burlap bag and dispose of them.

Rachel was downstairs, sleeping—he supposed—in Mrs. Nettles's room. She had come to the library after the sound of the shot, and had asked to see the face of the man who'd murdered Daniel. It was not Matthew's place to deny her. Though Matthew had previously explained to her how the murders were done, by whom, for what reason, and all the rest of it, Rachel yet had to see Johnstone for herself.

She had walked past Winston, Dr. Shields, and Bidwell without a glance. She had ignored Hiram Abercrombie and Malcolm Jennings, who'd rushed in at the shot, armed with their axes. Certainly she'd passed Green as if the red-bearded, gap-toothed giant was invisible. She had stood over the dead man, staring down into his open, sightless eyes. Matthew had watched her as she contemplated Johnstone's departure. At last, she had said very quietly, "I suppose . . . I should rant and rave that I spent so many days in a cell . . . and he has fled. But . . ." She had looked into Matthew's face, tears in her eyes now that it was over and she could allow them. "Someone that evil . . . that wretched . . . was locked in a cage of his own making, every day of his life, wasn't he?"

"He was," Matthew had said. "Even when he knew he'd found the key to escape it, all he did was move to a deeper dungeon."

Green had retrieved the pistol, which had belonged to Nicholas Paine. It occurred to Matthew that all the men he and the magistrate had met that first night of their arrival were accounted for in this room. "Thank you for your help, Mr. Green," Matthew had said. "You were invaluable."

"My pleasure, sir. Anythin' to help you." Green had taken to fawning at Matthew, as if the clerk had a giant's stature. "I *still* can't believe such a blow as you gave me!" He'd massaged his jaw at the memory of it. "I saw you cock the fist back, and then . . . my Lord, the stars!" He'd grunted and looked at Rachel. "It took a right champion to lay me out, I'll swear it did!"

"Um . . . yes." Matthew cast a quick glance at Mrs. Nettles, who stood nearby listening to this exchange, her face an unrevealing sculpture of granite. "Well, one never knows from where one will draw the necessary strength. Does one?"

Matthew had watched as Jennings and Abercrombie had lifted the corpse, placed it facedown on a ladder to prevent any further leakage, and then covered a sheet over the deceased. Its destination, Bidwell told Matthew, was the barn down in the slave quarters. Tomorrow, Bidwell said, the corpse—"foul bastard" were the exact words he used—would be taken into the swamp and dumped in a mudhole where the crows and vultures might applaud his performance.

To end up, Matthew realized, like the dead men in the muck at Shawcombe's tavern. Well: dust to dust, ashes to ashes, and mud to mud.

It was now the impending fact of another death that concerned him. Matthew had learned from Dr. Shields that the stimulating potion had finally reached the limit of its usefulness. Woodward's body had simply given out, and nothing could reverse the process. Matthew didn't bear a grudge against the doctor; Shields had done the best he could do, given the limited medicines at hand. Perhaps the bleeding had been excessive, or perhaps it had been a grievous error to make the magistrate attend his duties while so sick, or perhaps something else was done or not done . . . but today Matthew had come to accept the hard, cold truth.

Just as seasons and centuries must turn, so too must men— the bad and the good, equal in their frailty of flesh—pass away from this earth.

He heard a nightbird singing.

Out there. Out in one of the trees that stood around the pond. It was a noontime song, and presently it was joined by a second. For their kind, Matthew mused, night was not a time of sad longing, loneliness, and fear. For them the night was but a further opportunity to sing.

And such a sweetness in it, to hear these notes trilled as the land slept, as the stars hummed in the immense velvet black. Such a sweetness, to realize that even at this darkest hour there was yet joy to be known.

"*Matthew.*"

He heard the feeble gasp and immediately turned toward the bed.

It was very hard now to look upon the magistrate. To know what he had been, and to see what he had become in the space of six days. Time could be a ruthless and hungry beast. It had consumed the magistrate down to bones and angles.

"Yes, sir, I'm here." Matthew pulled his chair nearer the bed, and also moved the lantern closer. He sat down, leaning toward the skeletal figure. "I'm right here."

"Ah. Yes. I see you." Woodward's eyes had shrunken and re-treated. They had changed from their once energetic shade of ice-blue to a dull yellowish gray, the color of the fog and rain he had journeyed through to reach this town. Indeed, the only color about the magistrate that was not a shade of gray was the ruddy hue of the splotches on his scalp. Those jealous imperfections had maintained their dignity, even as the rest of Woodward's body had fallen to ruin.

"Would you . . . hold my hand?" the magistrate asked, and he reached out in search of comfort. Matthew took the hand. It was fragile and trembling, and hot with merciless fever. "I heard it," Woodward whispered, his head on the pillow. "Thunder. Does it rain?"

"No, sir." Perhaps it had been the shot he'd heard, Matthew thought. "Not yet."

"Ah. Well, then." He said nothing more, but stared past Matthew toward the lamp.

This was the first time the magistrate had surfaced from the waters of sleep since Matthew had been in the room. Matthew had come in several times during the day, but except for a few brief murmurs or a pained swallow the magistrate had been unresponsive.

"It's dark out," Woodward said.

"Yes, sir."

He nodded. Around his nose glistened the pine-oil–based liniment Shields had smeared there to clear his air passages. On his thin and sunken chest was a plaster, also soaked in the liniment. If Woodward noticed the clay dressing on Matthew's arm and the bandage—of cloth, which Dr. Shields had applied after Johnstone's departure—on his clerk's forever-to-be-scarred forehead, he made no mention of it. Matthew doubted the magistrate could see his face as anything but a blur, as the fever had almost destroyed the man's vision.

Woodward's fingers tightened. "She's gone, then."

"Sir?"

"The witch. Gone."

"Yes, sir," Matthew said, and didn't think he was telling an untruth. "The witch *is* gone."

Woodward sighed, his eyelids fluttering. "I . . . am glad . . . I didn't witness it. I might have to . . . pass the sentence . . . but . . . don't have to watch it . . . carried out. Ohhhhh, my throat! My throat! It closes up!"

"I'll get Dr. Shields." Matthew attempted to stand, but Woodward steadfastly refused to release him.

"No!" he said, tears of pain streaking his cheeks. "Stay seated. Just . . . listen."

"Don't try to talk, sir. You shouldn't—"

"I shouldn't!" Woodward blustered. "I shouldn't . . . I can't . . . mustn't! Those are the words that . . . that put you . . . six feet under!"

Matthew settled into his chair again, his hand still grasping the magistrate's. "You should refrain from speaking."

A grim smile moved quickly across Woodward's mouth and then was gone. "I shall have. Plenty of time . . . to refrain. When my . . . mouth is full of dirt."

"Don't say such as that!"

"Why not? It's true . . . isn't it? Matthew, what a short rope . . . I have been given!" He closed his eyes, breathing fitfully. Matthew would have thought he'd drifted to sleep again, but the pressure on his hand had not relaxed. Then Woodward spoke again with his eyes still closed. "The witch," he whispered. "The case . . . pains me. Still pains me." His fog-colored eyes opened. "Was I right, Matthew? Tell me. Was I right?"

Matthew answered, "You were correct."

"Ahhhhh," he said, like an exhalation of relief. "Thank you. I needed . . . to hear that, from you." He squeezed Matthew's hand more firmly. "Listen, now. My hourglass . . . is broken. All my sand is running out. I will die soon."

"Nonsense, sir!" Matthew's voice cracked and betrayed him. "You're just tired, that's all!"

"Yes. And I shall . . . soon sleep . . . for a very long time. Please . . . I may be dying, but I have not . . . become *stupid*. Now . . . just hush . . . and listen to me." He tried to sit up but his body had shut that particular door to him. "In Manhattan," he said. "Go see . . . Magistrate Powers. Nathaniel Powers. A very . . . very good man. He knows me. You tell him. He will find a place for you."

"Please, sir. Don't do this."

"I fear . . . I have no choice. The judgment has been . . . has been passed down . . . from a much higher court. Than ever I presided over. Magistrate Nathaniel Powers. In Manhattan. Yes?" Matthew was silent, the blood thrumming through his veins. "This will be . . . my final command to you," Woodward said. "Say *yes*."

Matthew looked into the near-sightless eyes. Into the face that seemed to be aging and crumbling even as he regarded it.

Seasons, and centuries, and men. The bad and the good. Frailty of flesh.

Must pass away. Must.

A nightbird, singing outside. In the dark. Singing as at full sunlit noon.

This one word, so simple, was almost impossible to speak.

But the magistrate was waiting, and the word must be spoken. "Yes." His own throat felt near closing up. "Sir."

"That's my boy," Woodward whispered. His fingers released Matthew's hand. He lay staring up toward the ceiling, a half-smile playing around the corners of his mouth. "I remember . . . my own father," he said after a moment of reflection. "He liked to dance. I can see them . . . in the house . . . dancing before the fire. No music. But my father . . . humming a tune. He picked my mother up. Twirled her . . . and she laughed. So . . . there *was* music . . . after all."

Matthew heard the nightbird, whose soft song may have reawakened this memory.

"My father," the magistrate said. "Grew sick. I watched him . . . in bed, like this. Watched him fade. One day . . . I asked my mother . . . why Papa didn't stand up. Get out of bed. And dance a jig . . . to make himself feel better. I always said . . . always to myself . . . that when I was old . . . very old . . . and I lay dying. I would stand up. Dance a jig, so that . . . I might feel better. Matthew?"

"Yes, sir?"

"Would it . . . sound very strange to you . . . if . . . I said I was ready to dance?"

"No, sir, it would not."

"I am. Ready. I am."

"Sir?" Matthew said. "I have something for you." He reached down to the floor beside the bed and picked up the package he had put there this afternoon. Mrs. Nettles had found some brown wrapping paper, and decorated it with yellow twine. "Here, sir." He put the package into the magistrate's hands. "Can you open it?"

"I shall try." After a moment of struggling, however, he could not succeed in tearing the paper. "Well," he frowned, "I am . . . lower on sand . . . than I thought."

"Allow me." Matthew leaned toward the bed, tore the paper with his good hand, and drew what was inside out into the lamplight. The gold threads caught that light, and shone their illumination in stripes across the magistrate's face.

His hands closed into the cloth that was as brown as rich French chocolate, and he drew the waistcoat to him even as the tears ran from his dying eyes.

It was, indeed, a gift of fantastic worth.

"Where?" the magistrate whispered. *"How?"*

"Shawcombe was found," Matthew said, and saw no need to elaborate.

Woodward pressed the waistcoat against his face, as if trying to inhale from it the fragrance of a past life. Matthew saw the magistrate smile. Who was to say that Woodward did not smell the sun shining in a garden graced by a fountain of green Italian tiles? Who was to say he did not see the candlelight that glowed golden on the face of a beautiful young woman named Ann, or hear her soprano voice on a warm Sunday afternoon? Who was to say he did not feel the small hand of his son, clutching to that of a good father?

Matthew believed he did.

"I have always been proud of you," Woodward said. "Always. I knew from the first. When I saw you . . . at the almshouse. The way you carried yourself. Something . . . different . . . and indefinable. But *special.* You will make your mark. Somewhere. You will make . . . a profound difference to someone . . . just by being alive."

"Thank you, sir," Matthew answered, as best he could. "I . . . also . . . thank you for the care you have shown to me. You have . . . always been temperate and fair."

"I'm supposed to be," Woodward said, and managed a frail smile though his eyes were wet. "I am a judge." He reached out for Matthew and the boy took his hand. They sat together in silence, as beyond the window the nightbird spoke of joy seized from despair, of a new beginning reached only at an ending.

Dawn had begun to light the sky when the magistrate's body became rigid, after a difficult final hour of suffering.

"He's going," Dr. Shields said, the lamplight aglow in the lenses of his spectacles. Bidwell stood at the foot of the bed, and Winston just within the door. Matthew still sat holding Woodward's hand, his head bowed and the Bible in his lap.

The magistrate's speech on this last portion of his journey had become barely intelligible, when he *could* speak through the pain. It had been mostly murmurs of torment, as his earthly clay transfigured itself. But now, as the silence lingered, the dying man seemed to stretch his body toward some unknown portal, the golden stripes of the waistcoat he wore shining on his chest. His head pressed back against the pillow, and he spoke three unmistakable words.

"Why? Why?" he whispered, the second fainter than the first.

And the last and most faint, barely the cloud of a breath: *"Why?"*

A great question had been asked, Matthew thought. The ultimate question, which might be asked only by explorers who would not return to share their knowledge of a new world.

The magistrate's body poised on the point of tension . . . paused . . . paused . . . and then, at last, it appeared to Matthew that an answer had been given.

And understood.

There was a soft, all but imperceptible exhalation. A sigh, perhaps, of rest.

Woodward's empty clay settled. His hand relaxed.

The night was over.

forty-four

A S SOON AS MATTHEW KNOCKED on the study's door, Bid-well said, "Come in!"

Matthew opened the door and saw Bidwell seated at his massive mahogany desk, with Winston sitting in a chair before it. The window's shutters were open, allowing in the warm breeze and early afternoon sun. "Mrs. Nettles told me you wanted to see me."

"Exactly. Come in, please! Draw up a chair." He motioned toward another that was in the room. Matthew sat down, not failing to notice the empty space on the wall where the map of the Florida country had been displayed.

"We are taking account of things. Edward and I," Bidwell said. He was dressed in a cardinal-red suit with a ruffled shirt, but he had forgone the wearing of his lavish wigs. On the desktop was a rectangular wooden box about nine inches long and seven inches wide. "I've been trying to locate you. Were you out for a walk?"

"Yes. Just walking and thinking."

"Well, it's a pleasant day for such." Bidwell folded his hands before him and regarded Matthew with an expression of genuine concern. "Are you all right?"

"I am. Or . . . I shall be presently."

"Good. You're a young man, strong and fit. And I have to say, you have the most determined constitution of any man I've ever met. How are your injuries?"

"My ribs still ache, but I can endure it. My arm is . . . deceased, I think. Dr. Shields says I may regain some feeling in it, but the outlook is uncertain." Matthew shrugged one shoulder. "He says he knows a doctor in New York who is doing amazing things for damaged limbs with a new surgical technique, so . . . who can say?"

"Yes, I hear those New York doctors are quite . . . um . . . radical. And they charge wholly radical prices, as well. What of your head wound?"

Matthew touched the fresh dressing Shields had applied just that morning. In the course of treatment, the doctor had been appalled at the Indians' method of tobacco-leaf and herb-potion healing, but also intrigued by the positive progress. "My scar, unfortunately, will be a subject of discussion for the rest of my life."

"That may be so." Bidwell leaned back in his chair. "Ah, but women love a dashing scar! And I daresay so will the grandchildren."

Matthew had to give a guarded smile at this flattery. "You leap ahead more years than I care to lose."

"Speaking of your years ahead," Winston said, "what are your immediate plans?"

"I haven't given them much thought," Matthew had to admit. "Other than returning to Charles Town. The magistrate gave me the name of a colleague in Manhattan, and said I would find a position with him, but . . . I really haven't decided."

Bidwell nodded. "That's understandable, with so much on your mind. Tell me: do you approve of where I placed Isaac's grave?"

"I do, sir. As a matter of fact, I just came from there. It's a very lovely, shaded spot."

"Good. And you don't think he would mind that he . . . uh . . . sleeps apart from the others in the cemetery?"

"Not at all. He always enjoyed his privacy."

"I shall endeavor, at some point in the future, to erect a picket fence around it and a suitable marker for his excellent service to Fount Royal."

Matthew was taken aback. "Wait," he said. "You mean . . . you're *staying* here?"

"I am. Winston will be returning to England, to work in the offices there, and I'll be going back and forth as the situation warrants, but I plan on reviving Fount Royal and making it just as grand—no, *thrice* as grand—as ever I'd planned before."

"But . . . the town is *dead*. There's hardly twenty people here!"

"Twenty citizens!" Bidwell thumped the desktop, his eyes bright with renewed purpose. "Then it's *not* dead, is it?"

"Perhaps not in fact, but it seems to me that—"

"If not in fact, then not at all!" Bidwell interrupted, displaying some of his old brusque self. He was aware of his slippage, and so immediately sought to soothe the friction burns. "What I mean is, I will not give up on Fount Royal. Not when I have invested so heavily in the venture, and particularly as I still fervently believe a southernmost naval station is not only practical, but essential for the future of these colonies."

"How will you go about reviving the town, then?"

"The same as I originally began it. With having advertising placards placed in Charles Town and other cities up the seaboard. I shall also advertise in London. And I am getting to it sooner than later, as I understand I will be having competition from my own family!"

"Competition? How so?" Matthew asked.

"My youngest sister! Who was sick all the time, and for whom I bought medicine!" Bidwell scowled. "When Winston and I went to Charles Town to find the maskers, we also looked in on the supply situation at the harbor. Come to find out there was a whole load of supplies there those dogs had hidden from me! Luckily, Mr. Winston convinced a watchman to unlock a certain door—and imagine how I near fell to the ground to see all those crates with my name on them! Anyway, we also procured a packet of mail." He made a queasy face. "Tell him, Edward! I can't bear to think of it!"

"Mr. Bidwell's sister married a land speculator," Winston said. "In the letter she wrote, she indicated he has purchased a sizeable amount of territory between here and the Florida country, and has hopes to begin a port settlement of his own."

"You don't say!" Matthew said.

"Yes, it's damnably true!" Bidwell started to hammer his fist on the desk, and then decided it was not proper for his new age of enlightenment. "It'll never work, of course. That swampland down there makes ours look like a manicured showpark. And do you really think the Spanish are just going to sit still and let a half-pint, weasly milksop of a land speculator threaten their Florida country? No! He has no business sense! I told Savannah when she married that man she'd weep a tear for every pearl on her dress!" He stabbed a finger in the air like a rapier's thrust. "Mark my words, she'll regret such a folly as she's about to enter into!"

"Uh . . . shall I get you something to drink?" Winston asked. "To calm your nerves?" To Matthew, he confided, "Mr. Bidwell's sister never fails. To antagonize, I mean."

"No, no! I'm all right. Just let me get my breath. Oh, my heart gallops like a wild horse." Bidwell spent a moment in an exercise of slow and steady deep breathing, and gradually the red whorls that had surfaced on his cheeks faded away. "The point of my asking you here, Matthew," he said, "is to offer you a position with my company."

Matthew didn't respond; in truth, he was too shocked to speak.

"A position of not small responsibility," Bidwell went on. "I need a good, trustworthy man in Charles Town. Someone to make sure the supplies keep flowing, and to make certain such dirtiness as has been done to me in the past is not repeated. A . . . uh . . . a private investigator, you might say. Does that sound at all of interest to you?"

It took a little while longer for Matthew to find his voice. "I do appreciate your offer, sir. I do. But, to be perfectly honest, you and I would eventually come to blows and our fight might knock the earth off its tilt. Therefore I must decline, as I would hate to be responsible for the death of mankind."

"Ah. Yes. Well spoken, that." Bidwell did appear much relieved. "I felt I should at least offer you a future, since my actions—and stupidity—have so endangered your present."

"I have a future," Matthew said firmly. "In New York, I believe. And thank you for helping me come to that conclusion."

"Now! That's out of the way!" Bidwell heaved a sigh. "I wanted you to see something." He pushed the wooden box across the desk toward Matthew. "We searched through the foul bastard's house, just as you suggested, and found all the items you said would be there. That five-bladed device was still nasty with dried blood. And we discovered the book on ancient Egypt, as well. This box was placed in the bottom of a trunk. Open it, if you please."

Matthew leaned forward and lifted the lid, which rose smoothly on a well-oiled hinge.

Within the box were three charcoal pencils, a writing tablet, a folded sheet of paper, a gum eraser . . . and . . .

"What he found in the spring," Bidwell said.

Indeed. The sapphire brooch and ruby ring were there, along with a gold crucifix on a chain, seven gold doubloons, three silver coins, and a little black velvet bag.

"You will find the bag's contents of interest," Bidwell promised.

Matthew took it out and emptied it on the desktop. In the sunlight that streamed through the window, the room was suddenly colored by the shine of four dark green emeralds, two deep purple amethysts, two pearls, and an amber stone. The jewels were raw and yet to be professionally polished, but even so were obviously of excellent quality. Matthew surmised they had been captured at sea from vessels shuttling between tropical mines and the marketplace.

"The folded paper is also worth a glance," said Bidwell.

Matthew unfolded it. It was a drawing, in charcoal pencil, of a good-sized building. Some time had been spent in attending to the details. Present were bricks, windows, and a bell steeple.

"It appears," Bidwell said, "the foul bastard . . . intended to build his next schoolhouse of a less flammable material."

"I see." Matthew gazed at the drawing—a sad sight, really—and then refolded the paper and returned it to the box.

Bidwell put the gemstones back into the bag. He removed from the box the pencils, the writing tablet, the eraser, and the drawing of the new schoolhouse.

"I own the spring, of course," Bidwell said. "I own the water and the mud. By the rights of ownership—and the hell I have gone through—I also claim for myself these gems and jewelry, which came from that mud. Agreed?"

"It makes no matter to me," Matthew answered. "Do with them as you please."

"I shall." Bidwell placed the little bag into the box, beside the coins, the brooch, the ring, and the crucifix and chain. He closed the lid.

Then he pushed the box toward Matthew. "It pleases me . . . for you to take this to the person who has suffered far more hell than I."

Matthew couldn't fathom what he'd just heard. "Pardon me?"

"You heard correctly. Take them to—" He interrupted himself as he snapped the first charcoal pencil between his hands. "—her. It is the very least I can do, and certainly it can't bring back her husband or those months spent in the gaol." In spite of his good intentions, he couldn't help but regard the box with a wanton eye. "Go ahead. Take it"—the second pencil was picked up and broken—"before I regain my senses."

"Why don't you take it to her yourself! It would mean much more."

"It would mean much *less*," he corrected. "She hates me. I've tried to speak to her, tried to explain my position . . . but she turns away every time. Therefore you take the box." *Snap*, died the third pencil. "Tell her you found it."

Realizing that indeed Bidwell must be half-crazed with humanity to let such wealth slip through his fingers, Matthew picked up the box and held it to his chest. "I will take it to her directly. Do you know where she is?"

"I saw her an hour ago," Winston said. "She was drawing water." Matthew nodded; he had an idea where she might be found.

"We must put ourselves back in business here." Bidwell picked up the drawing that Johnstone had done—the bad man's dream of an Oxford of his own—and began to methodically tear it to pieces. "Put ourselves back in order, and consign this disgraceful . . . insane . . . blot on my town to the trash heap. I can do nothing more for the woman than what I've done today. And neither can you. Therefore, I must ask: how much longer shall you grace us with your presence?"

"As a matter of fact, I have decided it's time to get on with my own life. I might leave in the morning, at first light."

"I'll have Green take you to Charles Town in a wagon. Will you be ready by six?"

"I shall be," Matthew said. "But I'd prefer you give me a horse, a saddle and tack, and some food, and I'll get myself to Charles Town. I am not an invalid, and therefore I refuse to be carted about like one."

"*Give* you a horse?" Bidwell glowered at him. "Horses cost money, aren't you aware of that? And saddles don't grow on trees, either!"

"You might wish for saddle-trees, sir!" Matthew fired back at him. "As that might be the only crop your farmers can grow here!"

"You don't concern yourself with our crops, thank you! I'll have you know I'm bringing in a botanist—the finest money can buy—to set our growing affairs straight! So stick that in your damned theory hole and—"

"Excuse me, gentlemen!" Winston said calmly, and the wranglers fell quiet. "I shall be glad to pay for a horse and saddle for

Mr. Corbett, though I think it unwise of you, Matthew, to travel unaccompanied. But I wish to offer my best regards and hope that you find much success in the future."

"Write him a love letter while you're at it!" Bidwell steamed.

"My thanks, sir," Matthew said. "As for travelling alone, I feel confident I won't be in any danger." The demise of Shawcombe and Jack One Eye, he suspected, had made the backroads of the entire Southern colonies at least safer than Manhattan's harbor. "Oh. While I am thinking of it: Mr. Bidwell, there is one final rope that remains unknotted in this situation."

"You mean Dr. Shields?" Bidwell crumpled the torn pieces of Johnstone's drawing in his fist. "I haven't decided what to do with him yet. And don't rush me!"

"No, not Dr. Shields. The burning of the schoolhouse, and who was responsible for the other fires as well."

"*What?*" Winston blanched.

"Well, it wasn't Johnstone, obviously," Matthew explained. "Even someone so preoccupied with his own affairs as Mr. Bidwell can understand *that*. And, in time, I'm sure Mr. Bidwell might begin to wonder, as well he should."

"You're right!" Bidwell agreed, his eyes narrowing. "What son of a bitch tried to burn down my town?"

"Early this morning I had a thought about this burning business, and I went to Lancaster's house. The place is still a wreck, as you're aware. Has anyone else been through it?"

"No one would go within a hundred yards of that damn murder house!"

"I thought not, though I did appreciate the fact that the corpse has been disposed of. Anyway, I decided to search a little more thoroughly . . . and I discovered a very strange bucket in the debris. Evidently it was something Johnstone didn't bother himself with, since it simply appears to be a regular bucket. Perhaps he thought it was full of rat bait or some such."

"Well, then? What was in it?"

"I'm not sure. It appears to be tar. It has a brimstone smell. I decided to leave it where I found it . . . as I didn't know if it might be flammable, or explode, or what might occur if it were jostled too severely."

"Tar? A brimstone smell?" Alarmed, Bidwell looked at Winston. "By God. I don't like the sound of *that!*"

"I'm sure it's worth going there to get," Matthew continued. "Or Mr. Winston might want to go and look at it, and then . . . I don't know, bury it or something. Would you be able to tell what it was if you saw it, Mr. Winston?"

"Possibly," Winston answered, his voice tight. "But I'll tell you right now . . . as you describe it, the stuff sounds like . . . possibly . . . infernal fire, Mr. Bidwell?"

"Infernal fire? My God!" Now Bidwell did hammer his desk. "So that's who was burning the houses! But where was he getting the stuff from?"

"He was a very capable man," Matthew said. "Perhaps he had sulphur for his rat baits or candles or something. Perhaps he cooked some tar and mixed it himself. I have a feeling Lancaster was trying to hurry the process of emptying the town without telling his accomplice. Who knows why?" Matthew shrugged. "There is no honor among thieves, and even less among murderers."

"I'll be damned!" Bidwell looked as if he'd taken a punch to his ponderous gut. "Was there no end to their treacheries, even against each other?"

"It does appear a dangerous bucket, Mr. Winston," Matthew said. "Very dangerous indeed. If it were up to me, I wouldn't dare bring it back to the mansion for fear of explosion. You might just want to bring a small sample to show Mr. Bidwell. Then by all means bury it and forget where you turned the shovel."

"Excellent advice." Winston gave a slight bow of his head. "I shall attend to it this afternoon. And I am very gratified, sir, that you did not leave this particular rope unknotted."

"Mr. Winston is a useful man," Matthew said to Bidwell. "You should be pleased to have him in your employ."

Bidwell puffed his cheeks and blew out. "Whew! Don't I know it!"

As Matthew turned away and started out with the treasure box, the master of Fount Royal had to ask one last question: "Matthew?" he said. "Uh . . . is there any way . . . any possible way at all . . . that . . . the fortune might be recovered?"

Matthew made a display of thought. "As it has flowed along a river to the center of the earth," he said, "I would think it extremely unlikely. But how long can you hold your breath?"

"Ha!" Bidwell smiled grimly, but there was some good humor in it. "Just because I build ships and I'm going to station a grand navy here . . . does not mean I can *swim*. Now go along with you, and if Edward thinks he's going to convince me to give you a free horse and saddle, he is a sadly mistaken duke!"

Matthew left the mansion and walked past the still waters of the spring on his way to the conjunction of streets. Before he reached the turn to Truth, however, he saw ahead of him the approach of a black-clad, black-tricorned, spidery, and wholly loathsome figure.

"Ho, there!" Exodus Jerusalem called, lifting a hand. On this deserted street, the sound fairly echoed. Matthew was sorely tempted to run, but the preacher picked up his pace and met him. Blocked his way, actually.

"What do *you* want?" Matthew asked.

"A truce, please." Jerusalem showed both palms, and Matthew unconsciously held more securely to the treasure box. "We are packed and ready to leave, and I am on my way to give my regards to Mr. Bidwell."

"Art thou?" Matthew lifted his eyebrows. "Thy speech has suddenly become more common, Preacher. Why is that?"

"My speech? Oh . . . that!" Jerusalem grinned broadly, his face seamed with wrinkles in the sunlight. "It's an *effort* to keep that up. Too many *thee*s and *thou*s in one day and my lips near fall off."

"It's part of your performance, you mean?"

"No, it's real enough. My father spoke such, and his father

before him. And my son—if I ever have a son—shall as well.
Also, however, the widow Lassiter detests it. Gently, of course.
She is a very gentle, very warm, very giving woman."

"The widow Lassiter? Your latest conquest?"

"My latest *convert,*" he corrected. "There is quite a difference.
Ah yes, she's a wonderfully warm woman. She ought to be warm,
since she weighs almost two hundred pounds. But she has a
lovely face and she can surely mend a shirt!" He leaned in a little
closer, his grin lecherous. "*And* she has quite the roll in her skirt, if
you catch my meaning!"

"I would prefer not to, thank you."

"Well, as my father always said, beauty is in the eye of the beholder. The one-eyed, stiff beholder, I mean."

"You are a piece of work, aren't you?" Matthew said, amazed
at such audacity. "Do you do all your thinking with your private
parts?"

"Let us be friends. Brothers under the warming sun. I have
heard all about your triumph. I don't fully understand how such a
thing was done—the Satan play, I mean—but I am gratified to
know that a righteous and innocent woman has been cleared, and
that you are also found guiltless. Besides, it would be a damn sin
for a looker like that to burn, eh?"

"Excuse me," Matthew said. "And farewell to you."

"Ah, you may say farewell, but not goodbye, young man!
Perchance we'll meet again, further along life's twisting road."

"We might meet again, at that. Except I might be a judge
and you might be at the end of a twisting rope."

"Ha, ha! An excellent joke!" Now, however, a serious cast
came over the wizened face. "Your magistrate. I—honestly—am
very sorry. He fought death to the end, I understand."

"No," Matthew said. "In the end he accepted it. As I did."

"Yes, of course. That, too. But he did seem a decent man. Too
bad he died in a hole like this."

Matthew stared at the ground, a muscle working in his
jaw.

"If you like, before I leave I might go to his grave and speak a few words for his eternal soul."

"Preacher," Matthew said in a strained voice, "all is well with his eternal soul. I suggest you go give your regards to Mr. Bidwell, get in your wagon with your witless brood, and go to—wherever you choose to go. Just leave my sight." He lifted his fierce gaze to the man, and saw the preacher flinch. "And let me tell you that if I but see you walking in the direction of Magistrate Woodward's grave, I will forget the laws of God and man and do my damnedest to put my boot so far up your ass I will kick your teeth out from the inner side. Do you understand me?"

Jerusalem backed away a few steps. "It was only a thought!"

"Good day, goodbye, and good riddance." Matthew sidestepped him and continued on his way.

"Ohhhhh, not goodbye!" Jerusalem called. "Farewell, perhaps! But not goodbye! I have a feeling thou shalt lay eyes on me at some future unknown date, as I travel this ungodly, debased, and corrupted land in the continual—continual, I say—battle against the foul seed of Satan! So I say to thee, brother Matthew, farewell . . . but never goodbye!"

The voice—which Matthew thought could strip paint off wood if Jerusalem really let it bray—was fading behind him as he turned onto Truth Street. He dared not look back, for he didn't care to become a pillar of salt today.

He passed the gaol. He did not give the odious place a single glance, though his gut tightened as he stepped on its shadow.

And then he came to her house.

Rachel had been busy. She had pulled into the yard much of the furniture, and a washtub of soapy water stood at the ready. Also brought into the cleansing sun were clothes, bedsheets, a mattress, kettles and skillets, shoes, and just about everything else a household contained.

The door was wide open, as were all the shutters. Airing the place out, he thought. Intending to move in again, and make it a home. Indeed, Rachel was more like Bidwell in her tenacity—one might say foolhearted stubbornness—than ever he'd imagined. Still, if elbow grease alone could transform that rat-whiskered shack to a livable cottage again, she would have a mansion of her own.

He crossed the yard, winding between the accumulated belongings. Suddenly his progress was interrupted by a small chestnut-brown dog that sprang up from its drowsing posture beside the washtub, took a stance that threatened attack, and began to bark in a voice that surely rivalled the preacher's for sheer volume.

Rachel came to the threshold and saw who her visitor was. "Hush!" she commanded. "Hush!" She clapped her hands to get the mongrel's attention. The dog ceased its alarms and, with a quick wag of its tail and a wide-mouthed yawn, plopped itself down on the sun-warmed ground again.

"Well!" Matthew said. "It seems you have a sentinel."

"She took up with me this morning." Rachel wiped her dirty hands on an equally dirty rag. "I gave her one of the ham biscuits Mrs. Nettles made for me, and we are suddenly sisters."

Matthew looked around at the furniture and other items. "You have your labors ahead of you, I see."

"It won't be so bad, once I finish scrubbing the house."

"Rachel!" Matthew said. "You don't really plan on staying here, do you?"

"It's my home," she answered, spearing him with those intense amber eyes. She wore a blue-printed scarf around her head, and her face was streaked with grime. The gray dress and white apron she wore were equally filthy. "Why should I leave it?"

"Because . . ." He hesitated, and showed her the box. "Because I have something for you. May I come in?"

"Yes. Mind the mess, though."

As Matthew approached the door, he heard a *whuff* of wind behind him and thought the mighty sentinel had decided to take a bite from his ankle. He turned in time to see the brown dog go tearing off across the field, where it seized one of two fleeing rats and shook the rodent between its jaws in a crushing deathgrip.

"She does like to chase them," Rachel said.

Within the bare house, Matthew saw that Rachel had been scraping yellow lichens from the floorboards with an axeblade. The fungus and mildew that had spread across the walls had bloomed into strange purple and green hues only otherwise to be seen in fever dreams. However, Matthew saw that where the sunlight touched, the growths had turned ashen. A broom leaned against the wall, next to a pile of dust, dirt, rat pellets, and bones. Nearby was a bucket of more soapy water, in which a scrub brush was immersed.

"You know, there are plenty of houses available," Matthew said. "If you really insist on staying here, you might move into one only recently abandoned and save yourself all this work. As a matter of fact, I know a very comfortable place, and the only labor involved would be clearing out a wasp's nest."

"*This* is my home," she answered.

"Well . . . yes . . . but still, don't you think—"

She turned away from him and picked up a rolling pin that lay on the floor near the broom. Then she walked to a wall and put her ear against it. Following that, she whacked the boards three times and Matthew could hear the panicked squeaking and scurrying from within.

"Those defy me," Rachel said. "I've run out most of them, but those—right there—defy me. I swear I'll clean them out. Every last one of them."

And at that moment Matthew understood.

Rachel, he believed, was still in a state of shock. And who could fault her? The loss of her husband, the loss of her home, the loss of her freedom. Even—for a time at least, as she prepared herself for the fires—the loss of her will to live. And now, faced with the daunting—and perhaps impossible—task of rebuilding, she must concentrate on and conquer what she perceived as the last obstacle to a return to normality.

But who, having walked through such flames, could ever erase the memory of being singed?

"I regret I have nothing to offer you," she said, and now that he was looking for it he could see a certain burnt blankness in her eyes. "It will be a time before my cupboard is restocked."

"Yes," Matthew said. He gave her a sad but gentle smile. "I'm sure. But . . . nonetheless, it *will* be restocked, won't it?"

"You may put faith in it," she answered, and then she pressed her ear to the wall again.

"Let me show you what I've brought." He approached her and offered the box. "Take it and look inside." Rachel laid down the rolling pin, accepted the box, and lifted its lid.

Matthew saw no reaction on her face, as she viewed the coins and the other items. "The little bag. Open that too." She shook the gems out into the box. Again, there was no reaction.

"Those were found in Johnstone's house." He had already decided to tell her the truth. "Mr. Bidwell asked me to give them to you."

"Mr. Bidwell," Rachel repeated, without emotion. She closed the lid and held the box out. "You take them. I have already received from Mr. Bidwell all the gifts that I can stand."

"Listen to me. Please. I know how you must feel, but—"

"No. You do not, nor can you ever."

"Of course you're right." He nodded. "But surely you must realize you're holding a true fortune. I daresay with the kind of money you could get in Charles Town from the sale of those jewels, you might live in Mr. Bidwell's style in some larger, more populous city."

"I see what his style is," she countered, "and I detest it. Take the box."

"Rachel, let me point out something to you. Bidwell did not murder your husband. Nor did he create this scheme. I don't particularly care for his . . . um . . . motivations, either, but he was reacting to a crisis that he thought would destroy Fount Royal. In that regard," Matthew said, "he acted properly. You know, he might have hanged you without waiting for the magistrate. I'm sure he could have somehow justified it."

"So *you're* justifying *him,* is that right?"

"Since he now faces a guilty verdict from you in a tragedy for which he was not wholly responsible," Matthew said, "I am simply pleading his case."

Rachel stared at him in silence, still holding out the box to him. He made no move to accept it.

"Daniel is gone," Matthew told her. "You know that. Gone, too, are the men who murdered him. But Fount Royal—such as it may be—is still here, and so is Bidwell. It appears he intends to do his best to rebuild the town. That is his main concern. It seems to be yours as well. Don't you think this common ground is larger than hatred?"

"I shall take this box," Rachel said calmly, "and dump it into the spring if you refuse it."

"Then go ahead," he answered, "because I do refuse it. Oh: except for one gold piece. The one that Johnstone stole from my room. Before you throw your fortune and future away to prove your devotion to Daniel in continued poverty and suffering, I *will* take the one gold piece." There was no response from her, though perhaps she did flinch just a little.

"I understand Bidwell's position," Matthew said. "The evidence against you was overwhelming. I too might have pressed for your execution, if I believed firmly enough in witchcraft. And . . . if I hadn't fallen in love with you."

Now she did blink; her eyes, so powerful a second before, had become dazed.

"Of course you recognized it. You didn't want me to. In fact, you asked me to—as you put it—go on about my life. You said— there in the gaol, after I'd read the magistrate's decree—that the time had come to embrace reality." He disguised his melancholy with a faint smile. "That time has now come for both of us."

Rachel looked down at the floor. She had taken hold of the box with both hands, and Matthew saw an ocean's worth of conflicting tides move across her face.

He said, "I'm leaving in the morning. I will be in Charles Town for a few weeks. Then most likely I will be travelling to New York. At that time I can be reached through Magistrate Nathaniel Powers, if you ever have need of me."

She lifted her gaze to his, her eyes wet and glistening. "I can never repay you for my life, Matthew. How can I even begin?"

"Oh . . . one gold coin will do, I think."

She opened the box, and he took the coin. "Take another," she offered. "Take as many as you like. And some of the jewels, too."

"One gold coin," he said. "That's my due." He put the coin into his pocket, never to be spent. He looked around the house and sighed. He had the feeling that once the rats were run out and her home was truly hers again, she might embrace the reality of moving to a better abode—further away from that wretched gaol.

Rachel took a step toward him. "Do you believe me . . . when I say I'll remember you when I'm an old, old woman?"

"I do. And please remember me, if at that point you're seeking the excitement of a younger man."

She smiled, in spite of her sadness. Then she grasped his chin, leaned forward—and kissed him very softly on the forehead, below the bandage that covered what would be his grandchildren's favorite story.

Now was the moment, he realized. It was now or never.

To ask her. Had she actually entered that smoke-palled medicine lodge? Or had it been only his feverish—and wishful—fantasy?

Was he still a virgin, or not?

He made his decision, and he thought it was the right one.

"Why are you smiling that way?" Rachel asked.

"Oh . . . I am remembering a dream I think I had. One more thing: you said to me once that your heart was used up." Matthew looked into her dirt-streaked, determined face, forevermore locking her remarkable beauty of form and spirit in his memory vault. "I believe . . . it is a cupboard that only need be restocked." He leaned forward and kissed her cheek, and then he had to go.

Had to.

As Matthew left the house, Rachel followed him to the door.

She stood there, on the threshold of her home and her own new beginning. "Goodbye!" she called, and perhaps her voice was tremulous. "Goodbye!"

He glanced back. His eyes were stinging, and she was blurred to his sight. "Farewell!" he answered. And then he went on, as Rachel's sentinel sniffed his shoes and then returned to its rat-catching duties.

MATTHEW SLEPT THAT NIGHT like a man who had rediscovered the meaning of peace.

At five-thirty, Mrs. Nettles came to awaken him as he'd asked, though the town's remaining roosters had already performed that function. Matthew shaved, washed his face, and dressed in a pair of cinnamon-colored breeches and a fresh white shirt with the left sleeve cut away. He pulled up his white stockings and slid his feet into the square-toed shoes. If Bidwell wanted back the clothes he had loaned, the man would have to rip them off himself.

Before he descended the stairs for the last time, Matthew went into the magistrate's room. No, that was wrong. The room was Bidwell's again, now. He stood there for a while, staring at the perfectly made bed. He looked at the candle stubs and the lantern. He looked at the clothes Woodward had worn, now draped over the back of a chair. All save the gold-striped waistcoat, which had gone with the magistrate to worlds unknown.

Yesterday, when he'd gone to the graveside, he'd had a difficult time until he'd realized the magistrate no longer suffered, either in body or mind. Perhaps, in some more perfect place, the just were richly rewarded for their tribulations. Perhaps, in that place, a father might find a lost son, both of them gone home to a garden.

Matthew lowered his head and wiped his eyes.

Then he let his sadness go, like a nightbird.

Downstairs, Mrs. Nettles had prepared him a breakfast that might have crippled the horse he was to ride. Bidwell was absent, obviously preferring to sleep late rather than share the clerk's meal. But with the final cup of tea, Mrs. Nettles brought Matthew an envelope, upon which was written *Concerning the Character and Abilities of Master Matthew Corbett, Esq.* Matthew turned it over and saw it was sealed with a red blob of wax in which was impressed an imperial *B.*

"He asked I give it to ye," Mrs. Nettles explained. "For your future references, he said. I'd be might pleased, for compliments from Mr. Bidwell are as rare as snowballs in Hell."

"I am pleased," Matthew said. "Tell him I thank him very much for his kindness."

The breakfast done, Mrs. Nettles walked outside with Matthew. The sun was well up, the sky blue, and a few lacy clouds drifting like the sailing ships Bidwell hoped to launch from this future port. John Goode had brought an excellent-looking roan horse with a saddle that might not raise too many sores between here and Charles Town. Mrs. Nettles opened the saddlebags to show him the food she'd packed for him, as well as a leather waterflask. It occurred to Matthew that, now that his usefulness was done to the master of Fount Royal, it was up to the servants to send him off.

Matthew shook Goode's hand, and Goode thanked him for coming to take that "bumb" out of his house. Matthew returned the thanks, for giving him the opportunity to taste some absolutely wonderful turtle soup.

Mrs. Nettles only had to help him a little to climb up on the horse. Then Matthew situated himself and grasped the reins. He was ready.

"Young sir?" Mrs. Nettles said. "May I give ye a word of advice?"

"Of course."

"Find y'self a good, strong Scottish lass."

He smiled. "I shall certainly take it under consideration."

"Good luck to ye," she said. "And a good life."

Matthew guided his horse toward the gate and began his journey. He passed the spring, where a woman in a green bonnet was already drawing water for the day. He saw in a field a farmer, breaking earth with a wooden hoe. Another farmer was walking amid fresh furrows, tossing seeds from one side to the other.

Good luck, Fount Royal! Matthew thought. And good life to all those who lived here, both on this day and on the day tomorrow.

At the gate, Mr. Green was waiting to lift the locking timber. "Goodbye, sir!" he called, and displayed a gap-toothed grin.

Matthew rode through. He was not very far along the sunlit road when he reined the horse in and paused to look back. The gate was closing. Slowly, slowly . . . then shut. Over the singing of birds in the forest, Matthew heard the sound of the locking timber slide back into place.

He had a sure destination.

New York. But not just because Magistrate Nathaniel Powers was there. It was also because the almshouse was there, and Headmaster Eben Ausley. Matthew recalled what that insidious, child-brutalizing villain had said to him, five years ago: *Consider that your education concerning the real world has been furthered. Be of excellent service to the magistrate, be of good cheer and good will, and live a long and happy life. And never—never—plot a war you have no hope of winning.*

Well, Matthew mused, perhaps the boy of five years ago could neither plot a war nor win it. But the man of today might find a method to end Ausley's reign of terror.

It was worth putting one's thoughts to, wasn't it?

Matthew stared for a moment at the closed gate, beyond which lay both an ending and a beginning. Then he turned his mount, his face, and his mind toward the century of wonders.

POCKET BOOKS
PROUDLY PRESENTS

THE

QUEEN

OF

BEDLAM

ROBERT McCAMMON

Available October 2007
From Pocket Books

Turn the page for a preview of
The Queen of Bedlam . . .

one

The Masker

'Twas said better to light a candle than to curse the dark, but in the town of New York in the summer of 1702 one might do both, for the candles were small and the dark was large. True, there were the town-appointed constables and watchmen. Yet often between Dock Street and the Broad Way these heroes of the nocturne lost their courage to a flask of John Barleycorn and the other temptations that beckoned so flagrantly on the midsummer breeze, be it the sound of merriment from the harbor taverns or the intoxicating scent of perfume from the rose-colored house of Polly Blossom.

The nightlife was, in a word, lively. Though the town awakened before sunrise to the industrious bells of mercantile and farming labors, there were still many who preferred to apply their sleeping hours to the avocations of drinking, gambling and what mischief might follow those troublesome twins. The sun would certainly rise on the morrow, but tonight was always a temptation. Why else would this brash and eager, Dutch-groomed and now English-dressed town boast more than a dozen taverns, if not for the joy of intemperate companionship?

But the young man who sat alone at a table in the back room of the Old Admiral was not there to seek companions, be they of humankind or brewer's yeast. He did have before him a tankard of strong dark ale, which he sipped at every so often, but this was a prop to blend into the scene. One watching him would see how he winced and frowned at the drinking, for it took a true hardgut to down the Old Admiral's keel-cleaner. This was not his usual haunt. In fact he was well-known at the Trot Then Gallop, up on Crown Street, but here he was within a coin's throw of the Great Dock on the East River, where the masted ships whispered and groaned on the night currents and the flambeaux from fishermen's skiffs burned red against the eddies. Here in the Old Admiral the blue smoke of clay pipes whirled through the lamplight as men bellowed for more ale or wine and the crack of dice hitting tables sounded like the pistols of little wars. That noise never failed to remind Matthew Corbett of the pistol shot that had blown out the brains of . . . well, it had been three years ago, it was best not to linger on such a foregone picture. He was only twenty-three years old, but something about him was elder than his span. Perhaps it was his grave seriousness, his austere demeanor, or the fact that he could always forecast rain from the aching in his bones like those of a toothless senior muttering in his pudding. Or, to be more correct, the ache of ribs below his heart and left arm at the shoulder, bones broken courtesy of a bear known as Jack One Eye. The bear had also left Matthew with a crescent scar that began just above his right eyebrow and curved into the hairline. A doctor in the Carolina colony had once said to him that ladies liked a young man with a dashing scar, but this one seemed to warn the ladies that he'd come close to a cropper with Death, and perhaps the chill of the mausoleum lingered in his soul. His left arm had been almost without life for over a year after that incident. He'd expected to live on the starboard for the rest of his days but a good and rather unorthodox doctor here in New York had given him arm exercises—self-inflicted torture involving an iron bar to which horseshoes were chained on either end—to do daily, along with hot compresses and stretching. At last came the miracle morning when he could rotate his shoulder all the way around, and with further treatment he nearly had all his strength returned. Thus passed away one of the last acts of Jack One Eye upon the earth, gone now but surely never forgotten.

Matthew's cool gray eyes, flecked with dark blue like smoke at twilight, were aimed toward a certain table on the other side of the room. He was careful, though, not to stare too pointedly, but only to graze and jab and look into his ale, shift his shoulders and graze and jab again. No matter, really; the object of his interest would have to be blind and dumb not to know he was there, and true evil was neither. No, true evil just continued to talk and grin and sip with puckered lips at a greasy glass of wine, puff a smoke ring from a black clay pipe and then talk and grin some more, all while the gaming went on with its hollerings and dice-shots and shadowy men yelling as if to scare the dawn from ever happening. But Matthew knew it was more than the humor and drinking and gaming of a tavern in a young town with the sea at its chest and wilderness to its back that brought out this festivity. It was the Thing That No One Spoke Of. The Incident. The Unfortunate Happenstance. It was the Masker, is what it was. So drink up wine from those fresh casks and blow your smoke to the moon, Matthew thought. Howl like wolves and grin like thieves. We've all got to walk a dark street home tonight.

And the Masker could be any one of them, he mused. Or the Masker could be gone the way he'd come, never to pass this way again. Who could know? Certainly not the idiots who these days called themselves constables and were empowered by the town council to patrol the streets. He reasoned they were probably all indoors somewhere as well, though the weather be warm and the moon half on the hang; they were stupid, yes, but not foolish.

Matthew took another drink of his ale and flicked his gaze again toward that far table. The pipe smoke hung in blue layers, shifting with the wind of motion or exhalation. At the table sat three men. One elder, fat and bloated, two younger with the look of ruffians. But to be sure, this was a rumpot of ruffians, so that in itself was not surprising. Matthew hadn't seen either of the men with the fat bloatarian before. They were dressed in rustic style, both with well-used leather waistcoats over white shirts and one with leather patches on the knees of his breeches. Who were they? he wondered. And what business did they have with Eben Ausley?

Only very seldom and just for a quick flash did Matthew catch the glint of Ausley's small black eyes aimed at him, but just as swiftly the man angled his white-wigged head away and continued the conversation with his two juniors. Anyone looking on would not realize that the young Corbett—with his lean long-jawed face, his unruly thatch of fine black hair and his pale candlelit countenance—

was a crusader whose quest had slowly night upon night turned to obsession. In his brown boots, gray breeches and simple white shirt, frayed at the collar and cuffs but scrupulously laundered, he appeared to be no more than his occupation of magistrate's clerk demanded. Certainly Magistrate Powers wouldn't approve of these nightly travels, but travel Matthew must, for the deepest desire of his heart was to see Eben Ausley hanged from the town gallows.

Now Ausley put down his pipe and drew the table's lamp nearer. The companion on his left—a dark-haired, sunken-eyed man perhaps nine or ten years elder than Matthew—was speaking quietly and seriously. Ausley, a heavy-jowled pig in his mid-fifties, listened intently. At length Matthew saw him nod and reach into the coat of his vulgar wine-purple suit, the frills on his shirt quivering with the belly-strain. The white wig on Ausley's head was adorned with elaborate curls, which perhaps in London was the fashion of the moment but here in New York was only a fop's topping. Ausley brought from within his coat a string-wrapped lead pencil and a palm-sized black notebook Matthew had seen him produce a score of times. There was some kind of gold-leaf ornamentation on the cover. Matthew had already mused upon the thought that Ausley was as addicted to his note-taking as to his games of Ombre and Ticktack, both of which seemed to have a hold on the man's mind and wallet. He could imagine with a faint smile the notes scribbled down on those pages: *Dropped a loaf this morning . . . a fig or two into the bucket . . . dear me, only a nugget today . . .* Ausley touched the pencil to his tongue and began to write. Three or four lines were set down, or so it appeared to Matthew. Then the notebook was closed and put away and finally the pencil as well. Ausley spoke again to the dark-haired young man, while the other one—sandy-haired and thick-set, with a slow oxen-like blinking of his heavy eyelids—appraised the noisy game of Bone-Ace going on over in the corner. Ausley grinned; the yellow lamplight fairly leaped off his teeth. A group of drinkers stumbled past between Matthew and his objects of interest. Just that fast Ausley and the other two men were standing up, reaching for their hats on the wallhooks. Ausley's tricorn displayed a dyed crimson feather, while the dark-haired man with the leather-patched breeches wore a wide-brimmed leather hat and the third gent a common short-billed cap. The group strolled to the tavern-keeper at the bar to settle their bills. Matthew waited. When the coins were down in the moneybox and the three men going out onto Dock Street, Matthew put on his own brown linen cap and stood up. He was a little light-headed. The strong ale, currents of smoke and raucous noise had unhinged his senses. He quickly paid his due and walked into the night.

Ah, what a relief out here! A warm breeze in the face was cool compared to the heated confines of a crowded tavern. The Old Admiral always had such an effect on him. He'd tracked Ausley here on many earlier occasions so he ought to be immune to such, but his idea of an excellent evening was a drink of polite wine and a quiet game of chess with the regulars at the Gallop. He smelled on the breeze the pungence of harbor tarbuckets and dead fish. But there on the very same breeze, wafting past, was quite another scent Matthew had expected: Eben Ausley wore a heavy cologne that smelled of cloves. He nearly bathed in the stuff. The man might as well have carried a torch with him, to illuminate his comings and goings; it certainly helped to follow Ausley by on these nights. But tonight, it seemed, Ausley and his companions were in no hurry, for there they were strolling up ahead. They walked past the glow of a lantern that hung from a wooden post to mark the intersection of Dock Street and Broad Street, and Matthew saw their intent was to go west onto Bridge Street. Well, he thought, this was a new path. Usually Ausley headed directly back the six blocks north to the orphanage on King Street. Better keep back a bit more, he decided. Better just walk quietly and keep watch.

Matthew followed, crossing the cobblestoned street. He was tall and thin but not frail, and he walked with a long stride that he had to restrain lest he get up the back of his bull's-eye. The smells of the Great Dock faded, to be replaced by the heady aromas of hay and livestock. In this section of town were several stables and fenced enclosures for pigs and cows. Warehouses held maritime and animal supplies in stacks of crates and barrels. Occasionally Matthew caught a glimpse of candlelight through a shutter, as someone moved about inside a countinghouse or stable. Never let it be said that all the residents of New York gamboled or slept at night, as some might rather labor clock-round if physical strength would allow.

A horse clopped past, its rider wearing polished boots.

Matthew saw Ausley and the two others turn right at the next corner, onto the Broad Way near the Governor's House. He made the turn at a cautious pace. His quarry walked a block ahead, still just ambling. Matthew took note of candlelight in several upper windows of the white-bricked governor's abode beyond the walls of Fort William Henry. The new man, Lord Cornbury, had arrived from England only a few days ago. Matthew hadn't yet seen him, nor had anyone else of his acquaintance, but the notices plastered up announced a meeting in the town hall tomorrow afternoon so he expected to soon have a look at the gent who'd been awarded the reins of New York by Queen Anne. It would be good to have someone in charge of things, since the constables were in such disarray and the town's mayor, Thomas Hood, had died in June.

Matthew saw that the red-feathered cockatoo and his companions were approaching another tavern, the Thorn Bush. That nasty little place was even gamier than the Admiral, in all senses of the word. Matthew had been witness in there last November when Ausley had lost what must have been a small fortune on the game of Bankafalet. He decided he wasn't up to anymore tavern-sitting tonight. Let them go in and drink themselves blue, if they liked. It was time to go home and abed.

But Ausley and the two men kept walking past the Thorn Bush, not even pausing to look in the door. As Matthew neared the place, a drunk young man—Andrew Kippering, Matthew saw in the bloom of lamplight—and a dark-haired girl with a heavily-painted face staggered out into the street, laughing at some shared amusement. They brushed past Matthew and went on in the direction of the harbor. Kippering was an attorney of some renown and could be a serious sort, but was not unknown to tip the bottle and frequent Madam Blossom's household.

Ausley and the others turned right onto Beaver Street and crossed Broad Street once again, heading west toward the riverfront. Here and there lanterns burned on corner posts, and every seventh dwelling was required by law to show a light. A dog barked fiercely behind a white picket fence and another echoed off in the distance. A man wearing a gold-trimmed tricorn and carrying a walking-stick suddenly turned a corner in front of Matthew and almost scared him witless, but with a quick nod the man was striding away, the stick tap-tapping on the brick sidewalk. Matthew picked up his pace to keep Ausley in sight, but making certain to step carefully lest he mar his boots with any of the animal dung that often littered both bricks and cobbles. A horse-cart trundled past with a single figure hunched over the reins. Matthew walked on a narrow street between two walls of white stone. Ahead, by the illumination of a dying post-lamp, Ausley and the others turned right onto Sloat Lane. A fire had broken out here at the first of the summer and consumed several houses. The odor of ashes and flame-wrack still lingered in the air commingled with rotten cloves and the smell of a pig that needed to be roasted. Matthew stopped and carefully peered around the corner. His quarry had slipped out of sight, between darkened wooden houses and squat little red brick buildings. Some of the houses further on were blackened ruins. The lantern on the cornerpost ahead flickered, about to give up its ghost. A little prickling of the skin on the back of Matthew's neck made him look around the way he'd come. Standing a distance behind him was a figure in dark clothes and hat, washed by the candlelight on the cornerpost he'd just passed. This was not his area of habitation, and it struck him suddenly that he was very far from home.

The figure just stood there, seemingly staring at him though Matthew was unable to make out a face beneath that tricorn. Matthew couldn't help but lay fingers upon his throat. His heart had begun to hammer in his chest. If this was the Masker, he thought, then damned if he'd give up his life without a fight. Good thinking there boy, he told himself with a twinge of morbid humor. Fists against a throat-slashing blade always won the day.

Matthew was about to call to the figure—and say what? he asked himself. *Fine night for a walk, isn't it sir? And by the by would you please spare my life?*—but abruptly the mystery man turned away, strode purposefully out of the lantern's realm and was gone. The breath hissed out of him. He felt the chill of sweat at his temples. That wasn't the Masker! he told himself with a little stupid fury. Of course not! It might have been a constable, or someone just out walking, the same as himself! Only he was not out just walking, he thought. He was a sheep, tracking a wolf.

Ausley and his tavern companions had gone. There was no sight of them whatsoever. Now the question was, did Matthew continue along this ashen-reeking lane or retrace his way back to where the Masker was waiting? Stop it, idiot! he commanded. That wasn't the Masker because the Masker has left New York! Why should anyone think the Masker was still lurking in these streets? Because they hadn't caught him, Matthew thought grimly. That's why.

He decided to go ahead, but with a watchful eye at his back in case a piece of darkness separated itself from the night and rushed upon him. And he had gone perhaps ten paces further when a piece of darkness shifted not at his back, but directly in front of him.

He stopped and stood stone-still. He was a dried husk, all the blood and breath gone from him on a summer night suddenly turned winter's eve.

A spark leapt, setting fire to cotton in a little tinderbox, and from it a match was lighted.

"Corbett," said the man as he touched flame to pipe bowl, "if you're so intent on following me I ought to give you an audience. Don't you think?" Matthew didn't reply. Actually his tongue was still petrified.

Eben Ausley took a moment lighting his pipe to satisfaction. Behind him was a fire-blacked brick wall. His corpulent face seethed red. "What a wonder you are, boy," he said in his crackly high-pitched voice. "Laboring at papers and pots all day long and following me about the town at night. When do you sleep?"

"I manage," Matthew answered.

"I think you ought to get more sleep than you do. I think you are in need of a long rest. Don't you agree with that, Mr. Carver?"

Too late, Matthew heard the movement behind him. Too late, he realized the other two men had been hiding in the burned rubble on either side of—

A lumberboard whacked him square in the back of the head, stopping all further speculations. It sounded so loud to him that surely the militia would think a cannon had fired, but then the force of the blow knocked him off his feet and the pain roared up and everything was shooting stars and flaming pinwheels. He was on his knees and made an effort of sheer willpower not to go down flat on the street. His teeth were gritted, his senses blowsy. It came to him through the haze that Ausley had led him a merry traipse to this sheep-trap. "Oh, that's enough, I think," Ausley was say-ing. "We don't want to *kill* him now, do we? How does that feel, Corbett? Clear your noggin out for you?"

Matthew heard the voice as if an echo from a great distance, which he wished were the truth. Something pressed down hard upon the center of his back. A boot, he realized. About to slam him to the ground.

"He's all right where he is," Ausley said, in a flat tone of non-chalance. The boot left Matthew's back. "I don't think he's going anywhere. Are you, Corbett?" He didn't wait for a reply, which wouldn't have arrived anyway. "Do you know who this young man is, my friends? Do you know he's been trailing me hither and yon, 'round and about for . . . how long has it been, Corbett? Two *years*?"

Two years haphazardly, Matthew thought. Only the last six months with any sense of purpose.

"This young man was one of my dearest students," Ausley went on, smirking now. "One of my boys, yes. Raised up right there at the orphanage. Now I didn't take him off the street myself, my predecessor Staunton did that, you see. That poor old fool saw him as a worthwhile project. Wretched urchin into educated gentleman, if you please. Gave him *books* to read, and taught him . . . what was it he taught you, Corbett? How to be a damned fool, like he was?" He continued merrily along his crooked road. "Now this young man has gone a far travel from his beginnings. Oh yes, he has. Went into the employ of Magistrate Issac Woodward, who chose him as a clerk-in-training and took him out into the world. Gave him a chance to continue his education, to learn to live a gentleman's life and to *be* someone of value." There was a pause as Ausley relit his pipe. "And *then,* my friends," Ausley said between puffs, "and *then,* he betrayed his benefactor by falling in with a woman accused of witchcraft in a little hole of a town down in the Carolina colony. A murderess, I understood her to be. A common tramp and a con-niver, who pulled the wool over this young man's eyes and caused the death of that noble Magistrate Woodward, God rest his soul."

"Lie," Matthew was able to say. Or rather, to whisper. He tried again: "That's . . . a lie."

"Did he speak? Did he say something?" Ausley asked.

"He mumbled," said the man standing behind Matthew.

"Well might he mumble," Ausley said. "He mumbled and grumbled quite a lot at the orphanage. Didn't you, Corbett? If I had killed my benefactor by first exposing him to a wet tempest that half robbed his life and then breaking his heart by treachery, I'd be reduced to a mumbling wretch too. Tell me, how does Magistrate Powers trust you enough to turn his back on you? Or have you learned a bewitching spell from your ladyfriend?"

"If he knows witchcraft," another voice said, "it hasn't done him any good tonight."

"No," Ausley answered, "he doesn't know witchcraft. If he did, he'd at least make himself into an invisible pest instead of a pest I have to look at everytime I venture out into the street. Corbett!!"

It had been a demand for Matthew's full attention, which he was able to give only by lifting his throbbing brain-pan on its weakened stalk. He blinked, trying to focus on Ausley's repugnant visage.

The headmaster of King Street's orphanage for boys, he of the jaunty cockatoo and the swollen belly, said with quiet contempt, "I know what you're about. I've always known. When you came back here, I knew it would start. And I warned you, did I not? Your last night at the orphanage? Have you forgotten? *Answer me!*"

"I haven't forgotten," Matthew said.

"Never plot a war you cannot win. Isn't that right?"

Matthew didn't respond. He tensed, expecting the boot to come down on his back again, but he was spared.

"This young man . . . boy . . . *fool,*" Ausley corrected himself, speaking now to his two companions, "decided he didn't approve of my correctional methods. All those boys, all those grievous *attitudes*. Some of them like animals wild from the woods, even a barn was too good for them. They'd bite your arm off and piss on your leg. The churches and the public hospital daily bringing them to my door. Family perished on the voyage over, no one to take responsibility, so what was I to do with them? Indians massacred this one's family, or that one was stubborn and would not work, or this one was a young drunkard living in the street. What was I to *do* with them, except give them some discipline? And yes, I did take many of them in hand. Many of them I had to discipline in the most strict of manners, because they would abide no—"

"Not discipline," Matthew interrupted, gathering strength into his voice. His face had reddened, his eyes glistening with anger in their swollen sockets. "Your methods . . . might make the church elders and the hospital council think twice . . . about the charity they give you. And the money the town pays you. Do they know you're confusing discipline with sodomy?"

Ausley was quiet. In this silence, the world and time seemed to hang suspended.

"I've heard them scream, late at night," Matthew went on. "Many nights. I've seen them, afterward. Some of them . . . didn't want to live. All of them were changed. And you only went after the *youngest* ones. The ones who couldn't fight back." He felt the burn of tears, and even after eight years the impact of this emotion stunned him. He pulled in a breath and the next words tumbled out of him: "I'm fighting back for them, you jackal sonofabitch."

Ausley's laugh cracked the dark. "Oh ho! Oh ho, my friends! View the avenging angel! Down on the ground and fighting the air!" He came forward a few steps. In the next pull of the pipe and the red wash of cinder-light, Matthew saw a face upon the man that would have scared even the winged Michael. "You make me *sick,* Corbett! With your stupidity and your fucking *honor.* With your following me, trying to get under my feet and trip me up. Because that's what you're doing, isn't it? Trying to *find out* things? To *spy* on me? Which tells me one very important thing: you have nothing. If you had something—*anything*—beyond your ridiculous suppositions and made-up memories, you would have first fetched your dear dead magistrate Woodward upon me, or now your new dog Powers. Am I not correct in this?" His voice suddenly changed; when he spoke again he sounded like a nettled old woman: "Look what you've made me step in!"

Then, after a meditative pause: "Mr. Bromfield, drag Corbett over here, won't you?"

A hand grabbed Matthew's collar and another took hold of his shirt low on his back. He was dragged fast and sure by a man who knew how to move a body. Matthew tensed and tried to convulse himself, but a knuckled fist—Carver's, he presumed—jammed into his ribs just enough to tell him that pride led to breakage.

"You have a filthy mind," Ausley said, standing closer with his odors of cloves and smoke. "I think we should scrub it a bit, beginning with your face. Mr. Bromfield, clean him up for me, please."

"My pleasure," said the man who'd seized Matthew, and with diabolical relish he took hold of the back of Matthew's head and thrust his face down into the fly-blown mass of horse manure that Ausley's boot had found.

Matthew had seen what was coming. There was no way to avoid it. He was able to seal his mouth shut and close his eyes, and then his face went into the pile. It was, by reason of the analytical part of Matthew's brain that took the cool measure of all things, distressingly fresh.

Almost velvety, really. Like putting one's face into a velvet bag. Warm, still. The stuff was up his nostrils, but the breath was stuck hard in his lungs. He didn't fight, even when he felt the sole of a boot press upon the back of his head and his face was jammed through the wretched excess near down to the cobblestones. They wanted him to fight, so they could break him. So he would not fight, even as the air stuttered in his lungs and his face remained pressed down into the filth under a whoreson's boot. He would not fight, so he might fight the better on his feet some other day.

Ausley said, "Pull him up."

Bromfield obeyed.

"Get some air in his lungs, Carver," Ausley commanded.

The flat of a hand slapped Matthew in the center of his chest. The air whooshed out of his mouth and nostrils, spraying manure.

"Shit!" Carver hollered. "He's got it on my shirt!"

"Step back then, step back. Give him room to smell himself."

Matthew did. The stuff was still jammed up his nose. It caked his face like swamp mud and had the vomitous odor of sour grass, decayed feed and . . . well, and stinking *manure* straight from the rump. He retched and tried to clear his eyes but Bromfield had hold of his arms as strong as a picaroon's rope.

Ausley gave a short, high and giddy laugh. "Oh, look at him now! The avenger has turned scarecrow! You might even scare the carrion birds away with that face, Corbett!"

Matthew spat and shook his head violently back and forth; unfortunately some of this unpalatable meal had gotten past his lips.

"You can let him go now," Ausley said. Bromfield released Matthew and at the same time gave him a solid shove that put him on the ground again. Then, as Matthew struggled up to his knees and rubbed the mess out of his eyes, Ausley stood over him and said quietly, the menace in his voice commingled with boredom, "You are not to follow me again. Understand? Mind me well, or the next time we meet shall not go so kindly for you." To the others: "Shall we leave the young man to his contemplations?"

There was the sound of phlegm being hawked up. Matthew felt the gob of spit hit his shirt at the left shoulder. Carver or Bromfield, showing their good breeding. After that, the noise of boots striding away. Ausley said something and one of the others laughed. Then they were gone.

Matthew sat in the street, cleaning his face with his sleeves. Sickness bubbled and lurched in his stomach. The heat of anger and the burn of shame made him feel as if he were sitting aboil under the noonday sun. His head was still killing him, his eyes streaming. Then his stomach turned over and out of him flooded the Old Admiral's ale and most of the salmagundi he'd put down for his supper. It came to him that he was going to be laboring over a washpot tonight.

Finally, after what seemed a terrible hour, he was able to get up off the ground and think about how to get home. His roost on the Broad Way, up over Hiram Stokely's pottery shop, was going to be a good twenty-minute walk. Probably a long, malodorous twenty minutes, at that. But there was nothing to be done but to get to doing it; and so he started off, seething and weaving and stinking and altogether miserable in his wretched skin. He searched for a horse trough. He would get himself a bath in it, and so cleanse his face and clear his mind.

And tomorrow? To be so impetuous as to once more haunt the dark outside the King's Street orphanage, waiting for Ausley to appear on his jaunt to the gambling dens and so spy on him in hopes of . . . what, exactly? Or to stay home in his small room and embrace cold fact, that Ausley was right; he had absolutely nothing, and was unlikely to get anything at this pace. But to give up . . . to give up . . . was abandoning them all. Abandoning the reason for his solemn rage, abandoning the quest that he felt set him apart from every other citizen of this town. It gave him a purpose. Without it, who would he be?

He would be a magistrate's clerk and a pottery sweeper, he thought as he went along the silent Broad Way. Only a young man who held sway over a quill and a broom, and whose mind was tormented by the vision of injustice to the innocent. It was what had made him stand up against Magistrate Woodward—his mentor and almost father, truth be told—to proclaim Rachel Howarth innocent of witchcraft in the town of Fount Royal three years ago. Had that decision helped to carry the ailing magistrate to his death? Possibly so. It was another torment, like the hot strike of a bullwhip ever endlessly repeating, that lay upon Matthew's soul in every hour lit by sun or candle.

He came upon a horse trough at Trinity Church, where Wall Street met the Broad Way. Here the sturdy Dutch cobblestones ended and the streets were plain hard-packed English earth. As Matthew leaned down into the trough and began to wash his face with dirty water, he almost felt like weeping. Yet to weep took too much energy, and he had none of that to spare.

But tomorrow was tomorrow, was it not? A new beginning, as they said? What a day might change, who could ever know? Yet some things would never change in himself, and of this he was certain: he must bring Eben Ausley to justice somehow, for those crimes of wanton evil and brutality against the innocent. Somehow, he must; or he feared that if he did not, he would be consumed by this quest, by its futility, and he would wither into slack-jawed acceptance of what could never in his mind be acceptable.

At last he was suitable to proceed home, yet still a ragamuffin's nightmare. He still had his cap, that was a good thing. He still had his life, that was another. And so he straightened his shoulders and counted his blessings and went on his way through the midnight town, one young man alone.